D0837257

AHEAD WAS THE LAND OF PROMISE . . .
A LAND THAT SOME OF THEM WOULD NEVER SEE . . .

A ship's officer was herding the people on deck down a deep stairway leading to the enclosed lower decks. When he looked at Sean and Nora's manifest cards, he ordered them in opposite directions.

Suddenly terrified, Nora screamed, "No, I want to be with my brother! Why are you separating us?"

The officer looked at her condescendingly. "Men and women do not bunk together."

With that Nora was swept down the narrow, steep, slippery stairs. She was carrying bundles of food, a comforter, a little bottle of the poteen, and a large bottle of water given to her by Peggy O'Riordan.

She suddenly realized she was in a line in front of the storeroom, and the next thing she knew, a blanket was thrust at her. In it was a tin pan, a dipper cup, a spoon and a fork. A very fat woman behind her commented, "You notice, deary, there's no knife. Me husband wrote 'twas because you're ready to murder by the end of the trip." She laughed, showing a mouth full of black and decaying teeth.

Nora moved away from her as quickly as she could, down the steep stairs to Compartment J. A feeling of despair was rising in her, but she didn't want to give in to it. She stared at the mayhem. There were already over one hundred women in the room. She shuddered as a pervasive feeling of isolation, even amidst hundreds, swept over her. . . .

The IRISH

Doris Flood Ladd

The IRISH

A Dell/Banbury Book

Published by
Banbury Books, Inc.
37 West Avenue
Wayne, Pennsylvania 19087

Copyright © 1982 by Doris Flood Ladd

All rights reserved. No part of this book may be
reproduced in any form or by any means without the
prior written permission of the Publisher,
excepting brief quotes used in connection
with reviews written specifically for inclusion
in a magazine or newspaper.

Dell ® TM 681510, Dell Publishing Co., Inc.

ISBN: 0-440-04845-1

Printed in the United States of America

First printing—January 1983

Prologue

Nora O'Sullivan and her dearest friend, Molly Macgeehan, met early in the morning to go berry picking. As always, the two young girls used this opportunity to sneak away to see Grandma Eileen, chattering with one another as they walked along.

"Does your ma kiss your pa, Molly?" Nora asked. Her deep violet eyes flashed with excitement.

"No, but they're yelling a lot," Molly replied. She was a dimpled, freckled, laughing, red-haired girl.

"Well, last night I got up to get a drink of water and I saw my pa pick up Ma, kiss her and carry her to their bedroom," Nora confided. She pushed a wayward lock of her raven-black hair back off the soft paleness of her forehead.

Molly looked puzzled. "Maybe she was sick and couldn't be walking on her own."

"Maybe, but she seemed cheerful and in fine health this morning. I think I'll ask Grandma Eileen."

Nora and Molly had made friends with old lady Murphy on the next farm. Everyone called her Grandma Eileen. It seemed natural, for she was sweet and kind. She was also a glorious spinner of tales, and all the Irish folklore came alive as she told them of the fairies and what they'd do to Nora and Molly if they were naughty, of the spirits, the pookies, the changelings, the wise women, and all the charms, curses, and cures. She was a regular encyclopedia of the other world. Nora and Molly would skip down the road holding hands, talking, laughing, still free of the responsibilities of chores and school, and find Grandma Eileen with her big black eyes and her matching big black shawl sitting, endlessly stoking the fire that had never been allowed to go out on their hearth for over a century. Grandma never left it alone, for it was considered that the fairies would be displeased if there were no fire for them at night. Her eyes lit up when she saw them, for she didn't have any other audience as attentive as these two, and often no other audience at all.

Nora was wondering about school, which she'd be starting in a week. She envied the older children who went off each year to this mysterious place, and often asked them about what to expect. Their answers never quite satisfied her, so she decided to ask Grandma Eileen, whom she considered an authority on everything.

"I'll be going to school soon, Grandma Eileen, and what is it I'll be learning there?" Nora asked.

"You'll be learning your letters and how to be reading and counting."

"I already know my letters and I'm already reading and counting. So what else will there be?"

Grandma Eileen looked at her strangely. "Now, how would you be knowing those things? Well, then, are you in the fairies, child?"

Nora was confused and looked inquiringly at Molly,

who just shrugged. "I don't know what you mean, Grandma Eileen. What is being in the fairies?"

"It means, bright child, that you talk to them, see them and hear them. Otherwise, how could you be knowing your letters and how to read and count already?"

"I know how to do those things because my ma and my older sister and brothers taught me. I don't know any fairies." Tears of fear welled in her eyes.

"Oh, don't you be worrying," Grandma Eileen said quickly, pulling her into her arms and comforting her. "It will be all right, all right. Most of the fairies are good, you know, and they've taken a shine to you. I can tell. Perhaps some day they'll grant you a great wish." Grandma Eileen's old eyes brightened. "Perhaps they'll send you to America."

"Oh, Nora, America." Molly repeated the word as if it were sacred.

The word sent a thrill down Nora's spine. " 'Twould be wonderful," she whispered.

"Can you read, Molly?" Nora asked as they held hands and huddled together, walking homeward along the hedgerows.

"No, Nora, I can't."

Nora was silent for a few moments and then said, "Perhaps Grandma Eileen is right. Perhaps I *am* in the fairies then, for why should I be reading when you're not?" And they trudged home in gloomy silence.

That evening she asked her mother if it was possible that she might be in the fairies.

"Good Lord, child, why are you asking such a question?"

"Grandma Eileen says I must be because I know how to read and count, and I've not been to school yet."

Mary O'Sullivan was exasperated, for she discouraged her daughter from these beliefs. Such superstitions were not discussed often in their home, except in a joking way. "Nora, darling, some of those stories are very quaint and even fun sometimes, but they are all superstitions, which are beliefs that are not based on anything real, so you mustn't be worried about fairies or spirits. There are none. Some of the older people believe in them because that's what they were taught, but we know they're not real, don't we?" Mary wasn't altogether convinced that Nora believed her.

She was relieved that Nora was starting school soon, for she and Molly wouldn't be visiting Grandma Eileen as often. God love her, Mary thought, she's ignorant, but a sweet woman for all that.

Nora's eyes had a faraway look in them. She gently stroked the back of her mother's hand with her own. "But Ma," she said in a hushed voice, "Grandma Eileen promised that the fairies will grant me a great wish some day, that they might even send me off to America!"

Mary took her daughter's head tenderly to her bosom, and she held her as she gently swayed back and forth. "There, there, child. I had no intention to dash your hopes, to spoil your dreams. Perhaps you *will* go to America some day."

Aye, and why not? Mary thought to herself. Why shouldn't my daughter go to a land where she wouldn't have to suffer the hardships and heartbreaks that a place such as Ireland offers in such abundance? Mary's thoughts drifted back to a time in her own life when the rift between the British gentry and the Irish poor had caused her more pain than she would ever know again.

She was then seventeen, and her dark beauty was breathtaking. Once anyone looked into those intense blue-violet eyes, they would be captivated. Her figure was slight and beautifully proportioned. She was somewhat taller than most of her friends. The profile was aristocratic, even elegant, but she was never haughty, for there was always warmth and understanding in her demeanor. The young men from Trinity enjoyed not only her beauty, but her wit and vivacious manner. But, just as she remembered they were Protestant, they never forgot that she was Catholic, and no young man could press his suit past friendship. For years it had been forbidden by law for Catholics and Protestants to marry, and while that was the case no longer, the old ways died hard. A young Protestant man or woman would be disinherited; a young Catholic man or woman would be ostracized. And Mary knew how her father felt about the Protestant Brits.

One evening, as was her habit in those days, Mary had gone to Tim's pub near Trinity College to sing old ballads for the student patrons who frequented the place. It was a way for her to make a few shillings in tips. She had a fine, lilting soprano voice, and she never failed to turn all eyes teary in a crowd of sentimental young men.

She had just finished singing "Purty Molly Brailaghan," a wonderful old ballad of love and desertion, when her eyes met and held for a moment those of a young man with fair, wavy hair, perfectly chiseled features and pale, searching green eyes. She had never seen such eyes. She looked away and tried not to look in his direction again. When she finally did, he was gone. But the next evening he was there again. Always alone, never approaching her, just watching quietly. She was uncomfortable, but intrigued. At last, she asked Tim, the proprietor, to find out who he was.

"He's manor born, lass, and one day will be Anthony, Lord Howard."

One evening, as she finished a ballad, he approached

her. She was certain he could hear her heart pounding, that no voice would come from her throat.

"Miss Matthews, your singing is as sweet as any I've heard, ever. Do you know any Schubert lieder?" She looked hard at him to see if he was teasing her, but he looked serious enough.

"Yes, Mr. Howard. Would 'Das Erlking' do?"

"Please sing it."

As she sang, her eyes flashed, her cheeks glowed, her hair tumbled about her shoulders in a blue-black cascade. Her voice was clear and bell-like. Mr. Howard was enchanted.

"How beautiful, Miss Matthews," he said when she had finished. "Where did you learn your German?"

"At the Convent of Mount Anville," she told him. " 'Tis where I attended school."

"Your accent is impeccable."

She acknowledged his compliment with a smile.

"May I see you sometime? Perhaps you would walk with me tomorrow?" His forwardness was disconcerting, but he seemed kind and honest.

Her heart raced. She knew she shouldn't even be speaking to him, much less meeting him for a walk. But just this once she wanted to forget all the obstacles of religion and class distinction to meet with him as if they were living in another world.

"Yes, Mr. Howard, I would like that. Shall we meet in St. Stephen's Green?" She smiled, suddenly feeling very youthful.

They met often the next few months, and her heart ached for him when she found out that he had lost his young wife and infant son in childbirth a year and a half earlier. In turn, she told him how her father had been killed by a fanatic's bomb at a political rally, and how her brother, Jim, had then gone to America, leaving her to live with a wretched, miserly old aunt. As they talked together for hours, they had a meeting of mind and heart, and it seemed as if they had known each other always. It was a glorious feeling for both of them. As they lay in their separate beds across the city from one another, forgetting that more than boulevards separated them, they each dreamed an impossible dream of being together forever.

One evening, he kissed her long and passionately. It was not her first kiss, but it was the first one that mattered. For a few weeks, the delight, the love and the warmth of the relationship enveloped them. She never anticipated it would go this far or that they would feel this strongly. She suddenly became frightened when one evening in St. Stephen's Green he asked her to be his wife.

She felt as if her heart would break, even though these were the words she so desperately wanted to hear. She couldn't believe that he actually thought they could become man and wife. They talked for hours, until the shadows lengthened, and finally she began to believe as he did. His arguments were very convincing.

She walked to the pub as happy as she had ever been, or ever would be again in her life. She burst in through the entrance. The early-evening patrons were gathering, and Tim met her as she started up the stairs.

"Where have you been, lass? There's a grand lady waiting for you in your room."

Mary paled. She wondered if perhaps it was Anthony's mother. She opened the door. Sitting on the one rickety wicker chair in her room was a girl not much older than she, but as different as two people could be. She was dressed in the finest and most expensive laces and silks. Her green silk moiré pumps shined like emeralds against the dingy grey floor. Mary suddenly became aware of the coarseness of her own cape, and she smoothed her hands down her mended and patched woolen skirt. It was a study in contrasts.

"Are you the girl who sings in this pub?" the young aristocrat asked in icy tones.

"That I am. My name is Mary Matthews, and may I ask yours?"

"I am Elizabeth Howard, daughter of Lord Anthony Howard," she said haughtily.

"Oh, how wonderful then, you're no stranger. You're Anthony's sister. I'm pleased to meet you." She stepped forward to offer her hand, but Elizabeth's gloved hand remained firmly fixed in her lap.

"Your little game is over. I've been sent by my father to ask how much money you want to leave my brother alone."

Mary reeled back as if she had been struck. "But you don't understand. It's no game. We love each other and we're to be married."

The contemptuous expression changed to one of disbelief. "Poor girl. I do think you actually believe this."

"I do believe it, because it's true."

"So, you actually believe Anthony will come to his father, who'll joyfully give his permission, and allow his son, descendant of one of the finest names in England, heir to a great estate in County Cork, to marry the daughter of an Irish peasant who makes bombs for a living? And do you also believe it's true that when Anthony takes you into Irish society that you would be accepted? Perhaps you think he'll present a pub singer to the queen, or that as Lady Howard, perhaps you can entertain your bog-trotting friends at Ballygarry Castle?" She paused a moment for breath. "Well, my dear, I'll tell you what the truth is. He'll be stripped of a title that has been handed down for generations of a life he was born to live. He'll have no family, no friends. All doors will be closed to him. He'll have no money. He'll have to seek common employment to which he is ill suited. Can you really do this to him? He will be friendless and penniless and this is what your love will have done for him."

Mary had covered her face with her hands as if to shut out the words. As cruel as it all sounded, she knew it was the truth.

Elizabeth rose to leave, and as she passed Mary, she said, "If you really love him, you won't ruin his life. And don't delude yourself that you have a choice, for there are no choices here." She paused. "You look like a sensible girl. Take the money, dear."

Mary took her hands away from her face, drew herself up with her inborn dignity and said quietly, "I love your brother, so I would no more ruin his life than I would take your money. But if the world he'll move in contains the cruelty you have exhibited to me, it will be ruined anyway. And, perhaps, it's not a life I'm wanting to be a part of." She stared hard into Elizabeth's eyes. "Kindly leave, Miss Howard, and may the good Lord grant you compassion before you die." Mary opened the door and Elizabeth whisked out.

Mary sat quietly that night in front of her window. She stared at the rooftops of Dublin until the sky grew lighter with the early morning. No tears had come. A part of her had died that evening and she would never be the same, for she knew that if she loved him, she would see him once more and once more only, to tell him that they would never be together again.

At their next meeting, Mary pulled away from Anthony as he tried to caress her.

"It's no use. It can't be, Anthony. It can't be. We'll need to stop seeing one another. There is no place in this

world for us. Your sister made me see that." Her voice
was sad, spiritless.

"Damn my sister, what can she know of our love?
My God, Mary, I've just found you. Don't ask me to let
you go. I love you. I need you." Again and again he
begged her to change her mind, but though he pleaded
and pleaded, she knew she couldn't give in. Finally he
gave up and left, sullen and dejected.

The next day Mary found this brief note slipped under
her door. "I'll always love you. I'll never forget you."
She carried it next to her heart for a long time. Then she
hid it in a little ivory box he had given her, for when she
decided she hadn't the heart to follow her brother to
America, she had found herself a local farmer to marry:
Frank O'Sullivan.

Oh, Frank was a good man, and she knew he loved
her dearly, but she could never find it within herself to
hold for him the same kind of passion that had once been
aroused in her by Lord Anthony Howard. So she made a
comfortable life for herself, tending to her husband and
making fancy linen lace, which she sold to the local
gentry. Some was even purchased by Anthony's new young
wife, an aristocrat from London.

By and by, Mary gave birth to a brood of three boys
and two girls. Terence was the oldest, a rowdy lad with a
broad smile that could turn into an angry scowl in an
instant. Then came Danny, taciturn and withdrawn except
when he was offered the opportunity to fight with his older
brother. After him came Bridget, a shy homebody, and
finally Nora and Sean, Mary's favorites. Sean loved music,
tales and poetry, and always gave his mother the most
charming smiles. He was a delight to have around. But
Nora was the most special of all.

Nora had inherited all of her mother's looks and
temperament. In fact, she and her mother were so close

that Mary sometimes felt as if she were reliving her own life through her daughter's. So now, as she held little Nora tightly against her, the thought of sending her daughter to America one day sparked a flame in her spirit, a burning determination to give her little girl a chance to have a better life, a chance Mary never had.

Chapter 1

The cutting of the turf was almost finished. The peat from the bogs was cut in oblong sods and piled high to dry, looking for all the world like huge black beasts. The clouds were hanging low, motionless, full to bursting with rain, waiting to dump torrents on the countryside. Mary paused for breath. Everything was still except for the pines dripping. The mist surrounded her. Even though it was midday, it seemed like an eerie night. She sighed a resigned, weary sigh. If she was going to reach Frank before the storm broke, she had to hurry. Knowing he would be against her decision, she sighed again, drew her shawl around her more tightly and shifted her basket to the other arm. Her shoes were already soaked through from the wet ground. Wet, she thought, and cold, always wet and cold and tired, always. Not for my Nora to be always wet, cold and tired. Nora was eighteen now and old enough to go to America. "Yes," Mary said to herself firmly. "It will be Nora and Sean who will go."

She stiffened, not just from the damp, but to harden

herself against the resistance she knew she'd meet from her husband. First, though, she had to find him. She wasn't sure just which part of the land he was working, and with the mists closing in, she could hardly see in front of her. She shifted her direction and began to climb the nearest dark, glistening rocks. Cold, wet, tired and sharp, like these rocks, is my life, Mary thought. No, not for my Nora, or my Sean. Dear God, where can you be, Frank?

As if he had heard her silent question, she heard Frank shout "Halloo, halloo, aye, Mary, I'm here. Stay there. I'll come to you. Don't try to come down through this weather." She could hear him coming toward her, even though she couldn't see him. "There you are, dear Mary," he said, patting her as he pulled himself up beside her. Where she was wet from cold and damp, he was perspiring as though the sun were out. "Thanks, love, for bringing lunch. It's hard work, the cutting and the stacking. Let's have a look at what you brought in the basket." He turned to her and smiled. His smile always warmed her, but today she could not soften her heart to him. He didn't seem to notice that she didn't return his smile. He simply went on talking.

Talk, talk, she thought. Nothing changes, but we talk and talk. There he sits, happy as the fool, mindless of how hard he works and how little we'll ever have. Frank *was* happy. He didn't mind the chopping, the milking, the plowing; he just loved the land. But Mary did not share that love. She heard a soft whinnying. Peering closely, she saw two of their farm horses huddling together for warmth. "Even the animals are always cold in this bleak place. I cannot let him condemn Nora and Sean to this life."

"Mary, Joseph and Patrick, why have you come out in this weather?" Frank asked.

"I need to talk to you. It's important and I didn't

want the children to hear." With seven of them, privacy was rare in the cottage.

"Well, what is it that's so important, love? Come sit down."

" 'Tis about the children going to America. We have passage for two now, thanks to Jim, so we need to be making plans," she said nervously.

"Jim is a good man, Mary, even if he drinks a bit too much. He's been a generous brother to you, and he can't be all that well-off himself what with Nellie and raising his own three children."

"He is good, bless him, for all his faults." She fidgeted with the fringe on her shawl.

"I've often wondered if Terence has inherited his love of the poteen from his Uncle Jim," Frank mused.

"Oh, nonsense, Frank. The love of drink isn't inherited," she answered impatiently.

Frank's musing look turned into a frown, and she realized she was antagonizing her husband instead of putting him in the proper mood to receive her news. Faith, she thought, I should know how to handle him after all these years. Then she changed her approach.

"Terence is a good boy, Frank. He's a bit spirited, is all. They're all good children, really. We've been lucky." She reached for his hand and added, "I've been lucky too." They sat silently for a moment. Her fondness for Frank was real. If it wasn't the love she had felt but once in her life, it was nevertheless a warm and caring relationship.

She continued nervously. "I'll not beat about the bush, Frank. The two children I want to send to America are none of our three oldest. I want to send Nora and Sean."

He gave her a long look to be certain he had heard her right.

"Yes, I said Sean and Nora," she said, and she hurried on, "they're our smartest and most ambitious."

He looked her right in the eye and said, "Have you taken total leave of your senses, woman? They're too young to go alone."

"They're not that young, Frank, and they have Jim and Nellie waiting in America."

"I don't understand what you're thinking. What kind of opportunities will there be for a sixteen-year-old boy and an eighteen-year-old girl?"

"That's the point, Frank. They're not yet set in their ways. If any of our children can make their own opportunities, it is those two." She had spoken as calmly as possible.

He sat very still for a few moments. She was lulled into thinking she was making progress, but when he turned his eyes to her, they were blazing with anger. "You talk of opportunities. I've heard of the so-called opportunities in America. They work in the sweatshops, twelve, thirteen hours a day, the women and children along with the men. And think what could happen to a young, lonely woman like Nora. She'd be easy prey for men. She could become something awful, she'd be taken advantage of." He was hiding his real fears of prostitution or rape in vague, general terms, afraid even to voice them; but Mary knew what he meant. She had thought of these very real possibilities and had weighed them in her heart.

"Frank, please. It's not so bad as you think. Yes, they will work long hours. We do here too, but here there is no opportunity for anything else. Our only opportunity is to survive. I want more for them and more for us. Nora has learned to make the loveliest lace in the county. Her talent will stand her well in America."

"Thousands of Irish lace-makers have gone to America. They live crowded in cellars with the company of rats and there are those *gombeen* men who take advantage of immigrants, steal their money and fool them.''

"Frank, much of what you're saying was true for those who fled from famine years ago, but it's 1900. Things are better now. Jim says so in his letter to us." She hadn't known how opposite their views of America were. She saw it as the land of opportunity, and he as a hellhole of ruin.

"Terence is the oldest, and it's usually the oldest or next oldest who goes," he persisted. "Why do you want to change the right order of things?"

"You know why Terence wouldn't be right, don't you?" she asked softly.

He shook his head and a cowlick of red hair fell on his forehead. She wanted to brush it back tenderly, but she knew he was too angry.

"You're right about that, Mary, at least till he's calming down some, till he stops his drinking and brawling. But even for all that he's a good farmer."

"Frank, he is a great farmer. He's the one who should inherit the farm. You need him here." She had seen her opening.

"So, then it's Danny and Bridget who should be going. They're next in line. That's how it should be, and by God, Mary, that's the way it will be!" he shouted. "Woman, hear me, that's the way it will be, and I'm not wanting to hear more on the subject."

"Bridget will be marrying soon, and Danny has never expressed a desire to leave Ireland. But Sean wants to be a writer, Frank, and you know how poorly writers fare here under the mean eye of the British censors. I only want what is best for all our children."

"You know what's best," he hissed. "You always know, you always have the answer, don't you? I've always known, Mary Matthews, why you married me." His voice rushed on, almost menacing. "It was to escape your Aunt Ella's farm and all her meanness. After your father was killed, your Dublin life ended. You had no money so you couldn't stay there or emigrate. When I came along, I was to you the best of a bad lot. I could read, I was kind, I wasn't bad-looking and I could get you out of that hellhole. So, even though I wasn't of your station, you said yes when I asked you to marry me. I could get you out of Kilclare, but you've never thought me your equal, Mary, never." His voice trailed off, spent and weary. His words were like a cold, hard slap across the face.

My God, how he has resented me, she thought, and I've been blind to it all these years. She knew Frank loved her deeply, but his anger and frustrations were coming out for the first time.

"Frank, you can't believe that I married you for those reasons. I married you because you were kind and sensitive and loving. 'Tis true you haven't my schooling, Frank, but that's an accident of fate, and you are more than my equal in many other more important ways, like patience, understanding and loyalty. And Frank," she continued, "remember that I came to the marriage with some money from my weaving and lace-making. That money was going to take me to America. I was planning on going, and then I met you. I married you for love, Frank, not for escape." She stopped talking and put her hand over his. He didn't pull away. They sat quietly for a few moments. "Frank, I didn't mean that I was the only one knowing the right thing to do. I'm sorry. I guess I'm so desperately wanting them to have a better life, a richer life, that I've lost my sense of balance. I know you want to do the right thing as much as I."

A heavy silence engulfed them. She spoke again. "I'm just trying to point out my reasons." Still he made no answer. "Bridget will be a wonderful wife and mother.

'Tis what she's wanting from life. She's after being very fond of Kevin O'Riordan, and he of her. She'll get the dowry, Frank, and then what's to happen to Nora? She'll have nothing. And Nora is driven. You know how ambitious she is and how she wants more out of life than there is here."

He turned to her with a strange look on his face. "So do you, Mary, so do you. It's why you work with the Sisters of Charity, educate your children, and embroider the lace at night to sell to strangers. You want more than you think I can provide. And you're always filling Nora's head with that uppity nonsense about wanting her to be better than she is."

Mary remained quiet. He knew her very well, better than she had ever realized. "Is that so wrong then, Frank?"

He looked long and hard at her. The color had drained from his face. The anger had diminished somewhat. "I'm guessing not, Mary, but it seems hopeless. If we'll be trying, we'll be needing to try another way, for I'll not allow Sean and Nora to be the ones to go." And with that, he jumped down from the rock and strode into the fields.

Chapter 2

Yellow gorse and purple and red wildflowers covered the hills like a beautiful patchwork quilt. Nora's heart leapt with joy. Teardrop, her favorite mount, was ready for a run and was letting her know. She bridled the filly as she watched Barney and Kevin, Lord Anthony's stableboys, ride double back to the stables. As they disappeared from sight, she gave the horse full rein and rode wild and free. Adding to the heady feeling of freedom was the knowledge that the rest of the day was hers to do what she pleased. School was out, chores were done and she had laid the groundwork for her absence. She thanked God in her prayers for these moments, and as she rode, she thought fondly of that day seven years before when Terence had arranged for these secret rides she took on horses belonging to the local British gentry.

At sixteen Terence had been almost six feet tall, broad-shouldered and slender, with his mother's dark hair. His eyes were a muted grey about which he was often teased, because no one else in the family had that strange grey color. But his eyes had the O'Sullivan mischief in them, and in combination with his romantic profile and open, winning smile, he was a handsome lad, whom people took to at once. His brothers and sisters knew, though, that when the soft grey eyes smoldered and became like steel, they'd best be getting out of his way, for the sparks were sure to fly.

This day Terence had been sent by his father to the village to see about a wheel repair, and his little sister Nora had badgered him into taking her with him. As Gareth, their big grey workhorse, pulled them in the common cart along the hedgerows brilliant with fuchsia, they passed the southernmost tip of Lord Anthony's vast estate. Nora suddenly caught sight of the most thrilling thing she had ever seen. A group of Lord Anthony's guests were riding to the hounds. Their red jackets stood out against the misty sky and dazzled Nora's eyes. The sleekness and speed of the horses, so different from old Gareth, and the beauty of the sight, made her catch her breath. She bolted out of the wagon and ran to watch.

"Terence, what would they be doing? Look at those wonderful animals. They don't look like our horses. And the women sitting on the side of their saddles. Is it dangerous? What are they chasing? Why are they dressed in those beautiful red jackets? Oh, Terence, could I ever be doing that? Would I be allowed to do it?" The words flew from her mouth breathlessly.

"Faith, Nora, one question at a time. I didn't know you hadn't seen the hunt before."

He explained as much as he knew about riding to the hounds, but added bitterly, "Sure, for the gentry, horses are more important than anything else in this country, even over farming the land. It seems they're always chasing after something: foxes, hares, stag, otters and anything else that moves. The damnable Brits would hunt us down too, if it weren't against the law."

In her excitement, she missed the bitterness in his voice. Her violet eyes blazed as she turned to him, and he had never seen her look so intense. "Could I be riding like that, Terence, on a beautiful horse like that? Not like old Gareth, though I do love him. Is there anywhere I could be riding? I'll die if I don't." She rambled on with the life-and-death passion only a ten-year-old could know.

Treating her outburst with respect, he answered slowly and thoughtfully. "Well, my treasure, I don't know. I'll have to be thinking on it. Is it that important to you?"

"Oh, yes, yes. I really want to ride. You can't call sitting on Gareth as he moves his old joints along riding. I've never seen anything so beautiful. I'd be good, I know I would."

He looked at her, seeing beyond the excitement of the moment. "Yes, I think you would."

After all, why couldn't his darling sister be riding to the hounds like the fancy Ascendancy group of ladies? Why couldn't she indeed? Terence thought. A plan began to form in his mind. While it was not likely for Nora to ride to the hounds, it might be possible for her to ride a fine horse, one of Lord Anthony's own. He chuckled, and mischief replaced the anger in his intelligent grey eyes as he looked at her fondly.

"Nora, me dear, I've an idea that will get you a horse to ride, but you're to tell no one, no one ever. Understand?"

Her eyes glistened with excitement. "I understand, Terence, sure upon my soul. You have my word."

For all his hatred of Lord Anthony and all his ilk, Terence had befriended many of the lord's stable hands over the years. He spoke to two of them, Barney and Kevin, about his idea to let Nora secretly take a horse out for a run now and then. " 'Tis a shame not to have these beautiful mounts exercised as often as they should be."

Kevin and Barney agreed, but were quite anxious at first about Nora's riding. Terence calmed their fears, and perhaps a little of the rebel that is in every Irishman spurred them on. They were responsible for exercising the animals, and it was planned that they would take out two horses, meet Nora on a distant moor, let her ride one horse, and meet her later to return the horse. It was a simple plan, and it worked admirably, for there were so many comings and goings and activities at the stables that one horse couldn't be missed easily.

"She's only ridden our old plow horse, so she'll be needing some instruction," Terence told them.

"We'll be taking care of her, and we'll teach her what we know," Barney volunteered.

They were both good riders. "Fine, fine, Barney," Terence replied. "Be careful with her, and I needn't be telling you to keep it under your hats."

"Faith, no, our lips are sealed," Kevin said, and he gave little Nora a wink.

Her thoughts snapped back to the present, for as she gained her stride, she suddenly became aware that someone was riding behind her. Maybe it's just Barney or Kevin, she thought nervously, but they had never ridden after her, and they would have called out. She braced her shoulders and held her head high. There was nothing to do but try and carry it off as best she could. The other rider came alongside. She turned to meet the steady gaze and curious smile of William Howard, Lord Anthony's only son. She recognized him instantly, although she had only seen him from a distance on a couple of occasions.

"What a glorious day, Miss O'Sullivan," he said, staring at her boldly.

"How do you know my name?" she asked.

"You ride superbly. It is a pleasure watching you," he continued, ignoring her question, but thinking, this is a pleasant surprise, the skinny little O'Sullivan girl has grown up to be a beauty.

She thanked him and waited for him to confront her regarding the horse. But she sensed immediately that he was not going to broach the subject. That's what being a gentleman must mean, she thought thankfully. He does not want to embarrass me. His presence intrigued her. She could see he was slender and tall, over six feet, as he held himself erect in the saddle. His blond hair was tousled, his pale green eyes alert and curious. His profile was aristocratic. He had a long, aquiline nose, high cheekbones, and a sharp chin. He was handsome in that ancient, lordly, Saxon way.

She smiled at him in spite of her nervousness. " 'Tis truly a glorious day, Lord William, and I'm pleased to be meeting you finally," she said with great warmth and a hint of amusement.

"And I you. Please call me William, forget the title. May I ride with you for a while, Miss O'Sullivan?" It was more of a command than a question. As they rode along, he glanced at her from the corner of his eye. By God, she was beautiful! And to think that just this morning he'd wondered what he'd do to keep from being bored to death this summer. There was nothing William liked more than a pretty face.

" 'Twould be my pleasure, William. Please do." She had quite charmed him, that she knew. He was a fine rider, she observed. She was enjoying the undercurrent of excitement, the thrill of a handsome new acquaintance, and the thwarting, if only for a moment, of the whole Irish social structure.

They stopped after a while and rested near a stream,

letting the horses drink. She had brought some bread and cheese. "William, you must be famished. Are you as hungry as I am? If you are, fetch some water and I'll divide the cheese." She bustled about, never doubting for a moment that he would not join her.

He protested, but she insisted.

" 'Tis more fun to be sharing, so don't be a goose, sit down and eat."

He laughed. She's an amusing little thing, he thought.

Conversation flowed. They laughed and talked and forgot all else. How easy he was to talk to, she thought, how interesting. And he seemed not to recognize Teardrop as a horse from his own stables, or at least he was gentleman enough not to mention it.

Suddenly, she looked at the sun low in the sky. "Good Lord, how time has passed. I must be getting back." She was nervous that Kevin would be waiting, that he'd be discovered, that the whole plan was finally about to fall apart. She wasn't sure how to handle the moment, so she spoke with her characteristic directness. "I'll be needing to ride back alone, William."

He didn't disagree. He grabbed her arm, almost roughly, and said just as directly, "I'd like very much to see you again, Nora." He gazed steadily into her eyes.

She stared back at him, withdrew her arm. "I think not. It's not suitable, you being who you are."

The need for secrecy was obvious to both of them, and she found she resented that fact. He sensed her warmth disappear, and curiosity made him want desperately to see her again. He didn't even know why, but somehow she had made a powerful impression on him. Her beauty was one thing, but what he had been unprepared for was her wit and warmth. No one had ever asked such questions of him, or listened so intently to his answers. Most people recognized him for the shallow person he was, but she had made him feel interesting. He liked that. It was an encounter like no other he had ever had. The superficial London and Dublin girls, with their endless talk of new dresses, balls, and who was marrying whom, bored him. But he had accepted the fact that, quite by accident, he had met another kind of girl. By God, he thought, she's fascinating. I must have her.

"Nora, you're right, I know we shouldn't meet. It is difficult, but I find I like you very much. I've never spoken to a girl like you before. I want to talk to you again. Whatever difficulties there may be, I want to see you again."

"Oh William, what blarney you're speaking," she said, softening, for she felt a flush of pleasure and was finding him attractive.

He seized the moment of weakening. "It's no blarney. That's only for you Irish. It's the truth, plain and simple."

She sensed that he meant it. And she realized she wanted to see him, too. Am I to pile one deception on another? she wondered. As if answering herself, she said, "Yes," trying to keep her voice from quavering.

"Yes what, Nora? Yes, it's the blarney, or yes, you'll see me again?"

"Yes, I'll see you again. Tuesday at the Fairies' Cave. You bring the lunch this time." Nora laughed, then gathered her skirts, swung up into the saddle, spun around and rode off without looking back.

Chapter 3

The following Tuesday, Nora approached the Fairies' Cave with her heart racing, her cheeks glowing and her hair flying wild and shimmering behind her. She was worried both that he wouldn't come, and at the same time that he would. Many young men had tried to court her, and she had attended several of the village crossroad dances with them, but none of the callow village boys had captured her imagination, or given her the excitement she had felt during the few hours spent with William. As she approached the cave, she saw him sitting on the grass. He was more handsome than she remembered. He jumped up when he saw Teardrop approaching, and caught his breath at the beauty of her. They were both awkward, but delighted to see one another.

"Nora, how glad I am you came," he greeted, surprising himself at how much he meant it.

"Faith, William, wasn't I after telling you I'd be here?" She was straightforward. " 'Twasn't easy, but I'm a woman of my word." She smiled down at him. He helped her off Teardrop, and as he did so, she saw that he had laid the most beautiful picnic on the grass. A green and blue tartan plaid blanket covered the ground. Two lovely Lowestoft plates, real Georgian silver and two smoky antique crystal glasses were set on the blanket. There was smoked turkey, ham, chutney and beaten biscuit, almost all of which Nora had never eaten before.

"Saints preserve us, William, 'tis a feast. What a lot of trouble you've gone to." They ate and drank, talked and laughed, forgetting about the time. As they ate, he told her of a wedding he had attended that weekend.

"Nora, it was quite the most amusing thing. The grandson of Lord Scott suddenly rushed out of church just as the vows were being said. Everyone thought he was a brokenhearted reject of the bride's, but he wasn't. Actually, he happened to see a young boy teasing a goat standing on the side of the road. He trounced the young boy, gave the goat a tidbit, came back in and resumed his place. Of course, all eyes were on him and the ceremony had stopped, but he seemed apparently quite satisfied with his deed. The minister then said, 'I believe we may now resume, am I correct, since justice has been done?' There was laughter, but also many looks of disapproval. But Nora, I thought it helped liven the usual tedious ceremony with all those silly promises. Personally, I think it will be the last thing the groom will find to laugh about for some time to come."

She laughed, mistaking his cynicism for a joke. No one else had ever laughed at his stories, for he was considered quite humorless, too preoccupied with himself.

"Well, those with the looks of disapproval are often those who feel disapproval is expected of them, and you know, William, they miss a great deal of the fun in life. I like the unexpected, don't you?"

"I do, Nora, very much," he replied, suddenly aware

that he did, never having thought of it before. He paused for a moment. "Our meeting was unexpected. You are unexpected. I am very much enjoying the unexpected at this moment." He gazed at her with his pale, penetrating eyes. He enjoyed the feeling that he was saying something significant, and he knew that she was the cause of it.

She felt things were becoming a trifle serious, so she jumped up and ran to the horse. "I'll race you to O'Riordan's still."

He jumped up after her, and they raced hard and fast to the still. They arrived neck and neck.

" 'Tis a tie," she exclaimed. "I'll be beating you next time, wait and see." She blushed for a moment, fearing that she was being too forward by talking about meeting again.

But he answered, "I was hoping there'd be a next time, Nora."

Whenever they could arrange these meetings, they did. Other things in her life now seemed inconsequential. She only cared about that next time they would meet. Nora worried about their meetings. Why do I do this? she wondered. He's not of my class. If we're found out, I'll be in all kinds of trouble about riding the horses and seeing William. Oh, why am I doing it?

On his part, all William knew was that this was a wonderful new feeling for him. When they were together, he felt interesting and amusing. She didn't brush him aside, as did the others who knew him as the spoiled child he was, and because she loved him, she didn't see him as he was. The feeling of importance she gave him went to his head and he wanted to keep seeing her, at least until he had his way with her. She hadn't responded to his advances, which alternately irritated and intrigued him. Plainly, his title and position had not made her give in to his advances, as many of the village girls had done. Nor had all his flattery moved her, so he decided to try another tactic.

One day when they were riding through the woods, he asked, "Nora, have you seen Champion, our show horse?"

"Oh yes, but from a distance. What a glorious animal, William. You are lucky to have him,"

"Would you like to ride him, Nora?"

"Oh, you're daft. I couldn't be riding him," she answered, but she felt a surge of excitement at the thought.

"Yes, you can. I can arrange it. I would like to see you ride him. You are such a fine rider, and he needs an expert with a gentle touch."

"William, I'll not be fooling with you. Of course, I can think of almost nothing I'd like better." She thought to herself, why shouldn't I ride him? I *am* a fine rider. I'll not even ask how he intends to go about it.

"We'll meet day after tomorrow, Nora, and I'll have Champion with me, I promise," he said.

"I'll be liking that, William, very much," she returned, failing to mask her excitement.

She rode back to Kevin almost in a frenzy. He noticed her excitement, but when he asked her if all was well, she reassured him.

" 'Tis nothing, Kevin dear. Just a wonderful ride, a really wonderful ride. Thank you, and Barney too, for your kindness." She smiled at him affectionately. "No wonder my sister is liking you."

He blushed.

Her mother noticed her mood of exhilaration as well as her preoccupation. "Nora, you're not with us lately. What is it?"

"Oh, Ma, it's nothing, I'm just happy school is finished and I have some free time, that's all. Am I neglecting anything?"

"No, no, you're not neglecting anything. You're just different, that's all," Mary said, suddenly noticing how very beautiful and vibrant Nora looked.

Mary thought, she must have a beau. What else could make her look so radiant? She made a mental note to find out. The thought worried her, because a young man in her life might make her wish to stay here instead of go to America. And Mary felt the time was drawing near.

"I'm trembling like a silly child," Nora said to herself as she caught sight of William and Champion some days later.

"Faith, and he's beautiful, William. I've never seen a more beautiful horse. He has a proud, regal bearing, and by the look of him, he must be the descendant of Kings." They laughed, and as she mounted Champion, she looked at him very seriously. "William, this is an honor. I want you to know I appreciate it. I do."

And they rode off. It was the ride of her lifetime. Champion responded to her as if they had been horse and rider for years.

As she galloped up, William remarked, "I never saw such a glorious sight. You were made for that horse, Nora. He knows it too. He responded to you. He gave you everything he had. He's never done it for me."

"Do you think so?" Nora was beside herself.

Now, whenever they met, Champion was with him. One day William said, "Nora, I've hurt my foot. Take Champion for a good run. I'll rest, and set up the picnic." He suddenly seized her by the shoulders. "I love to see you happy like this. You've become very dear to me, darling Nora."

She stared back at him with her violet eyes burning into his. "And you to me, sweet William. But I hate it that no one can know we're friends. It's crazy, isn't it?"

"We're not crazy," he said reassuringly. "Go ride, Nora."

William felt slightly out of control. Could I actually care for this girl? he wondered. He'd meant this only as an interesting diversion. He wanted to make sure it didn't turn into anything else.

Nora took Champion for a long ride and tried to deal with her tangled emotions. When she returned, it was starting to rain heavily. They moved everything into the cave and stood shivering. As William put his arms around her, she flinched.

"What's wrong, dear Nora?" he asked.

"Oh William, I'm frightened. We shouldn't be together. It's wrong. You know it too. We both know it. Why are we doing it?" she asked innocently.

His eyes had an amused look. "Because, beautiful one, we're very fond of one another. It happens now and then, you know. Haven't you been enjoying it?"

"Aye and nay, William. I cry in my pillow at night, one moment for happiness and the next for misery. Aye, I am so fond of you, and nay, because it's hopeless, William."

He didn't like it when she cried. It made him feel guilty when she started thinking they had any kind of future together. "Don't say such things, dear girl," he whispered. "Nothing is hopeless. Believe me."

"Oh, I do. I do. That is, I want to."

His response had put her somewhat at ease. Seeing she was more relaxed, he turned her head to his and bent down and kissed her. At first his lips barely met hers, but then they were locked in a long, wild, passionate kiss. Nora responded with all the desire of youth, and then breathlessly pulled away from him.

"It's too confusing, William. I'm caring too much." She ran out of the cave, tore the reins from the low bush, swung, jumped on Teardrop and rode off. Tears streamed down her cheeks. The rain pelted her face, her jacket and her hair.

"Little Teardrop," she sobbed, "my name should be yours today."

One evening at dinner, a few days later, Terence, who had obviously stopped at Mulligan's on the way home, had a story about Kevin.

"Well, his high and mighty lordship has fired Kevin from the stables."

"Why, Terence?" Bridget asked, very upset. "He's been there since he could barely reach the stirrups. Why would he be fired? He's such a good person, so responsible." She liked him very much, and had been walking out with him lately.

Nora just sat silently, looking at Terence. She had always been afraid he might blurt out the truth one day after he had had a few drinks, but bless him, he never had. She waited for his answer.

"Well, it seems their show horse Champion is Kevin's responsibility, and he was seen being ridden by a stranger without Lord Anthony's permission." Nora felt a surge of panic. She dropped her fork.

"What's wrong, Nora? You're often acting so queerly lately. I'm not knowing you anymore," Bridget remarked. Both girls were upset about Kevin for different reasons.

"I'm, I'm sorry," she stammered. "I haven't been feeling well." She sat staring at her plate. It's my fault that Kevin's been fired, she thought miserably. I've only been interested in myself, and even now I was only concerned about whether I had been found out.

Bridget spoke up with tears in her eyes. "What will the O'Riordans do? Kevin's pa has the fever and Kevin's pay was putting the food on their table."

Terence interrupted her. "It seems no great crime since the horse was returned and is in fine fettle. I'm hard put to understand the harm done. Why take a lad's job for no reason?" But he added sarcastically, "Sure, the landed gentry are knowing best when 'tis right to fire a fine, loyal stableboy."

Nora excused herself and left the table.

Mary was perturbed at Terence's comments. "If 'twas Kevin's responsibility, then he has to pay the price, Terence. Anything the gentry does is wrong in your eyes. You need a little balance in your thinking. Don't be so quick to condemn, lad. Have a little compassion."

His face, already flushed from drink, now burned red. "Compassion!" he shouted. "Tell me of compassion, what compassion did they have for you? Ma, you're defending them always. How can you, after what they did to your parents? Of all people, how can you be, as you say, fair? They murdered your mother, your father, your brothers, and still you take their side. It's beyond me, totally beyond me!"

Frank and the boys had entered from the fields and had heard Terence's outburst.

"Young man, take your anger out of this house," Frank commanded. "How dare you cause your mother such pain. Go fight your radical fight somewhere else. I'll not be having you tear our lives apart. Get out and sober up!"

"I was intending to do just that," Terence replied angrily, and he pushed past them and left the house.

The rest of the family sat silently. Mary was crying as she went to her room, and Frank followed her. Bridget and Danny and Sean bustled about, trying to keep busy, trying to forget the incident. Nora listened to everything in abject misery. She felt it was all her fault, and she vowed that, at the very least, she'd get Kevin's job back for him. She would meet with William tomorrow. He would know what to do.

William was waiting for her, and as she dismounted, she confronted him immediately.

"Do you know, William, that your father ordered Kevin fired because someone saw me riding Champion alone that day?"

"Yes, Nora, I heard. Don't worry. No one knows it was you," he said, misunderstanding her concern.

"William, an innocent person was fired because of me. You need to explain the situation to your father and get Kevin his job back."

He could see she was upset. "Nora, darling, calm down. He'll get another job. I can't tell Father that I allowed someone to ride Champion. *I'm* not even supposed to ride him without permission."

She was disturbed, because she was seeing for the first time another side of William that she didn't know. "William, did Kevin saddle Champion for you each time you rode him?"

"Yes, Nora. Why are you asking that?"

"Well, it means that he released the horse to you, is that right?"

"Yes, it is, but what are you getting at?" He was annoyed at the turn the conversation had taken.

"I'm getting at the fact that obviously Kevin covered up for you and never brought your name into it. He probably knew you were not supposed to ride without permission and so, for doing you a favor, he lost his job." Nora stood with her hands on her hips and looked at William.

He could see she was gravely concerned, but he tried to make light of it. "Nora, you are so beautiful when you're angry."

"Never be minding that," she snapped at him. "I'm asking you, William, to confess to your father that it was you who took Champion and let a friend ride him, so that Kevin may be getting his job back."

"I can't do that, Nora," he said coldly, "for he'll want to know who the friend was. And it won't do either of us any good if I tell him."

Nora looked at him curiously. "May I not even be your friend, William? Am I not good enough even for that?"

William was apprehensive. He had never seen her like this. "Nora, now calm down. We are fools to make such a commotion over a stableboy's job," he answered, becoming angry at her for making him uncomfortable.

At that moment, all the differences between them came rushing at her. She saw that he didn't understand what she was trying to tell him. He didn't care at all about Kevin's job or whether Kevin's family had food on the table or a roof over their heads. All she knew at that moment was that he couldn't see her point, or how important it was to her. She thought of the radical ideas Terence was always expounding and suddenly knew what he meant. Knowing that argument was useless, she looked hard at him and, risking everything, she delivered her ultimatum. "William, I'm sorry you're feeling this way. I see it differently from you. To me, 'tis not just a stableboy's job. 'Tis not even that it's a friend who'll be losing everything without the pay. It's just that we can't let someone else take the blame for what we've done."

William remained sullen and silent. Nora's heart ached as she continued. "If you're not telling your father, William, then I'll be needing to do it. Which would you prefer?" Her voice was soft but firm.

"My God, I can't believe this, Nora. Don't be such a

righteous goose. I'll pay off Kevin. We can't tell the world about us. Do you think I want my father to know I've been seeing you?"

She felt a shudder course through her entire body, but the words she had dreaded were out in the open.

He remained angrily silent for a few moments and finally replied. "All right, Nora, you win. I'll explain to my father. If he asks who my friend is, I'll tell him. If he doesn't, I won't. I'll ask him to reinstate Kevin." He knew that he was defeated and that she would do as she said, for she was stronger and far more courageous than he was. This was partly why she appealed to him.

"Thank you, William. I'm sorry to cause you pain, but it was necessary. We can't let someone else suffer for our wrongdoing." Her victory was hollow. Their relationship was subtly altered, for she had shamed him into doing the right thing. But she also knew that she had to do it.

Later that evening, William entered his father's study anxiously. His hands were trembling. How had he ever gotten into such a situation? he wondered. Surely no village girl was worth all this. He had an urge to bolt the room. Too late now. If he didn't tell his father, Nora would. He was determined not to stutter. He always stuttered when he had to tell the truth. He didn't like being in trouble. He had decided early in life that lying was easier. No way out of this, he decided.

"Father, I need to ask you a favor."

"Yes, William?" Anthony looked up at his only son. "How can I help you?"

"Father, I would like to ask you to reinstate Kevin, the stableboy."

"May I ask why?" Anthony said, alerted by this unusual behavior. He had never known his son to show concern for anyone other than himself.

"Because it was I who ordered Champion out of the stable. It was I who took him out riding several times without your permission." He paused for a moment. "I should have told you sooner," he added weakly.

"Yes, you should have," Anthony said, thinking how exceptional it was for William to be doing this. It was not like him at all. Anthony, a good judge of character, had been disappointed in his only son. He was charming and intelligent enough. And he performed his few duties reasonably well, but Anthony felt there was no real substance to the boy, no depth of character. And he had seen evidence of William's weakness in diverse ways. Here he was, however, doing something out of character. Anthony was intrigued. Could anyone change his personality at age twenty-two? He hardly thought so. "However, William, it's better to do it at this late date than not at all." He didn't want to discourage whatever noble acts which might follow this one. "Under the circumstances, I will, of course, reinstate Kevin O'Riordan. I always liked the young man, and now I like him even better, for his loyalty to you. As a matter of fact, a small raise in salary might be in order."

William relaxed, assuming his usual arrogant pose, and was surprised at how well things had gone. Perhaps this wasn't so bad after all. He smiled, thanked his father, and rose to leave the study.

"One moment, William," his father called after him.

"Yes, Father?"

"I know you're telling the truth about your taking Champion, but who was the stranger riding him?"

Anthony's question made William stop in his tracks, and he suddenly wished he had let the damned boy be fired. Nora and her lofty ideals. Well, I'm in for it now, he thought. "A friend," he stammered. "A very fine rider, so I thought it would be all right, sir."

"If it's not all right for you to ride him without permission, how did you arrive at the conclusion that it would be acceptable for a stranger to ride him? William, please answer me that."

"My friend is a better rider than I," he said, his voice becoming shakier by the minute.

"And this friend is also a woman? Is that not correct, lad? At least the description seemed to imply that," Anthony persisted.

"Yes, a woman, Father, but, but a very fine rider," he repeated, stammering again. "I'm sorry, I won't do it again." He thought to himself, if you'll just let me go now and leave me alone, I'll never, ever see Nora for one moment, ever for the rest of my life. I knew I should have lied. His feeling of smugness over how well things had gone at the beginning of the conversation evaporated. He was perspiring, and now he knew he'd stutter for sure.

Anthony sat staring at William for a time, and then he looked down at his folded hands. "I'm waiting, son."

William's color paled, but he answered with as much casualness as he could muster. "My friend is Nora O'Sullivan. I had seen her ride several times, and she was so good, I thought it would be good for Champion to have a gentle, consistent rider instead of incompetent stableboys."

Anthony was shocked. He was afraid to look up, fearing his eyes would betray him. He remained silent for a long time. His son was obviously smitten with Mary's own daughter. What a devilishly strange world, he thought. "I think I better meet your friend Nora, son. Please bring her to see me," he ordered, wanting to meet Mary's daughter.

"Oh, Father, she's done no harm. Please, I am the only one to blame," William said, uttering one of his first really courageous remarks.

"Yes, I'm certain of that. But I'd like to meet the young woman, William, nevertheless. Good day." He looked down at the papers on his desk and resumed his work.

Chapter 4

"Aye, so you want me to meet your father, William? Of course, I'll be going." Nora had steeled herself against William, shocked as she had been by his lack of strength and ashamed that he didn't want to admit he knew her. But she loved him, and in the way of girls in love, she excused his every fault and forgave him. He is proud of me, she reasoned. Doesn't he want his father to meet me? She decided she must have wronged him, thinking that he didn't care about Kevin. Wasn't he her darling William, and hadn't he done the thing that had saved Kevin's job?

Though she had lost some respect for William, she thought she had judged him harshly, for he had indeed done a noble thing. Her passion for him was burning as strongly as ever. She would respond to his touch, his caress, his embrace, as if her other life had never been, for when she was with him, *he* was her life. It amazed her that she had been able to thwart him for what she believed in. She only knew she could behave in no other way.

He looked at her admiringly. "You're a plucky lass,

Nora. You seem to be afraid of nothing. I'm not quite that way," he confessed miserably, as if she hadn't already discovered that, or as if by saying it, it would somehow seem more acceptable. Why, he thought, do I want this girl so badly? Other girls are so easy to bed, so eager for me. He knew why, as he looked at her. This is no simple farm girl. This one's different. She's a challenge.

"Yes, I know darling, but we're all different. We're having different ways of doing things, and you have other good points," she said tactfully, almost believing it, as she slipped into his arms, enjoying his kisses and caresses. Through William, Nora was discovering another part of herself, the sensual side.

She arrived at the big house one rainy afternoon, and Emerson showed her into a lovely sitting room. The walls were light green with darker trim at the joints. At one end of the room was a large picture window. She thought that what she had seen of the rest of the mansion had been heavy and dreary in comparison.

Lord Anthony entered, tall, attractive and imposing. His blond hair was greying, but he had the same sensitive, pale eyes that she loved in William.

"Young woman, I've seen you from a distance from time to time, and I'm now happy to have the pleasure of meeting you in person," he said gallantly. His eyes drank in her beauty. She looked so much like Mary that he couldn't take his eyes from her face.

"Thank you, Lord Anthony. I am pleased to meet you too."

"Nora, I understand you are an excellent rider. My son tells me that is why he allowed you to ride Champion."

She felt so at ease with him that she answered him with no shyness or reserve. "I hope you'll forgive me for riding him. I know what he means to you. He's a wonderful horse, sir."

He noted that while she had asked his forgiveness, she hadn't actually said she was sorry. "I'm sure you're sorry about Champion," he ventured, pressing for a more thorough apology.

"Oh, no sir, I'm not sorry. They were the best rides of my life, and I believe in my heart I may be the best rider he has ever had on his back. Forgive my boldness, Lord Anthony, but if it was good for me, it was better for Champion."

He was astonished by her assertion, but found himself quite willing to believe it. "Well, you're nothing if not honest, young woman. I admire that," he remarked with an amused look.

"Thank you, Lord Anthony. While I'm happy to meet you, I'm wondering why it is your wish to meet me?"

She had caught him off guard, but he smiled at her forthright approach. She is her mother's daughter, he thought to himself. "I wanted to meet William's friend, whom he told me was such a fine rider." He wanted to ask if she and William were more than friends, but somehow he couldn't. He was afraid she would tell him the truth, and he knew he couldn't handle the truth. William might be taking advantage of this beautiful, spirited person, he thought painfully. "Nora, whether you know it or not, you have challenged me. You have asserted that you are the best rider who's ever been on Champion. I would like to see you ride him. May we arrange it?"

"Oh, aye, of course. I'd love to, I'd really love to."

He smiled at her, for she was suddenly acting like a delightful child instead of a very assured, very perceptive woman. I shouldn't condemn my son for wanting this girl, he thought. God, how he had wanted the mother! If only he had been braver, and not given up so easily, this child could be his daughter. He knew without a doubt that she was the reason William had, for once in his life, acted in a noble manner, and he blessed her for it, but shuddered at the possibility that she might not know William for what he really was. As wise as she seemed, had she resisted his charms? Dear Lord, let the answer be yes.

As they said good-bye, he took her hands in his. "You're very beautiful, Nora, and a very special girl."

"Good-bye, Lord Anthony. It's been wonderful meeting you. And I'll be riding Champion for you as soon as you wish it. Thank you."

Her thoughts were reeling as she walked home. What a fine, kind man was Lord Anthony. I never met anyone quite like him before. Life certainly takes odd twists. Who would have ever thought that I would have Lord Anthony's permission to ride the finest horse in County Cork? Sure, and won't Terence be hating all this.

Next time they met, Nora greeted William gaily, throwing herself into his arms. She decided that she had completely misjudged him. Because she loved him, she saw him as she wanted him to be. She had a forgiving nature, so his cruelty and denial were already forgotten. Her eyes were sparkling and confident. "I liked your father, William, and I guess you know he wants to see me ride."

"He likes you too, Nora. After your meeting, he said to me, rather stuffily, 'Your friend, Miss O'Sullivan, has a great deal of charm and wit.' That's a lot for him to say in the way of a compliment, honestly." He paused and looked at her. He couldn't believe that she had not yet succumbed to him. His lust for her was mixed with frustration. It continuously puzzled him that he didn't just abandon his pursuit of her. He could have chosen any other village girl for his summer amusement. But William was not used to anyone saying no to him. He was determined to have her.

"Nora, I've never seen you look so radiant, so beautiful." He felt desire coursing through his body.

His look was a little frightening and at the same time thrilling to her. As he reached to pull her to him, the heavy raindrops of a sudden storm started to fall on them.

"Quickly," Nora urged as the storm grew more violent. "We must ride for cover. Hurry, hurry, we must get to the cave."

It was quite dark in the cave. William lit a candle from his saddlebag, and by the light, he could see that Nora was shivering. Her wet clothes clung to her body.

William wrapped his jacket around her and let his arms remain on her shoulders. She didn't resist. His touch was all she wanted. They stood quietly for some time. He remembered how she had pulled away the last time he kissed her, so he reminded himself to go easy. "Nora, I have some wine. Take a sip," he urged. "It will warm you."

"Oh, I'm afraid of the liquor. I've only had a sip of the poteen now and then, never wine. I remember when we were little, Bridget told me the poteen made men into beasts, and I quite believed I'd see the men at Mulligan's pub coming out as goats or donkeys." She smiled.

"It won't hurt you. I promise," he laughed.

She took a sip and felt it warm her almost immediately, but it hurt her tongue. The taste was pleasant, like fruit, and the next sip was more to her liking.

They relaxed and talked. The rain beat against the mouth of the cave. Nora felt safe and loved. William was gentle. He held her close to him. He pushed back tendrils of damp hair from her forehead, and kissed her cheeks and the palms of her hands. She was warm and relaxed. And then suddenly William covered her mouth with warm, ardent kisses. She resisted at first, felt a moment of panic, and made an attempt to pull away. But he calmed her and she let go all restraint. She returned his kisses, his embrace.

"Nora, oh God, how I love you. I've wanted to hold you in my arms from the first moment. You are so beautiful." He cupped her face in his hands. "Too beautiful, you know." He ran his hands through her blue-black tresses.

Her mind was filled with wild thoughts. She had no experience with passion. A few awkward kisses from the farm boys was all she had known, and she had rejected their advances. Though unsure and frightened, she was now caught up in a desire so intense that she could barely breathe. All she wanted at this moment was his kisses on her lips, her ears, her throat. She couldn't even protest. Finally she gasped, "And I love you. Is this then what love is like?"

"Yes, my darling. This must be what it's like." He ran his hand down her blouse and gently cupped her breast. While one part of Nora's mind wanted to push his hand away, another wanted it to caress her entire body. William carefully unbuttoned her blouse.

"Oh no, William," she uttered softly. "Oh no."

"We were meant for this, Nora," he murmured. He lowered his lips to her breast and began to caress the lovely small nipple. She shuddered with joy, for she had never felt anything so glorious. Her own sensuality had been a mystery to her. She didn't, *couldn't*, resist him. He took off her blouse, revealing her beautiful white skin, her small, firm, pointed breasts, her tiny waist.

He drew in his breath at the sight of her beauty. "You are exquisite, darling," he whispered, covering her breasts, her stomach, her throat with wild, abandoned kisses. She gave in to the moment, and when he began to take the rest of her clothes off, she did not protest. He quickly pulled off his own clothes and stood tall in front of her. His slender body, fine legs and wide shoulders were a revelation to her, and she instinctively pulled him to her. She kissed him with love and desire. It suddenly occurred to him she might be a virgin, so he was gentle with her. At first she uttered a slight cry, but then she responded to his lovemaking, pulling him close.

"Oh William, I love you." Pain and pleasure mingled, but she felt pure passion as the mysteries of love were unlocked.

Afterward, as they lay in one another's embrace, they gazed into each other's eyes. William had slept with many women, and he had expected to feel only triumph, but right now he felt a rush of caring.

"Oh my darling, I love you."

She lifted her head and kissed him. "William, what will become of us?"

"It's all right, Nora. Everything will be all right." He rose and began to pull on his trousers.

She believed him. She reached out to touch him, but the moment of magic and tenderness was gone.

"Sweet Nora, I should be going now."

His tone reassured her momentarily, but she didn't want him to leave, not just yet. She needed comfort and words of affection, as she had never needed them before. Her virginity was lost, and suddenly she felt ashamed and alone. Oh God, what have I done? she asked herself.

"Will you be here tomorrow, pretty one?" he called, but he was already out the cave entrance and on his horse.

As she pulled on her stockings and buttoned her shirtwaist, the cave seemed much colder. She cried softly, wishing he had waited. At that moment, she felt like an abandoned child, not at all like the passionate woman of a few moments ago who had just lost her anchor to youth. She painfully mounted her horse, patting her. "Take me home, Teardrop."

When she returned Teardrop, she thought Kevin looked

at her strangely. Will everyone know? she wondered. Do I look that different from the girl who left home this morning? Will I ever be the same?

Chapter 5

After Lord Anthony saw Nora ride, he knew she was good. Damned good. An idea formed in his mind and he turned it over and over. By God, he thought, I want her to show Champion at the Dublin Horse Show.

He was almost afraid to risk it. He knew that part of the reason he wanted to do it was for Mary. For Nora too, of course, for he really believed her to be one of the finest riders he had seen, a natural. But he knew that, as much as Mary might want it, she might feel she had to fight it. He decided to take the risk. He sent a message for Mary that he needed to see her on business. No one would think that unusual. The gentry often did business with the local cottage industries, buying their handmade laces and reselling them on the Continent.

When Mary arrived, Lord Anthony ushered her into a large study with vaulting walls made of oak, and a great desk set near a broad window. She noted the grey in his hair, the slight stoop of his fine broad shoulders. When she saw they were alone, she became ill at ease.

"Don't worry, Mary," Lord Anthony soothed, noting her worried expression. "I couldn't have anyone here, for this concerns only us. I understand that anything else can never be." He bowed his head. "And I respect that." Then he grew more cheerful. "Mary, you are aware, of course, how beautifully Nora rides."

"What do you mean?" she said, surprised.

"I mean, I've seen her ride and she is grace in motion."

"Anthony, I'm hopelessly confused. How did you see her ride? What is all this?"

He told her the whole story. Mary remained silent for some time.

"And our children are friends. How interesting, Anthony. Don't you find that interesting?" She smiled at the irony.

"Yes, and somewhat unsettling," he replied, wishing he could share his fears and warn Mary that Nora and William might be more than just friends.

"But I asked you here for other reasons, Mary. I'll come to the point. I want Nora to ride Champion in the Dublin Horse Show in August, with your permission."

Mary was stunned. "You can't mean it," she said incredulously. "You want Nora? You can't be serious. You think a poor, Catholic girl could ride in the Dublin Horse Show? I don't think that can be, Anthony. You and I both know that only ladies of the aristocracy ride."

"I can and do mean it. There are a few Catholic members of the aristocracy, and besides, no one would have to know who she is. That's not important. I want Champion to win and she's the one who will make him win. Mary, she loves Champion, and she'd give anything to ride in the best show in Ireland. And I want her to have the chance. I give you my promise—this will work, Mary. No one will know. They'll think she's an entrant from England.

She's a brave girl and a fine rider. You know she'll want to do it. Let's give her a great adventure. It won't be easy, I know. I don't know how you will handle all the problems and questions. Frank, Father O'Rourke, the villagers, for it would be difficult to keep it secret around here. But if you want her to do it, I feel certain you will find a way. It would be a wonderful experience for her, Mary, to ride with the best, in one of the best horse shows in the world. Think about that.''

"Aye, faith, and I'll be needing to think about it, Anthony. But whatever I decide, I want you to know how very much I appreciate the thought, how very, very much.'' She knew that if they were found out, it would cause a stir among his Dublin friends. But he seemed willing to take that risk. She thought he was taking the risk as much for her as for Nora.

"I expected you'd need to think about it. I'll be waiting for your reply before asking Nora.'' He kissed her hand and she felt herself shudder.

"I'll be letting you know, Anthony, bless you.''

Mary walked home, supremely happy, but worried nevertheless. Can I let her do it? she wondered. What will I tell Frank? He'll accuse me again of encouraging her to put on airs, to be someone she's not. Terence will get drunk for a week. Oh dear God, help me. She prayed silently the rest of the way home.

No one was in the house except Terence, who had come up for some tools. She looked at him oddly for a few moments. He was her first-born, the spiritual image of her father Sean, and he was her dear, dear son despite his drinking and bad temper. Impulsively she told him what had happened, how Nora had stolen a ride on one of the lord's horses.

His reaction surprised her. "Faith, Ma,'' he said with

undisguised relief. " 'Twas I who started her on a life of deception." His eyes twinkled. He told her the story.

"Then you don't object at all?" she asked.

"No, Ma. Why shouldn't we use the Ascendancy folk if it suits our purposes? If they are the necessary instruments of our Nora getting out in the world and enjoying life a bit more, I'm all for it. After all, that was my reasoning when we first did it."

She was grateful for the response. "And your father, how would he be feeling about it, do you think?"

"Ah, but that's a tricky one, Ma. But why not be letting me tell him, since I'm the instigator. It's been seven long years I've been fearing we'd be found out. I can finally breathe free."

"Well, let's ask him together," Mary suggested. "I would think he'd be feeling proud, but I'm nervous."

Frank was reasonable. It was all in the past, he concluded, and he saw the humor in it. Mary guessed that he might even enjoy the idea of the long deception.

Terence never mentioned William, for the thought that this fop knew his sister filled him with a fury that had never been tapped before. I'll deal with him in time, he thought. It's not enough that they steal our land, they want to steal our women, too.

Mary never mentioned William either, just that Lord Anthony had seen Nora ride and thought she was superb.

"Mary, you're both smarter than I. Who's to say no?"

So a note was written to Lord Anthony, giving permission for Nora to ride in the horse show.

Nora entered the celadon green sitting room for the second time in a week. Lord Anthony asked her to be seated.

"I'm not a man to waste words, Nora. I want to train you for the next two months to ride Champion in the Dublin Horse Show in August."

Her eyes widened. She was certain she hadn't heard correctly. She knew that no girl of her station had ever ridden in the Dublin Horse Show.

"Faith, and I'm not sure I'm understanding what you're saying, Lord Anthony."

"Ah, Nora, I'm sorry if I've shocked you. William was right about you. You are a fine rider, better than any we have about. Better than Lady Harlow, who has ridden for me in the past. And so in the dressage and jumping events, I would like you to ride Champion at the show. Matt will polish your training, though I think you may already know more than he does, but he must feel he's a part of it."

Nora's equanimity returned slowly. She looked curiously at this handsome, middle-aged man standing in front of her, who was offering her a gift beyond belief. "Lord Anthony, how do you expect that to be happening? It just isn't possible. I won't be deceiving you. I'd like to be doing it. But I'm certain my family wouldn't be hearing of it. My father already thinks I'm too big for my britches. And besides, I'd never qualify if the officials knew who I was."

His smile was warm and knowing. "Nora, that is all settled. I've spoken to your mother and she sent me a note yesterday that she and your father agreed that it would be all right with them if you wanted to do it."

"Faith, Lord Anthony, I can't believe this. I don't know what to say." Nora sank into one of the soft, striped velvet chairs. How had all this come about? Her normal self-confidence retreated as the awesome thought of the responsibility became more of a reality.

"Say yes, Nora. We both know you can do it, and no one carries herself more like a lady than you do. I would like to have you do it. I believe we'd have a chance to win with someone as capable as you riding him in those events. And old Matt will help all he can."

Nora wondered if William knew anything about this, but she kept silent. Then suddenly she bounded out of the chair. "Sure, and I'll be doing it," she exclaimed. "And I'll do the best I can to see that Champion wins." The sheer miracle of it all was too much for her to resist. She ran over and grabbed Lord Anthony's hands and curtsied. "Lady Nora at your service, oh bless you, Lord Anthony, faith, and I'm excited."

"Yes, so I've noticed." He smiled a comfortable, wise smile. "Well, we've got work to do then, Nora."

They spent several hours making plans, seeing Matt and telling the other stableboys. Barney and Kevin stood there grinning broadly. Everyone joined the conspiracy with enthusiasm.

"Nora, we're busting with pride for you, sure and we are. Good luck to you, lass," Kevin encouraged her. "And Nora, no matter what happens, you're a winner to me, for I've always known 'twas you who got me job back. St. Patrick bless you."

She squeezed his hand. " 'Tis all right. Just be good to my sister."

Chapter 6

Frank had gone down to the fields, and Danny and Terence hurried after him to get the animals safely in their byres and stow the hay away. The rain began to fall in torrents. The brothers were arguing; lately they were always arguing. Terence had come in drunk the night before, and on their way down to the fields Danny couldn't contain himself any longer.

"Terence, it's acting like a child, you are. Are you thinking it's a delight for all of us to see you come reeling in after you've been with one of your women or talking your endless politics in the pub with the other radicals?"

Terence whirled around angrily, his eyes a cold, steel grey. "Shut your mouth. You're more and more telling me what I should and shouldn't be doing. You're a prig, Danny, a sullen prig. A little of the poteen might be helping you act a little more like a member of the human race instead of some damned preacher, and it wouldn't be hurting you either to learn about the injustices we suffer at the hands of those British bastards."

"And for what should I be learning? To be more miserable than I am?" Danny shot back. "There's nothing to be done about it."

"There is indeed something to be done about it," Terence spat out angrily. "You should be learning instead of just sitting around complaining of your lot. You're like most of the Irish. I'm thinking we are all victims."

At that moment they reached Frank, who barked instructions. "The damned wheel of the cart is stuck in the mud. Pull it out, Danny. Terence, pull the front of the cart with me and hold onto the horses."

As Danny was pulling on the wheel, a bolt of lightning lit the sky. The frightened horses reared. Terence lost his grip and the wagon lurched to the side, wobbled for a moment and then clattered over, falling on top of Danny. His leg was crushed beneath the huge iron wheel.

"Oh my God, Pa! Danny's under the wheel! See if we can pull it up!"

Frank looked down at his son, who was moaning in pain. Danny's eyes were closed. His face was as pale as death. After pulling and tugging, they finally lifted the wagon off Danny's leg. Terence hurried over to him.

"Danny, Danny, speak to me! Oh Danny, I'm so sorry. It was my fault," Terence cried. "I haven't had the wheel repaired. It's my fault. Forgive me, please."

Danny just moaned.

"Stop that," Frank grumbled. " 'Twas not your fault. 'Twas the rearing horses. Blaming yourself won't help Danny. We're needing to get him help."

They lifted him up onto the cart, reined in the horses and took off for the Murphys, whose farm was closer than their own.

Bridget and Nora were crocheting lace in front of the hearth, and Mary had just got up to stir the soup in the pot, when the door flew open and Terence, wide-eyed and breathless, filled the doorway. "Ma, Danny's been hurt. It's his leg. It was crushed by the wagon. The lightning frightened the horses, and they bolted and the wagon overturned. He's at Murphy's. Pa and I took him there. Barney's gone to Ballygarry to fetch the doctor. Ma, he's unconscious. Come with me."

"Oh, God have mercy on us. Is he alive, Terence?" She pulled her shawl off the peg. "Bridget and Nora, mind the pot. I'll be back as soon as I can."

Nora and Bridget were shocked and frightened.

"Oh, our poor Danny," Bridget said. "Let's pray, Nora."

And they knelt to pray, saying their beads, not knowing what else to do.

As Terence and Mary hurried down the path to the Murphys, awful thoughts went through her mind. She was sick with anxiety. My poor, quiet, sweet Danny. Oh dear Lord, please let him be alive. She thought of his sad, caring eyes, his serious nature, his steadiness. "Oh why, why do such things have to happen," she said aloud. The anger rose up in her throat.

"Ma, they just do," Terence told her. "If we had equipment that wasn't so rickety, so out of date, maybe it wouldn't have happened."

When they arrived, Meg Murphy opened the door and said, "He's conscious now, Mary, but it's a lot of pain he's in. Big Barney is after giving him some poteen to take the edge off the pain."

"Thank you, Barney," she said. "I hope it will help."

She went into the tiny alcove where her gentle second son was. Fear gripped her heart, for he had no color, and blood was everywhere. She was almost afraid to look, but she took his hand. "Danny, dear, I'm here. Ma is here. You'll be all right. They've gone to fetch the doctor."

He gave a groan.

She looked at Frank, who shook his head sadly.

"Let's be bathing him," she said, "so there will be no infection."

She and Meg chased the men out of the room, and with the warm water Meg had been heating, they cleansed him, changed the bedclothes and made him as comfortable as they could. It seemed to Mary that it was only his one leg that was crushed badly, but the bleeding kept her from seeing the extent of the damage. Dr. Malock Callaghan arrived hours later, wet, disheveled and a bit tipsy. Mary looked on as he treated Danny.

"He'll be all right, but he's lost a lot of blood. I wouldn't be moving him for a day or two," the doctor said, helping himself to the poteen they'd been using to dull Danny's pain.

Meg and Barney quickly reassured her it was fine for him to stay. Old Grandma Eileen was in the corner on the settlebed praying loudly and wailing about the fairies. Mary didn't think hearing that would help Danny, but there was nothing she could do. She told Frank and Terence to go home, and that she'd stay the night by Danny's side. They did as she asked, and she kept her vigil all night, praying and crying and listening for his breathing. He seemed somewhat better in the morning.

As he stirred, he opened his eyes and saw Mary sitting by his side. "Ma, Ma, what happened?"

She told him. His eyes looked so bad, so defeated. He nodded and dozed off again. His leg was bandaged and the doctor told her he thought the leg would heal but he would probably have a limp for the rest of his life.

They took him home a few days later, took his bed from the loft and placed it close to the fire so he could be warm and near everyone, for he had become depressed and quiet. Everyone tried to cheer him, but he barely smiled. Nora missed his being in charge, his advice, his common sense. How she missed him! Strange, she thought, she could miss someone who was there, but an essential part of him had gone. She felt an urgent need to break the wall of silence and despair that seemed to engulf him, and to that end she would run home after school, try to engage him in small talk, read to him, play games, and whatever she could think of.

He barely spoke, ate little and caused no trouble, but he wasn't really there. Mary, concerned about his withdrawal, sent a message to the doctor, but he answered with no words of help. Just that it sometimes happened, and he'd probably snap out of it soon, and that he'd be by in a few days to check his progress.

"And I'm not sure we're needing him to come by," Frank said. "He's on the poteen most of the time."

Terence, guilt-stricken and miserable at the argument he'd had with his brother just before the accident, tried to talk to Danny. This was hard, for they had very little in common except the farm. There had never been a camaraderie between these two brothers who were so different, and of late, the tension between them had built, so that they were arguing constantly. Still, Terence sat uncomfortably and tried to make small talk, or crack a joke to try to get a smile out of Danny. But he succeeded no better than the others.

Bridget, Nora and Sean took turns reading to him. One day Nora and Danny were alone. As she was trying to get him to talk, she suddenly felt anger rise in her. Why was he doing this? It wasn't like him to cause everyone grief. The only person he didn't get along with was Terence. Nora felt an urgency to say something, to be honest.

"Danny, you're just feeling sorry for yourself, and

what good is that doing you or any of us? Dr. Callaghan says you should be getting on the crutches or your strength will disappear and your muscles weaken. If you're not trying right now, I'll not be reading to you anymore." She was irritated, and slammed the book shut.

He looked at her, startled by her anger, and yet said nothing.

Then, very softly, close to his ear, Nora scolded her brother. "Sure, and it's a sad thing, a terrible thing, but you're alive, lad, you're alive. We need you, Danny, it's pure selfishness. Pa and Terence are overworked. You're not being fair to them or yourself. Or even to me. Sure, you won't be coming to see me in the Dublin Horse Show in the state you're in."

She struck some remote chord in his mind that made him react. "So, it's alive am I? That's how much you know, my sweet sister," he said with a bitter sarcasm she had never heard before. "I might as well be dead. I wish I had died that day, for I'm dead in my soul." His voice was filled with despair.

Nora did not expect such a reaction. "Danny, darling," she consoled softly. "What's wrong? How can you feel that way?"

She saw a tear glimmer in his eye. He looked at her, but she felt he wasn't seeing her. "I don't know," he finally answered in a whisper. "I only know, Nora, that I hate this life. I hate farming. I'd rather be dead. 'Tis why I've tried so often to get work in Limerick or Cork. Each time I failed, I wanted to die."

"Oh Danny, my God, don't even say such a thing. No one knows how you feel." She took his hand. "Why didn't you ever talk about it, get it off your chest like Terence does with his revolutionary ideas?"

"Terence," he almost spat. "As if his drinking and whoring aren't bad enough, now he's joined the Gaelic

League. He'll kill us all with his gunrunning, rabble-rousing, Irish Republican Brotherhood or whatever."

Nora knew about these groups and it frightened her to think of Terence being involved. "I didn't know," she said.

"No one knows. Keep quiet about it, Nora. It might kill Ma. 'Tis enough she lost her mother, her father, her brothers in the cause of Irish freedom. She doesn't need to lose a son."

She had finally penetrated his wall of silence, and she saw with great clarity that it was not just the crushed leg which had him in such despair. She sensed there was more to it.

And the rage and frustration he had hidden so successfully erupted, almost violently. "Because it means he'll be going off to Limerick or Dublin or Cork, or even America to raise money and guns, and I'll be left on the farm. I hate farming, Nora. I hate being here. I'm wanting to live in a city where there are some other chances at life. What is there here for me? Why has God done this to me? I hate my life. There's no reason to be living it." He was shaking. "Nora, I'm not wanting to inherit the farm and I'm thinking 'tis what Pa has in mind because of Terence's drinking and disappearing."

"Has Pa ever said that?"

"No, but I'm sure it's true. I'm the steady and dependable one," he said with evident sarcasm. "You know what Terence does when he disappears for days?" Danny asked.

Nora had assumed he was drunk in Limerick or Cork like many of the other young men. "No." She shook her head.

"He's going around raising money for the Irish Republican Brotherhood, for guns, Nora, for guns."

She was stunned. My God, she thought, how I've

been misjudging Terence. I've thought him not caring about anything but his drinking and girls. And he's into a bigger caring than any of us have. But she couldn't say that to Danny, to whom it seemed completely abhorrent. She wondered how Danny had found out. "Terence is believing strongly in Irish freedom, Danny, you know that," she said. "He has since I was too little to know what he was talking about. He may need to do what he can in his way. Why is that bothering you so, and anyway, you may be jumping to conclusions. And even if you haven't, why not find out, talk about it? It's been festering in your soul, Lord knows." She did not really understand his inability to deal with it directly, as she would have done.

"And now this accident takes care of it for sure. For what good am I for anything else?" he said self-pityingly.

"Well, nothing, if that's what you're wanting to think." Nora showed no sympathy. She glared as she faced him. "If you're half a man, Danny O'Sullivan, you'll get up on those crutches. Stop feeling the pity for yourself and take the first step you'll be needing to take to try to make your life what you're wanting it to be."

Mary had just entered the room and stood quietly, holding her breath, listening to Nora's words. Oh, dear God, the very words I couldn't say to him for fear of hurting him, she thought.

They noticed Mary standing there.

Danny looked at them both for a long moment and then spoke. "Nora, get me the crutches. You'll need to be giving me a hand. And expect to see me at the horse show."

A long, painful siege had ended. She had risked losing Danny's love, and had instead kept it and gained his respect. They became closer, for she had been the only one with the courage to tell him what he badly needed to hear. He rejoined the family, and even laughed now and then.

A few days later, Terence came home with a gift for Danny. He had seen a flute hanging on a hook in a Limerick shop and had bargained hard for it.

" 'Tis old and scratched but I'm sure it will play fine," he said as he handed it to Danny.

Danny's eyes glowed with pleasure. He touched it reverently and played some pleasant music almost immediately. Everyone was amazed except Terence.

Bridget said, "Why Terence, you must be in the fairies to have known what to buy him."

"No it's not the fairies I'm in," Terence smiled. "Sure, and old man Macgeehan used to let Danny play when he was a wee lad, and I remembered how he played it without even a lesson."

"I'm grateful to you, Terence, that I am," Danny said simply.

Danny was soon playing heavenly music for them. He had finally found a way to express himself. They all knew when he was about to start playing, for he'd rinse the flute out with water. His very soul was in it, and his melodies were enchanting. It was a delight to hear him play on long winter evenings with Mary accompanying him.

One evening in bed, Mary said, "There's a balance in life, Frank, or maybe it's an irony, but another kind of happiness came out of Danny's tragic accident."

Frank nodded gravely. "But I'm wondering if he'd exchange the limp for the flute."

"No," Mary said, "but I think his music has given him a lot of happiness he's never known before."

And they let the matter drop.

The day dawned fair in Dublin. It was planned that Nora, Matt and Kevin would arrive very early at the show grounds, and Nora, dressed in the fine habit Lord Anthony had purchased, would appear at the last moment on Champion just as the event was to begin. This way no one would have time to approach or question her.

Nora would always remember her first glance of the Royal Society of Dublin show grounds. The very stern, formal exterior of grey stones and Georgian design belied the interior with its charming, typically English Tudor buildings.

"Why, it looks almost like a city," Nora exclaimed.

"Aye, Miss Nora," Matt said. "There are many villages in England that look just like this, without, of course, the grandstands." Nora thought how much she would like to see such beautiful villages.

A gigantic tent had been set up for refreshments, and there was a large band, and beautiful flags flew everywhere. As the crowds milled about, excitement mounted. The family met under the clock tower. They were ill at ease, feeling they must look so conspicuous, but no one seemed to notice, and Mary was determined they should all have a wonderful time.

Nora, Matt and Kevin kept on the move, so no one would talk to them. Nora noticed that some of the entrants were foreign-born, and she smiled politely, as they did, when spoken to. Lord Anthony and William appeared later, and though Nora saw them, she didn't go near them. When William spotted her, he was stunned at her beauty and elegance. My God, he thought, she is more beautiful than anyone here. How I wish she were of my class.

The horses paraded around within the show area before and after each event. She did not know what she would have done without Matt to guide her. He handled every problem, staved off any inquiries and kept speaking words of encouragement to both her and his beloved Champion. As the call came for her first event, Matt said,

"Miss Nora, if anyone can do it, you can. Champion loves you, and he'll do whatever you want."

"Oh Matt, I hope so. Thank you so very much. If I win, it will be due to you as much as anyone."

She was never to forget the moment as the women's jumping event began. The thrill of the crowds dressed in their finest, the soft sunshine of an Irish day, the gaily colored flags, the smell of the turf, the pageantry of this ancient show, and the pounding of her own heart, created in her an ecstasy she had never known.

Both she and Champion performed brilliantly, and as she passed Lord Anthony's box, he waved to her proudly. William was waving too. When the judges announced their decision, Nora held her breath. She had received first prize, and Lord Anthony came down to the judges' stand to accept it for her. The crowd applauded, and looking over to the grandstands, she saw Terence perched on the rail, waving wildly. She waved back. It was a moment that brought back the memory of Terence's initial plan for her riding.

Preparing for the dressage event, she noticed some of the women pointing at her and chatting amongst themselves. She became a little uneasy, but more determined than ever to win. She was better than all of them, and she knew it.

In the meantime, in Lord Anthony's box, William, who was on his third bottle of champagne, delighted about Nora's success and always striving to be in the limelight, turned to Lady Harlow's daughter, Diana, to whom he had just become engaged, and announced drunkenly, "Isn't it ripping? Isn't it amusing? My father has dressed up one of his tenant farmer's daughters and passed her off as a lady, and she turns out to be the best damned rider in the show." Waving his glass in the air, he toasted Nora. "To my fine Lady Nora. Show them."

Lord Anthony, not believing he heard William correctly, turned to him in disgust. "William, you're drunk. Sit down and stop making a spectacle of yourself."

He didn't notice Lady Harlow disappear from the box in the direction of the judges' stand.

The dressage event had already started, and Nora was leading the field in points. She finished in triumph, only to hear the judges announce that Champion, due to a technicality, had been disqualified. She bore herself off the field regally, more a lady than any of the others. She did not understand what had happened.

When Terence heard the announcement, he raced to find her. He led her quickly from the stadium, with Matt and Kevin following.

"What happened, Terence? What was the technicality?" she asked. She could no longer hold back her tears.

"The technicality was the circumstances of your birth, I'm sure. We were fools to think the bastards would let you win." He glanced at her, and knew this was not the time for this kind of talk. "But you did get one prize, Nora, before you were found out," he said, his indignation turning to a kind of triumph. "We've got them on that, lass. You won the jumping event, and they'll not take that prize away." He put his comforting arms about her and led her away.

The most exciting day of her life had turned to ashes in a few short hours.

"Oh Terence, why, what does it matter to them if I win? Why would they disqualify me on some stupid technicality?" She was sobbing now.

"Because, dear girl, you're a threat. All of us Irish are threats. We've fought them all these years, never giving in, never becoming a subjected people. If they let even one of us win in a horse show, that might be admitting we are as good as they are. But don't cry. You won.

Everyone in that stadium knows you won. And most importantly, *you* know you won. Don't ever forget that, dear Nora. A poor Catholic farm girl took the blue ribbon at the Dublin Royal Society's show. Isn't that a wonder?''

Chapter 7

Nora awoke to a wave of nausea, the same nausea she'd had every morning since returning from Dublin. At first she blamed it on the excitement and change of routine. Soon there were other signs, however, and she knew without a doubt that she was carrying William's baby.

Oh dear God, she thought miserably, what will I do? What have I done? She lay in bed silently weeping, feeling alone and frightened. She finally looked at herself in the mirror and admitted she had to go into Cork to see a doctor and confirm the worst. She told her mother they needed more embroidery needles and left early the following morning. "I'll stay with Megen tonight, Ma, and I'll be home tomorrow." Megen was her old school friend who had moved to Cork, where she had found work in Roche's Specialty Store.

Nora had always loved going into Cork. The family didn't go very often, only for market day, or a horse fair now and then, but the canals and quays and bustle had always delighted her. But today her heart was heavy.

Megen welcomed her warmly. " 'Tis not enough I'm seeing of you, Nora. I'll be off work at seven. Here's my key, go wait for me. I'm going to a dance at the Guild Hall on Patrick's Hill this evening. We'll go together. There's some of the nicest young men I've met, Nora. You'll be liking them, I'm sure."

Nora could barely look at her. The thought of a dance seemed cruelly ironic, but she knew she had to carry it off as best she could. "Fine, Megen, that will be lovely," she answered.

She waited apprehensively in Dr. Egan's outer office, afraid to look at anyone. She had sought out a Protestant doctor in a Protestant section of Cork, for gossip could travel through all the Catholic community too quickly. He examined her, and as it was her first real examination, she didn't know what to expect. When she was ordered to undress, she was visibly shocked.

"Young lady, I can't examine you with your clothes on. Get on with it," the doctor said as he closed the door.

Get off with it he means, she thought wryly. The examination was the worst indignity she had known in her young life, and she had not a single soul to share her misery with. He confirmed her worst fears and predicted the baby would be born the following February. Dr. Egan was cold, aloof and efficient. All she wanted was a reassuring word, a smile, but she received only reserved contempt.

"Thank you, Dr. Egan, for all your kindness," she said. He was so preoccupied that he didn't notice the irony in her voice.

This feeling of abject misery, shame and hopelessness was new to her. She simply didn't know how to handle it.

I've sinned, she thought, and I'm now faced with the consequences. Oh, dear God, forgive me, what will I do? And then it occurred to her that to be forgiven she had first to confess. The thought made her tremble.

She let herself in Megen's tiny room in a small boarding house in a dingy, grey area of Cork City near the River Lee. She threw herself on Megen's bed and wept openly for the first time. Finally she stopped, wiped her tears, and allowed her basically optimistic nature to assert itself. She looked appraisingly in the mirror at her red, puffy eyes. She wondered what she could tell Megen about these red eyes.

By the time Megen arrived at the dreary boarding house, Nora had pulled herself together and tried to affect a cheer she didn't feel. Megen was so excited about going to the dance that she hardly noticed Nora's appearance. She just chattered gaily about this boy and that and what fun they'd have.

The stuffy hall the dance was being held in made Nora want to run. It was smoke-filled and full of stale odors, very unlike the platform outdoor dances held in the rural villages that Nora had attended. What *was* the same, she noted, were the boys on one side of the hall and the girls on the other.

"Nora, I met this boy, Terry, at a box tea a few weeks ago. He bought my picnic tea at the auction even though everyone knows I can't boil water for tea, so I was knowing right off that he liked me." She paused and grabbed Nora's arms and spun her around in the other direction. "Look, there he is coming in the door, the one with the blue shirt," she said excitedly.

Terry was very undistinguished-looking to Nora, but she praised him for Megen's sake. "Oh Megen, he's got a fine look about him. Look, he's coming this way."

Megen blushed, and for a few moments Nora forgot

her own torments in preoccupation with Megen's pleasant, simple infatuation. Terry came over looking very awkward. He was with another young man and introductions were made.

Seamus Gorman was the other young man's name, and Nora liked him immediately. He had sandy brown hair, the pale Irish freckled complexion and a wonderfully warm, friendly smile. Seamus was witty and smart, she thought, not at all like the rough village boys she knew and had spurned, but neither did he have William's aristocratic bearing.

In answer to a question of hers, he quoted a lovely line of poetry:

"Come away, O human child!
To the waters and the wild
With a faery, hand in hand,
For the worlds more full of weeping than you can
    understand."

Nora was quite entranced.

"Sure, and that's lovely. Is it Yeats?" she asked.

"Why lass, it is indeed. Are you knowing the poem then?" he queried.

"No, not that particular poem, but it was sounding like Yeats. The rhythm, I guess."

And the four of them talked for hours about poetry, and life, and danced now and again and laughed quite a bit at Seamus' humor.

The boys saw them home and Seamus asked if he might see her again. Reality suddenly intruded.

"Oh Seamus, as I've told you, I'm living in Ballygarry. It's a distance," she answered hesitantly, all of her miseries suddenly returning.

"Ah Nora, remember, ' 'Tis distance lends enchantment to the view,' " he smiled.

"Oh, you are something, Seamus Gorman," she laughed, "but I'll not be in Ballygarry long. I'll be going to work in Dublin soon, or maybe even to America." She was searching for some reason to keep him away.

"Well, we'll be seeing about all that, lass," he answered mysteriously. She had no way of knowing that he had decided to love her the rest of his life and had no intention of letting her go. Terry kissed Megen lightly on the cheek and the girls ran up the stairs.

"What a nice young man Seamus is, Nora. Are you liking him at all?" Megen asked.

"Aye, he's a fine young man, Megen. Intelligent, and with a strength I've not seen in any of the farm boys."

Megen didn't really know what Nora meant by strength, but she nodded affirmatively. "Sure, and he does have that."

Nora lay in the makeshift bed on the floor thinking about Seamus and William. How simple my life would be if I had met someone like Seamus earlier, she thought. He had warmth, strength, caring. There will be no one like Seamus in my future, she sighed. Until that evening, she thought William was the only intelligent, attractive man in the whole world, and so she had given her heart, her soul to him. She patted her stomach where she knew his child lay and wept herself to sleep.

It was the first time she would be seeing William since the Dublin Horse Show. He had been there cheering her on, looking as pleased as his father and her own family.

She thought of the thrills and excitement and disappointments of that incredible day.

'Tis not too bad, she thought, on balance, to be winning one event and being disqualified from another. "At least 'twas one we won," she said, patting Champion, whom she was now allowed to ride freely. Her disappointment and hurt that day had almost crushed her, but in perspective she saw it differently. It had made her see much in her world differently. All was not love and friendliness and understanding outside her small village. She had come to see that all too clearly.

As she reached the cave, she saw William waiting. Her heart pounded madly, her hands trembled. She pulled in the reins and dismounted.

He rushed to her and threw his arms around her. "You were magnificent, my treasure. You were the most beautiful sight there. The way you sat proudly in the saddle, your command of Champion, all of that made you look a winner."

"Aye," she said, trying to keep the bitterness from her voice. "Too bad the judges didn't think so."

"Oh Nora, never mind, you won the important event, and Father was really pleased about that. He knows the disqualification had nothing to do with you."

"Sure, but you're wrong, William. It had everything to do with me, with my being a farm girl, and a Catholic, and with my not knowing my place," she replied bitterly, as bitter as he had ever heard her.

William knew she was right and he knew it that day at the show. As usual, when he got what he wanted, he lost interest and looked ahead. Now he was thinking of the London social season and his fiancée, a fiancée Nora knew nothing of. "Nora, Nora, please, don't dwell on the unpleasant. Just think of having been a winner at the Dublin Horse Show!" He didn't want to pursue this discussion.

"Sure, and I'm pleased about that," she said, her

spirits lifting. "It was one of the great moments in my life, the thrill of the performance, the applause of the crowd. I'll never forget it, never. And it was all due to you, William. I won't forget that either." She realized that he was both the cause of her greatest joy and the cause of her greatest misery. How will he react? she thought apprehensively. He said we'd be all right, so maybe we will. But in her heart there was a gnawing fear.

"Oh, darling Nora, it was my pleasure, and besides, it was my father who had the idea about Dublin, not me." His unaccustomed honesty surprised her.

"Aye, but you were setting it in motion," she said quietly, attempting to give him credit for goodness.

He put his arms around her, and for the moment she felt loved and wanted and secure. Surely he'll want to acknowledge this child. 'Tis his as well as mine, she reminded herself. And that thought momentarily satisfied her.

"You look so melancholy, Nora. What's wrong?"

But he didn't wait for an answer. He kissed her red, waiting lips. When he lowered his head to kiss her throat, she pulled back slightly and tensed.

"Nora, it's all right. You know I care for you." He chose his words carefully so she wouldn't notice he didn't use the word love.

His words melted her feelings of fear, and she returned his kisses with a desperation she had never felt before. It was as though Nora knew in the recesses of her being that this was to be the last time. As he pulled off her blouse, she lost herself in love and passion and succumbed to his kisses, his caresses. "Oh William, sure, and I'm loving you."

And they lost track of time and place.

Later, as they were sipping a little wine, Nora started to tremble.

"Nora, are you chilled? What's wrong?" William asked as he threw his jacket over her.

" 'Tis not a jacket that will be helping, William. I have something important to tell you," she whispered.

"Yes, sweet girl, what is it?" Her manner made him uneasy.

Nora came directly to the point, as was her way. "William, I don't know how to be saying this any differently." She paused for a moment and then blurted out, "I'm having your baby."

The color drained from his face. He looked at her in disbelief. Then she suddenly realized that he was as frightened as she.

"My God, Nora, it can't be. Are you certain?" he asked hoarsely.

"Yes, I'm certain," she answered quietly. "I saw a doctor in Cork. There's no doubt about it, William, none at all."

His mind was in torment. What have I done? he wondered. Why wasn't I more careful? What can I do? It's impossible. "Oh Nora, what will happen to me? This is just awful, awful."

If she had ever wanted and needed strength and reassurance in her life, it was at this moment, and it was simply not there. She stared at him strangely for some moments and answered honestly. "I don't know, William. I was hoping you'd have some thoughts about what to do." She had wanted him to gather her in his arms, tell her not to worry. They would marry, perhaps go to America together, where they wouldn't be known. But as she looked up at him, she knew that none of this was to be. She remained silent.

"Oh my God, Nora, we're in trouble. It's just an impossible situation," he groaned. "What would my father say? He'd cut me off without a penny."

"Yes," she answered listlessly. She watched him, seeing clearly for the first time that he was interested only in himself. At this moment, she thought of Seamus' kind face. How would he have handled this? she wondered. Nora was very certain that Seamus would have acted quite differently.

William just wanted to get away. "Nora, let me think about this. I'm so upset right now that my mind isn't working. Let's give it a day," he said, distraught, never once acknowledging her or her feelings in any way. Never asking if she was frightened, ill or upset.

"Yes, William, I think that would be best," she responded sadly. "I'll see you tomorrow." And she left the cave without another word.

"Champion," she whispered to the horse, "take me home. I'm not seeing for the tears."

The next day she rode to the cave, her heart heavy. William helped her down but he didn't embrace her or take her hand. She shuddered.

"Nora, this is a difficult situation," he acknowledged with a composure that had not been evident the day before. He had decided that if news of this came out, he would lie about it, deny that he'd ever touched her. Who'd believe her? Lots of poor girls tried to blame their pregnancies on a boy of higher station, but how could they prove it? "Actually, Nora," he continued, "it's not only a difficult situation, it's impossible."

Was this the William who had told her not to worry, asked her to meet his father, told her everything would be all right, and told her he loved her? "Is it impossible, William? Why?" Anger had started to rise in her and she wanted to make him as miserable as she was.

"Well, ah, well," he stammered, "our religions, our worlds, are just too different. We can't marry, Nora."

"And just why can't we, William? There are no penal laws in effect now. 'Tis even possible now to go to Wales and be married in the Catholic Church. You said we were in love, surely God will forgive us."

"It isn't possible. Life for both of us would be miserable. My father wouldn't support us, and I'd have to go to work. I don't know how to work. I'd be miserable," he answered truthfully.

Nora knew he was right, but she felt desperate. She wanted to hurt him as he was hurting her. "But William, we don't have to stay in Ireland. We could go to America. It's a land of opportunity. You could learn to do something. We'd have a chance at happiness."

"Nora, I don't want to leave Ireland," he answered angrily. "These are to be my estates. My inheritance and opportunities are here."

"And where are my opportunities, William?" Nora asked indignantly. "Or am I not entitled to any? And our child, William, this baby in my womb is yours too. Where are his opportunities? You haven't mentioned the child, not even once."

"Oh Nora, Nora, let's not argue," he responded. "I'll take care of the child. That's the least of the problem," he said callously.

"Faith, and how do you propose to do that?" she asked.

"I've money for you, Nora. And when you need more, I'll send it."

She was silent. She looked hard at him, searching for what she had loved and trusted in him. "And where will you be sending this money to, William?"

"Nora, you must go away. You know that. To Dublin, or London. I don't know where. You don't want to shame your family."

"Or you yours, is that right?" she hissed.

He bowed his head. "Yes, that's right."

But she knew it was more than that. He'd lose his position, his friends, his entire comfortable, wealthy Protestant world of balls and hunts and fashionable schools and travel. He hadn't really loved her, certainly not enough to give up all that. And suddenly, with blinding clarity, she saw that it was as much her fault as his. She had been naive. She had seen signs of his weakness and ignored them. She shrugged as she realized that there was nothing more to be done, that there was no going back. As she looked at him, she knew that, since he couldn't be counted on, she had to count on herself, and herself alone.

She stood up with dignity, feeling a mixture of contempt and pity for William. His tousled blond hair made her heart ache. For a moment, she wanted to touch him, to reach out, but she dared not, knowing it would be a futile gesture. Her whole demeanor changed; her voice became calm and self-assured. His weakness had made her strong again, but in the process, something in her had died. She felt perhaps it was her youth.

"Aye, I will be needing to go away. You're right, William. I'll be figuring something out."

He breathed an audible sigh of relief. "Nora, that's the reasonable thing. Perhaps you can put the baby up for adoption and resume your life." He pulled a packet out of his pocket. "Nora, here's some money to see you through. Please take it." He hesitated, then held it out to her.

She wanted to throw it back at him or to rip it up, but her survival instincts were stronger than a few moments of revenge.

"And perhaps," he added, "I can see you when you return."

She knew what he meant. "No, I'll never see you again, but I *will* take the money. It's for our child," she answered, taking the envelope from him. "William, right now I hate you. You are a weak, pitiful person, but I hate myself all the more for not having seen that earlier. In a way, this is all for the best, finding out the truth as I did." She paused, feeling such intense hurt and pain that it became difficult to speak. "I hope I'll never see you again, and this child will never know your name." And with that, she left him.

Chapter 8

Two months had passed since Mary first told Frank of her wish to send Nora and Sean to America. He had remained angry and adamant, rarely speaking to Mary, remaining aloof from her even in bed. Her own misery clouded her vision, and because of it she sensed none of Nora's unhappiness. Yet she would not back down. If asked, she couldn't have explained her stubbornness in this matter. She had blind faith in her judgment and intended to have it happen the way she wanted it to. As they lay far from each other in bed, she spoke softly and desperately one more time. "Frank, I'm miserable about all this. I'm not doing it to make you unhappy, please believe me."

He rolled over to face her and asked, "What is it then, Mary? You know my wishes."

She spoke cautiously. "Terence is gone again. We don't know where he is. Out doing some mischief to the Brits, I imagine. You know he's not the one to be going to America. You must know that, Frank. I'm not thinking he wants to." Frank grunted. She pressed on. "And Danny's leg has gone limp from the accident. They'll never let him into America. They turn away the lame. You know that." Mary was quiet for a moment. Then she said, "What I'm really telling you, Frank, is that Sean must be the one to go. He longs to be a writer, a poet. The farm is not for him. What Catholic writers stay in Ireland? All the good ones leave. It's not the place for a Catholic writer, not yet." She could not hide her despair. "Not yet. I wonder if ever." Frank said nothing. She ached to touch him and feel his strong arms around her. They had never been so distant from one another. "And Bridget. Oh Frank, she's in love with young Kevin O'Riordan. With her dowry, they could marry. And she's an immense help to me in the cottage industry. She's so good at lace-making and she teaches well, too. I need her here."

"Is Nora no help to you, then?" he asked.

"Oh yes, I didn't mean that. It's just that she's been busy with the riding and training for the show. And the truth is, her lace-making is not as good as Bridget's. I think she has great talent, but it's for design, and she should go where that's appreciated. Bridget has more patience for the tedious hours lace-making takes," she explained. What she couldn't explain were her other feelings, her instincts about their ambitions, their drives and their intelligence. She knew she had to keep it on a practical level. "Frank darling, please, please help me. Can you agree with what I've said?"

He moved over close to her. Her heart raced as he gathered her in his arms. "Faith, Mary, I can't be holding out against you any longer. Sure, and it will destroy us. You're stronger than I am, woman. You win. My poor, poor Mary, this has been the most difficult thing you've ever had to do, isn't it?"

She nodded. "I'm sorry to cause you such grief Frank, I am."

"I know, Mary. For you to do this shows me how much it means to you, and what you just said is making a wee bit of sense. I'm still against it, but if you're wanting it so badly and you think it's so right, perhaps we'd better do it."

"Oh Frank, thank you. I do think it's right. Call it a premonition. I don't know. It's just a strong feeling about it I'm having." After a few moments of silence, she said, "Frank, I've a secret to confess. I'd like to go to America, too. Someday. Is that crazy?"

He held her close in his strong arms and smiled sadly. "No, it's not crazy. Some of us want and expect more from life. You're one of those people, Mary. Maybe someday."

She wiped away a tear. "Do I have your permission, Frank? Can I tell them?"

"Yes, I guess so, but there may be a lot of hurt feelings. We'll need to handle it carefully. The thing that worries me most is how frightened I am for Sean and Nora. They're strong, Mary, but they're young and inexperienced."

"I know, Frank, I know. But I think they can do it, and I know they will want to. And they won't be alone. Jim and Nellie will help take care of them. Let me handle the situation and you help me where you can."

Mary came from a long line of strong women who, despite the pattern of male domination in Ireland, were the strength and backbone of their families. They made important decisions. They held families together or split them up when needed. And now Mary had to face this heart-rending decision, the most important decision she ever had to make.

Bridget was chattering and helping Mary serve dinner. Frank watched his wife closely, knowing the torments she had to be going through.

Mary noticed that Nora was, as usual lately, very quiet and pale, not eating. What on earth is wrong with the girl? she wondered. Everyone was home except Terence. Mary wondered when he'd be home from Mulligan's. Frank and Danny also went to Mulligan's, or other pubs in town, but when they visited, they'd play some darts, have a drink, help settle the problems of the world and then come home for dinner. Terence drank more than they did, and he was always late. She wondered glumly if he had the failing, the Irish failing.

Halfway through dinner, Terence roared in, singing and quite drunk.

Frank looked disgusted.

Danny shouted at him, "Good God, you're a man now, not an irresponsible child."

" 'Tis remarkably priggish you're being, dear brother. I'm just happy right now." Terence grabbed Nora and spun her around, doing a jig.

"Stop it!" Mary commanded. "Just stop it! I'm tired of the drinking and the bickering. And I have some important things to discuss this evening with all of you. I told you that last night, Terence, and I would have appreciated your coming home sober just this once."

Mary rarely raised her voice, so everyone sat very still.

"I'm sorry, Ma," Terence said, shamefaced, "I was forgetting."

"Yes, I noticed," she said sarcastically, believing more than ever that her decision to exclude Terence was a sound one. He was always sober for his radical activities, she knew, and could remain so, apparently, for whatever was important to him. In a more conciliatory tone, she said, "Terence, have some tea, 'twill take the edge off."

They all sat around the peat fire, as they often did. This time, however, they weren't listening to Danny play his lovely melodies on the flute or Mary singing a melancholy Irish ballad or one of the children reading poetry or history or legend. Everyone sensed something important was about to happen. They waited quietly for Mary to speak.

"Children," she started, "your pa and I have saved some money, and your uncle Jim in America has just sent one steamship ticket, so we now have passage for two of you to go to America." She paused. Everyone was silent. "We've thought this out carefully, and because of circumstances, we feel at this point in time the two who should be going are"—she hesitated, taking a deep breath—"Nora and Sean."

Terence's voice shattered the silence that greeted Mary's announcement. "Sean and Nora? 'Tis madness! 'Tis the oldest who should go," he shouted drunkenly.

Frank stood up with great presence. "Terence, you're needed on the farm, and what would your Irish Republican Brotherhood be doing without you? And Danny too is needed on the farm for the time being. It's a crucial time for us. The crops have been bad and we need experienced hands. Sean has just finished school and hasn't the experience you two oldest do."

Mary looked at him grimly. She knew he still disagreed with her, but knew too that they needed a united voice.

Nora was afraid to look at Danny. She kept her head down, remembering his utter devastation after his accident, fearing it would keep him forever bound to the farm work he hated. She remembered how she tried to reassure him about his future, and here *she* was the one who'd be leaving, not him. She lifted her head and stole a glance. The pain and despair were evident in his eyes. Yet she knew he wouldn't whine about his rights like Terence. He would accept the decision passively. No one else in the room knew how passionately he hated the farm. Danny, she thought, of all of us, is the one who really wants to go to America, maybe the only one. What a strange twist. She wondered if her mother had known and if she would still have made this decision. God, how I wish I could run over to him and say, Danny, go in my place, but I can't. I've been a fool and sinned against God, so I'm the one who needs to go, for the shame I'd bring to Ma and Pa would be worse than Danny's temporary unhappiness. 'Twas as though Father O'Rourke knew about this when he told me to do nothing foolish.

Sean was thunderstruck that he had been chosen. He had heard his father give a reason, but he still couldn't believe it.

"America," he whispered, hardly able to believe what had been said. "Faith, and maybe I could become a writer there and tell them in America what the Brits have done to us here."

He wasn't aware of Danny's hatred of farm life, so it didn't occur to him to offer him his place. Also, he wouldn't question his father and mother's decision even if he had thought it unfair. He was sorry Terence was so upset, but thought it was just his pride. He couldn't imagine Terence giving up his hard-earned position with the Brotherhood.

Bridget, who sat motionless, finally blurted out, "Why does Nora get the best of everything? Why shouldn't I go? Kevin could raise the money and we could go together and start a new—"

"Bridget," Mary interrupted, "since you are about to become engaged to Kevin, and with a wedding to be planning, we thought you wouldn't want to be going just yet. Maybe you and Kevin will go later." Mary had instinctively answered all the questions Bridget had in her mind, and thrown in a compliment that made her feel needed in Ballygarry.

Bridget's resentment passed quickly, as it always did. "Yes, Ma. I understand," she said quietly.

Terence had already stormed from the cottage, as was his wont when drunk and displeased.

Danny said nothing.

"How are you feeling about this, Danny?" Mary asked softly.

His voice was very low as he spoke. "I know, Ma, Pa, that you're needing me here for the crops. It's, it's all right." He paused. "Maybe I'll go later," he said sadly.

For Nora, the thought of America, of leaving her family, friends and home, was awesome and terrifying. Yet she felt a strange exhilaration at the prospect of starting a new life, escaping from the past and the shame she felt. At that moment, she didn't consider what would happen when she arrived or how she could hide her pregnancy from Uncle Jim and Aunt Nellie. None of that was real yet.

"Oh, Sean, and Nora," Danny said, a sudden cheerfulness replacing his sorrow, "what a wonderful, grand thing to be going to America. You'll be seeing cowboys and buffalo and firemen."

Sean smiled. "I think there are no cowboys and buffalo in New York City, but plenty of firemen, I'll wager. I'll be sending you pictures, count on it."

"Sean, you haven't said how you're feeling about this," his father said.

"Faith, and I'm overwhelmed. My feelings will be needing sorting out. I was going to apply to Trinity College, Pa, if we could have afforded it. Mr. O'Brien at school told me 'tis possible for Catholics to get in if we pass their tests, but now that won't be."

"So, you're wishing more education, are you?"

"Aye, Pa, but maybe I'll get it there. 'Tis sure I'd like it. Surely America has schools too."

Mary stared at him. "Sure, and I didn't know you were hoping for anything like Trinity, Sean. It's just been always out of the question for Catholics," she said quietly. She wanted desperately at that moment to take everything back she had said. But she had made her move and it seemed irreversible.

"And you, Nora, you haven't been your usual cheerful self lately. Was it thinking about going to America?" Frank asked.

"Oh no, no" she said hastily, afraid Danny might think she had known about it for some time. "It's just that I've been a little unhappy since Dublin," she lied. " 'Tis a grand opportunity, of course, Pa. There's not much of that here, sure. You know I've always dreamt of faraway places."

Then, with a forced cheerfulness, Mary said, "Well, 'tis settled then. We'll be booking your passage, and you'll be going from Queenstown Harbor."

"When, Ma?" Nora asked, holding her breath. Perhaps it was still six months in the future, she thought uncertainly.

"In a few weeks. I don't want you making a winter crossing."

Sean and Nora looked at one another. Only a few weeks. It was now a reality.

They all knew that many of those who left Ireland never saw their families again. No one spoke for a few moments. A quiet despair hung over them.

"We'd best be going to bed," Frank broke the silence.

Danny rose and said, "I'm needing some fresh air."

"May I walk with you, Danny?" Nora asked.

Danny had wanted to be alone with his thoughts, but he nodded.

They walked silently for a while. The moon was full. The mountains shimmered in the distance on this lovely Irish summer evening.

"Danny, I'm sorry," Nora murmured. "Because you're good and you're responsible, you have to stay."

He wouldn't look at her, fearing he would start to cry.

"Danny O'Sullivan, listen to me. I'm not sure how, but I'll have you in America no more than year or two after I arrive. That is the truth, and you must believe me. Know that I'm telling you the truth. Trust me."

She had spoken with such conviction and determination that he found himself wanting to believe her. "But how—" he started to ask.

"Never you mind. Just know it will happen. It will be making your life happier here. You'll have a goal. Wait and see."

"Oh, I hope, Nora." He paused, then said, "I hated you for a moment in there. I thought, why she's so much younger, and a woman to boot. I'm sorry."

"Just know that I mean it. Have I ever told you anything but the truth?"

"No, but this may be something over which you have no control."

Her voice had a hard edge as she said, "It will come to pass. I'll have control, Danny. Count on it."

Chapter 9

Queenstown, Cork City's bustling harbor, was humming with activity when the O'Sullivan family arrived to say their farewells to Nora and Sean. They had made the trip from Ballygarry with heavy sadness in their hearts. When Lord Anthony had heard that Nora and Sean were leaving for America, he had insisted on sending them to Queenstown in his carriage. Nora wondered bitterly as she stared out the window of the elegant black-and-gold lacquered carriage, if William had any part in sending them off in comfort. But she thought she would never really know, and more realistically, what did it really matter? She thought too of the friends and neighbors who had come with gifts: a half dozen loaves of fresh bread, pots of honey, and a jug of poteen. They had sung the old songs, drunk the poteen and offered advice on everything from how to avoid seasickness to how to look for jobs in America, and which of their relatives to look up. Everything had been packed in the wagon, including a rather large black trunk especially packed by Mary, who explained to Nora and

Sean that they must guard it carefully. It contained some of the most beautiful laces of the region and was more valuable than mere money. Bridget commented that Mary had indeed saved some of the most exquisite laces for this trunk. Nora was thrilled with the gift, but wondered if it was practical, since they were carrying bundles of clothing, food, cooking untensils, and comforters and blankets. She sensed, however, that it would serve some need, and hugged her mother, knowing well that years and years of her toil were in that black trunk.

"I'll guard it well, Ma, and I'll be knowing when to use it."

Mary smiled, knowing that Nora wasn't sure what it meant now, but believed its purpose would come to her in time. She knew her daughter well, and counted on her ingenuity and foresight. After all, she thought, isn't this why I'm sending her?

Danny was hanging out the window of the coach, his hair blown wild by the wind, his sharp eyes taking everything in. " 'Tis but two and a half more miles," he said excitedly.

Everyone took turns at the windows and watched with interest as signs of life began to appear. The road curved up the hillside with the harbor off to their right. It was a large, beautiful, busy harbor, with mountains on the other side and houses nestled in the hills. Carts, donkeys and horses could be seen. People on foot carrying bundles walked along the road, all heading toward the town and the quays. From a mile away they could see the cathedral spire, and then, suddenly, they were in Queenstown. The harbor was full of ships and boats and barges of all sizes and descriptions.

The sight was astonishing, for the town was lovely, perched as it was on a hill overlooking the harbor and the quays. The four-storied attached houses in greens and whites and pinks and blues sat above the main quay, the graceful Gothic cathedral spire piercing the sky behind them. The houses looked out over the harbor as if their windows were so many eyes staring westward to America, the next parish. For most of the emigrants, this would be their last look at Ireland. Nora stared hard as if to etch in her mind forever the look of Ireland, its people and houses, its skies and trees and flowers, its mists and mountains and lakes.

Mary, sensing something of what her daughter was thinking, put her arms around her, trying to comfort her.

Nora patted her hand gently and reassuringly. "It's all right, Ma. We'll be fine, really we will, and we'll soon be sending for all of you."

But Mary saw a look in Nora's eyes that belied the gentle voice. It was saying something else, and Mary didn't understand what. For Nora had already decided that her life and that of her family would to be better. She didn't know how exactly, but she knew that it was her purpose. Part of the reason for her determination was that doors had been unlocked for her to things she never knew existed, and then closed again abruptly. And she wanted them opened again.

Sean was excited. He was experiencing the departure differently from Nora, who was carrying her secret with her, looking forward with the enthusiasm of youth to a new adventure. Not that he wasn't sad about leaving his family, but he was full of optimism and, of course, poetry. He had been devouring Walt Whitman's poetry since he had found out he was going to America. Knowing that comic relief was needed at the moment, he jumped up on a barrel, smiled, opened his arms in a dramatic gesture and quoted, "Henceforth; I ask now good-fortune, I myself am good-fortune. Strong and content, I travel the open road." And he bowed low to their applause.

Everyone laughed, but that was actually the way he

felt. This trip was a great adventure. He was full of optimism and ready to test the world.

Mary hoped in her heart that this spirit would never be defeated, and as she looked at them, there came to her the sadness, the memories, the tears that always come with parting, but also a buoyant hope that life would be wonderful enough to make up for all the pains of parting with one's family, friends and country forever.

Sean and Nora went through the process of showing tickets, acquiring passports from the local consul and answering the questions that offered a concise history of both of them. Then medical examinations followed, and Nora was terrified when her mother insisted on going in to the doctor with her. What if he can tell, she thought naively, by looking? And her heart was in her mouth the entire time she was with the doctor. The doctor, however, suspected nothing, and wouldn't have cared that she was pregnant, for he was looking for contagious diseases. The steamship lines were responsible for making sure that the ill or lame or unfit did not make the trip, for the line would be required to bring them back to Ireland, free of charge. After the examination, they were vaccinated, and their baggage was disinfected. The routine was strange and frightening to many, especially to the uneducated and superstitious. They received their manifest numbers and headed to the main quay where the bandstand stood. The people were wailing, bustling about, arms loaded with bundles, boxes, baskets, crying farewells and pushing through other crowds of people doing the same. The uniformed band members were climbing up the stairs of the gay octagonal fenced bandstand. They began playing an old emigration ballad called "Noreen Bawn." Mary knew it well and thought it was a most unfortunate choice, for the lyrics told of "Noreen Bawn who sailed off, to that place where the Missouri, with the Mississippi flows," and then told of how she returned to Ireland, died, and her weeping mother sang, " 'Twas the shame of emigration, laid you low, my Noreen Bawn.''

"No wonder they have that group fenced in," Sean laughed, "for otherwise they'd be attacked with shillelagh cudgels for sure."

More people were arriving, for the train had come in a little earlier and the tracks dead-ended at the quay. The time of departure was nearing. The tender had already begun making its trips back and forth to the big steamship of the Inman Line, *Victoria*. People were loading by manifest number and it was then that Nora noticed that she and Sean had totally different manifest numbers. Fear gripped her. What did that mean?

The family moved off to a less crowded place, where each person had a few private moments, first with Sean, then with Nora.

Terence took Nora's hands in his. "I'm sorry, lass, that I blew up that night when Ma told us you and Sean were going to America. 'Tis not for me to go, Nora. 'Tis here that I'm needed, and truth is, 'tis here I'm wanting to be. I have a single goal in life, like a horse with blinders, and I believe I must have been put on this earth to pursue it, and that is to fight for Irish freedom, in whatever place, whatever way." She had seldom seen him so serious. "So forgive me, my treasure, do. I suppose my pride was hurt, but Ma and Pa are smart to be sending you two." He embraced her warmly. "Very smart. Good luck, lass, and be remembering your brother Terence when you're far from us."

"I'll never forget you, Terence. When I was a little girl, I said to myself that you were the best brother a girl could have. If it hadn't been for you, I would never have ridden, and you know what that has meant to me. And I'll never forget our Irish cause. You know you can count on

Sean, and I'll be helping you too. Just give me some time and I will, I promise."

"Aye, lass." He stared hard at her, remembering that day in the field years ago when they had peered through the hedgerows at the hunt, and she told him that she knew she'd be a good rider if she just had the chance. He had known then that she would fulfill that promise, as he now knew that she would fulfill this one. "Bless you, Nora. I'll be missing you." And they clung to one another.

Danny had his usual mournful look all day, but Sean joked with him, and he finally smiled. As Nora embraced him, she whispered that she'd be sending for him soon.

Bridget wept and hugged them both, repeating over and over how she'd be missing them and how she and Kevin would be seeing them in America soon. Kevin just stood shuffling from one foot to another, sad and uncomfortable, for he felt like his own brother and sister were leaving.

Their father stood looking desolate. These were the children he hadn't wanted to send, that he'd fought so hard to keep in Ireland, but Mary had won, and he was wondering how Mary felt at this moment. They were leaving, and he was only too aware that he might never see them again. His voice stuck in his throat. "Good-bye Nora. May God go with you. I love you, lass. You're a daughter any father would be proud of."

He had never said that much to her in her entire life, though she knew he felt it, and she buried her face in his rough tweed jacket.

And to Sean he said, "I expect great things, lad. I know you'll make us proud of you. Be careful, and take care of your sister."

Sean shook his father's hand solemnly, then threw his arms around him.

"Pa, I will," he said, trying to hold back the tears. "I will for sure."

Mary stood watching, numb with grief, but she attempted a smile and some words of love and advice. "Nora, dearest daughter, be careful, write often. Have faith. And remember what I've told you about the lace. You'll know when to use it." She paused to dab at her teary eyes. She threw her arms around Nora. "Oh God, how I'll be praying for you. Nora, Nora, you're our hope, you know that, don't you? And child, remember, there is in this life a law of compensation, I promise you there is. There has been for me."

Nora held her mother at arm's length and gazed into the blue eyes that had seen such sadness and grief. What were her compensations? she thought. Are they us, my father, what? And now more sadness for her. What will be the compensation for that. "Yes, Ma, I know. I've known for a long time. Don't worry. I'll see to it. I will." Her face carried a look of purpose that almost frightened Mary.

Now Sean embraced her. "And Sean darling," she told him, "write your lovely words. You'll add some beauty to this world, I know."

Terence grasped Sean's hands. "And lad, write your words for your country, too. That way you'll be adding some justice to this world."

Their eyes met, and Sean, now very serious, promised, "You can count on me, Terence. 'Tis important to me too. You know that."

"Some of us will be lighting the bonfire for you," Terence added. Sean knew it was a symbolic gesture, and would be the last thing they would see as Ireland faded from their view.

There were the final embraces and tears and farewells as Nora and Sean climbed down the ladder into the tender.

Oh God, hear me please, please take care of them,

Mary prayed silently, and aloud she called, "We love you, we love you, we love you."

Those were the last words Sean and Nora heard as the sailor closed the doors of the tender. They sat in stricken silence as people shoved and cried.

When they arrived at the ship, they found out that the different manifest numbers meant they would be in different places on the ship. Some of the married couples, noticing the differences in their manifest numbers, started wailing. Nora and Sean just stared at each other sadly. Nora asked if they would be able to see each other during their journey, and the young sailor explained they could meet on deck sometimes.

They pushed and found a place on the rail. A huge bonfire was burning and they knew it was Terence's.

" 'Tis the last thing we'll see," Nora said sadly.

"Aye," Sean replied, his excitement dimmed for the moment, as the enormity of what was happening dawned on him. The ship's whistles blew and the huge steamer started to pull slowly out of the harbor.

Nora clutched the rail to drink in the sight, the last sight of Ireland. She spoke softly, to herself, but Sean heard and knew the poem and they recited it together as a litany. " 'Long, long be my heart with such memories filled, As the vase in which roses have once been distilled, You may break, you may shatter the vase if you will, But the scent of the roses will hang around still.' " They held hands and watched their country fade into the distance. Mostly it was green, but Nora thought of the brown of the bogs and the grey of the rocks in the west. They watched the sea bathing the Emerald Isle and the mists blowing and the clouds floating. Terence's bonfire was bigger than the others, and its soaring flames and tall columns of smoke were the last things they could see as the shoreline disappeared from sight. The ship headed westward to the next parish. America.

On shore the family stared and waved until the ship was out of sight, and then they stood a little longer. The bonfires were now only smoldering ashes.

The ride home had been almost silent. No one had the heart to speak. The only sound was the women crying and the men clearing their throats to hold back their own tears. Though leaving for America had been Mary's idea, she was filled with doubt and sorrow. Oh, what have I sent them to? she agonized silently. How will those innocents make their way in a strange land? Thank the Lord for Jim and Nellie.

As they rounded the last curve, and the cottage came into view, they saw someone standing by the gate. It was hard to see with everything bouncing around from the motion of the cart, but soon they saw it was a man.

At the gate, Seamus Gorman was squinting, trying to pick out Nora's figure in the cart coming toward him. He had never in his life done such a bold thing as fall in love with a girl on first sight and then come without warning to ask if he might court her. In fact, he had taken a job and rented a room in Ballygarry so that he could be near her. This might have been folly in some people, but Seamus had that singleness and steadfastness of purpose that made him know his mind on the spot. Nora had known this intuitively and had called it a strength. He wasn't a foolish man with an eye for many girls. He knew what he wanted in life, and right now, that was to have Nora for his wife. He was sure he spotted her and he began to wave and run toward the cart. Frank stopped the horses as Seamus reached them, out of breath.

"Nora, Nora, it's me, girl." But it was not Nora. It was a woman who was an older, lovely version of his

Nora. He remembered his grandfather once telling him, "Before you marry, lad, look at the mother, for 'tis what your wife will be like in twenty years' time." He certainly liked what he saw.

"Oh, you must be Nora's ma. Mrs. O'Sullivan, I'm Seamus Gorman. I met your daughter in Cork." He pulled off his cap and thrust his hand up to Frank.

"Aye, Seamus, she told us about you, and good things she was saying about you."

"I should have let you know I was coming, I know, but I wanted it to be in the way of a surprise for Nora."

"I'm afraid, lad, it's you who's in for a surprise, for we've just put Nora and her brother Sean on the boat for America. She's long gone by now, Seamus."

Seamus felt as if the wind had been knocked out of him. His knees buckled and he reached for the cart.

"Here, lad, are you all right?" Frank climbed down and helped Seamus walk to the house.

After he had had a drop, Seamus told Mary and Frank everything. He poured out his love for Nora and his hopes to marry her. He had never felt such desolation. He loved her so and now he might never see her again. They were all sorry, for they all liked Seamus instantly, much as Nora had. His rawboned good looks, his straightforwardness and his warmth were evident to everyone. He remembered what he had said to Nora when she had told him Ballygarry was quite a distance away, and he said it aloud. " 'Ah, 'tis distance lends enchantment to the view.' " But this time it was said without hope.

Mary looked at him sharply. My God, she thought, is he another Sean, then, what with his quoting poetry?

"Well, that's the way it is, and there's no help for it," Terence said, putting an arm around Seamus' shoulder. "You're here, and she's there, so you'd best be accepting it. Come on, man, let's saddle up. We'll go to

Mulligan's pub. You'll feel better after a few porters. We'll go by the castle and pick up my new brother-in-law, providing my sister will let him out of her sight."

Bridget let Kevin join them after she had heard Seamus' sad story. She insisted that he stay with Kevin in the head groom's quarters for as long as he could before returning to Cork. "I know we're a poor substitute, Seamus," she told him, "but we are Nora's family and we welcome anyone who loves her as you do."

He liked Bridget. While she was different in appearance and demeanor from Nora, he sensed that same caring about people that he had liked instantly in Nora.

Mulligan's was crowded, smoky and noisy, and Terence sensed the mood was ugly almost as soon as they came in the door. The Sinn Fein, an anti-British group of which he was a member, had been recruiting in the village, and tempers were running high. Looking around the room, Terence thought of the group's motto, "We Ourselves." He wished his people felt and responded more strongly to that creed, but most of the Irish seemed to like to talk more about the injustices done to them rather than do anything about them. Terence paid only lip service to the Sinn Fein in terms of loyalty, and this was due to his activist nature. The passive resistance encouraged by that group did not suit him at all. As open as he was about belonging to the Sinn Fein, he kept his activities within the Irish Republican Brotherhood—known as the IRB—completely secret, for his life depended on it. Gentle and amiable as Terence was most of the time, his fierce love of his country, coupled with his hatred of injustice, suited him perfectly for his undercover work with the Brotherhood. If the British wouldn't willingly give the land to the people it rightfully belonged to, then, Terence reasoned, they would have to force the issue by violence, if that's what it took. Ireland for the Irish was the creed that sustained him during the long hours he spent hidden away, learning to construct the bombs he felt would help restore righteousness in his country.

He roused himself from his own thoughts to listen to Seamus and Kevin's conversation with two villagers who had come from market that day in Limerick. To Terence, it was the same weekly recital of English wrongdoings. It was true that the English merchants came over to buy with every intention of taking advantage of us, he thought, hearing again the litany of injustices: how the best cattle, fed on the finest grain, were sold to the crafty English for whatever they had a mind to offer, how the firkins of the best butter brought pennies and were then resold in England for fancy prices.

"All their profits are made at our expense," said Seamus. "They'd buy our houses from under us and leave us homeless if they could find a buyer for them in England."

Those surrounding him murmured agreement, and Terence added, "A lad after my own heart, sure, and the bastards would drive us out of Ireland if they could." He paused thoughtfully for a moment. "Why, come to think of it, haven't they already done that? There are now more Irish men and women in America than there are left here." More assent. " 'Tis a sad thing, this emigration." He thought of Nora and Sean, then shook off the thought. "See, Kevin, there are others who feel as strongly as I. I'm not the only one who hates the Brits. Seamus, come, let's find us a table. I want to talk to you. And Kevin, you join us as well. It would do you good to get the stable hay out of your ears and listen to some straight talk. Lord Anthony, being the gentleman that he is, has lulled you into thinking you're getting a fair shake in life."

Life is never fair, Seamus thought in his dejection over losing Nora. But in that moment he swore to himself that he would find a way to go to America, and there he would seek out his Nora and make her his own.

A ship's officer was herding the people on deck down a deep stairway leading to the enclosed lower decks. When he looked at Sean and Nora's manifest cards, he ordered them in opposite directions.

Suddenly terrified, Nora screamed, "No, I want to be with my brother! Why are you separating us? Please don't separate us!"

The officer looked at her condescendingly and said, "Men and women do not bunk together."

"Oh Sean, Sean, please try to meet me on deck tomorrow at one o'clock."

"I will, Nora. I'll be getting to you somehow."

With that Nora was swept down the narrow, steep, slippery stairs. She was carrying bundles of food, a comforter, a little bottle of the poteen, and a large bottle of water given to her by Peggy O'Riordan. The water was heavy and she didn't see the sense to bringing it, but Peggy had told Nora that her brother had made the trip and had said it was absolutely essential. She suddenly realized she was in a line in front of a storeroom and some articles were being handed out. The next thing she knew was that a blanket was thrust at her. In it was a tin pan, a dipper cup, a spoon and a fork. A very fat woman behind her commented, "You notice, deary, there's no knife. Me husband wrote 'twas because you're ready to murder by the end of the trip." She laughed, showing a mouth full of black and decaying teeth. Nora moved away from her as quickly as she could, precariously balancing all her bundles as she continued down the steep stairs.

Her manifest compartment was J, and after much searching, someone finally directed her to the right place. Compartment J was a room that extended the entire breadth of the ship and about one third of its length. The ceiling was less than seven feet high. The floor was wooden. A framework of iron pipes formed a double tier of six-by-two-feet berths, uppers and lowers, with very little space in between left to serve as aisles. A strong, unpleasant smell of disinfectant assailed her nostrils. She had never been in such a large, ugly room, but all she wanted to do was set her bundles down somewhere. Women were rushing about, staking out their territories, and she thought she had better do the same. She looked about and, seeing where the toilets were, ran to the opposite end of the room, where the odor was not so bad. She chose a berth, threw down her belongings and sat down, not knowing what else to do. A feeling of despair was rising in her, but she didn't want to give in to it. She stared at the mayhem. There were already over one hundred women in the room, and it looked like there were bunks for as many as three hundred. She shuddered and wished Sean were with her, as a pervasive feeling of isolation, even amidst hundreds, swept over her. As she sat looking at the activity, wishing she could close her ears to the din of voices, tears involuntarily streamed down her face.

A woman dropped her belongings in a berth next to Nora and bent down and patted her. "There, there, child, don't be crying," she soothed. "Remember, anything worth having is worth suffering for."

Nora looked up into the kind, healthy peasant face of the speaker. She was embarrassed. "I'm sorry. I was just feeling sorry for myself."

" 'Tis natural, girl, but save the tears. You'll be using them enough in this life."

At that moment, Nora saw a flash of red hair across the room. The movement looked familiar. She stared hard to find the owner of the hair. Then she ran across the narrow aisle, down a second aisle and up to the girl, who turned around at that instant.

"Molly, is it you?" Nora asked, knowing it was, and the years fell away as they fell into each other's arms.

"Nora, Nora darling. I can't believe 'tis you. Let me look at you. Oh, you're wonderful, more beautiful than ever."

"Molly, where have you been? Whatever happened to you? I wrote and wrote you in Ballinasloe, but you never answered."

"Oh Nora, 'tis a long story. I'll tell you, but first meet my baby, Retta." A darling, red-haired baby, the image of Molly, gurgled at Nora. "She's not yet a year old, and her daddy hasn't seen her, but we're on our way."

Molly seemed so happy that Nora was reassured. Then she suddenly thought of the berths. "Come, Molly. The berth above me is empty. I'll take it and you take the bottom one because of the baby." She took Retta and ordered Molly to get her things and follow her.

"The same old Nora," she smiled, remembering how Nora had always told her what to do, and how she so willingly had done it.

They settled themselves and the baby, and then they started talking. They huddled together on the bottom berth, which, being against a bulkhead, acted as a back against which they stacked their blankets and comforters.

"Nora, 'tis like Father O'Rourke's rectory when we'd be listening to the glorious old tales."

"Aye, and it is that, Molly." Nora remembered that Molly's sunny disposition and outlook had made everyone fond of her. Nora thought, imagine her comparing this ugly, smelly place to Father O'Rourke's lovely little rectory. Well it's all in how you see it. I can be learning from her. Then she said, "Molly, Sean is with me, but, of course, he's fore in the men's section."

"Sure, and isn't that the way of it," Molly answered. "The men always fore and us always aft. Baby Sean, how is he? I can't wait to see him."

"Aye, Molly, but baby Sean is now sixteen, and six feet tall!"

They both laughed.

"Now Molly, I want you to tell me everything. What happened to you? Didn't you ever get my letters? Who is your husband? Is he handsome? How are your folks?"

The last question brought a sad look to Molly's face. "They're dead, Nora," she murmured, dropping her chin. "Killed in a factory fire."

"Oh Molly, I'm sorry." She put her arms around her childhood friend.

Nora thought of her own mother and the sorrows she had suffered, and saw the same unconquerable spirit in Molly. She hugged her again.

At that moment, several cooks came in with big iron pots of soup and started dishing it out. Nora now understood the reason for the dipper cup. The soup looked unappetizing and tasted worse, but they ate a little bit. Nora opened the bag and they shared some of the homemade soda bread. When they finished, they got up to find out where they washed their cup and tin plate. There were several basins full of salt water, and the line was long.

"Surely this can't be how we do it," Nora remarked to Molly, and a woman farther up in line said, "Ah, Your Majesty, how do you propose we be doing it, then?"

Nora was embarrassed, for some of the women began to snicker. "Well I had been informed that the basins were golden and each one of us would have a servant," she joked. "Isn't that true, then?"

More laughed. Nora knew instinctively in this crowd

that it would be best to play down her education and her innocence. Later, when she found out that this was the same water they would use to bathe themselves, she felt sick to her stomach. She and Molly talked and talked until a neighbor asked them to be quiet so she could sleep. They apologized and prepared their berths. The beds had no springs. They consisted of metal strips and a straw mattress with an awful smell. The mattress failed to cushion the hard feel of the metal below them. Their pillows were life preservers of hard cork. Nora had a comforter she used for padding, for it was so stifling that she didn't need to use it as a cover.

Everyone slept in their clothes.

As she tried to sleep, thoughts of her family, William, and Seamus floated through her mind. There was snoring and coughing. And there was crying. But she finally fell asleep to the deafening staccato of trembling steel railings. Nora was happy that she had found Molly again.

The next morning she awoke to find Molly standing over her. "Nora, if we're wanting to wash, we'll be needing to get on line."

And they did, waiting for a half-hour to use the foul-smelling toilets and then wipe off their hands and faces in the stagnant salt water. Nora thought of the bottle of water Peggy O'Riordan had insisted that she bring, and now she knew why. She would use a little each day to wash her face and give Molly a bit for herself and the baby. But would it last ten days? She thought not, but they would do the best they could.

The ship was now in the open seas, and the swells were beginning to wreak their havoc. Some had been seasick since stepping on board, but others were only now beginning to feel ill. Nora was somewhat ill, but she thought it was just her usual morning sickness. A piece of soda bread helped enormously. They were assigned a time to go up on deck to get some fresh air, but it wasn't one o'clock, the time she had arranged with Sean. She was feeling panicky that she might not see him at all. Molly reassured her that they would find a way.

"Perhaps," Nora said hopefully, "he'll be assigned the same time." They went up on deck, and they were situated in the worst part of the ship, where the motion was most violent. Dirt had settled from the stacks and sickening odors creeped up from the hold and galleys. Still, it was "fresh" air, something completely lacking below. Sean wasn't with the group of men there, and Nora was beginning to worry about him. At least she had Molly.

Chapter 10

By the third day, Nora was weaving and pale. Molly was concerned, and tried to calm her down. "You're just seasick. You'll be all right," she said reassuringly. But she saw that Nora's face was flushed and her hand was hot in hers. Dear God, Molly thought, she has the fever. I hope it's not dysentery. I wonder if the doctor will be by again today. He had made two quick cursory looks in the compartment, but that was all.

Nora lay on the bed as sick as she had ever been. After three days, the stench in the compartment was unbearable. There were odors of scattered orange peelings, garlic, tobacco, the smell of vomit that the disinfectants couldn't remove, stale soup, and the relentless odor from the toilets. Molly didn't want to waste their good water, so she stood in line to soak a cloth with cold sea water. Retta was fretting, and Molly was terrified that she would get sick, too. Dear God, help us, she prayed silently. Many of those who were not seasick were ill with dysentery, and while she nursed Nora, she watched a young woman several bunks down tend and lose her sister. Molly went on deck with her when they tossed her sister's body over the side into a watery grave.

Nora remained in a stupor and lay there quietly, sometimes retching into her tin plate. Molly would then empty it. She knew she couldn't succumb, though the huge waves were tossing the boat ferociously, and she too just wanted to lie in her berth. Heavy seas continued for another day, and the women just lay on their beds moaning and retching. 'Tis a nightmare, Molly thought. 'Tis better Nora doesn't know what's happening. And indeed Nora did not. She was delirious. Please God, don't let her die, Molly prayed.

Molly left the baby with a woman named Tess, who wasn't as sick as some of the others, and ran to fetch the doctor. She pleaded with him to come, but with some two thousand persons on the ship, many of whom were seasick or had dysentery, he had his work cut out for him. He promised her he would be there as soon as possible. She sat nursing Nora as best she could.

The weather began to improve and people started to move about again, but Nora seemed worse. She had been delirious for two days and showed no signs of improvement. Finally, on the sixth day out, the doctor came. He examined her, admitting it was dysentery, and gave her some medicine to take. Within a few hours, Molly noticed some improvement, but Nora was still delirious. She started to speak incoherently. At first Molly paid no mind, but then she began to listen, for Nora was raving about someone named William, and about a baby. It suddenly began to make sense, and Molly realized with a shock that Nora was having a baby out of wedlock, by someone named William. Her heart went out to Nora, and she wondered what plans, if any, Nora had made. She sat silently, sadly, guarding and nursing her old friend.

Nora began to get some color back and she said a few sentences to Molly that began to make some sense, but mostly she lay there in a stupor listening with a hazy brain to the talk, the music and the dancing. Despite the miserable conditions, life went on when the seas were calmer. There were constant card games, much music on accordions and harmonicas and even some dancing. By now, the men and women were moving about more freely and were coming into one another's compartments. Nora became more and more aware of what was going on around her, and she listened quietly to the endless conversations about past lives and present hopes. It seemed a miracle to her that people could talk of their glowing hopes for their futures amid the squalor of the dingy, crowded, confused jungle of steerage.

Molly finally got her to eat some stale bread with honey on it.

"Oh Molly, sure, and it tastes like manna."

Molly breathed a sigh of relief, feeling the worst was over. But Nora, weak and still very ill, began to feel that God was punishing her. Her guilt became overpowering. She remained quiet and listless.

"Are you wanting to see Sean now, darling Nora?" Molly asked.

Nora, believing she was dying, said she did.

Molly had taken honey from her scant savings to bribe one of the stewards into bringing Sean down.

Sean couldn't believe what he saw. His darling sister looked pale and wasted and she was speaking strangely.

"Oh Sean, I'm a terrible sinner and God is punishing me," she told him. She kept repeating this over and over.

Sean, not knowing about the baby, could make no sense of what she was saying. He had been in endless political discussions during the trip, which had reinforced his own radical political leanings. Misunderstanding what she was saying, he started to lecture her. "You have not sinned. You have been sinned against as we all have by the monstrous British."

She stared up at him and understood all too clearly that what he was saying applied on two levels, the political injustices of the last few hundred years, and the personal injustice of her own situation. She smiled weakly at him. "Aye, lad, you don't know how right you are." She sat up slightly to eat the bread that Molly proffered. Sean kissed her and left.

Nora regained her strength rapidly and made Molly sleep while she took care of Retta.

One of the women burst into their compartment one morning and shouted, "We're arriving tomorrow."

"It can't be. That's a day early."

"Sure, and I'm knowing that, but one of the ship's officers told several of the men on deck."

This caused great joy, and a fat, frowsy woman pulled out her harmonica and began to play. Singing started, and some of the children began to dance. "Glory be," Molly said happily.

But the trip had taken its toll. Many of the women were disoriented, and they babbled about having their papers in order. The lack of exercise and the stench had left them in a state of bewilderment. Many felt lonely and lost and trembled because of the strangeness and confusion. When Nora went on deck and met Sean, she told him wearily, "If we can endure what we have just been through, we can endure anything."

He quietly reached over to hold her hand.

Land was sighted the next afternoon. The boat slowed down and the pilot came on board from the Ambrose Lightship. People streamed up on deck to see their first sight of America, the shore of Long Island. Some broke into tears, wailing and keening. As they waited in quarantine in the lower bay of New York harbor, they tried to recognize relatives in the groups collected on the Brooklyn shore at Gravesend Bay. After the passengers were inspected for contagious diseases, the ship continued through the narrows, where rural shorelines gave way to the harbor itself. At that point in time, the tip of Manhattan Island was only six miles away. As the ship moved slowly through the narrows, one of the most spectacular views in the world came into sight: Manhattan Island. The immigrants were overwhelmed, for the first object they saw was the Statue of Liberty stretching her torch of freedom into the sky. They knew, down to the smallest child, what it meant. The crowds on the decks cheered and sobbed. About a half mile to the northwest was Ellis Island. Soon the buildings on the lower tip of Manhattan came clearly into view. Sean and Molly and Nora stared in awe and amazement.

"Why, some of those buildings must be twenty or twenty-five stories high," Nora said. The highest building she had ever seen was in Cork City, and it was six stories high. They couldn't stop staring.

"Faith, and it's a wonder!" Molly cried. Sean, for once, was speechless.

The ship finally docked, and they walked across the gangplank to the barge that would take them to the island. As they neared the island, they saw a building, oriental in appearance, with four cupolas. The crowds were pushing and shoving. Babies were screaming. Another ship had docked at the same time, disgorging its one thousand steerage passengers. Nora had never seen so many people in one place, or heard so many strange tongues.

The lines were snaking around through a maze. "Sean, look they're eating in there," Nora noted. They entered the restaurant, which was all white tile, and clean. They sat down, looking about. Someone brought them a bowl of soup and two sandwiches.

"Real food, Sean, real food," Nora said as they devoured their meal. "Maybe now we'll have the strength to go through the processing. It looks like a grim procedure. Did you see the doctors pulling up the eyelids? It looked so painful. But never mind, we're here, lad, we're in America. It's noisy and crowded, and they pull up eyelids, God knows looking for what. But Sean, we're here, and it doesn't smell." They both smiled.

They moved slowly through the line and received a cursory physical examination. As they were watching, they noticed that the doctors were making chalk marks on some of the immigrants' shoulders and were sending them in a different direction. One man had a large L written on his shoulder.

"What does it mean, I wonder," Sean said, looking at the man.

A large, cross-eyed woman behind them explained that it meant he was lame and would be detained. "I know," she said, "because they'll mark me. Me eyes, you know, but I've a note from me doctor in Galway."

A woman large with child was marked PG, and Nora started to tremble, for she concluded it meant pregnant. She thought of Danny and his limp, and she wondered if indeed she would ever be able to bring him here. And will they know about me? she thought to herself.

Despite their worries, both Nora and Sean passed the examination without a problem.

As they looked around the large, airy reception room, their admittance cards in their hands, they noticed, almost for the first time because they had been so preoccupied, the colorful throng of humanity. Many aliens had come in their native dress. There were Hungarians in rough jackets and top boots, Russians in cossack hats of fur or lambskin, and a guard told them that the Rumanians, no matter what the season, wore big sheepskin coats. And Nora and Sean saw the first black person they'd ever seen. They were fascinated. He was one of the clerks asking endless questions of the immigrants. Most of the men had beards or mustaches, and all the women had shawls of one kind or another. Many women were wearing aprons. Some had bedroom slippers on and still others were barefoot.

In the baggage area, Nora watched as the strange potpourri of people grabbed their bundles and baskets and battered cases bulging with their precious possessions. They'd packed religious objects, pictures of family and friends, bowls, vases, comforters, pillows, letters. One County Clare man—they knew his origin from his accent— had a pot of shamrock. "A piece of the old sod, you know," he beamed.

Somehow they got everything but one small bundle of Nora's. It was nowhere to be found. Nora, fatigued and weak, suddenly turned white. "Sean, 'twas the bundle I had with me the whole trip, the one with Uncle Jim's address in it."

"Oh no, Nora," he said worriedly. "Pray God he's here, but remember, we're a day early."

"Never mind. My husband, Tim, will find him if it comes to that," Molly said with a spark of optimism.

They piled onto a squat, many-windowed ferry that took them to the terminal at the battery. Excitement was mounting. They were actually going to set foot on American soil. They walked off the ferry with all their belongings, Sean helping Nora, Molly carrying Retta. And then Nora started to cry. The illness, the stress of the trip, the endless questions and the fear of having her pregnancy discovered, all took their toll. She couldn't stop. Indeed she seemed to have no control. Sean and Molly tried to comfort her, but the tears wouldn't stop.

Finally her weeping ended, as if she had been cleansed. They walked down the walks enclosed with wire netting, and on the other side of the netting was an expectant crowd of relatives and friends. The air was charged with excitement as greetings were shouted back and forth, questions were asked, names were called. The Italians were gesticulating wildly. One handsome man racing down the walk knocked a woman's straw hat off, and she hit him with her cardboard case. A fistfight was averted by a poor, put-upon guard who, Nora thought, must run to the pub every evening after dealing with this seething mass of humanity.

At that moment, the gates opened. Men and women ran into the arms of their loved ones, sobbing, laughing, embracing, kissing. The years fell away and the separation and sorrow were forgotten. This moment of joy replaced the past.

Molly screamed, "There he is, there's Tim!" She ran to him, sobbing.

He grabbed her, looked into her face. Then he covered her with kisses. "My Molly, my beautiful, dearest Molly." They hugged each other, crying and kissing.

Sean and Nora stood by awkwardly, for they didn't wish to intrude on this private moment. They looked the other way, but they were happy for Molly, and they thought Tim looked like a fine, strong Irishman. He had a crop of curly brown hair, strong, wide shoulders, and a more than obvious love for their friend.

At last Molly said, "And here is your baby daughter, Retta, and two of my oldest friends in the world, Sean and Nora O'Sullivan."

Tim took Retta proudly, gazed at her lovingly, and shook hands with Nora and Sean. "What a stroke of luck, her meeting you on the ship. Who is coming for you?"

"Well, our Uncle Jim, my mother's brother, should be here."

"I see. Well, you know your ship is a day early. I knew because my brother-in-law is working on the docks, but there will be many folks not knowing. You'll just have to go to his house."

Nora blanched. "We've lost his address." She explained that the small bundle containing his address had been lost.

"Well then," Tim said, as if it were no problem at all, "you'll be staying with us till this gets straightened out. We'll leave a note for him at the information desk."

"Oh Tim, thank you," Nora said gratefully, as did Sean.

" 'Tis happy I am to be doing it for old friends of my Molly," Tim returned, and Molly beamed happily at them.

Tim hailed a carriage. Sean looked impressed. Noting this, Tim said, "I'm splurging today for my wife and baby and honored friends."

As they drove through Lower Manhattan, Sean and Nora were speechless. Tim enjoyed being tour guide as he pointed out all the places of interest. The towering buildings on either side of the carriage were almost more than they could absorb.

"Ten stories, I can't believe it." Sean felt his fatigue and apprehensions giving way to curiosity and excitement. The carriage headed north on Broadway.

"Oh, I've read about Broadway, all the theaters and shops." Nora was so excited that she couldn't sit still. Tim detoured down Wall Street to show them the Stock Exchange. Then they went back to Broadway and northeast on Park Row past City Hall and Five Points, an area in which many of the Irish had settled.

"We're on the Bowery now, and to the left is Chinatown.'' By now they were hanging out of the carriage windows so as not to miss a single thing in this incredible city. The carriage then went west on Canal Street and made a right-hand turn on Mulberry Street.

Molly knew when she saw the street sign that this was their street. She squeezed Tim's hand excitedly. ''We're here, we're here.''

''Almost,'' he laughed, ''but I'm warning you, 'tis no palace.''

As they reached Hester Street, a sight greeted their eyes that might as well have been taking place on another planet. Pushcarts lined the streets and people were everywhere. The carriage could barely get through. As they hung out of the windows gaping at the sights, several boys in the street screamed at them derisively.

''Greenhorns, greenhorns!''

''Off with you!'' Tim shouted at them.

But they *were* greenhorns. Of that there was no doubt. He explained that it was a slang term meaning they were raw, inexperienced newcomers.

''Well, we could have told them that,'' Sean laughed.

They pulled up in front of a six-story tenement on Mulberry Street off Hester. They got out and threaded their way with the boxes and bundles and baby.

As they entered, the smell of cabbage and onions and frying fish, the sound of children and whirring sewing machines, and all the other smells and sounds of tenement houses, met them head-on. They climbed four flights of stairs. When they reached the top, they were huffing and breathless, for they were all weak from the trip. Tim bounded up the stairs and opened the door, and a group of about twenty-five Irish men and women greeted them loudly.

''Welcome to America,'' both banners and voices proclaimed.

Nora had heard of the custom of newcomers being

soundly greeted by cheering people, either friends, relatives or merely fellow countrymen. They were swept into the tiny but clean flat, and were embraced and welcomed. Tired as they were, they reacted warmly to this welcome, for it helped them to overcome the strangeness and the fear that everyone in the room had already experienced. A fiddler started to play, and some of the younger children started off the dancing. Drinks flowed freely, but not the familiar poteen of Ireland, though Irish whiskey was plentiful. The noise was deafening, and now she knew why it was called a kitchen racket party. Introductions were made and all kinds of questions were asked. Advice about everything from jobs to where to buy the best and cheapest bread was given.

Sean and Nora and Molly were overwhelmed but happy. Tim explained that they had two bedrooms because his boarders had just moved to Philadelphia. The rent was paid to the end of the month, so he had elected to stay till then.

" 'Twas providence, that's what it was, providence, so you two can have this room. There's only one bed, but I see you have comforters, and a fine strapping young man such as yourself should find the floor to his liking."

Some old gentleman from Limerick said he had known Nora's father "when he was a wee wain," and he danced off with her. She started smiling, and laughing, and joking, and took a sip of the brew. Some of the aching loneliness was leaving. She and Sean smiled across the room at one another. She hugged Molly, thanked Tim over and over, and then, not used to the drink, tired from the trip, and still weak from the fever, collapsed in Tim's arms.

When she opened her eyes, it was morning. She looked around at the tiny room, with its one wooden dresser, its frayed curtains and cracked mirror. It's a palace compared to the ship, she thought. Sean was snoring on the floor next to her. Then she looked up, and in the doorway a banner hung askew. It said in bold red, white and blue letters, WELCOME TO AMERICA. She smiled and thought, Dear God, we're here. We're really here.

Chapter 11

Gaelic and English were the only languages Nora had ever heard. Her ears now rang with the sound of Russian, German, Rumanian, Hungarian, Chinese and Italian. Her eyes saw customs and clothing and sights completely unfamiliar. It was fascinating. Still, she was a little homesick for Ireland. She missed the sweet country air, the mists on the purple mountains, and the voice of the cuckoo coming from some ancient hawthorn bush. Yet, there was something about this place which was exhilarating. She felt alive and full of hope.

She wandered the streets listening, watching, dreaming. Would she ever be part of this America? What would she do? She knew she had to work for a few weeks before leaving for Massachusetts. She was worried about Sean, as they had not heard from Uncle Jim. She knew that Molly and Tim would be good to him, for they already accepted him as they would a brother. She had written her mother immediately, telling her how they couldn't find Jim because of the ship's early arrival, and how they had lost his address. And now, Nora didn't know where she was supposed to go for a job. Nora made up her mind to go to Lowell and look for Father Mahoney, an old friend of Father O'Rourke's, her pastor in Ireland. How many Father Mahoneys could there be? She felt sure she could find him. As she wandered down Hester Street, she turned a corner and suddenly was in the midst of a large, noisy crowd. Curious to know what they were doing, she edged closer. A young, dark girl in a colorful peasant dress was involved in some strange activity that appeared to be a form of bartering. Nora asked her what was going on. With a strong Russian accent, she explained that it was the Khazzer Mark. When Nora stared blankly, the young girl searched her mind, for her English vocabulary was limited, and finally said, "I think it's what you call in English pig market." She went on to explain that these men were clothing contractors by trade and they were bidding furiously for workers.

"Where do they take you if you get the job?"

"Into these tenements. They call them sweatshops and that's what they are." She smiled ruefully. "But," she said, appraising Nora, "there aren't many of you Irish who do that. Most of you have already moved uptown."

"What do you have to be able to do to get one of these jobs in a sweatshop?" she asked, interested.

"Well, for one thing, you need to know how to run a sewing machine," the girl replied.

Nora watched the market for a while longer, fascinated by this crude method of hiring and firing people. So that's what the whirring sewing machines are doing in our building. She thanked the young girl and headed for Broadway, where she was going to cash her bank draft, the money from William, and deposit it in the Emigrant's Savings Bank. She thought that a bank with such a name was surely all right.

Nora, like most of the other immigrants, hadn't brought many clothes, and what she had was hopelessly out of style here. While many of the immigrants simply wore what they had worn in the old country, the ones who were wearing American clothes somehow looked more like they belonged here. From the time she was a child, Nora had always looked nice, no matter how simple her clothes had been, but right now she knew she wanted to look like an American, and not like an Irish country girl.

However, she thought, whatever I buy had better be big enough to last me until the baby is born.

They loaded Retta in a little cart and set off to where Tim had told them to go. Retta was barefoot on this hot late-August day, smiling, intrigued by what was going on. She gurgled and cooed as they walked along toward Orchard Street. As they turned the corner, an incredible sight greeted their eyes. Stretching southward for blocks, all one could see was the teeming market of pushcart stalls and sidewalk peddlers hawking their wares. Mostly they were selling articles of clothing, but there were carts with pots and pans and one peddler was selling books.

One old Jewish peddler spoke to them. "So why is the baby with no shoes? Two such pretty ladies can surely afford to put some shoes on those little feet."

They were embarrassed, but then they saw he was only teasing them.

"You pretty shiksas look for clothes?"

They didn't know what a shiksa was, but said yes, they were.

"You go four stalls down. My brother has good stuff, fine stuff. You like."

Neither Nora nor Molly had ever met a Jew before, and they were excited by the experience. Four stalls down, they stopped and looked at the clothes.

"Ah, ladies, have I got the dresses for you," a tall,

bearded, but fairly young man said. By this time they were in the spirit. Tim had told them to bargain, and that it was expected.

Nora jumped right in. "Yes, your brother told us you would, and that you would give us a marvelous price."

Molly looked at her in amazement. What a surprising girl Nora was. She was already bargaining for what she wanted as though it were second nature.

Nora was having a wonderful time holding up the dresses, checking the quality of the fabrics and laughing with the young man, whose name was Max. Max claimed, "Oy, it's a bargain. For one dollar it's the latest Paris style."

Nora laughed. " 'Tis more like the latest Orchard Street style, but I like it. Fifty cents and I'll wear it home." They finally settled on seventy-five cents, and Nora had a lovely blue cotton dress, large enough to hide anything. Molly observed this, admiring Nora all the more. She could laugh and joke with a street peddler even while faced with the dilemma of her child.

But what about the baby? Molly thought sadly, wanting to talk to her about it, but afraid to broach the subject. Several times she had started to and then restrained herself. She wondered what Nora was going to do. But now Molly knew it was time to confront her.

As they walked along eating a penny Italian ice, Molly said, " 'Tis a wonderful dress, Nora, and I think a bargain. 'Tis lovely with your eyes." She paused a moment. "And, 'twill hide your condition for quite a while."

Nora spun around and looked at Molly. She made no denial. "Molly, Molly, how on earth are you knowing?"

"Lass, you told me on the ship, when you were delirious."

In the middle of the street, Nora threw her arms around Molly and hugged her and Retta. "Oh Molly, are you thinking I'm awful? Does Tim know? I've been so miserable, but the truth be known, I'm glad you're knowing. 'Tis a relief.''

"No, I'm not thinking you're awful. I love you and want to help you. Does anyone else know?''

"Only Father O'Rourke, who has arranged for me to go to Lowell, Massachusetts, to work in the textile mills until I deliver, for no one must know. Do you understand, Molly? No one, especially Sean, for it would be such a shame for my family.''

"Aye, lass, I understand, but my Tim already knows.'' Molly looked at the ground.

"And he hasn't thrown us out?'' Nora exclaimed.

"Oh Nora, no, he's not like that. We were just wondering when you were going to tell us, or what you were going to do. And Nora, what will you be doing with the baby?'' Molly asked gently. "Surely you can't care for him yourself.''

Nora's face paled. "Molly, I have to put him up for adoption. There is no other way.'' She tried to hold back the tears.

"Well, we'll see about that,'' Molly answered somewhat vaguely. "But faith, Nora, tell me what happened.''

After gaining control of herself, Nora told her the whole story.

"So, the baby will be gentry. A lord for a father. Isn't that the devil?'' Molly remarked. "And I recall seeing his royal highness a few times, blond, and rather high and mighty as I remember.''

"Aye,'' said Nora, churning inside as she listened to Molly's appraisal, her heart pounding with anger as she thought of William.

By this time they had arrived at the tenement, Molly carrying Retta—now wearing her brand-new shoes—and they climbed the stairs. Nora tried to peek into the flats where she heard the machines clicking away. The tenement smell always nauseated her, but once in their own flat, which had some light and air, she felt a bit better.

"I'm wondering if Sean has had any luck today, finding a job," Nora mused.

"We'll be knowing soon enough. Tim thought his friend Paddy at the local Democratic Club would be helping," Molly replied.

That night at dinner Sean told them he hadn't gotten a job yet, but that he was going with Paddy's recommendation to the Fulton Fish Market the next day. "And," Sean informed them, with a grand sense of himself, "I'm going down to the Democratic Club tonight to help Paddy with some party business."

"Oh, well, aren't you the important one? You two O'Sullivans are really something," Molly laughed. "Nora's been busy bargaining with everyone on Orchard Street, and our Sean's already running for city hall." She smiled.

Nora asked Tim about the pig market and he explained to her how clothing contractors came there for what he called the "shape up," which simply meant the act of hiring and firing. "It saves the expense of overhead, because they use their own homes instead of having to rent space. It's called the sweating system, and it's awful, Nora, awful, a dozen people in one badly lit, poorly ventilated room sewing long, hard hours for starvation wages."

Nora looked pensive. She mentioned to Tim the conversation she had had with the young Russian girl. "What did she mean, Tim, that we Irish were already uptown?"

Tim shook his head. "You've learned a lot, lass, in a few short days." He continued, lighting his pipe. "We Irish were the first to occupy these tenements, settling in the Five Points area where the well-to-do lived until the houses began to sag, having been built over a pond. But we've been coming in large numbers since the famine, and as we made better wages, we moved on to better neighborhoods. Those who stayed here were those who couldn't make it in America, and here they remained, deep in poverty. As new groups of immigrants came in, poor and wretched, from Italy, Greece, Rumania, we left. Your Uncle Jim, Nora, is most likely living farther uptown, for he's been here a long time. If only we could know for sure. There used to be shantytowns, right down on Cherry Street, and uptown too, where Central Park is now."

"Then why are we still here, Tim?" Molly said wonderingly.

"Because, love, 'tis cheaper. And for the moment I wanted to save every penny for our future. There's still some Irish here, mostly the new ones like you three."

Sean and Nora listened with great interest, but soon Tim turned to Sean. "Lad, you'll be late meeting Paddy. You'd better be going."

After he'd gone, Nora and Molly and Tim sat quietly for a time, lost in their own thoughts.

Nora broke the silence. "Tim, I realize you know about my baby," she said, obviously ill at ease, but confronting the problem directly. "I'm greatly appreciating your kind treatment of me, of us, seeing as what I've done." She was groping for words.

He interrupted. "I'm no one to judge you, lass. You're my Molly's childhood friend, and besides," he continued, puffing on his pipe, "I like you. We want to help."

"God bless you, Tim. You've been more of a friend than I ever could have hoped for." She sat quietly for a few moments, and then told him of her plans. "I'll be leaving in a few weeks, before everyone can see I'm with child, for I'll be showing soon, and Sean can't know. He mustn't. What I'm needing to ask is, can he stay with you until we find Uncle Jim? He'll be no trouble and he'll pay his way. I'll tell him I'm going away because I have an excellent offer for a few months, that the money is so good, I can't refuse, that it will give us a head start.''

"That's a good plan, Nora," Tim answered. "As for Sean, you needn't even ask. It goes without saying that he'll be staying with us." He looked at Molly and she nodded her head. "Nora, we too have a favor to be asking of you. A very big, very important favor."

"Of course. I would do anything for you. What is it?"

Molly pulled her chair closer to Nora, and Tim puffed at his pipe. He reminded Nora of her father and the times she used to sit in his lap as he smoked his pipe, happy and content with the world.

"Darling friend, life takes strange twists." Molly spoke almost in a whisper.

"Aye," Nora said, puzzled by Molly's serious tone of voice. "That it does." She nodded, though she was unsure of what Molly meant.

"God has given you a baby you can't keep, and I can never have another one," Molly continued.

"Oh, Molly, I didn't know. I'm so sorry." Nora placed her hand on Molly's.

"Well, we must accept that. But Nora, what Tim and I want to know is if you will let us adopt your baby. It would be as close as we could come to having our own, for you're such a part of my life, and now of both our lives, that we think God must have sent you to us."

Nora couldn't believe what she was hearing. She murmured a silent prayer of thanks and aloud, in a gentle voice, said, "Oh Molly, Tim, of course, of course. In my wildest dreams I couldn't have thought of two people I would rather have bring up my baby." She burst into tears of relief and happiness.

Molly put her arms around her friend, and she instinctively knew what Nora was wondering. "You'll be able to see the baby any time you like, Nora, even though no one, including the child, will know we're not its real parents. Not even Retta."

For the first time in weeks, Nora felt peaceful as she lay in bed. My baby will have the best parents God could give, she thought. Soon she was fast asleep.

Nora worried about their money. They had precious little left, and she had been firm with Tim and Molly about paying their share of the rent. It never occurred to Nora to touch the money at the Emigrant's Savings Bank. She pretended it wasn't even there, for she remembered what her father had said about having to have money to start a business and how the wages in America were barely enough for rent and food.

A few days later, she decided to go to the Ludlow Street Khazzer Mark to try to find a job for the few weeks she would be staying in New York. This she did against Tim's advice.

"Please hold on, my friends at the Democratic Club will come up with something," he had pleaded. But days went by and nothing happened. Sean had gotten a job at the Fulton Fish Market as a clerk. He worked from four a.m. to four p.m., and on Fridays, a big fish day for all the Catholics in New York, he started at three a.m.

"And I can have all the fish I can eat," he joked, "so we'll be saving on my food."

She arrived at the "pig market." Dealing had already begun. She knew she was at a disadvantage because she didn't have her own sewing machine, but she decided to give it a try. The dealing went on at a furious, noisy pace. Contracts were made, people left, others came. No one seemed interested in Nora, for there were enough people with their own machines. Finally, one contractor, looking lecherously at her, asked what she could do. Missing the double meaning, she earnestly tried to sell herself.

"Okay. Come with me," he ordered.

She followed him up tenement stairs far worse than any she had seen. Added to the smell of frying foods was a stronger odor of backed-up toilets. She was already regretting having come when they reached the fifth-floor landing, and she heard the dissonant symphony of the Lower East Side, the clicking, whirring of sewing machines. The door opened, and he beckoned her to move in quickly. The room was stifling, and already at work were four men, two young women and two children no older than ten. They were working on knickerbockers, which they referred to as "knee pants." Everyone kept their heads bowed to their work. A pale, sickly baby was asleep in the corner, propped up by scraps of fabric left after the knee pants were finished. Half-sewn garments littered the floor, and a pile of pants ready for the finisher stood in another corner. Nora was visibly shocked.

"So what were you expecting, carpets and soft lights?" he spat sarcastically. "My bonny Irish colleen, are you too good for this?"

She ignored his question and asked instead, "Where is my machine and what am I to do?"

"Becky will show you. Remember your quotas for today, one hundred and fifty," he said gruffly, addressing the others. As he left, he whispered to her, "Do a good job and there will be a bit extra for you." She was embarrassed and pretended not to hear. Becky, one of the young women, got up and gave her some directions. They weren't too clear, but from the corner of her eyes she watched the man next to her. He seemed to know what he was doing. She knew she was making mistakes, but by noon she was satisfied with her first attempts.

They were allowed to take twenty minutes to eat, but

the smell was so overpowering that she could barely even look at the food. The two young children, a boy and a girl, were looking shyly at her lunch pail.

"Come here, little ones. What are your names?" she asked, offering them a bite of her biscuit and cheese. With mouths full, they told their names, but they spoke Yiddish and she couldn't understand them. Her kindness to the children made an impression on the others, and sullen Becky came over and, in broken English, asked if Nora had any questions. Nora mentioned a problem or two and Becky offered to help her. The day dragged on endlessly. She hated it, and wondered how the children could stand it, and how their parents could let them do it.

Poor babies, she thought, feeling more pity for them than for herself.

She returned day after day, and one by one the others began to talk to her. When one man had told her he had been there five years, her heart nearly broke. She was more determined than ever to escape the bonds of poverty.

Although she thought the week would never end, finally Saturday night came, and that meant they'd be paid. Everyone seemed a bit more cheerful, and they waited for Mr. Levinsky to come with their wages.

He finally arrived all dressed up in a pin-striped suit and a high, starched collar. To Nora, however, he still looked greasy and repulsive. He paid each of them and they left one by one. Nora was last.

"Becky tells me you work hard. That's fine, fine. You look like a smart girl. I can always tell. For girls like you, there are extras in life, if you get what I mean." He winked at her.

What a disgusting fool, she thought, but she said, "Yes." She edged nervously toward the door. "Well, extras are fine, but I only want what's coming to me."

As she reached for the money, he demanded, "Give me a kiss now, honey."

Suddenly, she grasped what he meant by extras. She twisted to one side, grabbed the money from his hands and ran down the stairs as fast as she could.

He screamed after her, "Come back here, you little mick, come back."

Nora hurried on, never looking back.

Chapter 12

Sean was intrigued by the political system in New York, for it was at this time run almost exclusively by the Irish in Tammany Hall. These were the sons and grandsons of men who had never been allowed to hold office in their own country. The second and third-generation Irish in America were as dedicated as ever to the perennial cause of Irish freedom.

Sean monitored the operations of the Tammany machine with fascination. Because the Irish knew the language and used it eloquently, were born organizers and understood the Anglo-Saxon middle-class culture they were living in, they naturally assumed the role of mediator between the Protestant ruling classes of America and the tens of thousands of Poles, Italians, Greeks, Lithuanians and Russians pouring into the country. While there were frictions between the different groups, prejudices and hatreds, the Irish were quick to learn that they had to work with all these groups to establish their own place in America.

Sean went to the local Democratic Club one evening a

week to teach English to a newly arrived group of Italian immigrants. He remembered how frightened he'd been of this strange new country. He thought how much worse it was for those who often didn't know more than a few words of English. He was their link to the alien environment, and they loved him. He was caught up in the adventure of his new country. He considered the long hours at the Fulton Fish Market part of the price he had to pay for admission to this land of opportunity and wonder.

He told everyone at dinner one evening, " 'Tis fine, I've even time to do my studying. The fish are leaving me alone most of the time."

On Sundays, Nora and Sean explored the city. This particular Sunday they walked along Fifth Avenue gawking at the lovely homes in Washington Square, and they saw a world very different from the Lower East Side. They wondered where Uncle Jim lived. At the same time, Nora knew she had to go away soon from Sean to have the baby. She had to tell him some excuse. Nora had quit her job at the pig market after her run-in with Mr. Levinsky. But she had not told anyone about it because she was still upset and didn't want to cause any trouble now that she had to leave.

"Don't worry, Sean. We should hear from Ma or Uncle Jim any time now." She paused, then continued. "By the way, Sean, I've met a man at the pig market from a fine mill in Massachusetts," she lied. "He's offered me a job, and the pay is so much better than here. I'm going to take it, for a while at least, so we can get some money ahead."

Sean was visibly upset. "Nora, Pa told me to be taking care of you, and how can I do that if you're far away? I'll go too. Can this man get me a job?"

"Sean, no, no. You have your job, your night classes, your Italians who depend on you to be teaching them English. I promise I'll only stay for a few months, just long enough to get some money ahead.''

He finally gave in, making her promise to come home the first of the year, but he wasn't happy about it. They walked home in silence.

Chapter 13

Each day Nora had waited anxiously for the letter from Father O'Rourke, but it hadn't come. She could wait no longer, so she made her plans to leave for Massachusetts. Sean, Tim and Molly went to see her off at Grand Central Station. Molly's heart was aching for her, knowing she would be all alone. She promised Nora she would come up to see her. As the train pulled out and she watched them waving until she could no longer distinguish them, she felt suddenly and terribly alone. The ship was nothing compared to this, for Sean had been with her, and they'd been expecting to meet Uncle Jim, and she had found Molly. But now she was going to a strange city where she knew no one. She was alone and pregnant. Thoughts of punishment entered her head. If one sins, one pays, Nora felt.

It was late October and the changing leaves of autumn, all red and gold and burnished orange, shimmered in the afternoon sun. She had never seen colors so brilliant. If the scenery is so beautiful, she reasoned, the towns must be lovely too, and that thought made her feel better for a while. She had to get off the train at Worcester and change lines to go to Lowell. She took out her sandwich, spread her napkin on her lap and ate, staring silently out the window.

"Lowell!" the conductor finally cried out.

Nora grabbed her battered case and jumped down from the train. She was certain the conductor had made a mistake. Pictures she had seen showed a lovely city with wide boulevards and trees, but she faced a slum city, dark with soot. It was no mistake. This was Lowell, Massachusetts, a noisy, crowded, dirty mill town. Others were being met by friends or relatives or societies. She saw the young couple she had seen on the train wearing cardboard signs pinned to their shabby clothes. They were giving their destination and their names. She had been worried about them because they had not eaten on the trip. She was relieved to see a man wearing a yarmulke rush up and greet them.

Suddenly she was standing alone on the platform. She looked around and found a carriage driver. "Please take me, sir, to the Catholic Church," she requested.

"Aye, lass," the Irish driver said. "Which one, St. Patrick's, St. Peter's or St. Mary's?"

"Why, why I don't know. Is there a Father Mahoney in any of them?"

The old driver didn't know, but suggested that she see Father Donovan at St. Patrick's.

They drove through the town. Huge five and six-story stately red-brick buildings, with large windows, sat along the canals and the river like they were castles on ancient moats. The main street was wide and congested with late-afternoon traffic. Along Market Street she looked through the steaming windows of coffee houses. Men were talking and gesturing wildly. She asked the driver about them.

"Aye," he spat. "Greeks. They pretend they don't have the liquor in those places, but we know they do." The Irish driver did not believe that men could meet and discuss politics without the brew. Nora smiled at his remark.

"Well, lass, here you are." As she descended from the carriage, she felt a lump in her throat. She hoped she could find Father Mahoney.

Nora rang the bell to the rectory and a sour-looking woman, obviously Father Donovan's housekeeper, showed her into a small waiting room.

Finally Father Donovan appeared. "Yes, miss, what can I do for you?"

She asked if Father Mahoney was at any of the churches in town.

"Father Mahoney was transferred over a month ago. He's in Boston, now. He may never have received your Father O'Rourke's letter."

Her heart sank. She hesitated for a moment and then asked if he could help her find a job or send her to someone who could.

"Lass, the mills are in trouble now. Strikes, unrest and a depression. It's a terrible time to be coming. You have a place to live, I presume?" he asked.

"No, Father. I came because I thought Father Mahoney would have arranged everything."

He stared at her somewhat quizzically. "Well, you'll need to find a place to stay first, won't you?"

She felt no warmth of interest from him, and she wanted to run and catch the next train out. But she sat hoping for small favors from the indifferent priest in this strange and unsettling city. He left the room and came back with an address.

"Go see Mrs. O'Riley. She'll likely be able to put you up. And here are names of some people to see at the mills. Maybe they can find a place for you."

He escorted her to the door. As an afterthought, he added, "Let me know how you make out."

Soon she had found Mrs. O'Riley's place, in a section called the Acre. An acre of land had been allotted to the famine immigrants of the 1840s, and that's where the name came from, she was told later. The tenements of New York were palaces compared to these filthy, wooden slums. But she was tired and it was getting dark.

Mrs. O'Riley sized her up when she opened the door. "I've a bed, if you'll be climbing three flights of stairs."

"Yes, yes," Nora said wearily.

They climbed three flights of rickety stairs that ran up the outside of the building. Inside, there was no light, and the odor of sewage was overpowering. Children were running and screaming, doors were slamming and people were arguing. She walked into a room with eight beds, where women were in various states of undress.

"I've one bed left in here. Take it or leave it," Mrs. O'Riley told her indifferently.

"I'll take it," Nora said, desperate for a place to lie down.

The women stared at her. She tried to smile, and she introduced herself. They were friendly enough, she thought, and asked them first about what the prospects were for jobs and then about where she could eat.

"Well, there's one kitchen on the floor above," one told her. "You have to mark your food, however, else it will be stolen." They seemed to take that for granted.

"What about now?" Nora asked. "I haven't eaten since lunch."

"You could go out, back down to Market and try one of the restaurants," a dark, wiry Greek girl suggested.

Nora was terrified to go out alone and said, "Oh no, I'll be all right, thanks."

She took her comforter out of her case and put it over

the filthy bedcovers and lay down. The girls kept talking and waves of despair rolled over her as she heard them chatter about unemployment, strikes and violence.

Nora was dozing off when one of the women came over to her bed. She was a tiny, plain little creature with a red face and a large, bulbous nose. Her eyes were kind as she spoke. "Honey, here, I've something for you."

Nora turned over, and the mousy young woman added, "You can't go to bed hungry." She offered Nora a piece of bread and sausage. Nora wanted to hug her for being so kind, but instead she just thanked her and promised to repay her the next day.

"It's all right honey, don't worry." Nora had her first friend. "I'm Maggie Burns," she introduced herself. "Irish, like you."

Nora fell asleep finally from fatigue, but she woke up only a few hours later. It was dark and quiet and she wondered why she had awakened, and in a moment she knew. She heard scurrying all around the room and she realized the sound was being made by rats! She lay there frozen with terror, unable to speak or move. She felt one scuttle across the bed, and she lay trembling with horror, thinking she was going to die at that instant. She lay awake, terrified, staring into the dark, feeling completely abandoned and frightened. If I live through this, she thought, I'll be able to live through anything. She fell asleep again, just as the first light came into the room. It seemed she had been asleep for only a few minutes when the sound of loud whistles woke her.

"The mill whistles blow every morning at six o'clock," Nora was informed by a Polish girl, who saw how startled she was.

Nora's eyes were red-rimmed, her neat green dress now soiled and crumpled, for she had been afraid to take off her clothing. She knew she had to get out of here. She changed to her only other dress, the blue cotton with the high collar. She wanted to look presentable, for she had to find another place to live, and then find a job.

The women streamed out at the sound of another whistle. They were going to work or going to look for work.

Nora asked about the rats, and they just shrugged. "They come up through the sink room and carry off anything they can eat. Apples, eggs, anything," Maggie said resignedly.

Nora decided she couldn't spend one more night at Mrs. O'Riley's. As she looked out the window, she found she was staring into another room across a narrow alley. The tenements were so close that she could have reached out and touched a woman who was hanging some kitchen utensils on the outside wall of the next building.

"Bit of a shock, eh, honey?" Maggie queried.

"Oh, Maggie, it's awful. How do you stand it?"

"I don't know," Maggie answered grimly. "I just don't know."

"Come on. Let's go to one of the coffee houses and have breakfast."

Maggie hadn't eaten out in such a long time that she kept saying, "Oh, but it's too expensive. I can't be letting you buy me breakfast." But she was pleased all the same. They sat in a coffee shop and Maggie told her about life in Lowell, offering to show her around, and suggesting which mills she might go to for work.

"But first, Maggie, I have to find another place to live," Nora insisted. "I'll die in the tenement."

All that day, Nora walked the streets. She finally walked down a street farther from the center of town. It had a cleaner, less crowded look, and she walked from door to door, asking for a room.

Nora eventually came upon a plump, pleasant-looking woman who said, "I've a room, lass. The other boarder just left yesterday. Ellen McCluskey got married last week, but stayed here because she and her Tom couldn't find a place to stay. God is with you. Come in. I'm Mrs. Clancy, and I do the best I can. You'll have to be sharing with four other girls, but 'tis the best you'll find."

Nora already knew that to be true. She took one look around and said yes quickly, before Mrs. Clancy changed her mind. The rooms were clean and neat. This was a better section of town, away from the slums of the central city where the newer immigrants from Poland and Greece and Italy were forced to live. Nora paid her three dollars for the month in advance and told Mrs. Clancy she would be back later, after she'd gotten her things. The room was more expensive, but rent included a meal in the evenings. She returned to the boarding house, paid Mrs. O'Riley and got her luggage. She left a note telling Maggie where she could be found.

The remainder of the day, she went from mill to mill. Some of the mills wouldn't even take her application. She went back to her boarding house when the closing whistle sounded. She was discouraged, but relieved that she didn't have to return to the rat-infested tenement.

The girls poured in from work, hungry and tired, but they were chatting and laughing. When they introduced themselves, she noticed that they were almost all Irish. When she asked the girls about this at dinner, Mrs. Clancy explained, "We don't mix much here. Them terrible slums Father Donovan sent you to—God knows why, I think he's gone round the bend—are the lot of the Greeks and those French Canucks."

Everyone was friendly, and over steaming Irish stew they told Nora all about Lowell. They spoke of the different kinds of jobs, the hours, the people and what to expect. She had plenty of leads for the following day, for what they had told her was that the Irish were preferred as laborers since most of the foremen who did the hiring were Irish themselves.

"They're not liking the Greeks and the Italians, nor do we," said Ann Duff, another recent immigrant. "Why, you just try to jest with them. You know you have to be joking to pass those long, monotonous hours, and if you're trying it with an Italian, he'd as soon slit your throat. Our foreman finally put all the Italians and Greeks in the spinning room. He says they can knife one another and leave us be." She added, "You can't be taking away the jokes from us Irish. It just doesn't set well. 'Tis what keeps us going."

The only other girls in the boarding house besides the Irish girls were the Germans and a Pole or two who seemed to be readily accepted. Nora pondered all this and wondered as she was falling asleep what had happened to her safe, secure world. Here she was, being buffeted about by things beyond her control. It was terrifying, and she wondered how anyone climbed out of the pit so many immigrants lived in. 'Tis better than last night, though, she thought, and fell into a deep, much needed sleep.

A few days later Nora had a job at Indian Mills. She was hired as a weaver even though she had never handled steam-powered looms. The foreman liked her looks and liked the fact that she was Irish. For years, she was told, the signs all over New England, Boston in particular, had announced "No Irish Need Apply." At least Nora wasn't hurt by being Irish here.

The foreman brought her into the longest room she had ever seen. The noise was shattering. The floor was vibrating as the machines spewed out their cloth. The metal-against-metal sound was ear-piercing and the light was dim despite the large windows. The workers were packed in so tightly that they were rarely more than a few inches from the machines. Nora was overwhelmed and terrified, but she knew she had to bluff her way through or lose the job. Philip Scanlon, the foreman, called a woman over to help Nora. Her name was Annie O'Leary, and being an experienced operator, she knew instantly that Nora had never worked a power loom before. Nora guessed this and they looked at each other for a long moment.

" 'Tis all right, girl, just watch me carefully."

Nora breathed a sigh of relief and watched as carefully as she had ever watched anything in her life. It was not that difficult, but Annie reminded her of the dangers. "You can't be off your guard for one moment, lass, not a single moment. Hands and sometimes whole arms are lost in these machines."

When the whistle blew and she could stop, Nora just sat silently, dully, at the big loom. She could barely move because her arms had been stretched out for many hours. She had a sudden contraction and the baby moved for the first time, as if it were protesting. The workers streamed out. She hadn't even seen who was working next to her because she'd been so afraid that she might take her eyes off the loom. The sudden quiet astonished her, and she jumped as Annie put her hand on her shoulder. "Come, lass, 'tis time to leave. You did very well. Get a good night's sleep and it will be easier tomorrow."

Nora found that she became fatigued sooner and sooner each day. Annie was worried because of the awful accidents that could happen if one wasn't on guard all the time. Even when you were on guard, things happened. Spindles flew off machines, hurtling across the room and destroying whatever was in their path. The smells of acid and the steam rising up could burn and disfigure.

Annie said to Nora one day, " 'Tis time you saw a

doctor. You're pregnant, aren't you? This work isn't good for you, Nora, to be standing all day, breathing these fumes.''

"I know, Annie. I'm afraid it will hurt my baby."

Annie had been a midwife in Ireland and told Nora not to worry; she would deliver the baby. Nora said yes, though she planned to have her baby in a New York hospital so that Molly could be with her. But she agreed, not wanting to hurt Annie's feelings.

One of the girls with whom Nora and Annie had made friends was a young, lovely, spirited Polish girl named Katya. She was full of fun and was always walking out with a new young man. She was pretty and had her pick of beaus, but was being seen more and more with Jamie Farrell.

On their way to the mill one morning, she confessed to Nora that she was more than fond of young Jamie. "Everyone will say I should stick to my own, Nora, but I don't love one of my own. I love Jamie."

"Has anyone said that to you, Katya, that you should stick to your own?" Nora asked.

"Well, yes." She hesitated. "Mr. Scanlon."

"Since when is it Mr. Scanlon's business to pry into our private lives?" Nora complained. "Isn't it enough that he dominates our lives in the mill, that he assigns us too many machines to tend, that he so unfairly shorts us on the amount we have woven? Now he's to be a marriage counselor. Katya, pay him no mind."

She hadn't liked Mr. Philip Scanlon from the first day. He took advantage of his position, badgered the men and pinched the women. He had tried to force his attentions on Nora, but she had set him straight with such intense anger that he had backed off and left her alone.

Sensing something was wrong, Nora asked Katya if he had tried to force his attentions on her.

She was embarrassed. "Ya, Nora, he says if I'm

giving it to the other men, he should get some too. Nora, I give nothing. I just try to have some fun, and if I go with many it's because I want to find the right young man, not because I'm a loose woman." She was almost in tears.

Nora was furious. "Don't worry, Katya. We'll see to him. Soon you'll be married, and he'll leave you alone."

This reassured Katya somewhat, but if Nora's pregnancy hadn't stopped Mr. Scanlon's advances, she knew Katya's marriage wouldn't either. She spoke to Annie about it.

"I know, I know," Annie said sympathetically. "What can we do? Everyone's afraid of him. He has the power to fire us. His word is law. And so, many of those poor women put up with all kinds of indignities. That is one of the things a good union could help with. And also, maybe we could stop him from kicking the doffers." The doffers were the young French-Canadian and Italian boys who removed the bobbins and stripped the fibers from them. While most salaries ranged from seven dollars for unskilled labor to thirteen dollars a week for skilled labor such as loom fixing, the doffers were lucky to get three dollars a week, and they got all the abuse they could handle. Nora's doffer was a fourteen-year-old French-Canadian boy named Jacques. She was always kind and polite to him, and one day she heard it was his birthday, so she gave him fifty cents. He would have knelt in the cotton dust and kissed the hem of her garment, but Scanlon was watching him.

"*Merci*, Madam Nora, *merci*," he said as he ran to the next loom.

Scanlon made a remark to Nora about her kindness to Jacques. "Why, you treat those Canucks as if they're human. Save your kindnesses for the right people, young woman." He leered at her.

"Mr. Scanlon," she answered, barely controlling her

anger, "I am giving my favors to the right people." She turned back to her loom.

Scanlon couldn't get to her as he got to the other women, and it annoyed him. Damned upstart, he thought, we'll see about you.

The Ancient Order of Hibernians had a clubhouse and the Irish met there for their dances and socials. One Saturday evening, Nora, Annie, Maggie, Katya, Jamie, and another worker named Colin, whom Nora had gotten to know fairly well, were gathered around talking and laughing. One of the men who worked on the looms near Nora and Katya came up, full of liquor, and asked, "Is Scanlon still after you, lass?"

Annie pulled him away, but Jamie asked what he had meant.

"Oh, it's nothing, nothing, Jamie," Nora replied. "He's just silly sometimes. He pesters all the girls." She could see Jamie's face flush.

"I'll kill the bastard if he lays a hand on you," Jamie grumbled.

Trying to break the tension of the moment, Nora said, "Don't worry, Jamie, we're all onto him." She didn't know what else to say.

Colin walked Nora home. "Has Scanlon ever bothered you, Nora?" he asked.

"Aye, but I scared him off," she smiled. Lately, Colin had been spending as much time as he could with Nora. "You've been very kind to me, Colin. I'm appreciating it, but you should be finding a lovely lass. I'm taking up all your time."

"Aye," he answered simply, "but it's you I'm liking."

"Well, off with you, lad. What will my husband say?" She felt he was becoming too serious.

"I'm not knowing, Nora, but I feel you need a man's protection. You're too beautiful to be here alone."

They were walking home past the big Atlantic Mill when they saw a group of Greeks sprinting down the middle of the street, followed closely by a group of drunken Irishmen hurling rocks and curses at them.

Colin and Nora flattened themselves against the building.

"Why are they doing that?" Nora gasped, shocked.

" 'Tis the same old thing," Colin answered. "When I see them attacking, it makes me so ashamed of my own kind. We hate them because we feel our jobs are threatened, but 'tis the mill owners who should have the rocks hurled at them for hiring Greeks to take our jobs when we try to strike. They'll work for lower wages and our own get thrown out on the streets. Where will it end?" he asked sadly. " 'Tis why we need so badly to organize, Nora. I'll be working to that end all my days, I feel."

"You're a fine man, Colin. I believe you'll make your mark."

They reached her boarding house, and he looked at her with affection. "Nora, if you're ever needing me, for whatever reason, I'll be there."

"Thank you, Colin. I'll remember. You're a dear." She quickly pecked him on the cheek.

As she lay in bed, she asked herself, will I ever again feel anything more than friendship for a man? I think not, she concluded sadly.

Now it took Nora a supreme effort to drag herself to the mills each morning. She was feeling heavy with child, and knew she couldn't be breathing the humid, dust-filled air that caused the tuberculosis and pneumonia that killed many of the mill people before they were forty. She was getting her loom ready when Jacques, the doffer, put a package on her machine and then scurried away. She opened it, and inside was a crusty, delicious pastry. Apparently his mother was saying thanks to her too. She smiled. "Bless him," she murmured.

The days wore on more and more slowly for her. As she took her break and was eating the pastry, she watched the falling snow. Christmas was fast approaching. She remembered what the holiday season had been like in Ireland and wondered what it would be like here. She was returning to her machine when she remembered that she hadn't asked Scanlon for permission to take an hour off the next day. She needed the hour to see the doctor.

Seeing Scanlon on the far side of the room leaning over Katya, Nora started toward him. But as she approached, she suddenly saw what he was doing and she paused in midstride, uncertain whether to go on or to cry out. Scanlon appeared to be helping Katya at her machine, but as he leaned over her, his hand moved downward, reaching for her breast.

Before Nora could intercede, Katya leapt up, a look of fear and anger in her face. She turned on Scanlon, writhing to free herself from his grasp. Her long chestnut hair came tumbling down as she stepped backward. A few strands became entwined in the whirling bobbin and suddenly she was jerked away from the man's grasp, her hair pinned and clawed by the whirling machine.

Nora's screams were drowned by the shrill, unearthly howl of Katya's voice.

"Oh my God, my God," Nora wailed.

Annie was there first, bent over Katya, trying to soothe the tortured woman. Nora rushed forward, then stopped, shuddering, her breath choked off by the horror of the sight. There was blood everywhere. Limp strands of chestnut hair whirled around the ghastly bobbin. And Katya, now limp and unconscious, twisted slowly on the floor, one foot moving in a steady, involuntary rhythm.

* * *

Long after Katya had been carried out of the room and the other women had returned to their machines, Nora remained standing, her fist clenched against her teeth. Limp with fatigue, her dress still spotted with blood, Annie tried to comfort her. But it wasn't until Dr. Flynn urged Annie to take Nora home that the two women moved away from the scene of the accident.

"Annie probably saved her life," Dr. Flynn said gently. "The scalp is torn, but I've seen such accidents before. It may heal." Nora trembled, feeling the man's hand touch her shoulder. "There's nothing you can do now. Go home."

Throughout the following day, Nora could not erase the horror of the accident from her mind. Each time the scene recurred, she was overcome by nausea. Annie came by to soothe her but there was little she could do. She was alarmed by Nora's look of anguish.

"We're taking you to Dr. Flynn today. You can't be staying here any longer girl. We'll be losing you too."

"Is she dead then, Annie?" Nora asked, looking pale and waxen.

"No, she'll be all right. I just came from the hospital. Jamie is beside himself with grief. She'll pull through. I know she will."

Somehow Annie's voice didn't sound convincing. Nora wept in her arms. "Annie, Annie, 'twas Scanlon who caused it."

"What are you saying, Nora?"

"He grabbed her. It startled her and she jumped up. 'Tis then that her hair got caught in the bobbin." Nora sobbed.

"Oh my God. Isn't it enough that it happens all too often for no reason at all? That, that bastard. If Jamie Farrell doesn't kill him, I will."

Soon Nora had settled down. "Annie, I pray God that he pays for this. I can't help it if that's an awful thing to say."

"Aye," Annie replied grimly.

Dr. Flynn examined Nora. He was a kind, gentle man, sensitive to the suffering he constantly treated in this immigrant city.

"Annie tells me you're a fine young lass," the doctor said. "If that's true, you'll listen to what I'm telling you. You've got to quit the mill. Fortunately, you're a strong girl and your baby seems fine, but you'll kill it and yourself unless you rest. You must be finding something else to do." He paused. "Annie and I may have a few ideas," he added.

"Yes, Dr. Flynn, I'll do as you say. I'll finish the week and leave on Saturday."

"Fine," he replied. "We have made an appointment for you with Tom O'Houlihan, who owns a clothing shop on Market Street. I've spoken to him, and if he likes you, he might let you clerk for him. Let's give it a try, anyway."

She thanked the kind doctor and asked how Katya was.

"Awful, Nora, awful. I don't think she'll live." He paused, and added sadly, "I don't think she wants to live."

Nora stared into the distance. "I'm so sorry. I hoped she'd be all right, but I think I understand. I'll pray for her."

Poor, dear Katya, she thought sadly, how I wish I could hurt Mr. Scanlon, hurt him in some terrible way. Tears streamed down her face. I'll get even for you, Katya, I promise. How she hated the Scanlons of the world, those with power who took advantage of those with none. And then she thought fleetingly of William. I'll get even with both of them, somehow, some way, I will, she vowed.

Mr. O'Houlihan hired her. He was a man of quick decisions, and he liked the way she talked and looked.

"Only one thing, lass," he said. "We can't pay ten dollars a week." This was what Nora had been earning at the mill. "We can only pay six dollars, but we offer room and board." Without waiting for her reply, he added, "I'll show you where you'll be staying."

Out behind the shop was an old, converted stable, and above was a large room, somewhat dark, but clean. The room was furnished with a bed, several wooden chairs, a table and a wood-burning stove in a kitchenlike alcove. An old, worn, brown velvet settee that had seen grander days sat in a corner. The bed was piled high with pillows crocheted with lace around the edges, and had a feather comforter that looked inviting.

"Who else lives here?" Nora asked.

"Just you. 'Tis good, you can just roll out of bed into the shop."

She could barely hide her enthusiasm. Privacy, she thought, real privacy. No more snoring to keep me awake, no more getting undressed in front of others, no more waiting in line to wash. Quiet when I need it. Oh thank you, dear Lord. She said, "Well, Mr. O'Houlihan, that seems agreeable. I can start next Monday. I'll need to finish the week at the mill." And finish some business with Scanlon, she thought.

Chapter 14

It was always a shock to Nora to enter the door of the mill. No matter how many times she did it, the deafening noise always stunned her, almost as if she'd been struck. She squared her shoulders and started to make her way through the mass of machines and people. It's awful to have to look for someone you don't want to find, she thought as she headed for Scanlon's office.

Before she started up the rickety stairs, a whiny voice said, "Looking for me, Your Highness?"

Nora turned and faced Scanlon. His slick, greasy hair looked dirtier than ever, and his soiled clothes smelled, even at a distance.

"Yes, I *am* looking for you, Mr. Scanlon. I want to have a word with you."

Scanlon narrowed his eyes and looked her up and down. Even though she was uppity and pregnant and too smart for her own good, he had a yen for her. Perhaps she liked him better than she let on but was just shy. Yes, shy, that's probably it, he reasoned, and she didn't like other people around when she felt friendly. Finally he spoke. "Well, you can't see me now, but you can see me in my office when the mill closes down."

Nora nodded, turned, and walked toward her work station.

When the machinery shut off, the silence was shocking. The workers, anxious to leave, streamed out of the building. Nora stayed until the last rays of light caught the whirling dust in the air. Then that too settled and all was still. She gathered her lunch pail and her shawl and climbed the stairs to Scanlon's office. He was waiting at the doorway, a bottle of whiskey in one hand and two grimy glasses in the others.

"Come in, come in," he gestured with the bottle.

Nora refused the glass he thrust at her. "I'm not here to socialize, Mr. Scanlon. I'm here to tell you that I'm leaving. Saturday will be my last day."

"Come now, take the drink. What's the matter, are you too good to work here? Maybe you're too good to have a drink with me, is that it?"

"I'm leaving because I know it was you who caused Katya's accident." She wanted to frighten him and make him think she was going to report him.

"Now, that just ain't so, Mrs. O'Sullivan. She slipped and you know it. What you saw was me trying to catch her. Yeah, by God, that's what it was. I was trying to catch her. Come on, now, have a drink. I've been wanting to talk to you for a fact, about giving you a raise, making life a little easier for you. What do you say to that, now?"

"I'll be having nothing else to say to you, Mr. Scanlon, except that you are a horrible man to take advantage of women." She was suddenly afraid of him. Feeling the urge to leave, she started toward the office door.

He quickly set down the whiskey and the glasses and

stepped in front of her. "Come now, what's your hurry? We're just getting acquainted."

"I've no wish to become better acquainted with you, Mr. Scanlon. What I already know of you sickens me. Please get out of my way. I came only to tell you that I'm leaving the mill." Nora suddenly knew it had been a mistake to come here alone. Instead of getting out of her way, he reached out and clutched her wrist.

"Now, you just be nice to me, colleen, or you'll regret it."

Nora drew in a breath, and he reeked of whiskey. "Step out of my way, Mr. Scanlon. I'll be leaving now."

"Oh, I don't think you will. Didn't I tell you we were going to get acquainted? Yessir, we're going to get to know each other a whole lot better, yes we are." With his hand still locked around her wrist, he twisted her arm behind her and pulled her to him. The combination of his foul breath and the filth of his clothes produced a foul odor. Nora was terrified, but Scanlon didn't look strong, for he wasn't a big man. Yet he was very powerful, and she couldn't move at all. He pulled her by the arm across the room, and she thought to herself, Oh my God, my baby, my baby.

"Here, girl, stop your fighting," he hissed in her ear. "It won't do you no good. I'm going to have you." She spat into his face. In return, he slapped her with his free hand, slapped her so hard that her ears rang and she could only see him mouthing his threatening words. The look in his mean eyes terrified her. Each time she tried to move, he wrenched her arm painfully higher and higher behind her.

Why can't I scream? Oh, God, let me scream. But no sound seemed to come from her throat as he slapped her again. Even though she couldn't hear anything, she knew she was making noise, because she saw that he was shouting, "Shut up, you Irish whore. Shut up!"

He was on top of her now, tearing at her clothes. As he ripped off her petticoat, he let go of her pinned arm so he could tug at his trousers. Nora tried to twist away, but he struck her again.

"Don't care how you fight. I'm going to have you," he snarled drunkenly. "Keep fighting. Don't matter to me." He tried to kiss her. Nora fought to turn her face away, but his slimy mouth was on her throat as his hands tore at her blouse. The ringing in her ears had stopped, and she begged him to let her go.

"Beg, that's good," he howled. "I want to give you what you need."

Nora swung out, attempting to strike him, and her hand touched something. She grabbed it, not knowing or caring what it was. As she drove the object into his face, she saw that it was an empty bobbin. Suddenly, *he* was screaming, his face bloody. Her cries mixed with his as he let go of her to grasp his face with his hands.

"I'll kill you for this!" He struck her again with his blood-drenched hand, but Nora slipped out from underneath him, and his hands were too slippery with blood to hold on to her.

She was sobbing, struggling to get to her feet, when the door burst open and Jacques came in. He just stood there, frozen with horror at the sight in front of him. Then he remembered seeing Colin fixing a loom on the floor below, and he raced down the stairs to find him.

"Colin, Colin, come, hurry. *Mon Dieu, mon Dieu,* hurry."

Nora was on her knees and Scanlon was howling in pain when Colin burst into the room. He and Jacques knelt by Nora. Colin lifted her head and put his arms about her. Jacques put a cloth to her head.

"Jacques, call a doctor," Colin instructed. "No, no, we'll take her there. It'll be quicker. Nora, Nora, can you speak to me? Are you hurt badly, girl?"

"Thank God you're here, Colin," Nora murmured. "Get Scanlon, please, get him."

"I'll take care of him in a minute," he assured her. "Here, Jacques, help me get her up. Can you walk, Nora? Don't bother with that," he said as she tried to gather her clothes about her. "Come on, we'll carry her down. Don't even try to walk, Nora. Now, now, you'll be all right. We're here. We're here. Here, hold her, Jacques."

Colin walked to Scanlon and stood over him, glaring. "I know what's happened here, Scanlon. I've always suspected why the girls hated you, but they're silent for fear of losing their jobs. This time you've gotten what you deserve. I'm taking Nora to the doctor, and when I come back, you'd better be gone. If you're not, I swear, I'll kill you. Get out of this mill, get out of this *town!*"

Scanlon backed out the door, bleeding and terrified. As he ran down the stairs, he hissed, "I'll get her. I'll get her if it's the last thing I do." He ran out into the night.

Dr. Flynn came and assured her that her baby would be fine. Mrs. Clancy smoothed Nora's sheets and rearranged the pillow under her sprained arm. Dr. Flynn said she could take the sling off in a few days.

"You have some visitors, lass," Mrs. Clancy announced.

Colin and Annie then entered. They told her that Scanlon was gone from the mill and from the town.

"And Nora, he saw a doctor at the infirmary before he left," Colin informed. "He'll have quite a scar for the rest of his life."

"I know it's not Christian of me to be feeling satisfied, but that I am, Colin," Nora said. "Somehow, it's justice. He suffered just like Katya. And yet Katya is still suffering from what he did to her.'' She shook her head.

"He'll be thinking twice before trying to have his way with a woman again," Annie put in.

"I'm glad I did it," Nora declared, surprised at the fury in her own voice. "Colin, please thank Jacques for me and give him this." She pressed a dollar into Colin's hands. "Maybe it's true. Maybe Scanlon won't be hurting anyone again."

Colin looked at her admiringly and said, "I think you're made of steel, Nora. You'll always survive."

A few days later, Annie and Colin helped her move into her new quarters over the stable and she started working at O'Houlihan's Clothing Store.

Mr. and Mrs. O'Houlihan were hard workers and expected their help to be the same, but they were kind and fair. Nora's job was to sell. She had to learn the stock and the prices and the customers' names, but it all came easily and she enjoyed it. One day a gigantic Italian woman was trying on a dress, and she asked Nora how she thought it looked on her.

"Mrs. Capucci, I think I've seen dresses that would be more flattering on you. Let me keep my eyes open for just the right thing."

Mr. O'Houlihan glowered at her, and later said, "We've plenty of competition. 'Tis to them you're sending her."

"I think you're wrong, Mr. O'Houlihan. People appreciate honesty. I think she'll become our customer. And besides, I wouldn't have felt right selling her that. It was ugly on her."

"Ugly on her, indeed. Who cares? I need to sell clothes to make a living and pay your salary, not for some woman to look good," he ranted. Nora looked at him sharply and he turned away, slightly embarrassed. "Well, don't do it again," he sulked.

The next week, Mrs. Capucci was back. Nora had found a suitable dress, and she showed it to her. It trimmed down the voluminous figure, and even Mrs. Capucci could see the difference. The print was small and the vertical pleats scaled her down. She was pleased and bought the dress.

"I would also like to see some clothes for my bambini," she said. They had made a friend and gained a customer.

"You're all right, Nora," Mr. O'Houlihan conceded.

The store was crowded, for Christmas was drawing near. In the midst of the bustle, Nora received a letter from Molly. It was full of good news. She was coming to visit Nora after Christmas, and the long-awaited letter with Uncle Jim's address had arrived, and with it came the news that Kevin and Bridget had married.

Nora's letters to them were cheerful, and though she described some of the horrors of mill life to them, she did not let them know of her part in things.

Sean spent as much time with Tim and her as possible with his busy schedule, Molly wrote, and he was very happy with his Uncle Jim and Aunt Nellie. She told Nora she knew she would like them and how much they looked forward to her return to New York.

The season took on a new excitement as Nora prepared for Molly's visit. She had been crocheting lace pieces to give as gifts and Mr. O'Houlihan was extremely interested in her work.

Annie came by every evening, and they sat and talked while Nora crocheted.

"How is Katya?" Nora asked. "I didn't go by today, what with this Christmas rush."

"Not good, Nora, not good. Poor Jamie sits outside

her room for endless hours. She still hasn't spoken a word since the accident."

The next day she went in to see Katya. Her friend looked up at her sadly with eyes that couldn't conceal the terror that still remained within her. Nora held Katya's limp hand.

"Katya, please talk to me. I know you can hear what I'm saying to you. Please, please try to get well. We all love you and Jamie is suffering so. Will you try, dearest friend, for heaven's sake. Please, Katya, I'm begging you."

But the next evening, word came that Katya was dead. Jamie was in such grief that he couldn't talk coherently. He just kept saying over and over, "My little sparrow, my beautiful little sparrow." It was Nora who finally led him from the room, blinded as he was by tears. She knew he would never forget Katya. And neither would she.

Chapter 15

Snow was falling softly. The last rays of sun were slipping away as dusk cast its gentle shadows over the Middlesex Street Depot. Nora hadn't been there since she had arrived alone last fall. She remembered how frightened she was with no one to meet her, no place to go, no one to help. However, today it all looked kinder, more like an ordinary city in this light, covered by a blanket of white. The steeples on top of the mills looked like lovely old churches from a distance, until one saw that their weather vanes were made from bobbins.

Molly, dear Molly, was coming. Nora hadn't realized how isolated she had been, how much had happened to her in such a short time, how much she had changed. As she stood watching for the lights of the 5:15 from Worcester, her thoughts strayed to what had been her first Christmas in America.

Since Nora had been the only one with a place of her own after moving into quarters above Mr. O'Houlihan's stable, she decided to have Christmas dinner. Annie brought the turkey, Colin brought the wine, and Maggie brought the potatoes, which she had promised would taste just like the ones at home. Nora had decorated a Christmas tree and set the table. The room was filled with holly branches and pine cones, and ornaments made of scraps from the mill and odds and ends from O'Houlihan's store. It looked festive. They insisted that Jamie come, for they didn't want him sitting alone brooding, as he had been doing since Katya died. Some of the union people were invited, and they ended up with ten altogether. Everyone brought some gift of food or drink. It was a grand party. The wine flowed freely, everyone was cheerful, and even Jamie had a few smiles. Maggie Burns sat next to him, fussed over him and comforted him several times during the evening. Sometimes tears gleamed in his eyes, but he responded to her affections and seemed to be leaning on her for solace. Nora noticed he had been doing this often lately. Maybe, in the way of plain women, Maggie saw herself only in the role of comforter, but perhaps in time, if Jamie needed her enough, he would seek more than comfort from her. They might even marry for companionship. It might be best for both of them, Nora thought, because poor Maggie will never expect as much as she has a right to expect, and poor Jamie will never forget his beautiful little sparrow.

Colin and the others were engaged in their favorite topic of conversation: organizing the mill towns. But as more and more wine was drunk, they drifted to other topics and other times. Nora suggested that each person tell of a Christmas they particularly remembered, whether good or bad. As she suggested it, she realized it had once been her mother's idea. As the family had sat around the fire on long winter evenings, Mary would get everyone to tell a story, pretend or real, and Nora had loved that as much as she had loved reading aloud. The person telling the story always had everyone's undivided attention.

Some of the stories were funny, some were happy, some were sad. Nora thought she would never forget this Christmas, having spent it with such fine friends. She kissed everyone good night and saw them off into the falling snow.

Colin insisted on staying. "I'm the clean-up crew, remember? That was the agreement." Colin and Nora stood in the doorway waving good-bye. As the happy voices faded, Nora shivered, and she closed the door.

"Nora, I hope you don't mind my staying after the others have gone. Here, let me help you with those." Colin took the platters from her.

Nora put her hands to the small of her back. As the baby grew, she was bothered more and more by her back, and the truth was, she was glad of Colin's help. He was such a good friend. She treasured his company and she watched fondly as he moved the chairs back into place around the room. He's actually quite attractive, she thought. He was tall and angular, with wisps of brown hair continually falling down over his serious, perceptive eyes. Wire glasses perched on a long, straight nose gave him a scholarly look.

"You had a grand party, Nora, that you did, but I've never seen so many dirty dishes," Colin said, rolling up his sleeves. "I'll wash and you do the drying, and we'll have this mess cleaned up in no time."

"Colin, you should have let Annie stay to help me. She always does. This is no job for you."

"And why isn't it? Aren't men supposed to dirty their hands in soapy water? Is that supposed to be only women's work?"

"Well, I—I don't know," she stammered, not knowing whether he was being serious. "I guess I haven't thought about that."

"You should be thinking of those things, Nora. A

smart girl like you should be thinking of those things. If you're interested in advances for the working class, you should be interested in what happens to women too."

Nora was fascinated by what he had said. In the seven months she had been in America, her beliefs had already altered radically, and here was a new thought for her to ponder. She wanted to help better the conditions of the working class. Wasn't she, after all, one of them? Her experiences in the mill and the sweatshops had awakened her own social conscience and appealed to her own moral code. But women having rights apart from such movements was something she hadn't considered. Women *are* working to make life better, she thought.

Colin interrupted her thoughts. "Why, I'm the best dishwasher in this city, maybe the state. Besides, I didn't know any other way to be able to see you alone." Suddenly he was serious again. He took his hands from the soapy water and dried them with the towel she was holding. "Let's sit down, Nora. I want to talk to you. You've told me so little about yourself. I want to hear about your plans, now that you've left the mill. We miss you. You were one of the few bright spots in that place, but I'm glad you have a chance now to do something easier and to pursue your lace-making."

"Colin, I owe that all to you. You saved me from Scanlon and the mill. It seems I'm always thanking you, Colin, for all the good you bring to my life."

Nora's eyes glistened with tears, and Colin thought she was the most beautiful sight he had ever seen. He admired Nora. She was a fine, brave woman, and she was also open and honest. He had begun to suspect that her refusal to discuss her husband, who was forever delayed in joining her, was because he was never going to appear or that he didn't even exist. Colin thought that if Nora truly had a husband, she would at least have his pictures, for she had pictures of the rest of her family. And why didn't she talk about him often, lovingly, as Annie talked about her Tom? But Nora made only the vaguest remarks about her husband's reasons for not being able to come to America. Except when pressed, she never mentioned his existence. No, thought Colin, there isn't a husband. She's in trouble and she has no one to help her. She's ashamed to tell the truth. I can feel it in my bones.

He decided to broach the subject. "Nora, now what I have to say may be difficult, and God forgive me if I'm wrong, but I think you're needing a husband and a father for that baby." He paused, steeling himself so he could continue. "And I want to be that person. I'm asking you to marry me, Nora."

"Why, Colin," Nora stammered, "how can I be marrying you when I already have a husband? Would you be wanting me to have two husbands, now?" She couldn't meet his eyes. Needing some time to answer him, she chattered on gaily. "I don't know what he'd be saying when he got here if I told him I'd taken another." She turned away, pulled herself up with effort and started toward the kitchen. "Come on, let's finish the washing and drying. I'm too tired for your jokes."

Suddenly, her strength seemed to leave her and she swayed, putting out her arms as if to steady herself. Colin reached her before she fell and once again held her to comfort her, as he had on the awful day when Scanlon had attacked her. She began to cry, and he stroked her beautiful black hair and said, "There, there, dear Nora, you've had so much to bear. Come on, let it all out now. I'm here and I'll make it all right. I promise."

His arms were comforting, and Nora felt weary and alone in her secret. Between her sobs, she tearfully told him her story, and he murmured consoling words. Finally, he gave her his handkerchief and sat her very close to him on the settee. "Nora, don't you see how much I want to take care of you and the baby? You don't have to be alone. You don't want to send your baby away and you don't have to. No one need ever know it isn't ours, and I promise you I will love it as my own until the day I die. Please, Nora, say yes to being my wife and you'll never regret it."

As he talked, Nora felt more and more at ease. Yes, she thought, I wouldn't have to worry. I wouldn't go back to see anyone until a suitable time went by and everyone would believe it was Colin's baby. This way I can keep my child with me. Colin is saving me again. But then his last words registered. "You'll never regret it."

"Oh, Colin, it's you who'd be regretting it. Now hush." She put her fingers on his lips. "And listen to me. I'll never forget your kindness to me and to my baby, but Colin, dear, I don't love you as a woman should love her husband. I'm not sure I can ever love like that again. You deserve a wife who'll give you all her heart, and children who are really yours. Don't you see that in time you'd be the one with regrets, with neither a wife nor a child who truly belonged to you?"

And now it was Nora who comforted Colin in his tears of hopeless love. She felt as if she had finally made the decision to face life alone. Her child would be provided for and would never suffer for her foolish act and, pray God, would not be like its father.

The whistle interrupted her reverie and the 5:15 train chugged into the depot. She searched for Molly and finally spotted her at the other end of the platform. They ran toward one another, Molly quickly and Nora slowly, and they threw their arms about each other, crying and kissing.

"Oh, let me look at you, Nora. You're a little pale, are you all right?" she asked anxiously.

"Yes, yes, Molly. I'm, *we're*, fine. And you?"

They chatted all the way to Nora's, filling each other in on every detail of their lives.

"Oh, Nora, is the baby moving? I mean, will I be able to hear him, feel him?"

"Of course. He has a mighty kick." Nora began to laugh, and then she said with a smile, "How are you knowing it's a he?"

"Because I have a girl already," Molly said simply.

"I see," Nora replied. "That makes sense." And they giggled like two schoolgirls.

"Oh Nora, I had the worst time keeping Sean away. I don't know how I finally did, but I think it had something to do with the return train being too late for him to get to work on time. Their working six days a week made it difficult, too. Oh, and Christmas was the worst. Both he and your uncle wanted to come up. Fortunately, they had only one day off, and it didn't work out. I should get a medal."

They talked until early morning. Nora told her more of life here than she had dared put in letters, and Molly was in tears several times, especially when Nora told her of Katya.

"Oh Nora, to think you've had to suffer so. Life's not fair. You've already had more than your share of troubles."

"Sometimes I think the sadness I feel is punishment for what I did, Molly."

"Nonsense, Nora. It's just the way things happen."

They finally fell asleep, and when they woke, they were happy to be with each other. Molly kept right on talking, as if they hadn't slept at all, and she told Nora all about Retta's antics and how darling she was.

"She's like her mommy," Nora laughed.

Molly became serious. "Nora, there's something I have to be telling you."

Nora searched her eyes and began to feel frightened. "What is it, Molly? You're looking so serious."

"Aye, 'tis serious. Tim has a new job, a good one."

"How wonderful."

"Well, yes and no." Molly bowed her head and folded her hands in her lap. "We have to move to Chicago."

The shock of her announcement made Nora dizzy. She was speechless for a few moments. Finally she said, "Oh no, Molly, how will I see the baby?"

"I don't know, Nora. Just whenever you can come to Chicago, and maybe when he's older, he can visit you in New York."

Nora sat very still. "My baby will grow up without ever knowing me," she murmured.

"I'm so sorry, Nora, not only because of your not being able to see the baby, but because I'll miss you so. I know now how very much you mean to me. You're the only family I have." Tears were streaming down Molly's face.

Nora put her arms around her, desperately trying to believe that things would be all right. "We'll manage, Molly. I'll find a way to visit. And perhaps in some ways it's God's will. I might want to be interfering, and it will be, after all, your child."

They sat quietly, each absorbed in thought, when suddenly Molly leapt up. "How selfish! I've just been jabbering. I forgot there's a letter from your mother. It's an old one, for it had been sent to Uncle Jim's."

Nora's heart raced as she clutched at the letter. It had been written months ago. Her mother's fine script looked so beautifully familiar that she almost burst into tears. Mary told all the news of Bridget's wedding, hoped they were well, and hoped she would hear from Sean and Nora regularly. Then, as Nora read on, Molly saw her face slip into a frown.

"What is it, Nora? Is something wrong?"

"Molly, do you remember I told you about Seamus Gorman?"

"Yes, the nice young man you met in Cork who recited all the lovely poetry."

"Aye, well he came looking for me. He was there when they arrived home from putting us on the ship. He was wanting to declare himself, to, to court me," she stammered.

"Oh Nora. Poor lad. And poor Nora. Life could have been very different for you if he had come on time."

"I don't know, Molly. It's hard to say. I couldn't have let him court me without telling him about the baby. I just couldn't. Anyway, Ma tells me that he's great friends with Terence, Bridget and Kevin, that he's trying to get Kevin a job in Cork and that they'll live together there. Isn't that something? Also, she says he and Terence are fighting for the same cause. I know what that means, and it's dangerous business. It would be like him, though," she mused. "She also says he's bent on coming to America. I can't believe all this." Nora paused. "I keep wondering, Molly, what my life would have been like if I had met him before William." She had been charmed by Seamus, but recognized that he too might have been a trap to keep her from her new resolve in life. She would never love again, for loving meant a broken heart, betrayal and abandonment. Somehow, at that moment in her room over a stable in Lowell, Massachusetts, she determined that money would protect her from ever being hurt like this again. I'm going to be rich, and William will be sorry one day, she vowed.

* * *

Annie came by because Nora wanted her dear old friend to meet her dear new one, and she also asked Colin to come by, though she didn't tell Molly about his proposal. She just couldn't talk about that.

They had a nice visit and everyone went with Nora to see Molly off. She and Molly agreed to meet in New York for the birth of the baby. Molly wanted to be with her. They both cried, but knew it wouldn't be long before they were together again.

Nora found that she liked working in retailing. Mr. O'Houlihan said she had a knack for it.

"You've got a good eye, girl. You know what's right and what's wrong." She was also crocheting some laces for Mrs. Bingley and her friends, who paid quite handsomely.

She had convinced Mr. O'Houlihan to buy a better class of merchandise. In the latest shipment, he unpacked a wonderful woolen suit made for a woman. It was lavender and well cut, with leg-of-mutton sleeves and a deeper lavender velvet collar. Mr. O'Houlihan was buying the new kind of merchandise because he was interested in appealing more to Mrs. Bingley's group.

Nora fell in love with it on the spot. "I want to buy this. It will fit me after the baby. I know it will."

Mrs. O'Houilhan held it up and everyone admired it, for it was indeed breathtaking with her dark hair, fair skin and violet eyes.

"She has to have it, 'twas made for her," Mrs. O'Houilhan said, her eyes twinkling.

"Aye, I guess it was," her husband agreed. It became Nora's first important purchase.

A few days later, Mr. O'Houilhan offered Nora a more extensive job at the shop.

"Why don't you do some of the buying for all the

fancy ladies who come in and ask your advice?'' he said in his gruff but kindly way.

"Thank you for the offer, you're both dear, but I will be returning to New York after my baby is born to set up an apartment for my husband, who will be coming from Ireland."

"Well, Nora, we'll be sorry to lose you, but I'll give you a fine reference, lass, don't you worry."

Nora realized that each passing day brought her closer to having to part from her baby. She thought of it sadly. According to her calculations, the baby was due the second week in February, and she had arranged to leave Lowell on the fifth of February so she could deliver her baby at Flower Fifth Avenue Hospital. Molly would come to New York for the delivery and take the baby back with her. Nora was already beginning to anticipate her new life.

On January 26, 1901, at midnight, four days after her nineteenth birthday, she woke with terrible pains.

Oh, what have I eaten? she thought. As the pains grew worse, she started to become nervous. Can I have miscalculated by so much? Can this be the baby coming?

When the pains were coming at regular intervals, she got out of bed, put on her coat and went to get Mr. O'Houlihan. Mrs. O'Houlihan was visiting her sister in Lawrence. She banged and banged on his door, and he sleepily came to the door.

"Please, please get Annie. The baby's coming."

"Oh child, I will. Don't worry. I've had a few myself." He put his coat on backwards as he rushed off to get Annie.

Nora knew enough to start boiling water, and she prepared as best she could.

Annie rushed in. "Oh, Nora, are you early or did you just figure wrong?"

"I don't know, Annie. I only know it hurts."

"Sure, and it does, love, but it will be worth it." She got busy and settled Nora in bed, holding her hand, saying words of comfort and wiping her brow after each labor pain. "I have a little something for you. If it gets too bad, just say the word."

Knowing that made Nora feel a bit better, but the pains became worse. She thought she must be dying.

"No, you're not dying. 'Tis the way we all come into the world," Annie assured her.

"Annie, I'm not married," Nora suddenly confessed, feeling miserable and guilty.

"Aye, Nora, I'm knowing that," Annie answered matter-of-factly.

"How, Annie?"

"Well, for a smart young woman, you tell a silly story. Husbands come to America first, darling, then send for their wives. Not the reverse. I figured you'd tell me when you were ready."

Nora managed a smile. "Annie, you know everything."

"Not everything, not quite," she smiled back. "Tell me about it."

And Nora did. It kept her mind off her misery, and she told her secret to Annie in between the labor pains. "I trust you, Annie," she whispered.

" 'Tis a secret I'll keep to my dying day," Annie promised.

As the story unfolded, Annie just held Nora's hand and comforted her, wiping the perspiration from her brow. "So the little one is of noble blood," Annie mused.

"I suppose so, Annie, I suppose so." The pains were coming every few seconds. Annie knew the birth was imminent. She told Nora to bear down, and as Nora gave one last scream, her beautiful baby boy was born.

Nora had told Annie that if it was a boy, she was

going to name him after his father. That much, after all, was his right.

Nora raised herself up to look at Annie slap breath into her baby, and as she did, Annie said, "Lord William Howard, meet your mother."

Before Nora drifted off to sleep, she mumbled groggily, "He'll be Billy, not William."

"Yes, love, he's a fine lad."

When Nora woke, Annie put Billy in her arms and said, "Well, this lord of the Howard clan had a most unceremonious birth—in a room over a stable, behind a dry goods store in the mill town of Lowell, Massachusetts."

They both laughed.

Nora's plans had gone awry, but she realized she would have a little extra time to spend with Billy before she left for New York to meet Molly. Annie was apprehensive about this, thinking she might not want to give the baby up. She voiced her fears to Nora.

"I don't have that choice, Annie, and anyway I'll be able to see him from time to time, so I might as well get used to it."

Even as she said that to Annie, she knew she had another choice. Colin had offered to marry her and adopt the baby. But she couldn't do it, not even to keep Billy. She could keep her child and have a decent husband in the bargain, but she knew what she wanted from life, and it wasn't a simple existence in a poor mill town in northeastern Massachusetts. No, what she wanted was the same power that the Williams of this world wielded. And she concluded that this power came from money and property. She had ambitions to be something besides a poor farm girl. She knew how to make beautiful lace, she had a flair for design, and somehow she was going to make those dreams come true. No matter how hard she had to work, she would succeed.

She couldn't even tell Annie about Colin's proposal. She was too ashamed. Annie wouldn't have understood why she didn't do anything to keep her baby. Nora knew only that her life was going to be different, and she had no intentions of being buried alive. Dear God forgive me, Nora prayed, I can't do it. I can't stay here. Billy, please, forgive me. And she fell asleep with Billy in her arms.

Annie and Colin took her to the train. She kissed them both and thanked them for their love and support. Mr. and Mrs. O'Houlihan had made her promise to write.

As Colin put her bags on the train, Nora looked lovingly at Annie. "Annie," she said, gazing at her fiercely, "you'll be hearing from me. I'll be sending for you before you know it. I need you. You've been like an anchor for me. We'll meet soon."

Colin reminded her that he'd be there for her if she ever needed him. She embraced him silently with the baby in her arms. "Perhaps we'll meet again one day, Colin. I hope so."

As the train pulled out of the station and their figures faded in the dusk, Nora looked at the baby in her arms and whispered to him, "Lad, I'm leaving a different person than I was before I came here."

Chapter 16

Nora sat staring straight ahead. It was Sunday, and the coffee shop was quiet. Grand Central Station was resting before the onslaught of Monday traffic. Molly and Nora had met as planned, and were able to spend three hours before Molly had to leave for Chicago. Mostly Nora stared at Billy, as if to imprint his face in her mind forever. She wanted desperately to call off the whole thing, confess her sin and bring up her own baby. But as she looked at Molly, she knew she couldn't do it. She had given her word and she'd keep it. Besides, she thought, Molly looks so right holding him, and she wants him so much. Maybe, Nora thought, someday I'll have another baby. Molly never can.

They walked together to the train. Molly promised that Nora could visit whenever she wanted. They wanted her to come often. "And," Molly said, "perhaps you might want to move to Chicago. Then you could see him all the time."

But Nora knew that was not wise. " 'Tis better this

way, Molly, for many reasons." She took the baby from Molly's arms and held him one more time. Molly said nothing as Nora hugged little Billy. "He'll have the best mother and father in the whole world," Nora said. "He's a lucky boy." She knew she was speaking the truth. "How many women who need to give up their babies have any say over who their parents will be? *I'm* lucky too." Taking Molly's hand, she said, "Write me often, tell me what he does, and tell me when he starts to crawl and what he's like." She gazed lovingly at the baby. "I hope he'll be more like Lord Anthony than like William," she added wistfully.

"I hope he'll be like his mother," Molly said firmly. They embraced one final time. Nora took one last look.

She walked slowly back to the coffee shop and sat down. Only one other person was there, and the counterman was sweeping up. He didn't seem to mind her sitting there. She needed time to think, to readjust before going to Uncle Jim's. Another painful wrench. Is my life to be one painful parting after another? Would Seamus or Colin have been the answer? Of course they wouldn't have the answer. "I'm my own answer," she said to herself. I'll work hard, make my own way, my own success and my own happiness.

After a long time, the counterman spoke to her. "Miss, I'm closing up. Sorry."

"Oh, it's all right. You have been very kind to let me sit here. I really need to be going now anyway as I have a very important appointment."

An appointment with the rest of my life, she thought.

Some of the grief had subsided and she began to look forward to seeing Sean and meeting Uncle Jim and Aunt Nellie. She had to start a new life, right this minute, she resolved, and she needed to start it with her chin up. She ran out of Grand Central south to Third Avenue and ran up the "el" stairs. The wretched months in Lowell were over; her beautiful, healthy Billy was safe in the capable and loving hands of her oldest friend; she was going to see her beloved Sean, from whom she had never been separated before; and she was finally going to meet Uncle Jim and Aunt Nellie.

The train jerked and vibrated into Twenty-third Street and she bounded out and raced down the stairs with a new spirit. She wrapped the scarf around her neck to keep out the icy winds. Her small, worn-out leather suitcase was clutched in one hand and her purse, her only purse, brown, ugly and threadbare, was clutched in the other. Her simple dark blue worsted coat contrasted with her sorry-looking accessories. She had made the coat herself before she had experienced her first American winter.

She remembered how she and Sean had looked into the windows of big New York department stores like Altman's, Macy's, and Lord and Taylor's. It was after seeing a fashionable coat in an Altman's window that she had made the one she now wore.

This area, she knew, was called the Gashouse District. Tim had been right. It did turn out to be the neighborhood in which Uncle Jim lived, and now Sean was living here too. It was new and a little intimidating, quite different from the Lower East Side and Mulberry Street.

It seems quite a bit nicer, though, she thought happily. But where were the familiar awnings, the pushcarts of fruit and clothing, the barrels of pickles in front of the stores? Then she realized it was February and bitter cold for the pushcarts.

At that moment she spotted a policeman walking ahead and rushed to catch him. It was a quiet Sunday and there were only a few people about. She stopped breathlessly in front of him and asked directions. He pointed her in the right direction and said, "Faith, lass, 'tis a raw and miserable day to be lost."

"Oh, I'm not lost." A hint of mischief was in her eyes. "I've just not been here before."

"And who would you be looking for?" he asked, smiling at her obvious good cheer.

"My Uncle Jim, Jim Matthews. Are you knowing him?"

"Aye, I am indeed, He's a grand and fine friend of mine and all the neighborhood. I'll not be leaving his very own niece unaccompanied. I'll take you myself."

A simple wooden sign hung over the door of Matthew's Pub. She had known that Uncle Jim was a saloon-keeper, but she didn't expect that his flat would be over the saloon.

The officer, whose name was Mulcahy, rang the bell and said, "Nora, I'll be going. I'm not wanting to be intruding."

"Thank you kindly, Officer Mulcahy. My uncle will be grateful, as am I. Good-bye. I'll be seeing you again."

The door opened and a tall, broad-shouldered man with a shock of white hair and penetrating blue eyes like her mother's looked at her with great pleasure. His leonine face broke into a warm, welcoming smile that instantly melted her heart.

"If it isn't my sister Mary standing before me, as she was twenty-five years ago! Oh darling Nora, welcome, welcome." He swept her up into his muscular arms.

"Uncle Jim, I can't tell you how happy I am to be here." She began to cry.

"I know, darling. I know." His words comforted her.

"I feel like I'm home."

"And that you are, lass. But why didn't you tell us you were coming? We were planning to meet you."

"I wanted it to be a surprise," she lied, "and besides, I was able to get away a few days earlier than I had expected."

"Well, never mind. You're here. Come meet my Nellie. Sean is out. He's always at the local Democratic Club when he's not working. Takes to politics just like his uncle." Uncle Jim sounded proud of his nephew.

They climbed a flight of stairs to the right of the door leading to the saloon. Nora took a quick peek, but she caught only the flash of brass and mirrors along the long mahogany bar.

Nellie stood at the top of the stairs, filling the entire space with her ample girth. Her grey hair was pulled back in a bun and her plump face wreathed in a smile of welcome. Her hazel eyes twinkled, and she embraced Nora with such warmth that she immediately felt as if she belonged there.

"So this is our Nora. Bless you, darling. You're a beauty. We've been so worried about you up there in Massachusetts. They don't like us Irish. We're not welcome still after all these years, as we are in New York."

"Oh Nellie, stop," said Uncle Jim. "It's not so bad now. Times have changed since your brother Mike ran into his troubles there."

"Well, never mind. We're glad you're here and out of that awful place," Nellie said, making sure to have the last word.

"So am I, Aunt Nellie. It was awful, but not for the reasons you're saying. Anyway, I'm happy to be with my family."

Nellie gave her warm soup, fussed over her and showed her to her small bedroom. Nora was thrilled. The room had cheerful wallpaper with tiny yellow roses on it. On the bed were some pillows. She recognized her mother's lacework on them. And there was a comfortable chair in the corner near the window.

" 'Tis beautiful, Aunt Nellie. I love it. A room of my very own. Oh, thank you."

"It was your cousin Johanna's room, but now she lives in a fancy house on Long Island."

The flat was quite large and very comfortable. Nellie had a great deal of overstuffed furniture. It was homey and pleasant. Nora thought it was a marvelous place, quite the contrast to the cold-water flat on the Lower East Side, where she and Sean first stayed with Tim and Molly.

"Nellie, 'tis the grandest place I've ever lived in," Nora said, and indeed it was. She unpacked her meager belongings and noticed that her black trunk was sitting under the window. She thought wistfully of Mary. Her family pictures traveled wherever she went, and she was arranging them on the bureau when Jim walked in. He looked at them with great interest.

"My sister is as beautiful as ever, perhaps more so, for the character that was a promise when I saw her last is now a reality."

"Why Uncle Jim, what a nice thing to say." Nora was pleased that he recognized what a special person her mother was.

They heard a racket downstairs and she knew it was Sean. Her heart raced as she ran out to meet him.

"Nora, me love, where are you?"

She ran into his arms and they held one another in a long, tender embrace.

" 'Tis she who taught me how to speak, you know, sass and all."

Jim and Nellie laughed at his joke. Nora could see that they thought Sean was the salt of the earth.

"Oh Sean, how I've missed you. Are you well?" As she pulled herself away, she looked into his mischievous eyes and smiled. "Oh, I've missed those eyes, lad. And look how you've filled out. You're quite grown up."

"And you, Nora? You look a little pale, a little thinner. Are you well, then? I've worried so. Several times Uncle Jim and I were going to go up and drag you home. But you were so firm about it, we decided it was important to you and couldn't be as bad as we had heard."

"No, no it wasn't that bad. I made some nice friends, and the money was good. We'll be able to send for Danny soon."

Then they all sat and talked and reminisced for hours. Finally Nellie reminded them that Sean had to report for work at four a.m., and that Nora looked like she too needed a good night's rest.

Nora kissed them all good night, and when she had prepared to retire and had turned the light off, she knelt at the side of the bed, much as she had done when she was younger, and prayed. Her strength and resolve and maturity were drained from her, and for a few moments she was a little girl again.

"Thank you God for Nellie and Jim, and being with Sean again, and Molly having Billy, and my kind new friends, and for never having to have rats in my bedroom again. No matter how awful a job I might have to take, I've got this to come home to."

She climbed into bed feeling safe and secure in the bosom of family, a feeling she hadn't had for a long time. She fell asleep dreaming of Ireland, and her mother and father, her brothers and sisters, and the mists on the mountains.

*   *   *

The next morning dawned clear and cold. The sun glimmered through her rosebud curtains, and it took a few minutes before she realized she was at Uncle Jim's. She smiled and stretched luxuriously, feeling rested and happy. Nellie had a huge breakfast waiting for her. They had let her sleep late.

"Aunt Nellie, I don't remember the last time I slept until nine o'clock. It's positively sinful." She devoured the breakfast of wheatcakes and sausage and strong black coffee. "I'm wanting to get right out and find a job."

"Oh lass, will a few days' rest be hurting you, now? 'Tis no sin to be resting. Even God took a day off. And heaven knows you're needing it."

She hugged Nellie. "Aye, I do need it. But I'm feeling wonderful. I feel like the world is to be mine for the asking."

Nellie laughed. "And let's be hoping it is. And what do you plan to be doing?"

At that moment Jim came in red-faced and smiling. "Lass, you're looking good this morning, even more beautiful now that you've had some rest."

"Uncle Jim, I really enjoyed my last job at Lowell, selling at O'Houlihan's. I liked all of the things about selling. Being with people, trying to help them, helping to choose the nice designs. Why, I even enjoyed taking stock. Mr. O'Houlihan said I had a good eye, that I was a natural, so I'm thinking I'd like to try working in one of the big department stores. You know we don't have anything like them in Ireland, not even in Dublin. The whole idea of these gigantic bazaars of goods is so wonderfully American. I love them. I want to try finding a job in one of them. What do you think?"

They discussed all the possibilities. Jim told her where

all the different stores were located, and she set off happily with a full sense of adventure. She tried a few small stores in the area to get some experience in job application and interviewing. As she was walking along Madison Square, she noticed a huge sign painted on the side wall of one of the buildings. She had noticed this same sign as she had ridden on the "el" the day before. It proclaimed in bold letters: ALL CARS TRANSFER AT BLOOMINGDALE'S.

Maybe this is God's way of telling me that this is where I'm supposed to go. Well, if all cars transfer there, why shouldn't I? she thought to herself, heading for the Third Avenue "el." Her heart raced with anticipation as she descended the stairs at Fifty-ninth Street Station. The neighborhood was full of saloons and crowded tenements, but across the street stood the majestic entrance to Bloomingdale's, the Great East Side Bazaar. The six-story building, with its arched entrance soaring up two stories, bustled with shoppers. An unbroken line of display windows was full of all kinds of merchandise, both ordinary and exotic. The window-shoppers were gawking at a beautiful, wildly colored live parrot, who seemed to be an important part of a display of oriental jewelry and fabrics. Oh, how grand, she thought as she rushed into the store, certain that this was the place she wanted to work.

The main floor took her breath away. It was spacious and airy with columns dividing the departments. Lovely upholstered leather stools sat in front of the dress goods counter, so that the women could be comfortable while they chose a French silk, or an Italian gabardine. The jewelry counter captivated her for longer than she intended, and it seemed that one could find any book one wanted in the well-stocked book department. She finally came to laces, and when she browsed about this department, she looked at the goods with the eye of an expert. She asked questions of the salesgirls about price and design, and was somewhat disappointed in the selection and quality of the lace. Finally, she found out that the personnel department was on the fifth floor, and she was instructed to take one of the "sky-carriages." Before doing that, however, she rode for fun on the "inclined elevator" to the second floor. The elevators, all four of them, were mirrored. Fine mahogany doors and ceilings and little upholstered red velvet seats made them look like miniature drawing rooms.

In the personnel office, she was directed to fill out an application form. She waited for some time, and finally, a Miss Helen Fennell interviewed her.

After the interview, Miss Fennell said they didn't have too many openings at the moment, but perhaps they could call her.

"Oh, Miss Fennell, I have had experience, and I think I could be of great assistance in the lace department, and I would certainly appreciate an opportunity."

Miss Fennell, very interested, liked what she saw. What an attractive, well-behaved young woman with an engaging manner, and a cultured way of speaking, despite the still evident brogue. She asked Nora, "Young woman, do you know what a floater is?"

"Not exactly, but I imagine it means someone who doesn't have a permanent assignment."

"Exactly," said Miss Fennell. Nora's logic impressed her. "Until a regular opening occurs, you'll go from department to department, wherever you're needed. How does that sound?"

It sounded wonderful to Nora, who thought it was even better than a regular assignment. "Does that mean I have the job?" she asked.

"You can start tomorrow."

"Thank you, Miss Fennell. Thank you so much."

She left, walking on air.

*   *   *

For the next few months, Nora "floated" from department to department. No opening ever occurred in the lace department, so she decided to take matters into her own hands. She visited the department whenever she had a few free moments. She made friends with the salesgirls, and also with Mrs. Ruche, the buyer. It worked, for the next time one of the girls was ill, Mrs. Ruche requested Nora. Nora learned where the laces came from, learned about pricing, quality and demand in the first few weeks. But then the girl who had been ill finally returned, and Nora was floating again.

A week later, she was summoned to Miss Fennell's office.

"Nora, I've had good reports about you from both your customers and your coworkers." Helen Fennell came right to the point. "Now that a permanent assignment has opened up, I've recommended you for it. It's in ladies' underwear and corsets, and I think you're well suited for it."

Nora had hoped to be sent to laces, but lingerie might be interesting, and she was delighted to have a permanent assignment.

Ladies' underwear and corsets was a large, rambling department on the second floor. Her first impression was that the merchandise was not displayed as attractively as it could have been, and after a few days, she asked Mr. Hadley, a kindly salesman who had been in the department for fifteen years, what he thought about it.

"I don't think much about it one way or the other, young lady. I just sell the stuff."

Well, at least he's honest, she thought. No one seemed very interested in attractive display, including Mrs. Fitzwilliams, the large, big-bosomed buyer, who was often tipsy.

"If you have any ideas, Nora," Mrs. Fitzwilliams said to her one day after returning from a long lunch, "ask me, and we'll decide if it makes any sense. And, of course, we both know," she added, smiling, "it won't make any sense if it costs any money."

None of this discouraged Nora, who was determined that the department needed upgrading badly. The salesmen gathered in little groups and chatted when there weren't any customers. There were no other saleswomen in the department. Nora was extremely busy one afternoon, taking care of three customers at one time, running back and forth from the stockroom, when she suddenly noticed that the three salesmen were gathered in a corner chatting and laughing, without one customer among the three of them.

She said to one woman, "Excuse me, I'll call Mr. Hadley or Mr. Burrows. They can help you, and you won't have to wait."

"Oh, oh, never mind miss, never mind. I don't mind waiting. I really don't," the woman answered. She turned to the other waiting women, who said the same thing. At that moment, she realized that they did not want the men waiting on them.

But of course, she thought, neither would I. Why didn't I think of that sooner? What woman wants a man showing her intimate apparel? And she made a note to see Miss Fennell about that.

Miss Fennell was extremely interested in what Nora had to say, and saw the sense in it. "I'm going to send you in to see Mr. Bloomingdale. You should tell him this yourself."

Nora showed up for her appointment with Mr. Lyman Bloomingdale in her lovely lavender woolen suit, her only fine piece of clothing. Her hair was swept back simply, and she made an immediate impression on the man who, with his brother Joseph, had founded Bloomingdale's thirty years earlier. They both were good promoters. They advertised more than any other New York store, and they were still open to ideas which would help advance sales in any way.

Good heavens, he thought, what a beauty. And he asked the nature of her business.

"Mr. Bloomingdale, I work in corsets and ladies' underwear. I have been there for quite a while now, and I have noticed something that I think should be brought to your attention." Her manner was business-like and direct.

"Yes, and what is that?" He smiled at her approach, which was not at all timid or deferential.

"I'm the only woman waiting on the customers in the department, and I believe that is hurting sales. You are driving customers away, Mr. Bloomingdale. I know that for a fact. I often have three customers lined up waiting for me, while the three men stand around without a customer. Women simply do not want men helping them buy intimate apparel."

He looked at her and knew instantly that she was right. He became very interested in this spunky, beautiful, and obviously smart young Irish girl. "I don't know why no one, including me, thought of that before, Miss O'Sullivan. It probably does drive away customers. We'll see about changing that immediately." He added, "Thank you for calling it to my attention. Miss Fennell was right about you."

Nora thanked him and left his office, wondering what it was that Miss Fennell had said to him.

Within days, the department's personnel had been changed. Three women were brought from other departments, and the three men were reassigned. Nora met Mr.

Hadley in the elevator a few days later, and he moaned about having been sent to umbrellas. She smiled to herself, but was very solicitious to him. She was given more and more responsibility, and made many changes. The first thing she did was change the displays to show the lingerie in more attractive ways. She noticed that the department seemed to have more customers, and wondered whether this was just her imagination or if indeed sales had risen.

One lunch hour she took the elevator to the executive offices and entered the accounting department. She was determined to find out if this departmental change had made any difference in sales. A very striking young woman with olive skin, huge glittering brown eyes, pointed features and a deep throaty voice asked if she could help Nora. Somehow, her voice and manner made Nora feel comfortable immediately.

"I'm Rachel Friedman." She extended her hand.

"And I'm Nora O'Sullivan, and happy I am to be meeting you." Rachel was enchanted by Nora's brogue. She proceeded to tell Rachel what had happened, and Rachel seemed very interested.

She looked up the sales figures, did some calculating on a pad, and said, "It seems to me, Nora, that sales are up. I can't tell exactly how much, but I'll check later. Have you had lunch yet? If not, will you join me?"

Nora, elated at the news, cheerily replied, "Why, I'd love to be having lunch."

They went to the ladies' dining room on the fourth floor, chatting all the way.

A few months later, Nora was promoted to assistant buyer. She ran to accounting to tell Rachel, who had become her best friend and confidante.

Rachel was thrilled for Nora. "Oh Nora, that's wonderful, and in such a short time. Let's celebrate this eve-

ning and have supper out." They had become friends quickly.
Not only were they the same age, but they were similar in
temperament. They seemed to spark one another, and they
thought alike about so many things that they felt it was
uncanny. One would often anticipate what the other was
thinking. They were different in ways that were comple-
mentary. Nora was interested in the aesthetics of a situation, and Rachel would question the purpose. So, while
Nora would spend hours making the department look attractive, Rachel would spend hours checking out the sales
figures.

One afternoon, they were shopping for a new shirtwaist for Rachel. Nora had told her that pink would be a
lovely color on her. Rachel already knew that Nora's
instincts about these things were not to be questioned, so
she agreed. They looked through the rack of $1.98 blouses
and were frustrated by the time it took to find Rachel's
size.

Nora looked at Rachel. "Are you thinking what I'm
thinking?"

Rachel laughed, saying, "I believe I am." And over
lunch they discussed a scheme that Nora decided had to be
presented to Mr. Bloomingdale. She made an appointment
for the following day.

"May I see Mr. Bloomingdale, please?"

"Mr. Bloomingdale is in a meeting and cannot be
disturbed," the secretary said, not even looking up at
Nora.

"Well then, I'll just wait until he's finished." Nora
could not understand why a man of such optimism could
employ such a dour woman. She could hear Mr. Bloomingdale's voice through the closed door of his office, then
laughter as the door opened and he saw her.

"There you are, Miss O'Sullivan. I was just telling
how you banished male sales clerks from the lingerie

department. Poor Hadley hasn't smiled since we sent him to umbrellas. I think he misses corsets!''

"Miss O'Sullivan's idea is no laughing matter, Mr. Bloomingdale. Sales are up twenty-five percent in lingerie since the clerks became all women." Jess Jacobson, Bloomingdale's treasurer, waved sheets of sales graphs to illustrate his point.

"I never laugh at profits, Jess, but Hadley does look as if he's been banished to a desert island. Just see for yourself on your way to lunch.''

"Oh, Mr. Bloomingdale, I never meant to cause anyone to be unhappy, but I just couldn't keep still when I knew myself that I'd want no man to measure me for my chemise," Nora smiled. She felt so comfortable with Mr. Bloomingdale that she revealed her Irish humor to him, and as always, he showed his appreciation by throwing back his head and roaring with laughter.

"You're a treasure, Miss O'Sullivan. You make my day! Come into my office. I'm sure you have another idea for improving the store. Won't be long before you'll want my job, no doubt.''

"You're right, Mr. Bloomingdale. Not about wanting your job of course," she said, a mischievous twinkle in her eye, "but about changing something else, and I'm hoping you'll think it's a good idea.''

"Jess, you better sit in on this. She's probably going to change your sales figures for the coming year, so you might as well hear about it now.''

Nora wanted to be taken seriously, for she had a good idea and she knew it. "Mr. Bloomingdale, we group all our merchandise by price and I want to change that, and group it by size.''

Jess Jacobson interrupted. "That doesn't make sense. If I want a $1.95 shirt, I want to go right to the $1.95

stack. That's the way our customers are used to doing it, and I think it should stay that way."

"Well, may I please explain. For one thing, it's inconvenient to go through all the $1.95 merchandise to find your size, but more important, the customer never even sees the more expensive merchandise." Nora was firm about it, absolutely certain she was right.

"So what, Miss O'Sullivan?" Mr. Bloomingdale asked, stroking his beard and looking at her intently. "Our customers know what price they want to pay, and we make it easy for them by grouping the goods by price."

"The 'so what,' Mr. Bloomingdale, is that I think if a customer sees an item in his size for the dollar he intended to spend, but in going through all the goods in his size sees another item he likes much more for two dollars, I think he'll spend the dollar more. And the store would make more money." She sounded absolutely certain.

"You're saying that if he only sees the dollar merchandise, then a dollar is all he's going to spend, is that correct?"

Suddenly Jess Jacobson was excited. "Mr. Bloomingdale, she may have something. She may really have something there. I think she could be right. If we expose the customer, in his size, to two, three, and even five-dollar selections, he might spend five times as much money!" He looked at Nora as if he wanted to hug her, for profit was his major goal in life.

"Well, well, Miss O'Sullivan, it looks as if you have the makings of a merchant prince, or should I say, princess." Mr. Bloomingdale smiled. "I won't argue with you. Your idea is certainly novel, but it has possibilities. We'll try it out in your department and see how the customers react to it. By the way," he added, "I want you to take over more of the buying. Mrs. Fitzwilliams is, well, ah, losing her grip. Don't make it too obvious. She has given us many good years, and I'll not let her go.''

"I'm already doing most of it, Mr. Bloomingdale," she confessed, since he obviously knew about Mrs. Fitzwilliams' drinking problem. "And you can be sure I'll not let on."

"Good girl." He smiled warmly at her. "And good luck. Let's see how this new scheme works."

The reaction was more profitable than anyone could have imagined. Mr. Bloomingdale and Mr. Jacobson were pleased with her innovative ideas, and instituted the new method of presenting merchandise in all departments where sizes were essential. Nora received a small raise, but before accepting it, she gave part of the credit to Rachel. Mr. Bloomingdale had laughed, saying to Jess Jacobson, "Give the Friedman girl a small increase also. When this one makes up her mind, what's a poor man to do?"

Rachel was surprised, but pleased. "You needn't have told him I had anything to do with it, Nora," she told her friend later.

"Oh yes I did," she answered firmly. "Yes I did."

She and Rachel spent many hours talking about Bloomingdale's and the other things they would change if it were their store. One day, Rachel laughingly said, "You know, with all our wonderful ideas, maybe we should have our own shop. Then we could run it just as we pleased."

"Oh, Rachel, I wish that more than anything. When I see the quality of lace sold here at the store that the customers pay a lot of money for, and I think of the exquisite pieces handmade by my people, I just know there's a market for that work. But," she sighed, "I don't know how to present it to the public. A shop would be a good idea for sure, but do you think there's a way we could ever make that happen?''

"Nora, the lingerie you design and make for yourself is far superior to anything here. Better even than some of the lovely new things you've bought for the department. I think your talent is just wasted as a buyer and salesgirl. You shouldn't be buying other people's designs. You should be selling your own.''

"I don't know how to do that, Rachel. It's one thing for you and Aunt Nellie and Uncle Jim and Sean, everyone who loves me, to tell me how much you like my work, but who knows if anyone else would?''

"Well, then, it's time to find out, isn't it? I think what we need is a plan. If we want our own shop, we have to start right now, or we'll never make it happen. We already know that I know the business end and can keep the books. We both have good retailing ideas, and you design exquisite lingerie. I think everyone who could afford them would want to wear your beautiful things. So, what else do we need?''

"Oh, Rachel, you're wonderful! But, Miss Practical Business Mind, what we need is money! And to find out if people would buy what I make.''

"First things first, then. Would you be willing to give up your lunch time to take your designs and samples of some of the lace to the exclusive shops?''

"Rachel, I would gladly give up my lunch hour. What a good idea. And first, I want to try Jacques Mandel's. I spend hours on the way home staring in those windows. He makes the most exquisite clothes in New York. If he liked my designs, then I would believe that I have talent.''

"Might as well start at the top.'' Rachel smiled. "A few minutes ago you didn't know how we could do it, and now we're going right to Jacques Mandel. Well, why not,

Nora? That's the way to think, and that's where you should go, and, as your prospective business partner, I'll go with you. But first, Nora, we need a plan. I've been wanting you to meet my parents, so plan on coming to dinner tomorrow evening. I would trust my father's judgment on something like this. We obviously need advice.''

Chapter 17

Nora's exposure to the way people actually lived was very limited. She knew what the cottages and a country castle looked like, and she had been exposed to the grim, crowded conditions of tenements. She viewed with awe the mansions along Fifth Avenue, and she could not understand that one house could occupy an entire block, even though she had seen pictures of their gaudily ornate rooms in the *New York Weekly*.

So, when she entered Rachel's home in the Dakota apartments on the West Side of Manhattan right off Central Park, she was entering a new world. In the library where they gathered, a fire was burning cheerfully in a fireplace topped by a simple marble mantel. High ceilings with lovely moldings, and beautifully carved mahogany furniture upholstered in subdued velvets and brocades delighted her aesthetic sensibilities. Oriental rugs in jewellike tones covered the gleaming parquet floor, and the walls were lined with bookcases filled with handsome leather-bound books. Nora got an impression of refinement, of restrained taste. These words also described the occupants of the room. Both of Rachel's parents were of notable birth and were products of excellent educations. They had each lived an upper-class existence before fleeing the persecution of their homeland. They, fortunately, had escaped with some of their money and possessions, unlike so many other Eastern European Jews who were now reduced to working in sweatshops.

Mrs. Friedman's stunning white hair was piled high on her head. Her complexion was flawless and unlined, and her walk was erect and graceful as she crossed the room to meet Nora. "Welcome, Nora," she greeted in a soft voice. "Welcome to our home. Our Rachel has told us so much about you, and we have eagerly awaited meeting you. May I offer you a sherry?"

Rachel's father snapped shut the book he had been reading when the girls entered the room. He was shorter than his wife, and stocky, with the same snow-white hair. His hair stuck out in tufts from under the skullcap he wore. Nora thought he had the most vital, intelligent eyes she had ever seen. They fairly crackled with humorous curiosity. He was a world-renowned Talmudic scholar, but he had a practical side as well.

"Maybe she doesn't drink, Rebecca," he said to his wife. "Just because our Rachel considers herself a modern woman doesn't mean this lovely creature should be corrupted, too."

"Mr. Friedman, I think you're teasing me. I've never had a sherry, but if you are having a glass, then I'd like to try one too." Nora sensed these people were different from any she'd known—brilliant, cultured, and with a religious heritage as old as time itself.

"I don't approve of many things in the world today, Miss O'Sullivan," Rachel's father imparted. "I stay here, safe among my books and papers, clinging to the traditions

I was born under. We're not wealthy, but we have a happy life.''

Nora accepted the glass of sherry from Mrs. Friedman. She liked the warm feeling in her throat as she swallowed it, and was beginning to like the taste. "It's very nice, ah, excellent really. Who knows, I may become corrupted too.'' She smiled.

"We have another daughter—Sarah. Did you know?'' Mrs. Freidman asked her.

"Yes, Rachel has told me of her little sister,'' Nora replied.

"She's away at school, you know,'' Mr. Friedman interrupted. "She is a shy, retiring, obedient girl. But Rachel, she is our brave one. She has chosen to work to be a part of today. She has a head for figures. Unusual for a girl. She's restless. She dashes in and out like a bright tropical bird. Even though she embraces a world her mother and I try to escape from by staying within these walls, we are very proud of her.''

Mrs. Friedman then told her husband, "Dear, she knows all about our Rachel.''

After a sip of sherry, he continued speaking. "And now she tells us of you and how the two of you want to take the New York retailing world by storm with a shop of your own. I don't understand for the life of me why two beautiful girls want a shop instead of a husband! My Rebecca's life's work has always been caring for me, our home and our children.''

"Oh Daddy, please,'' Rachel said.

"Ah, but times change, and Rebecca says I should try to change too. Let's discuss all this after dinner,'' he suggested.

As conversation flowed, and Nora got to know these lovely people, she said a silent thanks to her mother, who had provided her with her own very fine education. She thought sadly, this is the kind of home my mother should have. How well she would suit it. Nora felt comfortable and conversed about everything with confidence and wit. Mr. Friedman liked her for her quickness of mind and her probing curiosity. Mrs. Friedman, for her part, thought she had never seen anyone as beautiful.

After dinner, once again settled in the library, Mr. Friedman returned to discussing Rachel and Nora's plans. "Girls, I think what you are proposing has merit. I do believe you both need more experience, however."

"Oh, Daddy," Rachel interrupted, "we're planning on that. I want Nora to take her designs to one of the fine fashion houses, and her laces too, to see if she can find work in one of those places. We don't mean to run right out and open the shop tomorrow. And I'll be continuing at Bloomingdale's. I learn a great deal there that will be helpful for us. As a matter of fact, Nora is getting her portfolio ready, and when it's completed, we're going to launch an attack on all those fancy emporiums."

"Well, I see you have already worked out your ideas. I can't say that I'm not impressed. And Rebecca and I were also impressed with some of the designs that Rachel has shown us. They're good, Nora. Even a sheltered Biblical scholar such as I can see that."

"Thank you both. I'm so delighted you liked them." Nora's enthusiasm was infectious. "We'll prepare ourselves well, Mr. Friedman, don't worry."

Mr. Friedman looked at them for a few moments and then said, "If you and Rachel want your shop, I want to help you. Rachel says that that lovely head of yours is full of good ideas and talent, and I must say, I think she's right. So, Mrs. Friedman and I want to lend you and Rachel the money for your shop."

The girls were delighted, but Nora said, "Oh, you are both so kind. Thank you so much. I love Rachel and I know we'll have a fine partnership. But I have my own money. It's in the Emigrant's Savings Bank, just waiting for the right opportinity. But I'll never forget that you and Mrs. Friedman wanted to help me just as you'd help Rachel. I'll be forever grateful.'' She hugged both of them.

Rachel was curious about Nora's account in the bank, knowing she was from a poor Irish background. Although, Rachel thought, Nora is so marvelously unpredictable, always full of surprises.

As Nora returned home that evening, her spirits soared. She felt a momentary clutch of sadness as she thought of how she had come by the money to do this, but banished it almost immediately. Molly wrote weekly that Billy was well and growing and happy. She tried not to think of William and his betrayal.

As she entered the door on the side of the saloon, she saw Uncle Jim and Aunt Nellie tending bar. The bar was jammed, for it was Saturday evening, and many of the men were spending small chunks of their paychecks in Jim's bar. There was a great deal of noise and singing and arguing. Smoke hung heavy in the air, and the mirrors and mahogany and brass glimmered. She ran up the stairs two at a time and went into the kitchen to make a cup of tea. She was surprised to find Sean sitting there. When he was home, he was usually in the bar. While he drank little, which had made him somewhat suspect in the eyes of his countrymen, he loved the political talk that always abounded, and he sometimes went so far as ending the talk in fisticuffs. His head was bowed over the table and there was a discernible look of sadness about him. He turned as she entered.

''Why Sean, what in heaven's name is wrong?'' The sorrow in his eyes was apparent.

"Oh Nora, read this," he murmured.

She recognized Danny's writing and began to tremble. "Sean, is everyone all right?"

"Yes, Nora, but the news is upsetting all the same."

She sat down and read the letter, trying to keep her hands steady.

Dear Nora and Sean,

I received your letter enclosing my passage money for America. Dear ones, I thank you with all my heart. You are the dearest sister and brother anyone could have, and I would do anything in my power to please you, you must know that. I don't want to hurt you, as I have hurt Ma and Pa, but I must tell you that I will not be joining you in America, now or ever. I seem to be disappointing everyone I love; Ma and Pa because I won't accept responsibility for the farm now that Terence has renounced his birthright to give his life to the Brotherhood and our country's freedom, but I cannot accept the farm and I cannot accept your gift of America, either. I am placing all my hopes in you to understand what I must do; perhaps you can help the rest of the family to accept my decision. For you see, dearest ones, I have decided to give my life to God and become a priest.

You, Nora, above all the others, know that my life has never been happy; I just never seemed to have a place like all the rest of you did. Terence had his Ireland, you and Sean had your new life in America. Bridget had her lace-making, and Kevin his horses. But, Nora, I felt it; there was just nowhere I fit. When I had my accident, I honestly wanted to die. Why would I have wanted to go on, with no purpose and nothing but the feelings of unhappiness and hopelessness that I had? Nora, you saved me then; I wasn't especially grateful at the time, but I am now, for I know why my life was spared. You gave me the first glimmer of hope that my dark feelings could be helped, but when you left, I again fell into the deepest despair. Father O'Rourke saw this, and asked me to come see him. Soon, I was going to the rectory every day, and slowly, but surely, I began to feel God's love and comfort. All my despair He understood, and He eased my pain. Suddenly, I knew why I had been born—to serve Him. And, Nora, Sean, I knew a joy I did not know was possible. My faith has set me free! If only I were not causing others sorrow, my happiness would be complete.

I have, with God's help, begun to understand Ma and Pa's disapproval. Each of them approach their faith in a different way. I think Ma feels I am giving up on life by entering the Seminary. You know, Nora, I think Ma is too intellectual for Mother Church; when she is in trouble, she solves it herself; I've never known her not to get her way. Perhaps, some day she will have to learn the lesson of humility. Pa, for his part, is a Catholic because he was born one, just as he was born Irish and a farmer; he just accepts it all as a way of life. So, they cannot understand how God has called me to serve Him. Terence actually called me "another passive, gutless Irishman," daring me to be a man and fight with him for freedom. Oh that was a sad day; I almost felt I couldn't stand alone against them, but again, God spoke to me, calmed me, and

called me for His own. And, Father O'Rourke
helped, even knowing Ma's feelings. Bless him.

In ten days, I will enter Maynooth Seminary
and I feel my life will begin, at last. If only you
both were here to see how happy I am, you
would know that I have made the one and only
right choice for me. Just as Terence is sure of his
calling, and you and Sean are undoubtedly shap-
ing your own destinies, I am firm in my conviction and hope that in your heart you can accept
that which our parents and brother would deny me.

> Your loving brother,
> Danny

Nora slumped into a chair, staring at Danny's words
over and over, as if by staring hard enough they would
change. "Oh, Sean, Sean. Danny a priest. Who'll help Pa
on the farm now that both Terence and Danny are leaving?
Oh, my God, he's not coming," she cried.

Sean put his arms about her. " 'Tis a shock, isn't
it?"

"Oh Sean, I knew about his deep despair when none
of the rest of you did, but I didn't think this would be his
solution." She paused a moment. "I'm so ashamed. Why
am I, why are we upset, when he says he has finally tasted
happiness? Why aren't we happy for him?"

"I'll tell you why, sister, because he's not coming to
America. We want our family here with us. We thought
that would start to happen, and the first one to come has
decided against it. It's a heavy blow for us."

She looked up at Sean. He suddenly seemed older,
more mature. He no longer seemed like her little brother,
but more of an equal, with strengths and insights that she
welcomed.

"Isn't it interesting, that Ma and Pa are upset too. It's

the dream of every Irish mother to have one son go into the priesthood, every Irish mother but ours. Perhaps Danny is right about her being too intellectual for Mother Church. And Pa, naturally, is worried about the farm. We're all concerned about Danny's choice for selfish reasons. I'm thinking he needs a letter of encouragement, Nora, we owe him that." Sean patted her shoulder comfortingly.

"Oh Sean," she cried, burying her face in his chest. "I'm so thankful you're here with me. I miss them so." As she looked up at his strong, reassuring face, she thought, my God, he's already a man.

Chapter 18

Two years in America had made a man of Sean O'Sullivan. His thick mane of golden red hair, his ever mischievous, sparkling eyes, his wild, wonderful wit and his soft, lilting brogue embodied the essence of the Irish spirit. His tall, slender physique, broad shoulders, warm, inviting smile and deep intelligence set him apart as a man to be reckoned with.

"He's as handsome an Irishman as has ever walked off the boat," Nellie told everyone who would listen, openly admiring his manly, attractive good looks. "Not at all unlike my Jim at that age."

Jim's face flushed. "That'll be enough of that kind of talk, woman." He was, however, obviously pleased.

Sean would as quickly make a joke or a pun as it took him to wink. He teased Aunt Nellie constantly, telling her far-fetched stories and crazy anecdotes that she always believed. When she would catch on, she'd say, "Aye, well it could have happened now, don't you know?" She fell into his trap every time. Nora and Uncle Jim always knew when he was teasing, but Nellie rarely did. She loved him though and thought he was the smartest man she had ever known.

He could imitate anyone he had ever heard with uncanny accuracy, and amused his family and friends with his wonderful impersonations of famous people.

Uncle Jim never tired of hearing him discuss politics in the pub; his arguments were forceful and compelling. They agreed on a great many things. Both of them, of course, were very interested in the Irish Nationalist cause in America, and Jim often said, "The lad can be explaining anything to anybody. Mary, Joseph and Patrick, the lad could give tongue to a stone."

Nora's assessment of her beloved brother was that "he could charm the skin off a snake." She adored him, and always had, for no matter what the circumstances, he could always make her laugh.

His professors at City College liked him and respected his intelligence and drive. The Italian immigrants, to whom he taught English at the Delancey Street Democratic Club, would have laid down their lives for him. The ward leader was smart enough to be grooming him for more important things. Everyone loved Sean, even when he became argumentative, because he'd end the most heated debate with a joke that made its mark, even when he was being quixotic and idealistic. He believed fervently that good would triumph over evil with a little push.

He worked long hours at the Fulton Fish Market with nary a complaint, never missing school, and never letting his Italian students down. Nora often wondered how he managed all those things *and* homework, for high grades were essential, but his boundless energy never seemed to wane. People sensed this energy when he entered a room and they responded to it.

*   *   *

One Sunday, Nora invited Rachel to dinner. Rachel looked lovely in a pale green suit with big balloon sleeves, a pinched waist and wide lapels of a darker green. The same dark green of the lapels circled the bottom of the skirt in a braid. A big soft pink bow at the neck completed the picture. Her green, high-buttoned boots peeked daintily out from the skirt. Nora thought she looked striking. Her lush brown hair was swept up in the Gibson girl look.

"Rachel, you look positively beautiful. Come meet everyone."

Nora thought of the differences in their apartments, but wasn't embarrassed, for she knew that Rachel was basically an unpretentious girl who judged people for what they were, not what they had.

When Nora introduced her to Sean, Rachel's smoky eyes flashed. He was charming and witty, attentive and interested. She glowed as he told her his amusing stories and performed his superb impersonations.

"You are an incredible mimic, Sean," Rachel proclaimed. "You could be on the stage. I have seen many impersonators and none come close to being as talented as you. Do your John L. Sullivan again, please. It's wonderful."

He was flattered and pleased. He genuinely liked Rachel, finding her bright and interesting with a shy, sophisticated wit. "Nora, your friend is absolutely delightful," he said. "And so lovely, with eyes like the dark lady of the sonnets." As he helped her into her coat, he added, " 'A lovely lady, garmented in light, which frames her own beauty.' "

Rachel blushed and graciously acknowledged his compliment.

Rachel and Sean became fast friends, and they and Nora would take Sunday outings to Coney Island or Central Park or Riverside Drive to watch all the young swells riding their horses and parading their finery.

Though Rachel longed for more than friendship, she gave no outward indication to Sean, fearful of rejection. They had long talks and, while he respected her ideas and opinions, he never looked at her in any other light than friendship. She loved his high jinks and his spirit, but kept her thoughts to herself. She was just happy being with him.

The *Irish World* was the newspaper that furthered the Irish Nationalist cause in America. Its successful and gifted editor, Patrick Ford, was responsible for raising huge sums of money for the "revolutionary chieftains" of Ireland, as he called them, and for rallying the Irish in America behind this cause. He seemed to recognize that the cause was the glue that held the Irish in America together, and he also knew that the movement in Ireland was extremely dependent on the funds raised in America, so his paper was an important part of the Irish fight.

Sean couldn't believe his luck. He had been hired. It was a lowly job and he'd have to advance on his merit and talent. He wrote Terence immediately, proud that he could feel he was still part of a struggle that had been inborn in both of them. When Terence wrote back, it was a glowing letter, part of which read:

> Leave it to our poet to find the right spot. You couldn't be with a better paper or a better man. Sure, and he's the one who wrote that 'America is Ireland's base of operations.' He wrote that back in '74, lad, but it may be even truer now. I'll write often so you have the latest facts at your fingertips, perhaps that will help you get what you call a scoop. Just keep writing. They'll have to notice you someday.

Sean needed the encouragement, for he had taken a

slight cut in salary, but he, like Nora, did what he had to do. He worked hard, longer hours than they asked, and kept trying to get someone to read his articles. No one paid him any mind, of course, dismissing him as a callow youth.

On one of their outings, Sean told Nora and Rachel how discouraged he was becoming. "I've been writing some really good pieces about the fight for home rule in Ireland. I know they're good, damnit, straight from the source too, but they keep being handed back, unread, I'm sure. Jaysus," he said, slipping into his Irish brogue, "it's dreadful out entirely."

Nora laughed.

Rachel looked puzzled. "What does that mean, Sean?"

"It means it's damned awful, Rachel." He started to laugh, realizing what he had said. "It's just not the same in English somehow, which just goes to show you there's something Irish worth saving besides tradition."

"Sean," Rachel asked, "to whom do you give your articles?"

"Well, there's this crusty editor, Frank Brady, who's hard to get to. He's a tough customer. He puts the reporters through their paces, and he demands nothing less than perfection." Sean shrugged, looking discouraged again.

"Do you actually hand the articles to him?" Rachel persisted.

"Well no, not exactly, I give them to his battle-axe of a secretary, Lulie O'Hara. She's even crustier than he is, and he's her domain."

"I think, Sean, that you need to think about handing something, something very good, directly to him, not to old Lulie O'Hara," Rachel advised.

"Rachel, you're a wonder. Why didn't I ever think of that? But, of course, it's easier said than done now, isn't it?"

"Yes, it is, but I'm sure you'll find a way."

He liked her assurance, and merely nodded assent, his mind already focusing on a possible plan.

Some months later, as Sean was delivering copy, he heard one of the editors, Pat Connelly, screaming for a reporter. Sean looked around and saw that no one was there. He dropped the copy and asked Pat if he could help.

Pat was totally exasperated. "I need someone immediately to cover a fire in the Bowery."

"I'm your man," Sean assured him confidently. "I can leave now. And Pat, you've no choice but to send me, for there's no one else here."

Pat frowned and looked at him. "Okay kid, get to 10 East Sixth Street as fast as you can. I'll get someone to take care of your copy. Get the hell out, fast, before it's all over."

Sean covered the fire. Several families were out on the street, but no one had been killed. It looked routine, so the other reporters left. Sean saw the chief talking to various people, and he became curious. He stood near them, and heard the word arson. He listened as discreetly as he could but could hear nothing else.

"Chief," he said, bluffing it out, "this fire has the earmarks of being intentionally set. Is there anything to that?"

The chief told him that it had been the third one in this area in the last few weeks and that they all looked suspicious. He admitted they were puzzled, and that the police were investigating.

When Sean returned to the paper, he told Connelly the whole story. "Maybe, Pat, you'll want to print that, since the other papers won't have it. But maybe you'll want to send someone to police headquarters first and see what's going on. It could be something hot."

Pat missed the pun, but the new young woman recently hired as a copy editor didn't. "Oh," she moaned. "That's awful."

"Nobody appreciates my wit," Sean said with a mock pout.

"O'Sullivan!" Pat screamed, demanding Sean's attention, "you may be onto something. Get on it. I'll ask Brady if you can cub. But move on it fast."

Sean had gone down to headquarters several times with some of the other reporters, so it wasn't a completely alien territory. He began inquiring, and concluded that they didn't really know all that much. He began checking the facts to see if he could come up with something. Despite the fact that all three blazes had started identically and appeared to have been set, they had nothing else in common, or so it seemed. He found the names of various people who had lived in the three tenements and interviewed them, still digging for a lead. Finally, as he began to piece things together, one fact claimed his attention. Several of the residents described a man who collected the rents, and the descriptions, from people in different tenements, were amazingly alike. It sounded like the same man, but when Sean checked, he found that the buildings were owned by three different parties.

"Pat," he reported, "something is really strange here. Why would the same man be collecting rents for three different owners?"

"I don't know, kid," Pat replied brusquely. "Why don't you find out? Get Johnny O'Brien to help you. He has sources everywhere."

Johnny took Sean from the buildings and housing department to various unsavory bars, and then back to the department. Sean was fascinated by his methods and the strange assortment of people he knew. Gradually the pieces began to fall into place.

Sean rushed into Connelly's office.

"Pat, they're owned by the same man, and he's collected insurance on all of them. He's a slum landlord, name's Telmack, who must have needed some quick cash. He's smart. Made it look like there were three different owners."

"Good work, kid. Call headquarters with your information, and then write your story," he ordered, with a trace of a smile. "We'll make tomorrow's morning edition, and you'll have a good story going for some time. The old man is impressed. If the story is half as good as your footwork, he'll probably put you on as a permanent cub reporter, so go to it, lad." Connelly slapped him on the back.

Sean had finally made a breakthrough. The story turned out to be a significant one, leading to an indictment of the landlord. Connelly told him that Brady had given him the new assignment. It wasn't the high-level political reporting he wanted to do, but he boasted to the family at dinner, "It's better than running copy." Nora hugged him, proud of him. Uncle Jim bragged to everyone in the pub.

When he introduced Sean, he beamed. "Meet me nephew, Sean O'Sullivan, reporter with the *Irish World*. Have you been reading of the Telmack arson case? Well, 'tis his story now, and that it is."

Sean got slapped on the back often, and toasted. He told Nora, "If I were an imbiber, lass, I'd be with drink taken, as Ma used to say about Terence."

They laughed at what they now considered quaint old country expressions, and both of them were working hard at taking them out of their speech, because they wanted to be accepted as Americans. Rachel was helping them, although now she said jokingly, as she often did, " 'tis a shame now, faith, and it is." And they laughed at her perfect mimicry.

"Even your accent couldn't be improved," Sean told her.

"Well, I've learned that from you, lad. It isn't dreadful out entirely then?" Rachel asked, smiling.

"No, lass, 'tis fine and grand and beautiful," Sean replied.

Rachel thought, if only he'd say that about me.

One afternoon Connelly called Sean in.

"I need someone to interview some hotsy-totsy actress. Name's Fiona McQueen. We've been trying to get an interview for months, and wouldn't you know, just when her manager calls and sets it up for tomorrow, Franny's on another theatrical assignment in New Haven. It's all yours, kid."

"Do I need to be wearing roses on my hat?" Sean quipped sarcastically, thinking it was a woman's assignment.

"Never mind, wise guy, just do it. Here are two tickets to see her show tonight. That's so you'll know what to talk to her about." Connelly too could be sarcastic.

Sean was waiting outside Bloomingdale's for Nora when Rachel came out and told him that the dress buyer had offered to stay and help Nora with her portfolio.

"She's been trying to pin him down for some time, Sean, I think she'll be quite late," Rachel informed him.

"Well, Miss Friedman, then you are going with me to see Miss Fiona McQueen in *The Almighty Dollar*. Are you free?" He made a mock bow.

"Well now, Mr. O'Sullivan. I don't know. I did have plans for dinner at Delmonico's and an invitation to the opera." They both broke into laughter. "What is all this about?" She knew he couldn't afford theater tickets.

He explained, and offered to pick her up later at the Dakota.

"Oh Sean, we don't have time for me to change. Just come home with me so I can tell my parents."

They rushed to her apartment and she made hurried introductions. Sean was as impressed with Rachel's parents and home as Nora had been, but his reception was not as warm and friendly as hers had been. Mrs. Friedman was gracious as always, but he sensed Mr. Friedman's coolness, and he employed all his charm, but to no avail. Rachel didn't really notice as she was pouring sherry, but Mr. Friedman had correctly surmised that Rachel had more than a friendly interest in Sean, and it was, in his mind, an impossible choice. Sean didn't understand that Mr. Friedman had two things against him. He was not Jewish, and he was a newspaper reporter. But since Sean was not interested in Rachel in any romantic way, he was baffled by Mr. Friedman's curtness.

Sean said nothing to Rachel, and he forgot all about it soon enough in the bustle and excitement of the theater. He was happy to be with Rachel, for she was much more worldly than he, and she knew what to do. Sean didn't admit to her that he had never been to the theater before, but she knew, and she tried to lead the way without being obvious.

He was absolutely awestruck when the curtain went up, revealing an incredible drawing room set. The audience applauded, and he followed what Rachel did, not quite knowing why they were applauding since nothing had happened as yet. Except for Rachel's home, he had never seen anything so beautiful.

He watched with interest as a door opened, and the most exquisite creature he had ever seen walked on stage. The audience went wild before she spoke a word. She swept to the center of the stage, saying in a deep, throaty, sensuous voice, "Why is that bumpkin of a maid never here when I need her? I know she disappears to annoy me.''

Her emerald-green, low-cut satin gown swished imperiously about her. The audience tittered. Sean stared at this vision as if she were from another world. The gown revealed a perfect figure, her marvelous bosom white and inviting, her luxuriant, brilliant red hair piled high on her head as in pictures he had seen by Charles Dana Gibson. Even from where he was sitting, he could see her green eyes flashing as she smiled her wicked smile.

My God, he thought, how will I ever interview such a creature. For the first time in his life, he felt inadequate to the task.

Rachel observed him with amusement.

''Rachel, it was fabulous. I've never seen anything like it. What did you think of the play?'' What he was really asking was, ''What did you think of Fiona McQueen?'' And somehow she knew this.

The next morning, he did his homework. He found out everything about the beautiful actress, and his mind spun at the stories about her. She was the toast of many of the wealthy young men about town, and the older ones as well. She walked her bejeweled pet cheetah along Fifth Avenue. She had fabulous jewels and a suite at the Waldorf-Astoria. She had been named in a scandalous divorce trial.

He approached her dressing room with trepidation, but the moment he entered, the nervousness faded, the O'Sullivan charm asserted itself, and his own handsome looks made a good first impression.

She peered out from behind the screen and, liking what she saw, smiled at him and pointed toward the chair in front of her dressing table.

''Darling, hand me my robe,'' she drawled.

He leapt up eagerly, sweeping up the robe and almost overturning the chair.

"I was expecting one of those reporters with a hat cocked back on his head and a cigar in his mouth. You're a pleasant change of pace."

"Why, I might say the same of you, Miss McQueen, but it would have been a surprise for you if our usual theatrical reporter had showed up with a cigar, for her name is Franny Murphy."

"I smoke cigars, Mr. O'Sullivan, when the mood strikes me." She grinned suggestively.

"With or without your hat on, Miss McQueen?"

"Sometimes with nothing but my hat on, Mr. O'Sullivan."

The interview continued for several hours, and the repartee was witty and open. Sean didn't know how he managed it, but his natural sense of the ridiculous, wedded to what he had been learning as a cub reporter, produced a dynamic combination.

"Mr. O'Sullivan," Fiona said, leaning toward him, "dine with me Monday, after the show. I find you to be most refreshing, and witty to boot. So few men are witty these days, darling, it's a rare gift."

Sean left exhausted, his mind reeling. Good God, how will I ever pay for dinner? he wondered. But he didn't consider for a moment declining the invitation. He was barely able to get through the next day, for he was trembling with anticipation. The article on Fiona McQueen sparkled. After all, it was a labor of love. He had even quoted Byron to describe her. "She walks in beauty like the night."

Connelly congratulated him on it, balancing the compliment with a good deal of sarcasm. "And I thought you were only interested in the hard stuff. You've a talent for this, even Miss McQueen should be pleased. The poetry will slay her. We're running it in Sunday's weekly magazine."

What timing, Sean thought, smiling. He was counting on her loving it.

His mind was somewhere else all day Monday. He couldn't concentrate on the story he was doing on a local school problem. He could only think of Fiona and that evening.

He watched the end of the play from backstage, his heart pounding. After she took her final bow, and two dozen long-stemmed yellow roses were put in her arms, she swept regally offstage.

I can't believe it, he thought. She's more beautiful than I remember, more beautiful than any woman I've ever seen.

"Darling, how lovely to see you. I'm delighted you could come. Come in, come in." He and a half dozen others entered the tiny dressing room. His heart sank. Had all these people been invited for a midnight supper? She introduced him as she disappeared behind the screen.

"This is the sweet young man who wrote that delightful interview in the *Irish World*. Sean, meet all my hangers-on."

Ooh, nasty, he thought. Three of them, he deduced, were what he had heard called stage-door Johnnies. They brought flowers, champagne and paid court to the obvious queen of Broadway.

"Thank you for everything, dears. Now, let us be. Mr. O'Sullivan is doing a two, or maybe three-part interview, and we need to be alone. Don't we, Mr. O'Sullivan?"

"That's the only way I do interviews, Miss McQueen. There are too many conflicting opinions otherwise. When I do your biography, then I'll talk to these gentlemen." He was needling her subtly, yet playing the game.

Fiona peeked around the side of the gold lacquered oriental screen, obviously intrigued by the thought of a biography. She wondered why she hadn't thought of that, or why Dan hadn't. "Yes, why yes, a biography, what a perfectly marvelous idea."

At that moment, Dan, a harried-looking man in a black tie walked in. He was short, bald and most unprepossessing. "All right, fellows, good night, good night," he said, ushering the Johnnies out of the room. When they were gone, he said, "Sorry I'm late, Fiona, another charity ball with Muriel. Young man, Miss McQueen needs to rest now." He motioned for Sean to leave.

"No, Dan, no, this is the young journalist who did the story you liked so well." Finally she came out from behind the screen. "Mr. O'Sullivan, meet Dan Welch, my manager. He manages my affairs. Well," she chuckled, "not all my affairs, lad, just the business ones."

Sean was somewhat taken aback, and he could feel his face redden. Damnit, he thought, she'll think I'm some country jake, still a greenhorn. So he quickly turned to Dan, acknowledging the introduction. "Didn't you manage the careers of the Lolly Sisters and the Flying Redenzas?" he asked, naming two big acts of recent years. Sean had indeed done his homework on Fiona McQueen.

Dan was flattered. No one ever acknowledged him, much less knew who he was. "I did. They were wonderful acts. Marvelous people, too. The Redenzas were a little high-strung, but who wouldn't be, flying around on those trapezes without nets under them."

"High-strung indeed," Sean said, laughing at Dan's unintentional pun.

As Dan started reminiscing, Fiona interrupted him. "Now darling, Mr. O'Sullivan hasn't come to hear about the Lollipop Sisters or the Flying Redenzas," she pouted, shifting her sharp gaze from Dan to Sean and breaking into a knowing smile. "Have you, Mr. O'Sullivan?"

He ignored her question and turned instead to Dan.

He liked the little man, and besides, he instinctively knew not to allow Fiona to dominate him completely. "Mr. Welch, I imagine you have some really wonderful stories to tell. I'd like to ask the paper if I might do a story on you. May I?" Sean's interest in doing a story was sincere.

"Yes, why yes. I'd like that." He was flustered, but pleased. "Well then, if you no longer need me, Fiona, it's back to the ball. It's come to that, young man. Charity balls instead of the courts of Europe."

Fiona didn't like being neglected, not even for a second, so she reasserted herself. "Go now, dear, enjoy your ball. Give Muriel a kiss." She smirked, knowing that he and Muriel barely spoke anymore. "We've a lovely supper coming in from Delmonico's."

The most beautiful table was wheeled in, complete with fresh spring flowers, candles and steaming, silver-covered platters. Another waiter brought in champagne in the largest bottle Sean had ever seen.

Fiona watched Sean's face with unconcealed amusement.

"It's called a jeroboam, darling lad. It's the largest bottle champagne comes in. I thought we'd need that to toast your wonderful interview, and"—she paused to take a sip, looking provocatively over the rim of her glass—"our wonderful new friendship."

"Jeroboam," he mused, quoting the Bible. "Miss McQueen, Jeroboam was a 'mighty man of valor' who 'made Israel to sin.' "

She looked seductively at him and said, "Why, darling Sean, how marvelously appropriate. Take a sip. We have our work cut out for us. But lad, no more Miss McQueen. It's Fiona." Her voice was a throaty whisper. "Fiona," she repeated as she chucked him playfully under the chin.

Sean had his first taste of expensive champagne, oysters, terrapin, duck and a Grand Marnier soufflé. He tried to sip the champagne slowly because a glass or two of stout was all he ever drank. Despite his precautions, he quickly became quite drunk. They bantered and laughed, his outrageous humor totally delighting this earthy beauty of the Broadway stage.

She applauded his impersonations. "Oh lad, you've missed your calling. You'd be a divine actor. Recite another funny Irish poem for me."

"This one is a warning against sin, Fiona." He stood, leaning tipsily against the door.

"Children and wife and honour and fame,
True love and goodness and grace,
He sold them all for a life of shame,
For a vulgar, venal face.
His name must pass and his memory slip,
From the scenes where it shone so high,
It was all for the little curve of a lip,
And the glance of a cunning eye."

He bowed, swooping the napkin in front of him in a regal gesture. "You've a cunning eye, Fiona, do you know that?" He giddily poured himself another glass of champagne. "This stuff is from heaven for sure."

Fiona's loose-fitting pale green satin peignoir made her exquisite white skin more luminous than ever. Her laughing green eyes, so tantalizing, seemed to look right through him. As she tossed her head back, laughing at the poem, one of her emerald earrings fell to the floor. They both got down on their knees, still laughing, to search for it.

"Don't worry darling, there are more where that came from." She laughed her throaty laugh. Her peignoir hung away from her body as she crawled along the floor,

groping about, and as he glimpsed at her full, provocative
breasts and her dazzling white skin, his head spun. He
pulled her to him and kissed her hard and passionately on
her half-parted lips. They tumbled to the floor in a fiery
embrace.

At that moment, there was a knock on the door.

"Who the hell is it?" she cried.

"Miss McQueen, I'm sorry to bother you, but the
theater's closing. Officer Lacy wants to know why we
haven't already closed." It was old Ed, the stage-door
guard. He was always nervous about bothering her, for she
had a gargantuan temper, but the producer had ordered him
to get everyone out by one a.m.

They looked at each other helplessly, and then started
laughing again, for they were both very drunk. She put her
fingers on his lips to quiet him.

"Shush, never mind, lad. Saturday night at the
Waldorf. Suite 1008. We'll have two jeroboams, and who
knows what else."

Her suggestive chuckle sent shivers through him.

He lurched out into the night, but Ed ran after him.

"Get into the carriage," he instructed. "Miss McQueen
will see to it you get home. We're not wanting you
arrested, now."

Sean obeyed, and old Ed shook his head as the carriage drove away. "There goes another one," he murmured. "Wonder how long he'll last."

The week was an agony of longing. Connelly barked
at him more than once.

"What's wrong with you, kid? You're dreaming half
the time. Brady wants your story on the St. Patrick's Day
Parade by noon."

"Fires, and parades, and luncheons and interviews,

that's all I get," Sean grumbled. "I can do more than that, Pat. Give me a chance to do more."

"You'll get a chance one of these days. Just do as you're told and learn your goddamned trade. For starters, get your copy in on time." Connelly was exasperated.

As he walked into his office, he grumbled, "I'm a goddamned nursemaid to these prima donnas."

Sean couldn't eat or sleep. He paced in the kitchen every night, and to take his mind off Fiona, he wrote article after article on the Irish Nationalist cause the paper espoused.

They're good, damned good, he thought. Why won't Brady read any? Then he realized that he had never again tried to get one to him. Terence had sent some news that gave new insights to the Land League problems, and he had written about them with a new slant.

"What good does it do, old Lulie won't give it to him." And he paced some more, for his mind kept returning to the wonder of Fiona.

Nora came out sleepy and curious. "Sean, I've heard you out here every night. What is wrong with you? Can I help?"

"No, I'm just trying to write about Ireland, not about every damned parade, or fire, or horse race. Jaysus I'm sick of the petty stuff," he grumbled. He didn't sound like the old Sean. No jokes, no teasing.

"Oh Sean, don't be so impatient. You can't start out at the top. No one does. The other things you're writing are good. I thought the article on Fiona McQueen was excellent. It was an exceptional interview. It gave a good feel for what she's like, bizarre but interesting." She laughed.

"She did like it," he answered distractedly.

"Why, how do you know?" Nora asked.

He hadn't meant to let on that he had seen her again.

"Ah, well she sent a note, asked me over to meet her manager. I may do an interview with him. Connelly thinks it's a good idea and has suggested some other personalities."

"That's exciting, Sean. Why didn't you tell us? Doing interviews could be fascinating. You could get to meet all kinds of famous people." Nora paused. "Did you like Fiona McQueen?"

"Well she's beautiful and actually quite funny. Has a kind of low charm. She browbeats and manipulates, but she's gorgeous."

Nora became curious. "Who does she browbeat?"

"Oh, her manager, and the stage-door Johnnies, and I imagine anyone who will let her."

Nora looked at him strangely. "That didn't really come out in the interview."

"Yes, well, I don't know that for a fact. It's just an impression. So I couldn't say it." Sean felt trapped. "Darling sister, I'm exhausted. I must go to bed. You go to bed too. You need to run that damned department store, and I need to run the *Irish World*, so we'd better get some sleep."

Nora knew now why he wasn't sleeping. Sean was smitten badly. It may not have been the first time, she thought, but I bet it's the first time he's ever lost any sleep over it. My little brother thinks he's in love.

It was the first time he had walked into the Waldorf on these terms. This hotel, haven and showplace of the Four Hundred, of the wealthy climbers and the pretenders, of the famous and infamous, was off limits for a poor, struggling reporter. Money was a god here. He thought of how he, Rachel and Nora had walked down Peacock Alley acting as if they belonged, and tonight, even if only for tonight, he felt he did belong. The other times had been for a lark. He had known he was an outsider, and it hadn't mattered. But tonight it mattered, for he was seeing things with different eyes.

His Peacock Alley walks and Nora's keen eye had helped him see what was fashionable in that other world, and he had turned himself out well, if not grandly. He had made no obtrusive or embarrassing mistakes. Nora had asked him about getting some decent clothes, and he had allowed her to take him shopping at Bloomingdale's. Her discount had made a slightly better purchase possible. When he had asked her to meet him to help choose a suit, she knew for sure what she had guessed the other night. She didn't like it, but she thought it was really none of her business.

As he entered through the glittering Thirty-fourth Street carriage entrance, he watched the incredible array of people coming and going in elegant carriages. All were splendidly dressed. The Saturday night crowds were grander than any he had seen. He suddenly felt like the greenhorn he wanted so desperately not to be. But the glances his way were made by sleek and well-tended women who appreciated a handsome man when they saw one. He sauntered through the Alley, being eagerly early, peering casually into one room after another. The dining room, with its Italian Renaissance carved pilasters and columns of midnight-sun marble imported from Russia, dazzled his eyes. He walked through an archway to a smaller court of palms. He sat in this grey terra cotta haven for a quiet moment. It was all quite spectacular. He entered the much talked about four-sided mahogany men's bar and ordered a stout.

As he stood drinking and enjoying the sights and sounds, acting as if he stopped by every evening for a nightcap, a rather drunk young man, a dandy if he had ever seen one, turned to him and said, "I'm stood up again. It's three times. Do you think she's trying to tell me something?'' His voice was sarcastic.

''I think that is a deduction you could safely make,'' Sean answered, smiling, now feeling a little calmer and more self-assured, for the young swell had addressed him as an equal.

''Yes, I thought so. Well never mind, old friend, have a drink on me.''

''Thanks, I will. I'm Sean O'Sullivan, and you are—?'' Sean extended his hand.

''I'm a very drunken, very miserable, heartsick Alfred Douglas Von Ende. Pleased to meet you, Mr. O'Sullivan. I'm one who doesn't mind the Irish. They've got wit, I'll say that for them. Have you been stood up too?'' He peered curiously into Sean's face.

''No, at least not yet, Mr. Von Ende.'' He did not take offense to Alfred's comment about the Irish, for he was used to such remarks, knowing the Irish were still considered second-class citizens.

''You know, O'Donovan—'' Alfred began.

''O'Sullivan, O'Sullivan,'' Sean corrected him.

''That's what I said.'' Alfred blathered on. ''The Royal Suite is all done up in tiger skins. I've seen it—well, just the entry, but it's swell.''

Sean nervously asked what time it was, his heart pounding with excitement and anticipation. He excused himself and walked back to the lobby. As he glanced about at this delirium of wealth, he ached to belong, and he ached to belong in style. He finally saw Fiona swoop in with her retinue. He unobtrusively remained behind a column and waited until she waved the last man off and entered the elevator. His hands were trembling as he knocked at the door to Suite 1008. He took a deep breath. Fiona's maid, Mattie, opened the door and showed him into a room. Its opulence made him gasp. Renaissance tapestries

from French chateaux hung on the wall and Pompadour
silk draperies from Paris graced the windows. Delicate
Louis XVI settees and chairs plumped with lush down
cushions looked too beautiful to sit on. He sank into deep,
soft carpeting. Sparkling chandeliers and sconces bathed
the room in a warm glow. Duck and champagne Monday
night, Saturday night the world. He smiled to himself.

Fiona entered. Her lustrous red hair was pinned loosely
back. Her peignoir, a wonderful peach silk moiré with
matching feathers, framed her glorious face. The arch of
her eyebrows gave her a perennially inquisitive look. Sean
took her hand and kissed it gallantly.

He knew something extravagant was called for. He
could afford no flowers, no gifts.

"You are a vision, Fiona,
a vision who 'walks in beauty like the night,
of cloudless climes and starry skies:
And all that's best of dark and bright
meet in your aspect and your eyes,
thus mellowed to that tender light
which heaven to gaudy day denies.' "

She smiled with delight, the coarseness gone from her
voice for a few soft moments. "I wondered how the rest
went. I love it. I want you to repeat it over and over. No
one I know describes me in poetry. It's a part of my
schooling that's been neglected. Sad, isn't it? But, you've
been sent to teach me, haven't you, darling lad? I know
you have."

Another wonderful supper arrived with a jeroboam of
champagne. They dined and sipped the wine, chatted and
laughed. Her throaty laugh intoxicated him as much as the
champagne.

He wanted to hold her in his arms, kiss her as he had

the other night. As if reading his thoughts, she whispered, "Darling lad, we have unfinished business, don't we?" She took him by the hand. "Come with me." He had never been seduced before, and he followed her, as if in a trance.

They stepped into her bedroom, all soft green silks and satins, Cupids and scented candles. He couldn't believe any of what he saw, but he watched as she unclasped her warm jewels and handed them to him. She loosened her fragrant silk peignoir slowly, and it rustled as it fell to the floor. As she pulled the combs out, her flaming hair tumbled about her lovely shoulders. She stood before him, her white skin shimmering in the flickering candlelight, her voluptuous breasts and the curve of her stomach a promise of heaven here and now. He pulled her urgently into his arms and covered her with kisses. As he shed his clothes, she gazed at his lean, taut body, graceful but strong. He fell onto the canopied bed, and his lips coursed over her body, lingering slowly, sensually on her breasts.

She moaned as he stroked her soft flesh. "Take me, lad, take me, for God's sake."

Her lips searched for his in a frenzy of passion. They knew all the fire and beauty of youth, and in their union they trembled and thundered. They made love all night, slept a little, awoke Sunday and made love again. They drank more champagne, frolicked, ate and found themselves locked in passionate union again. He forgot his date with Rachel and Nora. He forgot his Irish cause. He forgot the rest of the world. Sean O'Sullivan was in love.

Chapter 19

It had already been two years since Nora had seen Billy on that lonely day in Grand Central Station. Nora had finally visited Billy in Chicago. Molly and Tim had kept asking her to come, but Nora made excuses, telling them that her money was low and she couldn't take time off from Bloomingdale's.

Actually, she was afraid to see the child because she might do something foolish. Nora was tormented by the guilt of not raising the child herself. Molly and Tim made her feel welcome. And they were wonderful parents to Billy. Billy was such a handsome, happy child that Nora found a new peace of mind with her decision. The visit was delightful.

Billy had the tousled blond hair and pale green eyes of William. He had her classic cheekbones. And Molly insisted that Billy had Nora's personality.

As she stared out the window of the train on her way back to New York, she thought how she would look forward to seeing Billy again now that she had made the trip once.

*   *   *

Nora's portfolio was completed and ready to show. She had worked on it every spare moment she had. She thumbed through the pages of the portfolio with satisfaction. She had assembled the finest laces from the black trunk her mother had packed. As she reviewed them, her thoughts drifted to home.

Mary's letters came regularly. Danny was doing well at Maynooth and he was as happy as he had ever been. Some of the tension between Danny and Mary seemed to have diminished with time. Bridget and Kevin were living in Cork, and Mary didn't feel that Kevin liked it all that well. He missed the horses and his uncomplicated life, but Bridget loved it. She had had a miscarriage, so there were still no grandchildren. Terence and Seamus were still working for the Brotherhood, but, while Seamus continued to pursue his law studies, Mary wrote that Terence was pursuing danger. Nora heard from Seamus now and then. When they were on some assignment, she wouldn't hear anything for months. Then a letter would come. They were lively, warm letters, full of love and poetry, but it all seemed so distant to her. He was there, and Nora was here, and who knew what the future held.

Nora had gone out with some young men, but there had never been anything serious. Her heart was dead, she felt. She gave all her love to her family and friends, and believed that she had a grand design to her life that would take all her energy to make happen.

Aunt Nellie and Uncle Jim tactfully tried to introduce her to young men, and to please them, she would go out with the men or invite them to Sunday dinner. But nothing ever came of the well-intentioned matchmaking attempts.

She had decided that Jacques Mandel's was the shop to which she wanted to go. He was her favorite designer.

He seemed to be the only one who didn't go in for
excesses. She had so few dresses, but as she was getting
ready for her interview with him, she tried on each one at
least twice. No dress she owned seemed right to impress
the man she thought was a genius. She hoped he would
look at her designs, instead of what she had on. She settled
on the lavender wool suit she had bought from Mr.
O'Houlihan. Its simplicity had helped keep it from being
too outdated.

As they approached Mandel's the next day during the
lunch hour, Rachel was being very encouraging, for Nora
had lost her nerve.

"I can't do it, Rachel. He'll think I'm a fool, bringing
designs to him," she said as they stood outside his shop.

Rachel put her hands on Nora's shoulders. "I can't
believe what I'm hearing! Can this be the same girl who
Mr. Bloomingdale calls his merchant princess? You weren't
afraid to tell him your suggestions, and he took them too.
So, in you go. I won't hear another word from you." She
pushed Nora toward the door of polished brass and etched
glass.

Once inside, the activity astounded Nora. Jacques
Mandel himself, a small, dark man in a morning coat, was
unfurling bolts of fabric with a flourish. Encouraged by the
oohs and aahs of a stately dowager and a younger replica
of her, he continued his performance until the floor was a
sea of brightly colored satins and silks. Nora stood fascinated. A lovely young girl, dressed in a simple grey dress
and white apron, came down the stairs with a completed
garment, and Monsieur Mandel took the garment from the
girl and presented it to the older woman. It was an evening
gown of yellow satin, the bodice of lace, the full, sweeping skirt with bias bands of the same lace. The dress
shimmered like a canary diamond, a rather large canary
diamond, Nora thought, since it had to fit its ample owner.

Even from a distance she could tell that the workmanship of the lace and adornment were inferior to what she had in the satchel she was clutching.

Monsieur Mandel noticed Nora's presence. "What are you doing here?" She felt him looking disdainfully at her plain lavender suit. "Deliveries are made to the rear, so see that you take yourself there immediately."

Nora was so flustered that she backed out the door, right into Rachel, who stood waiting.

"Why are you out so soon? Didn't he like your things?"

"I didn't even get to show them to him. He thinks I'm a delivery girl and told me to go to the rear entrance."

"Then, that's what we'll do," Rachel replied, undaunted. "If you can't meet him in the front, you'll meet him in the back. Let's go!"

The rear of the shop was more frantic than Nora could have imagined. Fifteen young women were busily at work. Tables overflowed with satin, lace, pearls and feathers. Except for their chatter, the room was quiet. There was no sewing machine clatter here, for the work was all done by hand. Into the room burst Monsieur Mandel, the yellow gown in his hand and his face almost purple with rage. He flung the dress at one of the young women, screaming, "Denise, you do the worst lace applique in New York. No, in America. No, in the world! Do you think I would let Mrs. Ashleigh take this disgusting mess home with her? What good does it do for me to design a beautiful garment if I do not have a single competent seamstress to execute it?" He continued, "Not one of you does my work justice. I should fire the lot of you. And you, yes you." He was glaring at Nora. "What are you doing here, as if I don't have enough problems today? Every time I turn around I see you staring at me. What do you have in that suitcase, a bomb? I told you to get out! I don't want to buy anything today. Out of my sight!''

Everyone in the room was now staring at Nora, needles poised in midair, except the unfortunate Denise, who was still buried under the yards of yellow satin which had been thrown at her.

''Mr. Mandel, I don't want to sell you anything,'' Nora told him. ''I just want to show my work to the man I consider the most brilliant designer alive today!'' She knew she had to get his attention or fail altogether. Jacques turned to the staring faces. ''At last, someone appreciates me. Not one of you cares enough for me to do your best, but this stranger acknowledges me for what I am. My dear, forgive my rudeness, but you see what I have to put up with. Come, child, show what you have brought to Jacques Mandel.''

When Nora emerged a half-hour later, they were so late getting back to work that they had to run all the way to the ''el.'' Out of breath, Nora managed to tell Rachel that Mandel wanted to hire her as his assistant. He thought her laces were the finest he had seen, and he praised her lingerie sketches.

''Oh, Nora, it's your chance. You'll be working with the best. In time you'll be designing for him. It's wonderful, wonderful.''

''It's more than wonderful. It's a miracle. I'll work hard and learn everything I can. We'll use every bit he teaches us when we open our own shop, Rachel. This is just the first step toward our dream! He wants me to begin next Monday.''

Miss Fennell was pleased to see Nora. ''Sit down, Nora. I haven't seen you for a while, but I hear all the good things.''

Nora told her that she wanted to leave her job. While

she appreciated all the opportunities she had been given, they weren't in quite the direction she wanted to take. She emphasized that she liked working at Bloomingdale's, she respected Mr. Bloomingdale, and she had looked to Miss Fennell as her mentor.

Miss Fennell recognized how far this bright young Irish girl had come along in such a short time. She was pleased that Nora had lived up to her expectations. "You must, of course, take that position at Mandel's. While we have a fine store here, we don't cater to that type of clientele. Maybe someday, but not now. I see from your designs that you are creative and talented. We'll miss you, Nora. I have heard Jacques Mandel is a difficult employer, but I am sure you can handle him."

"Miss Fennell, you've been wonderful. Thank you for everything. You gave me my first chance, and I'll never forget that. Do you think Mr. Bloomingdale will understand? He's been so kind and supportive."

Helen Fennell smiled. "I think so, Nora." They shook hands and she added, "Although you'll be impossible to replace."

If Nora had only known that Mandel's assistants came and went like the seasons, she might not have left Bloomingdale's. Monsieur Mandel was impossible to work for. Not only did he have a terrible temper, but he was unreasonably demanding of his help. She had worked hard on the dress she was wearing. She had paid a lot for the London smoke cloth for her dress, but she envisioned this as her work uniform, and she wanted Monsieur Mandel's approval. Nora's excellent taste was evident in this simple, elegant design. The skirt was unadorned, the bodice buttoned to one side with jet buttons. She had fashioned a capelet effect over the leg-of-mutton sleeves, the material slashed in places and banded with Mary's lace. The lace was repeated at the neck. Otherwise, there was no decoration. Every head turned as she walked down the street. Her stunning beauty was accentuated by the simple, striking design of her dress.

The workroom was busy. Monsieur Mandel was inspecting each woman's work critically. Then he saw Nora.

"Ah, there you are. Punctual. Good, good. I like that. Follow me. We'll get a uniform for you."

Nora trailed behind him. She frequently stooped to pick up the pins he scattered behind him.

"First of all," Monsieur Mandel started to explain, "I only dress the best and my ladies demand, and indeed they deserve, perfection. I do not bother with ladies of lesser fortunes. My ladies will spend here a minimum of ten thousand dollars a year. If they were to spend only five thousand, I simply couldn't take them seriously as clients. I am concerned only with their gowns. I don't bother with hats or boots. I leave that to those with less imagination, and I have never considered lingerie for my ladies, but I find your things quite amusing, and, we shall see, maybe my ladies will as well. I insist on absolute courtesy at all times, to them and to me. Your opinion does not exist here. Only the client's and, of course, mine." He drew a grey dress from an alcove and thrust it at Nora. "Put this on, and we'll begin."

"Thank you, sir, but I prefer to wear my own dress. I hope you find it suitable."

"I do not care what you prefer, and I do not find it suitable. You will dress as all my assistants dress. Put this on! Now, look what your stubbornness has done. Here comes Mrs. Stelling, and you're not changed. Stay as you are. You'll put on the uniform when she's gone or look for other employment."

Mrs. Ava Pierce Stelling epitomized the fashionable figure of the day. She was big-busted with a generously curved front and back. She was swathed in yards of expensive fabric cinched at the waist, and trumpeting out from there was an extravagant lace bodice. On her head was an elaborate creation of ribbons, feathers and flowers.

"A vision, a perfect vision, Mrs. Stelling," Mandel gushed. "Take Madam's parasol, Nora."

As Mrs. Stelling handed over a parasol, which was also laden with lace, her glance lingered on Nora's dress. "Jacques, I like your new salon uniform," she commented. "It's most attractive. Really very, very nice. I must compliment you. I didn't know you did this sort of thing. But this is quite exceptional. I didn't know what I was going to do for the staff of the summer house, but I can see you've solved that problem for me. I absolutely insist that you do their uniforms just like this one."

"You're too kind, Mrs. Stelling, but really, don't you think this garment is too plain, too severe for your staff?" Jacques gave Nora a furious look. Nora struggled to suppress a smile.

"Nonsense! I think it's perfect. I must insist that you do this favor for me. After all, I have chosen you to do my Louise's wedding dress and all those dear bridesmaids'. Now you wouldn't want to disappoint me, would you?" A veiled threat lurked in her question.

"No, no, of course not. I will do your uniforms. Miss O'Sullivan, my new assistant, will be in charge. She will handle all the details, while I concentrate on the wedding gown for your beautiful daughter." All the while, he kept glaring at Nora, who had by then lost her restraint and was smiling graciously.

When Mrs. Stelling's list of her staff was brought around to the shop, Jacques thrust it in Nora's face. "Your highhandedness got me into this mess, now you get me out," he hissed.

Nora had heard the word summer house, so she had

pictured a simple scene. She knew nothing of Newport. The Vanderbilts, Astors and other members of New York's "Four Hundred," the name given to New York's high society, had unlimited amounts to spend on summer pastimes. Hostesses of the day thought nothing of spending twenty thousand dollars for a single party. There was no limit to overindulgence. One famous sportsman's horses slept on sheets embroidered with the family crest. Nora couldn't believe her eyes as she read the list, complete with their measurements: one private secretary, one tutor, one governess, two nurses, one housekeeper, five maids, one head coachman, two assistant coachmen, one chauffeur, one butler, one second butler, one head gardener, four helpers.

"Twenty-two uniforms! How will I ever do this?"

"I don't know, Nora, and I don't care how you do it. Just make sure you do it!" Monsieur Mandel ordered.

Even after she'd been there only a few days, the seamstresses loved Nora. She was kind to them, and besides, she stood up to Monsieur Mandel. She was worried about the assignment thrust on her, but Denise and the rest were determined that she wouldn't fail. They helped her find the wholesale outlets that sold the fabric, braid, machine-made lace and everything else that she needed. When Nora sketched the various uniforms, they compared the measurements of each servant and advised her how much fabric she would need. They gladly stayed extra hours to do the sewing and it became as much of a challenge to them as it was to her. Nora couldn't believe the extra time they were willing to give her. They already worked eighty hours a week for as little as six dollars.

"Don't you worry about that, Miss O'Sullivan," one worker told her. "We'll show that slave driver what you can do."

And they did. Monsieur Mandel had given Mrs. Stelling

a seemingly impossible deadline to complete the work, virtually guaranteeing Nora's failure, but she and the girls finished the uniforms by the promised day.

Mrs. Stelling was ecstatic with the uniforms. "Jacques, no one will have livery this smart. I can just see everyone's face now, green with envy."

Jacques Mandel was a tyrant who abused the people who worked for him. Nora had never heard him say a kind word to an employee, but when Mrs. Stelling had triumphantly departed, he turned and said with a forced spitefulness, "Well, Miss O'Sullivan, you seem to have put me in the uniform business. Why are the rest of you gawking? Don't we have the Stelling wedding in less than two months? Get back to work immediately."

Tyrant though he was, Nora was in awe of the beauty of his work. His exquisite attention to detail enthralled Nora. It had been said that his garments were so perfectly made that they could have been worn inside out. He also enjoyed the role of teacher to such an apt pupil, and shared his knowledge while encouraging her. Nora's taste was more refined than his, but his style was that of the day. Every time she turned in a design of elegant simplicity, he added the yards of trim, beads, pearls, and the profusion of lace his clients insisted on.

"My ladies want to show that they are very, very wealthy. You would have them without a single adornment. How can you design such provocative lingerie and prefer such severity in your dress?" Begrudgingly he added, "Perhaps that face of yours is all the adornment you need, and I grant you the things you do for yourself have some merit, but not for my ladies. Jacques Mandel is what they want, and Jacques Mandel is what they get!"

Nora could tolerate the frustration of her rejected designs because she was learning so much. She had even managed to endure his temper tantrums and verbal abuse, but the one thing she couldn't bear was his treatment of the seamstresses. When she had suggested that their working hours were cruelly long, he had told her to mind her own business. The girls appreciated her concern, but they reminded her that jobs were hard to find and they had families depending on their income. The situation seemed to be getting worse as the Stelling wedding approached. Monsieur Mandel had accepted the shop's first lingerie commission, and Nora was now deeply involved in the lavish lingerie trousseau, or as Sean referred to it, her "undercover" work.

Denise was working on the bride's dress, which was embroidered with thousands of tiny seed pearls. When she began to cough frequently, Nora realized she was burning with fever. Nora sent her home, promising to cover for her. When Monsieur Mandel returned from a house call to Mrs. Stelling to show her one of the seven elaborate bridesmaids' dresses, he was furious with Nora and sent her to bring Denise back. Nora left, but when she reached Denise's living quarters, she was crying tears of hurt and anger and she begged Denise to stay in bed.

"Nora, as you see, there are five of us in this one room, living on top of one another, and we can barely afford this. If I lose my job, I might not get another for weeks. Don't worry. I'll be all right. Don't cry. He's cruel, I know, but not much different from other bosses, I hear."

That night, they all worked until three in the morning. Nora dragged herself home. Sean wasn't in yet. She was now worried about him. He rarely came home lately and when he did, he was preoccupied. Nellie and Jim were worried too, but they remained silent. She knew Pa wouldn't have remained silent about it, but Sean was a man now, making his way in the world, and she was too weary and preoccupied herself to talk to him.

She slept as best she could until her alarm rang, and she dragged herself back to work at eight. This continued for four nights in a row. There seemed to be no way to avoid it, because the gowns had to be finished. Nora wondered why he didn't hire more seamstresses, even temporarily, but she realized that would have cost more money. Nora was frantic when Denise was sick again with fever and shaking with chills. She begged Monsieur Mandel to let Denise go home.

"Of course, she can go home to be sick. I can easily get another girl to take her place."

That night around midnight, Denise fainted, and Nora sent one of the other girls for a doctor, who arrived and announced that Denise was critically ill and had to be hospitalized. Nora went with her and guaranteed that she'd pay the bill. She was terribly exhausted when she returned to the shop, and she could hear Monsieur Mandel shouting before she opened the door. She couldn't believe her ears. He was cursing Denise and blaming her for the work being slowed down, and said that he was firing her and anyone else who caused trouble.

As she stepped inside, her control snapped, and she looked at him with cold fury in her eyes. "You are the cruelest man I've ever met, and I've met my share of monsters. Denise may be dying, and all you can think of is your damned money and that damned wedding," she sputtered, almost in tears. "She happens to be one of the finest seamstresses I've ever seen. So you're not only cruel, but also stupid. No one should work for you. Come on, girls. Let's go."

There was a terrible silence and they stared at her with stricken faces "Where can we go, Nora? Hush now, or we'll all lose our jobs."

"Anyone who wants to go, leave right now!" Mandel shouted. He felt that he had the upper hand. Then he looked at Nora. ''I think it is you who'd better leave, Miss O'Sullivan. You are obviously upsetting these girls who would like to get to work. You're a rebellious, ungrateful girl, and I insist you take your troublemaking ideas somewhere else.''

He was secretly sorry to lose Nora. The lingerie trousseau hadn't been completed, and he knew that she had a rare design talent. However, he feared that she might try to bring a union into his shop, so he decided to take the stand he did.

Outside, Nora lifted her chin, squared her shoulders and thought with a rueful smile how proud Terence would have been. She also thought, it's now time to open our own shop.

Chapter 20

Several months later, Nora and Rachel were in their own shop. Nora had paid Denise's hospital expenses and put her to work making the designs from Nora's sketches. What was Mandel's loss was Nora's gain. She and Rachel had decided to put Denise on salary so that they would have an inventory when they opened. Denise, for her part, was the happiest girl alive. They couldn't pay her much more than she had been making at Mandel's, but Denise was so grateful to Nora that she would have worked for nothing. She worked day and night, as did they, getting everything ready. Nora remembered how Mandel had treated his girls, and she vowed, no matter what, never to take away an employee's dignity, because most of the workers had precious little else.

The space they had rented was not at all large. They were very conscious of expenses. Rachel still lived free at home, but Nora insisted on paying Uncle Jim and Aunt Nellie room and board. They balked at this, knowing she needed every cent to get started.

One evening, at dinner, Nellie vowed, "I'll not be taking a cent from you until your shop is open and the books are in the black. Then, lass, I'll take your money, and as interest," she added shyly, "there is one thing I'd like from you. Remember the ice-blue satin gown and peignoir like the sketch you showed me for the Stelling girl's wedding, the one with the ruffles on top and bottom? Well, I'd like a set like that."

"Oh Aunt Nellie, of course. You shall have the most beautiful ensemble I've ever made." Dear Aunt Nellie, she thought, wanting such a luxurious item. She probably never even had a dress as beautiful as this lingerie would be. Uncle Jim never said a word, pretending to be reading his paper.

"It's probably the secret desire of every woman to own luxurious lingerie, Rachel," she commented the next day. "Maybe someday we can make beautiful things in a price range that someone like Aunt Nellie could afford."

"Your mind never stops working, does it, Nora? I admit, it is a good idea. But for the moment, let's worry about the expensive clothes that the rich ladies can afford." As Rachel looked around the tiny room, she laughed. "Well, Father says that from small beginnings come great events. Certainly, if that's the case, we are destined for greatness, Nora."

Nora smiled. She lifted the lid of her lace trunk. "Did you see all the wonderfully dressed ladies going into the other shops on the street? I really like this location. It's so near all the theaters and there's so much going on. I just know we'll have exciting customers."

"Well, you'll have to wait on them, Nora. I'm just the bookkeeper."

The shop had previously been occupied by a milliner, and although the carpet was a bit threadbare, the drapes on the one large paned window were of good quality. There were a few shelves and Nora began to unpack and arrange the laces. She had used some of the work to trim handkerchiefs and some chemises. She had Denise make some of the lovely peignoirs to show in the shop. Mary had recently sent an extraordinarily large piece and Nora had fashioned it into a bridal veil and was lovingly arranging it in the window.

"Look, Rachel. Come and see. Here come two men carrying trays, and I think they are coming here."

Rachel swung open the door and two waiters entered with trays laden with dishes and linen, lifting silver domes to reveal steaming plates. One of the waiters presented a long-stemmed rose to Rachel and Nora, and bowed. "Luncheon, ladies, compliments of Mr. Gambini."

"Who in the world would that be, now, and why is he sending us lunch?"

"Mr. Gambini owns the establishment across the street. He saw you moving in this morning, and he thought you might appreciate a little something warm."

"Why, how very nice. We do appreciate it, very much, but this is more than a little something. Nora, I've never seen such food. I think this is pheasant, and . . . oh! Strawberries in winter! I can't believe it."

"Mr. Gambini insists on the best always. He'll be happy that you're pleased, ladies."

"Pleased? Pleased? Why tell Mr. Gambini that we'll come over to thank him, in person," Rachel volunteered.

"That won't be necessary. Ladies are not allowed in the establishment without an escort. I'll give Mr. Gambini your thanks, if you wish."

"Oh, yes, of course, we do indeed thank him."

Nora was standing in the window, looking across the street into another window where a man stood observing her. When he caught her eye, he raised the glass in his hand as if to toast her and bowed low.

Nora turned to the waiters. "Please tell Mr. Gambini we are most grateful for this feast, and we hope to meet him soon."

They all had a sip of champagne, including Denise, who had never seen anything like this before. She started giggling. "Very first day and there's a mystery man, and some queer bird under glass. Don't know as if I'm up to tasting it." But she did, and they returned the trays with every morsel gone.

"I'm thinking he'll be guessing we liked it," Denise chuckled, "and maybe he'll get the hint we'd be liking some more."

They all laughed, and Ballygarry's was launched.

The man in the window, Angelo Gambini, had been watching their comings and goings for the past week. The beautiful Nora had caught his attention, and he wanted to meet her. He owned one of the most successful gambling houses and restaurants in New York. Many New Yorkers considered him a man of mystery and intrigue, and he did nothing to dispel those notions.

What very few people knew was that Angelo Gambini had spent time in prison as a felon. As a child of four, he had emigrated from Italy with his parents. His father's skills as a shoemaker had gone unappreciated in the new world and the family lived in abject poverty. Angelo's father couldn't seem to find work and his mother began to take in laundry. As their modest savings diminished, so did the size of their lodgings, until Angelo could only remember the one room they all shared, with the lines of drying laundry strung from the ceiling and draped and hung all over the fire escape. Angelo hated being poor and also hated his father, who was, in his childish mind, the cause of all this misery. Angelo couldn't bear his mother's desperation. He loved her passionately and would do anything to make her happy. He wanted to get things she needed for living.

So he began to steal. At first he stole a single piece of fruit, an apple, which he shined to brilliance on his tattered trousers to give to his mother. As he became more proficient, he was soon putting real food on their table. He was clever and fast, and soon this came to the attention of those who were in the business of stealing for a living. By the time he was fourteen, he was one of a stable of boys who stole and were paid for it.

By the time his father died, two years later, Angelo had long since abandoned his feeble attempts at schooling, but street smart he was. He was so obviously talented at what he did that he soon became a runner for the racketeers. Angelo didn't care what job they gave him to do as long as they paid him. His hatred of being poor was an obsession, and his one goal was to leave the ghetto. To his dismay, he couldn't seem to earn money fast enough to reverse his mother's decline. Even when he moved them to three rooms, just on the outer edge of the west side Italian ghetto, she didn't seem to have the energy to care. She was totally exhausted from hardship and misery. When her husband died from hopelessness, her will to live died with him. At the time, Angelo didn't understand this. In his mind, his father had been a total failure. Angelo only liked survivors. He was almost frenzied in his efforts to make his mother want to live. He took more dangerous jobs to earn bigger money, but she accepted his offerings from these earnings with dull apathy, hardly ever moving from her chair by the window. Angelo, for a time, thought she sat there watching for him to come home, but one day she told him that she was waiting for her husband, his papa, to come and take her with him.

For the first time in his life, he was angry with her. How could she reject him when he was doing everything to make her happy, to sit there watching and waiting for a loser in death? "You stupid woman," he said angrily, "how can you love him? I want you to love me, love me, do you hear?" Suddenly he realized he was shaking his mother as if she were a rag doll. As he gathered her to him, sobbing, saying he was sorry, she lifted her head up from his shoulder and gazed at him with a look of despair he would never forget. She died in his arms.

Angelo's grief was extraordinary. He fully believed that he was responsible for her death. If he had made more money and had been able to make a better life for her sooner, he reasoned, she'd still be alive.

More money, more risky jobs, more danger formed the pattern of his life until finally he was caught, tried and sent to prison. He was nineteen years old and was sentenced for twenty-five years. As his cell door clanged shut behind him, Angelo looked around him and thought, back to one room again, back to one goddamned room!

When he threw himself down on the narrow cot, something poked him in the back and he reached under and pulled out a book. Angelo had no respect for the written word, so he tossed it across the room and it lay untouched. All that night he could not sleep, so great was his loathing of being confined to a small space. He thought he could never sleep again. As dawn was breaking the next morning, the pages of the book, open to where it had been thrown, seemed to glow in the dark.

With first light, he got up and looked at the book. It was about Flemish painters, and Angelo's eyes caught a painting by Jan van Eyck. He thought it was beautiful.

Money had been his idol, but now he was suddenly consumed by his unquenchable love of beauty. The prison library was limited in its collection. He asked to see the warden for books on painting and painters. Angelo pleaded and promised to do anything the warden wanted in exchange for getting him books on art.

"What can you do, Gambini?" the warden asked.

"I'm a first-class Sicilian cook, Warden, taught by my mother, who, God rest her soul, said I must learn a trade."

The warden agreed to try him in the kitchen, and soon he was preparing the meals for the warden's own table. It seemed an eternity before the books arrived. Until then, Angelo spent endless hours with that one volume and learned everything about Flemish art the book offered.

His conduct in prison was exemplary. When he was not performing routine prison duties, or cooking the warden's meals, he spent his time feverishly devouring the beauties on the pages of these books. This passion for art saved and formed his life.

He was recommended for an early parole. The warden came to see him and clapped him on the back. "Gambini, I need you out of here. I've gained so much weight on your cooking, I told them to get you the hell out."

Now out of prison, Angelo wanted to buy paintings of his own, and he had to find a job. On his first day of freedom, he took a job as a dishwasher during the day. At night, through an old underworld contact, he became a dealer at one of the gambling establishments that had bought police protection. He was determined to earn money and stay out of trouble. He absorbed everything he could about the restaurant business as he moved up from dishwasher to bus boy to waiter to assistant chef. By night, he learned that man is a greedy creature willing to risk large sums of money on a slim chance to feel the thrill of winning. If these men were willing to chance their meager earnings in a game, Angelo wondered what it must be like for men who had real money to bet. He didn't have to wonder for long. His employers kept a room in a hotel that catered to the wealthy, and every night there was a game for very high stakes.

Angelo had many attributes that qualified him for the big time. He was darkly handsome, prematurely greying, and a perfectionist in the way he dressed. His study of art had rubbed off on his personal maintenance until there was no trace of the boy from the slums. He moved easily and quietly among the wealthy men for whom he now dealt cards. Their obsession with winning, even though they knew the odds were stacked against them, constantly amazed him. Part of it, he reflected, must be the need for some element of danger and risk in their lives, a kind of perverted challenge. He smiled to himself, thinking he had enough danger in his life without betting a cent.

The hotel room had just the right degree of elegance to suit the tastes of these men, but Angelo felt stifled in one room, and thought the one-room flat in the slums and the one room in prison were all the single rooms he ever needed for a lifetime. An idea began to form in his mind. Perhaps there should be many rooms devoted to gambling, and a fine restaurant to take the place of the tray of stale sandwiches sent up to the room. He had the knowledge to run a successful kitchen and a profitable gambling game.

Angelo was well liked, for he praised the right people and kept his real thoughts to himself. He sent presents to the policemen with new wives or babies. They were the ones who were paid to turn their eyes away from the gambling rooms, and the personal touch was the icing on the cake. He was completely honest with the men who hired him, scrupulously turning in every penny of the night's winnings, never keeping even a small amount off the top for himself, as many dealers did. He cultivated both sides of the law, for he had a grand plan.

He also had a personal life. He no longer worked at the restaurant. His wages from dealing in the big games were more than adequate for his personal needs. He had a suite of rooms, and though they were small, they gave the feeling of space. Large windows and high ceilings, without the fashionable clutter, made the rooms light and airy. They were as immaculate as his few well-cut suits. On his walls was a growing collection of the best art he could afford. He justified his loss of salary at the restaurant because he could now spend a large part of the day at museums and galleries.

He had never had a sexual experience with a woman and had no interest pursuing women. He remembered with loathing the vulgar sounds of his father making love to his mother. Once he had parted the curtain around his parents' bed and had stood watching his father's motions over his mother. Before she looked up and saw him standing there, he thought he detected the look in her eyes of being cruelly assaulted. This was merely one more wrong his father committed against his long-suffering mother. After being released from prison, he had actually tried a prostitute. When she had taken him to her tiny room, almost at once he experienced the panicky feeling of being locked into a small space. His other phobia was also activated, for the woman was dirty and smelly. She swiftly undressed him and managed to bring him to erection. As he lowered himself into her, he fought his feeling of claustrophobia and revulsion of her filth. Suddenly, she turned her face and it looked like his mother's face as it had gazed at him from under the weight of his father. Crying out, he tore himself away from the woman, threw on his clothes and flew out of the room. He was so revolted by what happened that he bathed and changed his clothes constantly for days.

In the winter of his thirty-fifth year, he found a way to put his plan into action. He had served ten years of his prison sentence, and in the six years he had been free, he had established friendships with important people who had seen to it that he was now released from the restrictions of parole. This was very important to Angelo since he had to have a clean slate to apply for a gambling license. He intended to have his own establishment. He had permission from his underworld bosses. Of course, they would have a cut of his profits and they trusted him.

He had everything he needed for the gambling establishment except money. However, his problem was solved by a Miss Gina Nunzio. She was one of the plainest girls he had ever met, but also the richest. Her father, for his own years of service to the organization, had been awarded the largest prize in the city: control of all the gambling operations—horses, cards, anything on which a bet was placed. His power was enormous and so was his pocketbook. He had, in a way, adopted Angelo, for he trusted him as he trusted no one else, except for his wife. He included Angelo in many Nunzio family dinners. He always had a place at their table, as close to Gina as her father could arrange. It became clear to Angelo that his mentor's fondest wish was for him to be nice to his homely daughter. Angelo did his best, although Gina was so painfully shy that any conversation was always one-sided. Mr. Nunzio rewarded Angelo's slightest attentions to Gina with lavish praise and money. Angelo couldn't believe his ears on the day he took her to the Metropolitan Museum of Art and she excitedly began to comment on each painting. From that moment on, conversation was no longer a problem. If it had not been for her knowledge and love of art he would not have been able to bring himself to say yes to the proposal Mr. Nunzio made. Mr. Nunzio offered to give Angelo the money to set up his own gambling house if Angelo would marry the sad, plain Gina. It was less difficult than he had imagined, because marriage to Gina didn't change his life. He spent most of the first day after the ceremony ignoring her, except for a discussion now and then about art. He was completely absorbed by the plans and construction of his gambling house and restaurant. Gina was used to being pushed into the background, so she made no demands. She worshipped Angelo with her every breath, and the fact that this hand-some man had chosen her for his wife was a miracle she couldn't bring herself to believe.

On their wedding night, their attempted lovemaking ended in Angelo's furious frustration. Gina took the blame upon herself, begging Angelo's forgiveness, promising to try harder to be a better wife the next time. She didn't have to worry about fulfilling her wifly duties the next time, because there was no next time. He was studiously polite to her, asking her opinions on art acquisitions and being unfailingly kind. In fact, he treated her as kindly as he would have treated a child.

To his satisfaction, Gina preferred buying paintings rather than jewels. She was great help in decorating his new restaurant. In the winter of the fifth year of their marriage, he took her to Europe on an art hunt. They purchased a Monet, a Pissarro for only two hundred francs, several Manets, and a group of Degas pastels. Gina was momentarily happy.

Angelo was quite satisfied with his life, but poor Gina suffered a series of illnesses, brought on by nerves and depression, for she longed to be his wife in every way and to have children.

Mr. Nunzio let it be known that he wanted grandchildren, and Angelo, an honorable man, felt he had to repay his father-in-law for what he had done for him. One evening, after having a few drinks to mask his revulsion, he unexpectedly approached Gina. She couldn't believe what was happening and she responded with a wild passion. After the act was completed, he went into their marble bathroom and became sick to his stomach. This was the pattern of their existence for some months. Gina's bouts with nerves and depression disappeared, and she lost her look of woe. From the moment she ecstatically announced she was pregnant, he did not touch her again, except for a pat on the shoulder. This time, however, she was preoccupied with the child and thought he was being solicitous of her condition. A lovely baby girl, Angelina, was the result of their peculiar union. He worshipped Angelina, for she resembled his own mother, who had once been a stunningly beautiful Sicilian with dark, exotic looks and flashing eyes. Mr. Nunzio was thrilled.

Gina began to hope Angelo would make love to her again, but he couldn't bring himself to do it. She thought, of course, that *she* was entirely to blame. She felt she repulsed him, but whenever she begged him to tell her what she should do to please him, he patted her absently and rolled over, telling her to sleep well. The more frantic she became, the more frequent her bouts with hives and other rashes became. Finally, she believed that her plainness and her body covered with rashes were the reasons her handsome, elegant husband didn't want to touch her, and she gave up hoping.

The day Angelo laid eyes on Nora, moving into the building across the street, he experienced an emotion he had never felt. She was lovelier than any woman he had ever seen in painting or statue. Her figure, her carriage, the tilt of her chin, the way her black hair glistened, her perfect profile when she threw her head back to laugh, all these things enchanted him. He felt no sexual longing, but a passion of another kind, perhaps stronger. He wanted her to be part of his world and his collection so that he could gaze at her as he did his other treasures. From the moment he had lifted his glass to Nora and their eyes had met, he knew he adored her as a priceless treasure.

The man in the window, Angelo, several days later sent a gilt-edged invitation addressed very properly to both Rachel and Nora to join him at the opening of the Madison Square Garden horse show, which signaled the start of New York's social season. He couldn't have sent an invitation that would have excited Nora more than this one did.

Nora jumped up in the air excitedly, grabbed Rachel around the waist, spun her around and shrieked loudly, "Rachel, we're going to the horse show! One of the finest horse shows in the world, with the exception of Dublin, of course. You and I. We're going!"

Rachel thought Nora had lost her mind. Denise poked her head around the doorway out of the back room. "Miss Nora?" Denise looked concerned. "Shall I be fetching the doctor?"

"No, no, you silly goose. I'm just happy." Nora tossed the invitation at them.

"Miss Nora," Denise exclaimed, "you'll be needing a new outfit, and in only two weeks. Thank St. Patrick, Miss Rachel, that your parents gave you your lovely new beige suit for your birthday." Denise rambled on. "Well, I'll manage to make something for you in no time. I have a wonderful idea from a picture I saw in *Leslie's Ladies Gazette*. It's gorgeous. Joseph, Patrick and Mary, where did I put it?" Denise started rummaging through drawers and boxes.

Rachel clapped her hands. "Oh, how exciting, Nora, how very exciting. And I do have that lovely new outfit. What perfect timing." She looked at Nora curiously. "I don't think I've ever seen you so happy."

"Oh, well, Rachel, I ride. That is, I used to ride. I'm very interested in everything to do with horses." Nora did not mention the Dublin show. It was hard for her to think of that time without feeling pain.

As the day drew near, there was a frenzy of activity in the shop. More and more customers had been venturing in and buying, and Denise was working on Nora's outfit for the show every moment she could.

Right on time, Angelo picked them up in his stately carriage. Rachel was wearing a tailored beige suit with wide lapels and a ruffled satin shirt of the same color. Nora was attired in a magnificent periwinkle-blue suit with leg-of-mutton sleeves, and the blouse peeking out at the neck was of her mother's finest lace. Her eyes, complemented by the dramatic blue of the suit, sparkled. Both ladies looked elegant. Their attire was understated, a look that Angelo particularly admired. He wore a tuxedo and top hat, and Nora thought he looked incredibly handsome. She wondered how her father would look dressed like this, for he was a very handsome man.

Nora chatted gaily and Rachel smiled, thinking she had never seen her friend quite so lively.

Angelo was enchanted with her. Not only is she exquisitely beautiful, he mused, but she's charming and witty. He congratulated himself on his judgment. And her friend was also refined and quite lovely. He relished every moment with these two new treasures. Rachel knew instinctively that it was Nora he was interested in, but that suited her fine, for her heart belonged to Sean, who didn't even know it was his for the asking.

They occupied a front box and were the object of

many curious stares. Angelo enjoyed the admiring glances cast in their direction, proud to be with the most beautiful woman in the room. As the events proceeded, Nora made several remarks that indicated her great knowledge of horses and shows. He was intrigued. How would a poor Irish immigrant know of these things? he wondered. She had told him of her poor childhood as they rode along in the carriage.

Nora informed them that Pretty Maiden would win in the dressage event, and Floradora would win in the jumping event. She was right both times, and she laughed with delight when her choices were the same as those of the judges. Angelo thought she must be heaven-sent, and his adoring looks did not go unnoticed by Rachel.

After the show ended, he took them to Rector's, the favorite restaurant of the new sporting society. It was gay and colorful, and he ordered Dom Perignon champagne.

The bubbles tickled, and Nora laughed gaily. "It's wonderful, Mr. Gambini. Much better than the Irish poteen."

Angelo turned to her and said, "Now Nora, I, and I believe Rachel too, have a right to know how you know so much about horses and riding and shows. We feel it is a mystery we would like solved."

A momentary flicker of sadness crossed Nora's face. "I won two events in the Dublin Horse Show in 1900, just two months before I came to America."

Both Rachel and Angelo were stunned by her hidden talents and they pressed for details. The champagne had lightened her mood and loosened her tongue, so she told them about the whole incredible day and the events leading up to it. When she came to telling about her disqualification, the look of sadness returned, but fortified by another sip of champagne, she turned her frown into a smile.

"But never mind. I won. I know I won, and everyone

else knew I won, and that is what really matters.'' She felt
a surge of relief at speaking about it. Angelo and Rachel
found it all quite fascinating.

What a remarkable creature she is, Angelo reflected,
making a mental note to see to it that she had the opportunity to ride again. For the rest of the evening, he found he
couldn't take his eyes off her.

Chapter 21

Ballygarry's address was truly chic. Because Angelo's, the most favored restaurant and gambling house of the theater crowd, was right across the street, Ballygarry's was guaranteed customers. Rachel's father had lectured them on the importance of location. Over and over he had urged them to resist the downtown lower rents because, he insisted, New York was moving uptown, and he named all the establishments that were deserting their Twenty-third and Twenty-fourth Street addresses and moving to the Forties and Fifties. "Old Lyman Bloomingdale knew that over thirty years ago, when he opened the Great East Side Bazaar on Fifty-seventh Street in the middle of farmland with chickens scratching around," her father stated positively, ending the discussion. He was right, of course. The extra money they spent each month for rent was nothing compared to the many sales profits they would make from the bustling crowds of people coming and going on Forty-fourth Street, right off Broadway.

Angelo's was so popular and crowded that often there

was a wait for a favorite reserved table, and the restaurant's patrons would stroll up and down the street, window-shopping until the table was vacated. It wasn't long before these people discovered Ballygarry's.

Before that happened, Rachel and Nora had dusted and polished the shelves and rearranged their merchandise, hoping it would seem inviting to the curious eyes that glanced in the window. Nora fretted about the threadbare carpet, and one day Sean and Rachel appeared, carrying a rolled-up rug.

"At least our carpet worries are over, Nora," Rachel smiled. "My parents had this stored in the basement, and I asked if we could use it. Isn't it lovely?" They unfurled it over the threadbare area. "We wanted to surprise you. Sean helped me bring it down. I think he was hoping that this would be one of the days that Mr. Gambini would send over one of his fabulous lunches."

"Well, I'm wanting some kind of payment. I'm famished," Sean said with a grin.

"It's beautiful, Rachel. What a marvelous idea." Nora was delighted. "*Now* the customers will come in. I know it. When an establishment has an Oriental rug on the floor, one knows it's a success. It was probably just what they were waiting for."

Soon, more and more customers drifted in. The stars of that day were the members of high society—the Four Hundred—and the theater idols whose comings and goings were eagerly chronicled by the newspapers and weekly magazines. The patronage of one of these women could make or break an establishment, so they eagerly awaited the day when an Anna Held or Ethel Barrymore or a Mrs. Astor would cross the threshold.

"You know," Sean remarked, "I bet Connelly would let me run a little squib in the paper about the shop. You need some publicity so that people will talk." He was true to his word, and shortly after that, they were mentioned in print. Business soon became quite brisk. Nora and Rachel were delighted, and Denise just sniffed, saying she had quite enough work to do already.

Several days after the heady experience of the deliciously wicked dinner at Rector's, a huge box arrived for Nora from Saks. Her hands trembled as she unpacked the most beautiful riding outfit she had ever seen. It was a deep chocolate brown trimmed with suede, and the boots were of the softest and finest Italian leather. Rachel, Denise and Sean, who had stopped by, all admired the outfit. Rachel suspected who it was from.

Later, in private, Nora glanced at the gilt-edged card, which said simply, "Central Park, Sunday at 10. Angelo."

Soon Nora was riding again, thanks to Angelo. Her horsemanship was perfect, he observed, like everything else about her.

They also attended the opening of the Metropolitan Opera, art gallery openings, and dined at Sherry's, Delmonico's and the Waldorf. Nora wondered why they never dined at his own Angelo's.

The relationship that developed satisfied them both. Angelo, of course, made no sexual demands of any kind, and played a fatherly, concerned role. She knew that he, too, had come from humble beginnings, which made her feel comfortable with him. His success also showed her what was possible in America. He was gracious and kind, teaching her about fine food and wines, good manners and, of course, about art. Angelo noted that she had an instinctive understanding of good art. For his part, he realized she was not interested in a romantic liaison. This put him greatly at ease, due to his asexual nature. This friendship was perfect for them. She enjoyed his sophisticated lifestyle, his kindness and generosity, and his good taste in all things. He worshipped beauty and brains, and perfection in any form, and she was, to him, that perfection. She was the only woman he had ever adored the same as he had adored his mother. She had tapped a well of love that he had thought no longer existed, and she quickly became one of the most important parts of his life.

Rachel and Sean both worried a little about Nora's new, unusual relationship, but since Angelo's reputation seemed impeccable, though a bit mysterious, they said nothing for a while. Finally, though, Sean confronted her one day. "Nora, we're worried about you. Angelo is taking all your time. You see him practically every night, and besides, he's old enough to be your father. What are his intentions, and what are your feelings for him?"

"Oh, Sean!" She was amused. "You're being the protective brother."

"Nora," Rachel interjected, "perhaps you do need to meet more people your own age."

"I don't want to meet someone my own age. I don't want a romance. I want someone who is brilliant, handsome, sophisticated, someone who moves easily through life because of his power and position. I want someone who teaches me about opera and art and literature, and the other beautiful things of this world. I want someone I can respect, and someone who makes no other demands of me. That someone is Angelo. I hope you can understand and respect my feelings in this matter. I do appreciate your concern."

"Of course, Nora. We do understand. We were just worried, that's all." Sean said it, but he was uncertain about whether he really understood his sister.

Nora and Rachel had many orders to fill, but not

nearly enough as yet to use all the lace. Nora kept thinking about how to use the lace and expand the business. One day she asked Rachel what she thought of the idea of making and selling some of their designs to a few of the better specialty shops. "We could have two businesses, Rachel, and we know how much more beautiful our things are than the lingerie with the machine-made lace many of the manufacturers are using."

Rachel agreed. "You'll have to be the representative, though, Nora. I just wouldn't be as good at it. I'll mind the store and keep the books."

Denise turned out a whole line of lingerie, and Nora began her rounds. Within several weeks, she had a sizable order from Bergdorf Goodman. Rachel and Nora jumped up and down and hugged each other. Denise moaned.

"Denise, don't worry," Nora soothed. "We'll get another girl to help you, and I have one in mind. My old friend Annie O'Leary from Lowell."

"Oh thank the Lord, Miss Nora. 'Tis a big order."

"I had to promise, though, that other than in our shop, I wouldn't sell any of the designs to anyone else in New York."

"Oh dear, that will limit us, Nora."

"Yes, it will in New York, but there are lots of other cities, Rachel. I've decided to go to Chicago in a few weeks and see about Marshall Field, if that's agreeable with you, of course."

"Why, that's a marvelous idea, and your dear friends Molly and Tim are there. How perfect!"

Denise interrupted. "Make sure you get that Annie O'Leary here first, though. If she dropped from the sky this moment, it wouldn't be quick enough."

They laughed. "I'm going to be sending a telegram today, Miss Denise. Now don't worry!"

*   *   *

Annie arrived within the week, and Nora met her at Grand Central Station. Ever since she had landed in Lowell alone, she vowed that no one she loved would ever arrive anyplace unmet. The two old friends cried and hugged.

Annie held Nora at arm's length. "You're looking like a fashion plate, dear Nora." She sniffled. "I can't believe this is happening. You know I actually believed you when you said you'd send for me. And it's what kept me going for a long time."

They talked of everything. Lowell, the O'Houlihans and, of course, Colin.

"Annie, how is Colin?"

"Good, Nora, good. He's become important in the union, and we're making strides in Lowell. We are doing that. Why, they're treating us a bit better just because of the threat of unionization."

"Does he have a girlfriend, Annie?"

"Aye, one of the new union members. Nice lass, very dedicated to the union and to him. He's cautious, though, but I think they'll end up getting married. And Billy. How is Billy, Nora?"

"Oh, Annie, he's fine. He's a beautiful, happy child. I went to Chicago. I was terrified to go. I thought I would do something foolish, but it was wonderful. He calls me Aunt Nora and he took to me immediately." She gave Annie a long look, and then fell into her arms, crying.

"There, there, dear Nora. It's all right." Annie patted her gently.

"Annie, my heart almost broke when I saw him. I wanted him so badly, but I knew he could never be mine. Even if Tim and Molly would give him up, I couldn't do that to the child now. He loves them so."

"Aye, Nora, you're right. I wonder if it's good that

you know where he is and can see him from time to time. Each time will reopen the wound.''

"Yes, it probably will, Annie. But I must see him now and again. I'm so happy you're here. There's no one I can talk to about him. I sometimes cry into my pillow at night thinking about him. Look, here's a photograph of him." She proudly showed the picture to Annie.

"He is a handsome child." She took Nora's hands in hers. "You'll have to remain always as strong as you are now, because it won't be getting easier. Each time you see him, it may be more painful than the last. You should know that, Nora. And decide whether you should keep seeing him."

"Annie, I've already made that decision. I *must* see him."

They went to the shop first, and Annie was as excited as a child.

" 'Tis beautiful, beautiful, Nora. So this is your lovely Rachel." She hugged her. "And Denise, what a darling girl! You're all just as Nora described."

"Now, we've got to get you some clothes, Annie. We'll be doing that at Bloomingdale's. I have a soft spot in my heart for that store, Annie. They gave me my first opportunity."

Then Nora took Annie to where she would be living. Aunt Nellie had a friend living close to them who took in boarders, and she had made all the arrangements for Annie.

The flat was clean and pleasant, and Nora prettied Annie's room with some lace pillows and other homey touches. She was acutely conscious of how important pleasant surroundings were.

When Annie entered, she looked around and began to cry. Nora patted her, saying nothing.

* * *

Rachel and Denise were thrilled with Annie. She took over and began acting like shop manager immediately. She had an instinctive grasp of how to keep things running smoothly, and she freed Rachel to do her bookwork, Denise her sewing and Nora her designing and selling.

After several weeks, Annie made an announcement. "We need another seamstress and another salesperson, Rachel. Can we afford it? If we are to fill the orders we already have and take new ones, we must have more people."

Rachel did her calculations and reluctantly agreed that it was probably necessary.

"Annie, my sister Winnie sews almost as well as I. Please see her," Denise requested.

"I'll take your word, Denise. You know more about her abilities than I do. Tell her to report on Monday."

"Well, if we're hiring family members," Rachel began, "Nora, my sister Sarah is home from school. She graduated last week and has been talking about trying her hand at something. I'm afraid there's not much she can do, but she might make an excellent saleswoman. She's a pretty little thing and quite charming."

"Wonderful, Rachel. Let's try her. From what you've told me, she might be perfect. Ballygarry's is doing well, Rachel. Can I uncross my fingers now, for 'tis interfering with my designing." Nora smiled.

Ballygarry's was indeed doing well. It was frequently mentioned now in the society pages, and Nora and Rachel's names were often included as the owners.

They would, on occasion, take lingerie to the homes of wealthy patrons, and one day, as they were loading boxes into a carriage, Nora became aware of a man standing across the street staring at her. Before she got a good look at him, he turned away. Something about him, his shape, his walk, was disturbingly familiar to her, but she shook off the feeling and turned to her task. The next evening, as she was locking up the shop, she thought she saw the same man under the lamplight across the street. She quickly opened the drapes, which she had just closed, but there was no one there. She thought she was seeing things.

Nora was dining out and she dressed carefully for her dinner with Angelo, hoping that extra care taken with her appearance would mask the lines of fatigue around her eyes. Her taste in clothes was a combination of what was in fashion and her own individual style. She had a lovely figure. Her bosom and hips were gently curved, perfect for the cinched-waist, full-sleeved, hourglass style of the day. Tonight she had chosen a pale blue dress of rajah silk, the skirt and matching cape made up of rows and rows of fine pleats. The dress had a high-necked blouse of her favorite lace, which Mary had sent for her birthday. The full skirt was held out by petticoats, and her tightly laced corset thrust her body slightly forward, giving her an appealing, slightly swaying walk. After she had pinned her hair up, she reached for her beautiful hat, which had been Angelo's birthday gift to her. It was a slightly darker blue, made from the finest felt, adorned with navy velvet ribbons, mauve roses and a snow-white plumed feather.

Before putting on her long gloves, she pinched her cheeks for color. Going anywhere with Angelo was always exciting, but dining out was a particular pleasure. Since Angelo's was one of the most popular restaurants in New York, Angelo, as the owner, was always treated royally when he dined in any other eating establishment, as if his being there gave his stamp of approval to his rival. Nora knew that she created a stir when she entered the room, and Angelo knew it too. He was proud to have her on his arm. She was beautiful and elegant, two attributes he considered essential, and he treated her like the jewel he felt she was.

She particularly enjoyed Delmonico's across town on Fifth Avenue at Forty-fourth Street. The first time she had entered this lovely restaurant, she had looked at the exotic two-toned building crowned with small Turkish minarets, iron grillwork around the windows, and gay awnings, and thought it must be something out of the *Arabian Nights*. The interior had paneled walls and finely detailed coffered ceilings. Globed chandeliers hung gracefully from the ceilings, casting their flattering rosy glow. Round tables with crisp white linens to the floor and chairs both comfortable and simple in design completed the elegance. As the head-waiter led them to Angelo's favorite table by the window, many heads glanced their way. People tittered, wondering whether she might be his daughter.

After they had been seated, and their orders taken, he commented on the circles under her eyes and chided her for working so hard.

"Don't lecture me, Angelo. I admit you're right. I've even started imagining a man watching me. That's how tired I am."

"There, you see, I was right. You're exhausted, and I'm glad you admit it. I know just the thing for you. We'll go to Saratoga Springs this weekend. You'll sleep and eat and we'll watch the races, if you feel up to it, and by Monday you'll be good as new."

Nora sighed. "That would be wonderful, Angelo, but Rachel and I are taking stock this weekend."

"Oh no you're not. Both of you are coming with me. It will do the two of you good to get away from that shop. You know Annie can handle it, and it will do me good to have two beautiful women with me." He held up his hands to ward off her halfhearted protests. "I won't listen to any of your excuses. You're both going to take a couple of

days' vacation, and that's it!'' He had a way of charming
Nora, and she enjoyed his fussing over her. She wearily
agreed. Rachel would be delighted, she knew, so she
accepted for her. Angelo said he would pick them up at
noon the following day.

He returned to Angelo's to lock up the vast sums of
money taken in that night at his gambling casino. He
enjoyed the closing hours, with the last satisfied customer
gone, or at times a disgruntled loser still hanging around
complaining, the bus boys clearing away the last dirty
dishes, the cooks wearily sitting at the long chopping
tables drinking strong coffee, the pretty little hatcheck girl
saying good night to him and putting a rose from one of
the tables in his buttonhole. It's a good business, Angelo
thought, especially when it's over for the day. He went out
the front door whistling a little tune under his breath.

''Buona sera, Dominic, lock up tight, now, you hear!''
he said to his doorman. It was an unbroken tradition, this
phrase he had repeated every night for eight years. It
brought him luck, he thought, for he had never had a
robbery. Even when he was away, he had Tony, his
second in command, say the same words to Dominic. As
he was about to get into his carriage, he noticed a man in
the shadows across the street. He seemed to be hiding.
Angelo wondered what he could be doing out at this hour,
and he started across the street.

''Hey, you there, what are you doing?'' The man
turned to walk away, and as Angelo drew nearer, the
stranger quickened his step. As he started to run, Angelo
caught up to him and swung him around, grabbing at his
coat sleeve. The man struggled, still trying to run, and
Angelo could feel him beginning to slip out of his grasp.

''Stop it, you bastard, and tell me what you're up
to.''

As the man twisted out of his coat, he turned, and for one moment, Angelo saw his mean eyes staring, saw a face that had a hideous scar running from above the left eye down to the corner of his mouth, which had been drawn up into a strange grimace as the cut had healed. The face was full of such hatred that Angelo must have released his grip, for the next thing he knew, he was standing alone in the middle of the street, holding an empty overcoat. He started to toss it away, but changed his mind and thrust it at Dominic, who had come running to his aid.

"Who was it, Mr. Angelo? What did he want?"

"Just some bum, I guess. Here, take the coat. We'll keep it in the kitchen. Maybe somebody will get caught without a coat when it's raining some night. Might as well be good for something." Angelo shivered, remembering the twisted face. "Dominic, you lock up tight, now, you hear?" It couldn't hurt to say it twice in one night, he thought, as his carriage clattered away.

Angelo had been one of the first to acquire one of the new "horseless carriages." This new possession was giving him a great deal of pleasure, and he wanted to try it on its first long trip to Saratoga Springs. It was one of the finest motor cars available, a Franklin. He told Nora that they would travel in this marvel of transportation. Before the trip, he insisted that both Nora and Rachel had to be properly outfitted for the journey. They started the day by going to Saks, which was catering to this new fad by carrying more than a hundred and fifty items of motoring gear. Angelo was compulsive about wanting to buy presents for Nora, to adorn his perfect woman. He insisted that they purchase several hats, complete with veils, necessary to keep the dust from their faces. He laughed with pleasure as Nora and Rachel posed for him in various outfits.

The weekend was a blur of racing satins, dazzling

lights and sparkling diamonds. Angelo was a supreme host. They were very gay on the way home. Nothing could have prepared them for the sight that met them as they turned onto Forty-fourth Street.

Where their shop had been, there remained only charred ruins. Nora screamed and Angelo restrained her from getting out of the car, sending the driver to question the police standing by the smoking rubble.

The fire had begun, they were told, in the early hours of the morning. The policeman on the beat had smelled smoke, but by the time he had summoned the fire company, everything had been destroyed by the flames. The firemen had tried valiantly, but everything Nora and Rachel had in the shop was gone, lost to flames or firemen's hoses. The policeman thought he'd seen a man running away from the fire, but he couldn't be certain.

As the firemen poked through the charred, wet ruins, one of them shouted, "Look here! Look at this, chief!"

He held aloft a now broken bottle stuffed with a grimy rag. The chief put the contents to his nose, then motioned to Angelo, who left the crying, distraught girls and joined him.

"Kerosene, as sure as I'm standing here. Smell for yourself. Somebody started this here fire. Who do you think would want to do this thing to those two nice girls?"

Suddenly, a twisted face flashed into Angelo's memory. "Of course. The man who got away from me when I caught him loitering around the shop. That's got to be the man." Angelo spoke his thoughts aloud.

"Did you see him, did you recognize him, Mr. Gambini?" the chief asked.

"No, but I'd never forget that face. Wait, I've got his coat. When he got away, he twisted out of his coat. I've got it at the restaurant."

Nora, Rachel and the chief followed Angelo across

the street. Annie, Denise and Winnie were at the restaurant, dazed and crying, for this horrendous sight had greeted them a few hours earlier.

Annie threw her arms about Nora. "Oh darling girl, how awful. I was careful, Nora. I checked everything, honest I did." Her eyes were red from crying.

"Annie, I know, I know. None of you had anything to do with it. The chief suspects arson." She was trying to regain her composure. Denise and Winnie were sniffling, and Rachel fell into a chair, now openly sobbing. Dominic brought coffee in and tried to comfort them as best he could.

Angelo unlocked the door that led into the kitchen storage room. There on the peg hung the tattered coat. "Let's see if we can find out who did this," Angelo said. "Pray God, he's left something to tell who he is." He went through the pockets one by one. The chief, Nora, Rachel and Annie stared expectantly. "Damn, only this scrap, no name. Just says Indian Mills on the edge." He was obviously disappointed.

"What did you say?" Nora gasped. "Did you say Indian Mills? Oh, my God, what did you say he looked like?"

Annie paled visibly. "Oh, no, it can't be, it can't be."

As Angelo described the man, Nora's eyes widened. She was incredulous. "Scanlon, it was Scanlon," she cried. "He said he'd pay me back, and he has, he has. Oh Annie, Annie."

They looked at each other in disbelief. No one else knew what they were talking about.

"Who in heaven's name is Scanlon, Nora?" Angelo asked.

"Yeah," intruded the chief. "I have to file a report."

Through the long night, Angelo questioned Nora,

making her remember and tell him everything she could about Scanlon. She and Annie both were in shock, but by dawn, Angelo had given the description to his men, the men whose job it was to seek out, find and punish offenders without the aid of the police. Their kind of justice was swift and final. In addition, Angelo offered a large loan to Nora so the shop could be reopened.

By the next night, Scanlon knew he was being hunted. He felt as if his singed clothes gave his hunters his scent, so he discarded first his jacket, then his cap, leaving a fresh trail for his pursuers to follow. The more he dodged and hid, the closer he could feel them. They had tracked him to the Bowery on leads from various informants. As his pursuers searched for him in the Lower East Side tenements, he darted from alley to alley. He was frantic now as he began to smell smoke, just as he had when he started the fire at the shop. He ran, panting, to get away from the smell. He knew it wasn't the police. Who was after him? Why wouldn't they give up? That Irish bitch had deserved to be punished. Hadn't she ruined his life, disfigured him? So why was someone after him?

Like a frightened animal who senses fire in the forest, he began to climb. As he clambered up a fire escape littered with garbage and laundry, he saw someone coming up after him, holding a burning torch. He climbed higher, scrambling frantically, but the men with torches were gaining on him. He looked up, knowing he had to reach the roof. As he climbed over the rooftop, he stood for a moment to decide which way to run. The door to the roof swung open, and there stood another figure with a burning torch. He turned to run back down the fire escape, but another figure with a torch appeared. He was trapped. As they converged on him, he felt a wet splash. My God, he thought, smelling the strong fumes, it's kerosene. He heard, then felt, the flames envelope him. He was now a human torch, and in agony, he ran to the edge and jumped, screaming, from the tenement, his fiery form silhouetted against the black sky.

The men with the torches vanished as quickly as they had come. Their justice had been dispensed. An eye for an eye, a tooth for a tooth. The police were powerless against these underworld forces, and the case was closed.

Chapter 22

Days passed before the smoking ruins cooled enough for Nora and Rachel to sort through and find a few things that were water-soaked but not charred. They carefully packed them away. Nora was thankful that some of Mary's antique lace and a few other fine pieces were still in her black trunk at home. Every once in a while they looked at each other sadly.

"Oh Nora, it was such a lovely shop," Rachel said one day wistfully.

"Yes, Rachel, but we'll have another. You wait and see. And Rachel, this time we'll have insurance, no matter how expensive it is." Nora tried to sound more hopeful than she really felt.

After Rachel left, Nora showed Aunt Nellie the few remaining things undamaged by the fire. Then Uncle Jim came in. It was midafternoon and the bar downstairs was empty.

"Lass, there is someone to see you, one of your fine ladies, I'll wager, probably wants you to make house calls," Uncle Jim told Nora. "She's waiting in the bar. We're closed and I'm leaving now, so you'll be private. Just lock up when you're done."

Nora couldn't imagine who would be coming here to see her. She entered the darkened room, and standing near the side of the polished mahogany bar with its glistening brass was a woman all in black. Her face was covered by a heavy veil. Nora did not recognize her as a customer.

"May I help you? I'm Nora O'Sullivan." She peered at the woman, trying to place her.

"Yes, you can help," she answered quietly.

"How?" Nora asked, puzzled.

"You can help bring a husband and his wife together and restore their life to them."

"My dear lady," whispered Nora, her heart aching at the sad sight in front of her, "of course, I would do anything I could, but how can I possibly be of help to you?" Nora thought the woman must be mistaking her for someone else.

"You have stolen my husband's affections from me, and I'm here to beg you to give him up," the woman intoned.

"Madam, you must certainly have me confused with someone else. I would never dream of stealing a man's affections from his wife. I would never cause such heartache."

"I can't compete with someone as lovely and young as you. While you are in his life, he will never look at me with love." As she lifted her veil, she painfully uttered, "Look."

Nora gazed at a face ravaged with sores, and eyes as melancholy and hurt as she had ever seen. Her heart went out to the poor creature. "I'm so sorry. But you must think I'm someone else," Nora persisted.

"You know my husband very well. Please do not pretend. I love him. Give him back to me, I beg of you."

At that moment, Angelo burst into the room. "Here, Gina, it's all right. Come, come. I'll take you home," he said, as if addressing a child. "Nora, I'll explain this to you later."

The woman collapsed in a chair, refusing his arm. "My husband, whom you say you do not know, calls you by name. I came here in good faith. Why couldn't you tell me the truth?" She was now sobbing.

Nora stood in stunned silence. Angelo's wife? Angelo quickly moved Gina out the door into the waiting carriage. Nora couldn't move or speak.

As the carriage door closed, she ran into the street. "I didn't know!" she screamed after the carriage. "I didn't know! Oh God, believe me. I didn't know."

Aunt Nellie heard her screaming and came out and led her inside. Nora sobbed out the story, Gina's face lingering in her memory with all its hopelessness.

Nellie tried to comfort her.

"Oh Nellie, I've brought such misery to this pathetic woman. How could he not have told me?"

Nellie said, "I think he loved you so much that he had to be with you, no matter what. It doesn't seem to me that his friendship for you took anything away from his wife. Here, here, child. Maybe there's some explanation."

Nora sat quietly in her room. She had been despondent since the fire and Scanlon's death. The knowledge that she had been capable of causing a man to go berserk for revenge had filled her with fear. She had tried to shake these thoughts, to be brave and hopeful about the future. But now this had happened. She had calmed down after the revelation about Gina, but sat languishing day after day in her room. She thought of Angelo. Perhaps there was another explanation, as Nellie had suggested, but even if there were, she would not see him again. Another painful loss, for she would have to end their friendship. Again she felt she had been deceived and used by a man. Nellie, Jim and Sean tried to cheer her, to no avail. Sean had suggested that they allow her to work through this by herself. He understood her strengths and weaknesses as well as anyone, and knew that her strong, optimistic nature would reassert itself, given time.

"She's not a brooding person, Uncle Jim. She'll come to grips with this soon enough," Sean had advised.

And indeed, Nora had started to come to grips with it. She had gone to Bloomingdale's to ask Miss Fennell to take Annie and Denise on temporarily, and Miss Fennell had done so. But now the sudden appearance of Angelo's wife had unsettled everything. How could Angelo have betrayed me like that? she thought. She felt tainted somehow.

She decided that she could never see him again. And, of course, she could not accept the loan he had offered.

She began to wonder how she could ever make enough money to reopen Ballygarry's. Working for Bloomingdale's could not help her with the capital needed for the shop. In the meantime, she had to confront Angelo.

Dominic showed her into Angelo's beautiful, paneled office. She loved the paintings by those French impressionists on his walls.

He greeted her. "Nora, Nora, I'm sorry. I should have told you about my wife. But if you'll just listen, I think you'll understand why I didn't. Our marriage, from the first moment, was a mistake. A mistake I honor as an obligation, but not as a part of my day to day life. Gina has everything in the world she needs, but she's a very disturbed woman. Our lives are totally separate. In her mind, she harbors a hope that we will share a life together,

and it will never be so. Now do you see why my marriage
had no bearing on our relationship? Almost no one knows
I have a wife. I have an obligation to a woman I should
never have married and can never divorce. My relationship
with you has nothing to do with my being anybody's
husband, even in name only. It doesn't excuse me from
not having told you, I know, and that has upset you
greatly. For that, I apologize, but Nora, please understand
what I'm saying.''

"Angelo, what you're saying makes sense to me. My
heart grieves for you, and for me too, but you *do* have a
wife, and I can't see you under those circumstances.'' She
turned her head away, for unexpected tears had come to
her eyes. She no longer thought that this was another male
betrayal. However, she knew that the relationship had to
end.

"Nora, don't banish me from your life. I care for you
more than anything in the world.''

She heard his words and thought he was being truth-
ful. Nora was certain that he cared about what happened to
her and he probably loved her. On her part, she felt she
had given him very little in return. She suddenly felt
selfish, and she shuddered at this revelation. "I know,
Angelo, I know. I'm sorry. You've been wonderful; it's
all been wonderful, but now it's over. I can't see you
again. You're a married man. I'll never forget your wife's
face.'' She paused, lowering her eyes. "And you must
know, of course, that I can't accept a loan from you.''

He put his head in his hands and remained silent for a
few moments.

"Nora, I know you well enough to know that begging
will not help. I can even understand what you're doing.
You feel compromised, and probably betrayed. Perhaps in
the future you'll see it differently. I can only wait and
hope. But there is one thing I must insist on. You must

accept the loan. What, in God's name, will you do for money otherwise? How will you reopen the shop? Please be sensible. You'll pay me back in no time."

"I can't, Angelo, I just can't. I'll have to figure something else out. I'll have to get a job that pays a lot."

He could see there was no changing her mind. "Nora, you are punishing yourself unnecessarily." He spoke softly. "I don't know why, but you are. However, if you intend to remain adamant about the loan, let me at least help you find a job." He knew she was being unrealistic because she was upset, and he hoped that, in time, he could get her to accept the money, for she would never be able to reopen the shop otherwise. "There is one job that pays extremely well. I don't like to think of your doing it, but I know you want that money and want it fast."

"What, Angelo, what?"

"They are hiring banquet waitresses at the Waldorf-Astoria. That hotel has a liberal policy regarding women, not only employees, but women guests as well. They admit women without escorts, and they actually allow them to smoke in the public rooms. Now, they've started hiring women. That kind of waiting on tables, Nora, can mean big money. You wait on the very wealthy who are always trying to outdo one another in every way, including tipping. Even though I think most of them are fools, it might be the very thing for you to do." He paused. "I'm offended by the idea of your waiting on tables, but it's for you to decide."

"Oh Angelo, do you think I could do it, and could I get a job there with no experience?"

"Yes, of course, to both questions. Yes to the first, because I believe you can do anything you set your mind to, and yes to the second, because I know Oscar," he answered, mentioning the famous chef who was already legendary.

"Angelo, I'll do it. Thank you for your help. Thank you so much." She held out her hands to him. "I'll never forget your kindness, never." As she turned to leave, he pulled her to him and kissed her. She didn't resist. She liked the feeling of warmth, for it was warmth rather than passion.

He looked into her eyes. "I've never done that before for many reasons, but I can't let you walk out of my life without even one kiss. Remember, Nora. I'm here and I love you. And I'll do anything for you."

"There is one thing, Angelo." Her voice was sad.

"Yes, yes, anything."

"Be kind to Gina. None of what has happened is her fault." She swept out of the room.

A week and a half later, Nora reported to the Waldorf, not in one of her elegant gowns, but in a black uniform with the white apron and cap. Her hair was pulled back simply. Her family had been somewhat appalled at her going to work as a waitress, but she eased their fears by telling them how good the tips would be.

Then Nora explained her plans. "Besides, Aunt Nellie, Uncle Jim, it will give me time to redo my designs and start working toward opening the new shop. Denise will start working on things in her spare time, and so will Annie. I'll be running my own sweatshop," she joked. "When we all get enough money ahead, they'll quit and start working in earnest to begin where we left off. Annie wants to invest a little and I would like to have her do that. She should own a piece of the business. Rachel's parents will reinvest, but she wants to pay back some of what they invested before she asks for more. We just have to work it out." She paused and shuddered as she thought of the fire. "And I've learned a lesson I'll never forget. We'll have insurance next time."

Nora had been at the Waldorf-Astoria for a few weeks when she was assigned to work the Hadley-Trenton ball. Until that time, she had waited on groups like the Friendly Sons of St. Patrick, the Ancient Order of the Knights of Malta, several charity balls and innumerable luncheons and dinners. She was close enough to run home in between shifts and work on her designs and plans. The job, she thought, was perfect. She missed her friends, working as she did almost every evening, and she missed the life Angelo had introduced her to, but she didn't have much time to feel sorry for herself, and the tips were, as Angelo had promised, big, and often very big. She liked the excitement, and though it was hard work carrying the heavy trays, there was a great deal about it that she liked. With the Friendly Sons of St. Patrick, she could drop her newly acquired Americanized way of speaking and joke with all the Irishmen in her own lilting brogue, and they loved her. They asked her name so they could request her the following year. She could check out all the styles at the charity balls and luncheons, and she would, from time to time, wait on the famous and infamous. She thought of it as another school.

"If the sweatshops taught me one thing, this job teaches me another," she told Nellie and Jim and Sean one evening at dinner. "And, next week, I'll know what Versailles looks like, for there is going to be a replica of that palace at the Hadley-Trenton ball. They're already working on it. The waiters have to wear powdered wigs and knee breeches, and the few women assisting them, one of whom will be me, will also be wearing powdered wigs and eighteenth-century costumes. It's really quite exciting."

"Who'll be there?" Sean asked, interested, because he knew Fiona was attending a ball next week and was feverishly having fittings every time he had been to see her lately.

"Everyone, Sean, just everyone. The Four Hundred, of course, but there will be some Shoddies and Bouncers too."

"And who, may I ask, are Shoddies and Bouncers?"

"The new rich, many of them from cities all over America, the ones on the fringes of society. They've been called the little brothers of the rich, and they're trying to break into society themselves. Why, the Bouncers are going to have their own ball at Delmonico's. And, at the Versailles ball, everyone has to wear costumes. It should be great fun to see. I do have to run now. See you later."

"Yes, yes, it should," Sean answered, preoccupied with his own thoughts. That must be the ball Fiona's attending, he decided. A plan began to form in his mind.

From the moment their affair had begun, Sean had known that he amused her. He watched as expensive gifts arrived: the finest caviars and champagnes, rare orchids, strawberries and grapes in February, and of course the jewels. One evening, in a dressing room already overflowing with roses, a rare orchid plant arrived. Fiona barely looked at it, tossing the card into a heap of other cards on her dressing table. He knew he couldn't compete for her attentions on this level, so he used his wit instead.

He had to get used to sharing her attentions, not only with all the suitors, some of whom he now knew were Shoddies and Bouncers as well as high society, but with Caligula, her pet cheetah, who was always on a short chain, sitting and watching. Caligula always wore a jeweled collar.

One evening, Sean asked, "Fiona, is that collar real? I mean are there real rubies and diamonds in it?"

"Of course, darling, I wouldn't let precious Caligula wear some cheap paste imitation. Would I, darling baby?"

she cooed. "I was tired of it anyway. It's a bit gaudy, don't you think?"

He couldn't help but wonder about the man who had given it to her. Did he now know that it graced the neck of her pet cheetah?

When Sean had first met her, he found out immediately who his rivals were. One, of course, was Caligula, and the other was Randolph Belfant, one of the wealthiest young men about town. His father had made millions in steel, and Belfant Industries supplied the young prodigal with an enormous amount of cash. Lavish but often tasteless gifts for Fiona arrived weekly from him. The only gift Sean could give her was for him to keep her entertained. He thought up antics that would please her taste for the bizarre and amusing. Having access to Linotype machines helped him with his first "gift." One day he substituted his paper with the morning paper at her door. When Fiona opened the paper the maid had placed on her tray, the headlines glared, BELFANT INDUSTRIES GOES BANKRUPT. She stared at it for a moment, then broke out into her wonderful, throaty laugh.

"Mattie," she called to the maid, "come look at this."

"Why that poor Mr. Belfant, does he know, 'cause he just sent another two dozen of them long-stemmed roses?"

"Oh Mattie, it's a joke, silly," Fiona explained.

"Well, Mr. Belfant probably don't think it's much of a joke. It's no fun losing your money. You just ask me about that, Miss Fiona. It's no laughing matter at all."

"Never mind, Mattie." Fiona laughed again.

Mattie shook her head as she left the room.

When Dan arrived, she handed him the paper with a flourish. He reacted as she had, knowing at once that it was Sean's doing. They both started laughing, and just as they would stop, they would once again look at the headline and start laughing harder than before.

"He's just too marvelous, Dan. How ever does he think of these things?"

"Your young man has a wild and wonderful imagination." Dan liked Sean.

What appealed most to Fiona was Sean's fresh way of viewing things. She was older than he, and jaded from too much adulation, too much success, too much money. Anyone, she thought, could order two dozen roses, or a case of the finest caviar. It took only money. On the other hand, Fiona respected creativity and inventiveness in people. She loved the fact that Sean had dreamed up this crazy plan and executed it wonderfully. Fiona appreciated talent.

"I shall be very, very nice to him, Dan. I want to buy him something marvelous. Think about what it should be, darling, will you? If we put our two heads together, maybe we can come up with something half as clever as what he would think of."

Dan promised, thinking she probably cared about Sean for that moment as much as it was possible for her to care for anyone. Poor Sean, he thought, knowing her changeable moods only too well.

Chapter 23

The Hadley-Trenton ball was an extravaganza that even jaded, wealthy New York had never seen before. Nora couldn't believe anything she saw. The ballroom looked like pictures she had seen of Versailles, what with the curlicues, Cupids, baroque mirrors and the ornate throne on which Mrs. Trenton received her seven hundred guests dressed as Tudor Queen Mary Stuart. Nora wondered if Mrs. Trenton simply didn't know her history, that indeed she should have been Marie Antoinette rather than Mary Stuart, or perhaps she simply didn't want to be that obvious. She laughed to herself, because unfortunately Mrs. Trenton didn't look like a queen at all, but more like a rugged peasant just in from stacking the hay. However, she wore an ostentatious ruby necklace at her throat, which had in fact once adorned the neck of the queen she had chosen not to imitate. As the guests approached the platform, on which sat the "king" and "queen," a flunky called out their real names together with the historical characters they were supposed to be. Nora watched in utter fascination as one gentleman approached the "throne" in full Indian regalia, dangling several scalps; another, a Belmont, as it turned out, clanked in in a full suit of armor that had cost ten thousand dollars; and still another, Mrs. Astor herself, appeared simply as herself in a Paris creation. Well, the costumes were quite incredible and expensive, but what, she wondered, did they have to do with Versailles?

Many of the guests wore masks and didn't remove them the entire evening, which played right into Sean's hands. He had given a note to Nora, asking her to deliver it to Fiona McQueen at the ball. " 'Tis just a prank, darling. Do it for me, please." He handed her an elegant note with sealing wax and fancy scrolls.

"I will, Sean, if I have time. I will be working, not cavorting with the guests. And how will I know her?"

Sean laughed. "Do you think you'll be able to miss a flaming redhead being led by a cheetah with a diamond collar and a gold leash?" He knew that whatever costume she wore, Caligula would be with her.

"No, I'm guessing I won't be missing such a sight." She was suddenly intent. "Sean, are you in love with her?"

He was embarrassed. "I'm a mite taken, sister, but it's nothing serious," he said in a cavalier manner. "Don't worry about me, just give her the note."

She watched the guests arrive, and finally Fiona arrived with a young man who was announced as Randolph Belfant. He looked like a fop, Nora thought, but she could certainly understand what Sean saw in Fiona. She was a little flashy, but absolutely gorgeous. Her white bosom was nearly spilling out of her Empire costume. Nora asked one of the waiters to deliver Sean's note to her.

Fiona opened the note and looked around. Sean had discovered that she was going as Josephine and assumed that Belfant would be dressed as Napoleon. He wrote in the note, "Josephine, you are with an impostor. The real Napoleon is watching and waiting." She kept looking around, particularly at anyone with a mask on.

"What on earth is wrong with you, Fiona? Who are you looking for?" Randolph asked, exasperated at the lack of attention she was showing him.

"I'm looking for the real Napoleon, darling." He didn't understand her answer any better than he ever understood her, and so he gave up. She smiled at every stranger and wondered how Sean had ever gotten in, for she was sure he was there. Sean's intention had been to make her think of him the entire evening, and he had succeeded.

The guests paraded, danced, drank cases and cases of imported champagne, and dined. The last guests straggled out at 6:30 a.m. and Nora arrived home tired and disgusted. Sean had not as yet gone to work, and he was waiting for her.

"What was it like? Did you see Fiona?"

"Sean, it was awful. It was vulgar and ostentatious and outrageous. When I think of the tenements on the Lower East Side, with eight and nine people living and working in one room, with barely enough to eat, and then I see this expensive extravaganza, it makes me sick to my stomach." She collapsed into a chair, pulling the pins out of her hair to let it cascade down her back. She looked extremely unhappy.

"Good God, Nora, it couldn't have been that bad."

"I'm tired, Sean, and I suppose I'm being the righteous goose again. But there's something wrong, terribly wrong, in a society that allows such inequities."

He comforted her as best he could. In some ways, he thought, she was more upset by injustice than either he or Terence. But she was upset in a different way.

"I'm sorry. Ignore me. A few hours sleep and I'll be all right. I gave your note to Fiona. You devil, what did it say? She kept staring at everyone after she read it."

"Ah, good," he laughed. "If you've the heart for it, tell me about the ball."

Nora was not alone in her condemnation. The newspapers reported every detail, from the jeweled favors to the several hundred carriages the Hadley-Trentons had supplied for their guests to use. Feelings ran high and public indignation continued for weeks. Sean extracted every bit of information from Nora, and wrote an editorial for the *Irish World* from Nora's point of view. He called it an "idyll of extravagance and opulence" and went on to contrast it to the world Jacob Riis had written of in his famous exposé on slum conditions, *How the Other Half Lives*.

People were becoming aware, Nora thought, of the insensitivity of the wealthy who put on their charity balls more to display their wealth than help the poor and starving. It was estimated that more than $350,000 had been spent on the affair, $70,000 alone on Oscar's fabulous food. Nora and others felt somewhat vindicated when the city fathers, in indignation, doubled the Trenton's taxes. Truly believing that they had given this ball for the benefit of humanity, and not understanding the abuse hurled at them, the Trentons moved to England.

"And good riddance it is," Uncle Jim commented as he put the paper down. "Our Nora and Sean had their part in it, Nellie, that they did."

Sean's editorial received some notice and was reprinted in various other newspapers. Frank Brady, a veteran of many years at the *Irish World*, took note of the editorial, thinking the young cub reporter did indeed have some talent. Sean finally felt that he had written something worthy of his social conscience, and proudly sent a copy home to Terence. It was a different kind of injustice he was writing about, but in the long run, he thought, there were many of the same elements in both situations. The British were merely blessed with better taste, so that their self-indulgences and contempt for those below them, including the Irish, weren't as blatantly obvious. Sean had, in fact, pursued this line of thought, and that might have been why both Brady and Patrick Ford himself took note of the young man as someone worth watching and grooming.

Sean felt that his romance with Fiona was on the wane. She allowed him in her presence less and less, and to keep his heart from breaking, he threw himself into his work. He wrote her letter after letter and ended up tossing them in the wastebasket. He railed against himself, but he couldn't bring himself to end the bizarre liaison. Sean felt like a court jester when he entertained her. But he would be at her place whenever she beckoned, waiting for her favors and her notice, and the deep throaty laugh that rewarded his antics.

Some evenings earlier, Fiona had stood Sean up for a wealthy new fop about town from San Francisco. She had asked Dan to lie for her, but Dan, liking Sean as he did, told him the truth. "O'Sullivan, she's not worth it. Forget her. Half the time she's dazed on the laudanum, and the other half she's indulging every whim. Get out, while you're still whole." He advised further, "She's running around now with a whole new group, the new, vulgar rich, and they shower her with everything from jewels to a new horseless carriage. She loves that new toy more than she can love any person. I will say this for you, though. She cares more about you than she ever has anyone, and she respects you. But lad, face it. You can't afford her."

Sean left dazed. He hadn't known about her laudanum habit, but now he understood why she had such wild mood swings. He went back to the paper and wrote her another note, full of love and passion, and shoved it, unfinished, in his pocket. Then he walked into the Waldorf Bar and had a porter. He smiled to himself as he thought of the drunk he had talked to more than a year earlier, who had been stood up three times and wondered if that might indicate something. Lord, he thought, at least I haven't lost my sense of humor!

He received a letter from Terence, telling him of some new developments in the home rule discussions. To take his mind off Fiona, he wrote an article about it. He pondered how he could get it to Brady. He completed it, knew it was good, and put it in his pocket. When he went into the men's room that afternoon, old man Brady was there as big as life.

"Uh, hello, sir, my name is O'Sullivan. I've been at the paper for some time, sir." Suddenly he pulled the sheet of paper out from his pocket and thrust it into Brady's hands. "Please read this, sir. I think you'll like it." He exited quickly, before the surprised Brady could refuse.

He went back to his desk and removed his jacket, and as he put it over the back of his chair, he noticed a piece of paper sticking out of the pocket. He looked at it, and his face went white. It was the article on home rule that he thought he had given Brady. My God, I've given him the love note to Fiona. And he sat staring into space, not knowing what to do.

A few days later, Brady sent for him. Miss O'Hara showed him into the office, scowling all the while. Brady swung around in his chair with his shock of white hair standing straight up in front, and he looked at Sean with his piercing blue eyes.

"Sir, I'm sorry. I thought I had given you an article

on home rule. I . . . I . . ." he stammered. "It was a
mistake, Mr. Brady. I'd like to apologize."

"Are you trying to tell me, young man, that I'm no
longer the keeper of your heart? Are you trying to let me
down easy?" He let out a roar of laughter, pounding the
desk with his fist, enjoying himself thoroughly. For a
moment Sean was startled. Then he began to laugh too, so
infectious was Brady's laughter.

"O'Sullivan, word has it that you're a witty lad. I can
see that, for even when you're not trying, you're still
funny." He roared some more. "I haven't had such a
good laugh in years. Sit down, O'Sullivan. Tell me about
your home rule article. By the way, lad, I liked the poem
you wrote to whoever the hell the keeper of your heart
was."

Sean blushed. "Well, sir, I think she's no longer
interested in that job. Until I find a replacement, I'll
relieve you of the poem. It may come in handy again, who
knows." Sean smiled. He showed Brady the articles he
had been writing since he came to the paper. Brady started
to read them, puffing away at his pipe.

"They're good, O'Sullivan. I thought they would be,
especially after reading your exposé of the Hadley-Trenton
fiasco. How did you get in to the ball?"

"I didn't, sir. My sister is a banquet waitress at the
Waldorf, and she was one of the help that night. They had
her wearing a powdered wig and an expensive Versailles
ensemble. She looked perfectly breathtaking," he digressed.
"She clued me in on every detail. It had such a powerful
impact on her, sir. Her descriptions were quite vivid. If I
had attended myself, I would have only stared at the
keeper of my heart."

Brady chuckled again. "You're all right, young man,
all right." He swung around in the chair, all business.
"I'd like you to cover the State Assembly on an assign-

ment. Charles Evans Hughes is, as you probably know, conducting an investigation of the insurance industry. He believes malpractices abound. Dig around and see what you can find out. It may be a hot issue. Tell Connelly to see me. Isn't it ironic that he's been touting you for a long time now, thinks you have talent, and what gets my attention finally is a love letter." He laughed. "Good luck, O'Sullivan. I'm throwing you in with some big fish now."

"It's all right, sir. I can handle it. After all, I have a degree from the Fulton Fish Market." As he left, he heard Brady still guffawing loudly.

He breathed a sigh of relief. He was grateful to Connelly for putting in a good word for him. His spirits were as high as they had been in months.

Connelly informed him a few days later that the Assembly would be taking up the results of the insurance investigation in three weeks. "You had better take care of what needs to be taken care of here, kid, because you may be in Albany most of the time. You can come home on weekends if you can afford it."

"Pat," Sean said, looking at the perennially harassed "thanks for all the good words. My getting this is all thanks to you." He left quickly, before Connelly became flustered.

The family was delighted, and they opened a bottle of wine to celebrate his new assignment. Nora invited Rachel, who was like family, and Annie, whom she included in everything since she had no family of her own. She and Aunt Nellie had become fast friends.

Sean had not been able to bring himself to tell Nora of all his foolish escapades. Not only was he embarrassed, but he was afraid she would worry. The person he had chosen instead to tell was Rachel. Sometimes he would wait for her outside Bloomingdale's to pour out his misery and soak up her advice and solace. It nearly broke her heart to hear him tell of his yearnings and love for Fiona, but she never let on how she felt. She was happy that at least in some way he was part of her life. It was only Nora who knew the extent and depth of Rachel's feelings for Sean.

This evening, Rachel and Nora both noticed that Sean was almost his old self. The assignment had bolstered his morale, and he felt he was a young man on the way up. He was twenty-two years of age now, and he thought it was high time some good things began to happen to him. What they didn't know was that he had decided to ask Fiona to be his wife. Surely now that he had a decent job, it might be possible. He knew she loved him in her own peculiar way, and his old self-assurance and confidence had returned.

He informed them that he was leading a rally in Madison Square to raise money for the Irish Republican Brotherhood. It was a big push, he explained, and the torch-lit rally was expected to bring in a great deal of money. Rachel wanted to attend, but he dissuaded her because there might be some trouble. "The people living in the area don't like the idea. They feel we are def their sacred Madison Square. What it really amou a resurgence of anti-Irish feeling. I'll tell you all about it, ladies, I promise."

Sean planned to see Fiona later in the evening to ask her to marry him. She was his obsession. He was the life of the party, and when it neared ten, he offered to take Rachel home. As they departed, Nora thought how wonderful it was to have him back to normal again. How I wish he'd fall in love with Rachel, she thought.

At the theater, Fiona and Dan were discussing Sean. Dan was trying to find out how she felt about Sean.

"Darling, he's so amusing, but lately he's become a bore. All that spouting about home rule, whatever the hell that is, and insurance malpractice. I mean, darling, who cares? I think it's time for me to make a change, don't you think?''

"It's funny, Fiona. I thought you really cared about this one," he said casually.

She looked thoughtful for a moment and then replied seriously, as seriously as he had ever heard her, "Yes, you're right, Dan. This one's different. I think I may have fallen for him. Can you believe that?" His heart skipped a beat, but then she continued, "But, of course, he must go. You know, darling, I have to fill my coffers." She laughed.

A little while later, Sean burst into the dressing room. He was carrying a gaily wrapped package. He had never brought a gift before, other than a single rose or a piece of beautiful lace that his mother had sent.

"Why darling, what on earth is in there?" Fiona asked curiously.

"Open it and see, beautiful one," he replied.

As Dan unobtrusively left, she opened it. Inside was a lovely glass plaque, and etched on it were the words, large and clear, HOORAY FOR FIONA. She laughed and kissed him.

"It's wonderful, darling. Anyone can have a sable, but who can have a plaque like this? I love it." She kissed him again.

"Fiona, I'm going on assignment to the State Assembly. I'm finally out of the ranks of cub reporter. Love, I'm on my way. I'm a damned good writer, and they know it," he boasted happily.

"Yes, darling. I'm sure you are. And the very best thing you've written is the piece on me. Everyone loved it." She had brought the conversation back to herself, as she usually did.

He thought it best not to say that he no longer wanted

to do those frivolous kinds of articles. He gazed at
her while she brushed her luxurious hair and reached
to touch her. "Fiona, my God, how I love you. You
are the most beautiful creature I have ever seen."
Caligula snarled jealously and rattled his golden chain.
Sean noticed his collar was missing. He pulled her into
his arms and kissed her open lips. "This is what we
were meant for," he said, almost savagely. "Lock the
door, Fiona."

After she had locked the door, she turned to him and
dropped her dressing gown to the floor, beckoning him to
her. He dropped to his knees and kissed her stomach, the
inside of her thighs. As he kissed her breasts, she moaned
with pleasure.

"No one knows how to make love like you, darling.
You're a wonder. Take me, Sean. I'm made for love. That
may be my mission on this earth."

"Your mission, dearest, is to become my wife."
Before she could reply, he pulled her to him, kissing her
waiting lips. He thrust his tongue in her mouth, exploring
its mysteries.

She moaned, "Sean, oh Sean, take me, take me."
Their passion grew and grew, until finally he did take her,
and her wild hunger drove him to incredible peaks.

After they made love, they lay exhausted on the floor
of the dressing room. Finally he spoke. "Fiona, marry me.
I can ask you now. I'm no longer a cub reporter. I'm on
the verge of great things." He smiled at her, resting on
one elbow and looking into her languid eyes.

"Darling, you're sweet, but I don't want to talk of
marriage right now." She was obviously uncomfortable
with this kind of talk.

"Fiona, I have a future. I know that now. I'm a good
journalist. Why, I'm going to be covering the State Assembly. That's way up the ladder from fire stories."

"Be a sweetheart and get me a glass of champagne," she requested, ignoring his persistence.

He was frustrated. Someone knocked.

Fiona went to the door and asked, "Who is it?"

Sean could barely hear the voice that answered, but he knew it was a man's. "Oh, Randy, I'm getting dressed. Be a good boy and run and get some champagne. Come back with it soon."

Sean felt as though he had been slapped across the face.

"How could you, Fiona? I want to talk to you. This is serious."

"Yes, I know, darling. That's the problem now, isn't it?" she replied in her maddeningly offhand manner.

She had put her robe on and was running the brush through her hair when there was another knock at the door. She turned the key and opened the door, revealing several adoring young men, whom she welcomed. "Come in, you dears. You're just what the doctor ordered."

Caligula growled at them, and for the first time Sean felt a kinship with the jealous animal. Soon Randolph came bounding in with several bottles of champagne. Everyone started drinking, including Sean, who thought he'd wait them out. As to why exactly he was doing this, he wasn't sure, except that he still felt a compulsion to make her listen.

One of the young men said, "Well, Mr. Reporter, no jokes tonight, no witticisms or puns or clever lines?"

Sean glared at him, his sense of humor having deserted him completely.

Fiona guzzled some champagne and teasingly said to Sean, "Now pet, don't be cross. You are my pet, like Caligula. Only bigger and much, much better in bed. You are such a good pet. I'm going to put a collar on you. Won't that be fun?" She took Caligula's collar out of the dressing table drawer. "Here, this is for you. Let me put it on, darling." She had it around his neck in a flash. He tried to pull it off, but he couldn't. Everyone was laughing. The smart aleck reporter was being made a fool of, and the young swells relished every moment.

Sean was furious and humiliated. As he turned to leave, he looked at Fiona, who was teetering drunkenly with her empty glass of champagne in her hands.

"You, you slut." He ripped at the collar, but it wouldn't budge.

"It's yours, darling," she said. "To remember me by always."

He bundled his coat around his neck and went into the streets. He walked and walked, raging at the night. After several hours, he went back home.

In the morning Nora found him resting his head on the kitchen table. He was weeping.

"Sean, my God, what's wrong? What is it?" She put her arms around his shoulders. Then she patted him reassuringly. "Dear Sean, what can be so terrible?" Suddenly, she noticed the collar. "Sean, what in heaven's name is this around your neck?"

He looked up. "Oh Nora, take the damned thing off." As she unclasped it, he told her what had happened.

"Sean, Sean, she wasn't for you. Surely you must know that. I think for the last few months you've been in love with love. I don't mean to say it wasn't important. For everyone the first love, no matter how awful, is important. Because we learn from it. Sometimes the learning is painful, so painful we don't think we can live through it, but we do. We also emerge knowing more of the ways of the heart. Now, go to bed." Nora hugged him affectionately.

"Nora, I was so humiliated with that damned collar around my neck. I wanted to die."

"I know, I know." She stroked his hair. "You know, it's a beautiful collar. It looks real."

He stood up and held it up to the light. "It *is* real, Nora. These are real rubies and diamonds."

She gasped.

"It belonged to Caligula," he added with a hint of a smile, beginning to see the absurdity in the situation.

"I beg your pardon?" Nora answered.

"Caligula, her pet cheetah." He grinned.

"Oh Sean, what would Terence say?" They both started laughing. "It feels good to laugh again, Sean. I know your misery is right below the surface, but it's good that you can poke fun at yourself."

"Aye." He became serious again. "You know, sister, I'm thinking we've both had rather strange liaisons this past year. Do you suppose what appealed to both of us was that they represented exotic and forbidden worlds that we didn't even know existed?"

"Yes, Sean, I think so." Her face clouded as she thought of Angelo.

Brother and sister sat and talked some more.

Chapter 24

Though Sean was able to see some of the humor in his romance with Fiona McQueen, he remained melancholy and heartbroken. He filled his days with work to forget her beautiful, taunting face and her mocking laugh. He filled in for every sick reporter and wrote a prodigious number of articles.

He had tried to return the collar, but she wouldn't see him. Finally, ashamed, he contacted Dan and met him at The Stage Door bar. After he painfully told his story, he produced the collar and gave it to Dan.

"Sean, she doesn't want the collar back."

"I don't understand, Dan. What do you mean?"

"I mean she wants you to have it," Dan replied. "She told me she never wanted to see it again, and if you returned it, she was going to throw it in the trash."

"Dan, it's worth a great deal of money. These stones are real. What on earth is this all about?"

"Sean, I'm not sure. But she raved on about how it would always remind her of what she had done, and she didn't want to have anything to do with it again, ever. Take it, do with it what you will, but I don't want to have to throw it in the trash. You know that's what she'll make me do." Dan looked uncomfortable.

"This is crazy, Dan."

"Yes, but then so is she."

Sean put the collar back in his pocket. "I don't understand, but I'll figure something out. She's incredible, Dan. I could wring her neck, but for all that she's incredible."

"Look at it this way, Sean. If you're a lot sadder, you're also a lot wiser than when you went in." Dan knew that Fiona, in her own twisted way, wanted to repay him for the misery she had caused him. "Good luck, Sean."

They shook hands and parted.

He felt tired at the end of the day. He had done everything that needed doing for the rally coming up in Madison Square, and he was tired of the talk and smoke and drinking in Uncle Jim's bar. Nora worked almost every evening. He wished he could start his stint at the State Assembly, but that had been postponed for a month. Sean was restless. It occurred to him to take Rachel to dinner, and he headed for Bloomingdale's, where he waited for her outside the employees' entrance.

"Sean, what a delightful surprise," she called when she caught sight of him.

"May I have the honor of your company for a sumptuous repast this evening?" he asked, trying to seem light and cheerful.

"Oh, Sean, I'm sorry, I can't. Nora's coming to dinner this evening. My sister Sarah has been home from school for some time and Nora's really only met her fleetingly several times, so Mama and Papa decided it would be a good time for a visit. Because Nora has so few evenings off now, we decided to take advantage of this one.''

She saw the instant look of disappointment. She knew that his romance had ended. Nora had told her that, but she knew none of the details, knew only that he was miserable.

''You'll join us, of course. Come on.''

''Oh no, Rachel. I'd be intruding. No, thank you.'' He remembered his cool reception the last time and was reluctant to chance it again.

''Nonsense. Come. I want you to meet Sarah.'' She took his arm and pulled him toward a waiting horsecar.

He was so lonely and miserable that he agreed.

Mr. and Mrs. Friedman were very polite, but still he sensed Mr. Friedman's aloofness. Nora was already there, and they were all having sherry while they were waiting for Sarah.

Finally Sarah emerged from her room and Rachel took her arm and introduced her to Nora and Sean. ''I want my dearest friends in the world to meet my sister Sarah.''

The petite and charming Sarah, smiling and chattering gaily, quite won their hearts. She was tiny, slightly taller than five feet, and fragile. Her hair was much lighter than Rachel's and streaked in front with flashes of gold. Her eyes were the same dark brown, but without the smoky, exotic look of Rachel's. The planes of her face were surprisingly angular. Even the nose had a sharp point, and it was this feature that gave her some look of character, that made her more than just another pretty young woman.

As the evening wore on, Nora continued to ponder how different the sisters were. Rachel exuded a sense of purpose about her life that Sarah completely lacked. Rachel had a strength and an independence, whereas Sarah seemed to openly espouse the dependent role. Rachel was curious, mature and intelligent, while Sarah seemed innocent and childlike in contrast. Sarah was a charming and delightful creature, solicitous and accomplished. She played the piano delightfully. She seemed concerned only with things of the home and pleasing the men. It was obvious that Rachel adored her little sister.

Sean was enchanted with Sarah. She was so different from the earthy, demanding Fiona that he found her very easy to be with. He was charming and restrained at dinner, and Mr. Friedman begrudgingly admitted to himself that he was a nicer young man than he had originally thought. He warmed slightly to Sean out of deference to Nora because he and Mrs. Friedman were extremely fond of Sean's sister. Mrs. Friedman took her lead from her husband, and Sean began to feel much more comfortable.

Sarah liked Nora and Sean, for they seemed to respond to her and didn't talk down to her. Several times she looked up at Sean secretly and thought him an extremely attractive young man, and funny too. She flirted with him delightedly.

Nora noticed that Sarah was an accomplished coquette. She wondered if Rachel had noticed this too.

Sean, now feeling accepted, relaxed, and gradually his gentle charm asserted itself. This was not the company, he decided, for puns and impersonations, so he spoke of his job and his upcoming assignment in the state capitol. Mr. Friedman was happy to hear about this because if Sean was working out of town, then Rachel might get the fellow off her mind. He could read his daughter like a book, and her love for Sean was no secret to him.

The evening passed pleasantly, and as they were leaving, Sean said, "I've four tickets to the circus tomorrow. Mr. Friedman, may I take Rachel and Sarah?"

Sarah was enthusiastic and Rachel looked quite pleased

also. Mr. Friedman agreed. Sarah flashed Sean a radiant smile as she closed the door.

Nora was working, so the three of them attended the circus. Sarah was like an excited child. Sean found her amusing and attentive and enjoyed her company.

"She's a darling, Rachel," he said when Sarah had left to say hello to an old school chum. "So happy and uncomplicated."

"Yes," Rachel agreed, "and she has a good heart, too. Sean, tell me, isn't your big rally coming up soon?"

"We've had trouble getting a permit. It's been postponed, but it's been rescheduled for next Thursday. Rachel, everything I'm involved with lately has been postponed."

"Are you all right, Sean?" she suddenly asked, referring to Fiona.

"I'm getting there, Rachel." He knew what she meant. "Thanks for asking. You've sure lived through a lot with me." He looked steadily into her eyes. "Thanks for that too. You were a friend when I really needed one." He put his hand over hers. She hardly breathed and didn't dare move, afraid to spoil the moment. Just then, Sarah returned, bubbling with the latest gossip her friend had shared with her. He thought she was an enchanting little thing.

A heavy, insistent knocking woke Nora. It was one o'clock in the morning. She heard Uncle Jim and Aunt Nellie stirring, and then heard Uncle Jim's steps on the stairs. She roused herself and came out into the kitchen. She looked down the stairs and there stood Officer Mulcahy.

"Yes, three hours ago," he was saying. "I'm sorry to be bringing you this news, Jim."

Nora's heart almost stopped as she suddenly realized that Sean was not at home.

"What's wrong, Uncle Jim?" she asked, panic in her voice.

Jim looked very disturbed. "Lass, Sean's in jail!"

"Jail? Oh my God. What happened? Is he all right?"

"Aye, well, he was hit with a rock. But it's nothing serious. That's not the worst of it."

Officer Mulcahy followed Jim up the stairs, and when they reached the top, the officer turned to Nora. "Miss Nora, the rally to raise funds for Irish independence turned into a terrible free-for-all. We're thinking there were troublemakers sent to create diversions, and it turned into one gigantic brawl. The group was orderly. Oh, there were a few drunks. But mostly just speeches and cheering, like all those torch-lit gatherings, you know. Then someone upped and hurled a rock. That was all that was needed, and all hell broke loose. Oh, excuse me, Nellie, Miss Nora. I mean a big fight occurred. Some people were hurt bad. Your brother was bleeding and had a big gash on his head, but he's all right. I mean, it's not that serious," he reassured them quickly. "What *is* serious is that he's been booked for inciting to riot and assault. Those are bad charges, Jim."

"Oh no, no. How could they do that? Sean wouldn't start trouble," Nora insisted, coming to his defense.

"Well, he was in charge of the rally, Miss Nora. That part is true," Mulcahy observed. "And they've put a huge bond up for his bail. Looks funny to me. I'm not knowing what's going on. His boss on the paper will take care of it, I'm sure. Don't worry."

But Nora was beside herself. "Can we see him?"

"Not yet. Maybe tomorrow. I've some friends down there. I'll see what I can do." He turned to leave.

Jim was already thinking of what strings he could pull and which contacts he could use.

"Oh Uncle Jim, Aunt Nellie, how could this have

happened now, just when he's about to go to Albany in a couple of weeks? Will this ruin that for him? What if he's indicted? He'll have a police record. Oh dear God, what will we do?'' Nora started to cry.

"There, there, Nora, don't cry,'' Jim soothed. "Mulcahy's right. No doubt the paper *will* step in, and I've got plenty of good contacts. The best thing you can do is get a good night's sleep so that we can better handle all this tomorrow.''

Nellie put her arms around Nora. "Come on, lass. I'll get you a glass of warm milk.''

The next few days were an agony of waiting. Jim finally arranged to get them in to see Sean. As Nora was shown into the room where she would be able to see him, she shuddered. She did not like her Sean being locked up like a common criminal.

Sean was pale and drawn, and he had an ugly gash along the right side of his face.

She wanted to reach out, but there were bars between them. "Oh Sean, how awful!''

"Aye, Nora, 'tis that, but I'm better than I was. Don't fret. Brady and Ford at the paper are working on getting me out. They're baffled by all this. They think it's some kind of put-up job to discredit the cause. Nora, I never threw anything!''

"I know, I know, darling. It will be all right.'' She attempted to soothe him, but she was extremely worried. All attempts to free him were being met with obstacle after obstacle.

She went to see Brady at the *Irish World*.

"I'm delighted to meet you, Miss O'Sullivan. I wish the circumstances were different,'' he said, shaking his head sadly. He then proceeded to tell her of all the complications and dead ends they were running into.

"Our regular lawyer who handles cases like this is in Europe. We're using another, but he's gotten nowhere as yet. It's damned discouraging, Nora, I need to be honest with you."

Nora liked the craggy man with the shock of white hair and bright blue eyes. He was obviously trying to help.

"Thank you, Mr. Brady. Please keep me informed."

Nora returned to work since there seemed to be nothing she could do. She visited Sean every day, and also checked with Brady daily. Jim's contacts were doing no better. She felt a creeping despair, and tried hard to ward it off.

Rachel thought her father might be able to help Sean, but his response was quite negative. "He's a radical, and that's what happens to them," he informed her cruelly.

"Oh, Papa, please don't say that," she said angrily. "He believes in the cause of his homeland. You know how the Jews feel about theirs. Maybe we should be more like the Irish."

"Enough, young woman. I'm sure he has enough people trying to help him. What could I do?"

Rachel had begun to sense her father's disapproval of Sean and she knew why he felt this way. What's the use, she thought?

Sarah had been listening and was very upset. "Papa, you must help him. He's one of the very nicest young men I've ever met."

Rachel glanced sharply at her. Mr. Friedman instructed them both to leave him alone. It seemed to him that both his daughters were in league against him. What was this world coming to? Nice Jewish girls standing up for some young Irish radical. And then Rachel throwing in a barb about her own people. The Jews weren't powerful enough yet to help each other. He shook his head sadly. Mrs. Friedman just sat quietly, forever taking the lead from her husband, no matter what she herself might have felt.

Rachel found herself comforting Sarah.

"Oh Rachel, I like him so much," Sarah wept.

Rachel's heart sank, but she tried to ignore her feelings for now.

Nora had carried the last tray back to the kitchen when Sam, the pastry chef, told her someone was waiting to see her. She entered the employees' quarters and saw a man standing there. She had never seen him before. "May I help you, sir? Forgive my appearance. I've just finished working. I'm Nora O'Sullivan."

"Allow me to introduce myself. My name is Mike Desmond, and I'm an attorney. I am here to talk to you about the trouble your brother Sean seems to have gotten himself into."

Nora realized that she hadn't actually looked at the man—she was that preoccupied—until his last statement. Her eyes widened with surprise and she asked, "How in the world do you know about my brother?"

"Well, let's just say that you and I have a mutual friend who apparently cares very much about you and wants to help. I am his attorney and he thought I might be of assistance to you if you would allow it, and, Miss O'Sullivan, I hope you will."

Nora had been terribly worried, but the sound of this stranger's voice was so kind and comforting that she could feel the tears starting, and suddenly she was crying into a big handkerchief that he offered her.

"Come now, Miss O'Sullivan," he comforted her. "I'm sorry to have made you cry."

"Oh no, you haven't made me cry. It's only because Sean needs help and here you are offering that help. I'm just grateful, because even the *Irish World* people aren't able to help him." She paused to dab her eyes. "I don't know who you are, but I think I know who sent you. I believe you are a miracle." Impulsively, Nora threw her arms around him and hugged him. Then, startled by her impetuous gesture, she backed away, embarrassed, stammering an apology. She couldn't imagine that she had done such a thing, but he was very comforting, like a big, friendly bear.

In fact, Mike Desmond was bearlike in size, and he had soft brown wavy hair parted in the middle, soft, kind brown eyes, a bushy brown mustache, and a wonderful brown tweed suit, which smelled of good tobacco and spice cologne.

In all her life, she had never met anyone who looked as solid and dependable. She motioned him to a chair and smiled as he ambled over.

"Well now, I'm glad you're smiling."

Mike Desmond was a fine, conscientious lawyer. His mind was slow but methodical, nothing escaping his careful thinking. He was not flashy, but he was doggedly painstaking and thorough. He never gave up, even when other attorneys did, and had earned a reputation for saving even the most difficult cases. Because of this reputation, he had many important clients.

He carefully explained to her what he planned to do to get Sean out of jail, and the people he would contact to try to keep his name off the records. She confided her fears, which he had already anticipated, and he asked her to trust him. He confided that there seemed to be more to the case than met the eye, and he meant to find out about it.

"Mr. Desmond, we don't have much money," she admitted, worried about his fee.

"You are not to worry about that. It's all taken care of," he explained.

Uncle Jim had heard of Mike Desmond.

"A fine lawyer," he commented. "He helped the construction workers get a fair shake. Your cousin Jerry told me about him when their union was having some bad legal problems."

"Yes, well, I believe the *Irish World* has hired him to handle Sean's case," she fibbed, silently blessing Angelo.

"Sean's in good hands, lass."

But Nora had known that instinctively, for Angelo would only have the best.

Mike Desmond seemed certain of his success. He came to see Nora frequently, and Uncle Jim and Aunt Nellie thought he was the grandest person who had ever entered their home. He liked them immensely, being a man with simple, homey tastes.

Sean, too, felt relieved at Mike's handling of his case. Mike's cautious, thorough manner impressed Sean, and gave him hope for the first time. When Rachel and Sarah next visited him, some of his color and optimism had returned.

"Ford and Brady offered to pay Mr. Desmond for my defense," Sean explained, "but he told them that wasn't necessary. I didn't understand why he didn't care about his fee, until Uncle Jim told me he's been at the house quite often. I think he's interested in Nora, Rachel."

Nora blushed. "Oh, get on with you. He just knows we don't have much money and he's very kind."

Mike put together a first-class defense for Sean. He had uncovered evidence that a group called the "America for Americans" had instigated the riot. He called several witnesses, who discredited the group, telling how its members hated all the poor immigrant groups. Apparently, "America for Americans" believed immigrants were causing all kinds of economic and social problems in America. Johnny O'Brien, with whom Sean had worked on the Telmack arson case, was of enormous help to Mike. Connelly had sent him over, knowing that O'Brien had sources that Mike might not have known about.

"That O'Brien's a wonder, Sean," Mike told him. "I thought I had all the good sources possible, but he came up with some new ones."

The trial continued for several weeks, and near the end, Mike dramatically produced a witness who had been in on the plot, but who was promised immunity if he turned state's evidence. Sean was acquitted, and the "America for Americans" group was badly discredited.

The case had made headlines, and Sean sent copies home to Terence and the family—after he had been acquitted. He hadn't wanted to worry them. Now that it was all over, Sean was proud of having been arrested, for the publicity of the trial had helped swell the funds for Irish independence.

"All's well that ends well," Sean kept repeating at the party Brady threw for his homecoming. Everyone had been invited, and Nora was grateful to Mike, the hero of the evening. Mike felt like a hero himself and enjoyed the attention he got from Nora.

Mike began to see Nora every chance he could. She was very fond of him, and life was comfortable when he was around. He didn't take her to Sherry's and Delmonico's or the races at Saratoga Springs, but he was kind and gentle, and she came to enjoy the little restaurants they went to. As she had suspected, Angelo Gambini had been the one who had sent him. She'd found this out through artful questioning.

He chuckled when he realized she'd gotten the information out of him. "Now, just who is the lawyer here, Miss O'Sullivan?" He did tell her what she wanted to know, however, plus a little more. "His daughter was with him the day he asked me to take the case. Her name is Angelina, and she's a dark, flashing Sicilian beauty. Angelo adores her."

Nora smiled. Angelo had mentioned the child. Thank God she's beautiful, she thought.

After finding out for certain that Angelo was the one who had helped Sean, she could no longer stay away. His kindness had to be acknowledged, and so she went to see him.

"Nora, Nora, what a delight!" he greeted her when she arrived. "Thank you for coming. Thank you for breaking that dreadful silence."

"Angelo, I've come to thank you for what you did for Sean. Bless you for that. Your are as dear a friend as I'll ever have."

"I want always to help you, Nora. And speaking of help, you must realize by now that you will never reopen your shop if you don't allow me to lend you the money. It will take you years. Do you want to wait that long? Be sensible. I will not hear a refusal from you, Nora, and that's final."

"You'll be hearing no refusal from me. I'm ready to admit it can't be done, at least not for ten years or so, and I don't want to waste ten years. I've wasted enough time. So, I will take the loan, and I thank you for it, Angelo. You're always there when I need you. I'll pay back every cent with interest, I promise."

Angelo had his man bring tea, and they spent the next hour sharing every thought that had passed since they had last talked. It was as if they had never parted. They were happy to be back in each other's lives again, even though it was understood that they wouldn't see each other as they once had. There was no one who could fill Angelo's place in her life. He was her father, brother, teacher and best friend, all in one.

Nora and Rachel made plans to open their new shop. They had been hunting down locations and already had Denise and Annie working at home. Nora's tips were getting larger as she received better table assignments. Angelo had been right. The big spenders wanted everyone to know how wealthy they were, and Nora benefited from this foolishness. They would flash money and big tips, for that was how success was measured.

When Nora came home from work on the Tuesday before Christmas, Mike was there talking to Aunt Nellie.

"I've just asked your aunt if I can steal you for Christmas Eve, then bring you back for Christmas Day dinner. After all, I've met your family, you've never met mine. Will you come?"

Uncle Jim and Aunt Nellie exchanged knowing smiles.

"Of course, Mike. I'd be delighted."

It was a long drive to Corona in Queens County. Mike had warned Nora to dress warmly. He had hired a hansom cab so she could see a little of the rest of New York. She was nervous, even apprehensive, but excited too. She was going to meet Mike's parents, three of his five brothers, their wives and children. Snow was falling lightly. As the farm came into view, Mike put his hand over hers.

"Mike, why do your parents live so far away from the city?" she asked.

"Nora," Mike explained, "my family wants none of the bustling crowds, the horse cars, the traffic, the tall buildings, and the horse-drawn fire engines and thundering hoofbeats as they race through the streets. They're farming people. They like their peace and quiet. But you've become a city girl with New York in your blood, haven't you?''

"I guess I have, Mike. I love all the excitement.''

"Aye, because it's still new to you. But I think you'll find you'll soon want a more placid life. Well, we're here, little one." As he helped her out of the carriage, she glanced fondly at him. His plain talk, his direct way of telling a story and his simple approach to life appealed to her. He was not an exciting mind, but at this moment in her life, Nora didn't want that. She felt comfortable and secure with him, as she would with an older brother. She would like to care for a man like this, to cook for him and bring him his slippers.

Mike looked at her with obvious pleasure. Her black hair was pulled tightly back, and a brown velvet hat with a chiffon veil tied securely under the chin in a big bow sat on the back of her head. Nora's cheeks were flushed from the cold and the snow, and her glittering violet eyes seemed full of laughter. Her long brown coat with its velvet lapels and intricate pleating was smart and fashionable.

The house was a two-story wooden frame structure, with a narrow front door, and wooden slat siding painted egg-shell white. There was a small front yard, but much acreage behind the house. A pine wreath on the door welcomed them.

A large, heavyset man with bushy white hair and eyebrows, a reddish nose and the same brown eyes as Mike opened the door.

"Meet my brother, Stephen," Mike said.

"I could tell right off, there's such a strong resemblance." Mike had told her he was the youngest of five brothers, but she was unprepared for the sixty-year-old man who welcomed her. She had thought Stephen was his father.

"Nora, 'tis a joy to meet such a lovely lass. Now

come and meet the Desmond clan. They've been waiting for you.''

She was presented to all the brothers and their wives, then the children were introduced. The young ones immediately asked if she'd like to see the cat spun around on the Victrola. She tried to say no, but they paid her no mind, and the poor animal wobbled off drunkenly. There was no sign of Mike's parents.

Suddenly the front door opened and in walked a big broad-shouldered man who appeared to be at least eighty-five years of age. He still had a full head of white hair. Now there was no doubt in Nora's mind. This was Mike's father.

Brushing the snow off his black suit, he turned to the group. ''Where in St. Patrick is she?''

Nora knew whom he meant, and she rushed over to give him her hand. ''Here I am, Mr. Desmond. Nora O'Sullivan.''

''An O'Sullivan, is it? Faith, one of my mother's sisters married an O'Sullivan, and a fine lot they were. A little too taken by drink, but fine for all that. Most died in the famine.''

At that moment, the kitchen door swung open, and out poured all the wonderful smells of roast turkey, sweet potatoes and plum pudding. Mike's mother hobbled through the doorway on a cane. She was the one Nora had been waiting for.

''Never you mind about the famine now. More and more you've been living in the past,'' the old woman scolded.

Mike's mother was thin, with steel-grey hair, brilliant and penetrating blue eyes, and a strong, uncompromising way about her. A long nose gave her an aristocratic look, which not even her country dialect could dispel. A striped apron covered her simple black dress, the only adornment being a gold cross, which hung from her neck. Nora remembered Mike saying that one of her legs was gone from the knee down, but that hardly slowed her at all.

"So, this is our young colleen, faith, and a beauty for sure. Come with me, pretty wild bird. Come and tell me all about yourself." She took Nora by the hand and led her into the parlor. She almost tripped on the cat, who was still reeling around the room, and the youngest child snatched it quickly out of her path.

Nora didn't understand what she meant by wild bird, but she liked it, and she adored Mary from the first moment, so she gladly let herself be led away. The others all drifted in behind.

They talked for a very long time in the flickering light of the gas lamps. The Christmas tree was glowing with candles, and the Victrola shivered with Caruso's voice sobbing "Pagliacci." Nora had two glasses of port and observed that most of the others were consuming a great deal of the Irish liquor.

"Grandma Desmond, tell us a story, please," one of the younger children pleaded.

But rather than recite an old folk tale, Mary Catherine Desmond told of how she and her husband and young Stephen had fled the famine, and how they had come to America, and how the family had grown. Nora's admiration for her grew with every word. Through dinner Nora asked polite questions to keep the fascinating story going, and she would have listened for hours after their meal had not the old woman's voice begun to grow weak.

The memories of such sadness and struggle had tired Mary Desmond. When Nora was about to leave a short time later, she kissed Mike's mother gently on the cheek and said, "My mother's name is Mary too, and I'm missing her."

Mary squeezed her hand and smiled.

*   *   *

A month later Nora visited Billy in Chicago. Molly and Tim filled her in on every detail of Billy's day to day life, and she could see how much they loved him. Little Retta took care of Billy, much as Nora had once taken care of Sean.

"I love it when you're here, Aunt Nora," Billy said, and hugged her. Her heart ached. "I love you. Please come and live in Chicago so Retta and I can see you all the time." He cuddled in her arms and said, "Read me a story now." But he fell asleep immediately. She sat gazing at him for a very long time, then tucked him into his crib.

"Molly, I'm wanting a baby of my own," Nora confessed.

"Nora, you'll be needing a husband first," Molly teased.

"I have one in mind, dear Molly. He's very kind and gentle. You'll like him."

Molly embraced her. "I'm so happy, Nora. We thought you would never marry. Has he asked you yet?"

"Aye. Two months from now, I shall be called Mrs. Michael Desmond."

Chapter 25

The wedding was scheduled for eleven o'clock, and it was time for Nora to get dressed. She and Rachel went into her room. Denise had made an exquisite ivory satin gown. Antique lace stood up around the collar and on the cuffs, lace Nora's mother had made. Rachel, while kneeling to arrange Nora's veil, suddenly bowed her head and tried to muffle a sob.

"Rachel, dear, why are you crying? I thought only the bride and her mother were allowed to cry on her wedding day." Nora reached down and helped Rachel to her feet.

"Oh Nora. I'm so sorry. This is your day, and here you are having to comfort me."

Nora dabbed at Rachel's cheeks with her "something new" handkerchief for which Bridget had spun the most beautiful lace, like a gossamer cobweb.

"Oh, Nora, are you sure you want to get married today? It isn't a good idea to rush these things, you know. You can still change your mind. No one would think the less of you." Rachel's words were tumbling out between agonizing sobs.

"Why, Rachel, you really are upset. Come, let's sit down here." Nora held her friend's hand and patted the fresh tears away. "I'm not rushing into this marriage, and I won't be changing my mind. We've talked about it many times, Rachel. I feel I need a husband and family. And Mike's a good man and kind to me."

"Oh, I know he's good to you. But, Nora, I can't keep it inside any longer, even if you hate me for it. I don't think he's good for you! There, I've said it. Please, I beg you, reconsider."

"Rachel, your love for me allows you to speak your mind and I'm never going to hate you, but what can possibly make you feel this way?"

"I just think you're throwing yourself away. You and Mike are so different. He'll never be able to appreciate the finest things about you. Oh, Nora, can't you see? He wants a wife to cook and clean and wait with his slippers by the door at night. He might as well get a cocker spaniel or a maid. You're so clever and quick, and your talent is going to make you a great success. But not if he—" She paused a moment to blot her tears. "I know, I just know, he'll resent you for it, and you'll never be content staying home the way he will want you to, locked in a house doing nothing but rearranging the dust!"

Fresh sobs followed this outburst, and Nora gathered Rachel to her. "I know you believe every word you've said, and you're only saying all this because you love me. But Mike loves me too, and I believe that he wants what's best for me. Oh, he's not enthusiastic that I intend to keep working, but when he sees that I can care for him and our home too, I know he'll understand how important my work is to me."

"But, you don't really love him, Nora. Wait until

you meet the right man, please. Marriage is for a lifetime."

Nora felt a stab at her heart. "I'll never love anyone
again," she whispered hoarsely. "Romantic love isn't the
most important thing. Most marriages are for convenience
of one sort or another."

"I've never known you to be so cynical." Rachel
seemed resigned. "I only hope it will work out."

"It will. Now, dry your tears. We mustn't keep everyone waiting."

Nora's comforting smile covered her own feeling of
misgiving. She had to stop mourning her child, from
whom she was parted, and bear other children she could
hold to her bosom. She believed in her heart that all the
love she could feel for a man had been given to William
years ago. What she felt for Mike was respect and affection. She reasoned that since she would never love again,
she had wisely chosen a man who would be a loving father
and a loyal and caring husband.

All of Nora's cousins, Nellie and Jim's children and
grandchildren, all of Mike's family, Sean, the Friedmans,
Molly, Tim, Billy and Retta, Denise and Annie and other
New York friends, all attended the wedding at St. Pancras
Church. As she looked around, Nora wished Angelo were
there. Besides her family in Ireland, only he was missing
from among those she loved. She had wanted to invite
Angelo, but she decided against it. After all, she reasoned,
that was a closed chapter of her life.

Nora looked radiant in the dress made of her mother's
lovely antique lace. Her hair, piled high, was covered by a
veil her mother had also made and sent. Her skin seemed
luminous; her eyes glowed. Rachel was Nora's maid of
honor. This had taken some doing since she was Jewish,
but Uncle Jim, friend of priests and bishops, had interced-

ed, and the minor miracle was accomplished in the form of a special dispensation. Rachel cried again when the vows were spoken.

The reception was held at one of the private rooms at the Waldorf, catered lovingly by Oscar, who adored Nora, his favorite banquet waitress.

"My pet, this is my gift to you," he said expansively, winking at her. "Only the best for the best."

Most of those invited had never been to the Waldorf-Astoria. The air of opulence, combined with such a sumptuous and beautiful table of delicacies, was an unusual treat. The cake, four tiers high, was decorated with roses of all colors, and the traditional statuettes of bride and groom stood precariously on top.

Everyone stood around awkwardly until the dancing began. Uncle Jim danced with Nora first, waxing very sentimental, especially after a few drinks.

"I've given you away, lass, because we love you like our own child, but I felt the solemn duty of taking your father's place. I never met your father. But you're the picture of my sister Mary. I can still see her lovely young face, even after all these years."

Seeing a tear in his eye, Nora gave him a big hug. "I'll be fine, Uncle Jim. Don't worry. You've been wonderful to us." She then added, "You'd like Pa, you would. How I wish Ma and Pa were here."

Mike cut in and they danced their first waltz. Nora began to feel that everything would turn out for the best. Mike's parents sat with Nellie and Jim, and everyone chatted and laughed as if they had known one another for years. Nora noticed how often Sean danced with Sarah, and she searched Rachel's face for some sign of emotion, but there was none. He occasionally danced with Rachel too, and Nora decided they looked wonderful together.

The Friedmans, sitting rather stiffly by themselves,

looked surprised when Uncle Jim went to their table and asked Rebecca Friedman to dance. She was delighted and seemed light as a feather as Jim spun her around the floor. Nora smiled at Uncle Jim, her eyes silently thanking him. Frank Brady, of the *Irish World*, engaged Arthur Friedman in intellectual conversation, and it was soon obvious by the volume of their talk that they enjoyed each other's company.

When Nora finally went to change into her traveling dress, Rachel followed to help.

"Nora, I'm sorry for what I said earlier. It was just a case of nerves, I suppose. You look so nice together, so happy. You'll make it work, if anyone can."

"I'll try, Rachel, I'll really try." She gave Rachel a warm embrace.

As Nora stood ready to throw the bouquet from the doorway, she spotted Rachel, closed her eyes and threw it in that direction. Sarah caught it. Nora was dismayed for a moment, but quickly recovered. Rachel just smiled her inscrutable smile.

William had had many faults, but at least he had been an accomplished lover, and Nora had worshipped him in the fervor of first love. She did not worship the man who had just turned down the covers and climbed into bed beside her. William had driven her to passion with his lingering kisses and touches, but Mike knew none of that. His experiences with the girls at Fanny's place had taught him nothing of the subtleties of lovemaking. The girls there liked Mike because he was never cruel, and he never forgot to say thank you. But they often had a good laugh over his clumsiness when he had gone. Of course, he loved Nora and wanted to make her happy, but he knew only one kind of sex.

Nora was stunned when Mike, after a short kiss or two, suddenly pulled up her nightdress, which had been so lovingly detailed by Denise, and rolled on top of her. As he forced himself inside her, she cried out in pain. After a few thrusts, he let out a cry, fell away from her, kissed her perfunctorily, saying, "Good night, sweet one. Thank you," and instantly began to snore. Nora was so horrified that she couldn't fall asleep until almost dawn. It seemed she had just dozed off when she was awakened by Mike pulling her toward him, and she sensed the whole dismal performance was to be repeated. She was dimly aware of Mike telling her how much he loved her and that he was always going to take care of her. His large hands were fumbling with her nightdress again. She tore herself away, leapt out from the covers and stood shivering by the side of the bed.

"Nora, dear, what's wrong? Come back to bed. You'll catch pneumonia out there. Nora, darling, are you crying?" Mike got out of bed and gathered her in his arms. She found herself instantly flooded with a feeling of comfort and safety. The man who a moment ago had seemed to her a frightening stranger was once more the kind person she had envisioned as a good husband and father.

As he laid her gently to bed, Mike looked confused. Nora felt a sudden fear that he might try to mount her again, but he did not. Instead, he lay down and fell into a restless sleep. She knew that he would be harder to put off next time, and poor lover or not, he was within his rights to claim her. So she sniffled and wiped the tears out of her eyes, and promised herself that she would not disappoint him again. After all, he was a good man.

When they arrived home from their honeymoon, Nora looked tired and drawn. Mike felt a vague discontent. Although she no longer resisted, she still seemed to do no more than tolerate his lovemaking. Well, perhaps that was the way with wives, Mike thought.

"You look as if you don't feel well," he said. "Come, let me feel your forehead. Maybe you have a fever."

Nora let him fuss over her a moment, then said, "I'm fine, really, I just need a good night's sleep."

"Well, you can stay in bed in the morning and catch up on your rest."

Nora gave him an impatient glance. "Mike, you know that's impossible. Rachel and Annie have been handling the painters and carpenters while I've been gone. They need my help. We're opening the shop within a few weeks. I need to choose fabrics and colors. There's much to be done."

"Now, now, let's have none of that silly talk about the shop. You're a married woman now. You have a husband to take care of you, so there's no need for you to work. No woman in the Desmond family has ever worked. You just stay in bed in the morning and get your rest."

"Don't joke about this, Mike," she said in exasperation. "I can't neglect my business any more than you can yours."

"What do you mean, your business? Your business is staying home and looking out for the needs of your husband."

"Mike, I made it clear when you proposed that I would marry you only on the condition that you would accept my working. I know you never pretended to like it, but I told you I would not give up the shop when we got married. I never deceived you about it." Nora was standing with her arms akimbo and her eyes flashing.

Mike was a peace-loving man, and he couldn't stand scenes of this sort. It was true. She had told him she was going to work, but he hadn't taken her seriously. He had reasoned that once they were married she'd change her mind and stay at home like any decent wife. All women filled themselves with strange ideas in their youth. That was natural. What was unnatural was that matrimony seemed to have no domesticating effect on this particular woman. He sensed it would do him no good to command her to stay home. She was obviously too set in her ways to obey. He felt cheated, and unmanly, and angry.

Nora was spared his clumsy lovemaking that night, but again she lay wide-eyed, regretting the quarrel and still determined to be a good wife to a man she would never love. They barely spoke as they were dressing the next morning, but as they were leaving, Nora made an effort to be pleasant, telling Mike that she would miss him, standing on tiptoe to kiss his cheek.

His face broke into a wide smile. "Nora, I love you. Do whatever you want as long as you're happy. Play with your little shop. Just don't forget you have a husband."

When Mike got home that evening, he was feeling most convivial, having hoisted a few glasses with the boys at Paddy's Tavern on his way, but when he opened the door, the house was dark and cold. What kind of homecoming was this? He angrily started a fire, jabbing furiously at the logs with the poker. By the time Nora arrived home at ten, dead tired, Mike had fortified himself with a few more drinks of Jameson whiskey. Nora listened quietly as he raved on about her neglecting her wifely duties.

"Mike, I'm sorry. We had a water leak at the shop today." She indicated her water-stained skirt. "I honestly will try to be the kind of wife you want, but my being late today simply couldn't be helped."

"Where's my dinner?" he demanded as she turned toward the bedroom.

Nora was clearly startled. "Dinner? Oh, Mike, I'm sorry, I never gave it a thought. I'll fix you something."

"Never mind, I'll just take another drink."

Mike filled his glass, and Nora's heart ached at the

look of sadness on his face. She wondered if she could ever be what he wanted her to be. She had promised herself she would try, but now she wasn't at all sure trying would be worth the trouble.

An hour later, Mike stumbled into bed. He propped himself on one elbow and looked down at his wife's sleeping form. "Nora, Nora, please love me." He felt his tears hot on his face. Nora was fast asleep.

Chapter 26

Ballygarry's reopened uptown on Madison Avenue on a brisk winter day. The girls had been delighted when they finally found this location, and at a rent they could afford. Mr. Friedman had been so impressed by Rachel and Nora's hard work and unswerving efforts to rebuild that he offered to help in whatever way he could. Only Mike's objections to Nora's working clouded the scene as everyone helped them get ready for the grand opening. Mike had made it a point never to visit the store, which saddened Nora. Annie and Denise fussed with the windows while Rachel arranged the flowers, Sean iced the champagne and Nellie checked to see that all the glasses were spotless. Nora was arranging on a silver tray the hors d'ouevres that had been provided by Oscar of the Waldorf.

The shop was not terribly large. The main room would be used as a salon to greet customers and to display merchandise. Four smaller rooms would be made into discreet fitting rooms, and a narrow space across the back would serve as a workshop.

Nora had chosen the fabrics and colors for decorating the shop herself. For the salon walls, she selected a soft celadon green that picked up the pale hues in an exquisite Aubusson rug the Friedmans had given her. The Friedmans had also offered to share their French antique furnishings. She picked the pieces with great care, always asking Rachel's opinion, though the final decisions were made by Nora. She chose a pair of small chinoiserie side chairs to flank an elegant armoire, lined in pale apricot moiré, its drawers and shelves spilling out a wealth of satins, silks and laces. There were several lovely upholstered pieces, chairs, and a settee, all with gently striped down cushions. The room was lighted by an exquisite Waterford chandelier with matching sconces on the walls. This soft, enchanting room was repeated over and over in the oblique reflections of the collection of antique convex mirrors that had been Rachel's grandmother's. The salon seemed like an understated, but perfect, jewel.

As the time drew near for guests to arrive, a carriage pulled up outside and the driver entered, carrying a large, carefully wrapped package. Nora took the note he carried for her. It said simply: "A masterpiece for a masterpiece." She quickly put the paper in her pocket. As she lifted the quilted wrapping, she drew in a sharp breath of surprise, for it was a painting by Monet that she had admired in Angelo's outer office. She gazed at it rapturously, adoring every detail.

"How incredibly beautiful," she said aloud. No one suspected who the donor might be, and out of respect for her privacy, no one asked. Everyone admired it, though, and Sean went about hanging it immediately. Nora thought how very much she missed Angelo. I shall treasure this painting as I treasure him, she thought, remembering how much he had loved it too.

Her pleasant reverie was interrupted by the arrival of

guests. The champagne bubbled, the conversation flowed, laughter filled the air. They had invited all their old clients from the small shop on Forty-fifth Street, many friends, and some well-known names from the social register whose patronage they desired. Elegant carriages and autos pulled up and discharged their elegant passengers.

Nora and Rachel's faces shone with excitement as Mr. Bloomingdale entered with Miss Fennell. He smiled and nodded approvingly. "I should never have let you two get away," he exclaimed. Miss Fennell was beaming with pride for the two young women.

As everyone was making toasts to their success, who should have swept in grandly flourishing a cape and a cane but Monsieur Jacques Mandel. Nora knew she hadn't sent him an invitation, but there he was, nodding to everyone, appraising the shop, guests, and merchandise with his cool glance and all the while carrying on a running commentary.

When Monsieur Mandel finally saw Nora, he turned and bowed extravagantly. She wanted to giggle but kept a straight face as he said most seriously, "Darling girl, I forgive you. Anyone who can create such beauty deserves to be my friend." He grandly kissed her hand. "She's my protégée, you know," he announced to the assembled group. Before she could reply, he saw Denise and turned his attention to her. "Nora was probably right. I was stupid to let you go, dear Denise. But Nora profited by my mistake, didn't she?" he asked rather wickedly.

"Aye, as have I. I now know that some employers are able to treat their employees with respect and consideration, a wonderful thing to be finding out, Mr. Mandel." She blushed as she said it, but Nora and Rachel looked at her proudly, for it had taken courage to say what she had.

Mandel shrugged off the slight and swept away, eager to speak to anyone who looked as though they could afford his services.

Several people asked about Mike, and Nora made excuses for him. She was hurt by his absence, but she knew why he had not come. He's punishing me, she thought, embarrassing me by staying away. Sean and Rachel sensed her disappointment though she tried to carry on gaily. When at last the guests began to leave, however, a taxi pulled up and Mike fell out of it. He staggered into the shop, obviously drunk. When he began to bother the remaining guests by breathing into their faces and leaning on any available shoulder, Nora squared her shoulders and marched up to him. "Mike, you made it. How wonderful!" she said between clenched teeth. She tried to lead him away from her friends.

When he began to object, Sean took over immediately, leading him to a quiet corner and engaging him, as best he could, in conversation. Sean was fond of Mike and hated to see this happen, hated to see Mike's pain and his sister's hurt made public.

Finally, when the last guest had gone, Sean helped Nora and Mike into a taxi. Nora was furious and could barely contain her anger, but remained silent until they reached home. Mike was dozing and his head kept falling on her shoulder. She led him into the guest bedroom, turned down the covers, and began to walk out.

"Why did you do that? What am I doing here? I want to sleep in my own room. What does this mean?" Mike demanded.

"I'll not share my bed with a drunkard," Nora hissed.

"I'm sorry," he replied, sarcastically, "but I always get drunk on an empty stomach. Where's my dinner? You're never here to fix me dinner. Never!"

"We've discussed all this a million times, Mike. You know how dear you are to me, but you also know how important this shop is to me. And you had no right to embarrass me that way." With that she ran out of the room crying, but Mike followed her into the bedroom, now somewhat more sober.

"Nora, Nora, God, I'm sorry. Please, let's forget it. We'll work it out." He lurched to kiss her, but she turned away, repulsed by his drunkenness. Suddenly she felt a terrible guilt. Oh God, I never should have married him, she thought. I don't love him. I'll never love him. Why did I do it? I've done him a terrible turn. I've been selfish and stupid. Why did I ever think it would work? He was so kind and strong, and I so desperately wanted a baby and the security of a husband and a home. And so, here I am, with a man who disapproves of my ambitions, my dreams. Oh, Lord, help me.

"Come, Mike. Let's get you to bed," she said softly. "We can talk tomorrow."

When he fell into bed and rolled over, snoring, Nora buried her face in her arm and cried herself to sleep.

In New York, the ruling queen of society was Mrs. Cornelius Vanderbilt, and it was this august person who, one rainy day, appeared in the doorway of the Ballygarry Shop accompanied by a small, drab secretary. Mrs. Vanderbilt was simply attired in a black wool coat with collars and cuffs of velvet. She wore a large, plain hat adorned by a single jewel of black onyx. Her black shoes, made from the finest leather, protruded from the floor-length coat. Nothing about her appearance, save her manner, gave any indication that she was head of one of the most powerful families in America. But when she left, her secretary was carrying ten boxes of Nora's most expensive items.

Nora couldn't wait to tell Rachel. Annie and Denise had eavesdropped, and after Mrs. Vanderbilt had exited, they ran out chattering wildly about what this would mean to the success of the shop.

Rachel and Nora never quite knew how, but suddenly, Mrs. Vanderbilt would wear only their creations. They designed and made everything: from her handkerchiefs, to the lace for her pillowcases, to the trim for her maid's caps. Overnight, as if by magic, they had more customers than they could have ever imagined. If you were anyone who mattered in society, your lingerie simply had to come from Ballygarry's.

Soon the shop had a talented and dedicated group of seamstresses, and many of them had previously worked for Jacques Mandel.

Rachel and Nora were fair and kind employers. Nora never forgot for a moment her sweatshop and mill days, and was scrupulous about the treatment and conditions her employees received. As a consequence, their employees were fiercely loyal to them and did work as fine as could be found anywhere in New York.

The girls were very crowded in the workroom, and when business kept expanding, they took a room upstairs that had come up for rent. They hired five more girls and almost outgrew that room before they moved into it.

Nora's success in business, however, was not matched by success in marriage. Mike had never again created such a scene as he had at the opening a year earlier, but then neither had he ever acknowledged her achievement. Whenever she tried to discuss her business, he listened politely but shared none of her joys or problems. She realized that he was embarrassed to have a wife who worked, and more and more she had come to understand that his male pride was sorely threatened by her success. He had even refused to tell his family that she worked. She tried to talk to him about it, but he refused. One evening, at one of their infrequent dinners together, he finally admitted: "I'm humiliated about your working. What will my family think?

I'll tell you. They'll think I can't afford to maintain a household."

Nora saw the hopelessness of the situation and her guilt grew proportionately. "Mike, no one in your family would be so silly. I know your mother wouldn't. Why, a spirited woman such as she would probably think it was wonderful. Won't you please let me tell them? It is ridiculous for me to have to pretend the way I do when we see them."

"No, damnit!" he shouted, tossing his napkin on the table. "You are not to tell them you're working, is that clear?"

"Yes, it's clear, Mike, but it's also stupid. They'll find out one of these days," she answered angrily.

Mike stormed out of the house, slamming the door behind him. Nora knew he was going to the local saloon. Let him go, Nora told herself. She hadn't the heart to deny him even that.

Nora began to expand her social life. Mike didn't like to eat out, and he didn't care for the opera, ballet or theater, so she would go with Sean or Rachel or some other friend. She loved the opera especially. She went as often as she could, sometimes even alone. One evening at a performance of *La Bohème*, during intermission, she met Mrs. Trent-Williams, a handsome socialite widow who was a regular client of Ballygarry's. They chatted amiably. Mrs. Williams was delighted to find out about Nora's interest in opera.

"Where are you sitting, Mrs. Desmond?" She peered in the direction Nora pointed. "Why, you can't see or hear well from there. Why don't you get a box, dear girl? You must, if you come to the opera that often and like it that well."

"I honestly haven't thought about it."

As they parted, Mrs. Trent-Williams turned to her.

"If you're interested in the box, I'll be happy to do what I can about your membership."

Nora thanked her and decided to act on her suggestion. She applied for a box, and waited anxiously for several weeks, but finally, word came that she had been turned down by the committee. When Mike arrived home, she was sitting disconsolately in the living room.

"What's wrong, Nora?"

"Oh, Mike, I'm so disappointed. We've been turned down for a box at the Met. Mrs. Williams seemed so certain I'd be approved. I can't understand what happened."

"What happened, dear girl, is what happens all the time. The Metropolitan Opera Association is a bastion of high society, and Protestant society at that. Why would they allow an Irish Catholic shop girl into one of their boxes?"

"I see," Nora sat quietly. "I guess I hadn't thought of that."

"Well, it's a fact of life, Nora. You might as well get used to it. We're Irish. We can't belong to any of the country clubs. We can't have a box at the opera or the horse show."

When he mentioned the horse show, she paled. A rush of memories invaded her mind. The Dublin show seemed eons away, and so did the discrimination she had suffered through. But it wasn't much different here. We can earn money here, she thought bitterly, but we can't earn social acceptance.

"Cheer up, Nora," Mike prattled on. "While you may not own a box, still you're not kept out. If you've the money for a ticket, you are free to go. Of course, I can't imagine why you want to for the life of me. Opera's so damned boring." Mike picked up his newspaper.

Nora stared at him silently.

*   *   *

Sean had just been made an associate editor of the *Irish World*. His columns had become quite famous, and he had a loyal following. Today, at lunch with Nora, he was looking very debonair.

She smiled at him. "Baby brother, you look so handsome. Success agrees with you. I only wish Ma and Pa could see you. And Terence. How proud he is of you and your work. He says so in every letter. I'm proud of you too, Sean, sure, and I am," she said in a heavy brogue. They laughed. "But don't waste all your efforts on work, Sean. Make some time for the ladies. It would be a shame to let those blue eyes go unappreciated."

Sean blushed, averted his eyes, then said, "Nora, I think I'm in love."

She drew in a sharp breath. "With whom?"

"Can't you guess? With charming, delightful Sarah."

Her heart sank. First, flamboyant Fiona, and now, little childlike Sarah. Why not Rachel? Why isn't it ever Rachel? She tried to keep the disappointment out of her voice. "How do her parents feel about your seeing her?"

"Not good, Nora. They have never liked my being Irish, and, of course, Catholic. But she is so precious, and I love her dearly."

"Sean, please think about this carefully. She's such a child, and her parents not approving will make matters very difficult for both of you." Nora could see that none of this mattered to him, but she loved Sean and was bound to warn him. She wondered to herself if Rachel suspected how serious his attentions for her younger sister were.

As they rose to leave, Nora felt suddenly dizzy and had to sit down again. Sean was alarmed.

"You should see a doctor, right away."

"I'm all right. I think I've just been working too hard. A good night's sleep and I'll be fine. As a matter of fact, I may go home right now. Get me a cab, Sean, please.''

For several days, Nora had been waking up feeling terribly nauseated. She could barely climb out of bed. She remembered how she had felt when carrying Billy. Billy, darling Billy. Her thoughts strayed to her son. She was planning on visiting Chicago soon. She missed him so.

The doctor confirmed that she was pregnant.

''Oh, that's wonderful, Dr. Quinlan. Mike will be so happy.''

All the way home, she thought how the baby would change her marriage. Life with her husband would be better between them now, and she felt at peace with the world for the first time in many months.

Mike was thrilled beyond words. He seemed like his old self and insisted that they dine out. He even asked about Ballygarry's in an interested way, but ended the conversation saying, ''Of course, I don't know how you'll manage to care for a child if you're to continue working.''

Several weeks later, she received a letter from the Metropolitan Opera Association saying that they had reconsidered her application since a box had become available, and she had been approved for membership. She couldn't believe her eyes. What had changed their minds? she wondered. She was still Irish, and she was still Catholic, and she was not one of the very wealthy.

When Mike arrived home, she ran into his arms, telling him the news. He was genuinely pleased for her, but as puzzled as she. ''Maybe they don't know you're Irish. Or maybe they are becoming more liberal in their policies. Never mind, Nora, just enjoy your box.''

''I will, I will! As a matter of fact, *La Bohème* plays

tomorrow evening. Will you go with me?'' she asked excitedly.

''Nora, I told you yesterday I have the Hibernian dinner tomorrow.'' They had been getting on so well, and while he didn't want to break this truce, he was glad to have a legitimate excuse for not going.

''Of course,'' she said stiffly. ''I should have remembered.''

As she entered the box, looking radiantly lovely in her peach velvet gown, she glanced around. The sight never failed to thrill her. Though the exterior of the Metropolitan Opera House was ugly and unimposing, the interior was splendid. Massive chandeliers, heavy red velvet drapes, and beautiful gilt carvings and moldings made it look like a Renaissance palace. Her box was in the top tier, not as socially important as the lowest, but it had its advantages, one of which was being able to survey the entire scene without straining one's neck. People were staring at her, for not only was she a newcomer, but a very beautiful one. Women gossiped behind their fans, and men gave her appraising glances.

As she looked over the crowd, she suddenly saw Angelo. Their eyes met, and he bowed. She nodded. So it was he who had helped her get a box. While he had taken her to the opera a few times, he hadn't owned a box then. She hadn't thought of his being the one who had managed this miracle. She had mistakenly assumed that Mrs. Trent-Williams had been the instrument of her acceptance. Grateful, she flashed him a dazzling smile. Bless you Angelo, she thought, and settled back to enjoy the production.

A few days later, when she was telling Sean about the evening, he looked fondly at her. ''Good, Nora, good. Someone in that world of wealth likes you, that's certain.''

"Yes, Sean, and surprisingly enough, I think there's more than one. It was obviously Angelo who had the final word, but Mrs. Williams had already suggested me for membership. She knows I'm Irish and doesn't seem to care. As a matter of fact, she has invited me to one of her salons. I can't wait to attend. She has these fabulous afternoon teas to which artists, writers and people of the theater are invited. She told me to bring an escort if I wished. Would you come with me?" She was quite breathless.

"But, Nora, what about Mike?"

"I've asked him, like the dutiful wife I'm trying to be, and he made some excuse or other. He's uncomfortable in that sort of environment."

"Well then, Nora, I'm yours."

"Good, pick me up Sunday at one-thirty."

Nora was still able to camouflage her pregnancy, and she made a sensation in a tailored suit of bright lavender. Her stunning black hair was swept back into a chignon. When they arrived at Mrs. Williams', there was already a crowd there. People were mingling. One group was listening with rapt attention to a poet reading his latest work. Another group was having a rather heated political discussion, and still another was discussing the merits of the impressionist painters. When Nora introduced Sean, she made certain to mention his position on the *Irish World*. Mrs. Williams was obviously pleased with his credentials, and she swept him off, introducing him to a group of writers. Then Mrs. Trent-Williams approached Nora.

"My dear, you are lovely, and thank you for your thoughtful gift to me. You needn't have done that, but I adore the exquisite petticoat. I enjoyed proposing you for opera membership, you know. Heaven knows, we needed some spark, some zest in that fusty atmosphere, and you, my dear, have provided it." She smiled tantalizingly, as if she were about to reveal a delicious secret. "I was so disappointed when at first you were refused membership, but then suddenly, mysteriously, everything turned about." She looked slyly at Nora. "You obviously have friends in high places."

Nora returned a glance just as sly and answered, "Oh, Mrs. Williams, I do hope so."

Mrs. Williams threw her head back and laughed. "You're a clever one. And Nora, please call me Caroline."

Caroline and Nora chatted for some time. Finally, she confronted Nora directly. "I'm interested in you. You're beautiful and have great style. You're a successful businesswoman, and becoming more successful by the day. And," she added, smiling wryly, "you obviously have important friends. I sense, however, that you're not quite satisfied with your life. I think you need to engage that mind of yours in more than business and opera. Every intelligent woman needs a cause, don't you agree?" Her eyes were searching Nora's.

Nora found all this intriguing. This lovely, mature woman, with golden, upswept hair, aquamarine eyes and a tall, imposing bearing, was whisking Nora into another life, of that she was sure. What that life was she didn't know, but at this moment in time, she believed she would follow Caroline wherever she led.

"Yes, I do agree, but my life has been so busy with my business and my new marriage that I've just begun to look around me."

"Yes, dear, and you are young, too, but it's time for you to become involved. We are living in interesting times, times in which there are many battles to be fought and won." Her eyes moved to the door. "We'll talk more later. I must see to some new guests now, but I want you to meet Belle Moskowitz, Wanda De Young, Frances

Perkins. I think you'll find them stimulating. Come.''
Taking Nora's arm, Caroline led her to a group of men and
women animatedly debating women's suffrage. Nora became immediately absorbed in what they were saying. It
reminded her of the days in Lowell when Annie had
introduced her to union men and women who were fighting for the rights of the downtrodden immigrant workers.

Nora understood now that Caroline wanted her to
become involved in the struggle for women's rights. The
idea appealed to her, but she wanted to think it over. She
heard that afternoon how dedicated these people were and
how hard they worked for their cause. They had all been
delighted when they learned that Nora had initiated the
fifty-hour work week before it became law, and that now
her seamstresses were working only forty-seven hours a
week. When Nora and Sean were leaving, Nora asked
Caroline how she had known about her work policies.

Caroline smiled and replied, "I made it a point to
find out about you. I would never have sponsored you for
the Metropolitan, my dear, without having known something that significant about your character."

Nora took the handsome woman's hand. "Caroline,
this has been one of the most interesting afternoons of my
life. I feel my education is just beginning."

Caroline gazed back at her steadily and replied, "It
is, my dear. But I know you'll learn quickly."

Chapter 27

Two days later Nora's doorbell rang. Sean stood there red-eyed and mournful.

"Good God, Sean, what is it?"

He stumbled in. "This." He thrust a letter into her hand. "I guess Danny sent it to me so you wouldn't receive it while you were alone, in your condition." He started to cry. She sat down. Her hands shook as she read the letter.

Dearest Nora and Sean,

If only we were together instead of an ocean apart, somehow I think what I have to tell you might be less painful. There is no easy way to say this, but I must tell you that there has been a terrible tragedy. Kevin is dead and Seamus and Terence have disappeared. Kevin's body, cruelly mutilated, was dumped on his own doorstep yesterday morning. Fortunately, Bridget was not the one to discover him there, but of course she is brokenhearted. Because Terence and Seamus have not been found, we pray to God they are alive and in hiding.

I can hear your question: How did it happen? We know very little, I'm sorry to tell you. We are aware only that there was a secret meeting, that they were betrayed, that Kevin was taken prisoner and ultimately killed.

Our mother is doing what she can to console Bridget, and to care for Pa, who was ill when we received this terrible news and has worsened every day since. I don't know how Ma bears up as she does. She is frantically worried about Terence and Seamus. Monsignor has allowed me to come and stay here at home for as long as I feel I can be of use.

Frankly, I worry most about Bridget. We can only, with great effort, persuade her to eat or drink. Dr. Callaghan has been stopping by each day to see Pa and to check on Bridget. He assures us that because she is young and strong, in time she will recover. He is not so optimistic about Pa, who just seems tired of living. He has always worked so hard, it seems as if he is simply worn out.

I have discussed at length with Ma the idea of Bridget coming to America, and we both feel this would be best for her. Everything here is too painful a reminder of Kevin. I know that you will welcome her in all love, so as soon as we feel that she is strong enough to travel, I shall book her passage. I implore our Lord Jesus to keep Terence and Seamus safe in his care, and I shall get word to you the moment we have news of them.

Please know that you are in my prayers
many times a day. We are separated by distance,
but our love keeps us close.

Your brother in Christ,
Danny

Nora dissolved in sobs, clinging to Sean, who also
wept. "Dear God, please let our Terence and Seamus be
all right," she cried. "How dear Bridget must be suffering."

"Thank God she's coming to America," Sean said.
"We'll take care of her, you and I."

"We'll all take care of each other, won't we, Sean?"

"Aye, that we will. You, me, Bridget, and Sarah."

Sarah? Nora thought with sudden annoyance. What
has she to do with us, with our tragedy? Rachel was
obviously the girl for Sean, not little Sarah. And anyway,
this was a matter for family, not outsiders.

Apparently Sean read her thoughts in the expression
on her face. "I hope to make Sarah my bride," he said.

Chapter 28

Several weeks later, while Nora and Mike were having dinner, Sean burst in, obviously upset.

"I'm sorry, Mike, but may I please speak to Nora?"

"Sure, Sean," Mike said.

Nora had barely shut the library door when Sean blurted out, "I asked the Friedmans for Sarah's hand in marriage. I told them I was making good money, that I had prospects for the future and that we love each other. They told me to leave. They kept saying it would never work."

"Sean, calm down. Take your time. They may need to get used to the idea. A mixed marriage probably frightens them."

"It's more than that, Nora. It's like they think I'm some kind of criminal."

Though Nora was secretly relieved that Sarah's parents had forbidden him to see her, she felt great sympathy for Sean. "It will all work out I'm sure," she told him.

"We love each other so very much, Nora. She needs me."

So perhaps that was it, Nora reflected. Fiona hadn't needed him, but this sweet young girl did. She was eliciting in him all those urges to protect that men seemed to come by naturally. And she was pretty and easy to be with and so accommodating. The thought of her made Nora suddenly impatient. "Sean, Sarah is a fine girl and we all love her, but she is still very young. You are asking her to take upon herself a responsibility for which she may not be ready."

"Oh, Nora, you just don't understand. Perhaps you don't want to. I don't know why you're all against us. We're in love. We want to be together."

"All I can advise, brother, is that you allow yourself a little time to think all this over," Nora pleaded. She reached for his hand.

He pulled his hand away. "If I can't gain your support, Sarah and I will work this out ourselves." He left the house angrily.

Nora slumped heavily into the chair. At that moment, the baby kicked. A tired smile appeared on her face. Life always seemed to provide small compensations that made the difficult moments worthwhile. "Mike," she called, "come and feel your child. It's kicking."

Nora's body grew heavier and slower, but despite her condition she went to the shop every day. Rachel and Annie suggested that she rest now, but her spirit was too excited, and work kept her mind occupied. Mike had hoped she would abandon the shop soon after she became pregnant, and he still gently pleaded with her to stop, but he was smart enough not to force the issue and ruin the happiness that had slowly come to touch their lives.

In preparation for the baby's arrival, Mike and Nora

moved to a larger flat in a fashionable uptown neighborhood. Nora loved the place, which was quite close to the shop, and she threw herself into decorating it. She was hanging pictures on the parlor wall one evening when the doorbell rang.

"Whoever can that be at this time of night?" she said.

She heard Mike going to the front door. It was a telegram. Her heart raced with anxiety. Please God, she prayed, let nothing be wrong at home. They were expecting Bridget's arrival within the next few weeks, and she had been fearing that Bridget would decide not to come. Mike, looking troubled, handed her the message.

"It's all right, Nora. No one's ill," he quickly reassured her.

She grabbed the telegram from him and read it. SARAH AND I WED THIS AFTERNOON STOP WE ARE ON HOMEYMOON STOP PLEASE BE HAPPY FOR US STOP SEAN.

"Oh, Mike, they've eloped. I shouldn't be surprised. Sean was so determined. I only wish I could be happy about it." She sat, silently thinking for a few moments, then was struck by a thought. The Friedmans had probably received a telegram too. "Poor Rachel. Oh, Mike, I've got to get over there. Will you take me? Please. I must see her."

When they arrived at the Dakota, Nora told Mike not to worry, that she would be home in the morning.

Mrs. Friedman, disheveled and crying, opened the door. Nora put her arms about the older woman's shaking shoulders. "I'm so sorry," Nora said. "But you must believe that my brother will take good care of her."

Mrs. Friedman nodded. "I know, I know. But Rachel's taking it so hard, Nora, and I don't know why."

"I'll talk to her."

She opened the door to Rachel's room and saw her

lying across the bed in a posture of despair. Nora gathered her friend into her own arms and tried to wipe away her tears. "I know how it feels. There is nothing worse on earth," Nora said in a comforting voice.

"Oh Nora, I feel as if I had lost him to death. He had never given me any reason to hope, but I hoped anyway. I couldn't help myself. I've never loved anyone the way I loved Sean, and I never will," she cried.

"Please, dear Rachel, grieve if you must, but you must promise me not to close your heart to love. I've done that, and I know it's wrong." Her voice was almost desperate.

Rachel looked up at her through tear-filled eyes. "Nora, what should I do? It might not be so bad if she weren't my own sister, but I'll have to see them and pretend I'm happy for them. What will I do?"

"What you'll do is put your chin up and go on with your life. Somehow one lives through it. Just don't cut yourself off from love," Nora warned.

Rachel saw the worried look etched across Nora's face and knew that Nora was speaking from experience. She put her head on Nora's bosom and lay sobbing in her arms.

Two weeks later, with Aunt Nellie acting as midwife, Nora delivered a healthy baby girl with Mike's chestnut hair and Nora's violet eyes. They named her Mary after both their mothers. Her bedroom was full of flowers, and everyone came to see her, Sean and Sarah being among the first. Nora was pleased to see how happy they seemed together, and hoped with all her heart that the marriage would work.

When Rachel came, she told Nora of her parents' decision to close their hearts and home to Sarah and Sean.

"Maybe with time they'll soften," Nora suggested.

"It's possible, I suppose, but not likely."

Nora admired how Rachel had handled her heartbreak, and no one except Nora knew how much strength it had taken.

Annie bustled in with flowers from all the girls at the shop, and the most gorgeous peach satin peignoir, embroidered with a piece of Mary's old lace that Annie had found in Nora's black trunk.

"Annie, how beautiful! It's Denise's finest sewing. And my mother's lace. You darling! You knew this was the perfect time to use it. Bless you, and thank everyone."

Bridget arrived two weeks later. Nora had insisted that she travel cabin class. There was no need to send anyone steerage now. She shuddered as she thought of those awful days on the ship coming to America.

When at last Bridget was in her sister's arms, they both shed tears of grief over Kevin's death and of joy at being reunited. After Nora had held her tightly for several long minutes, she released Bridget and stood back to look at her. "You look wonderful, dearest Bridget."

The contrast in their appearance was startling. Nora had always been the beauty of the two, and her loveliness was accentuated by her fashionable hair style, her black tressed gathered up in a loose pouf and her slim figure encased in a stunning purple gown by Worth. Amethysts adorned her throat and ears. Nora bore no resemblance to the girl she had been when she left Ireland. But now, looking at Bridget, Nora was reminded of how she herself must have looked when she had arrived in America. Everything about Bridget was rural and sturdy. Her black leather shoes, heavy stockings and coarse brown dress, even her folded hands and face peeking out of a black lace shawl, were weathered and rough. It was as if they had been born in different worlds.

The journey seemed to have been a tonic for Bridget. People had been kind and pleasant to her, and being away from familiar places full of memories had eased her pain. While a sadness was present in her eyes, she was bearing up better than Nora had expected.

"Faith, Nora, 'tis beautiful here," she exclaimed enthusiastically. "Our own cottage has had many new repairs, an addition, and Ma found some grand pieces of furniture at the country auctions, but it's still just an old Irish country cottage. Since we've become so rich," she giggled. "Wouldn't Ma love to be seeing this? 'Tis beyond belief." She hugged Nora warmly.

As the sisters chatted, the enormous differences between them began to surface. Nora spoke of the ballet, of opera and theater, of social and political causes. Bridget was fast becoming awed by her younger sister, and she grew quieter by the minute.

Nora suddenly realized what was happening and hugged her. "Oh, Bridget, I'm sorry. Here I am chattering away, when you must be exhausted. Come, let's go to your room so you can have a nice hot bath. Afterward, I'll tuck you into bed and we can chat all we want."

It wasn't until she climbed into scented linen sheets with some of her very own lace decorating them that she realized in surprise, that instead of someone bringing hot water for her bath, it had come right out of the wall through a pipe!

"Nora, you just turned the handle, and there it was! 'Tis a grand house you have, with a fine husband and beautiful baby. I think you're the luckiest girl in the world!"

"Oh, Bridget, I want you to have a wonderful life too. I'm so happy to see you again. We'll have such good times. And, as soon as I'm strong enough, we'll go

to choose new clothes for your life in your new country."
While Nora was talking, she was also rubbing all kinds of
lotions and creams with marvelous fragrances over Bridget's
weathered skin.

"I feel like a princess," Bridget laughed.

"You are, dear girl. You are."

Bridget hadn't much time those first few weeks to
lose herself in the despair she had felt since Kevin's death.
She met Aunt Nellie and Uncle Jim and all her cousins,
talked hours and hours with Nora and Sean, loved Sarah,
adored Mike, and worshipped baby Mary. Nora was
delighted, not only because she would have her sister
nearby after so long a time, but also because there was
now someone to help with the baby.

Mike found her simplicity utterly entrancing and welcomed her to their home warmly and graciously. How
different these two sisters were, he thought. Yet there was
something alike about them, not so much in looks, but in
spirit. He sensed the same indomitable determination in
Bridget as in Nora, but it manifested itself in quite a
different way. Bridget reminded him more of his own
mother.

Not long after Bridget's arrival, Nora was up and
dressed when Mike was ready to leave for work. He
became curious. "Why are you up and dressed so early?"

As Nora pulled on her gloves, she said firmly, "I'm
going in to the shop for a few hours this morning."

Mike looked as if she had struck him. "You can't be
serious! Nora, have you lost your mind? You have a baby
now. Mary needs you. Do you know you're a nursing
mother? And your place is here at home taking care of her
and me. I won't hear of your returning to the shop this
morning, or any other morning. I won't allow it!" He
stood between Nora and the door, blocking her way. "I

thought you were going to take hold of your senses after Mary was born, that you would sell your interest in the shop and retire. What you're doing isn't natural. Why, it's immoral,'' he sputtered.

Nora tried to stay calm. She had hoped this wouldn't happen, but she wasn't surprised that it did. Mike had been behaving well because of her pregnancy and had bided his time, hoping she would want to stay at home once she had a taste of motherhood. How little he had come to know her, she thought sadly. ''Mike, please, it's unfair of you to try to make me feel guilty. I never promised you I wouldn't return to work. I've spent all these years struggling to achieve what I have, and I have no intention of giving that all up. Could you give up your own work so easily? Besides, the shop is a success. Business is getting better daily and it brings in extra money. I've met all kinds of interesting and dedicated people through the shop. It's my life. It's what I've always wanted. I had hoped you would see that and want it for me too. I don't know what else to say to you,'' she sighed resignedly.

''Why don't you say you love little Mary and want her to grow up having a mother? Why don't you say you want your husband to be happy, even show some interest in his work?''

''For God's sake, Mike, I adore our child, and she'll have the best mother in the world. My going to work is not the test of that. Do you consider that she's growing up without a father because you're at work all day?''

''That's different,'' he countered. ''That's what a man is supposed to do.''

''For a brilliant lawyer, your logic seems to lapse into stupidity quite easily. As for making my husband happy, how about my husband trying to make me happy? Are women only born to serve men?'' she asked, remembering words Mrs. Moskowitz had used at one of Caroline's gatherings. Nora was seething. All of the issues she had heard discussed by Belle Moskowitz, Caroline, Mrs. Perkins and some of the others were becoming very real to her now. It was not just an abstract cause to occupy one's free time, but a very real problem that had to be dealt with.

"I won't have a wife of mine working, and that's final," he stubbornly insisted. "It looks to the world like I can't afford to keep a family. It casts doubt on my abilities."

She shook her head sadly. "Mike, please be sensible. All anyone might think is that I'm a little daft. Furthermore, who cares what people think?"

"I care, I care," he said vehemently. "Isn't that enough for you? We can give up the box at the opera, do without some of your crazy friends and notions, fine apartments and expensive furniture and the like. We can live very nicely on my income without adding yours to the pot. Your place is here with your child."

She was very angry now. He's a narrow-minded, hard-headed man who means to have his way, she thought, no matter what. She was tired—tired of this endless argument, tired of it all. "I'm sorry you feel this way, Mike." She looked at him as coldly as an empress and continued in icy tones, "I'm not giving up my box at the opera, or my apartment, or my friends. Most important, I'm not giving up the shop. You obviously resent my success. I'm sorry for you if that's true, but I'll be a good wife and mother, no doubt a better wife and mother than if I were forced to give up what I've worked so hard for, dreamed of all these years." She sighed. "Mike, please move out of my way. I'm not abandoning my child forever. I'm just going to oversee my business for a few hours. I intend to be home for the noon feeding." He did not move. She put her hands on his shoulders. "Mike, just because my work is important to me, it doesn't mean I love you less. Let's don't quarrel. Everything's going to be fine, I promise you." She didn't want to leave in anger, despite everything, so she kissed him on the cheek and went out, leaving him to stare in misery after her.

Damn her, he thought. He walked over to the bar and poured himself a whiskey.

Bridget had heard the argument and sat nervously in her bedroom. From her arrival she had sensed tension in the house, but hadn't really understood until now what was wrong. She picked little Mary up and hugged her close. "I'll care for you, little darling. Don't you fret."

When Nora came home to feed the baby, her sister was singing with joy, rocking little Mary. After the feeding, Bridget held the baby deftly, putting her over her shoulder and patting her, while Nora told her excitedly of all the wonderful things happening at the shop.

"Why don't you go back this afternoon for a while. I'll take care of the little one. We'll be just fine."

"Oh, Bridget, thank you. You're so good to me, so understanding. Now I can finish my new designs." In a flurry, she was gone.

When Mike came home, the most wonderful aroma greeted him. The house was ablaze with light, and a fire was burning. There were fresh flowers and polished apples in a bowl on the table. He followed the delicious smell to the kitchen, and there he found Bridget, her cheeks flushed pink with pleasure as she leaned over the baby in the cradle. Mary was cooing in contentment. Mike stood in the doorway, touched by the tender scene. For the first time in months he felt a sense of balance, of rightness in his life. As he sat down to the wonderful meal of beef and boiled potatoes Bridget had prepared, she tucked a napkin under his chin.

This is more like a proper homecoming for a man after a day's work, he thought.

This was Bridget's way of bringing peace to a house badly in need of it, for as she judged the situation, both Nora and Mike were in need of a gentle, balancing hand.

A few evenings later Nora was attending the opera. The atmosphere in the house was still strained despite Bridget's gifts as a homemaker, and though Mike and Nora were coolly polite to each other, nothing had been resolved.

Bridget was crocheting a beautiful piece of intricate rose point lace for a special wedding trousseau commission, and Mike was sitting by the hearth, smoking his pipe and drinking his Irish whiskey.

"Mike," she said cautiously, "I'm wanting to talk to you. I heard most of your argument the other morning, so I know you've a problem here. Would you mind my discussing it with you? Maybe I can be helping. Lord knows, I've known my sister longer than you."

Mike looked away, a bit embarrassed, but found that he did indeed want to discuss it with someone. "No, Bridget. I don't mind."

"Well, Nora's an independent woman, Mike. I guess you're already knowing that. She always has been. If there was something Nora wanted, she always found a way to get it, believe me. She has strong feelings and was never satisfied with the ordinary pursuits the rest of us took for granted. She's plucky and determined, and I always admired that in her. She never cared much for girls' tasks. She'd always be off with Terence or Danny or to some horse show or other. And if what she wanted took money, she was willing to work hard to get it."

"Bridget, I can't help how I feel. It's different here. Women with some social station are not supposed to go out and work like men. They're supposed to take care of their homes and husbands and children."

"Aye, Mike, but you've had a fair chance to see how stubborn Nora is. Always has been."

"I think she'll come around, Bridget. She'll see that I'm right. I'll be patient."

"Didn't you two talk at all before you were married? Did she tell you she'd give up her business?"

"Well, no, but I always figured she would come to her senses."

"I see," Bridget answered slowly. "Mike, you're both such nice people. It would be a shame to go on so unhappily. You love each other. Why not try to compromise?"

Mike gave her suggestion a moment's thought. "Well, maybe. We'll see. Thank you, Bridget, for listening to me. You're a fine girl. You've brought some badly needed peace and order to this house."

Bridget blushed. "Thank you, Mike. I want to help, and the work helps me keep my mind off of Kevin. I miss him so." A tear shimmered in her eye. "If I hadn't insisted we move to Cork, maybe he'd be alive today. Oh Mike, I keep thinking it was my fault. I knew he'd be making more money there, so we'd have a nest egg that would pay our way to America. All he wanted to do was to stay at Lord Anthony's and tend the horses. And for us to have a good life together."

"Don't think that way, girl. God meant it to be. It wasn't your fault," Mike said paternally. "There, there." He put a comforting arm about her shoulder. "You were lucky to have had those years of happiness. Some people never even have that."

"Aye, I suppose that's true. Mike, I never asked how he died. If he suffered, I didn't want to know. Is that awful?"

"No, lass. Remember him as he was, as you were together. Don't put yourself through agonies like that."

As she fell asleep that night, she thought how very wise Mike was in some ways and what a dunce he was in others.

Chapter 29

Nora and Rachel had noticed that even though most of their clients were wealthy or famous, there would appear now and then a shop girl, an office worker, or a middle class woman looking for a gift. As a result, Nora designed a charming, relatively inexpensive petticoat with machine-made lace, an affordable purchase for a woman of limited funds. The shop made no money on the item, but Nora wanted to do this, and Rachel, as usual, indulged Nora in her concern for working girls.

One afternoon Nora asked Rachel to come into her office to chat.

"Rachel, I remember some years ago when Aunt Nellie wouldn't take money for my room and board, saying all she would like was a peignoir set like one I had designed for Jacques Mandel. I made it for her and presented it to her at Christmas. Well, she couldn't have been more pleased had it been a diamond necklace. She has nothing else like it, and probably never will." Nora seemed to lose her train of thought.

Rachel waited a moment or two for Nora to continue, then finally broke the silence. "Nora, that was a lovely gift. I remember when you made it. But may I ask if there is more to the story?"

"Good heavens! I'm sorry. I was so engrossed in a new idea that I forgot what I was saying. Well, in a way there is more to the story. Do you know *why* Nellie has nothing else like that peignoir?"

"Well, I suppose because it's so expensive," Rachel replied.

"Exactly. For women of modest means there is precious little in the stores that is both within their price range and beautiful as well. Lingerie in the department stores or specialty shops is usually either shoddy or severely functional. These women want something beautiful, Rachel, and they should be able to find it at a price they can afford."

"Nora, you're right about that. What are you thinking?" she asked, already getting the point.

"I'm thinking we'll design a line of pretty lingerie at an affordable price." Nora rose from her desk decisively.

"Nora, I've always gone along with your ideas, but this isn't the sort of shop that carries that kind of merchandise. I hate to say this, but it would hurt our other business. Mrs. Vanderbilt is not going to shop where working girls do. Those special petticoats in our window make me nervous enough."

"Rachel, dear, I don't mean to sell it here. It should be sold where those women normally shop—the big department stores like Bloomingdale's here or Marshall Field's in Chicago or John Wanamaker's in Philadelphia. Don't you see? There's a need. We've already seen that here at Ballygarry's. Do you know how much courage it takes for those women to enter a shop like this? Yet they're willing to do it, for we have an item that's both attractive and affordable.''

"Nora, you're a visionary. I worry about that. But you may have a point. I suppose you want me to figure out how, financially, we can carry this off." Rachel smiled.

"Now you're getting the idea." They laughed. "I already have some ideas, Rachel, and I'm going to start working them up immediately."

First stop on Nora's selling agenda was, of course, Bloomingdale's. Old Lyman Bloomingdale had died, and the store was being run by his sons. When Samuel saw her, he immediately called for the lingerie buyer, who could barely contain her excitement. At first they placed a modest order of thirty pieces to see how it would sell.

When Nora returned to the shop with the good news, Rachel insisted they break open a bottle of champagne.

Denise stood with her hand on her hips. "Well, you've done it at last, Nora. You've finally designed something that even I can afford."

Nora invited Rachel, Sarah and Sean for dinner. Bridget made a huge pot of Irish stew, and Nora planned to tell them over their meal about her new business venture. That way, Mike, whom she also had not yet informed, would at least have to pretend to be pleasant.

Sarah and Sean were blissfully happy, that was plain to see. He was attentive and deferential, and if a subject was discussed that Sarah didn't understand, he would patiently explain it to her. For her own part, Sarah was constantly chirping away about trivial things, but in such a pleasant manner that everyone enjoyed her company. Nevertheless, Nora couldn't help feeling a twinge of regret for Rachel.

Bridget and Sarah had become fast friends, and together they often took little Mary to the park or window-shopping. The only cloud on the newly married couple's horizon was the unyielding attitude of Sarah's parents. Rachel had recently told Nora that their names were not even allowed to pass anyone's lips at the Friedman house.

Before dinner, Sarah took Rachel aside and asked if her father's attitude was softening at all. She couldn't imagine that her beloved parents would do this to her, that they, who had given her everything she had ever wanted, would now refuse to give her even their love. She brushed a tear away. "I guess I just don't understand what is so terrible about what we did," she said to her sister. "Sean is a wonderful person."

Rachel couldn't shake her own sadness. She had never told anyone that the Friedmans, when Sarah married, had sat shiva, a ritual performed by Jews when someone dies.

But for those few moments, the evening was going well. Everyone's spirits were high, even Sarah's. Sean told of an offer he had had from the Hearst papers.

"Much as I love the *Irish World*, it is a small newspaper with a limited circulation. The Hearst papers reach an immense audience, and they've promised I could write the same sort of column I've been doing. Of course, my salary would be doubled. It's a hard offer to turn down. What do you think, Mike?"

"It sounds like a good offer, Sean, but I'd be wary about whether they'll really allow you to write the same caliber of column on the controversial subjects. They reach a different audience, so in their enthusiasm to hire you, they may be promising things that will not be possible. I don't know how to advise you, but I think that you should be aware of the dangers of the situation."

"Rachel and I have some good news too," Nora said. "You tell them, Rachel."

Rachel eagerly told them about their new low-priced line and their first order from Bloomingdale's. Everyone congratulated them, but Mike, who looked miserable and sat in silence.

Sarah stood up, her glass in her hand. "I'd like to propose a toast. First, to my darling Sean and his new job offer. Even if he doesn't take it, it's flattering that he was asked. And to Rachel and Nora's new project. May it bear the fruits of success. She paused, smiling. "I'd like to propose one more toast. I don't know if it is proper to toast myself, but since everyone here is related, I didn't think you all would mind." She giggled, a little tipsy from the wine. "Sean doesn't know this either, because I just found out today. We're going to have a baby."

Sean bounded out of his seat and took her in his arms.

"Oh Sarah, how wonderful! We're going to be a family. That makes the decision for me. William Randolph Hearst, here I come."

Even Mike's frozen stare turned into a smile, for he was very fond of Sean and Sarah.

That evening in bed Mike approached Nora. He hadn't done so for a long time, and she was hoping that he wouldn't. He said nothing, just kissed her. She dutifully accepted the kiss, but she seethed with resentment, for it meant that he expected her to forget all their arguments and his unkindnesses, and to be warm and open to his advances. She couldn't understand how anyone with any sensitivity could behave in this manner. She lay still and frigid, but either he didn't care or didn't notice. When he was satisfied, he rolled over and fell asleep. Nora crept quietly out into the living room and took a large drink of his Irish whiskey.

When she arrived at the shop the next morning, the phone on Nora's desk was ringing. "Will someone please answer it?'' Nora called as she squirmed to get her coat off.

"Nora, it's for you,'' Denise called.

Nora ran and took the receiver from her. "Hello, yes, who is it?''

It was Miss Terrell, from Bloomingdale's lingerie department. They had sold out of the back-up order Nora had shipped to them, and were sending a messenger down with a new order.

"Fine, fine. We'll fill it as quickly as we can,'' Nora said, hanging up and running into Rachel's office on the other side of the salon.

Rachel wasn't surprised. "The line was bound to be a success,'' she said, "but we're going to have problems. We'll have to hire more seamstresses immediately. This time they'll probably send an order for at least one hundred pieces.''

"Well, we'll just have to fill it. Where to store them is another problem. Let's discuss all this at the staff meeting.''

When the messenger arrived with the order, Annie signed for it and brought it in to Nora. Nora opened it. "Rachel was right. No more orders for thirty. This one is for one hundred.'' She looked at the order again. "Wait, Annie, I was wrong. It's not for a hundred. Run, get Rachel.''

"I'm here. How big is it?'' Rachel ran over.

"Rachel, sit down. Take a deep breath. It's for one thousand pieces.''

"Oh my God, are you sure?''

"Look for yourself.'' Nora handed over the order to Rachel.

"What are we going to do?''

"I think, young ladies,'' Annie answered, "we're

either going to have to move into a factory or go out of the low-priced lingerie business."

"Well, we're not going to go out of business," Nora stated, with a determined look. "We'll have to confirm this order immediately. Annie, find us some Queen's Lace stationery and order blanks. We'll want the name on that very first confirmation. That's good luck."

"Who says so?" Annie asked.

"I do," Rachel answered. "It's one of my personal superstitions. Guaranteed to work."

They rented an empty factory on Houston Street, and Nora soon found she was working nights and weekends. She couldn't even find time for the opera. She never missed going to any of Caroline's gatherings, however. She even brought Rachel with her once, and Caroline warmly invited her back.

Mike was constantly disgruntled and quite aloof, but because of Bridget's presence and her impeccable care of their home, he had been keeping his objections to himself.

One evening, when Nora had come in rather late, Bridget was waiting up for her, crocheting at the kitchen table. She fixed Nora a cup of cocoa, and sat down next to her. "Nora, as you know, I see Sarah all the time. 'Tis worried about her I am. She's not looking at all well. The doctor says that 'tis nothing, that she's just fragile, but I don't believe his hocus-pocus. I think Sean is worried too. We talked the other day, and he's feeling that if her parents would just lower that wall they've put up, she'd feel much better. I don't know if that would help, but Mary, Joseph and Patrick, it couldn't hurt." She paused. "Maybe you and Rachel could talk to the Friedmans."

"Oh, Bridget, I had no idea. Rachel and I have just been buried in work. I'll talk to Rachel tomorrow, and we'll try to figure something out. Thank you for telling me. I don't know, Bridget, how we ever managed without you." Nora put her arms about Bridget.

When Nora went to see the Friedmans, she felt awkward and anxious. Rachel said it would be better for Nora not to tell them in advance why she was coming, so they welcomed her cordially and offered her sherry. They both looked strained and unhappy, not at all charming and relaxed as they had been when she first met them. She remembered how bright and lively Mr. Friedman's eyes had looked then. Now they seemed dim, almost lifeless.

Not being one to avoid confrontation, she told them at once why she had come. "Mr. and Mrs. Friedman, I have a favor to ask of you. My sister Bridget has become a very good friend of your daughter Sarah's, and she informed me the other day that Sarah's pregnancy is not going well. She is weak and lethargic."

"Oh no," Mrs. Friedman whimpered involuntarily.

"Be quiet, Rebecca."

Nora watched her clutch the arms of her chair until the knuckles were white.

Rachel interrupted. "Father, I'm worried too. I've seen her. She looks pale and thin even though she's already showing. Her spirits are low because she misses your affection."

"This is all very interesting." Mr. Friedman's voice dripped with sarcasm. "But those two should have thought about losing our affection before they ran off as they did."

Nora persisted. "Mr. Friedman, they are young, and they are in love. I understand and respect your feelings about religion, but my brother is a fine man, and he adores your daughter. He treats her with all the love you could ever want for her. If you and Mrs. Friedman would at least see Sarah, perhaps her spirits would be lifted."

Mrs. Friedman sat on the edge of her chair. She pleaded with her eyes to her husband.

"Thank you for your interest Nora," he said abruptly, "but in our eyes, Sarah is dead." With that, he got up and left the room.

Nora looked imploringly at Mrs. Friedman. "Go see her. *Please* go see her. You must take matters into your own hands, I beg of you. And so does Rachel."

Rachel sat crying with her head in her hands. "Yes Mother, please. Before it's too late."

"I—I can't," she said, giving them an anguished look. "I can't go against my husband's wishes." Then she too left the room.

Chapter 30

Several weeks later the doorbell at the Friedmans' rang, and Mrs. Friedman opened the door to find Sean standing there, gaunt and harried. He pushed past her and into the study, where Mr. Friedman sat.

"I'm married to your daughter, Mr. Friedman. And I love her. I want her to be well and happy. If you'll just reconcile with her, you need never speak to me again, but you can't just abandon your own flesh and blood. She needs you." He paused, and Mr. Friedman walked over to the study door.

"You are not welcome in my home, Mr. O'Sullivan. Please leave and take your hysterical theatrics with you," he said coldly.

Sean stared at him in disbelief. "My God, are you not human? Have you no love for your child?" The door slammed closed in his face. He had no choice but to leave.

Later he told quite a different story to Sarah, who lay quietly in his arms. "I think they're coming around, darling. Nora and Rachel think so too. So sleep. You need your rest. You'll be seeing them any day now, believe me. It's sometimes difficult for proud people to admit they've been wrong. We need to give them a little time." He was smoldering inwardly with frustration.

Rachel hadn't spoken to her parents since the evening Nora had pleaded for Sarah. When she came home in the evenings, she went right to her room. If her father was intent on being such a fool, that was one thing, but she couldn't understand her mother.

As she lay awake one night, she heard a noise at her door. She got up and opened it. Rebecca Friedman was standing there in her nightgown, shivering, looking old, pathetic and beaten.

"Talk to me, Rachel. I can't endure your silence any longer," she whispered, her voice sodden with tears.

"Mother, what is wrong with him? What is wrong with you? I'll talk to you if you promise me you'll go to see her. Don't tell him if you don't want to, but you must see Sarah," Rachel demanded harshly.

"I don't know, Rachel. I thought he'd give in, but he just sits and reads the Talmud hour after hour. I'm frightened. If he were to catch me, I don't know what he would do." She looked around, frightened.

Rachel was losing patience. "Mother, what on earth could happen? Father would never hurt you. What could he do? Scold you? There are some decisions in your life that you have to make on your own, without him. How would you feel if something were to happen to Sarah? Could you ever forgive yourself?" She hated having to say these things.

Mrs. Friedman sat with her head bowed. "Take me to see her tomorrow, Rachel. I'll meet you for lunch, but don't say a word, please."

*　　*　　*

Mrs. Friedman appeared at the shop the next day looking haggard and frightened. Nora tried to comfort her by telling her she was doing the right thing.

When Rachel arrived with her mother at Sarah's, Bridget greeted them. " 'Tis happy I am, Mrs. Friedman, that you're here. The child needs her mother. No one else will do at a time like this."

Rebecca Friedman walked into the bedroom and saw her younger daughter propped up against the pillows, listless and pale. Rachel closed the door so they could be alone. Rebecca was shocked at her daughter's appearance. Oh my God, she thought, is it too late? "Darling Sarah, Mother's here." She swept her into her arms.

"Mother, I'm so happy to see you. I—we're so sorry to have caused you both grief. I'll make it up to you, I promise. You'll have a beautiful grandson. Everyone says I'm carrying a boy, and we've decided to name him Terence after Sean's older brother. But if it turns out to be a girl, we've decided to call her Rebecca, after you."

Rebecca Friedman's face brightened as it hadn't in a long time.

Sarah was up and about, and quite cheerful over the next few days. Bridget brought Mary over and stayed with her during the day until Sean returned home. One evening he asked Bridget if she would stay there all the time until Sarah delivered.

"Well, if Nora doesn't mind, I'll just bring Mary over and move in with you temporarily. It probably would be best." She took over the care of that household as well, and her presence cheered Sarah immensely. Rachel and Nora took turns visiting, and on weekends, Nora took Mary home with her. Mike felt lonely and rejected without Bridget, his only solace, and began behaving badly again.

But he knew better than to object too strenuously, for uppermost in everyone's mind was Sarah's well-being.

At midnight, two weeks after Bridget moved in, Sarah woke up with pains. Sean ran in and woke Bridget, begging her to come quickly.

My God, she's more than a month early, Bridget thought. It can't be the baby coming. But soon the pains settled into regular intervals. "Sean, we can't deliver the child here. We've got to get Sarah to the hospital immediately." Sean called Nora, who in turn called Rachel.

Nora's voice was stern over the telephone. "I don't care how you get your parents there, drag them if you have to, but get them there," Nora commanded. "Considering how poorly she's been looking, these early labor pains don't sound like a good sign."

Several hours later, Terence was born. And Sarah was dead.

Everyone was waiting silently in the solarium when Sean stumbled out of the recovery room.

"She's gone," he cried. "She's gone. My Sarah's dead. My God, she died in my arms." He slumped into a chair, sobbing.

"My baby, my baby," Mrs. Friedman screamed while Mr. Friedman dropped his head in a gesture of utter despair. He made no sound, but sat with his head bowed, staring at the floor. Nora and Rachel were crying, and Bridget was keening, a sound Nora hadn't heard since Ireland.

Sean was like a madman. He leapt up from the chair and confronted the Friedmans. "Are you happy now? My Sarah is dead. Her marriage to me was probably the first disobedient thing she had done in her life, and you couldn't forgive her for it," he railed.

Mr. Friedman looked away, tears streaming down his

face, while Mrs. Friedman moaned and wailed. Nora jumped up and tried to stop Sean, but he brushed her aside. He had to blame someone, and in his fury and grief, he poured his rage out at Mr. Friedman. "Is this what your Talmud teaches you? No forgiveness ever, for anything?"

"Stop it, Sean, that's enough. Listen to me. None of this will do anyone any good. Nothing can be undone. Do you understand that? Nothing!" Nora cried.

He spun around. His face was crimson and sweaty and twisted. "You, Nora, what do you know about love or commitment? You've never lost anything of value. You've never lost anyone you loved. Maybe because you've never loved anyone." He went raging out into the night.

Rachel started to run after him. "But your baby, Sean, your son."

He turned around and shrieked, "I don't want to see the child who killed my Sarah." He ran down the stairs.

Nora stopped Rachel from following him. "No, Rachel, let him go. It's the way he's handled grief or unhappiness all his life. He'll walk for hours until he's tired and numb. Let him go. It's best," she said wearily. "Believe me."

Rachel tried to comfort her father while Mrs. Friedman walked slowly into the room where Sarah lay lifeless. She sat staring at the sweet face whose eyes would never again sparkle, whose laughing mouth was forever silenced. She kissed her on the lips and sat holding her cold hand.

"I loved you so much, little one," she sobbed. "We wronged you greatly, your father and I."

Nora entered the room and put her arms around Mrs. Friedman. "I'm sorry, Mrs. Friedman. I'm so sorry about Sean. He didn't mean all those things. He was just beside himself with grief."

Mrs. Friedman looked at her strangely. "Everything he said was true, Nora. Every last word. I wanted to be reconciled with Sarah and Sean, but I was too weak to stand up to the anger in my husband's soul."

"We all do what we must, Mrs. Friedman. It's not your fault. It's not Mr. Friedman's fault either. Life and death are not matters that are in our hands. And remember, you did come to see Sarah, and you and she were reconciled. That made her so happy. Think of that," Nora comforted.

"All I can think of is that my daughter is dead." Mrs. Friedman wept.

Three days later, Sarah's funeral took place, and still Sean had not been heard from.

"Rachel, he's never before disappeared for so long a time," Nora said with concern. "I don't know what to think."

"Nothing this terrible has ever happened to him before, remember that."

"But where could he be? They've searched everywhere. If even Angelo's men can't find him, I'm really worried." Nora paused. Angelo, who seemed always to know what was going on in Nora's life, had heard about Sean's disappearance and had immediately sent a few of his employees to have a look around town for him.

Rachel took Nora's hand. "I'm worried too, Nora, but remember, I've cared dearly for Sean ever since I first met him, and I know he wouldn't do anything foolish."

"I hope you're right, Rachel. I do hope so."

Several evenings later, a pale, gaunt and disheveled Sean appeared at Nora's door. "Oh Sean, Sean, thank God you're safe." As Nora looked at him, she remembered her mother's story, told only once, about how Mary's father, Sean's grandfather, had disappeared for months after his wife and babies had been killed by a bomb in Belfast, and had as suddenly reappeared at Father O'Rourke's rectory door.

Bridget came running out of the kitchen. "Oh my God, look at the lad, 'tis barely alive he is." After making certain he wasn't hurt, she ran into the kitchen to warm some soup.

The sisters ministered to him, helping him out of his filthy clothes, running a hot bath, giving him a shot of Irish whiskey. "Ma says a shot of Irish whiskey now and then is better medicine than any the doctors prescribe," Bridget said, handing him the glass. "And I'm needing a drop myself. Good Lord, lad, where have you been?"

"I'm not sure. I'd rather not talk about it now," he replied, remembering only a haze of drunken days, and debauched nights full of painted women, the persistent recollection of trying to get out of a room. He also remembered having asked someone for more to drink, and then having been given bottle after bottle. Everything was a blank from that time until he woke up in Angelo's apartment. Angelo told him that he had been found in the gutter, drunk and wretched.

Apparently Sean had gone from bar to bar, drinking wildly to drown the grief and pain of losing Sarah. In one place, he was given a drugged drink and robbed. A prostitute found him outside the back door. She and the bartender, feeling sorry for him, took him to The Golden Lantern, a seedy whorehouse on the Lower East Side. One of the male bouncers recognized that he fit the description of the man for whom a rather large reward was being offered. Before the prostitute, Jenny, could do anything to help him, the bouncer told Reynaldo, a local pimp, who then kidnapped Sean and locked him in a room until he could figure out how to get the reward without going to the police. Reynaldo soon learned that Angelo Gambini's men were in on the search, and he appeared at Angelo's restaurant. His appearance was so disreputable, with a patch on one eye and flamboyant clothes, that Dominic tried to turn him away, but Reynaldo gave him the photograph and suggested menacingly that Angelo would want to see it. And Angelo did.

Reynaldo entered the elegant room. Angelo stared icily at him. "What do you want, Reynaldo?"

"I know the whereabouts of this man, and it seems you're interested in knowing them, too. I've come to make a deal."

"The reward offered is five hundred dollars. Deliver him within the hour and the money is yours. That's the deal."

Reynaldo began to snivel. "Ain't he worth more than that?"

Angelo grabbed him by the collar. "You scum, sure he's worth more than that, but I'm not paying you a cent more. As a matter of fact, if you don't deliver him within the hour, I'm going to hold you *very* responsible, do you understand?"

"Okay, okay, no harm in trying. He'll be here." And he left with a number of Angelo's men following him, just in case.

Reynaldo, frightened when he realized that Angelo meant business, delivered Sean as he said he would and collected the reward. Angelo was known to be a man of his word.

Angelo's valet had put Sean to bed and summoned the doctor, who confirmed that Sean had been repeatedly drugged.

When Sean awoke the next evening, Angelo was standing over the bed. "Get right home. They are all frantic with worry."

Sean thanked him and left.

"Just don't ever scare us like that again, please," Bridget pleaded.

Nora couldn't help staring at him. He looked so young, so vulnerable, but he had already lived through more tragedy than many men twice his age had. He and Bridget had both lost their beloved spouses, and Nora realized that if anyone could help him through this, it would be Bridget.

Sure enough, Bridget instinctively took over the job of comforter, and while Nora was reticent about mentioning his young son, Bridget came right to the point. "Your son is with the Friedmans. He's a fine, healthy lad. Looks a little like both of you. And Sean, they've named him Terence, just as you both wished. Everyone is already calling him Terry." Bridget just assumed that he'd want to know. Sean said nothing, so Bridget continued. "He's gaining weight daily, and within a week or two Rachel will be able to bring him over for you to see. Since he was premature, they're taking a few added precautions."

"Good," Sean said indifferently.

"Sean," Nora put in, "you cannot convince me you don't care about your own son."

"I thought I didn't want to see him," Sean said very softly. "I thought he was responsible for my Sarah's death, and that I'd hate him." He paused, putting his head in his hands. Nora put her hand on his shoulder. "I know better now. Sarah would want me to take care of him. But I couldn't see that at first."

"We know, lad," Bridget answered. "I'll tell you one thing, though. I'd give anything to have had a child by Kevin. Count your blessings." She wiped a tear from her eye.

That one comment helped Sean to see the situation clearly. "Do I really have to wait a week or two to see him? Is there any other way to see him sooner? I will have nothing to do with the Friedmans, so I can't go there."

"Rachel will work something out, don't worry," Nora told him.

"How is Rachel?" Sean asked, concerned.

"As worried about you as we were," Nora replied quickly. "We've been everywhere looking for you. Uncle Jim organized search parties, and so did Angelo. Rachel and I looked everywhere they didn't."

"Well, I'm back now."

Within a few weeks, Rachel arranged for Sean to come to the apartment to see his son by conspiring with Mrs. Friedman to get Mr. Friedman out of the house for a few hours. It was a touching scene. When Sean picked the child up and held him closely, silently rocking him, Rachel had to leave the room so Sean wouldn't see her tears. She promised they would work out ways for him to visit Terry when Mr. Friedman was out of the house.

"Besides, he's doing so well. I'll be able to take him out soon, and then there will be no problems. I can bring him to you."

For the time being, Sean was content with the arrangement, but Rachel anticipated that he was soon going to want his son back.

Nora was so grateful for Angelo's help in finding Sean that she decided to thank him in person. She sent a note to Angelo, asking to see him.

To her great surprise, the next afternoon his carriage appeared at the shop. The driver had instructions to bring her to the restaurant.

When Dominic showed her into the inner office, Angelo rose and hurried toward her. She was shocked by his appearance. He looked haggard, pale and fatigued.

He noticed her worried glance. "Your feelings always show in your eyes, Nora. I'm quite all right. Don't worry. It's just that I've had a few problems with Gina."

"Oh Angelo, I'm sorry. I didn't know."

"No one knows, Nora. Everyone thinks I'm ill, but I'm not. At least not in the way they think." Angelo quickly changed the subject. "You, my dear, look more beautiful each year. You are one of the few fortunate ones whose beauty grows with age. But, of course, you are still young. Not thirty yet, right?"

"Yes, not quite thirty yet," she smiled. "Angelo, I've missed you terribly. I probably shouldn't have written that note, but I wanted to thank you in person for all your help. I know it was you who arranged for the box at the opera, and I know that it was also you who found Sean and returned him home. Please accept my thanks."

"Your well-being is always of concern to me, Nora, and it always will be." He looked into those discerning violet eyes. "How I've missed you. I often think of those golden days we spent together."

"Angelo, what has happened to Gina?" Nora found the courage to ask.

He was silent for a moment, and as he looked down at his hands, she noted the fine lines of fatigue and worry etched on his forehead. They hadn't been there when she'd last seen him.

"It is very bad." He spoke so softly that she could barely hear him.

She said simply, "Tell me."

"She never leaves the house anymore. She can't, really, for she has no control over herself. She is always unwashed and half-dressed. She won't eat unless we force her. And she raves madly. When her father died two years ago, she wouldn't even go to the funeral. She insisted that he wasn't really her father, but some impostor."

"Oh Angelo, how awful. Where is she?"

"In our house on Long Island. I didn't want my daughter to be around her. We visit her once a week. That's all we can do. Angie can't grow up normally around a mad woman."

They talked long into the afternoon, two old friends catching up on each other's lives. As the last rays of the late afternoon sun disappeared, shadows flickered on the paneled walls, making the figures in the paintings seem alive in the warm, hazy glow. And still they were talking. Angelo learned about her unhappiness with Mike. It was a relief for Nora to be able to discuss it honestly and openly with him. She told him of her friendship with Caroline Trent-Williams and of her activities in the women's suffrage movement. He applauded her for her courage and for her business pursuits and success. In fact, she thought, he applauded all the things Mike berated her for. Angelo was a deeply sensitive man who knew that her intelligence and creativity needed outlets, that she was a woman with a dream, a hope, a driving ambition, and a sense of beauty, all things he respected and admired. Mike, on the other hand, was an average man with limited vision and sensibilities, so that the very traits in her that he should have nourished and encouraged became threats to him instead.

"I can't imagine, dear Nora, why you married him," Angelo ventured. "Please don't be angry at my saying that. You and I seem to be able to speak honestly with each other, and you must have had your reasons. I only hope that they were good enough to balance out all you've given up by living with a man you don't love."

She smiled sadly. "No, I don't think my reasons were good enough, but I did it, and I'll manage as best I can for as long as I can. And, of course," she added more brightly, "I have my little Mary. That helps more than anything."

"I know how you feel. Angie, my daughter, has helped me through a great deal too. She's a delightful girl, Nora. How I would love for you to meet her. Very realistic and sympathetic about her mother too. She accepts the situation without shame and is kind and gentle with her. I suppose children are compensations in unhappy marriages, aren't they?"

They parted sadly, knowing that it might be some time before they would get together again.

"Destiny has made us friends, and destiny will arrange our next meeting. Good-bye, Nora. And remember, I'm always here for you."

She held his hand tightly, kissed him gently on the cheek and left.

The carriage was waiting for her. As she stepped into its black, comfortable privacy, gaslights were beginning to twinkle, people were bustling homeward, carriages and cars were crowding the streets, and restaurants and theaters were opening as New York prepared for evening.

Chapter 31

"Nora! Nora, 'tis a letter from Danny!" Bridget shouted, waving the missive in her hands. "Pray God, 'tis good news we're getting of Seamus and Terence." Nora watched Bridget's trembling hands rip at the envelope to get it open. She pulled it out and the two sisters sat on the sofa, devouring its contents as fast as they could.

Dearest Nora and Bridget,

What a comfort to me to picture the two of you there together, and to know that you were both there to love and support Sean at the death of his beloved Sarah. I know that his grief must be as awful for him to bear as it is for you to behold. Though I never met Sarah, I learned to love her through your letters. Ma and I have both written to Sean, though I imagine our words are of small comfort to him at the moment. We have not told Pa of Sarah's death. He is so weak but he is overjoyed at the idea of a grandson. Don't be hurt, Nora. Granddaughters are precious, but a boy carries on the family name.

Little Terry's birth even brought his uncle out of hiding. He arrived in the middle of a stormy night, as if he'd been blown in by the wind, and he brought with him his own surprise, a wife! And, what a pair they are! Julia is almost as tall as he, has beautiful curly red hair and more freckles than Bridget. Ma and Pa loved her at once. I feel it's a sad way to begin a marriage, hiding from the authorities, but they are as happy as any two I've ever seen, Terence the more so, because of his new namesake. He's been proud as a peacock, toasting little Terry with every drop in the house. Next morning when we awoke, they were both gone.

Terence gave us news of Seamus too. It seems his name has been turned in by an informer, and the British have launched an intense search for him. Meanwhile, the Brotherhood is trying to smuggle him out of the country. I have a feeling he'll be showing up in America. No doubt he'll contact you when he finally arrives. May God be with him.

Our mother is bearing up well. Pa's care takes a lot out of her, but she is as brave as ever. She still gets out her books every Thursday, after dinner, as if we are all here to gather around, and how I wish we were!

Dear sisters, take care of yourselves. Bridget, your letters have cheered Ma and Pa enormously. It is so obvious that you love America and are doing well, but we miss you so. And Nora, we all just stared and stared at the beautiful portrait you sent us of you and little Mary. You are more beautiful than ever.

I hope you will rest easier after reading this letter. I feel I've been the bearer of too many sad tidings lately.

Yours in Christ,
Danny

Shortly after Danny's letter arrived, Sean received a letter, this one from Terence, addressed to him and sent to his office.

Dear Sean,

I know Danny has recently written, telling you the news of me and Seamus. We are needing to get him out of the country, for since he was seen, he is a marked man, and one ill equipped to be in hiding. My heart's breaking as I write. He went blind a short time after the incident. He must have been wounded in some way, though the doctors don't know exactly how. Probably a blow he got on the head in the melee. Sean, the Brotherhood has forged some documents to sneak him out of the country and has found a trustworthy captain of a large freighter who'll take him on his ship to America. It's too dangerous for Seamus to remain here a moment longer than he has to, and this captain, one Jeremy O'Neill, will be ready to leave Ireland in approximately a week. God willing, Seamus will be with him. We'll be needing you to meet the ship, the *Shamrock*, and get him safely to Philadelphia, where he has a brother. The name he'll be traveling under is Tim Kenny. Seamus is a fine, brave lad, and has worked hard for our cause. I'm enclosing a photograph of him so there will be no mistakes. We're plagued with informers, as you know, so we're on guard every moment, but I think we're pulling it off. If you'll take care of things on your end, we'll be very grateful.

One more thing. You're not to tell Nora. Seamus is adamant about that. He doesn't want her to know he's blind. I've pleaded, cajoled, even threatened him, but he won't budge. He finally agreed to allow you to meet him and get him safely to his family in Philadelphia. And I think he agreed to that only because he wants so badly to meet you.

He took your place with all of us, Sean, and he's become like a brother to me. Treat him well. Since he won't allow Nora to know about him and she is the one I was counting on to help him, it's up to you and this brother of his. He's so damned stubborn. Julia says I'm a fine one to talk. Sean, she's as much of a firebrand as I and the only kind of woman I could have married. I hope you'll meet her some day, and I am only sorry I never met your Sarah. When I was hearing that your baby son bears my name, I cried with happiness, for I don't know how Julia and I in good conscience can dare bring children into our kind of life, filled as it is with running and hiding, danger and death.

I must go now, but keep us in your heart. Take care, and don't lose hope.

> Yours for a free Ireland,
> your brother Terence

Three and a half weeks later, Sean watched Seamus being led down the gangplank of the *Shamrock*. What a fine-looking man, he thought, with his broad shoulders, strong look and tousled brown hair.

Sean rushed up to him. "Seamus, it's Sean. Jaysus, I'm happy you're here. I worried from the moment I received Terence's letter." They embraced warmly. "Are you all right, lad?"

"Aye, I'm well. 'Tis good to be here on free soil." He paused. "I'm thanking you, Sean, for meeting me. It was a great kindness."

"None at all. All that matters, Seamus, is that you're here safely. Let's go have a fine lunch and a few stouts, before we get the train to Philadelphia."

They talked as if they were old friends, finding they had so much in common. Sean felt no self-pity evident in Seamus' attitude, so he found it odd that the man didn't want Nora to know about it. Finally he broached the subject. "Seamus, I wish you'd stay in New York with us. You could live with me. I'm alone now. Nora talks so fondly of you; I know she'd want to see you and talk to you. Please reconsider."

Seamus was silent a few moments. A sad look came over his fine face. "No, Sean, don't ask me. I can't do it. I don't want her to see me like this, not ever, so please don't ask me. My brother will take care of me. Maybe I can find some kind of work. You know I've had legal training." This last he said wistfully, without hope.

"I'll respect your wishes, Seamus, but if you change your mind, I'm always here."

"Should I change my mind, I will call on you, I promise."

But Sean could see his mind was closed on the subject.

They took the train to Philadelphia, arriving at nine that evening. Seamus' older brother met them at the station. It was a warm reunion, but Sean couldn't help thinking that Seamus seemed more an O'Sullivan than a Gorman. Dave, Seamus' brother, thanked Sean, and invited him to come home with them, but Sean was catching the train back to New York in an hour. He and Seamus parted sadly.

Ballygarry's now occupied an entire building on Madison Avenue. The shop remained on the ground level, but the executive offices were located on the second floor, as were the seamstresses who worked on the handmade lingerie still sold at the shop. The factory downtown produced all the Queen's Lace lingerie, the new line introduced at Bloomingdale's. These items were now machine made, but still quite exquisite. Queen's Lace was becoming enormously successful. While Bloomingdale's had been its first buyer, other New York department stores soon followed suit. Macy's, Wanamaker's, Gimbel's and Gertz on Long Island were soon selling the line, and reordering faster than the articles could be produced.

Annie was in charge of the factory on Houston Street, and Denise was running Ballygarry's shop, which still turned out the loveliest, most sought after lingerie in New York.

Their office staff had also expanded, and Nora had suggested all the garment workers join the International Ladies' Garment Workers Union. She knew she was paying better wages than the union asked, but she felt it gave the workers dignity, allowing them as it did a say in their futures. Rachel knew how important this was to Nora, and gave in, though she wasn't as enthusiastic about unionization as Nora was.

Nora had begun traveling to other cities to show the line. At first, she went only to stores in New Jersey or Connecticut, but soon she was traveling farther and farther away from New York. She had received requests from

Marshall Field's in Chicago, the J.L. Hudson Company in Detroit, Hess's in Allentown, and McAlpin's in Cincinnati.

A decision was made that Nora should take a long selling trip to call on all these establishments. Nora was beside herself with excitement. She was going to see Billy. It had been over a year since Nora had been to Chicago, and she acted like a schoolgirl going on her first outing. But seeing Billy was only part of the reason for her excitement. She also relished the prospect of showing and selling the line. She was proud of it, and she enjoyed going to new places and meeting new people.

Nora was worried about telling Mike that she was taking a trip, but Bridget had assured her that there was no reason for concern. Bridget would take care of the baby, Mike and the apartment.

"Bridget, you know he'll be upset, but I must do it," Nora told her sister. "I can triple our business on this selling trip. If he would only just give in and stop creating scenes."

"Nora, he believes what you are doing is wrong. I make no such judgments, but I can understand his point of view. He wants a wife and a home life, and you can't seem to give that to him."

"Well, since I'm running the business and intend to keep right on running it, don't you think he'd at least stop fighting me? What good is it doing either of us? It changes nothing. In fact, it only brings us more hardship."

"Aye, I know. Poor Mike. He doesn't know how to handle this situation." Bridget shook her head.

"Poor Mike, indeed. If he would just stop nagging me, we could have a happy enough home life. Oh, how I wish I had never married him."

Bridget felt a great sadness. She was sorry to see Nora and Mike so unhappy. She cared deeply for Mike, understood his needs, and didn't think them unreasonable. But she also understood Nora's drives.

Mike was strangely quiet when Nora told him about the trip. "Nothing I have said seems to matter to you, Nora, so do what you must."

"Bridget will be taking care of Mary and the house and you. She loves doing it, Mike."

"I know." He seemed resigned. "When will you be back?"

"In two weeks. Sooner, if I can, but I do want to spend a few days with Molly and Tim."

"Yes, of course."

She didn't quite understand this new attitude of his. It confused her. She had expected another unpleasant confrontation. Perhaps he's changing his tactics to see if he'll get better results that way, she thought cynically. They were no longer sharing a bedroom, for Mike had moved some time ago into the other guest room. This had been a tremendous relief for Nora, who found it more and more difficult to respond to his lovemaking. Every so often, he'd have a few drinks and come to her at night to make love to her. She detested this, but continued to give in to his desires because she thought it was his right.

Nora was staring out the window, watching the rain pelt the windows, when her secretary announced that she had a visitor, a Mrs. Trent-Williams.

Nora was delighted. "Oh, Caroline," she greeted, "you are the proverbial sight for sore eyes. I need some cheering up at this moment."

Caroline looked at her sharply. "Trouble with Mike?"

"Yes, I don't seem to be handling things at all well. But never mind that, Caroline. Tell me what you've been up to."

"It's what I'm going to be up to, Nora. We're organizing a march to demand the vote for women. I want you to march with us. We'll be trudging up Fifth Avenue, with banners and determination, and we need everyone we can get. Please say yes.''

"Caroline, I'm going on a business trip.''

"When?''

"In a week and a half, and I'll be gone at least two weeks, probably more.''

Caroline pulled out a cigarette. "Do you mind?''

"No, of course not.'' She loved to see women smoke, although she didn't care to do it herself. Caroline inhaled deeply and, blowing out the smoke, looked at Nora.

"Maybe next time, then.''

"Yes, I promise you.'' She promised herself as well. Woman's suffrage was a cause she believed in and one she intended to fight for.

As she was getting ready to leave for Allentown, she went in to say good-bye to baby Mary, but as she came near the door, she saw Mike and Bridget kneeling at Mary's bedside, teaching her her prayers. Nora stepped away so as not to intrude. Why can't I be happy with those simple pleasures? she wondered, and then thought, what a perfect wife for him Bridget would have made.

A week later, she arrived in Chicago, Hess's had bought her line, and had given a sizable order. McAlpin's, a bit more cautious, had placed a smaller order, but Nora knew it was just a matter of time before they reordered, and J.L. Hudson's in Detroit had wined and dined her, recognizing a good thing when they saw it. Then she arrived in Chicago, obstensibly to meet with Mr. Selfridge of Marshall Field's, but most importantly, to see Molly and Retta and Tim and Billy. She wondered if Billy had changed much and if he'd be happy to see her now that he was older. When she stepped down from the platform, all four were waiting for her. They ran to her, smothering her with kisses and hugs.

"Aunt Nora, how beautiful you look." Retta shyly touched Nora's stunning traveling suit. "It's so soft. What is the fabric? And what do you call the color? It's not blue and it's not green." She rushed on with girlish enthusiasm. "Oh, and look at your beautiful jewelry, Aunt Nora. You're so, so elegant."

"Enough, Retta." Molly was smiling warmly at Nora. "But she's right. You *are* elegant. I guess you always were. Oh Nora, beside you, I feel like a country bumpkin."

"You always look wonderful to me, Molly. And Tim, you've put on some weight. Too much of Molly's good cooking, or too much success?" she teased.

"Both," he laughed.

"And Billy, you've gotten so handsome, so tall. I've missed you." She bent to kiss him. He blushed, but allowed it.

By the time they arrived at the house, Billy was chattering away, asking if she would like to watch them ride the following day.

"Better than that," Nora said. "I'll ride with you."

"Do you know how to ride, Aunt Nora? Ma didn't tell me that." He looked surprised.

"Oh, I manage," she smiled.

Molly broke in proudly. "Manage, is it? Why, Billy, your Aunt Nora has ridden in shows in Ireland. She even rode in the Dublin Horse Show, and she won in two events."

"You rode in the Dublin Horse Show, Aunt Nora?" He knew everything about every horse show in the world, for riding was an all-consuming interest of his. "Why, Dublin's the most famous one. It's the one I want to ride in. Tell me about it, please, Aunt Nora."

Nora watched with pleasure as his eyes glowed while

she described the show to him. Then she had an idea. She offered to take him to the Madison Square Garden Horse Show in September if his mother would allow it. Molly agreed.

"Oh, Aunt Nora, I can't wait," Billy cried enthusiastically.

As they rode along the next day, she showed him things he had never even seen.

"Why, it's just so easy for you, Aunt Nora. And you look so calm. I think I get a little scared sometimes."

"I know, Billy. I was the same way. It takes practice and time. You'll learn to handle your horse better each year. Take my word for it. You have a natural talent for riding."

"Really, Aunt Nora, honest?" He was thrilled with her compliment.

"Honest. Would one rider lie to another?" She smiled at his zeal and enthusiasm.

"No, I guess not. Will you come and see me ride in the Greater Chicago Horse Show? It's in July. Please, Aunt Nora. You could help me train," he begged.

"I wouldn't miss it, Billy, not for anything."

The following day, Nora had to go into town on business. Riding down State Street was always a thrill for her, and when she reached Marshall Field's and looked up at the two famous huge clocks on the exterior of this grand emporium, she smiled, remembering her first awesome impressions of such grandeur. Now, I'm here as a guest to show and sell my lingerie line. What a wonder America is! The Tiffany Dome in the south rotunda took her breath away, as the iridescent glass shimmered in the sunlight and cast rainbows of color on the walls.

As she turned toward the elevators, she saw dashing

in her direction a gentleman, about five foot eight, in his early forties, impeccably dressed, coattails flying, with an orchid in his buttonhole and another in his hand. His high, stiff collar gave him a military bearing, and his high-heeled boots clicked on the marble floors as he stopped at one counter, then another, saying good morning, giving orders, checking merchandise. She knew instantly that it must be "Mile-a-minute Harry" Selfridge, the man she had come to see. She walked right over to him and introduced herself.

"Mrs. Desmond, I'm delighted. This is for you." Handing the orchid to Nora, he bowed extravagantly. She was flattered by his courtliness, and liked his style.

"It's perfectly beautiful, Mr. Selfridge," she said, pinning the flower on her suit.

He smiled and led her to his office, a room decorated in so many colors that she grew a little dizzy. What a showman, she thought. As they discussed the business at hand, a butler brought tea in on silver trays. Selfridge lavished praise on the quality of the Queen's Lace line, but couldn't understand how it could be done at such moderate prices.

"Mrs. Robinson from lingerie will be in shortly, and you can be certain that whatever order she places should probably be doubled or tripled. Those people work hard but think small. Thinking big and thinking of good merchandise at fair prices, that's the secret of success. Always remember," he practically roared, "that there is no room here for yesterday's ideas." His voice dropped. "But then you seem to know that already." After a sumptuous lunch, Nora left with a very large order, and she felt she had made a new friend as well. As she left, he boomed at her. "You must visit us often. You brighten our fair city, for such beauty and vision are so rarely combined in one person."

*   *   *

When it came time to leave, Retta and Billy extracted promises that Nora would be there for the show in July. She promised, and invited not only Billy and Retta to the Madison Square Garden Horse Show, but Tim and Molly as well.

" 'Tis time for you to meet Mike and my Mary. And Bridget and Sean want so much to see you, Molly. Please say you'll come," Nora begged.

"Aye, we will, if Tim can get the time off. I haven't seen New York since—" She was about to say, "Since I picked up Billy, right after he was born," but caught herself in time. "Well, since we left eight years ago. I bet Sean has changed so much since then. And *Bridget*. I can't wait to see her. Nora, you had better watch out when we three redheads get together." Her freckled face glowed with warmth at the memories, and in truth, she was looking forward to going as much as the children.

"It's all settled then. We'll have a wonderful time. I'll be renting a house in Southampton for the summer, and we'll spend part of the time there if the weather is still good." Nora was excited at the thought of her loved ones being together.

As always, after leaving them, she experienced a feeling of loneliness, and sat staring out of the train window. There had been many times when she wanted to tell Bridget or Sean, or write her mother about Billy, but there seemed to be no reason to open old wounds, or create new ones. Billy was secure and happy and belonged to Tim and Molly. This was a very private part of her life that would serve no one the better for being known, but sometimes it took all in her power not to blurt it out to Bridget. She was thankful that Annie knew, for that gave her someone to pour her heart out to when she felt the need.

*   *   *

She lunched with Sean a few days later to tell him all the news about Molly and Tim.

"And, their Billy. He's a wonderful boy, Sean, very handsome. He rides so well. It seems natural for him, as if he had been born to it," she bragged.

"Just like you, sister. It was so natural for you. You were such a splendid rider. I'll never forget that day in Dublin, Nora. You were so beautiful, so precise, so perfect, so in control of your mount."

"Aye, it is a good memory. But, what do you mean I *was* a splendid rider? I still am! And I promise I'll teach little Terence, as soon as he's old enough. I've already had Mary on a pony several times in Central Park, and she loved it."

Sean became serious.

"Nora, I want my son back. I'm not satisfied seeing him once or twice a week, and it's difficult for me to avoid seeing the Friedmans." He paused. "Also, I don't want them to turn him against me, or bring him up to think as they do."

"Be fair, Sean. They've changed. I think if you made any move toward reconciliation, they would be willing. You know Mrs. Friedman likes you, and remember how she went against her husband's wishes and visited Sarah before she died. It would be so much easier if there were some kind of truce. How will you explain it all to Terence when he's older without hurting all of you?"

"I don't know, Nora. I'm not looking forward to that."

"Well, you had better start thinking about it. They grow up so fast." She thought of Billy. "And that might be the first step toward getting him back, although you must admit that he's in good hands. You would have to hire a nursemaid, and the child's own grandmother seems to me to be the better choice."

Sean was now working for the *Journal* as a syndicated columnist. The Hearst Company allowed him a great deal of freedom, because he was respected and well known, and the *Journal* had a wide Irish readership. Although some of Sean's more radical causes were not particularly popular with the readers of that daily, Hearst, who had recently been defeated in the race for mayor of New York City, decided to let him have his say, hoping to win over more Irish voters for the next election. Sean instinctively knew what was inappropriate for the *Journal*, so when he had an Irish axe to grind, he'd send his columns to the *Irish World*. Ford, publisher of the *Irish World*, admired his work and agreed with his nationalist and social reform ideas. There was a split between the more radical nationalists, who believed violence was necessary to achieve Irish freedom, and a more moderate group of nationalists who were more interested in helping the immigrants to a better life than furthering the revolutionary militancy of the Irish Republican Brotherhood. The United Irish League of America, a group Sean had joined, believed in full national self-government for Ireland, but through achieving home rule rather than blasting the British out of Ireland.

He wouldn't want Terence ever to think he had abandoned the cause, for he hadn't, but the real truth of the matter was that Sean had become an American. While he sympathized with Terence's fight, he began to see these political matters as would an outsider. It was after he had met Peter Doyle O'Reilly, editor of the *Boston Pilot*, that his opinions had begun to change. He respected this man, who was realistic enough to understand that the Irish in America needed leaders. With O'Reilly, it was a question of first things first. He understood that before any substantial help could be given to the Irish in Ireland, the Irish in America needed to help themselves. Many immigrants were still struggling for survival and acceptance. While most of the Irish in America wanted Ireland to be free, some of the radical doings of the militant nationalists were causing embarrassment to the majority of Irish, who so badly wanted to be part of American society. Furthermore, it seemed that the activists spent more time attacking the moderates than they did the British. So, while Sean began to shift to a more moderate political stance, he continued to raise money for the Brotherhood in Ireland. "Just don't give it to the radicals here," he advised those who asked. "Send it where we know it will help."

Sean, Nora noticed, seemed to become more attractive all the time. He dressed with taste and flair, had a warm and gracious manner with people, and sported a wit that was mature and finely honed. His red hair didn't look as wild as it used to, and the beard he had grown gave a strong, square look to his jaw. Still, there was an air of sadness about him since Sarah's death that sometimes almost made him seem aloof. Nora wondered if this was what made him so attractive and sought after. Or perhaps it was because of the sense of fearlessness he exuded. He always had the courage to say what he felt was right, and he scorned cowards and hypocrites of whatever kind. He now attended Caroline's gatherings with Nora and Rachel. His apartment was tastefully decorated, for he had made some profit in the stock market by investing the money he'd gotten when he sold Fiona's diamond collar.

Another interesting development had arisen in his life, Nora noted. Rachel had become his official hostess. In fact, she was managing a dinner for him this night, an affair for publishers and politicans, though family had been invited too.

Nora promised that she would try to come, and she really wanted to, for not only did she want to meet Sean's friends, but her interest was piqued to see Rachel playing Sean's hostess.

Mike and Bridget weren't interested in going to the dinner party, so Nora went alone. She enjoyed the party immensely, especially meeting Peter Doyle O'Reilly. The conversation was of politics, women's rights, social reform, and even the opera. She listened with great interest to Mr. O'Reilly's assessment of what he called the flaming radicals.

Rachel looked beautiful in her ivory satin gown. It contrasted with her olive skin and played up her dark, heavy, shining tresses and flashing dark eyes. She was quite breathtaking, Nora thought.

After the guests left, Rachel and Sean were alone. The help had already left. Rachel playfully straightened Sean's tie.

"It's been hanging at a very strange angle all evening," she teased.

Her face was very close to his; the delectable scent of her gardenia perfume struck some responsive chord in him, and suddenly he gazed at her as if he had never seen her before. Her beauty and serenity were so evident that they quite took his breath away. He bent down and kissed her tenderly on her full, warm lips. She responded so naturally that the kiss, first so tender, now became full of passion and searching.

"Oh Rachel, Rachel darling, have you always been here?" he asked, pressing his lips to her hair, holding her lovely head in his hands. "I've been so blind, so very blind. Forgive me."

They melted in an embrace of love that Rachel had been waiting for for over seven long years. "I knew you would come to me, darling," she whispered. "I just didn't know when. I would have waited forever."

Chapter 32

Little Mary was racing across the polished parquet floors when suddenly she heard Nora's key in the lock. She skidded into Nora, laughing and squealing, her chestnut curls bouncing wildly around her pretty oval-shaped face as she hugged her mother. "Mommy, Mommy, I have a new friend, and his name is Timmy, and he has a sister named Vickie, and she's older but she lets us play in her room, and they live on the ninth floor. They have a metal man standing in the corner as you go in, and he's scary, but he didn't scare me because I knew he wasn't real, and Timmy's mother"—she giggled—"gave us hot chocolate and biscuits, and—"

"Wait one moment, young lady. Catch your breath. Now, what is this about a metal man?" she asked, knowing full well what it was; suits of armor had come into fashion.

"Well, he's big, and he clanks when you push at him. But Timmy's mother says he guards the house. Why don't we have one?"

"We don't have one because *you* guard our house, so we don't need one."

"Oh, Mommy, I'm glad you're home." Climbing on Nora's lap, she coyly asked, "Do you have anything for me?"

"Open my purse, and take out the long white envelope."

Mary slid her socks across the floor again and quickly found the white envelope. She opened it and peeked in to discover hundreds of beautiful tiny red beads. "Oh Mommy, now I have four different colors. I can make something beautiful. Thank you, thank you." She hugged Nora once again.

Mary had accepted from infancy the fact that Nora was not an ordinary mother. She was only home in the evenings and on weekends, and she didn't do a lot of things that she knew other mommies did. In her childish mind, she felt her mother was the best there was because she was fun to be with and always looked so beautiful. Also, she brought home wonderful presents, such as stamp pads with star stamps, colored drawing pads, and lately, all these lovely colored beads. Mary had been gluing them in designs interesting enough that Nora thought she might have some talent. Many of the designs were in lovely shapes, not just in random clumps as might have been expected from a child so young. Mary took great delight in her mother's beautiful clothes and in the parties Nora gave from time to time, despite her father's objections. She was allowed to greet the guests, and they always made a fuss over her. She loved to see these exquisite satins and silks and lace and flowers that the ladies wore, and the top hats that the men presented to the butler. When Nora would go out for the evening, Mary would imagine her dancing away the night under twinkling stars, for she was much given to fantasy. Nora took her to the shop from time to time, for it was Mary's favorite place to go, even more so than the zoo.

Even Mike couldn't be angry or disgruntled long around his little daughter. Something about the child wouldn't allow it. He spent long hours with her, reading and playing games. In their different ways, both parents doted on her, and in her presence, all the dissension in the house between Nora and Mike seemed to vanish.

After Mary was tucked in bed this night, Nora announced that she would be traveling to Boston, and would be gone about a week. "I'm going to show the line to Filene's. I'm trying to pull Rachel out of her office to go with me, but she's superstitious about our both being gone at once."

"Uh," Mike grunted, still unable to hide his resentments. "I should think that by now you could hire someone to do your traveling."

His remark took her off guard. "It's not a matter of being able to hire someone. I like to travel with the line, and I sell it well." She felt annoyed at his implication that she still traveled just to annoy him.

He took another drink and turned away from her. Nora rose and poured a small sherry for herself.

Taking a deep breath, she turned to him, speaking softly. "Mike, you are miserable with me. I'm sorry, but this is nothing you could call a real marriage. Why do we pretend it is?" She stopped and looked at him. "I think I would like a—a divorce," she stammered. There. It was out. Oh, how long she had been wanting to say it.

He turned slowly and glared at her. His face was red with rage. "Now I know you are insane. Divorce!" he shrieked. "We are Catholics. Catholics don't divorce. Only those godless, immoral friends of yours get divorces. Those radicals and troublemakers, those anarchists and suffragettes. Who the hell do you think you are? Someone special that the pope will give a dispensation to?'' He paused for breath. Nora began to shake as he raged on. "Never, do you hear me, never mention that word again in this house."

Nora felt as though she had been struck hard across the face. Her usually calm façade began to crumble, and she tried to keep her hands from trembling. She remained seated, too afraid she would falter if she stood up. Her bearing remained proud and sure, however, and that disconcerted Mike. He had expected anger or tears.

"I am not your property, Mike. You didn't purchase me, and you have no right to forbid me anything. If I want to talk about divorce, I shall." Anger was seething in her voice as she continued. "Why in God's name do you wish to stay in a mockery of a marriage? To punish yourself and me? I don't understand. Maybe divorce would be difficult, but it's possible, do you hear me? It's possible. And if it's not to be divorce, then I think we need to talk about separating, for I shall no longer live by your rigid lace-curtain-Irish rules and regulations." She rose and swept quickly out of the room, no longer able to hide her tears.

Nora wept herself to sleep as she had so many times in her life, thinking over and over of all her mistakes. She slept restlessly, awaking at first dawn, sick to her stomach. The thought suddenly struck her that lately she had often been nauseated when she woke up. Perhaps I am pregnant again! Oh my God, if I'm pregnant, how ever will I be able to leave him? She thought of those unfulfilling sexual encounters with Mike that she had suffered through. She watched the sun rise over the city and heard the sounds of the day begin.

That morning, on the way to work, the doctor confirmed Nora's fears, and she arrived at the shop angry and upset. It wouldn't be so bad, she thought, if the child had been conceived in love, but the thought of how it had been conceived, without love or consideration, almost made her ill.

*   *   *

Sean and Rachel spent every possible moment together, laughing, talking, embracing, touching. The first few days after they recognized their love were a fever of discovery, for though Rachel had known for years that she loved Sean, her feelings had had to be repressed, ignored, even forgotten. Now all was in the open, and she became like a lovely, exotic, dark red rose whose petals were opening one by one until finally blossoming into a glorious flower in full bloom.

Sean, whenever he gazed at this alluring creature, wondered why he hadn't recognized this love before. How different she was from Fiona and Sarah. Fiona had been for play, Sarah had needed protecting, and Sean the boy had responded to their needs. But now Sean was a man, and he needed a mature woman with whom he could talk and share his life. He found that her quick mind and quiet wit made her even more desirable, for she could deal in the nuances and subtleties he thrived on. He had loved Sarah. He knew that. But it had been a youthful love. Now he discovered another kind of love, profound and peaceful and giving.

This evening they were going to the theater, and Rachel hurried to his apartment to meet him. His housekeeper, Tillie, opened the door with her coat on.

"Me daughter's about to deliver a baby. I've got to be running. I left a roast and a bottle of wine so you'll not go hungry at the theater. I hope I'll be in tomorrow." She slammed the door behind her. Sean arrived moments later. "Where's Tillie?"

As Rachel tried to explain, he grabbed her in his arms and swung her around dizzily. His exuberance was catching, and soon they fell laughing in a heap onto the living room floor.

"I'll not be fit to go to the theater with crumpled clothes, nor will you," she said with a laugh as she rose to her feet. He pulled her back down and kissed her warm, full lips. Desire rose in him as he touched her satin skin. Without saying a word, he pulled her up from the floor, swept her up and carried her to the bedroom. She lay limply in his arms. This was a moment she had dreamed of, thought about, and wished for for many long, lonely years. He gently undressed her, murmuring, "I love you, I love you, Rachel, my God how I love you." She was soon naked, and her dark beauty took his breath away. She surprised him by sitting up and helping him pull off his clothes, all the while kissing his back, his arms, his throat. He shuddered with pleasure. When he was completely undressed, he kissed her mouth and then ran his tongue down to her hard, waiting nipples. She moaned with pleasure, then responded by rubbing her hands up and down his back, slowly and sensually. At last they joined as one and reached the heavens of passion together in one glorious moment of ecstasy. It had been so easy, so exciting. He had felt no resistance of any kind, and he began to suspect that he was not her first lover.

"Darling," she whispered softly, "I'm not a virgin." She gave no further explanation but lay there. She seemed to know what he was wondering. This confession only served to intensify her mystery, but a feeling of jealousy swept over him. Who could it have been? When? Had she been in love? Questions swirled in his brain. He wanted desperately to ask her, but she seemed so calm and untroubled that he remained silent.

She'll tell me when she's ready, he thought, and he kissed her again.

Sean, with a bouquet of spring daffodils, tulips and irises in his hand, rushed into Rachel's office the next afternoon. After he had deposited them on her desk, he bounded across the hall to see Nora.

"Rachel tells me you're off to conquer Filene's and Boston," Sean told her. "Well, guess who's going with you?" Nora raised her eyebrows and pointed a finger at him. "That's right," he said. "Me. What a stroke of luck that you're going next week. I've been asked to speak at a political fund raiser there, and you know how I'm always willing to create a little fire where there's only been smoke."

Nora was delighted. They tried to persuade Rachel to join them, but she remained stubbornly unwilling for them both to be away at once from the shop.

Rachel saw them off at Grand Central Station, the first time she and Sean were to be parted.

"You two have embraced eighteen times. I've counted. Now, that's enough." Nora grinned playfully.

The train trip was relaxing for both of them. They lunched in the elegant dining car and then sat back and enjoyed each other's company as they hadn't had a chance to do for a long time.

Sean and Nora took rooms at the Plaza hotel and settled in for the night. Filene's sent a carriage for Nora the following morning. She looked forward to meeting the two Filene brothers who had built this great merchandising emporium, especially Edward, who was well-known outside the retailing world, for he was a humanitarian who was always working for social reforms.

She did get to meet Edward, but unfortunately, the store's buyer was ill, and therefore unable to meet with her.

Edward apologized. "We are sorry for this inconvenience, Mrs. Desmond. All of your expenses, of course, will be ours. In addition, a carriage will be at your disposal for sightseeing. We do hope the delay will only last a day or two. Can you stay the extra time?"

"Of course, Mr. Filene. I find Boston a delightful city and one that I know I'll enjoy exploring."

Nora was indeed looking forward to a few days' rest and sightseeing. She even thought of going to Lowell but decided against it. She didn't want to relive those painful memories.

She was especially looking forward to Sean's fund raiser that evening and sung happily as she was dressing. Her voice wasn't as beautiful as her mother's, but she loved to sing when no one was around.

Sean knocked on the door. "I heard you, Nora, and was suddenly feeling I was back home in Ireland. Sure, and it was haunting. It made me feel so homesick again." She paused as he looked at her. "You look so like Ma, I want to cry."

"Oh Sean." She embraced him. "I wish we could get them all here where they'd have an easier life."

"Aye, well, at least there's Bridget with us. Maybe Ma will come some day."

"There are so many reasons she hasn't been able to come. Now, with Pa sick, I'm afraid it will never happen. If—if he dies, Sean," she stammered, barely able to face that thought, "then she might come."

"Maybe, Nora, but don't count on it. Her roots there are strong." He stuffed his strong, large hands into his pockets. "Oh, Nora, I'm sorry. You were singing so happily, and I brought all these sad thoughts with me."

"They are sad thoughts, but we have happy memories, don't we?"

"Right, darling sister. Now get your beautiful self ready, and we'll be off. You know, you may look the spitting image of our mother, but you don't hold a candle to her singing." He left her so that she could finish dressing.

Nora laughed and patted her stomach. She had pushed

the thoughts of her pregnancy to the back of her mind, determined to enjoy the trip and worry about all that later, but now, for some reason, her worries came back. How can I separate from Mike, pregnant as I am? she thought. And how would Mike react to the news? for, of course, I'll have to tell him. He'll probably be happy about it, certain that of course this will finally end my foolish pursuits. But he will be wrong, as he always has been.

She finished putting on her make-up and met Sean in the hall. "You are breathtaking, Nora, more beautiful every day. I'm proud to have you by my side." Sean offered her his arm. "I'll have to be on guard every moment. Every man will want to steal you away."

She was stunning in a lilac-colored taffeta with intricate detail and a feminine softness. The dress enhanced her lovely pale skin and made her violet eyes sparkle. Her hair was swept up in the back and combed high off the forehead in front, and around her neck she wore a choker of pearls. Her hat was large with a matching lilac plume.

When they arrived at the Parker House, where Sean was to speak, they were met by Sean's old friend, Peter O'Reilly, and were immediately taken to a large private room on the second floor. Chairs were lined up in front of a speaker's podium, but people were walking around greeting one another, discussing politics and world affairs, and of course, gossiping.

"I'm delighted you could come, Mrs. Desmond." Peter O'Reilly escorted her around the room, making introductions.

"This is all quite exciting. I've never really heard Sean speak, but our grandfather, for whom he is named, was a famous speaker in Ireland."

"Really? Sean never told me."

"Oh yes. He traveled with the likes of O'Mahoney and Stephens."

O'Reilly was impressed. "I'll have to ask him about all that. You obviously have Irish history in your family."

As Nora's eyes roamed the room, studying the crowd, she suddenly noticed as handsome a man as she had ever seen. He was a commanding presence, over six feet tall with dark wavy hair, laughing dark eyes, a strong, square jaw and perfectly chiseled features. His face seemed to her full of character, intelligence and warmth. She drew in her breath and placed her hand on her brother's arm. "Sean, who is that? He looks familiar."

Sean turned to look. "Why, Nora, it's John Patrick Ryan, lieutenant governor of Massachusetts." He turned to O'Reilly. "I didn't know he was going to be here this evening." He turned back to Nora. "You've undoubtedly seen his picture in the newspaper. As a matter of fact, I think this morning's paper had a picture of him with the governor. I want you to meet him. He's a fascinating man and one of the finest and most unusual Irish-American politicians I've ever had the pleasure of meeting. He's honest and direct, with a great knowledge of history, politics and trends."

O'Reilly interrupted. "He's also quite controversial. He says what he believes, whether it's popular or not. That's hard for a politician to do, but somehow he gets away with it. At least he has so far."

"Wait till you hear him speak," Sean put in. "As Pa would say, he'd give tongue to a stone. I'll introduce you later if you like."

Over the crowd of chattering, smoking, scurrying spectators, Nora once again looked in Jack Ryan's direction. Their eyes met and locked for one short moment; his were smiling, almost intimate. Nora quickly averted hers, feeling a blush warm her fair skin. When she again found the courage to look his way, he was still staring at her, still smiling. This time, amazed at her own forwardness, she smiled back.

The program commenced, but his gaze never faltered from her.

At a short break for refreshments, he came over under the pretext of saying hello to Sean. Nora's heart raced and she felt weak at the knees. Sean turned to Nora. "My sister, Nora Desmond. Nora, Jack Ryan."

"We've already met, haven't we, Nora?" he teased.

"Oh, I didn't know," Sean answered, preoccupied with getting ready to make his speech.

"Mrs. Desmond, meeting you is a very great pleasure."

Nora blushed slightly. "For me also, Mr. Ryan. I understand I'll have the pleasure of hearing you speak this evening."

"I hope it *will* be a pleasure. Politicians do tend a bit toward boorishness sometimes."

"Sean says you are a masterful speaker," she said, and he smiled again. Even though his smile was warm and inviting, it also had an ironic and enigmatic quality that she found most intriguing.

"You will join us later in the Mermaid Room." He hadn't asked, but stated this.

Sean heard this part of the conversation and answered for her. "We'd be delighted. Now wish me luck."

The next thing Nora knew, Sean was leaving the podium to the sound of deafening applause. She smiled and clapped along with everyone else, but she had not heard a word, so taken was she with Mr. Ryan's attentions.

"Oh Sean, how I wish Ma and Pa could have heard you. It was grand," she said convincingly.

Next on the program was Jack Ryan, who began by promising that his speech would be mercifully short. The audience chuckled. Already he had the room full of people on his side, but none more so than Nora Desmond, who by now adored the sound of his voice as much as what he said.

The Mermaid Room was paneled with polished mahogany. Red plush settees and chairs, and luxurious ruby and blue Oriental rugs graced the room. Soft candlelight shimmered from the chandeliers, the tables and the sconces on the walls. Peter O'Reilly, Sean and Nora sat chatting while they waited for Jack.

"He'll have his entourage with him. They follow him everywhere," O'Reilly commented. Nora felt disappointed. How could she talk to him in a big crowd?

When Jack entered several minutes later, however, he entered alone.

"How did you manage to get rid of your shadows, Ryan?" O'Reilly asked, laughing.

"It wasn't easy. I made up some ghastly lie. So ghastly that I can't even remember it. It will probably trip me up sometime." He turned to Nora with his insinuating smile. "No matter. It was worth it."

"Why, thank you, Mr. Ryan. We're flattered that you would rather be alone with us than with a crowd of adoring followers."

Ryan sat with them, ordered drinks all around, and let the others prattle on about home rule and the plight of the immigrants while he talked with Nora about less political matters. "What brings you to Boston, Mrs. Desmond?"

"Oh, Mr. Ryan, I have a business in New York. A lingerie shop called Ballygarry's. I'm here to sell a new line to Filene's."

"How interesting. It's a bit unusual for a woman to own a business."

She went on to tell him how she had come to be an entrepreneur. As her story unfolded, she also mentioned her interest in unions and woman suffrage. "My friend Caroline Trent-Williams never tires of saying that the only people denied the vote are lunatics, idiots, criminals and women."

He laughed. "She's right, of course. I think women should be involved and I'm glad you are. My sisters are always getting on their soapboxes, and I've pledged to them my support, because it's a damned waste of brainpower that women can't vote."

"Mr. Ryan, you're my kind of politician."

"Are you interested in politics?"

She became a little flustered, unsure of her ground. "Well, no, probably not as much as I ought to be, except for the suffrage issue. But I would like to learn more."

"Why, we'll have to do something about that. Would you like your first lesson over dinner tomorrow night?"

Her heart was pounding. She gazed into his dark eyes. "Yes, I'd like that very much."

At that moment, Sean interrupted. "Darling sister, I'm exhausted. I'm speaking again tomorrow, and I do need to get some sleep. Shall we go?"

"Of course, Sean." She rose and turned to Jack as Sean stepped away with Peter O'Reilly.

"It has been a pleasure, Mr. Ryan. Good night." She offered him her hand.

He lifted it to his lips in a courtly gesture. "Tomorrow night, then. I'll pick you up at seven."

"But you don't know where I'm staying."

"Don't worry. I'll find you." He flashed her a brilliant smile as she left.

When she closed the door of her room, she leaned heavily against it for a moment, finally able to give in to the overwhelming sense of excitement. For the first time in years she felt young and vital. She danced gaily around the room, finally flinging herself across the bed. What a fascinating and attractive man he was! Thoughts like these tumbled wildly in her head until she finally dozed off, dreaming of romantic waltzes, shimmering chandeliers, candlelit dinners, and Jack Ryan's enigmatic smile as he said, "Don't worry, I'll find you."

Chapter 33

Nora thought she was still dreaming. A bell was ringing, but it seemed to be very far away. Suddenly her eyes opened wide, and she sat up on the edge of the bed. As she gathered her robe around her, the telephone rang insistently. The room was dark and Nora wondered who could be calling her before dawn's first light. She thought of Mary, hoping all was well at home. As she lifted the receiver to her ear, she heard a strong, deep voice.

"You see, I told you I'd find you."

"Mr. Ryan! Why, what time is it?" Nora rubbed her eyes and a delicious feeling came over her. He really had found her.

"I know I should apologize for waking you, but actually, I've been waiting for an hour to ring you up, so count yourself lucky. I'm only calling to tell you that you're beautiful and dazzling, and if you change your mind and refuse to dine with me tonight, I shall come and kidnap you. So, please say the answer is still yes."

Nora tingled with pleasure. "You won't have to kidnap me, Mr. Ryan. I'll be waiting at seven."

As she placed the phone back on the hook, she was astonished at how strongly she felt. The attraction she had for this man was almost overpowering. No one had ever affected her this way, not even William. She sank into a chair, lightheaded, and happier than she could ever remember being. She rose and pulled open the drapes. Dawn was just touching the horizon. It seemed the most beautiful sunrise she had ever seen. She sang as she dressed, and she found herself humming at the most unexpected moments during the rest of the day. Everyone seemed to be smiling at her as she went to her appointments, and she returned the smiles to one and all.

Wanting to look her best for the evening, she came back to the hotel early to rest. She carefully chose what to wear, a full-length orchid dress made of satin, and then took a scented bath and lay down. She couldn't lie still. Her mind was racing. But never once did she stop to consider that she was a married woman, and that her meeting with Jack Ryan might be seen as highly improper. She got up at least five times, changing her mind about her dress, getting out another gown, then another, until she finally abandoned the idea of resting and began to dress.

At seven, there was a knock on her door, and she opened it to find an enormous bouquet of while lilacs staring her in the face. "Ah," she exclaimed delightedly, "I see these lilacs have feet." The upper body of the bearer of these gorgeous flowers had been hidden, but the flowers were lowered and Jack Ryan was revealed. "How did you know my favorite flower, my favorite scent?"

The evening dazzled and enchanted her. Later she would try to recall the ride to the restaurant, what they said, laughed at, ordered or ate, but everything blurred into the background behind Jack's face, voice and touch. She did remember a great stir as they entered the restaurant, the maître d'hôtel recognizing Jack, bowing low, and with great self-importance, leading the way through the dining room to their reserved table. "Enjoy your meal, Mr. and Mrs. Ryan," he said.

"I'm flattered that he thought such an exquisite woman might be my wife," Ryan remarked.

Nora again experienced the same lightheaded sensation. The very thought of belonging to this man thrilled her.

Jack was suddenly serious. "Nora, I must be honest with you. I do have a wife, and children too. Our marriage seems to exist solely to make the two of us miserable, but until last night, I thought I had made my peace with my situation. I had given up on loving, had closed my heart to that possibility. But now that I've met you, nothing looks the same to me."

Can it be that our lives are so much alike? she thought.

"If only you knew" he continued, "how I felt when I first saw you. Do you recall how I put myself between you and the doorway? I did that because I was so afraid you would get away before I had found out who you were. God, I'm like a kid. I wanted to call you at five o'clock this morning. I lied to my staff and canceled a major speech tonight just to be alone with you. Now I'm pretending to everyone in this room that you are my wife."

Nora felt joyful, for, miracle of miracles, he felt as she did—that they belonged together. So she spoke loudly when the sommelier poured their wine. "Dear, which anniversary are we celebrating tonight? I forget. Is it our eleventh or twelfth? The time passes so quickly with you." The waiter couldn't understand why they laughed then, but he smiled with them, so infectious was their joy.

During the meal, they shared their lives: secrets they

had never told anyone else; how it felt to be poor growing up, she in Ireland and he in America; the shame of darned clothes and patched shoes. Although each had suffered the stigma of poverty and of class distinction, Nora thought there had been softness in her life, singular moments of joy, that Jack Ryan had never known in the rough slums of Boston.

His father had died when he was seven, and to raise the seven Ryan children, Jack's mother and grandmother began taking in laundry and selling homemade baked goods. The oldest and the youngest were boys, with five girls in between. Jack had been the baby.

"You know, Nora, we only bathed once a week. My brother bathed first, then the water was changed for my sisters, but not for me. Until I was fifteen, I bathed in the water that those five girls had used before me. I'll never forget the luxury of my first steaming tub that was drawn just for me. What an extravagance I thought that was."

To make matters worse, his mother, unable to afford new clothes, cut down his sisters' blouses and skirts to make shirts and pants for him. He never knew how the other children in the neighborhood could tell, but somehow they found out and teased him unmercifully. But soon he grew tall and strong, and he began to even the score all around. He seemed to be a born leader. He became captain of every sports team, was respected by men and adored by girls, and was voted president of every organization he joined, including some gangs in the slums. "But," he told Nora, "somehow I always knew I didn't belong there. I also knew that the only way out was to get an education. So I worked at odd jobs, until I had saved enough to get into Boston College. After I got my degree, I went into politics."

He told Nora how he had met his wife. Priscilla Noble was the daughter of a powerful shipyard owner, the granddaughter of an English duke on her mother's side, and the sole heir to huge fortunes on both sides of her family. And this girl, an American aristocrat, had fallen in love with John Patrick Ryan on sight, and had made up her mind to have him almost before he finished introducing himself. He explained to Nora that he knew all this because Priscilla, in her frank, outspoken way, had told him, without considering for a moment that he might not want to belong to her. "And," Jack said, "she was right. Had our courtship been longer, I think things would have turned out differently, but she was a good enough judge of her own character not to let that happen. She went on a hunger strike when her parents objected to her seeing 'Irish-Catholic riffraff.' On the third day of her refusal to eat, there was a stormy scene with her father. She vowed to starve herself to death unless she could see me, and rather than take the chance that she'd keep her promise, I was invited to dinner." He smiled sadly. "I had never met anyone like Priscilla, and I misjudged her traits, mistaking arrogance for spirit, and selfishness for enterprise. She was the girl I had always dreamed of: educated, wealthy, spoiled, beautiful. I can't tell you how flattered I was that she was attracted to me."

The story went on. Three months later, Jack had married Priscilla in the most lavish and talked about society wedding of the season. Shortly thereafter, Jack learned that childhood dream girls weren't for marrying, and Priscilla learned that she had finally met her match in strength of will. She was miserable in the tiny flat Jack had rented, and she begged him to accept her parents' gift of a small house on their estate, but he remained adamant. He would not become dependent on her father. For her part, she would have nothing to do with his family. The first time they went to his mother's for dinner, Priscilla feigned a headache and insisted on being taken home before dinner.

Jack confided to Nora that it was that one act that probably killed his love for Priscilla, for it had caused such a look of hurt on his mother's face.

Jack eventually became more successful in politics, and managed his investments well enough to amass a tidy little fortune, but his wife still wasn't satisfied. "How can you be so stubborn, sticking to your damned seamy Irish politics," she would say. "It's—it's so demeaning. Why can't you go into Daddy's business?"

Their lives went on this way until one drunken night he finally admitted to himself that he was married to a woman he could neither love nor respect. But, being a Catholic, Irish and a politician, he knew he had to play the game. So they lived together, had sex, children, wealth, power, everything, in fact, but love. His two sons became the only bright spots in his life at home.

In turn, Nora told him of her background. When they finally bade each other good-bye, dawn was breaking.

"Oh, Jack, we've both known poverty, and we've been without love all these years when it should have been our constant companion, but the last thing my mother promised me when I left for America was that there was a law of compensation. I now know what she meant."

The next afternoon, the hotel clerk handed Nora an envelope when she returned from a few hours of sightseeing and asked for her room key. It had been a stimulating day, and she was still full of the magic of the previous night. Every historical landmark was more interesting and every beautiful sight was made even more enchanting because of her gay mood. She caught herself humming again; since meeting Jack, it seemed she was always singing. She put her gloves, hat and parasol on the bed, rang for tea and opened the envelope. The paper was of the finest quality, heavily embossed with a coat of arms. The handwriting was elegant, the message surprising: an invitation to dine the next evening with Mr. and Mrs. John Ryan at their Beacon Hill town house, undersigned by Priscilla Winchester Noble Ryan. Nora was puzzled. If only she could talk to Jack.

As though he had read her mind, her telephone rang, and it was he. "Don't be surprised if you receive an invitation to dinner from the Ryans."

"I just opened it. It's sent by your wife."

"I had to see you again, before you left, so I suggested to Priscilla that we have my new speech writer to dinner and that he bring his sister along. Please, say you will come."

"Oh, Jack, I want to see you too. If you feel it's wise, of course we'll come."

The next evening Sean and Nora arrived at the Ryans' promptly at seven. A private courtyard buffered the heavy, ornately carved oak doors of the brownstone from the street. Flanking the entranceway were two urns filled with branches of flowering peach blossoms. The doors opened and a liveried servant ushered them in, taking their wraps. Nora had dressed very simply in a Worth black velvet gown with her beautiful pearl choker filling in the neckline.

The room they entered was a vision of beauty. Soft candlelight illuminated highly polished furniture, silk and satin coverings, and muted paintings on the walls. Elegantly gowned women talked in groups with men in evening dress. Nora saw Jack instantly. He broke away from his conversation and took the arm of a slender, elegant, but haughty blonde, and together they came to greet Sean and Nora.

"Welcome. Priscilla, may I present Sean O'Sullivan and his sister Mrs. Nora Desmond. Sean, Nora, this is my wife Priscilla."

Priscilla was gowned in a ruby red satin dress with

ropes and ropes of pearls. Her blonde hair was swept up rather too perfectly, and her brown eyes appraised Nora in a cold and unsettling way. It was not a beautiful face, being too angular, but it was made up to perfection. Her smile was forced, and her greeting mechanical. "Jack, be a good host and get our guests a glass of champagne while I introduce them around."

These words were delivered in a tone so disdainful that Nora inwardly flinched. Priscilla put a hand, which felt ice cold, on Nora's arm as she guided her around the room, making introductions. Most were Jack's political allies, but a few were members of Priscilla's family. Nora had become aware of a beautiful, fair young man lounging against the fireplace as she had moved about the room. Now they approached him and Priscilla said, "Last, but never least, my brother, Dennis. Pay no attention to anything he says or does. He's impossibly naughty." The butler signaled to Priscilla, and she moved away, leaving Nora without a word.

Dennis Noble laughed. "Alone at last! What's a gorgeous creature like you doing here with all these fossils?"

Nora smiled warmly at him. "I might ask you the same question." They both laughed.

"Beautiful and witty too. How divine. Come sit down, and I'll be impossibly naughty. I wouldn't want to disappoint my sister. By the time the evening is over, I'll do something awful. It's expected of me, you know."

"What a delightful reputation to have. It gives you carte blanche to do all kinds of things without apologizing." Nora found herself liking this handsome, charming young man. "If we ordinary mortals do those things, there's the deuce to pay."

"Tell me about yourself," he said, becoming more serious. "I rarely meet goddesses, you know."

Before she could answer, Jack joined them, bringing

a glass of champagne for Nora. "So, have you met everyone? Sorry to have neglected you, but I was cornered by a couple of cronies."

Nora felt herself flush at Jack's hand brushing hers as he handed the glass to her. How strange it was to try to behave normally, when all she could think about was how it had felt to be alone with him. When she looked up and caught Dennis' glance, he winked at her, a droll, knowing look in his eye. "Well," he said, "I can see you two have things to say to each other, and it makes me nervous to be away from the bar too long. If you'll forgive me, I'm going in search of more champagne."

His elegant figure moved away and Nora and Jack stood smiling noncommittally. Jack moved closer. "You are so beautiful," he whispered. "I was afraid I wouldn't see you again, but I've arranged for us to meet again on Sunday, and as often as we can after that, if you'll allow. This is only the beginning, Nora."

Nora could see Priscilla approaching, and she stepped back from Jack.

"You two must come along to dinner," Priscilla told them. "Mrs. Desmond, we mustn't let my husband monopolize you when so many others want to hear all about you. What part of Ireland did you say you were from?"

"I'm from Ballygarry, County Cork." Nora knew instinctively that Priscilla asked about her background to make her feel ill at ease. Had the woman guessed at her husband's feelings? Nora wondered.

Nora was seated between an uncle of Priscilla's, who she discovered, to her dismay, was quite deaf, and an alderman who seemed little interested in conversation with a stranger. She caught Priscilla giving her a gloating look from the head of the table. "Mrs. Desmond, I understand you're in business. How quaint! What is it you make? Ladies' underwear?" The guests laughed nervously. Before Nora could answer, Priscilla pressed on. "I would never be able to bring myself to leave Jack and the children while I went away on business trips. Don't you feel guilty about leaving your little ones?"

Jack jumped in, upset and embarrassed by his wife's attack. "Priscilla, I'm quite sure Mrs. Desmond has nothing to feel guilty about. I've heard she's a very accomplished businesswoman, and her brother tells me she's an equally good wife and mother."

"Of course she is. Mrs. Desmond knows I meant no offense. It was only a question from one mother to another. There go your touchy Irish feelings again, Jack. I swear, Mrs. Desmond, I have to watch every word I say around him."

Dennis came to Nora's defense. "I think it's quite fascinating that Mrs. Desmond is in business. How sensible for a woman to design women's lingerie. And, dear sister, there are worse things that keep women away from their children, don't you think? Like pleasure trips and shopping sprees." He smiled wickedly, sipping his champagne.

Priscilla glared at him furiously. Damn, she thought, he's already drunk.

Sean looked as if he were about to physically come to Nora's defense as he half rose, but he smiled charmingly. "We Irish are sensitive, Mrs. Ryan—especially to beauty such as yours." Priscilla flushed with pleasure and Sean raced on, turning the attention away from Nora, talking of the excellent food and the china on which it was served.

"Why, I'm so happy you noticed the china service. I've used it in your honor. It's handmade in Ireland and was given to my grandfather by the queen in appreciation for his loyal service in quelling rebellion there."

Nora saw Sean blanch at this statement, and she gave

thanks at that moment that it was Sean sitting there and not Terence.

"Uncle Lester," Priscilla shouted to the deaf old man on Nora's left, "you remember this china from Ireland, don't you?"

Without missing a mouthful, the old man shouted, "Damned Irish troublemakers."

Jack's voice was cold, but controlled. "The china is beautiful, but the way it was earned is not. The gratitude of the queen was measured against the number of Irish massacred by Priscilla's illustrious grandfather."

Priscilla laughed sarcastically. "There he goes again, the noble patriot. He acts this way every time I use this service. You're a grown man, Jack, too adult to be angry over a set of dishes, for heaven's sake!"

Nora wanted nothing more than to take Jack's hand and escape this dreadful evening.

Priscilla waved her hand for the last course served to be removed, and continued: "You'll have our guests thinking that I don't adore the Irish, and obviously I do, darling, since I married you." She raised her glass to Jack.

"Why, Mrs. Ryan, I'm flattered by your affection for my people," Nora interrupted. "And I would like to toast your gracious hospitality." The sarcasm was obvious, but several of the other guests, grateful for the break in the embarrassing tension, lifted their glasses and murmured, "Hear, hear."

"Besides," Priscilla went on, now lusting for the blood of this beautiful Irish upstart, "I have many friends in Ireland. I'm sure Mrs. Desmond would know them. In fact, she may have gone to school with some of them. Let's see, Mrs. Desmond, Lady Julia Harrington would be about your age. She attended Miss Harcourt's School for girls. And her sister, Margaret, she's the one who was presented at court. Then there is—"

Jack was about to speak when there was a terrible crash.

"Dennis, what have you done?" Priscilla cried shrilly.

"An accident, dearest sister, an accident! What a pity. One of your favorite historical plates. I do so hope it can be mended. Thank heavens, I didn't spoil your lovely dinner conversation. Damned considerate of me, I think, to wait till we were finished to break something. We are finished, aren't we? Good, I thought so." He rose without waiting for her answer. "As my penance for being so clumsy, I'm going to make amends by showing Mrs. Desmond your famous roof garden." He was already pulling back Nora's chair.

"Mrs. Desmond, do you trust yourself in the moonlight alone with someone of my obviously dubious character?"

Nora had never been so grateful. A hundred retorts had sprung to her lips at Priscilla's insulting sarcasm, but Nora didn't want to embarrass Jack more than he already had been. That was the only thing that held her tongue. I won't let her humiliate me like that again, Nora thought, Jack or no Jack.

When she looked across at Ryan, he was livid, but she flashed him a brilliant smile which said to him not to worry. Obviously upset, Priscilla was gathering up the pieces of the plate, looking to see if it could be mended.

"I don't know why you saved me," Nora whispered to Dennis, as they stepped into the foyer, "but I'm grateful."

He pushed open the door leading to a winding stairway. "I can't imagine why Jack threw a creature as lovely as you to that carnivorous she devil. Too bad we can't let those two go at it with pistols at dawn. I only say that because I know Jack is an excellent shot."

"But Dennis, she's your sister."

"I know, isn't it awful? She hates me because I'm

more beautiful than she. The boy she was madly in love with the winter of her debut ended up liking me better, and she's never forgiven me. He and I had quite a little fling. Oh dear, have I shocked you? You've gone positively white as a ghost. Sit down here on the stairs. I'm afraid this whole evening has been dreadful for you. What must you think of the Nobles?''

Nora had to laugh. He was irresistible, totally charming, and, she was sure, very kind. ''Well, there's no question about one thing,'' Nora placed her hand on his arm. ''You are definitely more beautiful than she is''—they both laughed—''and infinitely more likeable.''

He smiled warmly at Nora. ''I'll tell you what: let's skip the roof garden. It's really quite pretentious anyway. Quite like my sister. Let's sit right here, and you will tell me all about yourself.''

So, while Dennis drank vintage champagne from a bottle he produced from under his jacket, Nora told him about her childhood and her life since she'd been in America. They were like two school chums hiding from the adults and trading secrets.

''I admire you, Nora. You're certainly not afraid of hard work. I'm quite allergic to it, you know. As you can see, I do pretty much as I wish, and, dear girl, what I wish right now is to take you to lunch tomorrow. How's that for a splendid idea?''

''It *is* a splendid idea. Let's do it.'' Nora's spirits were much higher now.

''Then your knight in shining armor will arrive at one to carry you off. I suppose we must go back now and see whom Priscilla is dissecting.''

Some of the guests had departed. The rest were having coffee and cognac by the fireplace.

''There you are, you naughty Dennis,'' Priscilla chided. ''You've had Mrs. Desmond to yourself quite long enough. Mrs. Desmond, I've so enjoyed meeting you, and I absolutely insist that you join us this weekend at our country estate. Your brother has accepted for you, so it's all settled.''

Nora couldn't believe that Sean had done such a thing, but when she sneaked him a look, she could see that he was as surprised as she. Never mind, she thought, I'll go. Two can play this game.

Sean had had enough and pleaded an early engagement the next day. As they were being helped into their coats, Dennis whispered to Nora, who was now his friend and confidante, ''She must really be out to get you. I'll bet she probably has something up her sleeve that she's sure will make you look like a fool in front of Jack and the others. Don't take it too personally. It's one of her favorite games. Since you are beautiful as well as bright, she considers you fair game. Besides, you'll get to see Jack that way,'' he added mischievously. ''There, there, don't look so frightened. I won't tell a soul. I'm all for you.'' He lifted his glass in a mock toast.

''I'm praying you'll be there this weekend, Dennis. I have a feeling I'll need my Sir Lancelot.''

''Ordinarily, I avoid those tweedy bores Priscilla puts together, but for you sake, I'll be there. We'll plot our strategy tomorrow at lunch. Incidentally, if you've never ridden to the hunt, don't let my sister know. She'll make it hard on you.''

A fox hunt? Nora wondered, puzzled. She had had no inkling that they would be riding. Why surely Priscilla couldn't expect her to ride without the proper attire, but her interest was piqued, and a smile crossed her face at the idea of that particular challenge. She wondered if Sean had said something about the fact that she rode. As she rejoined the group by the front door, she surprised everyone, Jack in particular.

"Why Mrs. Ryan, I wouldn't miss it for the world. How very sweet of you to include us." Even Priscilla was a bit taken aback by Nora's seemingly gracious acceptance, though Sean, and now Dennis, knew that Nora was onto Priscilla's game.

Nora stayed in bed the next morning, for she didn't feel at all well. She was very tired. Everything was happening too quickly. Meeting Jack had changed her whole life, and last night, Priscilla's cruel attempts to humiliate her had set something vicious in motion within her. Old angers were stirring. How like William was Priscilla, with that same arrogance, that same lack of sensitivity, that same total self-centeredness. I hate them, she thought, and everyone like them. I can't help wanting to pay them back. A few errant tears rolled down her cheeks, and she quickly sat on the edge of the bed. There was no time for tears. She would have her chance to teach Priscilla a lesson, and to repay her for the life of misery she had given Jack. She would find that opportunity, she swore.

She took herself out of her reverie, realizing she would be late for her luncheon with Dennis if she didn't hurry. Dear Dennis, she thought, smiling to herself. How she wished all the gentry were more like him.

As she walked through the lobby to meet him, she noticed a small crowd gathering outside on the sidewalk, and as she stepped out the door, she instantly discovered what had captured their attention. It was a glorious sight. There was Dennis, elegantly handsome in a meticulously tailored white suit, and a flamboyant lavender scarf around his neck, at the wheel of the longest, most extraordinary white American underslung automobile with the top down. An enormous white fluffy dog sat beside him in the passenger seat. The entire back seat of the car was filled with flowers: tulips, daffodils, lilacs, flowering quince, irises, and a dozen other kinds.

"Ah, there you are, divine one!" He jumped from the car and came around to take her arm. There was applause from the gathered people, who were thoroughly enjoying the sight, and Dennis, opening the door for her, said, "These are your subjects come to pay you homage, as well they should. Move over, Arthur. Make room for our honored guest." Arthur followed these directions, but not before trying to sit in Nora's lap. She laughed all the way to the restaurant.

"Oh, Dennis, you're magical! And this car is absolutely fabulous. Why, you could fit four more of us in here easily."

"I could, and have, but not today. I want to be alone with you." He beamed at her.

She laughed. "Oh, Dennis, it feels so good to be around you."

"It's the least I could do to make amends for what Priscilla subjected you to last night. You mustn't go away thinking ill of all the Nobles. I only wish it were truly the days of King Arthur, so that I could sally forth to slay a dragon, or whatever they did, with your hankie tied to my lance as a sign of your favor."

"Thank heavens," she replied playfully. "I'm happy finally to have a champion to protect my honor, a knight to go running around the countryside slaying ogres."

"Like my sister."

She shrugged. "You said it, Dennis, not I."

Once lunch was ordered, Dennis told her about himself. "Moms insisted we be schooled abroad, so we never saw much of her or dear old Dad. I used to think I missed them, until I'd come home on vacation, and they tried to make a man of me. Ha. So much for that. You know"— he was suddenly, touchingly sad—"I never remember one person hugging or kissing me. Probably just not done in the 'right' families. Vulgar, you know." He paused a moment, a glimmer of loneliness in his eyes. "I had a bad time, even tried to do away with myself. Had the rope around my neck and was about to kick the chair out from under, when I caught a view of myself in the mirror. Damned funniest sight I ever saw. I guess I've been poking fun at life ever since. I do care, though, at least for the right people. I love Jack. He's all man, but he has a rare and marvelous sensitivity. He's always been kind to me, and I know he understands me. Poor man. Priscilla makes his life hell." He paused to light up a pipe. "If Jack weren't so damned fine and good, he'd have left her years ago. As it is, they lead almost completely separate lives. She loves New York, you know. She's there a great deal of the time. This may be just awful to say, and will no doubt shock you, but now that I've met you, I feel a sudden surge of hope. You and Jack look so right together. I can tell it's meant to be. Now, let's have some champagne, dear one, and let me just gaze at that glorious face of yours. You'll feast on this divine lunch, and I will feast on your beauty."

Dennis entertained her during the next two hours with his extravagant enthusiasms and ironic cynicisms. She knew he felt a terrible disappointment in himself and in the way his life had turned out, but he seemed powerless to alter it. Nora's heart went out to him. He was so vulnerable under all his outrageous actions and wicked humor.

She placed her hand on his and kissed his cheek. "I hope you don't think me vulgar," she said.

"No. Never." He silently took her hand in his, and Nora knew their friendship had been sealed.

Hours later, he dropped her at her hotel and grandly escorted her to the door. "I shall see you at Marblehead, my dear, protecting you as best I can, and after that, we shall next meet for lunch in New York. I can't wait to see all that lovely lace lingerie.'' He kissed her tenderly on both cheeks.

It took every man on duty to carry the flowers up to her room. Dennis departed with horns blowing and Arthur barking. To Nora, the sun seemed a little less bright with his departure.

Chapter 34

Sean and Nora motored up the curving ocean road to
Marblehead on an exhilarating September day, admiring
the lovely old mansions and summer estates of the wealthy
Bostonians along the way. Gingerbread Victorian houses
with cupolas, gables and large verandas, old stone mansions that were fortresslike in appearance, and an occa-
sional chateau in the French style commanded the ocean
view. When they finally reached Marblehead, they turned
off the main road onto a driveway that carried them out
onto a peninsula. This had been the Nobles' land since
before the Civil War. The drive wound through a large,
secluded, completely private woods of maples and oaks.

"Sean, it's just beautiful. It reminds me just a little of
the woods near Ballygarry and the one solitary road through
it."

The house suddenly loomed in front of them. It was a
large wooden structure, white with green shutters, surrounded by many verandas and porches, steeples and
cupolas.

"It's hard for me to believe they have anything this friendly-looking," Nora remarked. "Their Beacon Street home is so impersonal."

Dogs, children and adults bounded out to meet them. When Jack helped Nora from the car, she felt a strange sensation of forbidden excitement when he took her arm. There were other guests. Introductions were made, and everyone gathered on the porch for refreshments.

Dennis was already being enormously entertaining, and Sean was soon at his best. Even Priscilla was making an effort to be pleasant.

"I do recall, Mrs. Desmond, that at dinner the other evening your brother mentioned that you rode," Priscilla said to Nora. "Well, I have a lovely surprise for you. We'll all be riding a bit later. I insist you take part. We have extra outfits, so we'll hear no excuses from you. I've told everyone about the Irish rider who'll be joining us. We're off at once."

Jack realized at that moment that his wife was trying to humiliate Nora. Walking over to Nora, he quietly spoke to her. "I'm sorry. I didn't know anything about this. Of course, you needn't ride if you don't care to."

Nora inwardly laughed, secretly relishing the call to battle that Priscilla had issued, and reveling in the irony that Priscilla had chosen the arena in which Nora excelled. *That lady is in for a surprise!* "Why, Mr. Ryan, I wouldn't miss this for the world." Turning to Priscilla, she smiled. "Mrs. Ryan, what a lovely surprise. May I choose my mount?"

Priscilla seemed taken aback. "Why, of course. I'll show you where the riding habits are kept."

Jack took Nora by the arm. "Allow me, Mrs. Desmond." He turned to his wife. "You don't mind, do you?"

"Of course not," she said coldly.

Nora turned to Dennis. "Will you escort me to the stables when I'm dressed?"

"Of course, Mrs. Desmond." He smiled conspiratorially, then lowered his voice. "You knew not to let her pick your mount, didn't you?"

"Of course, Dennis. If I'm to be made a fool of, it won't be on an old nag."

He laughed delightedly. "Somehow, I don't think it's in the cards for you to be made a fool of, on or off an old nag."

Nora winked. "We little Irish girls are a force to be reckoned with."

"Meet me right here as soon as you're dressed. No doubt what she's chosen for you will be last year's riding habit, and ill-fitting at that."

She squared her shoulders. "Well there's nothing to be done about that. I'll make do."

Sean watched these proceedings with a suppressed smile. He purposely made no mention of Nora's equestrian abilities. He wasn't much of a rider himself, but Jack had asked him to ride along, just to view the property.

Dennis had been right about Priscilla's clothing choice for Nora. The outfits laid out for her were old and ill fitting, but Nora suddenly had an idea. She would hide them someplace, then innocently ask what she was supposed to wear. If Priscilla wanted all this to happen badly enough, she would have to lend Nora one of her own expensive, well-tailored habits. This was becoming more fun by the moment.

Nora peeked out. The hall was clear, so she ran, carrying the castoffs, into a large closet and stuffed them into a chest in the corner.

Priscilla was totally confused by the disappearance of

the clothes. She sent the help scurrying, but the garments were not to be found. Priscilla was furious, but just as Nora had hoped, she brought her an outfit from her own extensive collection.

"Why, Mrs. Ryan, this is really quite handsome—a trifle large in the waist, but I'm sure I can manage. I do feel that I am causing you a great deal of trouble. Why don't you let me sit out? I'd be happy to do that if it would make matters simpler."

"Oh, no, no, no, absolutely not! It's no trouble at all, my dear. You'll enjoy the ride immensely." She gave Nora a sly look and walked out of the room.

Nora and Dennis carefully chose her mount, a handsome gelding of fine breeding and good spirit, named Halley's Comet. Jack Ryan relaxed, taking his cue from Nora and Sean, neither of whom seemed to be in the least concerned. The rules of the hunt were explained, the master of the hunt blew his horn, and the riders and dogs took off. Nora rode like the wind, jumping the fences and bushes with an authority and beauty that even the most seasoned horsemen there had never seen before. Priscilla was livid as the other riders gathered around after the hunt to compliment Nora and to chat with her. Dennis, Jack and Sean congratulated her heartily.

Sean, no longer able to resist, remarked innocently to Priscilla, "I don't believe I mentioned the other evening at dinner that Nora had taken prizes at the Dublin Horse Show."

Meanwhile Jack saved her from the unstoppable enthusiasm of her well-wishers. "Sean's already seen the estate, Mrs. Desmond. If you would care to join Dennis and me, we'll show you parts you couldn't have seen on the hunt."

"My pleasure, Mr. Ryan."

The three of them rode off and toward the lovely woods they had driven through earlier. The air was getting crisp, and sunlight flickered on the leaves of trees that formed a bower over their heads.

"I can't remember a more glorious day," Nora exclaimed, still exultant over her triumph, "or a more beautiful place, except, of course, in our County Cork." Her eyes were full of mischief.

Dennis purposely fell behind them. "Go ahead, you two. I haven't had a good gallop all day, and neither has Blackbird. I'll return shortly." Dennis gave his horse rein and rode off.

Nora and Jack were alone. Nora's heart began to race. Jack reached for her hand. "You were absolutely superb today," he said in a low, trembling voice.

"Was I?" She gazed up at him. Their eyes locked as they had during that first moment across a crowded room. Words were not needed. Jack swept Nora into his arms and kissed her warm, moist, waiting lips—lips that had been waiting all her life for just this kiss. She responded with all the pent-up passion she had once thought forever dead.

"Oh, Nora, I never believed I could be so happy." He kissed her again, a long, lingering kiss, in this quiet forest on this soft, golden day of Indian summer, and her yearning lips yielded to his.

They could hear Dennis returning now, and Jack quickly whispered, "Till tomorrow, my love. We'll have time alone again. I promise."

When they returned to the house, a party was in progress. More people had arrived, and Nora excused herself to change her clothing. She had left the hubbub as much to think delicious thoughts as to dress. She found herself standing in a small, quiet hallway. While looking in the ornate, gilt mirror to adjust her pearls, she thought how different she looked from the girl who had arrived some hours ago. Suddenly Jack Ryan was standing behind her. They stared at each other in the mirror. He gently put his hands on her shoulders.

"Nora." Then, even more softly, "Nora, darling, we are looking at our other selves, our other life, when we will be together forever."

Her eyes glistened with longing for him. There was a profound silence in the quiet hallway as they both thought of the extraordinary promise of that other world.

"We'll never forget this moment, Nora."

She could hear her heart pounding and wondered if he could too. She stared back at him, her violet eyes alive with hope. "Is this life in the mirror to be ours, then?" she asked softly.

"Yes, Nora, it is."

At that moment, they heard the door down the hall open, and they parted as wordlessly as they had come together.

Nora pretended to be asleep on the journey back to the hotel so that she could savor the memories of this incredible day. She still felt his touch, his mouth on hers, her passion stirring, rising again, like the phoenix, out of its own ashes.

Why do I always choose a man who is unavailable to me? she thought. One who cannot be mine because of his station in life or because he belongs to another? But she could not help her feelings.

She moved around the hotel room that night as if in a dream, wanting only to stay awake thinking of every moment, or asleep dreaming of every moment.

She finally fell asleep, but the dreams were not the ones she wanted. Her dreams were of her falling off precipices, of William scornfully handing her the envelope of money, of Mike hiding little Mary from her, of her mother asking again and again if there was anything wrong, of trying to break a frightening mirror, of fleeing the ravaged face of Gina Gambini.

Nora awoke in a cold sweat. Oh, my God, what does this all mean? But she knew. Where hours earlier she had felt only joy, she now felt guilt and fears.

I can't do this. I mustn't. I was a fool to let myself love again. I'll be hurt just as I was before. Jack has a wife, just as I have a husband. And he has his career as well. He could never be divorced; it would ruin him. She suddenly had the awful realization that she had set herself up to be rejected. I can't do it again. How do I know I can trust Jack's promises? I trusted William and Angelo. The old wounds had reopened, and panic overcame her. She frantically packed her bags, telling Sean she must leave immediately, creating a story that she had received a telegram from Rachel, that there was trouble at the factory. She hurriedly stopped at Filene's to pick up the lingerie order and to thank them, and sent flowers to Priscilla Ryan with a note, thanking her for her gracious hospitality. To Jack she sent only a short message: *It can never be. I'm sorry.*

On the train, she resolved again to try to make her marriage work, so real had been her dream of losing Mary. I can't risk losing another child, or ruining my life again. And good God, I'm pregnant. I owe it to Mary, to this baby and to Mike to bring some order into our lives. Jack will be far better off if I never see him again.

When she entered her apartment, Mary, Bridget, and even Mike seemed happy to see her, and she felt she had made the right decision. This was her life, a good life, she thought as she looked around the table, and she was determined to live it as best she could. But that night when she turned Mike away on the pretexts of fatigue and an upset stomach, he cursed her for being an unloving wife, and the reality of her misery returned. Once again she softly cried herself to sleep.

Jack returned to Boston the evening Nora left. He immediately ducked out of a staff meeting and went to meet her at the Copley Plaza. He rang her room, but there was no answer. When he asked for Mrs. Desmond at the desk, they told him she had checked out. He stood there in disbelief, arguing with the clerk, saying it wasn't possible, insisting that there was a mistake.

When he admitted the truth to himself, he was furious. You fool, he thought, you've frightened her away, for he couldn't bring himself to believe after the intensity of their shared moments that there could be any other reason for her running away. What have I done? Have I lost her, just as I found her? He walked into the bar and slumped spiritlessly into a corner chair. For the past week his life had seemed as bright and happy as it had ever been. He thought of his loveless existence with Priscilla and of how his mother had tried to talk him out of marrying her. "You'll be needing one of your own kind, Jack," she had counseled him. "Otherwise, count on misery all the remaining days of your life." Nora would have met his mother's requirements, being Irish and Catholic, but she was even more his own kind in other ways. She was someone with whom he could talk, someone who could understand him and accept his career, who would have the vivaciousness and wit to make life the pleasure it should be. He thought of the enthusiasm and the mischief sparkling in those lovely lavender eyes. He thought again of Priscilla, of her cold, regal manner, which had not the slightest touch of caring or humanity, of her self-centeredness and arrogance. Why did I ever marry her, why, why? He pounded his hand on the table, startled the waiter, and ordered his fifth drink. As with anyone in love, Jack couldn't think of one thing about Nora he wouldn't cherish. By the time he finished his drink, however, he had become angry with her. How could she give up so easily, after so many years of denial? How could she run away without even trying? She must not care he thought. So he would forget her, forget the whole interlude! "By God, I will forget her," he said aloud. "I will!"

To keep up with demand, plans were made to open a second Queen's Lace factory, and Nora threw herself body and mind into the preparations. She needed to forget Jack and the flame he had kindled in her soul. She and Annie and Rachel worked day and night. One evening after work, Nora and Annie sat alone drinking coffee.

"Nora, you're not looking well since you returned from Boston. What is it, girl?"

Nora wanted desperately to tell her about Jack, but knew she couldn't. "I'm just tired, Annie. That, and I'm pregnant again."

"Faith, what a surprise," Annie answered. She knew what a mixed blessing a child would be for Nora right now. "How are you feeling about having another baby?"

"Confused. I don't want to have a child now, but I don't have much to say about that, do I?"

Annie saw a tear drop from Nora's eye. "Ah, lass, there, there. Cry if you wish. It will make you feel better."

"Oh, Annie." Nora's voice was filled with anger. "I was going to separate from Mike. And now, this."

Annie hadn't realized the extent of Nora's misery.

"Separate? But Nora, what about Mary? 'Tis a terrible big step to be taking. Please think about it, be really sure what you're doing."

"I think Mary would be better off in the long run. Our unhappiness will become apparent to her only too soon."

Annie just shook her head, knowing only that she wanted Nora to be happy, however she could manage it. She would support her in whatever decision she made.

"Forget it for now, Annie," Nora said in a lighter vein. "We have work to do."

Shortly after Sean arrived home from Boston, he and Rachel announced their wedding plans. He had already spoken to her about how afraid he was that their marriage would alienate her from her parents, but Rachel had quieted his fears.

"Darling, it will be all right," she had told him. "I believe they learned a lesson from what happened to Sarah, and I think they'll support my decision. Oh, Sean, I can only hope so, for as much as I love them, I must live my own life. And you are my life."

Rachel was right. The Friedmans did not want to repeat their mistake, and they did not want to lose her. They told her they were happy for her, and if Sean could find it in his heart to forgive them, they would welcome him as their son-in-law. If Mr. Friedman had objected, Rebecca Friedman was ready to take her stand, but the old man had suffered enough for one lifetime. His only fear now was that Sean would have nothing to do with them, would never forgive them. Sean did struggle with his feelings for some time. Rachel knew the battle raging in his soul, and told him she would understand if he could not bring himself to forgive and forget. But forgive he did, more for Rachel's and baby Terry's sake than for his own.

Nora insisted on planning their wedding and having the reception in her beautiful apartment, which Nora had filled with masses of irises and daffodils and poppies, and Oscar of the Waldorf had done the catering, which was both beautiful and delectable. The family and guests mingled, sipping the fine Dom Perignon champagne that Nora had been introduced to by Angelo, talking and wishing the bride and groom happiness, and complimenting Nora on her beautiful home. Rachel looked vibrant, dressed in the ivory satin she so loved. Her eyes were aglow with happiness.

Just before she left on her honeymoon, Rachel threw the bouquet, and Bridget caught it. Bridget began thinking of her own wedding and of Kevin. As she brushed away a tear, she glanced over at Nora, who was crouching over on the settee. Bridget rushed over to her. "You're looking dreadful, Nora. What is it?"

"I—I don't know, Bridget. I have terrible pains. I'm afraid to move. I don't want to spoil the reception. Please don't let anyone know."

"Here, stand up and take my arm. We'll get you to the bedroom. Don't be worrying about the guests. Most of them have left."

Nora lay down on the bed and Bridget undressed her, fearing the tight corset was causing pain. Nora's undergarments were covered with blood. Bridget became alarmed then. Nora quickly fell into semiconsciousness. Bridget rushed to get Mike.

A few moments later, Bridget and Mike and Annie had Nora in a carriage on the way to the hospital. Annie knew that Nora hadn't told her family yet about the pregnancy, so she remained silent. Joseph, Mary and Patrick, she thought, she must be losing the baby.

*   *   *

Annie's worst fears were realized, for when the doctor came out from the examination room, he called Mike aside. "I'm terribly sorry, Mr. Desmond. She lost your child. But your wife will be all right. Don't worry about her. She's a strong girl."

Mike looked like he had been struck. Bridget stood at his side. "I—I didn't even know she was pregnant," he repeated over and over.

Bridget tried to comfort him. "She may not have known, Mike. Sometimes you just don't know. Isn't that so, Annie?"

"Aye, often. That often happens."

"She knew," he whispered hoarsely. "And she killed it."

"That's nonsense," Bridget said harshly. "Don't say such a horrible thing."

"Oh, maybe she didn't intend to"—his voice was now full of fury—"but it's all the same. Running to the shop and the factory, working all hours, traveling to Chicago and Boston and everywhere else. She killed my child."

Annie looked at him strangely. "Mike, you should know that's not what causes miscarriages. I've seen women in the fields, working twelve hours a day until their time, then deliver their babies, get up and continue working. You mustn't blame her." Her comment sounded more like a warning.

But all of Mike's frustrations and suppressed anger spilled out in recriminations. "She didn't want this child. Otherwise, why wouldn't she have told me about him? Why wouldn't she tell her own husband she was pregnant, answer me that?"

"Mike, please, don't act this way. She's a very sick woman. She needs comfort and kind words. Imagine how she must feel losing a baby." Bridget couldn't imagine anything more terrible than that, having long wanted one so desperately.

He shrugged her away and walked down the hall into Nora's room. Nora sat up weakly. Her eyes were red from crying, for she had been thinking much the same as Mike, only she was convinced that riding in the hunt and taking the jumps had done it. When he strode in, she held out her hand.

He ignored the gesture. "Nora, this is the final straw. You've killed our baby, a baby I didn't even know existed. You've killed it running and working, when you should have been home taking care of yourself. I can't take this any longer." He was obviously overwhelmed by his own frustration and anger. "I'm leaving you." He turned his back on her and walked out.

"No, no, Mike," she managed weakly. "Please don't say such things. I—" But she didn't finish her sentence because he was already gone. She stared at the door. I wanted him to leave, she thought, but not like this. She sat in quiet desperation, not knowing what to think. She felt no emotions, no anger, fear, relief, or sadness. One thing she did know was that she could never forgive him for what he had just done. The one time she had needed him, needed to hear some words of comfort, he had failed her. There was nothing left between them.

Bridget and Annie appeared at the door, and Nora put her arms out to embrace them. "Thank God you're here." She broke down and wept.

They comforted her, reassured her, even made her smile a little. Bridget took her hand. "Mike's overwrought about losing the baby, Nora. Don't worry, it will be all right."

Nora smiled wanly. "I don't think so, Bridget. I really don't think it will be all right ever again."

The nurse shooed the women away, for Nora needed to rest. They left reluctantly, promising to return the next day. As twilight fell, and Nora could no longer see out the window, she fell into a deep, dreamless sleep. Later she awoke and slowly opened her eyes, becoming aware of a figure sitting on the chair in the dark room, barely visible from the dim light filtering in from the hallway. She tried to make out who it was. Was it Mike? It couldn't be Sean, she concluded. He didn't even know. But she knew it was a man. She lifted her head and then saw the walking stick.

"Angelo, Angelo, is it you?"

"Yes, dearest Nora. I didn't want to disturb you. I just had to see with my own eyes if you were all right."

"Oh Angelo." She extended her hand to him. "Thank you for being here when I needed you." This man, who made no claim on her and wasn't even really a part of her life, was always there when she needed him. I shall never forget this, she thought. Someday he will need me, and I will be there for him. "How did you know?" she asked.

He shrugged. "One hears. Are you feeling stronger?"

"Oh yes, much stronger."

"I also heard that Mike walked out, that he's leaving you. Is that true?"

Nora bowed her head. When she looked back up at him, there were tears in her eyes. "Yes. He seems to think I tried to kill the child."

"My God. Did he actually say that to you?"

She shook her head, unable at that moment to speak.

Angelo sat silently for a few moments. Finally he said, "Nora, you are wasted on a man like Mike Desmond. You're a priceless jewel, and he's a dimwitted peasant."

She had rarely seen Angelo angry, but he was angry now. It was a quiet, intense, controlled anger, but it frightened her nonetheless, for she suddenly had a sense of his enormous power. "Angelo, I'll work this out. Don't worry about it. There are some things you cannot do for me, must not do. I have gotten myself into this misery, and I will get out somehow. Perhaps it's just as well that he left." She was quiet for a moment. "It's as much my fault as his for having married him, Angelo. You must understand that."

Angelo was losing patience. "All right, Nora. You made a mistake. But does that one mistake make it all right for him to drag you down to his level, to walk out on you when you're suffering this way? Why, good Lord, didn't he take the same vows you took, for richer or poorer, better or for worse? All right, so you shouldn't have married him. But you don't have to spend a lifetime placating him. You have got to come to grips with all this, Nora . . . or you'll be destroyed." They sat silently for a few moments.

"Also among those vows it says, 'till death do us part,' " she whispered hoarsely.

"Well," Angelo said slowly, "it doesn't seem that that is going to be, does it?"

"I had asked for a divorce, and he flew into a rage, forbidding me to ever mention the word again. Now he says he's leaving me."

"He'll be back!" Angelo roared, filled with disgust. "That kind always comes back. And you'll need to decide what you are going to do before your life is ruined."

"I know, Angelo. I will. I'm just tired and confused. I didn't want another child, but I didn't want to lose the baby either. I'm so very tired and confused. I can't seem to think at all."

He pressed her hand tightly. "Good night, dear Nora. I'll try to come again, but I don't want to cause trouble. Remember, I'm always there for you."

She gazed up at him gratefully. "I know Angelo, I know." Then she closed her eyes and fell into a deep, restoring sleep.

"You're strong as an ox, Nora," Bridget commented. "Just four days out of the hospital, and you're already off to work." She paused. "Mike will be back soon, I'm sure."

"No, Bridget. He said he's never returning. He's at his mother's, and there he'll stay." She pulled her gloves on and went to kiss Mary good-bye.

"Where's Daddy, Mommy?"

"On a trip, remember? Mommy told you," she answered nervously, trying to change the subject. "Mommy will try to be home early, love. Be good for Aunt Bridget."

Nora left hurriedly before Mary could ask any more questions. The postman was stuffing her mailbox, and she intercepted him, taking the correspondence. There were a few bills, a letter for Bridget from Kevin's mother, and a letter for Nora from Danny.

When she arrived at work, she took the coffee offered her by her secretary, Miss White, and asked not to be disturbed. She settled into her favorite chair and opened Danny's letter.

Dearest Nora,

Sorry I haven't written sooner. The Bishop sent me on a tour of the counties to take care of some complicated Church matters recently, and I was gone for several weeks.

The news here, I'm sorry to say, is not as happy as I'd like. Pa has taken a turn for the worse. He no longer is able to work in the fields and needs a great deal of rest and care. If he follows the doctor's orders, he should be with us for a long time yet, at least that's what old Doctor Callaghan says. Pa's not happy about being kept out of the fields, but Doc says if he does no heavy work, he can soon go down to supervise at least. That, of course, improved his mood.

We've had word through the grapevine that Terence and Julia are fine, although still in hiding. That may forever be their fate, I'm thinking, but we all travel different roads, and if that's the one they have chosen, I can only wish them well. I've also heard that Seamus is now safe in America, having sailed with forged papers, all arranged, of course, by the Brotherhood. You'll probably be hearing from him before too long, if you haven't already.

Dear Nora, if there is any chance that you or Sean might return home for a visit, now is the time, while Pa is still alive. How it would gladden his heart if such a thing were possible. Ma goes to Lord Anthony's with Father O'Rourke. Lord Anthony had also been quite ill, and Ma goes over twice a week to the big house to read to him, though one would think his own daughter-in-law could do it, but he asked for Mary, and she loves to do it. They have become fine friends.

Well, time is dear, and I must go now. You are always in my prayers, and don't forget to keep Ma and Pa in yours.

Love,
Danny

That evening at dinner, Bridget noticed that Nora was quiet and preoccupied. "What's wrong, Nora? Can I help?"

Nora told Bridget the news about their father and Seamus.

Bridget was not surprised that their father was ill, but she was very upset about Seamus. "If he's here Nora, it's strange that he wouldn't let us know."

"Perhaps he's with his family here. He has a brother."

"Yes," Bridget said. "In Philadelphia."

"I'm scheduled to make a trip to Philadelphia to show the line to Wanamaker's. Perhaps I can look into the matter." She lapsed back into silence.

Bridget tried again. "Nora, darling, don't worry about Mike. He'll be back. Sure, and he didn't mean what he said."

Nora looked at her steadily. "I think that even if he returns, I won't allow him to stay."

Bridget turned pale. "Nora, you can't do that. He's your husband. This is his home, and Mary is his child."

"We can no longer live together, Bridget. He disapproves of everything about me. And frankly, there's little about him of which I approve."

Bridget started to cry. "Nora, please reconsider. He's a good man. He means well."

Nora stood up, not wanting to continue the conversation. "Yes, he is a good man. But he's not good for me."

Two weeks later, Mike appeared at the shop, contrite and miserable. He asked Nora if she would join him for lunch, to talk about their future. Though she had decided that separation was their only alternative, he seemed so lost and lonely that she began to soften her heart, believing he would change as he promised he would.

He apologized for all his harsh words at the hospital. "Nora, I was overwrought about losing our baby."

"Yes, so was I," Nora quietly answered. Tempted as she was to say more, she remained silent, thinking perhaps she needed to give their relationship one more try. Later, when she looked back on this decision, she thought she must have been in the grip of some madness, for this had been the perfect time and the perfect reason. "Well, Mike, perhaps we should try for Mary's sake. I won't make any promises, but yes, you may come home."

He took her hand across the table. "It will be better, I promise. We'll talk over our life together and start anew."

Nora smiled strangely at all these promises.

Chapter 35

"Saints alive! Is this the same pale young lady we sent away just two weeks ago? Rachel, you look positively radiant. Married life seems to agree with you." Nora hugged her enthusiastically. "Welcome back."

"Oh Nora, I can't begin to tell you how wonderful it was. We're both so happy. But Nora, how are you?" Rachel's voice was full of concern. "We just heard about your miscarriage when we arrived home late last evening. Why didn't you let us know?"

"Why? What could you have done? I wouldn't have dreamed of interrupting your honeymoon. I'm fine, Rachel, really I am, though it was difficult with Mike's leaving. He actually suggested that I was responsible for the baby's death because I was working and traveling."

Rachel's face blanched. "Oh Nora, how could he?"

"The poor man was grief stricken. He didn't know what he was saying. Rachel, I did some hard horseback riding when Sean and I were in Boston. I couldn't resist, because some priggish, proper Bostonian was out to make a fool of this little Irish-Catholic girl, and I, of course, accepted the challenge. To tell you the truth, I put aside the fact that I was pregnant, in all the excitement. It was almost as though I wanted to forget.''

Rachel shook her head. ''I can't believe the riding did it. What did the doctor say?''

''He assured me that wasn't the cause, but I'm not convinced it wasn't. Mike may have been very close to the truth.''

''You mustn't think that, Nora. You'll only torture yourself.''

''No, I suppose I mustn't. But Rachel, I'll be honest with you. I didn't want a child now, because I had finally made up my mind to separate from Mike. When I found out, I was miserable. That's why I worry that somehow I was responsible.''

''Now, stop that this instant. For an intelligent woman, you sometimes astonish me.''

Nora smiled ruefully. ''Well, it's probably my Catholic upbringing. The guilt is stronger than the good sense. Anyway, I'd rather talk about what's ahead than to dwell on the past. Rachel, you know we've been wanting to capture the Wanamaker market. I think it's time we made that move. We've discussed my going to Philadelphia in the next few months. I'd like to go now.''

''Shouldn't you be taking it easy for a while?''

''Rachel, Seamus Gorman is in America and hasn't contacted either Bridget or me, but he has a brother in Philadelphia who might know something. Bridget is very upset. She thinks that Seamus believes he was responsible for Kevin's death and is afraid to see her. I just need to find out where he is for my own peace of mind.''

''Of course, Nora, go ahead. I suppose we are ready for Wanamaker's.''

"Without having to open another factory?"

"Yes, we'll manage. See what you can find out about your Seamus."

The Grand Court in the new John Wanamaker store in Philadelphia was very grand indeed. Nora lifted her eyes to gaze up at the tiers of galleries that soared one hundred fifty feet to the ceiling. The immense eagle perched in the center of the Court took her breath away.

Her appointment was for noon, and as she was making her way to the elevators, the thunderous sound of organ music greeted her ears. Of course, the organ. She had heard about the gigantic organ, second largest in the world. She craned her neck to see it. It was located in a gallery high over the Court.

The day proved to be an exciting one. The buyers had been more enthusiastic over her line than she could ever have hoped. It was almost dark as she was repacking her sample cases.

"Mrs. Desmond, I'm afraid that in our enthusiasm for the beautiful items you brought to show us, we've kept you far too long. Look at the time, we've caused you to miss your train." It was Mr. Wanamaker himself making an apology.

"It's no problem, Mr. Wanamaker. I have an old friend who has just recently emigrated to America. I believe he's living here with his brother. In fact, I'm very cross with him, for I haven't had even a postal card from him since his arrival, so I think I'll just try to find him to give him a piece of my mind."

"Then I insist you use my car and driver on your search."

"Thank you. I'm most grateful. If I can't find my friend, of if he isn't home, perhaps the driver can take me to the train station. Good-bye, Mr. Wanamaker, and thank you for everything.''

The driver loaded Nora's cases into the car, and she gave him an address that Sean's secretary, Miss Kinney, had given her quite by accident. When Miss Kinney learned that Nora was going to Philadelphia, she said, ''Well, then, you'll be wanting Mr. Gorman's address.'' Nora had been surprised, but figured that Sean had probably just found out.

Now, as she settled back under the fur lap-warmer, she thought about Seamus. How long it had been. She wasn't really angry with him, just hurt and puzzled. Of course, he had probably been busy getting settled and finding work. Still, she felt he could have found time to drop a note, for he must have known how much Bridget would want to hear from him.

The driver interrupted her thoughts. ''This is the address, but it's dark. Looks like no one's home, Mrs. Desmond. Shall we go on?''

''No, at least I'd like to leave a note on the door. I'll be back in a moment.''

As Nora went up the walk, she thought for a moment she saw a figure inside, silhouetted against the window. She rang the bell, but there was no response. She gathered her skirts and stepped to the sill to peer in. She had been right. There was a man, seated in a chair, staring straight ahead. She went back to the door and knocked. As she did, she heard a voice behind her say, ''Can I help you?''

''Oh, yes, I'm looking for my friend, Seamus Gorman. I can see someone inside, but no one answers. Forgive me, my name is Nora Desmond.''

''Why, Nora, I'm happy to meet you. I am Seamus' brother, David. I'm so glad to see you. He talks of you often. Please come in.'' He turned the key, opened the door and stepped aside for her to enter. As he lit the lamp, the man in the chair did not turn around. Even from the back, Nora knew it was Seamus.

She ran to him and knelt beside him. "Seamus, oh Seamus, how happy I am to see you. Why didn't you answer when I knocked?"

Seamus didn't move at first, but when he did, his eyes looked straight through her, as if she weren't there.

She felt fear grip her. "Seamus, speak to me. Why won't you look at me? What have I done?"

She felt David's hand on her shoulder. "Nora, has no one told you? He can't see you. He's blind."

Nora's breath caught in her throat. She put her arms around Seamus, kissed his cheek and whispered, "Seamus, dear Seamus, it's Nora. Please speak to me."

Suddenly, he came alive and pushed her away. "How did you find me? Sean swore he'd never tell. Dear God, go away. I can't stand for you to see me this way!"

"Seamus, don't send me away. How could you make Sean promise such a thing? I want to be with you. What happened? How did this happen to you? I knew Kevin had been killed, but I heard nothing of this. Oh Lord, why didn't someone tell me?" She was crying, and Seamus was crying too.

"I wish I had died with Kevin, for it was all my fault. Terence and I pushed him into it." He put his head in his hands. "I made Sean swear he'd never tell you. I don't want to be a burden. What good am I? Oh, Nora, I wish I were dead."

Nora turned to David in anguish. "How did this happen? Please tell me."

"No one knows. Even the doctors don't know what's wrong. There seems to be no physical injury, but blind he is." He lowered his voice. "Please talk to him. You mean the world to him. I'll fix us some tea."

Nora pulled a chair up close to Seamus and took his

hands in hers, speaking softly, urging him to tell her what had happened. She was shocked at his appearance. His ruddy good looks had turned pale, his shoulders were stooped, and his warm smile was gone.

"Oh Nora, my life is over. I wish I had died along with Kevin."

"But dearest Seamus, I want you to live, and so does Bridget. How upset she was when she thought you were here and hadn't been in touch with us. You're her only link to Kevin, the only one here who knew him as well as she. She needs to talk to you."

"Nora, if you had seen what I saw, you'd want to die too." Slowly, painfully, Seamus unfolded the story of that terrible night. "Terence had arranged a secret meeting so that Michael Collins, that firebrand who was rallying so many Irishmen to the cause of freedom, could speak to them. Kevin, as you know, didn't care much for politics. Nonetheless, he admired Collins, and came to hear him. We met secretly in a barn, even brought the horses inside with us so there would be no sign of us outside, but all our precautions were useless, for in the group that night was an informer." He paused, and she saw a look of unutterable pain on his face. "Had we ever found the bastard, we would have killed him in cold blood. He'll never be safe as long as Terence is alive, and that's the only consolation I have, for Kevin had become like a dear brother to me, and I'm so useless now that I have no hope of avenging his death, ever."

Nora's attention was riveted on his face as he continued. "Collins was talking to us, when suddenly from outside there was someone shouting for us to come out with our hands on our heads. Collins shouted back that we'd never come out, we'd never surrender. Our group began firing through the closed doors. Lord knows where all the guns came from. The man who owned the barn was moving bales of hay away from a spot in the middle of the floor. At first we thought he was daft, but then he opened a trap door. Here was our chance to escape, so all the men started down into the tunnel. Suddenly, we smelled smoke, then saw the flames all around us. The Brits had set fire to the barn. In seconds the place turned into an inferno. Our men hurriedly scrambled down the escape hatch. The horses were in a panic, kicking and screaming and wildly looking for a way out. Kevin was poised to go down the tunnel when a burning beam fell, barely missing the horses. Before we could stop him, he ran to his mare, caught her bridle and ran with her to the barn doors. He lifted the bar, kicked open the doors and led her out, with the rest of the horses following. He—he ran right into the hands of the soldiers.'' Seamus stopped, as though reliving that awful moment. He gripped her hand tightly. ''I swear, Nora, I didn't think I had the strength to force Terence back down the hatch, he was wanting so badly to go after Kevin, but down we went just as the burning barn roof crashed in where we'd been standing moments before. We crawled along in the dark for what seemed like hours. There wasn't enough air and I thought we were going to suffocate, but we finally emerged, though we still weren't safe. The soldiers were so close, I couldn't believe they didn't see. They must have thought we were all burning alive. And Nora, they had Kevin, that dear, kind, simple young man who had never hurt a living thing, and, my God, the things they were doing to him.'' By now he was sobbing, the memories racking him. ''I'll hear his screams until the day I die. They were trying to make him tell the names of the men who were with him at that meeting, but he wouldn't, so they tied his hands together, and one of the soldiers tied the rope to his saddle. Then they all mounted. When Terence saw that they were going to drag him, he could stand it no more and started toward them, but we pulled him back down to our hiding place in the brush. Collins and his men twisted rags into both our mouths, and held us tightly so we couldn't speak or move. We were all nearly wild from helplessness, but if we revealed ourselves, we would all have soon been dead. With the butt of a pistol, Collins knocked Terence out, and thank God he did, for your brother wasn't able to see them ride off with his old friend's body dragging behind them, screaming like a banshee." Seamus was now dry-eyed, telling his tale of horror, but Nora, holding him, was quietly sobbing.

"Poor, poor, dear Kevin," she cried. "But how did you lose your sight?"

He shook himself out of that terrible past. "I don't know. One of Collins' men may have hit me too, or perhaps I hit my head. I can't remember."

"Can't the doctors do anything?"

He shook his head. "I'll be sitting here, in my own dark for the rest of my life. Oh God, why didn't I die instead of Kevin?"

Nora stood up. "Nothing is hopeless, Seamus. You're young, you're healthy, and you have an education. You needn't sit in your own dark. Oh, I know the despair and horror that are seared into your brain, but—"

"No, I don't think you do," Seamus interrupted. "No one can know who hasn't lived through it."

She realized she had that rebuke coming. He was right. How could she know? How could anyone but Seamus? "Please, I didn't mean it that way," she said. "I'm sorry."

He took her hand. "I know." His voice was tender.

She was treading a difficult path with him, she knew. If she left him in his trough of despair, he'd soon go under. "Seamus, I'm not letting you stay here. I'm taking you to New York with me tonight. We'll go to the best doctors. I won't let you abandon hope. And even if you can't see ever again, well, I've heard of a doctor who can teach you to read with your fingers. It's a system called Braille, and Seamus, if you learned that, you could finish law school."

Seamus reached out for her, a flicker of a smile across his face. "Nora, you haven't changed a bit. In a matter of seconds you have a blind man graduating from law school. You're so strong and courageous that you think everyone else is too. But you do almost make me believe it could happen."

"It *is* going to happen." She turned to David, who had come in with tea and cake. "What do you think?"

"I think you should try it, Seamus. There's nothing here for you, no friends, no job, just me and I'm away so much."

"Well—" Seamus still sounded unsure.

"Well, nothing. Let's get him packed, David."

They talked and talked, filling each other in on ten years of dreams and hopes, accomplishments and failures.

"How I wanted to come to America and claim you, Nora. I loved you, but I wanted to have money before I came, so I worked, and waited, and I lost you. Losing you has been the other regret that haunts me, but I suppose I just wasn't meant to have you."

"Dear Seamus, how wonderful it would have been. But I guess you're right, it wasn't meant to be. Perhaps there will be sweeter things still in your life."

"I'd like to believe that. I've tried to believe that. But I can't forget Kevin."

"You must believe." Nora squeezed his hand. "Only hope for a better future keeps any of us going."

During the next few weeks, the change in Seamus was startling. He quickly came to love Nellie and Jim, who opened not only their home to him, but their hearts as well. He and Bridget had an emotional reunion from which Nora quietly withdrew, for she could see there was a very special bond between them, both of friendship and of their shared love for Kevin.

Sean and Seamus became good friends. They would laugh and drink together, and would sit, quoting poetry at each other by the hour.

Nora took him to the finest specialists, who privately told her that though they could find no physical cause, Seamus was totally blind, and suggested that he learn Braille. He became so involved, so eager to learn, that he had to be forced to come to meals. He loved learning, and Braille brought him back to life. He learned quickly and was soon reading everything the Braille library had to offer.

In less than a year, Seamus was enrolled in law classes. Nora dropped him off at New York University in the morning, and Bridget gathered him up when she took the children out to the park in the afternoon.

Baby Terence was now living with Sean and Rachel, and Bridget insisted on taking care of him as well as Mary. She would bring Seamus home to Uncle Jim and Aunt Nellie's, or Mike and Nora's, and Bridget and Seamus would talk while she prepared dinner. It seemed to both of them much like their days in Cork City, where they had lived under the same roof as close friends. Through the winter afternoons they helped to heal each other's wounds, and together they learned to bear the pain of Kevin's death.

Bridget and Seamus had something else in common—an admiration, almost an awe, of Nora. She was a source of strength in both their lives. Though Bridget was well aware of Nora's great fault, the demon in her that drove her to accomplish more and more at the expense of her personal life, Nora's strengths still gave her a stability that she used to help everyone she cared about.

By now Seamus had sensed the unhappiness in Nora's life, but he never probed. Mike was good to Seamus, helping him in the late afternoons with his studies. Mike, the patient and good soul, was at his best as a teacher. In his gentle way, he explained every problem that Seamus met with in his studies. Bridget constantly hovered about, filling Mike's teacup and tamping his pipe. Although he couldn't see her, Seamus knew she was different when Mike came home. Her voice and her step were lighter. She laughed more often, and she seemed very girlish. As time went by, Seamus began to suspect what Bridget herself didn't, that she was in love with her brother-in-law. Mike talked only of the law, so there was no way to know if he shared her feelings. What Seamus felt most intensely, however, was how strained moods became when Nora was around.

Nora is just too much for him, Seamus thought. They're all wrong for each other. How sad. No wonder Bridget says Nora can do everything but be happy. She's always away on business, while her sister cares for her husband and child.

It was a dangerous situation, he decided, but there was nothing to do or say. He only knew that Nora was the focal point of all their lives in differing ways, bright, beautiful, glittering like a star among them, and he hoped that star didn't crash to earth one day.

Nora stared at the pile of mail on her desk. She had been finding it increasingly difficult to concentrate on her business. She was worried about her father and miserable with Mike. She realized now that it had been a mistake to agree to let her husband return home, despite all their sincere attempts to work out the differences between them.

And lately she had begun to think about Jack Ryan again. Just last week, she had received an amusing letter from Dennis, who was coming to New York and wanted her to lunch with him. She enjoyed him immensely, but their friendship somehow didn't allow the door to close on Jack. Thank God, she thought, that Seamus, at least, was doing well. And, of course, Mary. How she loved that child! But she couldn't help feeling she wronged her daughter by being away so much. Maybe someday she would slow down and stay home more, but she just couldn't now. There was too much work to be done.

She finally plunged into the mail, and felt a surge of excitement as she ripped open a letter from Harry Gordon Selfridge, return address, Oxford Street, London. She read with amazement. He remembered her from Marshall Field's, reminded her that he was now owner of Selfridge's Department Store in London, one of the largest in the world, and thought it was high time that she entered the European market. Her hands trembled as she read further. "And so, Mrs. Desmond, we wish to invite you to London, as our guest, as soon as you can find the time in your busy schedule." Enclosed were first-class steamship tickets on the *Lusitania* with the date left open.

Nora's depression lifted instantly, and she ran into Rachel's office with the news. "Selfridge's wants the line, Rachel! Can you imagine breaking into the European market with a plum like that?" They hugged one another, dancing around joyfully. "Now I can go home to see my family. Oh God, Rachel, I hope Pa's all right till I arrive."

"Nora, it's wonderful. As Bridget would say, 'tis a gift of God."

Nora stood looking thoughtfully at Rachel for a moment. "If Sean can get the time off, why don't you two come? Sean should see Pa, and they should all meet you. Then you two could come home, and I'd go on to London." She was excited and sensed that Rachel shared her enthusiasm.

"I just don't know. I'd like to, and I'm certain Sean would, as well. But you know how I am about the two of us being gone at the same time."

Nora laughed. "You've been superstitious about that ever since the fire. We now have a large, capable staff, and they would probably be delighted to be rid of us for a while. Let's call Sean immediately."

Rachel was pleased to see Nora so happy, but said, "Please let me tell him at home this evening. Then I can share his excitement, too."

"You're right, of course. Oh Rachel, you'll meet our ma and pa, Terence, and Danny and . . ." She paused, a faraway look in her eyes. "You'll see the mists on the mountains." Her only regret was that she had to cancel Billy's trip east to see the horse show. She hoped he wouldn't be too disappointed.

Several days later Nora was balancing precariously on a ladder, trying to locate a box of antique lace that she and Rachel had saved from the fire.

Rachel was holding the ladder steady. "Nora, why don't we let Ralph get it down? I'm afraid you'll fall. This is what we have stock boys for."

A man's voice interrupted. "I'm no stock boy, but I *am* a bit taller than Mrs. Desmond. Perhaps I can help."

Nora swung around. Jack Ryan stood in the doorway, handsome and smiling, all six feet two inches of him.

"Why—why, Mr. Ryan, how very nice to see you." She was flustered and embarrassed at being trapped on the ladder, stunned at seeing him and completely delighted as well.

"This, I imagine, is Mrs. O'Sullivan." He turned to the surprised Rachel, briefly took her hand, then helped

Nora from the ladder, lifting her deftly down. "Now if you'll tell me what the box looks like, I'll do my best to find it," he offered wryly.

"Why, thank you, Mr. Ryan," Rachel replied. "We'd be much obliged. It's a big grey one. We think it's stuck behind the white box you're touching."

He pulled it out, handed it down to them and jumped off the ladder. "You understand, ladies, that I have taken this job on a temporary basis only, so Ralph needn't worry. However, I do insist that in payment you both join me for lunch at Sherry's."

Though Nora had regained some of her composure, she was sure they both could hear her heart pounding wildly. She smiled and took his hand. "Mr. Ryan, I'd be delighted. How about you, Rachel?"

Nora had told Rachel how she met Jack Ryan, lieutenant governor of Massachusetts, that he was a fine speaker, and that she had spent an afternoon with him at Marblehead, but nothing more. Rachel, however, sensed immediately that there was something more. She thought she had never seen a man so handsome, imposing, and with such charm—except, of course, her Sean. She instinctively felt that he had unsettled business with Nora. "Mr. Ryan," she said, "it is a pleasure to meet you, and I would like nothing better than to join you, but I've already made a luncheon date."

"I'm sorry to hear that," Ryan replied, but somehow, Rachel didn't believe he was.

When Nora and Jack were safely in his carriage, he turned to her, suddenly serious. "Why, Nora? Why did you leave without a word? When I came to the hotel and found you gone, I went into the bar and got good and drunk. That's not like me, but that's how hurt I was. We had a glimpse in that mirror of a paradise that we could have together. How could you close your eyes to it?"

"Jack, I had to. I'm sorry, but I was frightened of such intensity. I'm a married woman. You're a married man. It's wrong."

At Sherry's, they were shown to a private corner booth, where they felt safe from the world's prying eyes. They talked for hours. She told him of her miscarriage, of being separated from Mike, of their reconciliation. "I went back, I realize now, out of guilt. I thought I really had killed the baby by riding that day at Marblehead, and I was overcome with remorse." She hesitated for a moment. "Mike's coming back was a mistake for both him and me. I'm not right for him. I never have been. I'm happiest when either one or the other of us is out of town. I'm happy now, for example, because he's gone for a few days to Buffalo on some insurance case." She sat silently for a moment, then looked cautiously up at Jack. "And I'm happy too, because I'm sitting here with you."

"Thank you for saying that, Nora. I worried that you left because you never wanted to see me again. I was going to forget you, but found I couldn't. I wish time would stop at this moment, and that we could sit across from each other forever. I don't want to have you disappear from my life ever again."

"Well, I'm afraid I *am* planning to disappear, for six weeks at least." She told him of her invitation from Selfridge's in London. As she talked, her eyes sparkled with excitement.

"You're even more beautiful when you're happy," Jack told her. "Stay happy, Nora." She became uneasy as she felt his steady, intense gaze. Does he know what power he has over me? she wondered. How I want him to hold me. Oh, God, it's as well I'll be leaving soon.

They suddenly realized that they were the last people

in the restaurant. Their waiter stood discreetly across the room, while the bus boys quietly cleared the other tables.

"I must go, Jack. It has been a lovely afternoon. I shall always cherish it."

"I don't like the finality of that remark." He smiled that knowing smile. "See me tonight, please. Please, beautiful Nora." As he spoke, he had to restrain himself from touching her. "We have so little time. I return to Boston tomorrow, and you'll soon be off to Europe. You've said Mike is in Buffalo. Please."

She returned his gaze, feeling the magical attraction between them. "Yes. I'll see you this evening." In that moment she felt as if she had no power to refuse him.

That evening was full of mystery and enchantment and unspoken desire. They dined by candlelight at Antoine's, a charming French restaurant in Greenwich Village, where they talked, and laughed, and waltzed under sparkling chandeliers. They took a hansom cab through Central Park, delighting in that night of seemingly endless beauties, and hoping in the whispered promise of tomorrow.

"Nora," Jack said softly, turning her face with his hand toward his, "we will have tomorrows. You must remember that." The intensity of that moment could lead to nothing but mutual surrender, and he gathered her in his arms, kissing her lips, lips that had been waiting to be touched for what seemed like eternity. She could summon no refusal, utter no objection, for she already felt the power of a love so great it would not be denied. As they neared her apartment house, he held her face, beautiful and serene, in his strong, commanding hands.

Nora tried to shake off the spell. "Jack, we must never meet again. Never." He gazed at her, and she saw that ironic, mocking glance that in some strange manner eased her fears.

"Yes," he answered, gazing steadily into her eyes, "we will meet again. We *must* meet again. We are meant to."

"Caroline, how good to hear from you," Nora said into the phone. "Of course, I'd love to lunch with you. Today? Well, yes, I can rearrange some appointments."

Miss Burke, Nora's secretary, grimaced, for it had taken a long time for her to set them up.

Caroline always preferred Delmonico's, and Nora loved its elegance. She never walked in the door without remembering when she had first dined there with Angelo.

Caroline was waiting. "I know how busy you are, Nora, but I've missed you. And," she added mysteriously, "I have something important to discuss with you."

Caroline always had something important to discuss, Nora thought, smiling to herself. Perhaps that's why I drop everything when she summons me. Soon they were seated, and Nora could wait no longer for what Caroline had to say. "Tell me." She leaned toward her friend conspiratorially.

"Nora, there are some women I would like you to meet. Belle has arranged a gathering Thursday evening at her place. You know how we've all worked for the vote for women. Well, it's time for us to stop marching and start acting."

Nora knew that Caroline, having been involved in the suffragette movement for over twenty years, had done far more than talk. She had numbered among her personal friends women such as Elizabeth Cady Stanton and Susan B. Anthony, who together had founded the National American Woman Suffrage Association and had tirelessly worked, organized and lectured for many years.

Though Nora had contributed generously, she was still not actively involved in the movement. She rationalized that she hadn't the time, what with her business and the cares of her family. She felt different today. She listened intently as Caroline spoke.

"Nora, you've become an important force in this city. You run two large businesses and employ hundreds, mostly women. You have a responsibility to these women. Oh, I know that you treat them well, that you've organized your shop and factory, but there's more to it than that. How are working women ever to achieve their rights until people like you, their employers and models, encourage them to make use of those rights." She paused and smiled. "Oh, I'm on my soapbox again. I'm sorry, Nora, but we need you. The National American Woman Suffrage Association is having a meeting Thursday evening, and we want you as a guest speaker."

"Me, a speaker? What on earth would I talk about?"

"About what you do in your business, about what your problems and policies are, about what reforms you've initiated."

"But I'm leaving for Europe in two weeks." Nora was stalling for time.

"Nora, dear, you're always leaving for some place or other. I'm used to that. Right now, I'm only asking you for Thursday night."

Nora sat quietly for a few moments, watching Caroline puff on her cigarette, searching her face for an answer. Nora felt a surge of excitement and knew at that moment she would make this commitment. "All right, Caroline. I've never really spoken before a large group before, but I'll do it if you think I can make a worthwhile contribution."

"I do. Besides, I want you to meet these women. They're interesting, intelligent and dedicated. And we haven't seen you for a while. I'm so pleased you'll attend. But I must warn you of one thing."

"What is that?"

"You'll never again be the same after one of our meetings."

As she rode home, Nora's thoughts were tumultuous. She hadn't stopped thinking of Jack. The forthcoming European trip was much on her mind. And now this. Doors that had been closed for a long time were now opening. Why were all these things happening at once? Perhaps, she thought, it's because I've finally opened my mind to change in my life.

Mike wasn't home from Buffalo yet, but he had called to say he hoped to be back later that evening. Bridget had a dinner of ham and cabbage prepared, and Nora enjoyed every morsel.

"Mary, Joseph and Patrick," Bridget exclaimed, "you've been looking marvelous, Nora. Happy and as content as I've ever seen you. What is it, lass?"

Nora told her about the speech she was going to make, and at the same time noticed that Bridget had become wary. Little Mary was beside herself at the news.

"Oh, Ma, what will you speak about?" she asked excitedly.

Bridget had a reproving look on her face. "Why Nora, why are you wanting to get mixed up in that silliness? We women stand to lose a great deal. The men are putting us on pedestals now, but if we're able to vote like they do, it's down to earth we'll be coming."

For all her common sense, Bridget had never been able to understand why women should have the vote.

"It is out of your cage you'll be coming," Nora said patiently.

Mary jumped off her chair and ran to her mother. "Ma, I want to vote. I do."

Nora smiled at her and lifted her into her lap. "You will, darling. Someday, you will."

Mike came in later that evening and Bridget happily warmed his meal, while Nora asked about his trip. He was feeling expansive, for he felt the insurance case was just about won, and he liked to come home to two admiring women, his happy Mary and a delicious meal. This surely must be what God had meant life to be, he thought.

Nora's happiness over the forthcoming European trip and the invitation to speak to such an important group had made her feel good too, so she was kind to Mike, and asked him all kinds of questions. This puffed up his self-esteem enormously.

Mary heard them talking and came sleepily out of her bedroom in her nightgown to welcome her father home. "Daddy, Mommy is going to talk to the ladies about voting. I'm going to vote too. Mommy promised."

The smile disappeared from his face. "What is all this?" he asked, turning to Nora.

Bridget, sensing that a battle was brewing, swept Mary up into her arms, saying, "Kiss Mommy and Daddy good night, darling. 'Tis late for you to be up. We're taking Seamus to the library tomorrow, remember?"

Mike repeated his question. "What is she talking about?"

"I've been invited to speak to the National American Association for Woman Suffrage," Nora told him. "It seems I'm what they call an enlightened employer who understands the needs of—"

"I don't want you to go," he interrupted. "I don't want you to have anything to do with those harpies and harridans. They're nothing but rabble-rousers, what with their parades and carryings-on, bent on destroying family life. They don't seem to realize that women are incapable of dealing with important civic issues."

Nora winced. Bridget was a simple farm girl whose lack of sophistication in these matters was understandable, but his was unforgivable. She felt strong and calm and self-assured as she replied, "I, for one, am as capable of dealing with important civic issues as any man. And how on earth giving women the vote will destroy family life, I am hard pressed to understand. I find your objections both juvenile and uninformed, and I intend to speak to the group, whether you approve or not. Furthermore, I have no intention of arguing about my political views or my business ever again."

She watched dispassionately as the rage colored his face. This is the last such scene I'll endure, she thought calmly.

"You'll damned well do as I say," he sputtered. "You're my wife, and you will obey me. It's bad enough you're running off to Europe alone. Now this!"

She remained silent for a few moments. How senseless all this anger was, she thought. When she again spoke, her voice was soft and calm. "Mike, I am sorry to cause you such grief. I am not the woman you should have married. We both have known that for a long time. I thought we should try to make our marriage succeed for Mary's sake, but I see now what a foolish hope that was. I wish for us to legally separate, since divorce is out of the question for you. I hope we can do it as amicably as possible. Otherwise, Mary will be the one to suffer most. I am serious about this. I shall, of course, allow you to see Mary whenever you wish."

He sat listening with his head in his hands. His rage had dissipated now.

Nora felt a lump form in her throat as she watched

him, for he was crying. "Mike, this will be better for both of us. Believe me."

He looked up, sad and bewildered.

"Mike, we're too different. You have many fine qualities, and so do I, but our qualities are mismatched." He sat numbly and she kept talking, persuading. "You can stay in the house with Mary until I return from Europe if you like." He nodded sadly. "I've been thinking of moving farther uptown, so perhaps you can keep this apartment. Then separating won't be such a big wrench for you." He nodded again. "Thank you, Mike. This will be better for all of us." She patted his hand as if he were a hurt child.

That night she slept soundly for the first time in many months.

Belle Moskowitz welcomed Nora and Rachel into her spacious West Side apartment. She was married to Henry Moskowitz, who was director of the Madison Street Settlement House and had recently served as market commissioner in the mayor's administration. Belle was a graduate of Columbia Teacher's College, a professional social worker and a tireless supporter in labor rights and woman suffrage. Caroline, dressed in a grey tweed suit fashioned after a man's, introduced Nora and Rachel all around. Nora had never seen such an illustrious gathering, even at Caroline's salons. Frances Perkins was there, as were Mrs. Dodge, Emma Goldman and many others.

Caroline took Nora's hand. "I've a special treat for you, Nora. Come along." She led her to the other side of the room, where a fierce-looking woman of at least eighty years sat chatting. Caroline introduced Nora to Mary Harris Jones, better known as Mother Jones, a labor heroine, who had come from Ireland as a young woman and had risen in the labor ranks as a radical organizer.

"Mrs. Jones, you're from my very own Cork, and I've admired your work for years," Nora said. "It's a very great pleasure to be meeting you."

"Well, I've heard of your company, lass, but we've had no labor grievances from your workers, so I haven't had the pleasure of meeting you before this."

The two women got along famously, and made small talk until it was time for Nora to speak.

Nora began her speech with a quote of Mr. Dooley's, a fictitious Irish philosopher created by newspaperman Finley Peter Dunne, to illustrate the prevailing attitude about the vote for women:

"Speaking of women, Mr. Dooley concedes that 'they haven't th' right to vote, but they have th' priv'lege iv controllin' th' man ye ilicit. They haven't th' right to make laws, but they have th' priv'lege iv breakin' thim, which is betther. They haven't the right iv a fair thrile be a jury iv their peers; but they have th' priv'lege iv an unfair thrile be a jury iv their admirin' infeeryors. If I cud fly d'ye think I'd want to walk?' "

She brought the house down. The rest of her speech covered topics from women in business to women in politics.

As she was leaving, Caroline drew her aside. "You have the gift, Nora. I knew you did. Are you with us? You know, this time it's for more than a march up Fifth Avenue."

Nora, flushed with success, committed herself. "Indeed I am, Caroline. I'm with you to the end."

Chapter 36

The ship's whistles blew. People embraced and waved their last farewells as the ship's officers hurriedly ushered everyone aboard.

"Good-bye, Mary," Nora said with a tear in her eye. "Be a good girl. Mommy will bring you something wonderful. Take good care of Aunt Bridget, now."

Bridget had come down with influenza several days before they were to leave, and her going was now out of the question. She had been teary-eyed as she held Nora's hand and made her farewells. "Please give everyone my love, Nora, and kiss Pa for me. Will you do that?" She began crying in earnest.

"I shall, Bridget, I shall."

Mike stood uncomfortably by Mary's side, not really knowing what to say. He waved unenthusiastically as Nora ran up the gangplank, followed by Sean and Rachel. Little Terry had been left with his grandparents. Mary was jumping up and down, excited by the whistles and the ship and the crowd. She blew kisses to Nora, yelling, "I love you,

I love you!'' Nora smiled at her lovely little Mary, who adored her no matter what, and blew kisses back.

When the figures on the shoreline grew too small to recognize, the passengers retired to their staterooms. As Nora began unpacking, she thought bitterly of the people in steerage, huddled together in misery. Had there been lovely staterooms like this on board the *Victoria*? she wondered, and a wave of memories swept over her. She recalled how many women she had seen die of dysentery, and how everyone's lips and skin had been cracked and bleeding from washing in the salt water, and how fever had racked her own body.

The memories upset her so much that she jumped up from her bed and ran to see if there was steerage class on the ship. A polite ship's officer informed her that steerage was reserved for packages and animals. She smiled. Of course, she thought. Conditions would be better for people traveling *back* to Europe. The poor only traveled one way.

The ship's dining room was gracious and old-world. Victorian. A string quartet played Mozart, and the diners were handsome: the women in their fashionable dresses and sparkling jewels, the men in black tie.

''Oh Sean, what a far cry from the kitchen helpers serving us slop from a big iron bucket back on the *Victoria*.'' Nora laughed, then held up her champagne glass and offered a toast. ''To Ma, who saw the possibilities.''

''To Ma,'' Sean repeated. He turned to Rachel. ''Our ma is very special, as you'll find out soon enough.''

After dinner, Nora joined a group of young people in the lounge for conversation and drink. One fellow, named Andrade, was obviously smitten with her immediately. Nora found his attentions amusing, so she allowed him to see her to her stateroom, where he made her promise to join him for cocktails and dinner the following evening.

At breakfast the next morning, she told Sean and Rachel about him. "A charming young man. I hope I haven't encouraged him."

"Don't worry, Nora," Sean said. "From all I've heard, a ship romance never lasts beyond the first port of call."

Nora blushed girlishly. "I certainly wouldn't presume a romance with him before we've even shared dessert."

She arrived in the captain's lounge for cocktails looking breathtaking in a long black chiffon dress with a Burgundy ruffle around the neck. By the look he gave her, she judged that the captain was as smitten with her as young Andrade was. The rest of the group she found interesting and amusing because of the diversity of the people. There was a stuffy rich American, Mrs. Bigelow Packard, who let it be known immediately that she was listed in the social register. Her husband, a gentle, henpecked soul, had made his fortune in the railroads. She immediately liked the portly, red-faced Irishman across from her named Fitzsimmons, and though it was obvious to Nora that he was a member of the gentry, Mrs. Packard was undone at his strident Irish brogue, certain that he must be riffraff. To Nora's right was seated Lord Ian Rexford. He was an entertaining and amusing old gentleman, obviously delighted to be sitting next to a lovely young woman.

"What part of the world is responsible for producing such a beautiful creature?" he asked her with a friendly sparkle in his eye.

She smiled back at him. "Ballygarry, Ireland. Do you know it?"

"County Cork. I should have known. Loveliest girls in all Ireland come from Cork." He winked. "I've been there, Mrs. Desmond. A dear friend of mine, Lord Anthony Howard, resides there. Yes, I've ridden to the hounds on his estate. Lovely man. Do you happen to know him?''

Nora, fully aware of the impact her words would have on Mrs. Packard, allowed herself the pleasure of deflating the pompous windbag. "Aye, he was our landlord, Lord Rexford. My father was his tenant. He is a fine man, well liked by all.''

If Lord Rexford objected to sitting next to a former Irish peasant girl, he showed it not at all. A true gentleman, she thought. However, she noticed that Mrs. Packard avoided looking at her at all.

"If only the same could be said of his son,'' Lord Rexford observed. "He's a sad disappointment to his father, what with his drinking and gambling. Arrogant too.''

Nora's heart almost stopped beating, and she barely dared to breathe. "I'm sorry to hear that,'' she said as casually as she could. "Lord Anthony deserves better. Does William squander money, then?''

"Oh, Lord, yes, and his wife, Margaret, is even worse. And the girls—there are three of them, you know—show promise of completely depleting the family fortune if they ever get their hands on it. Well, that's true of two of them, anyway. The third is a nice young girl, actually.'' Lord Rexford struck a match and lit a fragrant cheroot. "Lord Anthony could have been a bitter man, Mrs. Desmond, reclusive and pitiful. But he didn't allow that to happen.''

Nora found she was becoming extremely interested in Lord Anthony's story, and the old gentleman apparently knew a great deal about him. "Why should he be bitter?'' she asked. After all, she thought, everyone has disappointments, even the rich.

"Well, I've known him many years. Our families were old friends. I knew his first wife, a fine young woman, from my own native Kent. She died in childbirth, and the baby, a son, lived for only a few hours. It was a terrible blow for Anthony, as you can imagine. He returned to Trinity College to study law, and while in Dublin, he met a young woman with whom he fell deeply in love. Alas, she was Irish and Catholic, and the situation was impossible.'' He offered no apology. That was the way of the world and both he and Nora knew it. ''Well, he told me of the young woman one night at our club in Belgravia. 'A true Irish beauty,' he said, 'with hair like the night and eyes of deepest violet. Altogether she is the loveliest, brightest, sweetest and gentlest girl in all the world!' I had't seen him so happy in years, for after the loss of his family, he led a melancholy, lonely existence. This girl gave him hope, and a love the likes of which I, for one, have never known.'' He was silent for a moment.

''Who was she?'' Nora pressed.

''I don't remember the name, but they were everything to each other. I tried to warn him, but he wouldn't listen, so sure was he that his ancient family doors would swing open for this beautiful girl, whom he called his nightingale, for she had a voice as lovely as her being.''

Suddenly Nora felt her throat constrict, and when she tried to speak, she had to struggle to find her voice. ''Was she a singer, then?''

''In a pub in Dublin, The Three Feathers or the Two Larks, something like that.''

Nora was clutching the edge of her seat. ''Was it called, by any chance, The Three Pigeons?''

''Yes, yes, that's it. How on earth did you know?''

''Ah, my grandfather once mentioned it to me. It's on Dame Street, if I remember rightly.''

''It is indeed. Fancy that.''

Nora's head was spinning. There was no doubt of it; Lord Anthony had been in love with her mother. She strove to pull herself together, for Lord Rexford was chatting on.

"His sister Elizabeth visited the young woman, and told her the affair had to end—offered her money, in fact, to break it off. Anthony was furious with Elizabeth, argued violently with his father, who vowed to disinherit him. He promised the girl that he would marry her no matter what, but she refused. How much she must have loved him, Mrs. Desmond, to refuse, for she knew his life would be ruined if she became his wife." He shook his head sadly. "So he took a wife he didn't love, and she also died in childbirth, but this time he was left with a weak bounder for a son."

Nora wanted to cry. She felt stifled, as if she were choking. No wonder her mother had wanted so much more for her children, for Nora. No wonder she had struggled— so some of them, at least, would have something of what she was forced to give up. She had been so close to finding happiness. Oh, Ma, where is the law of compensation for you?

Chapter 37

As the tender drew close to the Queenstown dock, Sean screamed, "I see Ma, and I'm sure it's Danny with her!"

"Where, where?" Nora cried out. They were like two children scrambling to the rail, and they waved furiously.

Nora was dressed in the latest New York fashion. By 1913, the entire silhouette of women's dresses had changed. Skirts had become straight and smaller at the hemline, giving them a sleek sophisticated look that was much more to Nora's liking and was extremely flattering on her. Her deep rich purple broadcloth suit was simply tailored, and a deeper purple silk braid banded the jacket and cuffs. A belt cinched in her waistline, and a ruffled white blouse completed the look. Rachel looked stunning in a pale green suit and a beret-like hat with a single falcon's feather.

Nora was the first one down the gangplank, and she ran into her mother's waiting arms. They held each other tightly, until finally Nora found her voice. "Oh Ma, Ma, how are you?" She sobbed with joy. "You look as beautiful as ever." But streaks of grey in her hair, and fine lines etched in her mother's translucent skin, told of the passing years.

Sean came running down next, and Mary was crying with joy as her son held her so tightly she could barely breathe.

"Faith, lad, you're a man, and a mighty strong one too. And this must be our Rachel. Welcome to Ireland, dear girl. We've been waiting to meet you." She embraced her daughter-in-law warmly. "Where is Bridget?" she suddenly asked, looking around.

"Oh, Ma, she's come down with influenza. She couldn't come, but she sends her love."

Mary couldn't conceal her look of disappointment.

"And Father Daniel O'Sullivan. Well, I'll be." Nora was amazed at the change in Danny's appearance. "Look now, aren't you the fine gentlemen?" Danny had put on weight that came from good living, and his priestly garments were well tailored. His face was wreathed in smiles as he embraced his brother and sister, and he shook Rachel's hand, telling her what a pleasure it was for all of them that she could come.

"Oh Danny, 'tis pleased I am to see you happy and content," Nora said. "God has been good to you."

"That He has, Nora, that He has."

"How is Seamus?" Mary put in with sudden seriousness.

"Oh Ma, he's doing well," Nora replied. "I'll tell you all about it. And we will be seeing Terence, won't we? And his Julie?"

"We will indeed. I'm not quite certain how or when, but you know they'll be here," Danny assured them.

"And Pa," Sean asked, "is he any better?"

"Not much," Mary answered sadly. "But knowing you were coming has given him strength I didn't think he possessed. He's talked of nothing else since your letter arrived.''

"And now, let's get the luggage and be off," Danny said. "You came to Queenstown thirteen years ago in Lord Howard's carriage, and you'll be leaving this time in Bishop Quinn's limousine. This family travels in style.''

"Oh, Danny, 'tis a wonderful machine," Nora exclaimed.

They all drank in the sights and sounds of the countryside, gently sloping fields and rolling hills, meadow flowers and beech trees covered with moss and ivy along the softly flowing river, clothes drying on the potato plants in the fields, wildflowers growing from the roofs of thatched cottages. Rachel was overwhelmed. She had heard that Ireland was beautiful, but she was unprepared for this.

Sean and Nora were amazed at the change in the cottage. New fences surrounded it, and a flagstone walk now led to the entrance. The walls were whitewashed, and a profusion of flowers lined the walk and the entire front of the house. A new room, added just one year ago, made the cottage look very grand indeed.

Frank appeared at the doorway. They ran to him and smothered him with hugs and kisses.

"Pa, Pa, how we missed you," Sean cried.

Frank smiled happily. "Ah, lad, and I have missed you. And my little princess is now a queen, I see. How grand you are.''

"Pa, 'tis how we all look in America." Nora was slightly embarrassed.

Frank looked thin and weak, but his present joy seemed to give him strength. When he was introduced to Rachel, he took her hand. "Faith! Another queen, I see. I've been surrounded by female royalty all my life.''

They talked and laughed and cried till very late that

evening, then finally they all went to bed, fatigued, but happier than they had been for a long time.

Sean and Nora, happy though they were to see their family, found life in Ireland somewhat dull and behind the times. Comparisons were inevitable, and as neither of them lived under the protective cloak of an Irish neighborhood, they were now unquestionably Americans. The two countries tugged at them for allegiance, and though their roots were on this plot of ground in County Cork, their new ties were in the New World, for America had allowed them to prosper as Ireland would never have.

As they were finishing dinner one evening, a knock sounded at the door. Danny released the latch and opened the door, and there stood Terence, as grand a sight as Nora had ever seen. Julia, standing almost as tall as her husband, her flaming hair wild, curly and beautiful about her pale, freckled face, smiled a smile so lovely that it nearly made Nora's heart break.

"Terence, Terence, Terence!" Nora screamed as he swooped her into his arms and swung her into the air.

"Aye, lass, 'tis me."

Then he and Sean embraced away their thirteen-year separation. Tears were in everyone's eyes. Terence turned to Julia and said, "Here they are, lass. What do you think?"

"Oh, faith, I'm happy to be meeting you all."

Terence broke open the first bottle to start the celebration, and Rachel had her first taste of poteen and her first earful of an Irish kitchen racket. They drank and talked into the night. Terence told them the whole sad story of Kevin, their escape, and Seamus' blindness. And he swore revenge before them all.

Sean stayed up after the others had retired to spend some time with his father. He dearly loved the old man, and the sight of that pale, worn face saddened him. You're not long for this world, Pa, he thought to himself. But at least I have you for these few minutes. Even when his father fell asleep in the rocker, Sean stayed a long time just staring at him.

When Sean finally climbed into bed, Rachel stirred. He was full of frustration, lost memories, old sadnesses, and this new sadness of seeing that his father was dying. He gathered Rachel in his arms, almost desperately, and covered her with kisses. She held him tenderly, stroking him, comforting him. He kissed her again and whispered, "I love you, Rachel. I love you, and I need you." He took her with a deeper passion than she had ever known from him. As they lay in each other's arms, listening to each other's heatbeats, thinking the same thoughts, Rachel and Sean both knew that a change had occurred in their love, that it had become deeper and more piquant, so that even in their sadness, there was joy.

Chapter 38

When Mary returned home from an errand the following day, Nora noticed she looked flushed and excited.

"Ma, what is it?"

"We have an invitation to tca at Lord Anthony's, you and I and Sean and Rachel, if they're interested in coming. Lord Anthony wants to see you, Nora. I guess I've bragged a bit, and he's interested in hearing all about you and America. Will you go?"

Nora's heart had pounded wildly at the mention of Lord Anthony. She tried to keep the emotion out of her voice as she asked, "Will anyone else be there?"

"Why yes, I suppose William will be there, and perhaps his family, though one can never depend upon the girls. They flit about quite a bit. Lord knows, when they're older they'll be something to deal with."

Nora felt a constriction in her chest. Wasn't this the moment she had been waiting for all these years? "Why, that will be very nice, Ma."

That night, Nora lay in a fever of anticipation. What

would William be like? What would they say to each other? What were his wife and daughters like?

When Sean was told of the invitation, he laughed. "Everyone wants to take a look at us. We're a little like circus freaks, I think. Rachel, I never had an invitation to his house before I went to America. Oh, well. It will be interesting, I suppose. I always liked Lord Anthony. But that foppish son of his, William—Lord, it will be difficult for me to keep a straight face."

"Never mind, Sean, maybe he's changed for the better," Nora suggested.

Mary shook her head. "I'm not sure about that. He causes them all a great deal of pain, I'm afraid. But we're not going for the purpose of seeing William, so take him in your stride, Sean."

That's why I'm going, Nora thought, to see him and to show him I'm a lady.

An older, more stooped Emerson opened the door.

"Oh, Emerson," Nora said, "how very nice to see you."

He smiled. "Thank you, Miss Nora, and it's a pleasure seeing you. Please, please, come this way." He led them into the celadon-green study. It was virtually unchanged from the last time Nora had seen it.

Lord Anthony appeared promptly and graciously welcomed them. He, too, looked much older. Nora looked at him now with very different eyes, this man who had been so in love with her mother that he was willing to give up a great fortune for her. Does he love her still? she wondered. Perhaps they still loved each other. The thought didn't disturb her as it once might have, for they obviously had come to peace with their emotions.

Tea was served on the heavily ornate Georgian service that Nora remembered, and by the look of Rachel, Nora knew she was enjoying every moment of this rather un-usual visit. Lord Anthony was charming, asking them all sorts of questions about America. They had been there nearly half an hour, and Nora was fast losing hope of seeing William when Lord Anthony said, "My son asked me not to let you leave. He'll be along shortly and wants to visit."

Nora felt breathless and weak, but turning to Rachel she said pleasantly, "William let me ride their show horse, Champion, many years ago. I believe I've mentioned it to you, Rachel."

"Yes, of course," Rachel replied, and quickly checked to make sure Sean wasn't about to burst into mocking laughter as he had threatened.

Just then the door opened, and William stood on the threshold, a very different man than the one Nora had last seen in the Fairies' Cave thirteen long years ago. His wonderful shock of blond hair was thinning and already showing streaks of grey, his face had a florid cast from too much drinking, and his once lean, muscular body had gone soft, with a paunch attesting to too much good living. Only his green eyes, pale and penetrating, seemed the same.

Nora took a deep breath, rose and went over to extend her hand. "William, it has been so long."

William's eyes drank in Nora's beauty. She had on her favorite lavender suit, which showed off her glistening violet eyes. A ruffled blouse softly framed her classic face. And her hair was swept back in the lovely new full fash-ion. At her throat and ears were amethysts, and on her finger a diamond ring. "Nora, how wonderful to see you. You are even more beautiful, if such a thing is possible. But how have you been? You must tell me all about yourself."

After introductions were made, he led her to a sofa in front of the window where they could chat. She noticed that while everyone else was having tea, he was brought a whiskey. She had gradually relaxed and found that she was enjoying the encounter. Time had treated her well and him poorly, and there was a satisfaction about it that she couldn't deny.

"William, will I meet Margaret and your daughters?"

"Why, yes. They are off somewhere, but I hope they will be back before you leave." As if they heard the summons, there was a commotion at the door, and Margaret and the three girls came in to be introduced. Margaret was a plain, plump, frowzy woman with a high, squeaky voice. The two oldest girls looked like miniatures of her, but the youngest girl, Sybil, was a lovely child, blonde and green-eyed, with a flashing smile. She was much like William had been, and, Nora realized with a start, much like Billy. William looked slightly uncomfortable, as if he was embarrassed by his family.

He immediately turned the conversation to horses. Did Nora still ride? She told him she did whenever she had the opportunity.

"Well, then, you must meet and ride Champion's granddaughter, Starfire. She's almost as good a horse as Champion was, and we're thinking of entering her in a small show at Cork. Do come see her, please. Perhaps you would like to ride her tomorrow."

"I would indeed," Nora laughed. "Dear Champion, I know how you must miss him."

Much to William's chagrin, everyone wanted to see Starfire, so he wasn't able to speak to Nora alone. In desperation before they parted that afternoon, he pulled Nora aside.

"Nora, may I arrange for you to ride tomorrow? If so, we'll have the groom ready her."

It was obvious he wanted to speak to her. What about? she wondered. Did he want to know about the child, what had happened to her and the baby? She hesitated a moment, looked at him strangely, then decided she was curious enough to want to know what he wanted. "Yes," she finally answered. "It would be wonderful to ride Starfire."

The following day they met at the stables, and William was more like his old, gracious, charming self. He can still be endearing, she thought. Memories rushed in on her as they rode across the meadows, her hair flowing free, her cheeks flushed with excitement. Starfire was perfect as Champion had been, and handled as if she and the horse were old friends.

They finally stopped under a tree to have a drink.

"It is a glorious day," William said amiably. "And you still ride like the wind."

She confronted him candidly. "What is it you wanted to discuss with me?"

He looked a little uneasy. That pleased her. She couldn't remember him ever looking uneasy.

"Nora, I wanted to say I'm sorry for all I did to you in the past. I made a mistake, and I've thought about you often. I want to ask your forgiveness."

"Yes, you did make a mistake, and because of it I had to leave my beloved family and go to a world where I was often treated as an unwelcome stranger. But we were both young, and it's past. I can even say now that it has all turned out for the best." She purposely did not mention Billy.

"Nora, what about the child?" he asked in obvious frustration.

"What child, William? I miscarried on the crossing."

"Please, don't play that game," he said. "Our son, where is he?"

"What are you talking about?" She was momentarily stunned. How did he know? "We have no son. You and I have nothing together."

"Nora, I want to know where he is."

She answered in a fury. "Why are you suddenly so interested? And how did you find out, William? I demand to know." Her cheeks were flushed and her eyes blazed with anger.

"Please, Nora, don't be angry. Some years ago, shortly after Sybil was born, Margaret found out she could have no more children. That meant I would have no male heir, no one to inherit the title and estates, no one to carry on the family name. So I had my solicitor hire a detective in America. I knew, of course, where you had gone, for my father and your mother are very good friends. It was quite simple to find the birth certificate in Lowell, Massachusetts, but after that, all trace of the child disappeared. You have an obligation to tell me where he is. He's my own flesh and blood, after all."

"I see," she answered softly. Old wounds were opening. So now he wanted to claim the child, to offer it his lands and title. It was almost too much to comprehend.

"You forfeited your right to that child, William, and mine, also. I gave him up, I had to." She bowed her head in silence, reliving those awful moments when she handed Billy to another to raise.

"Ah, I see. Well, that's no problem. I can get him back."

"No problem?" She was incredulous. "Billy is happy. He has parents who love him. Would you destroy his life just so he can have some damned English title?" Her voice was trembling with long-suppressed rage. "Do you think you can simply reappear after all these years and take him away from the loving people who have given him everything you would not? Do you have any idea how I've suffered, how I've cried, and prayed, and wanted him back? But how could you know any of that, for you're the one who tossed me a packet of money for him.''

William looked stunned by the passion of her outburst. He leaned toward her. ''Nora, please calm down. I had no idea. I'm sorry. I only meant that since I had so much to offer him that—'' He stopped, seeing that what he was saying was only making her angrier.

''You have never understood common decency.''

William put his arms about her. ''Oh, Nora, I love you. I've always loved you.'' He grabbed and kissed her.

She pulled away abruptly. ''You fool, stop that. You think your class and social position give you the privilege of doing whatever you have a notion to. Well, it doesn't. Not only will you not have me, but you will never have your son. Never, do you hear me?''

She turned away from him, mounted Starfire and rode away, leaving him staring after her disappearing figure.

Nora had always looked forward to her moment of revenge. She had thought that moment, whenever and however it would come, would be so sweet, but it had been bitter and heartbreaking, and opened doors she wished now had remained forever shut.

She was very quiet that evening, and both Mary and Rachel suspected something had happened. Mary asked her to go for a walk. ''Come, child, smell the hawthorn and the roses.''

They walked along quietly, hand in hand. ''Darling Nora, I've missed you so. I'm so proud of you, but I know, too, that you've suffered. A mother knows these things instinctively. I've always felt the closest tie with you of all my children, since the first moment Maggie Gargan put you in my arms. I've always known what you were thinking, what you were wanting, when you were in trouble." She paused. "And I sense trouble now. Do you want to tell me, child?"

"Oh Ma." With tears streaming down her face, she embraced her mother. In that moment she almost told her about William and Billy, but found she couldn't find the courage. Instead she said, "Ma, my marriage is failing. We're separating."

Mary held her tightly. "Oh lass, I'm so sorry. What's wrong?" She told Mary all about their problems. "It's just not working, Ma. It's not fair for him, either."

May tried to understand and to give Nora comfort, but she was heartsick. She didn't admonish her, for her daughter needed understanding and sympathy at a time like this. So they talked for hours.

"I won't tell your father," Mary said sadly as they walked back to the cottage. "I'm afraid he hasn't much time left, and I want him to be happy."

"Of course, Ma." They moved on silently for a few moments, each lost in her own thoughts. "Ma, it will be lonely for you when he's gone. Will you come to America? You can see Bridget and your grandchildren."

"Nora, there was a time when that was a dream of mine, but now, I don't know. I'm happy here. I feel useful and respected, and I have dear old friends. I just don't know."

"Old friends like Lord Anthony, Ma?"

Mary looked her straight in the eye. "Aye, lass." She smiled. "He is one of my dearest old friends."

"That's wonderful, Ma. He's a very special man. It's too bad his son isn't more like him."

Again Mary sensed that there was something more

bothering Nora than what was being said. "It *is* too bad, but at least there is Sybil. She's the only one Anthony cares about."

"That was quite obvious. She's a delightful child."

"Aye, and quite like her grandfather," Mary answered.

And quite like her half brother, Nora thought.

"I'm glad we talked, Nora. I still worry, you know. I want to know when any of my children has a problem. Not that I can always help, for I can't, but just so they can know there is someone to whom they can unburden themselves. Keeping a hurt hidden in the soul can give birth to bigger problems. Please, tell me when you need to talk."

"I will, Ma, thank you. But you're not to worry. I have Sean and Bridget and many wonderful friends in America. Little Mary and I will be fine. Bridget has been wonderful with her, and Mike loves her dearly. Whatever is wrong between us hasn't affected her. She'll always have her daddy, don't worry."

Mary smiled. "How did you know I was thinking that?"

Nora's eyes were twinkling. "We're very much alike, Ma. So I know a great deal about you."

They walked slowly back along the path, arm in arm, feeling the love and understanding between them, smelling the delicious scent of the hawthorn on the hedges along the lane, and savoring the special bond between mother and daughter.

It was soon time for them to leave Ireland, and they made their farewells. Life here was still harsher than the life Sean and Nora knew in America, but the memories of the warm and mutual love had remained and would remain forever with these children who had left. They said sad good-byes to everyone.

Frank had been so happy seeing them that he felt almost well again. He said to Mary, "You were right, weren't you? The gombeen men didn't get them."

They all laughed, and kissed him warmly, tenderly, fearing in their hearts it would be the last time. He clung to each of them. They thanked Danny for being a patient, dependable letter writer, and told him to be sure to telegram as soon as he became a monsignor. And Terence, how they loved this handsome, mercurial man of monumental principles and rages, who had given his life to the cause of Irish freedom.

"Terence, promise one day you'll come to America," Sean said. "You'll raise as much money as Parnell did, I'll wager."

"You raise the money, Sean. I'll raise the hell," Terence replied.

Everyone had loved gentle, lovely, wise Rachel, and wished her and Sean well. "Promise to come again soon, and bring the children," Mary said to her.

"Why, we only have little Terry."

"Yes, but by the time you're coming again, there'll be more."

Rachel blushed. "It's been so wonderful for me to see Ireland, and meet all of you."

"Aye," Terence replied. "And good to have you as one of us."

Danny and Mary drove them to the train that would take them to Dublin. From there Nora would catch the ferry to England, Sean and Rachel would leave by ship for America. As they boarded the train, Mary couldn't help but think of their last farewell, their patched clothes, pathetic bundles, the black trunk, and the awful fear that they would never see one another again.

These children of mine have done well, she thought, despite much sadness and overwhelming odds. They have done well, just as I knew they would. As they waved and shouted, ''We love you,'' she whispered under her breath, ''Thank you, God, for hearing my prayers.'' And they were gone.

Chapter 39

As the white cliffs of Dover came into view, Nora suffered conflicting and confusing thoughts. It had been an enemy of Ireland for hundreds of years, yet here Nora was, hoping to make friends of old foes. She had never confessed to anyone how much she wanted to see England, especially London, and when she had been younger, she pored over books containing pictures of that city. She thought she had detected disapproval in Terence's eye when he learned of her plans to come here, but he at least hadn't exploded in anger.

When she disembarked, there was a young man holding up a sign that said "Mrs. Desmond." She walked over to him and he handled everything for her, having been sent by Selfridge's to assure her an uncomplicated arrival. It felt good to her to be treated this way. He packed the limousine and they were off to London. The drive was simply beautiful. The little British hamlets were so different from the Irish villages, being better kept and more picturesque. Well, she thought, had we the wealth, ours would be as beautiful.

London was more entrancing to her than all the picture books she had ever seen. "Mr. Wentworth," she said, addressing the driver, "would you mind driving by the Houses of Parliament and Westminster Abbey?"

"Of course, madam. I shall point out numerous places of interest, if you please."

She smiled to herself. He's too young to be so stuffy, she thought. He assured her there would be much more time for sightseeing, for he had been assigned as her driver until she left London. How like Mr. Selfridge, she thought. So courteous and considerate.

Her suite at Claridge's was furnished with a blue-and-rose striped, canopied bed, antique French chairs, and Venetian mirrors. Mr. Selfridge had sent flowers and fruit, and it seemed everyone hovered around trying to meet her every need. I'm sorry, Terence, she thought wryly, but England is quite marvelous.

That evening the lingerie buyer for Selfridge's and two other executives took her to dinner. It was a formal but pleasant affair, and they all made plans to meet the following day, when she was to show them Queen's Lace.

Mr. Wentworth picked Nora up promptly at nine-thirty. She had been in the lobby, browsing in the beautiful shops while she waited. Oh, I can't wait to see more of this city, she thought excitedly.

When they arrived at the store, even Nora was awed. The building covered two full city blocks, and the entire front was colonnaded like an ancient Greek temple. A multitude of flags waved along the entire façade welcoming people of all different nationalities. She smiled. What a great showman, she thought.

Mr. Selfridge, holding for her an exotic white orchid, greeted her as a long-time friend. She then emptied the cases containing the lovely creations offered by Queen's Lace, and Mr. Selfridge was extremely enthusiastic.

"I believe that fantasy is an important part of shopping, especially for women. Now this"—he picked up a gorgeous pale blue satin petticoat with subtle touches of lace along a side slit—"would make them sit up and take notice. This is fantasy."

Nora smiled indulgently. "Thank you, Mr. Selfridge. Your compliments make me feel all the hard work was worthwhile."

"Of course it was! You know, Mrs. Desmond, I feel I have an important role to play in the emancipation of women. You prove my point. Women like you want to be on their own now, not just the chattels of their men, and I feel I can help them. I've even written newspaper essays about it." He was becoming more and more enthusiastic.

He's almost evangelical about his beliefs, she thought, but she liked that about him. The buyer placed one of the largest orders she had ever received, and she left feeling better than she had for some days.

When she opened the door to her suite, she was met by a sight so spectacular that she stepped back quickly, thinking she must be in the wrong room. The scent of lilacs filled the air, but there were roses and lilies and irises and daffodils in such profusion that the place looked like a manicured garden. Jack, she thought, you darling. You sent these flowers. Who else would? At that moment she noticed a book covered in lilac moiré with tiny flowers on it. As she reached for it, a knock sounded on the door. She laughed delightedly, wondering if she needed to explain to the bellboy—who was obviously bringing up her sample cases—why the room was in such a state. But when she opened the door, there stood Jack Ryan, looking roguish and handsome, and smiling that smile that always made her tremble. She was speechless with surprise.

"May I come in?" he asked, closing the door behind him. The next moment she was in his arms, laughing, crying, asking questions, and finally kissing him.

"Jack, I can't believe it. How did you get here? I'm so happy to see you. You look wonderful. When did you arrive?"

"Hold on, catch your breath, darling girl. I came on Her Majesty's ship, *City of London*. I arrived in Southampton late yesterday and took the train up this morning, and it *is* perfectly marvelous to be here, you're right. But you haven't asked me *why* I'm here."

She stepped back from him, and with a bewitching smile, asked, "Jack, why are you here?"

"To see you, Nora. To see the woman I have waited for all these years." He gathered her in his arms and kissed her. They clung desperately to each other, as though all the lost love of both their lives had been found in that kiss.

"Jack, I still can't believe it. I must be dreaming."

"You're not." He pinched her playfully on her cheek. "See, you're awake, and we're together. Nora, I knew I couldn't let this opportunity pass. From the moment I heard you would be in London, I knew I would come to you." He laughed. "It was difficult to arrange, what with broken speaking engagements, a curious staff, and a furious Priscilla. Unfortunately, I had to miss one of her pet charity balls. Despite hating politics, she loves having the lieutenant governor on her arm. Otherwise, she loves it when I'm gone." He paused thoughtfully. "You know, Nora, I think she has a lover. I've thought so for years, and to be honest, have hoped it was true. But never mind all that. We'll have hours and hours to talk."

She had a momentary twinge of guilt, but no more

than that. She knew at that moment as she gazed into his eyes that she loved him. It was crystal clear, and she knew nothing could ever keep her from him.

"Now," he said, "have you looked at the book?"

"No, darling. I just noticed it as you knocked on the door."

She picked it up and opened it. In his strong, bold hand he had lovingly outlined how they were going to spend every day of their stay, and on each day's page there was a secret message hidden by a strip of paper.

"Jack, it's marvelous. May I see what today's secret message is?" she asked, delighted as a child.

"Not till tonight after we return. Now, get some rest. I'll be back at seven." He turned to leave, and then walked back to her. "Nora, our lives will never be the same after tonight."

She gazed at him steadily, lovingly. "I know," she whispered.

As soon as he left, Nora dozed off, dreaming of lilacs and waltzes and crystal chandeliers. When she awoke, it was dark. She turned on the light, took a steaming hot bath and put on an ivory dress. She placed her pearls at her neck and stared at an expression in the mirror that she had never seen: one brightened by joy and contentment and anticipation.

As they were shown to their booth at the Royale, heads turned to stare. Who was this handsome couple? You could see the question on the face of every stranger. Jack and Nora chatted and laughed all through dinner. The champagne was making Nora delightfully giddy, as if she were riding on a floating cloud. Oh, she thought, how I want to tell him I love him, how I want his arms about me, his lips on mine. His every movement, every gesture, every word filled her with longings she had never felt, yearnings she had never known. They gazed lovingly into each other's eyes as the candlelight began to flicker low, and their voices became whispers of love. Afterward they rode through Regent's Park hand in hand.

In the suite of flowers they fell into each other's arms. Nora was trembling with anxiousness, for she had never known such passion, not even with William. Jack kissed her gently, touching her nose and ears and cheeks with his lips, slowly and gently, until he roused within her a response so deep, so intense, it was almost savage. Lifting her in his arms, he took her to the soft satin pillows and coverlets of the canopied bed. His lips moved down her dove-white throat as he undid her dress, button by button.

Nora stood up, and her chemise fell off her shoulders, rustling as it fell to the floor. Jack nearly shed tears of joy and desire when he saw her naked. The soft arch of her back, the sensual curve of her stomach, the full and pointed breasts made him ache with passion. He touched her shoulders, her breasts, her thighs, and she shuddered with pleasure. He ran his lips over every part of her body and she cried out in a sweet agony of desire.

"Jack," she whispered, "I want you." She fondled him, lovingly gazing at his strong, firm body.

"My Nora, my love," he murmured as he gently thrust himself into her. They made love in a quickening sensual rhythm, both crying for joy as they climaxed together and for a long moment their bodies shuddered as their passion spent itself.

"I shall never forget this moment," she whispered softly.

He gazed into her eyes. "I love you, Nora. I love you as I have never loved anyone, and I will always love you."

They fell asleep together, and when she woke and saw his strong arms around her, she quietly wept with joy.

Then she got out of bed and pulled the strip from the diary of lilacs to find out the secret message. It said, "We were meant to be."

Beautiful days and nights were theirs. They did everything Jack had planned out in the diary: boat rides on the Thames, long horseback rides in the countryside, evenings at the opera and theater, dancing till dawn. They were oblivious to everything except each other. Each day Nora would pull the strip off the appropriate page in the diary to reveal the message. Jack laughed at the delight it gave her. On Saturday, as they were getting ready to go to a wonderful inn in the country, Nora discovered this message: "A vow of love." This intrigued her. As she dressed, feeling as gay and young as she had ever felt, she hummed happily. Each message had meant something important to them as the day unfolded.

The Wings of the Dove Inn, set in the beautiful countryside of Kent, had been built during the sixteenth century. The owners had lovingly restored it, but had added modern conveniences to make it comfortable. Their room, furnished with Jacobean pieces, was warm and cozy, for the fire in the hearth was kept burning all day until bedtime.

The first morning they were there, they mounted their horses and rode, taking along a picnic lunch, which they spread out near a small river. When they returned to the room, they fell into bed laughing, and made love gently and lingeringly, like the very tempo of the day, and fell asleep.

Nora awoke suddenly and shook Jack. "We'll miss dinner, and I'm famished. Come on, now." She tickled and poked him. "This inn is supposed to have some of the best food in England, and I don't want to miss it."

He laughed. "We won't, darling. I won't allow you to miss anything that makes you happy."

The dining room glowed with candlelight, and Mr. Burbridge, the owner, was kind enough to place them at a very private table. "Please allow me to order for you," he offered. "I want you to have our very finest cuisine and a meal you will never forget."

"By all means," Jack answered. "We are in your hands." He looked at Nora and smiled. "We certainly want to enjoy the finest on our honeymoon."

Nora blushed and smiled shyly as Mr. Burbridge left for the kitchen. "There's so much for us to talk about. Will we ever learn everything there is to know about each other?" she asked.

"We'll be finding out things till we're old and grey and deaf and tottering around." Jack told her. "And I'll never tire of your voice, I promise."

"Oh Jack, if it could only be forever." Her eyes grew misty.

"Darling, it *will* be forever. It will just be a different kind of forever for us. Tonight, we'll make a vow that will ensure our being together forever."

She remembered the diary. "What, Jack? What vow?"

"Nora, we can't marry. Mike won't give you a divorce, and—"

Nora interrupted, "And your career would be ruined. Our situation is hopeless, darling."

"I don't ever want to hear you use that word again," he commanded.

"What would you call it?"

"I would call it difficult, unusual, even dangerous in some ways, but never hopeless. We have waited all our lives for each other, and we must find a way to be together." He paused, looking thoughtful. "You know, if Mike would give you a divorce, I'd say to hell with my career."

Nora gazed lovingly at him, and took his hand in hers. "Darling, I couldn't allow that to happen. Your constituents need you. So you are not to even think of such a thing, please. It wouldn't make me happy. In fact, I couldn't live with myself." As an afterthought, she added, "Besides, the question is academic. Mike will never consent to a divorce, you are right, so we must find another way to share our lives."

Suddenly Jack reached into his coat pocket. "Dearest Nora, if we can't have a normal life, I want you to know that I still cherish you as I would a wife. I want to make a vow with you here and now that we will belong to each other always, that I will always be here for you no matter what, that we will love each other until death do us part. I offer you this as a symbol of my pledge." Opening the black velvet box, he revealed a diamond pin so bright that she gasped. It was in the shape of a heart, and set with hundreds of tiny stones.

"Oh Jack, it's the most beautiful thing I've ever seen."

"It's very old, and the only property of worth that has survived in our family. My mother gave it to me. It had been given to her by her grandmother, and so on to the time before the famine, when my great grandfather's family had estates and wealth. My mother wanted me to have it, and now I want you to have it. It's our wedding ring."

Tears glistened in Nora's eyes. She knew what this pin must mean to him.

"I never loved Priscilla enough to give her something so special, so meaningful." He paused. "She always hated my family. She would never visit them for any reason. So I could never give it to her. She's even seen it," he added, "but she's never questioned me about it."

"Jack, I accept it with love. And I make the same vow. I shall always be there for you, darling. Always. I love you." They kissed across the table, and toasted their vow.

"To us," Jack finally said, "to our happiness, wherever we can find it. And we will, Nora. Don't doubt that for a moment, not a single moment." He put the pin on the ruffle of her dress. It glittered against the black velvet.

Never had Nora trusted anyone so much in her life, and she told Jack her most secret thoughts, ambitions and beliefs. Only one fact of her life was left untold, and that was about Billy. At that moment she couldn't bring herself to tell him. She would someday, but not now. She knew he would love her still and understand, but she thought to herself, I'll recognize the right moment when it arrives. So it went unspoken.

The night before Nora was to leave for America, they remained in the suite through the dinner hour. They wanted nothing to intrude on these last few hours, for they didn't know when they would be together again. They lay in each other's arms, talking, making plans, whispering oaths of love for each other. When they made love, Nora thought that if she died that instant, she could do so happily. She smiled at the thought.

"What is funny, my princess?"

She told him, and pulling her powerfully into his arms, Jack covered her face with kisses.

Jack took Nora to the ship the following day. She was sailing on the *Lusitania,* and he was sailing two days later. They had almost considered going on the same ship, so they could have ten more days together, but decided that it would be too risky. Though they tried to be gay, their parting was difficult for both of them.

They kissed good-bye in her stateroom, in an embrace of bittersweet tenderness, and then moved outside among the crowds of well-wishers and passengers. As he walked down the gangplank, a woman stopped him. He looked a little startled, and Nora heard him say, "Oh, I was just seeing off a friend, Mattie. I'm here on business. My best to George and have a good trip.'' He didn't look back at Nora.

"Yes, Jack, you too,'' the woman replied.

Nora didn't move. She dared not wave at him. Had they been seen together? Her throat was dry. When the ship finally began to move, she felt it safe to wave, for no one could see to whom she was waving and blowing kisses. No one could see who it was that had brought tears to her eyes.

Chapter 40

"Bridget, you and I are having dinner out Saturday night," Mike said. "Get your very best outfit ready."

"Faith, we're not needing to eat at a restaurant, Mike. I can cook as well as anyone in this city."

"You can indeed, Bridget, but I want you to have a night off, and some fun. We'll send Mary to Jim and Nellie's for the weekend."

Secretly, she liked the idea. Nora had often invited her to the theater and out to dinner, but Bridget had always said no, afraid of testing the waters of that world. When Mike offered, however, she found the prospect exciting.

On Saturday they took a hansom ride in Central Park, visited the Museum of Natural History, and had dinner at a charming restaurant on the West side called Des Artistes, which one of Mike's clients had recommended. They had a lovely meal of lobster cooked in whiskey, and candied vegetables, and a chablis that loosened their tongues. They talked of everything from the law of marriage to life in Ireland.

" 'Twas a grand dinner, Mike," Bridget said when she finished her meal. "I can't remember when last I enjoyed an evening so much."

Mike was glowing with pleasure. What a charming girl Bridget is, he thought. So open and friendly. Her sweet, simple nature was in sharp contrast to Nora's aggressive one. Mike understood that his wife was quicker and brighter than he, and he found that unacceptable. It wasn't her fault; he knew that now. They were both caught in a web of sorry circumstance. He had fallen in love with a beautiful, intelligent, ambitious woman, and had forever after spent all his time trying to change her, to make her fit the mold in which he thought all women belonged. But Nora could no more change her own nature than she could stop breathing.

He raised his head and looked at Bridget, who was smiling at him, and he felt a wave of tenderness flow over him. This woman, he thought, treats me more like a husband than Nora ever did. She's concerned about me, listens to me, and knows what makes me happy.

Bridget was sorry for Mike, sorry about the trouble between him and Nora, sorry his life wasn't going well, and she cared a great deal for him. He's such a good man, she thought. What a pity he's so unhappy. Her heart was lighter when she was with him, for she could talk to him without feeling tongue-tied or stupid. He made her feel happy and comfortable.

They rode home slowly in a carriage, laughing and chatting. Suddenly, she felt Mike's hand on hers. She sat very still, barely breathing. It felt so wonderful to have a man touch her again. It had been so long, so very long. She didn't move her hand away, but sat quietly, enjoying the moment.

When they closed the door of the apartment behind them, they fell into each other's arms. Mike kissed her as he had never kissed Nora. He wasn't as clumsy with Bridget, for she brought out a tenderness in him, a loving consideration.

"Oh Bridget," he whispered, "I want you. I need you more than I've ever needed anyone."

Bridget felt such stirrings of desire and love that nothing else entered her mind at that moment, not Nora, not Kevin, not sin, nothing except the sudden realization that she had loved Mike since she first set foot in his home. "Mike, I love you. I've always loved you from the day I first saw you."

He picked her up in his strong arms and carried her to her bedroom. He undressed her with a finesse he didn't know he had, while murmuring words of tenderness and love. Her white, freckled skin delighted him, and after kissing her throat and breasts, he entered her willing, waiting body. If he wasn't a master lover, Bridget didn't know, for she experienced great peaks of ecstasy, and her pleasure made him feel very self-confident. Maybe women *can* enjoy sex, he thought in surprise, and said aloud, "I love you, Bridget."

Something had begun between them that was beyond their power to deny. They were two lonely souls who had found solace, warmth and love. They had both been deprived of their mates, one by death, the other by misunderstandings. As the days went by, they grew happy and settled in their love and contentment. There were sober moments, however, for both were good Catholics and each would have bouts of guilt and depression and soul-searching. Most of the time, they were like two children who felt they were doing no wrong. After all, wasn't Mike about to be legally separated from Nora, and wasn't Bridget a widow? And there was so much laughter and fun around the house that little Mary thought it was all just wonderful.

"Seven weeks of happiness, Bridget, I'm thankful for that. How I wish it could last forever."

"Aye, how nice that would be," Bridget murmured sadly. She kept her eyes averted to the lace shawl she was embroidering so that he wouldn't see her tears. "Could it ever be?" she stammered, knowing that Nora wouldn't be hurt.

Mike stared at her. "You mean divorce?" he asked incredulously.

"Well," she answered timidly, "you and Nora are going to separate. It's the next logical step."

"Never, Bridget. It's against the laws of the Church." And so he blindly closed the door to any possibility of lasting happiness.

Bridget was crushed by his rejection, but she wasn't capable of the sophisticated arguments Nora would have given. She knew only that divorce was impossible for him. She thought to herself that he might be willing to continue their present relationship, which, in his mind, was somehow less sinful than divorce. But she wanted a man to call her own, to take care of, to have a child by, to marry. When Mike closed the door to any of those things that day, Bridget's heart became heavy, and her spirit miserable.

The day before Nora arrived home, a telegram came bearing the news of Frank O'Sullivan's death. He had passed away peacefully in his sleep, thankful and happy that he had gotten to see Sean and Nora again. Bridget locked herself in her room and cried herself to sleep. She had lost her father to his death, and the man she loved to his own insensitivity all in the same week.

When Nora arrived home, they greeted her as cheerfully as they could. But when Nora retired to her room to unpack, Bridget knocked on her door and handed her the telegram. Nora sank into the comforter, tears streaming down her face. "He's gone, he's really gone," she sobbed. "Does Sean know?" Bridget nodded mutely. He had been saddened but not surprised. "You poor darling," Nora whispered. "I wish you could have been with us to see him one last time. He was so happy, and he wanted to know all about you. Hearing that we were content and doing well in America gave him a great satisfaction." The two sisters wept together for their pa, and secretly for their own recent losses in love.

"Bridget, you still aren't well, are you? I don't like the way you are looking at all."

"I'll be all right," she answered cheerlessly. Nora almost didn't know this girl who stood before her, listless and pale.

Several days later, the phone on Nora's desk rang. Jack's voice was on the other end. "Darling Nora, I'm home and dear heavens how I've missed you."

"And I you. I've been wondering when I'd see you again," she replied.

"I'm trying to figure something out, darling. Be patient."

She told him of her father's death, and he comforted her as best he could. "Thank God," he told her, "that He allowed you to see him once more."

She admitted to him that that thought had given her great solace. He then asked if on the ship she had met the couple who had recognized him coming down the gangplank.

"I saw them a few times, and I must say I thought they were pointing a finger at me the entire time, but luckily I avoided meeting them."

He was glad to hear that, for the woman was a friend of Priscilla's whom he had always detested. She was a terribly cruel gossip. "Nora, I don't think they suspected anything. Please don't worry, darling."

"I'll try not to, I promise. Oh, how I want to see you, Jack. I love you."

"And I love you, darling. I will find a way. Trust me."

A few moments after she hung up, a messenger delivered a huge white bouquet of lilacs.

Nora invited everyone in the family to dinner a week later. She had sensed Bridget's constant unhappiness and thought this might help her. Indeed, she did perk up a little as she always did at the thought of a party.

The night of the gathering came. Rachel and Sean looked wonderful, Bridget commented, and she had never seen Nora look so radiant. Little Terry and Mary were playing hide-and-seek, and Uncle Jim played right along with them. Seamus asked endless questions about Terence and the old country. Annie had also come. Mike was unusually pleasant, Nora thought, though he was drinking too much, as usual.

Sean and Rachel delightedly announced in the middle of dinner that the were expecting a child. Nora proposed a toast, but as she looked across the table, she caught that unmistakable look of sadness in Bridget's eyes. Nora longed to go to her. How dear Bridget had wanted children of her own. Her only happiness now lay in taking care of Mary and Terry.

Sean's column had just been syndicated nationwide, and he was telling everyone of all the offers he's gotten to speak at political functions. In fact, he had recently accepted an invitation to go to San Francisco.

Nora insisted that Rachel leave the business to her so that she could accompany her husband on the cross-country trip.

Nellie shook her head in wonder. "Imagine, you'll be seeing real palm trees, and you'll be picking the lemons and oranges right off the trees outside your window. I've seen pictures, you know.''

"Yes, Aunt Nellie." Sean smiled at her. "We promise to bring a whole crate of lemons and oranges home for you.''

Uncle Jim was anxious about getting back late to the pub, so he and Nellie said their good nights. Then Mike and Bridget volunteered to take Seamus home. Annie, Sean, Rachel and Nora were talking and having a nightcap when there was a knock at the door.

"Who on earth can that be?" Nora wondered aloud. "Bridget and Mike couldn't be back so soon.''

A telegraph messenger handed Nora a telegram, which she accepted with trembling hands after giving the boy a quarter tip. An awful premonition seized her. She hesitated a moment before opening it. Sean had come up and was standing close behind her.

The telegram read: MOLLY AND TIM SHANNON KILLED IN CAR ACCIDENT STOP WILL STIPULATES TWO SURVIVING CHILDREN BILLY AND RETTA TO BE PLACED IN YOUR CARE STOP PLEASE CONTACT LEWIS MARTIN OF MARTIN BELLEWS AND FALLOWS CHICAGO STOP.

Nora let out a cry and collapsed into Sean's arms.

"They're dead," she sobbed. "Molly and Tim are dead.''

Annie and Rachel ran to them, and Annie took the telegram and read it. Her face went white. "Oh, dear Lord," she muttered. "Dear Lord.''

Rachel tried to calm Nora, while Sean brought her a shot of Irish whiskey, but she was sobbing, talking incoherently. Annie held her, stroking her hair, until finally Nora's sobbing abated. Then Annie took Nora's arm. "Let's go to your room for a few moments. We'll wash you face with a cool cloth," She led Nora into her room, closing the door. "Nora, are you all right now? You must be careful not to say anything about Billy, at least not now."

"I won't, Annie. I'll be all right." She fell into Annie's comforting arms, thankful to have such a dear friend.

"My God, Annie, Billy and Retta are all alone. Those children need me, Annie, they need me right away. Ask Sean to make a train reservation for me, would you please?" She dried her eyes.

"I will, Nora, and I'll be going with you."

"Oh yes, Annie. I'd like that."

Sean booked passage for both of them, at ten-thirty that night. When Bridget and Mike returned, Nora and Annie were already packed and ready to leave. Sean explained to them what had happened, and Bridget began crying. Mike collapsed into a chair. He had no idea that Nora was in the will as guardian of Tim and Molly's children.

"Nora, how can you take care of two more children?" he asked.

"I don't know, but we will. Won't we, Bridget?" She started to cry again.

"Of course, Nora, of course we will."

Mary had heard the commotion and sleepy-eyed, had padded out of her bedroom. "What is it? Mommy, where are you going?"

Nora took her in her arms. "Darling, something has happened, and I need to go get Billy and Retta. They'll be coming to live with us. You'll have your very own brother and sister, won't that be wonderful?"

Mary stared at her wide-eyed. "I will?"

"Yes, sweetheart, but go to bed now. I'll be back just as soon as I can."

* * *

Lewis Martin met them at the station in Chicago and directed them to the neighbor's house where Billy and Retta were staying. It was early in the morning, but as soon as they knocked, a portly woman in a robe and slippers let them into the gloomy foyer of the two-story brownstone. Mrs. Hennessy filled them in as best she could on what had happened. The family had been coming home from a Sunday outing, and the children had pleaded to be allowed to ride home in another car with some friends. Molly and Tim had agreed, taking instead the grandmother of one of the other children. As they had been rounding a curve, another car was speeding toward them, partially in their lane. Tim tried to swerve, but it was too late. They met head-on. Everyone was killed instantly.

Nora considered with horror that Billy too would have been dead, but for a fortuitous circumstance. She thanked God for sparing her son. He mind was a mass of conflicting emotions. She was happy that Billy was still alive, but sad about the death of her dearest friend, who had taken Billy to her heart and brought him up. Now she would have Billy back, but not as her son. That couldn't be. And Retta. God was now giving her Molly's child to bring up. "Oh Molly," she whispered, looking heavenward, "I shall do the very best I can with your little girl." She began crying again.

"The children are upstairs," Mrs. Hennessy said.

Nora took a deep breath before opening the door. The children were sitting quietly on the bed, holding each other's hands. They didn't know what was going to happen to them. When they saw Nora they immediately ran to her.

"Oh, Aunt Nora, Aunt Nora," they cried.

"I'm here, children. I'm here. I'll take care of you, don't worry."

Annie poked her head in the door. "Retta, can you come downstairs a moment?"

Billy and Nora were left along. He looked at her with such sadness in his eyes that she averted her own, unable to bear his pain. "Aunt Nora, why did it happen?" he asked. Then this twelve-year-old boy, who was trying so hard to be a man, climbed on her lap and sobbed as if his heart would break. She held him and let him cry, gently comforting him, and answered his questions as best she could. She realized that he hadn't been able to break down while Retta was around, for he was trying to be brave and strong for her. Bless his heart, she thought.

When Nora went downstairs, she discovered Retta in Annie's arms, crying.

Having the children in the household gave Bridget a new interest, and for a while her spirits seemed to have returned to normal. She fussed over them, doing everything she could to make them comfortable and at ease, but with six people living together, the apartment was proving to be too small.

As they gathered at dinner one night, Nora announced, "We really do have to move, as everyone knows, and I've been looking at a wonderful apartment on Beekman Place. It's beautiful—elegant, as you are so fond of saying Retta— and we'll each have our own bedroom."

"Why? I like sharing with Aunt Bridget," Retta exclaimed, her bright green eyes showing annoyance. Billy said nothing, for he had to sleep in a tiny maid's room behind the kitchen and was quite willing to move to larger quarters.

"Well, you can still do that, Retta, if Aunt Bridget doesn't mind," Nora said. "But we do have to get Billy out of the closet."

Billy was pleased. "Can we see the new place right away?"

"Of course. I'll take you all tomorrow. We'll have lunch and then go over."

Mike sat quietly. He feared that this meant he would finally have to move out. Nora sensed what he was thinking, and she knew she hadn't the heart to turn him out now. He was wonderful with Billy, for whom a household of all women might not be best at his age. Mike took him to the park, where they played ball and taught him other things that boys need to learn at that age, and Retta learned along with him. Mary was delighted with her new big brother and sister. They were kind to her, taking her out, playing with her, reading to her. Nora often took Billy riding. It was a major passion in both their lives and sharing it brought them very close to each other.

That night, after the children were in bed, Nora interrupted Mike's reading. "Mike, if you don't want to leave for a while, it's all right with me. The children love you, and I'm afraid of one more painful loss for them."

He looked surprised. They actually got along quite well when they weren't attempting to be married. "I don't mind staying, Nora. You know I'm a family man at heart. I'm glad I'm able to be of some help with Billy and Retta."

"Well, then, if it's all right with you, let's put aside our own problems for a while. The separation can wait a bit, I think."

"Yes," he answered, feeling relieved, for he wanted to be near Bridget. He had tried to approach her from time to time, but she was too ashamed and fearful to respond to him with Nora back. When they took the children out, he would steal a kiss now and again, which succeeded only in making her more miserable and guilty.

Billy was becoming very interested in Sean's newspaper

work, and followed him around asking endless questions until Sean finally suggested that Billy come to work with him one day to see just how a big city newspaper was run. Billy was so excited with anticipation that he could talk of nothing else for days. When Sean picked him up at Nora's office, Billy was poring over that morning's paper. Sean walked into Nora's office and stood watching the boy. "He reminds me of someone, I don't know who. Does he remind you of anyone, Nora?"

Nora froze. "Why, no, Sean, I can't think of anyone," she answered, trying to keep her voice steady. "Except sometimes, he has some of Tim's mannerisms, like the way he brushes his hair from his eyes."

"Maybe that's it," Sean acknowledged. "We'll see you later. We have a big day ahead of us."

Nora sank down in her chair. My God, she thought, did Sean suspect? Billy was growing more and more to look like William as each day went by. The same pale green eyes, the same tousled blond hair, the same aristocratic nose. None of this had occurred to her before, but the resemblance was striking, actually unmistakable, for anyone who knew them both.

She shook the thought away as the phone rang. It was Angelo Gambini, inviting her to lunch.

They met at Delmonico's. She hadn't been there for some time, but it was still her favorite restaurant. Angelo greeted her, and they sat down at his regular table. She was delighted to see him again.

"Nora, I've been worried about you. I know how saddened you must have been by the deaths of your two friends."

She told him what had happened, told him about the children living with her. "It's not easy living in such a big household," she laughed, "but I love it, Angelo. I love having them. They are delightful children. Billy rides with me, and Retta shops with me. She loves clothes, always has. Funny, because Molly wore the plainest things. She's interested in design, almost as if she were *my* daughter instead of Molly's.'' She was silent a moment. ''How I shall miss Molly. But don't be concerned. I'm doing just fine.''

''Nora, do you remember when I gave you the names of those doctors for Seamus, to see if he could be helped?''

''Why, yes, of course. They were all very nice, but they told us nothing could be done.''

''Yes, I know, but there have been some interesting developments in the new field of psychoanalysis. You've heard of Dr. Sigmund Freud?''

''Of course. Why?''

''Well, he has treated all kinds of cases, and there is a man here from Vienna who has studied with him, a Dr. Schmidt. The reason I think you might be interested is because he had made a study of what he calls hysterical blindness. A doctor I know, Dr. Keppler, through our mutual interest in art, mentioned this the other night at a dinner party I attended. I immediately thought of Seamus, for the doctors have been able to give no reason for his blindness, and he doesn't remember falling or being hit. I guess it's a slim chance, but I wanted you to know.''

Nora was fascinated. ''Hysterical blindness. How would such a thing happen?''

''Well, Dr. Keppler says it is often caused by someone seeing something so terrible that his mind simply cannot accept the horror of it.''

Nora shuddered as she remembered Seamus' description of Kevin's death. ''Angelo, could we take Seamus to see this Dr. Schmidt?''

''Yes, of course. Keppler will arrange it.''

''Angelo, thank you so much for telling me about this.''

"Seamus is a fine man. He deserves to have any chance he can get."

The following week, Bridget and Nora took Seamus to see Dr. Schmidt, a short, precise man with a heavy German accept. He examined Seamus, talked to him, and concluded that his blindness might very well be psychosomatic in nature. Seamus asked him what it meant, and what could be done about it.

"It is difficult to say, young man, but I would venture the guess that you feel a terrible guilt and responsibility over the death of your young comrade and dear friend. When that happens, one often shuts it out by denying oneself sight. What you saw was too awful, too painful to confront. I can tell you it was not your fault. Everyone, including the young man himself, could tell you that it was not your fault, but until your subconscious mind tells you that, and frees you from your bondage of blindness, there is nothing to be done."

"How do I go about freeing myself from this bondage, Doctor?" Seamus asked in desperation. "Please, help me!"

"Well, Dr. Freud uses hypnosis in cases such as yours, and that has often been helpful, but it is a new therapy and somewhat controversial. It's expensive and time-consuming as well. You are welcome to see me again if you wish to try hypnosis, but remember, there is no guarantee."

"Dr. Schmidt, at present I am studying for the bar, but I would like to consider trying after I pass the examination."

"Very well, then." Schmidt turned away. "My secretary will schedule an appointment for you when you are ready. With help, perhaps you will someday find a reason to see."

The words Dr. Schmidt had used, "Perhaps you will someday find a reason to see," puzzled Seamus, for he felt he had many compelling reasons to see, but he obviously had as many compelling reasons not to see. It was new and frightening territory, pondering the doctor's words about guilt and responsibilty. He wondered if he himself could change any of that. It sounded so simple. If he just stopped feeling guilty he would see again, but he suspected it would not actually be so simple. "I do want to see," he said to himself. "Dear God, help me, please."

Chapter 41

Lilacs and love letters from Jack arrived at the shop weekly, and he called Nora almost every day. Twice that year
they managed to slip away and meet for a few brief, stolen
hours in a haze of love and promises, reaffirming the
undeniable bond between them.

In fact, everything seemed to be going well for Nora.
The business was still expanding, Billy and Retta had
enrolled in school, and Sean and Rachel had a baby girl.
Only Bridget, with her sad moodiness, and Mike, who had
become fat from so much drinking, disturbed Nora's tran-
quillity. She didn't like Mike's drinking, but she was used
to it. It was only when his habits began to affect Mary that
Nora really got angry.

Mary had been attending catechism classes regularly,
and she was ready to receive her first Holy Communion. It
was a very important day for her, and trying on the lovely
white organza dress that Denise had made for her, she
paraded and preened in front of the mirror.

"Oh, Mommy, it will be the most beautiful dress in church."

"Darling, it *is* a beautiful dress, but that is not the most important thing. You are about to receive, in the form of a wafer, the body and blood of our Lord Jesus Christ. That is what is important about your first communion," Nora explained.

"I know, Mommy, but I want to look pretty, too."

Nora turned away to keep from smiling.

Blessed Sacrament Church was crowded with proud families. The children, excited and happy, fussed with flowers and prayer books as they stood in the front pews waiting for Mass to begin. Nora, Bridget, Retta, Billy, Seamus, Sean and Rachel with Terry and the baby, Uncle Jim and Aunt Nellie, and all of Mike's family were there. Annie, Denise, and other friends all came too. Only Mike had not appeared yet. Nora looked around but didn't see him. He had not been home when they left for church that morning, but Nora had assumed he had gone out for a stroll and that he would show up at the Mass. As the organ began to play, Nora looked once again toward the back of the church, and there she finally saw Mike. His tie was askew, his face unshaven. Oh my God, she thought, he's drunk. Bridget spotted him at the same time. Nora, worried that Mary would see him, was becoming frantic. Bridget put her hand on Nora's.

"I'll take care of him. You don't want to miss Mary's big day." She quickly moved out of the pew.

Bridget led Mike outside. "You can't do this to the child, Mike. What in God's name is wrong with you? How dare you come here, looking this way? You had best leave, and I'll tell Mary you're sick."

"But I'm not drunk, Bridget," he slurred. "I jush

want to see my baby girl make her first communion. Ish a big day, you know, very big. I need to see her.''

"Sure, and you're cold sober, are you now? Faith, Mike Desmond, you're drink taken. I've seen enough drunken men in my time to know. Now go someplace to sober up, or you'll be sorry.''

"Well, I guesh I know where I'm not wanted.'' He turned and lurched away.

A tear came to her eye as she watched him stumbling up the street. Whenever Nora was gone on a business trip, Bridget had allowed Mike into her bed. Now she was beginning to feel nauseated in the mornings. She was pregnant, and the father of her child was a sot.

The ceremony was underway when Bridget re-entered the pew. "He's left,'' she whispered to Nora.

Oh God, help me. What can I tell her about her father? Nora thought in despair. Mary so wanted her daddy to be here.

Outside, all the families were kissing the children and taking photographs. Mary always loved being the center of attention, but now she realized her father wasn't there.

"Mommy, I don't see Daddy. Where is he?''

"He was here, darling, but he got sick and went home. He felt just awful about not being able to stay, but he just couldn't,'' Nora lied.

Just then Mary looked across the street, and balancing crookedly against an apartment building to support himself stood Mike.

"Oh, Mommy, he must be feeling better already. There he is.'' She broke away from her mother and ran across the street to him.

"Daddy, why do you look this way?'' she asked when she saw him up close.

"What way, little angel? You look jush like a little angel, Daddy's little angel,'' he blubbered.

Mary was frightened. "Daddy, I don't like you this way." She started crying. "Why are you like this?"

"Here, here, angel, ish all right."

"No, Mike, it is not all right," Nora said, coming up behind them. She had never before allowed him near Mary when he was drunk. "How could you do this?" she hissed under her breath so her daughter wouldn't hear. "Get out of here right now, before anyone else sees you. And don't come near her again till you're sober. Find youself a room, or sleep in the street, for all I care, but stay away from my home." She took Mary's hand. "Let's go back, darling. Daddy will be feeling better tomorrow, and everyone wants to see you." Nora led her away.

"But Mommy, what is wrong with him?" Mary cried, a hopeless look in her eyes. Nora knew that Mary would never forget that disappointing, confusing moment as long as she lived, but there was nothing Nora could do about it. What was done could not be undone. Oh Lord, she thought, where will this all end?

When they returned to the apartment for Mary's party, Mary temporarily forgot the unpleasantness with Mike as she became the center of everyone's attention. Sean lifted her onto his shoulders, and she was gleefully patting everyone on the tops of their heads when the front door opened and Mike stumbled into the room. There was a hush.

"Here's Daddy. Did you think Daddy would mish your party? Come give Daddy a kiss." As Mike reached for Mary, Sean lost his grip, and she almost fell. She began to cry. Nora took Mike's arm, firmly propelling him down the hallway into the library. She shut the door behind them.

"You were never much of a husband, but until now I always believed you were at least a decent parent," she said angrily.

Mike lurched toward her and Nora put out her hands to steady him, to keep him from falling.

"I *am* a decent parent!" he retorted. "She never had a mother there when she came home from school. I was always the one there when she was sick and feverish, while you were at the office, or in Boston or Philadelphia, or God knows where else. So don't lecture me!"

Mike's face was bright red, all his angers and resentments spewed out. Suddenly, a great shudder shook his body, and he sagged. Even his facial features dropped. He was trying to talk, his eyes still full of anger, but his mouth was contorted and his words came out twisted and confused.

To Nora, the moment seemed frozen in time. She knew that she must reach him, but she seemed incapable of moving. She was reaching for him, calling to him. Then he was on the floor, and she was holding him and crying for help. At once, the room was full of people. Mary saw her father, screamed and clutched at Rachel, who tried to lead her from the room.

"Sean, go for help!" Nora's face was full of terror. "Someone, do something. We must get him to the hospital. Mary, darling, it's going to be all right. Don't cry, dear. Daddy just feels sick. Go with Aunt Rachel. Daddy will be fine in a minute." Rachel led her from the room. "Sean, help me lift his head. Undo his tie. Oh God, what's wrong?"

Sean and Seamus were helping her, while Bridget stood rigidly behind them, all color drained from her face. She finally bent down and softly spoke to Mike. "You'll be all right. Help is on the way. You must be all right." She kept repeating those words, as if to convince herself.

An ambulance arrived. Mike was carried out on a stretcher and was put in the back. His eyes opened wide in terror and he cried out.

Nora bent close. "What is it, Mike? Tell me, what is it?"

Mike made the same sound over and over, finally quieting when Bridget, who had climbed into the ambulance with Nora just as the doors were being closed shut, took his hand. His eyes lost their frightened look, he sighed heavily and stared up at her. He then lost consciousness, and remained that way even after they arrived at the hospital. Nora and Bridget waited in the hallway, Nora pacing the floor, Bridget quietly crying and saying her rosary.

When the doctor appeared, his face was grave. "Mrs. Desmond, your husband has suffered a heart attack. I'm sorry, but there isn't much hope."

Bridget let out a cry of anguish. Nora rushed to her side and held her sister in her arms.

"May we see him, Doctor?" Nora asked.

"Of course. He is unconscious, but certainly you may see him."

"When will he wake up, Doctor?" Bridget inquired, her tone pleading. "Please, when will he awaken?" She grasped the doctor's arm.

"My dear lady, that's impossible to say. He may never regain consciousness. Of course, I don't know that for certain, but you must be prepared for the worst."

Bridget sobbed. "But there is something I must tell him. He must wake up!"

Nora took her arm. "Come, dear, let's go in to see Mike. You can tell him whatever you want. I'm sure he'll hear you." How close he and Bridget have become, Nora thought.

The room was dark except for the small circle of light where the nurse read over the instructions on Mike's chart. Mike was still and pale. Bridget rushed to the bedside and Nora stood behind her. Bridget began to call his name over and over, pleading for him to hear her until the nurse came over and gently took her arm as if to lead her away.

"Now, now, Mrs. Desmond, you mustn't upset yourself so. Come, sit down, calm yourself."

Suddenly, it dawned on Nora that Bridget was grieving as if it were her own husband who was so gravely ill. No wonder the nurse had called her Mrs. Desmond. Bridget seemed to care more for Mike than she did. Nora looked closely at her sister and for the first time recognized the genuine love she showed. How good she would have been for him, Nora thought. She would have made a wonderful home, borne him many children, been a dutiful, adoring wife. All I ever did was to frustrate and upset him. Poor Mike!

As if he had heard Nora silently speak his name, Mike opened his eyes and glanced at her, then at Bridget. His face lit up briefly, and he clearly called out, "Bridget, Bridget, I—" He sighed, closed his eyes and was gone.

Nothing could comfort Bridget. Her tears were unceasing. Nora, on the other hand, went throught the days before the funeral dry-eyed and full of guilt. She had never truly loved Mike. To mourn his passing would be a mockery. She felt as if she had used Mike, had trapped him into a marriage she had never really cared about, even at the beginning. Now he was gone and she shamefully had to admit to herself that she was relieved. At the same time she was gratified that Bridget, at least, was there to mourn his passing. He deserved that much.

Angelo accompanied Nora to the funeral. She leaned heavily on his arm as they entered Blessed Sacrament Church. She left Mary to walk with Sean and Rachel. Nora had not slept or eaten for two days and she was so consumed with guilt that she had come to believe she had somehow brought about her husband's death by her willful, selfish ambition. Angelo tried to convince her that she had honestly presented herself to Mike from the day she first met him, but she would not listen, and after endless hours, Angelo gave up. She was not yet ready for logic.

Nora did not at first see Jack sitting in the shadows in the back pew. He half rose as she almost stumbled in the aisle, but Angelo caught her and supported her, and she lifted her veiled face to his in gratitude.

A noise at the back of the church caused Nora to turn around. She saw Jack. Dear God, thank you for letting him be here.

It seemed to Nora that the service would never end, but finally she found herself stepping up to the casket for a final farewell. As Bridget leaned close to Mike, Nora heard her whisper, "Oh, Mike, you went away before I could tell you, but I'm tellin' you now and I pray you can hear me. Mike, oh Mike, I love you."

As Nora heard the words, the weight of her guilt bore down on her until she could no longer stand, and she collapsed into Angelo's arms. Jack slipped out of the church, weeping for his Nora.

Bridget felt numb and helpless. If only she had been able to wail and keen as she would have in Ireland, but that just wasn't done in America—it might annoy the neighbors. So she held in her misery by day, and she lay awake staring at the ceiling night after sleepless night. Oh dear God, she would pray, take me too. I don't want to live, please don't make me live. I've lost the only two men I've ever loved. But she could not let herself die. She was pregnant with Mike's child. Mike's death, she was convinced, had been punishment for her committing adultery, treason against her own sister. I'll never again receive God's blessing, she thought. A miserable sinner such as I dare not even ask His forgiveness. Poor Mike, I led him astray, and made him miserable, and now he's dead! It's all my fault.

Bridget shared her feelings with no one, not even a priest. Soon the sickness of her soul manifested itself in a sickness of her body, and she quietly took to her bed. Nora and the children did all they could to cheer her, but she would not be consoled.

One night, as she lay silently suffering, a thought occurred to her: If God cannot forgive me, and if I am doomed to hell anyway, then what is the point of living? Why should I not end my own life with my own hand? The moment she thought of this, she began to feel better. If she were dead, all would be solved. No guilt, no sadness, no baby. But how to do it? She had no gun, and hanging was messy. She decided to turn on the gas stove, then climb into bed and wait for death. To accomplish this, she would have to talk Nora into taking the children to Southampton for a weekend in the vacation house Nora had recently rented. She would tell Nora that she needed to be alone for a few days to rest and regain her strength. When Bridget made the suggestion that afternoon, Mary jumped up and down with delight. "Oh, Ma, could we? Could we, please?"

"Why not? Aunt Bridget is right. A change might be best for all of us." It seemed as though Nora had been waiting for someone to make that very suggestion. She packed and helped Mary to get ready. They would leave that night, but first Nora called Seamus and told him where they were going. "Seamus, please call or come by, won't you? Bridget seems better, but I'd feel easier if I knew you were around. You're the only one she listens to at all. Even Sean gets nowhere with her lately. Anyway, Sean and Rachel will be in Albany for a couple of days, and I'm taking Terry with me, so there will be no one else for her to talk with."

"Of course, Nora. I'll call and stop by to check on her, don't worry. And you have a good time."

The apartment was quiet for the first time in weeks. Bridget sat despondently in the living room, able at last to surrender to the misery in her soul. An even deeper depression settled on her as she sat quietly for hours, reliving her entire life. She left the lights off and ate nothing. The phone rang, but she did not answer it. It rang for five minutes before it finally stopped. At last, she arose from the couch and walked slowly toward the kitchen as if she were in a dream. Then she put on her nightgown and took the phone off the hook. Returning to bed, she lay down, staring at the ceiling, waiting, waiting.

Seamus thought it odd that no one had answered when he had called a few hours after Nora left. He tried again but this time received a busy signal. He rang again a few moments later. Still busy. After a half-hour of busy signals, he began to feel uneasy, so he checked with the operator. He was told there was no one on the line. Without another thought, he grabbed his jacket, felt for his cane and called to Jinx, his new Seeing Eye dog.

When he reached the apartment, the doorman smiled. "Good evening, Mr. Gorman. 'Tis fine summer weather, isn't it now?"

"Yes, it is. John, have you seen Mrs. O'Riordan?"

"No, sir, she hasn't been out since I've been on duty."

Jinx began to whine, sensing his master's anxiety. Seamus rang the bell insistently, but received no answer, so he fumbled in his pocket for the key he always carried. He finally opened the door. The odor of gas was strong. What has she done? he thought in a panic. "Bridget!" he screamed. "Bridget, where are you?"

Jinx went into a fit of whining and barking.

"Jinx, find Bridget, find her." This new apartment was so large, and Seamus didn't know it as well as he had known the other one.

Oh Lord, how can I save her when I don't know where she is? God help me, please, please! Jinx ran off, then came back and pulled at Seamus' leg. Seamus tried to follow, but it was slow going. If I don't find her, he thought, we'll both die. If I could only see. I've got to save her. I must force my eyes to see. I couldn't save Kevin, but I can save his wife.

Seamus could feel something against his legs. Jinx had pulled him to the bed. "Bridget, are you there? Can you hear me?"

He heard a low moan. My God, she's still alive. If I can get her to a window, maybe I can help her. Lifting his head toward heaven, he screamed, "God, how can I save her if I can't see!"

In a flash, as he opened his eyes, he could make out the outline of the bed and Bridget's body. "I can see, Bridget, I can see! I'll help you!" he screamed deliriously. He grabbed Bridget, dragged her to the window and opened it. The cool night air blew in. Seamus propped her over the sill, then ran back into the kitchen and turned off the gas, then threw open the rest of the windows. When he ran back to the bedroom, Bridget was gasping in the night air. "Bridget, dear, it's Seamus. You're all right. Please speak to me."

She moaned again and opened her eyes. "Seamus, go away and let me die. Please let me die."

"Stop that. What kind of nonsense is that? You're all right, now." He carried her to the bed. In her dazed condition, she didn't realize that he could see where he was going. He held her in his arms, soothing her. "You'll be all right. Just rest."

At first she was sobbing and incoherent, but finally her words began to make some sense. "Seamus, how did you get here?" she sobbed. "Why didn't you let me die? I don't deserve to live. You don't know what I've done. I can never be forgiven."

"Bridget, I think I do know what you've done. You had an affair with Mike. It's long been obvious how you felt about him."

She nodded mutely.

"Well, now, that's not so bad."

"My sister's husband, Seamus. How can you say it's not bad?"

"Bridget, stop it, now. Listen to me. It would be better if it had never happened, but you were two lonely people needing affection and love. Mike was no longer Nora's husband. They hadn't been man and wife for a long time. You know that. God can forgive you, Bridget. He has forgiven far worse sins than yours."

Bridget looked into Seamus face, and knew she could trust this gentle blind man with her deepest secrets. "But, that is not all, Seamus," she sobbed. "I'm carrying his child."

He put his arms around her. "Hush, now. That too will be all right, woman, for you and I will be married and no one will be the wiser. There are worse reasons for marriage than this."

"You would do that for me, Seamus?"

"I would do anything for you, dear Bridget. Anything."

She finally looked up at him. "Oh, dear, dear Seamus."

He got up from the bed and closed the curtains. She stared after him, a realization beginning to grip her. "Seamus, how did you do all this? You closed the cur-

tains. You walked right to them. My God, you can see!''
She ran into his arms.

"Aye, lass, I can see. The doctor was right. I had
denied myself sight after I saw Kevin killed, but to save
you, I had to see again. You're so lovely, dear Bridget.
Your lovely face is just as I remembered.''

They held each other very closely and spoke no words.

Seamus did not know if he was in love with her. He
had never allowed himself to think about it before. But
holding her in his arms made him feel more content than
he had felt for a long, long time.

Chapter 42

Jack had introduced Nora to Southampton. It was a fashionable resort where the Irish were welcome. It had all the attributes of a great summer retreat: miles of beautiful white sand beaches and rolling dunes, balmy breezes and beautiful summer days. Some of the wealthy Irish families were already buying property there, for they couldn't buy real estate in wealthy Protestant resorts like Newport.

Nora had loved Southampton at once, even though she first saw it on a bleak November day. The sea had been rough, the sky grey and the wind chilly, but she and Jack had shared a quiet, loving stay at a marvelous old home on the water. She often thought later that perhaps her love of Southampton might be partially due to the happy memories of that November weekend by the sea. She had rented a house on the spot, intending to spend as much of the following summer there as she could. Perhaps she would even send Bridget and the children to stay all summer.

Now, finally, she was pulling up in front of the

two-story frame house, which was located a short distance from the water. The children piled out, racing down to the beach. Nora opened the house up, pulled sheets off the furniture, unpacked the groceries and put bouquets of flowers on every table. Her spirits were lifting for the first time since Mike's death. The children were happy to be there too, and after exploring the beach, they discovered every secret nook and cranny of the house. Nora was delighted that Bridget had insisted they come, but wished that she were there with them to share these happy moments. Nora even managed to cook a dinner, a feat she hadn't performed in a long time. Just as they were sitting down to eat, the phone rang. It was Jack. "Why, you sound as if you are right here in Southampton."

"I am, love. I called your office and they told me where I could find you." In a more serious tone, he added, "It has been too long, Nora. I must see you."

"Of course. Come now. Come to dinner."

"Is that wise?" he asked.

"Nothing could be wiser. I'd like you to meet the children."

The children were enchanted with Jack. Mary climbed all over him, asking him to read her a bedtime story. As Nora watched, she realized how much the child missed Mike. Billy took to Jack, too, for Jack treated him as an adult, an equal.

Retta was the only one who held back, and Nora suspected that she had probably guessed this might be someone who cared for Nora as more than a friend. So Nora was very careful to include her in conversations with Jack, and Retta finally began to warm to him.

After the children were all in bed, Jack and Nora shared a long embrace, then went in to sit before the fire.

They sat quietly for a few moments, and Jack turned to her. "Nora, are you all right? You have been through a monstrous time. I wanted to help, and to be near you. When I sat in the back row at the funeral, it was like watching a stranger. You were surrounded by your children, none of whom I had ever met, and your sister, and brother, and family, none of whom I knew. I was the outsider. And there was Angelo Gambini sitting next to you. Why, Nora, I didn't even know you knew that man.''

"Angelo is an old friend, Jack, one of my oldest friends in America. He has always been there when I needed him, when I was alone and miserable. And he knew Mike quite well.''

"I see." He considered for a moment. "I know you had a life before you met me, Nora, but I worry about friends like that one. Did you know he was being investigated by a senate committee?''

"Yes, Jack, I do know, but none of that matters to me. I hope I don't shock you, but even if they found something unsavory about him, which I know they won't, it wouldn't matter to me. He will always be my friend.''

"Of course, Nora. Anyone would be lucky to have such a loyal friend as you.''

"Well," she smiled, "you have me.''

He grinned back at her. "It was just seeing him there next to you, Nora, while I was relegated to the rear that was—well, it was hard for me.''

"I know, darling. I'm sorry. But you'll never know how much it meant to me just having you there so close by.''

They were quiet and pensive. The grandfather clock in the hall chimed midnight.

"How your sister, Bridget, sobbed. She must have cared a great deal for Mike.''

"Yes, she did," Nora replied, remembering how Mike's last words had been for Bridget.

"You know, Jack, she was kind to him. In fact, she

knew him better than I did.'' Tears began to form in Nora's eyes as she thought of Bridget leaning over Mike in the casket and whispering her love to him. ''Jack, I still feel responsible for his death. We had a terrible argument about his coming to Mary's first communion drunk and unruly. I—I—'' she stammered. ''Oh, Jack, I feel that I killed him as surely as if I had taken a knife to his heart.''

''Nora, stop that. You didn't kill him. If anything, he killed himself with his drinking. You can't torture yourself. It was bound to happen, and at least he was with all of you when it did.''

''But in a sense,'' she said more calmly, ''I did rob him of his life by marrying him. How happy he would have been with someone like Bridget. They would have been perfect together. He wanted a wife, a home, simple family pleasures—all the things I couldn't give him.'' She was crying again softly.

''Yes, Nora. Cry, darling. Cry all you must until this poison of self-accusation is purged.''

''You're right, I know you're right, Jack. I can't pretend I was a good wife to Mike.''

''Nor was he a good husband to you, Nora. He never understood you, and he never tried to. He never liked you working and he took your success as a sign of his own weakness. You were mismatched from the moment you met.'' As he was speaking, she began to realize he was saying all the same things Angelo had said, trying to comfort her. Now, however, she was more ready for logic.

''Yes,'' she replied quietly. ''Yes, I did try to tell him. I guess I thought it would all work out, that he would come to see things my way.'' She smiled. ''I'm wiser now. It was a mistake to expect him to change.''

''Of course, darling. In youth we make so many mistakes that affect the rest of our lives and sometimes even destroy our souls." He stared into the fire. "But Nora, we can't waste our lives regretting the past."

That made her think of Billy. She looked at Jack uncertainly. Dare she tell him? "Jack," she said quietly, without emotion, "there is something else, something you don't know about that has been with me for a long time."

He sensed by her voice and manner that it was something very important, and he held her hand tightly, attempting by his touch to give her the emotional support she needed. "Yes, Nora, what is it, dear one? Tell me. We must not keep secrets from each other."

She was silent for a few moments longer, and then looked away, into the fire. "Jack, Billy—Billy is my child," she stammered.

Jack sat motionless. "Your child, Nora? How can that be?" He put his arms about her shoulders in a gesture of compassion.

"I was pregnant when I left Ireland, unmarried and pregnant. I carried him in secret. That's why I went to Lowell, and when he was born, Molly and Tim adopted him." So few words to explain so much heartbreak. "His father was the local lord of the manor, so it was perfectly acceptable for him to abandon a peasant girl."

Jack detected a bitterness in her voice that he had never heard before. "My darling Nora, I'm sorry. I'm so sorry, not that you are Billy's mother, but that you must have suffered so. What a strong, brave woman you are, Nora, and were. Then, you were but a girl." He gathered her into his arms, and she wept.

As the evening wore on, and the fire flickered and died, she told him everything. He never let her go for a single moment, and she knew that they had never been closer, for finally she had trusted him. "I have struggled with the idea of telling Billy the truth, but it seems too cruel. Perhaps some day I'll tell him, but I don't think now is the right time. He's so young.''

"I'll keep your secret. Don't worry, darling.''

As he left that evening, Nora felt a lightness, a joy, a renewal of life. Here, at last, was a man to love and trust. A man who understood her darkest secret, but loved her nonetheless. She slept long and peacefully, and had glorious dreams.

The next few days were full of sunshine and long walks on the beach and toasting marshmallows over the fire in the evenings. At times she caught Jack studying Billy. My burden is lighter because he knows, Nora thought. Billy and Mary adored Jack, and Terry thought of him as his very own plaything, but Retta still remained strangely aloof; polite always, but aloof.

As they sat on the veranda one evening, Nora told him about a call she had made to Seamus. "I tried several times to call Bridget and got no answer, but Seamus told me she's fine, feeling better and out and about. I can hardly believe it, she was so sick, both in her mind and her body.''

"Thank God she's all right now.'' They sat listening to the sound of the surf, watching the children running way down the beach. "Nora, I haven't told you, but some of my misdirected fellow politicians have it in their minds that I should run for the Senate next year—in Washington, not the state senate.''

"Why, Jack, how wonderful. What an honor for you. I'm delighted.'' Leaping from her chair, she threw her arms about him. "Senator Ryan, I demand a kiss. I may not be one of your constituents, but I carry a lot of weight, nonetheless.''

He picked her up in his arms, saying jokingly, "That you do, lass, that you do.''

"Oh Jack, put me down. What if the children see?''

"I'll tell them you've fainted from sheer happiness."

"Now, tell me about it. Will you run? I must know everything."

He told her of the plans, the pressures for him to accept, what was involved, and she listened intently, asking questions here and there.

"But now, Nora, I have other plans I want to talk to you about. We're going to take a trip! A friend of mine has a yacht berthed in the harbor, and it and the crew are at my disposal. We can leave the children with friends in Easthampton for a few days. I'll make all the arrangements. We'll be alone, darling." His voice was raw with emotion, and she felt a desire so strong that she couldn't speak for a few moments.

"Oh Jack, how wonderful, how divine. I don't know that we should, though. I can't help but worry."

"There's nothing to worry about. This is a perfect plan. I want to hear nothing further from you. It's a fait accompli."

The children raced back to the house, their feet full of sand, their clothes wet and their arms filled with shells— beautiful shells, ugly shells, broken shells.

"What is all this?" Nora asked, laughing.

"We're going into business," Billy answered seriously.

"Mommy," Mary interrupted, "we are going to paint them and sell them."

"Well, that's very interesting, but who do you think is going to buy a broken shell, painted or not? You need perfectly formed shells if you're to sell them."

"Not necessarily so," Retta began in a haughty, grown-up manner.

Little Terry excitedly interrupted. "We're going to make garages with the broken pieces, that's what."

"Garages?" Nora asked incredulously.

"Terry, it's collages, not garages," Mary corrected him impatiently.

"Yes, Aunt Nora," Retta patiently explained, "we plan to use the broken pieces to make collages."

"Collages? How interesting." Nora was surprised that Retta knew the word.

"Yes, Aunt Nora, they are pieces of art made from pasting all kinds of different objects on them. We've done them in art class at school."

"I see," Nora answered, properly chastised. "Well, that should be great fun. I'll help you in the morning, if you like, but for now, I want to see you all in bed. It's very late. The latest you have ever stayed up, Mary."

"Yes, Mommy, but I had to stay up. They couldn't have collected all these without me."

"I'm sure, but now, off to bed with you."

When the children were tucked in and all was quiet, Jack and Nora returned to the veranda. The children had accepted his presence as normal and had completely accepted him as a new friend. Even Retta had become a little less distant toward him, for which Nora was thankful.

"Darling," Jack said, "let's take a walk down the beach. The children will be fine. We won't go far."

They walked down the beach, hand in hand, strolling on the water's edge, jumping back just as the surf would roll in.

"Oh Jack, we're worse than the children. If we're going to live dangerously, let's take off our shoes."

Jack pulled her to him. "You're beautiful, my Nora, you're the most beautiful, wonderful thing that has ever happened to me." He kissed her hungrily. She returned his kisses with wild abandon. They ran back to the dunes and fell into the sand, and into each other's arms with a passion and fire that was beyond their control. She helped him pull off her clothes, then his own, laughing with love

and delight. He covered her face and throat and breasts
with his kisses, then she smothered his face with her
kisses. She felt him harden under her, and suddenly he
was inside her. She was on top of him, throwing her head
back in dizzy rapture. She moved slowly, ecstatically on
him, climaxing as she never had before. "Oh Jack, Jack!"
She shuddered with joy and passion as incredible pleasure
swept through her body. "I love you, I love you."

"And I love you, darling Nora," he moaned as his
own release matched hers.

They lay quietly staring into each other's eyes and
listened to the waves rolling in to shore.

Jack had been making plans for their trip, and the
children were chattering away, getting ready for their own
trip to Easthampton. Laurie Welch, Retta's friend from
Sacred Heart School in New York, had invited all four
children to her summer home in Easthampton. Nora was
delighted to have Retta and Billy go, but was worried
about little Mary and Terry, who were so much younger.

Mrs. Welch, anticipating Nora's worry, called her.
"Faith, they'll be having a grand time, Mrs. Desmond.
My little Honora is just Mary's age, and her brother Pat is
just a little younger than Terry. They're not having that
many friends here. Hard to make friends with these high
and mighty Protestants, so we're looking forward to seeing
some decent Irish-Catholic children. Please let them come."

Nora smiled. She liked Mrs. Welch's friendly voice
and agreed that Mary and Terry could go. Mary leapt
around dancing, jumping on furniture, and Nora realized
that the child needed some friends her own age. "Oh
Mommy, Mommy, I'm so excited. Thank you, thank you."
She raced up to Nora, hugging and kissing her.

Jack's chauffeur came up and drove them all to
Easthampton. All the Welch children provided friends the

same age for Nora's children, so she returned home happy, full of plans for their yacht trip the following day.

She and Jack sat on the veranda having cocktails before dinner.

"Much as I love all your children," Jack said, "I want you alone." He kissed her cheek. "When we return, I must go back to Boston. I will have been gone almost two weeks, and the party can't run a phantom for the Senate."

"Jack, this is so exciting for you. Washington is where you should be. The Senate is where your talents will be best used."

"Nora, darling," he laughed, "I'm not elected yet. That's a whole year away."

"You'll be elected. I know you will."

At that moment, the phone rang. Nora went into the kitchen to answer it. When she returned, she was white as death.

"My God, Nora, what is it?"

"It was Annie. Something has happened to Angelo. He needs me. Jack, I must go. There's been a terrible tragedy. Annie wouldn't tell me what has happened, but I cannot imagine anything so dreadful that would cause her to call me away from you."

"Is he alive, Nora?"

"Yes, he's alive, but something terrible is going on."

"Nora, darling, what can you possibly do? Please, try to call. Don't leave."

"I must go. I will not abandon Angelo if he is calling for me. Please try to understand."

"But this will be our only time alone for God knows how long."

"Oh, Jack, if you can't understand this, you can't truly understand me. Please don't ask me to abandon one of my dearest friends. I can't do that."

Jack was trying to hide his anger and jealousy behind a mask of concern for her reputation. "Nora, don't do this to us. I don't want you involved with a gangster. Please don't go."

"He's not a gangster." She was crying now. "And I've told you that even if he was he would still be my friend. I must go." She abruptly ran upstairs, leaving Jack looking angrily after her. He grabbed his jacket and, slamming the door, left the house.

The trip was an agony for Nora, as thoughts of Angelo and Jack confused her. She cried tears of fear for Angelo during most of the drive into the city, and tears of agony that she might have lost Jack. She was terribly afraid and those fears were heightened by the police cars and the crowd gathered in front of Angelo's restaurant. The police had obviously been waiting for her, for they immediately helped her from her car and led her through the crowd into the restaurant and up the stairs to Angelo's private living quarters.

Annie and Dominic rushed toward her, talking at once, until Annie took charge. "They're in there, Nora. Mr. Gambini and her, Mrs. Gambini. The door is locked, and he won't let us in, no matter how we beg."

"Oh, my God, Annie what's happened here?"

"Something awful, Nora. Mr. and Mrs. Gambini have had a terrible row. Mrs. Gambini, she had arrived and demanded to see her husband. Dominic took her up and the minute that door closed behind them, she started to scream like you wouldn't believe."

Dominic interrupted. "That she did, Mrs. Desmond. I never heard such a sound. I was pounding on the door and Mr. Gambini was telling me to go away, but I didn't. I stayed right here. You wouldn't believe, Mrs. Desmond, all the awful things she said to him, like a madwoman she was. I could hear things being broken. It was like a hurricane was in that room blowing things around. And, all the time I could hear Mr. Gambini talking low and calm to her and then there'd be more screaming and crashing.'' Dominic stopped a moment to mop his forehead. ''Finally—I'll never forget it—there was a wail from her that wasn't like a human sound. Then I heard him call out her name. 'Gina, Gina,' like he was desperate, and then it was quiet. I was banging on the door and begging him to answer me. When he didn't I called the police. He never let nobody have a key to his rooms, and it would take six men to break down this door. While we was waitin', I thought I could hear a sound. At first I couldn't make it out, but then I realized it was your name, Mrs. Desmond, so I sent for you. Oh, Mrs. Desmond, why won't he let us in?''

''Let me stand by the door, Dominic. Don't worry. It will be all right.'' Inwardly she was terrified at the thought of what might have happened. She could hear movement inside, she was sure. ''Angelo, it's Nora. Please unlock the door. I'm here now, and I want to see you.''

There was no sound for agonizing moments, then the key was turned in the lock. Nora turned the knob and stepped into a scene of horror. Angelo stood before her, his left arm hanging useless, blood smeared all over his jacket. There was broken glass everywhere, overturned furniture, and in the debris at Angelo's feet lay Cina's body, a knife by her side.

''Nora, lock the door behind you. No one must come in.''

His tone was so desperate that Nora obeyed, closing the door on the anxious faces of Dominic, Annie and the police. Nora tried to remain calm.

''Angelo, what's happened here? Gina, is she—?'' Nora couldn't bring herself to say it.

Angelo slowly knelt down beside Gina's lifeless form, stroking the wild hair of his mad wife.

"She's dead. She came to kill me. She said that God had sent her to punish me for taking our daughter as my lover. I tried to calm her, but she was like a wild animal. She came at me with the knife, slashing at my arm when I put it up to defend myself. My God, she had the strength of ten men." He rose to his feet slowly. "I called out to her and suddenly she stopped and looked at me bleeding in front of her. There seemed to be a moment, only a moment, when she realized that she had meant to kill me. Sanity flickered in her eyes, and as I reached for her, she turned the knife on herself, thrusting it into her heart." His voice faltered and became a whisper. "See, I pulled it from her heart, her poor, tortured, broken heart. We mustn't tell anyone. This is a terrible thing. No one must know."

Nora could see that he was in a terrible state of shock, almost incoherent, and bleeding badly. She knelt beside him, holding him, speaking to him slowly, comfortingly, lovingly, trying to erase the horror and to bring him back to reality. He rocked back and forth, and she rocked with him, cradling him as one would a child. He began to cry, softly at first, but then he began to utter cries of agony. Nora never let go of him, and she still held him tightly as she opened the door and led him out to the waiting ambulance. The horror was over.

Nora stayed by his bedside at the hospital through the long night, until she knew that he was out of danger physically. She worried about how the police would view all this, but wiped it from her mind for the moment. She was too tired, too drained. When at last he opened his eyes, he smiled at her and with obvious effort, and said softly, "Nora, you are wearing violet. Good. Very good. That is your best color."

She smiled, knowing that he was out of danger, and she left the hospital as the first rays of dawn slit the sky.

As she got out of a cab in front of her Beekman Place apartment at four in the morning, she heard her name being called. She walked up to a limousine parked at the curb.

"Oh Jack, Jack."

"Get in, please, Nora."

They fell into each other's arms.

"I'm so sorry, Nora. You needed me to be understanding, and I wasn't. Please forgive me. I don't like Gambini, but I can't let it come between us. He's your friend, and I have to respect that. I'm sorry to have added to your misery. Were you able to help him?"

"I'd like to think I did. You know, there are just times when you need to talk to someone you can trust, and Jack, he does trust me."

They parted an hour later, making plans to see each other as soon as they could. Nora watched the limousine drive away down the quiet city street. He was leaving her life again. Dawn was breaking as she entered the apartment house lobby. She was weary, so very weary, and she climbed into her bed, not waking until eleven the next morning.

The apartment was still when she got up. Where was Bridget? Her sister was nowhere to be found. She dressed and went to the shop. Rachel would be surprised to see her, she thought, and indeed she was.

Sean had arranged to pick Rachel up at work that evening and planned to take her to the movies. They asked Nora to join them, and though she loved the new movies, she was too exhausted from the emotional events of the last few days to go. They insisted on seeing her home.

On the way to her apartment, she asked if they had

seen Bridget, suddenly realizing that she hadn't spoken to her since she had returned.

"Why no, Nora, we thought she was with you," Sean replied.

"No, she wanted some time alone, and Seamus told me she was very busy when I called his office. That's good news, I think, as I was beginning to fear that she would never come out of her depression. But she wasn't at home this morning when I left, nor was Seamus at his office. Well, never mind. I'm sure she'll be home by now."

As they entered the apartment, they heard noises in the living room.

"Bridget, dear, is that you?" Nora asked as they headed toward the living room.

"Aye, Seamus and I are here."

"Bridget, you look so much better. You were right about needing some time to yourself. It's agreed with you. But I was concerned because I couldn't reach you by phone."

Seamus and Bridget exchanged glances that went unnoticed by Sean and Nora. "I've been busy, Nora," Bridget answered mysteriously.

Seamus just sat quietly on the chair, drinking in Nora's loveliness. He hadn't seen her since that June night in Cork over thirteen years ago. How marvelous she looks, he thought. Oh God, how I had loved and longed for her, dreamed of her. He took a deep breath, for now he was married to her sister. It's time they found out all that has happened, he thought, smiling to himself.

"What shall we all have to drink?" Nora asked, walking to the mirrored bar.

"Champagne is in order, I believe, Nora. Bridget and I were married three days ago, and have just returned from a short honeymoon."

Nora dropped a glass, and Sean spun around to look at them.

"Married? Married!" they screamed in unison. "Why, how wonderful!" They rushed over to embrace them.

"But I could have given you a beautiful wedding, you two. Why did you just sneak off?" Nora scolded.

"We wanted no fuss. Please, we are happy just the way it is," Bridget replied.

"Of course. Oh, how wonderful. Let me see if we have champagne."

At that moment Seamus stood up. "It's in the icebox chilling, Nora. I'll see to it."

Nora and Sean looked at him strangely as he headed toward the refrigerator without a hesitation of any sort.

"Seamus," Sean warned, "be careful." Seamus continued, sure of foot and without his cane. Bridget was smiling. Sean and Nora and Rachel exchanged glances, running in after him, watching as he opened the icebox door, retrieved the champagne and turned around to look at them.

"My God, Seamus, you can see!" Nora cried out. She collapsed into a chair, tears of joy streaming down her face.

"That I can, lass. You are as beautiful as I remembered, even more so."

Sean put his hand on his new brother-in-law's shoulder. "Thank God, Seamus. How did it happen?"

"Come," Seamus answered, "let's open the champagne and we'll tell you."

Bridget shot him a glance, but he just smiled back a smile that said he wouldn't tell them the truth. "Your Dr. Schmidt, Nora, was the one who worked the miracle. He tried hypnosis, and after a few trials and errors, it finally worked. And, as for Bridget and me, we suddenly realized that we belonged together. I wanted that long ago, but not without my eyes to be able to see her.'' He put his arms about Bridget's shoulders tenderly.

"Bless you both. We're very happy for you,'' Nora smiled.

Similar thoughts were going through both Sean and Nora's minds. How wonderful for both of them! Bridget would finally have a life of her own, and Seamus could see.

Seamus and Bridget were like old friends. Their honeymoon had been platonic, for Seamus, knowing that she still loved Mike, had not tried to make love to her. She was grateful that he understood. They didn't even think about love in the traditional sense, but they were extremely fond of each other. As he had said, there were worse reasons to be married.

Chapter 43

Bridget suffered a miscarriage a month after she married Seamus. She was saddened by the loss, but her husband, kind and sensitive as always, helped her through the crisis. In a way, she thought it was better not to have that constant reminder of Mike in her life.

As fall turned into a cold, blustery winter, then winter into spring, Bridget also began to come to grips with her own sense of guilt. She had even gone to confession and had found that God could forgive her, and that she could forgive herself. Dear Seamus, she thought, he must be the best man in the world. He had helped her so much. Her feelings for him were gradually growing. What had begun as gratitude was becoming something much more.

Nora and Jack stole moments together whenever they could. They planned to spend six weeks in Southampton during the summer. Nora rented the same house she had the year before, and Jack rented a cottage down the beach a short distance away. Both houses were isolated from the main community, for Jack's public reputation had to be protected.

Jack was bringing his sons with him: Patrick, handsome and blonde like Priscilla, and Brian, fourteen, a replica of his father. Brian and Billy, who were the same age, became great friends, but Patrick, being older, didn't bother much with the younger children. Instead he found friends in town closer to his own age. Retta immediately developed a crush on Patrick, as did most of the other girls in Southampton.

One afternoon they were all invited to swim at the Welch's gigantic salt water pool. Retta watched as Patrick dived off the high diving board with a crown of daisies on his head; one of the girls had gushingly placed it there. Why won't he pay attention to me? Retta wondered. Little Mary was also dazzled by him and announced to her mother that she was going to marry Patrick when she grew up.

Retta spun around when she heard her. "Don't be a silly goose, Mary. He's far too old for you. He's not even aware that silly little seven-year-old girls exist, for goodness sakes."

Mary retreated, hurt by Retta's remark.

"I think, perhaps, Retta, that you owe Mary an apology."

Retta saw that Nora was angry. "I won't. She is silly, and she is seven, so what is there to apologize for?" She broken into tears and ran from the group at the pool.

Billy just sat quietly, miserably taking in the whole episode, for he was sick with confused emotions. As long as he could remember, he had protected Retta, loved her. Though he was almost a year younger, he had always felt that she was his responsibility, and as he entered his adolescent years, he had no inkling of the underlying feelings that were making him so miserable. He was jealous of Retta. He had dreams of her and thought she belonged to him, so when she paid attention to other boys on the beach or at parties, he was unable to understand or control his jumbled emotions.

Retta was sobbing in her bedroom. Her young heart was breaking with frustrated love for Patrick, that unavailable god.

Nora opened the doors. "Retta, what is this all about?"

"Leave me alone, please, just leave me alone!"

"Retta, what is wrong with you? You've been impossible for days."

"Nothing is wrong with me. I just want to be left alone. I'll apologize to Mary, if you'll only get out."

Nora, seeing how upset she was, quietly turned away and closed the door. She would talk to Retta later. Adolescence is such a difficult time, she mused.

Brian came in at that moment and saw Mary sitting despondently on the sofa. "Come on, Mary. Last one into the water is a rotten egg."

Mary forgot her sadness in a flash and sped out the door.

"Billy, aren't you going with them?" Nora asked.

"Yeah, I guess so." He pulled himself out of the chair and ambled after them.

Bless Brian, Nora thought. He's as sensitive as his father.

Jack was coming for the weekend, and Nora was getting the house ready. The boys had been staying with a housekeeper so far, but Jack always came whenever he could find time. He had told Nora that Priscilla had been thrilled when Patrick and Brian went on vacation with their father, for while she never said as much, he knew that she didn't really enjoy having them around.

Late Friday afternoon, there was a knocking on the

front door. Expecting to see Jack, Nora ran to answer it, but when she opened the door, there leaning against the column was Dennis, in white yachting clothes, balancing a tray with two glasses of champagne on it.

"Special delivery. Dom Perignon for Mrs. Nora Desmond."

"Dennis, you charming idiot. How perfectly wonderful to see you. Come in, come in."

"One moment." He handed her the tray, ran to the car and brought in the bottle of champagne and a delectable-looking tray of canapés. She laughed happily.

He sipped the champagne, then proposed a toast. "To the most beautiful woman I know."

She held up her glass. "To the most enchanting man I know."

"What is this?" A voice called to them. "A mutual admiration society?" It was Jack, who had come in the open front door. "I can't leave Dennis alone for a single moment."

"Jack, I'm so happy you're here." She held out her hand.

"Don't bother about me, you two," Dennis chucked. "Pretend I don't exist."

"Stop that now, Dennis," Nora said with a blush.

"Seriously, it seems I've come at a bad time."

"Nonsense," Jack put in. "You're always welcome."

"In fact, I insist you stay for dinner," Nora said.

"Of course, providing you have pheasant under glass, and caviar first."

She looked at Dennis with a smile, her head cocked to one side. "No, but I can put some fresh fish under a glass tumbler if you like."

"Just point me to the kitchen," Dennis said. "I'll show you what to do with that fish to make it utterly divine."

After Dennis found his way into the kitchen, Jack kissed Nora quickly. "Darling, I've missed you. I'm sorry I couldn't be here sooner, but there's so much going on. We're planning our campaign strategy, and I've been making speeches all over Massachusetts."

At that moment the children returned from the beach, wet and sunburned and hungry. They were introduced to Dennis, and he delighted them instantly by insisting they all pile into his American underslung, the car he had first taken Nora out in two years earlier, and promising to get them ice cream.

"Oh, no," Nora said. "You'll spoil their appetites."

Dennis shrugged. "I'm afraid that won't matter. I ruined the fish."

The summer was passing lazily by, and the house was always full of people. Rachel and Sean and Seamus and Bridget came out whenever they could, and Bridget shyly announced one weekend that she was pregnant. They threw a party for her.

Another time, Angelo Gambini came out to rest for a couple of days. Fortunately, Nora thought, Jack had to be out on the campaign trail, so there was no tension on that score.

The evenings were filled with cocktail parties and other social gatherings, and Jack and Nora went boating or swimming every chance they got during the long summer days. They laughed and dined and danced. They sailed, played and swam as they would never do in quite the same carefree way again.

Only one dark cloud cast its shadow over that idyll. Ever since Archduke Francis Ferdinand of Austria-Hungary had been assassinated on June 28, by a Serbian fanatic, everyone had expected the inevitable. By July 28, Austria-Hungary had declared war on Serbia. Sean predicted that the whole world would soon be at war, and as it turned out, Germany declared war on Russia within days, then declared war on France. When Britain entered the war, the die was cast. All of Europe would be dragged into the fighting.

America, however, remained strongly isolationist, and life continued on much as it had for a while. Dennis came out to Southampton quite frequently, and he and Nora became inseparable. He taught her to play tennis and insisted that she and the boys go golfing with him. Nora loved these times.

One weekend, he drove up with Brian and Patrick in the car. Nora and the three children also piled in, and they took a ride to Montauk Point. When they arrived home, tired but happy, Nora sent the children to bed, then she and Dennis sat by the fire.

"I have bad news for you, Nora," he said as he went to the hearth to stoke the coals.

"Why, what could that be, Dennis? You've never had anything but good news for me before." She smiled at him fondly.

"I'm serious. Priscilla is coming out on the weekend of the big McConnell Ball for the hospital benefit. Lorraine Quigley, the chairwoman, is a dear old friend of Priscilla's and has invited her and Jack as her guests." He puffed away at his cigarette.

"I see. Well, there's not much to be done about that, is there? I'm on the committee, and I have to attend, so we'll just have to grit our teeth and do the best we can."

"Good girl. I hear Mrs. Quigley is planning fireworks, and all that sort of thing."

"Yes. It's going to be an event to remember in many ways. But it's for a good cause. Will you be attending the ball?"

"It may be best if I don't. I'll go to New York that weekend. I can't abide being around her. But enough about my awful sister. Now, dear girl, we're going to the beach tomorrow. Get out your very best swimsuit, and we'll take a picnic lunch. Just make sure that whatever you pack for us goes with champagne.''

Nora's very best swimsuit was the latest fashion, much different from the heavy wool serge or sailor suits of past years. It was a one-piece tight-fitting knit suit, with a scoop neck and covered legs. With it she wore a little bathing cap with flowers on it.

At the moment Nora was totally absorbed by a covey of society women down the beach. "Look, Dennis, that marvelous-looking girl is smoking.''

"So she is, though not very well, I must say.''

"Caroline is the only woman I know who smokes, and she rarely does it in public.''

"Nora, we're living in a completely new world. Obviously all your protest marches up Fifth Avenue have paid off. You have a new kind of swimsuit, and women can smoke on the beach. Such progress! What will you girls think of next?''

"You dunce!'' she said with a laugh. "We still can't vote.''

"You will, darling, you will. Mark my word.''

Patrick had, at last, noticed Retta. He had discovered that she was a good swimmer and tennis player, two sports he excelled at, so they began spending quite a bit of time together. Billy became edgy and jealous when he saw them together, but he hid his feelings as well as he could. Fortunately, Brian always came up with some adventure to divert Billy's attention, and the two of them would be off for hours at a time. Mary had found some young friends, but she still worshipped Patrick from afar.

Nora and Jack were invited to many of the same cocktail parties, and so were often together in public. No one seemed to suspect that they were more than friends, though sometimes their eyes would meet across a room and relay messages that the most unimaginative person could have read.

Nora looked striking the night of the charity ball. Her gown was made of deep red silk taffeta with ruffles standing up around her neck. She pinned her diamond heart pin up near her shoulder. Her escort was a pleasant, middle-aged gentleman, a widower named Ted Buckley, who had bought a big estate a mile down the beach.

The ball was held at the Southampton Beach Club, a bayside building which had been festooned for the evening with garlands of flowers and ribbons. Huge bouquets adorned every table, and palm trees stood in all corners of the room. Nora didn't sit out a single dance.

She was twirling around the dance floor when she was spotted by Priscilla.

"Jack," Priscilla said, "isn't that the Irish girl who rode with us at Marblehead? What was her name? You know, the speechwriter's sister."

Jack's heart was pounding. "Where, Priscilla?"

Priscilla turned to him. "The one in red, see?"

"Yes, I believe it is she. I heard she had a place here."

Priscilla looked at him curiously. "I see," she said, then dropped the subject.

Soon the fireworks were announced, and the crowd assembled on the front veranda to watch the spectacle. By now Priscilla had lost Nora in the crowd but was trying to find her. Suddenly, she saw Nora with Ted Buckley on the west veranda, and she pushed through the throng of people with Jack in tow.

"Come, Jack, we must say hello, mustn't we?"

Before he could answer, she had come right up behind Nora and tapped her on the shoulder. Nora spun around.

"Mrs. Desmond, isn't it? It has been such a long time, but I would recognize you anywhere. You remember my husband, of course?"

"Mr. and Mrs. Ryan! Why, hello. Of course I remember you both. My escort, Mr. Ted Buckley."

There were a few silent, uncomfortable moments.

"This is a very popular resort with the Irish, isn't it?" Priscilla said. "I would prefer to go to Newport or Cape Cod, but Jack finds it much more to his liking here. He's here with our boys, you know."

"Yes, I do know. My children have met yours." Nora thought she should mention this in case the boys already had. Jack nodded approval.

"How very interesting."

At that moment, Priscilla's eyes came to rest on Nora's diamond heart pin. Why, that's Jack's mother's pin! she thought. What is this woman doing with it? Suddenly, everything fell into place. How stupid of me. Of course. She must be Jack's mistress. How fascinating! Jack's mother's pin, she mused. Priscilla hadn't seen the pin for years, but she would know it anywhere.

Her eyes were blazing at Nora. "Well, good night, Mrs. Desmond, Mr. Buckley. We must be getting back to our friends. Come, Jack."

Nora had a premonition that something was wrong. She watched them disappear into the crowd, her heart racing. Had Patrick or Brian said something? But what could they say? They didn't really know anything. Still, she couldn't shake the fear that somehow Priscilla knew. She asked Ted to take her home, explaining that she suddenly wasn't feeling well. They left hurriedly.

Later, when she was undressing, she automatically reached up to remove the diamond pin. Oh, my God! she thought. She saw it! Jack told me she had seen it once, and she must have recognized it. Of course she knows! Now what will we do? She lay awake the entire night, wondering if Priscilla had confronted Jack.

The following day she practically bit her nails waiting for the phone to ring. Jack finally called in the late morning.

"Darling, good news. Priscilla is leaving today. May I see you tonight?"

"Yes, of course, Jack. Let's ride into Easthampton for dinner." He sounded undaunted. Perhaps her imagination was playing tricks on her. But no, she knew she hadn't been wrong. Priscilla just wasn't ready to play her ace yet.

Nora told Jack of her fears over dinner. "It was so stupid of me, almost as if I wanted to get caught. I'm so sorry."

"Nora, calm down. She saw that pin so many years ago that it's hard for me to believe she would remember it now. Besides, she didn't say anything, so let's not borrow trouble. Now drink your champagne. I won't be seeing you for a while, so let's not talk of Priscilla. If it weren't for this damned Senate race, I'd walk out on her tomorrow. She hates me, and everything I stand for, but she covets the prestige she would enjoy as a senator's wife."

"You're probably right. Let's forget it."

They bade farewell on the dunes that night. They had slipped out of their shoes and walked down the beach hand in hand, barely talking, just enjoying each other for the little time they had.

From Southampton, Jack went on a campaign tour of small towns in Massachusetts. His staff had every moment accounted for, but finally, after three weeks of speechmaking, he was going home.

He entered their Beacon Hill home late at night. He was extremely weary. The butler took his coat and hat.

"Is anyone here, Grayson?"

"Mrs. Ryan returned from New York today, sir."

Jack had hoped she wouldn't be home. He needed time alone to think. Perhaps she would be asleep. But when he opened the door to his bedroom, there sat Priscilla. She never entered his room, so now he was completely taken aback. "What on earth are you doing up at such an hour?" he asked.

"Waiting for you. I telephoned your headquarters, and they said you would be home this evening. Of course, I wasn't quite certain whether that meant home here, or home in Southampton." Her voice was full of sarcasm.

Jack bristled. "What the hell difference does it make to you, Priscilla?"

"It makes a great deal of difference, my husband. You *are* my husband, isn't that correct?"

"Priscilla, say what's on your mind and then let me get to sleep. I've been campaigning hard, and I'm exhausted. I'm in no mood for one of your games."

"It seems you are in the mood for at least one game. It's called adultery, I believe."

His heart raced. There would be no point in denying it. "Priscilla, what the hell would that matter to you?"

"It matters a great deal. You are my husband, and I don't want to lose you. It would be most embarrassing for me."

He shrugged his shoulders. "How touching."

"Jack, our life suits me very well, and I don't want it altered in any way—other than moving to Washington. So dear, I want you to stop this sordid little romance. Is that clear?"

Jack's anger grew, but he knew that he had to control it, or it would make matters worse. "I'm in love with

Nora," he said between clenched teeth. "I'd prefer you didn't refer to this love as a sordid little romance."

"It makes no difference to me what you choose to call it. I want it to stop." She paused, gazing steadily at him. "If it doesn't, you won't be running for the Senate, I can assure you. I'll ruin your career. Believe me, Jack, in fifteen minutes I can destroy what you have spent fifteen years of your life building."

Jack glared at her. "What good would that do anyone?"

"It would give me satisfaction."

"Priscilla, get the hell out of my sight. I'll resign tomorrow from the campaign, and save you the trouble. Just get the hell out of my sight."

"Dear Jack, I'm afraid it's not that simple. I don't really want you out of the campaign, and I have one other trump card. I will expose your precious Nora. Her family will know, her children will know, her business associates will know. She too has climbed the ladder of success, and it can easily be pulled out from under her. I think the decision you must make is clear enough."

Jack couldn't believe his ears. "My God, you're a monster. I don't know how I ever could have believed there was anything good in you." He was shaking with anger and frustration.

"You married me, Jack, for my social position. Now I want to take advantage of *your* social position. You know, tit for tat." She smiled sweetly and kissed Jack on the cheek. "Good night, dear husband. Pleasant dreams."

Priscilla quickly left the room, and Jack stared after her. He knew she would do exactly as she said. He slumped into the chair, staring into space, remaining in that position until dawn flickered through the heavy draperies. He shook himself, rose and left the house. He walked every foot of the common, trying to sort out his thoughts and decide on some course of action, but there was no course of action but Priscilla's. Today he would call Nora and tell her they couldn't see each other. One thing he knew for certain was that he didn't want Nora hurt.

When Nora heard Jack's voice on the phone, she knew instantly that something was wrong. He confirmed her worst fears. "Nora, I want to call her bluff. She wants the prestige of being a senator's wife too much, but I'm afraid of what she'll do to you. So we mustn't meet for a while, darling, not until we think of something. We'll find a way, I know we will."

"Jack, right now you need to throw yourself into your campaign. We've had each other, and we must be satisfied with that."

"We'll have each other forever, Nora. You mustn't doubt that for a moment, not for a single moment."

As she hung up the telephone, she dropped her head on her desk. Through her sobs, she heard a light knock on the door. "Who is it?"

"It's Annie. Nora, is something wrong?"

"Come in, Annie, come in."

"Nora, are you crying? What's happened?"

Nora, sobbed the whole story to Annie.

"Dear, dear, girl," Annie said, "this is an impossible situation. I don't know what to say to you, how to comfort you. If you've really made up your mind not to see him again, you'll have to learn to live with that decision. I'm sorry. I wish there were something more hopeful to say, but there just isn't."

"I know, Annie. No one knows how hopeless it all is better than I do."

Chapter 44

The months Nora spent apart from Jack were an agony for her. Her children and her business gave a certain shape to her life, supporting the illusion that nothing had changed. When Nora crawled into bed at night, however, she would softly cry herself to sleep. She often thought of what her mother had sacrificed in the name of love. Now Nora knew the pain her mother must have felt at giving up the man she loved. Oh, Ma, how ever did you bear it?

Nora threw herself into the suffragette cause with new dedication, so she saw a great deal of Caroline. They had gone to Washington to march on the Capitol, and she had, for a few hours at least, forgotten her personal woes. The march was exhilarating. Ten bands played and fifty ladies rode on horseback behind platoons of government dignitaries. The suffragettes' unity of purpose was stronger than it had ever been.

Caroline dined with them the evening they arrived home from Washington. At the dinner table, Retta asked an endless stream of questions and showed great enthusiasm for the cause. "Aunt Nora, I want to march too. I'm fifteen years old, and I want to be able to vote when I come of age. Please, Mrs. Williams, can't I be in the next march?"

Caroline was not one to turn down any offer of help, young or old. "If your Aunt Nora agrees, I see nothing wrong with it. You young women are the ones whose lives and interests are most at stake."

Nora looked pensive. "I suppose you're right, Caroline. If she's interested, then let's give her a banner."

Billy had also became interested, and he admired Retta's determination. "Do men ever march in any of your parades?"

"Yes, indeed," Caroline answered. "Many enlightened and intelligent men have joined us." She smiled over his head at Nora.

"Well, then, I'd like to march, too. I don't know any men smarter than you three women."

They all turned to look at him, and started to laugh.

"Why, that's a wonderful compliment, Billy," Nora said.

"And very perceptive, too," Caroline added.

In November, 1914, Bridget was six months pregnant. She had also just turned thirty-four. Her doctor, concerned about her age, ordered her to spend the last three months of her pregnancy in bed. Bridget, normally very active, was dismayed at the thought of an enforced bed rest, but she wanted the baby so much that she willingly agreed to do it. Nora insisted that she and Seamus come to stay with her so Bridget wouldn't be alone during the day while Seamus was away at work. Nora felt that everything must be done to keep up Bridget's spirits, and she knew that Retta, Billy and Mary, with their childhood antics, would see to that.

The months passed. Christmas was celebrated at Nora's so that Bridget could be there, and Sean and Rachel brought Terry and little baby Sarah. Sean watched Nora moving rather too mechanically among her loved ones. He had always suspected, since first learning that Nora and Jack had become friends, that his sister was actually in love with the man. But lately she had not mentioned Ryan at all, so he followed her into the library where they could be alone, and he asked her about it outright.

"Sean, yes, I won't deny it, but now it's over." She told him the heartbreaking story.

"Why didn't you tell me, Nora?"

"What could you have done except worry? Anyway, it's all in the past. I speak to him from time to time, and there are lilacs on my desk every Monday, but I haven't seen him since that August evening in Southampton. I don't know if I'll ever see him again, Sean. I just don't know how."

"I'll be meeting him next week, Nora. I'm helping him write a campaign speech. Can I relay any message for you?"

"Tell him I love him, and I'll never forget him. No, you can't do that, but you can give him a note for me. I dare not write him, you know. There's no safe place to send a letter."

Sean agreed to carry the note, and held his sister in a warm, comforting embrace.

She stepped back, her eyes glistening with tears. "Come, dinner is ready. Let's join the others."

Christmas dinner was exuberant. Nora had a butler now, Frederick, who was extremely stiff and proper. When Mary and Terry first began throwing napkins at the table, Nora thought she would lose him forever. She laughed at the look of incredulity on his face as the children, wild

with enthusiasm and Christmas cheer, became totally un-
manageable. It was the first time she had laughed in many
months.

On February 15, Bridget delivered a healthy ten-pound
boy. Seamus was ecstatic. As he sat next to her in her
hospital room, he lovingly pushed the hair out of her eyes.
It had been a difficult and long labor, but mother and child
were doing well.

He bent over and kissed her. "I love you, Bridget,
darling. Thank you for our son. I love you very much."

She looked at him for a long time before replying. "I
love you too, Seamus Gorman." It was the first time
either of them had ever declared their feelings, which had
been slow in blossoming.

The phone on Nora's desk rang. Nora picked up the
receiver, and a voice at the other end asked, "Am I to be
banished from your life too?" It was Dennis.

"Dennis, oh how glad I am to hear your voice.
Where are you? When will I see you?"

"In exactly a half-hour, dear one. I'll pick you up."

Nora's spirits lifted. True to his word, in a half-hour,
Dennis Noble appeared at the front entrance of Ballygarry's
in a chauffeured limosine. He was carrying an extravagant
bouquet of orchids that he thrust into Nora's arms.

"There, dear Nora. Admire them, then put them
down, so I can give you a proper embrace."

They embraced warmly and chattered away as they
stepped into the limousine.

"You are such a tonic, Dennis. How I've missed
you."

"Well then, I serve some good purpose in this life."
He suddenly became serious. "Nora, this blackmail of
Priscilla's to keep you and Jack apart is so dreadful. When
I finally pried the facts out of Jack, he had to restrain me

from killing my dear, beloved sister. She doesn't want him, but she doesn't want you to have him either. And she doesn't want the inconvenience and scandal of a divorce now that he's on the trail of something big. Of course, if he loses the election, she probably won't look at him again. However''—he puffed thoughtfully at his cigarette—''we know he's not going to lose that election, don't we?''

''I think he will win, Dennis. I've been following every move he makes and every speech he gives, and I believe you're right, he's going to win. Walter Lippmann seems to think so too.''

''He deserves a victory. He's a good man. The country needs him in Washington. I don't think, however, we need Priscilla there.''

She had never seen Dennis quite so serious or so upset. ''Dennis, dear, there's nothing to be done. But tell me about Jack, please, you and Sean are my only links with him other than our brief telephone conversations.''

''Well, I have a note for you from him. Here, darling girl, read it when you're alone in bed this evening.''

They visited awhile longer, then Dennis said goodbye with his usual flourish, and the chauffeur opened the door to his limousine.

The luncheon crowd at Angelo's had gone, and the waiters were clearing the tables when Jack Ryan was ushered into Angelo's office. Jack was surprised at the quality of the paintings and furnishings in the room. He was gazing in admiration at a Pissarro when Angelo said quietly, ''We share a taste for fine art, I see.''

Jack turned sharply to his host. ''I'd like to know how in hell you found out I was in New York and how you managed to get a message to me past my staff?''

''It disturbs you to find that your affairs are not as

private and protected as you had imagined. I'm sorry. I should have known, but I'm glad that you've come."

"You knew I'd come when you said you needed to talk to me about Nora. Whatever else about you I may not like, I respect you for all you've done for her. So, what do you want, Gambini?"

"Your hostility is understandable, Mr. Ryan. It's soon to be Senator Ryan, is that correct?"

"If I win the election."

"It has been confided to me that you are no longer seeing Nora, though you still call her and would like to see her again."

"Did Nora tell you that?"

"No, she didn't, but trust me, I know."

It disturbed Jack that others knew, and it disturbed him to have a man of Angelo's unsavory reputation knowing so much about his personal life.

"No need to worry, Mr. Ryan. Nora's well-being has for years been the most important thing in my life. She has been to me like a daughter."

Jack looked intently at him. Perhaps he had been mistaken, perhaps Angelo's interest had been only paternal. He liked hearing it from Angelo.

Gambini went on. "Also, whether you believe it or not, I admire you, and I wish only the best for you." He paused a moment. "Are you sure you won't have a drink, Mr. Ryan?"

"Yes, I believe I will have a scotch, thank you." He felt less antagonistic now than when he'd arrived. He was intrigued by Angelo now and sensed something important was going to come of this meeting. What did Gambini have up his sleeve?

Angelo turned to him with the drink. "Most importantly, Mr. Ryan, you and Nora love each other. But something has gotten in the way of that. Your wife, perhaps? Has she perhaps learned of your relationship with Nora and threatened to expose you?'' He sipped his own drink slowly.

Jack was listening intently. There was beginning to form in his mind a different picture of the man before him. ''Everything you say is true, but I would gladly leave public office for Nora. Only that wouldn't stop Priscilla. She vows to ruin Nora's reputation unless we remain forever apart. I cannot bear her to humiliate Nora, so it's been months, almost a year, since we have seen each other.'' He stared dismally into his glass. ''You know Nora, Mr. Gambini, she says she doesn't care what Priscilla says or does, or what people will say. She actually told me she'd be proud for the world to know we are lovers, but I won't allow her to be publicly disgraced. I can't.''

Angelo noted that he had just become Mr. Gambini, rather than simply Gambini. This begrudging respect amused him. ''Well, Mr. Ryan, I'm going to ask you to trust me, to believe that I care for Nora, and yes, for you too, because you are the man she loves. Ask no questions please. Just come with me. We're going on a little ride to pay a surprise visit.''

Jack asked a few tentative questions from the back seat of Angelo's limousine, but Angelo only said time and again, ''Trust me, trust me.''

They drove up to the alley entrance of a prestigious Park Avenue apartment building. A nervous-looking little man opened the service entrance door without a word, motioning them into the delivery elevator. When the elevator stopped, he led them to a door, used his passkey to unlock it, took the money Angelo gave him and scurried off. Angelo stepped inside, and after a moment gave a sign for Jack to follow him. The living room was darkened, the heavy drapes pulled against the sun. At first Jack thought they were in an empty apartment, until he heard voices coming from another room. He and Angelo crossed the thick carpeting toward those voices, and as they drew nearer, Jack recognized one of the voices as Priscilla's, though it sounded as he had never heard it—husky with passion as she moaned with pleasure. Jack was stunned. At that moment, Angelo touched the wall switch, and the glaring light revealed Priscilla, her arms around another woman, their naked bodies entwined as one.

"My God, Priscilla, who are these people?" the other woman shrilled. She was a New York socialite friend of Priscilla's named Renee Martin. "I'll be ruined, ruined!"

Priscilla distractedly patted her as she would an excited dog while pulling the covers over her own nakedness. Her companion hid under the covers. Angelo quietly retreated from the room. Priscilla glared at Jack, who had been stunned into shocked, disbelieving silence. Priscilla spoke with an eerily calm, icy voice, her arrogance never deserting her for a moment. "Get out of here, Jack. This is my apartment, and you have no right to be here. I want you out of here *now*!"

Jack had regained his composure, though he still felt himself trembling. "Gladly, Priscilla, gladly." He turned to walk out, but not before glancing back once again. "Assure your friend Renee that her secret is safe with me, assuming of course, that the accounts between you and me are now balanced."

Priscilla nodded silently. For a moment, he almost felt sorry for her.

Angelo took Jack's arm and softly closed the door behind them. Jack didn't speak on the ride back to Angelo's.

"Come in, Mr. Ryan, I think you need a drink."

Jack gratefully accepted the whiskey. "How did you know all of this about my wife, that apartment, when she would be there?

"Let's just say I have friends who owed me a favor, Mr. Ryan."

Jack understood that he was never to know how Angelo had found out.

"I'm sorry to have caused you such a shock, but I do believe you will hear no more threats from Mrs. Ryan. Do you understand why I couldn't tell you? I was afraid you would refuse to come along and see for yourself."

Jack downed the entire glass of whiskey at once.

"Yes, yes, I understand. It's all right. You were right to do it. It's just that I never suspected such a thing."

They both sat silently for a few moments. "Now you and Nora can be together again. Your career and Nora's reputation are safe. Of course, you can never divorce Priscilla while you hold public office, but at least you and Nora can share a part of your lives with each other."

Jack nodded his head. This is a good friend, he thought. How distasteful all this must have been to him. "Mr. Gambini, I'm grateful. I see that Nora's right. You do take care of the people you care for. I want you to know that I appreciate how difficult this must have been for you, how unpleasant."

"Yes," Angelo replied, "but there seemed to be no other way. Believe me, I tried for eight long months to find another way to stop her, but beating her at her own awful game was the only way."

"I understand."

"So we did what had to be done, fight fire with fire, eh, Mr. Ryan?"

Jack clasped Angelo's hand. "Please call me Jack. All my friends do."

Nora followed the maître d'hôtel to a booth in the far corner of the restaurant. She hadn't seen Angelo for some time, but his invitation had been insistent. Lilacs were casually arranged in a beautiful vase, and she breathed in the delicious scent, a reminder of her beloved Jack.

The papers were full of news about the coming election, and through her reading, Nora followed Jack's every move. If elected, he would be in Washington for six full years. Well, she thought, it didn't really matter to her where he was because she couldn't be with him anyway. It was just too risky. He had pleaded several times to see her, and she had almost given in, but she believed that Priscilla would have detectives watching them. A woman like that didn't leave anything to chance. Of that, Nora was certain. Suddenly, she felt a hand on her shoulder, and turning around, she found she was staring up at Jack.

"Jack, oh my God, what are you doing here? Please, please leave immediately. Priscilla will think we planned this meeting."

He moved into the booth and sat down. "Darling, it's all right. I did plan this meeting."

"How can it be all right? Oh, Jack, my God, you look wonderful." Her emotions were in turmoil. She wanted him to be there, yet wanted him to leave.

He took her hand. "I'm sorry to upset you. I wanted this to be a wonderful surprise. Darling, it's all over. Priscilla played the wrong card, and she'll never threaten us again."

Nora was astonished. "But how can that be?"

"I guess you might say I've been fighting fire with fire. I'd rather not talk about it, Nora. Just remember that I wouldn't be here if it weren't all right. I promise you."

Nora wasn't completely assured. "We still must be careful. Don't forget, the election will be held in just five months."

"We'll be careful, don't worry. I couldn't have lived any longer without you. It just wouldn't have been possible."

"Jack, oh Jack." Tears filled her eyes. "I can't believe it. Say it's not a dream. I've had so many, but when I'd wake up, you'd be gone."

They dined and talked and gazed into each other's eyes.

Over the next few months, though Jack was now campaigning in earnest, he and Nora stole moments, sometimes entire weekends, together. Nora never questioned Jack further about Priscilla, for she could sense that he was not ready to discuss it. She believed he must have struck some bargain with her, a distasteful deal of some kind which he must have found demeaning.

By the summer of 1915 the country was a-flutter with talk of the war and how Wilson had pledged to keep America out of it. In a speech to Congress several weeks after the war had begun, Wilson had forcefully stated that "the United States must be neutral in fact as well as in name," and he implored the people of the United States to "put a curb upon their sentiments."

Nora and Jack had been in Southampton on their stolen reunion weekend in May when they heard the news that the *Lusitania* had been sunk. Nora had been stunned by the sad fate of the beautiful ship, for this had been the vessel on which she had traveled from England in 1912. Over twelve hundred lives were lost. More than a hundred had been Americans.

"Oh, Jack, what will this mean for us?"

"Nora, neutrality has always been unrealistic. Now it will be impossible. We'll be at war within the year."

He looked sad and thoughtful, and she knew what was worrying him. While her Billy was only fifteen, Patrick, Jack's seventeen-year-old son, would be old enough to join the army. And, if the war continued for long, Billy and Brian would be next. A cold chill shook her.

"Darling," she said, "maybe it will all end as quickly as it began. Maybe Wilson can help end it by negotiation. That's what he has been trying to do. Isn't it possible?"

He distractedly smoothed her hair. "Maybe, Nora. But somehow, I don't think so."

In his campaign speeches, Jack had taken a firm stand for woman suffrage. Members of his staff were worried that this would hurt him at the polls, but believing in women's rights as strongly as he did, he could not do otherwise. Nora was proud of him. She knew that his principles might very well cost him the election, but she also knew that morally and ethically it was a stand he felt compelled to take.

When he could free himself for a few days, he would come to Southampton, and sometimes they would meet in some small, out-of-the-way Massachusetts city where he was scheduled to speak. These meetings were difficult and painful because they had to be so secretive, but they accepted the situation as best they could. Jack promised it would get better, and Nora wanted to believe him.

That summer of 1915 was carefree for the children. Retta was blossoming into full womanhood and was very aware of the effect she had on the boys. Her glorious red hair, sparkling brown eyes and glowing skin drew glances from everyone. Her tall figure was already showing the promise of the soft and well-proportioned curves that would be hers in maturity. She had turned, almost overnight, from a rather quiet, withdrawn young girl to a vivacious, compelling spirit. There was a sense of purpose about her, an energy that was difficult to resist. Nora would gaze in amazement sometimes, surprised at this change. Retta's mother had been a happy, uncomplicated woman, but Retta was turning into something quite different, and Nora's own influence was unmistakable. She was ambitious, Nora

could already see that. She did well at school, threw
herself into causes and soaked up everything in her environment. She knew all about Ballygarry's and Queen's
Lace, read all of Sean's political columns and followed
Jack Ryan's campaign avidly. She knew as long ago as
last year what others just suspected—that Nora and Jack
were lovers. She had never seen or heard anything that led
her to believe this; somehow she just knew. At first she
had resented Jack, thinking that he was going to steal Nora
away from them, but she now considered him an ally, and
in fact, had even come to like him. She still adored
Patrick, as did all the girls, but now aware of the effect she
had on boys, she found she wasn't quite ready to waste it
all on one young man. She dressed with great taste and
style, and she was extremely impetuous, which had often
landed her in rough waters. Yet there was no doubt that
spontaneity was part of her charm. Her willfulness drove
Nora to such distraction at times that she found herself
sending Retta to her room more often than she cared to,
for that often made bad situations even worse. Retta had a
fiercely independent side to her nature which, when thwart-
ed, would send her into hours, sometimes days, of stubborn sulkiness. Then she would reappear sunnily, as if
nothing had happened. She protected Billy always, as he
did her, and while they often fought with each other
bitterly, the bond between them was deep.

Billy was becoming more and more handsome by the
day, with his blond hair falling over his forehead, his
mocking green eyes and his knowing smile. He was different from the others, quieter, with more exacting tastes in
clothes and foods. Billy loved horses, reading and tennis,
in that order. While his looks were very much like William's, his personality was very different. He had a nobil-
ity of spirit, much more like his grandfather, Lord Anthony.
There was the same generosity and humanity, and the

same calm manner. Still, Billy had firm opinions and beliefs, and when he was voicing or defending them, Nora was sometimes reminded of her brother Terence. Billy loved her, she knew, yet sometimes he seemed aloof, alone, unreachable. The only time she felt the gap between them was bridged was when they were riding together. Then their problems and differences dissipated, their friendship was unshakable, their understanding was perfect. She would ache sometimes to tell him that he was her real son, but she still believed that was not the right thing to do.

His aloofness, merely a facet of his personality, was never meant as a rebuff to those around him, least of all, Nora. And if there was something unreachable in him, perhaps it was better that way, for it concealed the terrible secret in his heart, the aching, desperate love for Retta, his own sister. His adolescent yearnings and sexual longings were embroiling him in passions he loathed and couldn't understand. Girls found him attractive, even irresistible, but none captured his imagination as did his own sister. He would die a thousand deaths when he saw Retta flirting outrageously with some other young man. In his mind, no one was ever good enough for her. Tensions were created, and tempers flared over his possessiveness and jealousy, which he masqueraded as brotherly interest and protection. Astute as Nora was, she recognized none of this, for even Billy himself couldn't call his feelings by their right name.

Mary was a sunny, effervescent, optimistic child who loved everyone and assumed the world loved her in return. At eight years of age, she was as outgoing, bright and charming as Nora had been at that age. She had a desire to please her elders, with an eagerness that would melt the coldest heart. Even difficult children enjoyed playing with her, because of her even temper and her willingness to compromise. She accepted people's quirks with interest, and was never threatened by the new and unusual.

Brian and Patrick Ryan were in Southampton once again, and Brian and Billy resumed their old friendship. They were quite different, but they liked each other enormously. Brian was more outgoing, laughed a great deal more and loved a good joke. He often teased Billy about being so serious, and Nora attributed some of Billy's emerging humor to his exposure to this congenial, attractive boy.

Patrick was strong, charming and incredibly handsome, if sometimes a bit arrogant, and appeared only now and then at Nora's, for he was running with an older crowd these days. Billy would always be himself when this older, self-assured young man appeared on the scene. Retta, with her independent spirit, outspoken opinions and strong will, intrigued Patrick greatly. His time with her was different from the times he spent with the other compliant girls, and he knew it. Patrick appreciated her high spirits, but in some strange way, he was vaguely aware of the complications they could cause him.

The summer passed pleasantly. Dances and fireworks and parties, picnics and walks on the beach, sunsets on the dunes, new friends and old friends, summer romances, agonies of new love and love lost, days melting one into another, all this was Southampton during that summer of 1915. But soon, too soon, it was over. Good-byes were said, promises to see each other in the city were made, and tears were shed in private.

As Nora locked up the house, she somehow knew that the face of the world was changing, that it might never again be quite the same. Jack had tried to guard against just that unspoken fear by buying a beautiful beachfront lot so they could build a house and be together. The thought was a tempting one, but she recognized its impracticality. Nevertheless, knowing that it was to him a symbol, a need for a place to anchor their love, she encouraged and supported him in the idea.

"One day, dearest Nora, this will be our home," he would say as though insisting against fate.

She would nod quietly and rest her head on his shoulder as together they listened to the lovely, timeless rhythm of the waves lapping at the shore.

"Yes, Jack, someday." But in her heart, she somehow believed that someday would never come.

Chapter 45

In November, 1915, Jack Ryan was elected to the Congress of the United States. Sean had gone into the kitchen to call his office at the *Journal* for the election returns, and he returned to the living room carrying a bottle of champagne.

"I propose a toast to Senator Jack Ryan."

"Oh, Sean, he won? He really won?" Nora jumped out of her chair, spinning happily around. "Oh, he's done it. Sean, he's done it!" She danced him merrily around the room.

A few moments later her phone rang. Sean answered and called to her. "Nora, someone wants to speak to you."

Nora ran to the phone. "Why, Senator Ryan, I'm so thrilled. So are Rachel and Sean. We all are! Yes, I can hear you, but it's so noisy. What? A gigantic party? Well, I should think so. Oh, of course, I'd love to be there."

They chatted happily, making plans to meet that following weekend at the tiny Southampton house on the beach he had first rented three years ago.

"Good-bye, Senator. I think it's a dream come true! I still can't believe it." As Nora put down the phone, she was jubilant. It had all been worth it. Jack had won. This second-generation Irishman had dreamed the American dream, and it had come true.

As they walked hand in hand along the windswept, desolate winter beach, they talked endlessly of what had been and what would be. They went back to the house and built a fire and sat quietly huddled together. She gazed up at his strong jawline, at the dark hair falling onto his forehead, at the shadow of his profile on the wall behind him.

He leaned over, kissing her tenderly.

"Jack, is there any place in this world for us to be together?"

"There will be, Nora. We'll make one somehow." They kissed again. "Darling Nora, it will be difficult for me to get away from Washington once I take my seat in Congress. I'm going to see about a vacation house in Virginia next week, and I want to know if you can get away to help me decide about it. After all, you'll be spending a great deal of time there. I'll keep an apartment in the Capitol, of course, but I want a place where we can be together, whenever possible." He stared into the fire quietly. "Priscilla and I have an agreement. She will come down when it's necessary for her to attend government functions or the like. Nora, I hate the thought of it. We have been able to live almost completely separate lives in Boston, but it will now be politically necessary for her to show up from time to time."

"I understand, darling. Don't worry, it's what you have to do."

He suddenly grabbed her and fiercely covered her face with kisses. "I love you so, Nora." Lifting her in his arms, he carried her to the bedroom, where, in a bevy of kisses and embraces, he slowly and lovingly undressed her. As he removed each article of clothing, he ran his lips and hands over her exposed silken white skin.

"You drive me quite mad, Nora. How I want you, darling."

"Jack, I'm yours. We belong to each other."

They made love slowly, passionately, then finally fell asleep in each other's arms.

Nora awoke the next morning, stretched luxuriously and opened her eyes to see Jack lying next to her, looking at her with such love, such passion in his eyes that she felt her breath catch in her throat.

"Do you know how very beautiful you are in your sleep?"

"Jack, how long have you been awake?" She rolled into his arms.

"Hours, wonderful hours of feasting on your loveliness."

"Well, good. If you've been feasting on that, then you won't want any breakfast, is that right, Senator?"

They laughed, and joyously made love again.

That night, over a candlelit dinner, Jack raised his glass to her. "To you, Nora, and to us."

She raised her glass, and as their eyes met, they touched glasses.

"I have something for you, Nora," he said soberly. Taking her left hand, he placed on her third finger a ruby ring, so magnificent that she was left momentarily speechless.

He raised his glass to her again. "To the wife of my heart."

*   *   *

Mary was nine years old on May 20, 1916, and Nora was planning a party for her. That morning the child raced up the stairs and flew into Nora's room, waving a letter.

"It's from Ireland, Mommy, from Uncle Danny. Open it, please, right away. Oh, how I wish I knew them all. Mommy, when can I go? When can I meet them all?" She was dancing happily around the room.

"Mary, as soon as the war is over in Europe, I promise you we'll go. They all want to meet *you* to, you know."

Nora settled in her favorite chair and opened the letter.

> Dearest Nora and Sean,
>
> Everyone here wishes you all well. Thank you for keeping us up to date on all your lives. Your letters are all eagerly awaited. I know little Mary will be nine soon, and we all join in wishing her a happy birthday. Ma said to tell you there is a gift on the way. How Ma wants to meet her namesake, and how she studies the pictures of little Terry and Sarah. Please ask Seamus and Bridget to send along a photo of little James. Ma is looking forward to seeing her newest grandchild.
>
> It seems I am once again the bearer of ill tidings. Terence is in prison. We can only thank God that he's still alive. As you must have guessed, he participated in the Easter Rebellion on Easter Sunday, when the Irish Volunteers took the General Post Office in Dublin, proclaiming an Irish Republic, and held it against impossible odds for a week. We all knew, of course, that Terence was in the thick of the uprising, and Ma was nearly crazy

with worry. 'Tis an irony, but she actually cried with relief when she heard that he had been imprisoned. We were in an agony of despair that he would be executed along with the fifteen leaders. Terence's dream of a free Irish Republic seemed almost within their grasp, but by week's end they had no choice but to surrender. What a sad day for Ireland. At first, the people almost unanimously condemned the revolt, but when the British court-martialed and cruelly executed the leaders, Connolly, Pearse, and the others, the rebels came to be accepted as heroes. Even I, who have never been one to side with the Irish Republican Brotherhood, feel an admiration for these men who cared so desperately for their country that they were willing to die for it. It seems, dear Nora and Sean, that after all these years I have finally come to understand Terence and his cause a little better.

We pray for him, and we worry even more now, because his Julia is here with Ma, and she is with child. We know you will rejoice in that news, and though Terence vowed never to bring children into an Ireland subjugated to the British, it seems he has done just that despite himself. When Julia was permitted to see him, and told him the news, he wept with joy. He swore to her that by the time the baby was a year old, Ireland would be free. You see, he still harbors hopes of a victory. Ma keeps Julia's spirits up as best she can, God bless her.

Please join us in our prayers that Terence be freed. We know that all Irish Americans have been incensed by these awful murders, and that is the reason the government of the United States is bringing pressure on the British to halt any further executions. Sean and others like him are the ones responsible for this, and have without a doubt been instrumental in saving Terence from that same fate. And so we hope for his speedy release, and pray to God that it be so.

Your brother in Jesus,
Danny

Nora sat numbly, stunned by the news of Terence in prison. She called Sean and read him the letter. He said he and Rachel would be right over, and hung up.

When they arrived, Sean slowly read the letter again, then handed it to Rachel.

"Danny has come a long way, Nora," Sean told her. "It took him long years to see that Terence's cause was just, that freedom is worth fighting for."

"Terence is a special breed," Rachel said, "as are you, Sean."

Nora, still preoccupied, couldn't stop thinking that Terence might be hanged. "Sean, he—he won't be executed, will he?"

"I think it unlikely. Danny is right, you know. Public opinion and the American government have indicated their horror over those executions, and believe me, the reactions of the American government are of supreme importance to the British right now. They're counting on our support in the war at some point in time. I think he'll eventually be freed." He put his arms about Nora. "If he isn't, remember, Nora, that he chose his life, and he is willing to die for his beliefs."

*　　*　　*

Sean had correctly assessed the situation in Ireland, and on Christmas Day, 1916, a cablegram arrived in the middle of dinner. Nora's hands shook so much that Sean took it away from her to open it. It contained good news. Terence had been freed and Julia had given birth to a nine-pound boy. Sean and Nora gave cries of joy, and the family ran from the table to join them at the front door to find out what had happened.

"Bridget, they've let Terence go."

Before Nora could tell about the baby's birth, Bridget interrupted. "Oh, thank God. Let's all be saying a prayer of thanks."

"One moment, sister. That will be two prayers of thanks, for we have a new O'Sullivan baby, a nine-pound boy. Terence is a father."

Bridget gave out a whoop of delight, and everyone else laughed and talked all at once.

"Terence a father. I can't believe it," Bridget said. "Why, many was the night we'd all sit round the kitchen table, drinking the poteen, listening to Terence expound on the foolishness of bringing children into a world where they would be little better than slaves. Well, it took a good woman to change his mind. I propose a toast to Julia O'Sullivan for making a good man better."

On April 6, 1917, America entered the "war to end all wars" on the side of the Allies. Thousands upon thousands of red-blooded boys, furious over the atrocities of German submarine warfare, were eager for the fight and enlisted. Public opinion was at fever pitch, and though America was woefully unprepared, not having fought a war in fifty years, the people threw themselves wholeheartedly into the effort. The draft quickly remedied the lack of manpower; food was diverted to the men in the trenches; civilians organized war bond rallies; women took over many men's jobs; and American industry attempted to get into production as fast as possible by having factories working around the clock.

Within a month of the declaration of war, the government had offered Nora and Rachel a contract for their Queen's Lace factories to produce uniforms, and they felt they could do no less. They worked day and night retooling, and by June they were turning out uniforms by the hundreds. They had even been asked to produce a few canvas parachutes. Queen's Lace had gone to war.

Nora went to Washington, D.C., in April to finalize the contract, and Jack picked her up at the station.

"Darling, I couldn't wait to see you."

"Oh, Jack, this is dangerous. You shouldn't have come." She smiled mischievously. "But I'm so glad you did."

"So, you've gone from lingerie to parachutes. That's quite a jump."

"Oh, Jack, that sounds just like one of Sean's terrible puns." She laughed. "Yes, we're converting right now. I don't know what the ladies will be wearing for underwear for the duration, but I do know that making uniforms is our patriotic duty."

"Sweetheart, I can't stand this another minute." With that, he turned a corner, slammed on the brakes and gathering Nora to him, kissed her with such love and warmth that she didn't even try to protest.

That evening, after all her meetings, she met him at her hotel, and they left for their retreat in Virginia. They drove through winding, wooded roads fresh with spring. Dogwood, lilac and cherry trees were in bloom.

The house was a charming, small Colonial built on a modest, secluded estate surrounded by woods. Burnished antiques filled the rooms, bouquets of flowers were everywhere, and a fire was lit in the fireplace.

"What would we do without Bessie?" She was the maid he had recently hired. "That woman works miracles. Look at the supper she's left for us."

They talked, ate by candlelight and sat by the fire for hours. Their conversation turned to the war.

"Nora, Patrick is enlisting. I've asked him to wait, but he won't." He paused. "I don't want him to go. I know he has to sometime, but, oh God, Nora, I just don't want him to."

"Oh, Jack, I'm sorry. Even my Billy is carrying on about enlisting, and he's barely seventeen. Won't Patrick even wait until he's drafted?"

"Not a chance. We can only pray this damned war is over soon."

Their weekend was an idyllic one. They rode, took walks through the woods, talking, holding each other through nights of love. They knew it would be many long weeks before they saw each other again, so they tried desperately not to waste one moment.

"Darling, I'll try to take some time in July in Southampton but it's going to be difficult. Rachel and I will be working night and day converting the other factories."

"Nora, we must find the time. The thought of seeing you is all that keeps me going."

"I'll try," she promised.

They fell asleep in each other's arms.

One week after Retta graduated from Sacred Heart High School, she was at work in a government gas mask factory.

"Retta, I could have used you making uniforms. Why didn't you tell me you were looking for work?" Nora asked her.

"Aunt Nora, I'm eighteen years old, and I need to be

on my own, to find out what I can do myself, without anyone's help.''

"Retta, you're right. I'm sorry. I wanted you to be where I can keep an eye on you. Is that so wrong?''

"Oh, no, Aunt Nora, it's not wrong. I know you mean well, but remember, you left Ireland by yourself when you were my age. Who kept an eye on you?''

Nora looked at her young, adopted daughter. Retta was right. "You win, Retta, dear. I'm properly chastised.''

Retta embraced Nora warmly. "I do love you, Aunt Nora.''

When Billy came home that evening and announced he had found a job delivering ice, Nora just stared at him. "Oh, Billy, surely you can find something better than that to do.''

"Aunt Nora, what would we do if we didn't receive our ice delivery? Most of the icemen have enlisted, and I want to do something to help.''

She smiled wearily. "I wonder what Mary will find to do for the war effort?'' While Nora had meant it as a joke, Mary indeed found something to do. She joined a group that knitted socks for the doughboys.

Late in July, Nora insisted they all go to Southampton for a long weekend. They arrived Friday evening, tired from the trip, but happy. Terry and Sarah were with them, and Dennis was expected Saturday with Jack's younger son, Brian. Nora was looking forward to seeing her darling Dennis, and she was hoping desperately that Jack would be able to take a few days off. She hadn't seen him since May, and she was lonely, yearning for his touch, his voice.

Everyone seemed to know they had to cram a whole summer's pleasure into these few days. Brian appeared early the next morning, and Mary opened the door for him. "Oh, Brian, how happy I am to see you!'' She threw her arms about him, and he picked her up, swinging her around as she giggled wildly.

"Why, Mary, you're so grown up, so beautiful. Is this the same little girl who pestered me all last summer?"

She stopped giggling and put on her very best young woman's manner—which she instantly forgot the moment he challenged her to race him into the water.

Billy and Retta hadn't seen much of each other at home lately, and he now became painfully aware of her presence once again. He found himself staring at her young loveliness, wanting desperately to touch her, reach out to her, talk to her. But the longings frightened him, because he now recognized them for what they were—sexual feelings for his own sister. Oh God, what kind of an unnatural monster am I? he wondered. It was agony for him to be around her, and he welcomed Brian's presence even more than usual. Brian always cheered him, made him laugh, made him forget his obsession. Unfortunately, every time Billy wanted to go off alone with him, Brian always invited Retta. One night the three of them were leaving for a dance at the Irving Hotel.

"I want to go, Mommy," Mary demanded.

"Darling, you can't, you're too young."

"Oh, Mommy, can you believe that I'm already nine years old, and I've never once been to a dance at the Irving?" She was almost in tears. Nora tried not to laugh.

Brian jumped in. "Mary, you and I will go alone tomorrow to have tea at the Irving on the veranda."

She looked up at him, holding back her tears. "Honest? You'll take me out for tea?"

"Of course, Miss Desmond. May I call for you tomorrow afternoon at four?"

"Oh, yes, Brian, yes, I'll be ready." She skipped off, her happiness completely restored. "Tea's better than dancing anyway!" she called back to them.

Dennis arrived the next evening, resplendent in a white suit, a marvelous white hat and a long red scarf. Cradled in his arms was a gigantic bouquet of yellow roses. He chatted about the latest city gossip while Nora arranged the flowers in a vase on top of the piano. "Jack hopes to be down tomorrow. He's hopelessly dreary, working every minute, but I suppose the war must be attended to by someone."

"Don't be so flip, Dennis," Nora returned. "I happen to know you're selling Liberty Bonds, and Jack told me you've become involved with the Red Cross, too."

"But of course, darling. Khaki is my best color, you know."

"Oh, Dennis, stop it. Admit you feel useful and wanted, that what you're doing counts for something."

"Perhaps, dear Nora, but you're forever giving me credit for lofty ideals, when the truth is that I've never been lofty about anything in my life—like most people."

"My, but we're cynical tonight."

He sidestepped the remark. "You know, Priscilla asked in a roundabout way whether you and Jack were still seeing each other. I, of course, gave her no satisfaction. You know she and Jack don't speak at all. She appears in Washington when she must, then she's back to Boston or New York. It's really quite an awful situation." He looked at Nora thoughtfully. "Nora, why won't you let him divorce her?"

"It would ruin his career. We manage, Dennis. Maybe some day things will be different."

After he had left, she sat alone thinking about what she had said. Would it really be different some day? She couldn't see how.

The following day the ocean was too rough for swimming, so everyone decided to go to the big salt water pool at the Welch house. Nora packed a picnic lunch, and the young people were in fine, high spirits—everyone, that is, except Billy, who was withdrawn and miserable.

Nora confided to Dennis that she didn't know what was wrong with the boy. "Dennis, he's so quiet and despondent, and he stays in his room too much. I'm at a total loss to explain his behavior. Be a dear, and try to cheer him up. You always make him laugh."

"It's just adolescence, Nora. I seem to recall having gone through it once myself. I couldn't abide the pimples. They were so frightfully ugly." Nora laughed. "Don't worry about him," Dennis said reassuringly. "He'll be all right."

But Nora wasn't convinced.

Retta ran to the bathhouse to change into her bathing suit, and the rest of the young people trooped after her. She was in one of the changing rooms, hurriedly pulling off her clothes, when Billy opened the door by mistake and caught a glimpse of her naked. Her face was covered with the dress she was pulling off, so she didn't see him. He was transfixed for a moment by the loveliness of her, the firm buttocks, the high, pointed breasts, the satiny freckled white skin. Then he quickly and quietly shut the door, flattening himself against the wall, trying to bring his emotions under control. He was in a frenzy of desire and wanted to run away as far and as fast as he could.

Just then, Brian came out of one of the rooms. "For Pete's sake, Billy, what the hell is taking you so long? Come on, get your bathing suit on. Everyone else is ready."

"You go ahead without me," he said in a husky voice. "I'm not feeling well. Go ahead. I'll be along in a minute."

He had worked himself into a cold sweat. I'm so ashamed. I want to touch her, kiss her, my own sister, for

God's sake. I've got to get away, leave home. I can't stand it any longer.''

Later that afternoon he began asking Brian questions about Patrick's letters home from the army.

"He says the food is awful. They drill with broomsticks, and they learn a lot about personal hygiene and care of the feet. He can't believe that learning about his feet is going to help make the world safe for democracy, but in case they know something he doesn't, he's willing to give it a try."

Billy laughed for the first time in days. "Brian, I want to enlist," he confided.

"You're still under age, Billy."

"I don't care. I'm almost eighteen. I can lie. I look eighteen, don't I?"

"Yes, I guess so, but why not wait? Who wants to drill with a broomstick, for God's sake?"

"I just want to get away."

Brian looked at him curiously. "They'll get us soon enough. Don't be crazy, Billy. Whatever problem you're having can be worked out." Brian too had lately noticed Billy's strange behavior, but even though they were best friends, he sensed he shouldn't pry.

"I don't think so, Brian. I just don't think so."

"Sure it can. Why, pretty soon you'll be going back to school. Maybe that will solve your problem."

Billy nodded. "Maybe."

It was worth a try. For the time being, Billy decided he'd go back to school early.

Chapter 46

Orange, red and golden leaves swirled around Jack and Nora as they they walked hand in hand through the glorious autumn woods. "Virginia is so beautiful in October, Nora. There's nowhere else quite like it."

The crisp autumn wind blew her hair into charming disarray. She pushed it out of her eyes, then took his arm. "Have you heard from Patrick?" she asked.

"Yes, he'll be going overseas soon. Oh Nora, how I want this war to end right now."

Her heart went out to him. "Does Brian talk of enlisting when he's old enough?"

"Yes, he does. He had been sensible about all that at first, but now he's as caught up in soldier fever as the rest of the young fools."

"Billy was driving me crazy with talk of enlisting. He's been so miserable this last year, so restless and unpredictable, I just don't know what's wrong. Dennis says it's only adolescence, and maybe he's right. Anyway, I talked Billy into going on to Georgetown rather than back to prep school. He's a year ahead of himself, but maybe that's the kind of challenge he needs. His letters have been a little more cheerful, and thank God he likes school. I was hoping to visit him this week, but I have to be in Boston on business.''

"Nora, what business do you have in Boston?''

"We still have some production of lingerie, and Filene's is having a promotion. I don't want to lose their business, so I said I'd be there. I'll be home Friday night, and Billy has promised to come in for the weekend.''

Jack looked thoughtful. "Nora, do you ever think about telling Billy?''

She tilted her head to one side. "All the time, Jack. It tears me apart because I don't know what's right. I guess I'm afraid of what would happen, that in claiming him, I might lose him. Maybe that's the real reason I don't tell him.''

He saw a look of despair in her eyes, and reached out to hold her hand. "You'll have to confront it one of these days, Nora. I think it's inevitable.''

She shook her head "Maybe it is, but not now." He held her tightly as she buried her face in the soft wool of his jacket. "No, not now," she whispered.

Retta answered the doorbell, and signed for a cable-gram. She was late for work, so without reading it, she quickly laid the message on a table in the foyer, then bounded out the door.

Billy bounded in happily an hour later. "Where is everyone?" he shouted, but silence was his only answer. He unpacked his suitcase, and hungrily raided the icebox. Finally, he checked through the mail on the entry-hall table to see if there was anything for him. He looked curiously at a letter from Maloney and Dougherty Solicitors, Dublin, Ireland. Must be for Mom, he thought, but no, it was very clearly addressed to Mr. Billy Shannon, care of Mrs. Nora Desmond. How strange. He opened the letter and read it, his mind unable to fully comprehend what it said. In shock, he sat down and read the message again. It became clear. There was no doubt. William Howard, heir to Ballygarry Estate, was deathly ill after a terrible fall from a horse and had instructed his solicitors to tell Billy that he was his real father. Since there were no other male heirs, Billy would now inherit his father's estate and be in line for his grandfather's estate and title when his grandfather, Lord Anthony, died. But most incredible of all, the message referred to Aunt Nora as his mother!

"Oh my God!" he cried aloud. His thoughts swirled in confusion. Aunt Nora was his mother. He started to weep with the sudden realization that she had abandoned him, given him away, and that his own mother and father weren't his real parents. He wept bitterly as he read the letter over and over. Retta was not his real sister. How could Aunt Nora have done this to him? Why hadn't she told him? After his initial shock, he sat silently trying to sort out his thoughts, but his mind was in too much turmoil, his emotions raw and exposed.

He heard the key turn in the lock. It was Nora. The apartment was in the shadows of late afternoon darkness.

"Is anyone here?" She turned on the hall light.

He didn't answer, but she saw his coat thrown over the chair.

"Billy? Are you here?"

Still he did not answer. She looked into the living room. As her eyes adjusted to the light, she saw him slumped in a chair.

"Is that you, Billy?"

Billy turned around slowly, his eyes red from weeping, his entire body trembling. "Yes, Mother, it's me!"

She stopped dead in her tracks. My God, she thought in a panic. *He knows*. "Billy—please—let me explain."

"Just tell me if it's true."

"Yes, I'm sorry, darling, but it's true. I became pregant in Ireland. Your father wouldn't acknowledge you or me. He told me I had to leave, that we couldn't tell anyone or he'd deny it."

"I don't know anything about him. All I know is that you gave me away."

She was trembling violently. How could William have done this? What had happened? Billy just sat in cruel silence. Her voice dropped almost to a whisper. "I had no choice but to put you up for adoption. I had no way of keeping you, Billy."

"You what?" The contempt in his voice was more than she could bear.

"I was working fourteen hours a day in a mill. It—"

She stopped, unable to continue under the glare of his contempt. "My God, Billy, you're my son. I love you. You must know that. I'm sorry, I wanted to tell you when Molly and Tim died, but—"

"But *what?* Why didn't you?"

"You won't let me talk, Billy. You won't let me explain. Please." With that she moved toward him, her arms outstretched.

"Stay away from me." He recoiled. "I hate you. You gave me away. I could never call you Mother." He was growing hysterical.

"Billy, please forgive me. I've made a mistake. Don't you think I wanted a thousand times to hear you call me your mother? I was a young girl, no older than you are now. Can't you find it in your heart to understand? I love you, Billy. I don't know what else to say."

"If you loved me, you would never have given me up."

His words ripped at her heart. Her eyes pleaded desperately for forgiveness. She had never felt so lost, so vulnerable.

Billy suddenly became calm. "I can't stay here. Maybe I can see my father before he dies. At least he was honest enough to finally tell me the truth. How could you deny my knowing my own father? How could you?"

"Billy, he wouldn't—"

Billy interrupted, screaming at her, "I never want to see you again. Never!"

Her eyes were blurred by tears, her mind numb from his rejection. First the father, now the son. When she looked up, he was rushing quickly past her.

"Please, don't." Her hand was on his arm. He pulled away violently, dashed out the door and slammed it shut. She stood as if paralyzed. "No, Billy, don't leave, please don't leave. I love you. I'm sorry." By now she was sobbing violently, but Billy heard none of it, for he was long gone.

She fell into a chair. He'll be back, she thought. It's just the shock that caused him to run off. She sat for hours, remembering the past. Finally she called Annie.

"Annie, Billy knows." Her voice was flat and emotionless. "He's found out. He knows everything."

"Stay there. I'll be right over."

Nora placed the phone back on the hook and slowly walked into her bedroom. Suddenly the cablegram caught her eye. In a trancelike state she opened it, and reading it, collapsed in a heap on the bed.

Annie found her lying there, and knelt beside her. "Nora, are you all right? Come, girl, sit up." Nora struggled to her feet. "That's it, now tell me what happened."

As Nora tearfully related the awful scene, Annie kept her warm, safe arms about her friend, offering words of reassurance and comfort over and over. Finally, she looked her straight in the eye. "Nora, you've got to tell them. Sean, Bridget, everyone. They're your family, and you need their support. You've carried this terrible secret around long enough. Besides, with Billy knowing, it's only a matter of time before the others do too."

"Maybe you're right, Annie. But I don't know if I have the courage."

The following evening Seamus and Bridget arrived at seven, followed a few minutes later by Sean and Rachel. Nora had asked them all over, as well as requesting that Retta stay home from work. Nora walked around aimlessly all day, trying to understand what had happened and wondering how to explain it all to everyone. She felt numb and dazed, but she knew Annie was right. Her secret was finally out.

Everyone was ill at ease, suspecting that something unpleasant was happening. They engaged in nervous small talk as they waited for Nora to appear. She finally came in and sat down.

"Nora, if this is an important family matter, why isn't Billy here?" Sean asked, looking at her quizzically.

She squared her shoulders. "He's not here . . . because he's left home. He may be back, but I doubt it." She looked weary and beaten.

"What on earth do you mean?" Bridget asked in alarm.

Nora couldn't bring herself to speak.

"Aunt Nora, what is it?" Retta persisted.

Nora turned to Retta, gazing at her pensively for a few moments. "Retta, Billy is not your brother."

Retta looked at her incredulously. Everyone sat perfectly still, waiting for Nora's next words. Nora didn't know how else to say it, so she blurted out the simple truth. "Billy is my son!"

They gasped. Sean finally broke the stunned silence.

"Nora, what are you saying? He's *Molly's* son. You were with me on the ship. How—" Then he realized what had happened. "Lowell! My God, then you were pregnant when you went alone to Massachusetts. Oh, Nora, why didn't you tell me? I'd have understood." He crossed over and put his arms about her. "Who is the father?"

Bridget putting her arms around a crying Retta, stared at Nora as if looking at a total stranger.

"The father is William Howard." She hung her head, feeling ashamed and alone.

Rachel rushed over and knelt at her feet. "Dearest Nora, we all understand. We even understand why you told no one, and I, for one, admire you for it. But how did Billy find out?"

Nora steeled herself and told them everything. Then, turning to Retta, who seemed in a daze, she said imploringly, "Retta, darling, I love you like my very own daughter. Please forgive me for not telling you. I may have made a mistake, but I thought my reasons were good. Please don't hate me. I couldn't bear it."

Retta ran to Nora and threw her arms about her. "I couldn't hate you, Aunt Nora. You've loved me as one of your own. You've treated me no differently from Mary and Billy. Oh, Aunt Nora, how could Billy hurt you like that?"

"I understand why he did, Retta, I really do. I can only hope that he'll forgive me in time."

"I'll try to track him down," Sean offered. "The people at the *Journal* can help. Don't worry, we'll find him."

Nora was aware that Bridget was the only one who hadn't spoken, and Nora ached for her to say something, but Bridget sat rigidly quiet. Seamus took Bridget's hand and patted it, but he had a puzzled look on his face. He obviously didn't understand his wife's reaction any more than Nora did.

At last Bridget spoke. "What will Ma say?"

So that was it. Nora looked at her, understanding at once what Bridget feared. "Who knows."

Bridget looked up. "And, how will you tell Mary?"

"I'll tell her when the time is right, Bridget. We'll need to be alone. It will be hard to explain to a child, but she too must know. I can only hope she'll understand."

"Oh, Nora, poor Nora." Bridget fell weeping into her sister's arms.

Nora waited anxiously for her mother's letter. What a shock it must have been for all of them. At last, the letter arrived. Nora opened it with trembling hands.

> My dearest daughter,
>
> I have been sitting here for hours, with pen in hand. The rain is beating against the eaves, and the greyness of the day has only added to my sadness. I have tried all morning to picture you, once more going up the gangplank of the ship that I believed was taking you to a bright new life of opportunity. I remember you looked so very small and alone. I almost cried out, "Come back, my precious little girl, come back." Had I known the terrible burden of the secret you were keeping, I would have gathered you to me and never have let you part from me. I know you must have suffered greatly, bearing so great a burden with no consolation from family or friends with a stranger delivering your son in a strange place, in a strange land. Then, how your heart must have broken to give him away, just to keep

from shaming us. But in that, darling Nora, you were wrong. My heart would not have cracked from shame, as you imagined, nor would have your father's. Indeed, all of us would have been at your side.

I have agonized over how this shocking news was delivered to Billy. The circumstances of his discovery could not, I'm sure, have been more traumatic. It appears that William was cruel and self-centered till the end, wishing only to cleanse his own soul, this time at Billy's expense.

However the disclosure was made, the truth is known now, and more than anything, I want somehow to be more of a mother to you, to make up for all the trials you bore alone for the sake of saving us grief and shame. I stand in awe of your sacrifice and will remember for the rest of my days that you cared more for the feelings of those you loved than you did for yourself. No mother could be more proud of a daughter.

You should know one thing. Anthony, though dismayed as I by the way this all happened, is thrilled that he has a grandson. It made him feel a little less pain at William's death. Bad son though William may have been, he was Anthony's only child. We both can't wait to welcome Billy to our hearts.

Come home to us soon. Let me enfold you in my arms—you and my grandson. And allow Billy to take his rightful place in his family.

> Your loving mother,
> Mary O'Sullivan

Nora's eyes were full of tears as she finished the last sentence. Her mother's letter was so full of love and hope. How sad Ma would be once again, and Anthony too, to find that Billy had left home, angry and unforgiving, and had probably run away to join the army.

Jack called and came over that afternoon. He came to New York often lately, for he knew the pain his beloved Nora was suffering. When she showed him the letter, instead of saying anything, he took her in his arms and held her for a long, long time.

Three weeks later, Sean arrived at the Queen's Lace factory with a letter in his hand.

"Nora, I've heard from Billy." He handed her the letter.

She was afraid to look at it, feeling out of control, a little dizzy. But finally she opened it. "Oh, Sean, thank God he's all right. He's joined the army. You have no idea where he is?"

"No. It was mailed in New York City. Doubtless someone mailed it for him, but Nora, he's all right, and you must admit, it was thoughtful of him. Although he says it was to keep the rest of us from worrying, it's obvious that he wants you to know he's all right." He paused. "It seems the kind of thing I might have done." He put his arms around Nora. "Nora, I'm sorry." Nora held on to the thought that Billy had cared enough to send the letter. She began to sleep more soundly, though she was still tense and worried.

Angelo called often, insisting that she take some time off, so they met at their old favorite restaurant, Delmonico's.

"I have some news for you, Nora," he told her over a piece of quiche. "Billy is at Camp Custer, Michigan. He's quite all right."

Nora was startled, but hadn't he always known everything? "Oh, Angelo, how did you find out?"

"Through an army contact, but I don't know what you'll do with the information. I just thought you would want to know."

Nora felt a surge of relief. "You're right. Just knowing where he is helps somehow." She looked steadily at him. "Dare I try to see him?"

Angelo shook his head. "I just don't know, Nora. You might only be hurt again. Maybe not enough time has passed yet."

A week later, Nora made up her mind. She went to Michigan. She didn't tell Jack or any of her family. Angelo had arranged for the camp commander to see her, and fearing the worst, he arrived on the next train. He did not want her to face this ordeal alone. She didn't tell Commander Wilson that Billy was underage, for she knew that her son would not forgive her for that, but she asked if she might be allowed to see him. The commander went to call him in. While she waited, Nora watched the drilling and marching parades of boys through the window. Her heart was full of fear. At last, she saw Billy approaching. She held her breath. How different he was. Practically overnight he had become a man. In uniform he looked even more handsome than usual. His blond hair was now combed slickly back and he stood tall and straight. She wanted to call to him through the window, but she remained still. She waited and waited until finally the door opened, and Commander Wilson walked in alone.

"I'm sorry, Mrs. Desmond. He won't see you."

Nora sat dazed for a moment, but then rushed to the window, knowing somehow that this would be the last time she would see her son for a very long time—perhaps forever. She watched his retreating figure with a melancholy in her heart she had never known. She whispered under her breath, "Billy, oh God, Billy, I love you. Please forgive me."

Angelo was waiting outside for her. She wasn't surprised. Wasn't he always there when she needed him? She gave him a look of such despair that he just took her arm and led her silently away.

Chapter 47

As Russia was crumbling on the Eastern Front, the first American doughboys landed in France in March, 1918. Patrick Ryan was among them. At Château-Thierry, fighting with French troops under Marshal Foch, he was wounded by shrapnel from the same hand grenade that killed his dearest friend. Under the force of the combined Allied drive, the desperate offensive launched by the Germans was smashed, but losses were great. Patrick, burdened by a leg injury, and in severe depression from having his buddy die in his arms, was sent to a hospital behind the lines.

When Dennis Noble heard the details of the battle in a letter from his nephew, he made up his mind to go to Europe with the Red Cross. Before catching his ship out of New York, he came to say good-bye to Nora.

"My God, Nora, I've been working for the Red Cross for two years, and what have I been doing? Sorting out books to send to the boys. I ask you, when do they have time to read books? Especially the kind people donate: catalogues of canine diseases, instruction manuals on how to do needlepoint. I felt so damned useless I decided I had to do more. Daddy has pull, you know, and he's gotten me assigned to a Red Cross unit in France. He says maybe it will make a man of me." He smiled wryly. "Who knows? Maybe I can do some good somewhere." He ground out the cigarette he'd been smoking. "Patrick's been wounded, you know. And now Brian's gone too. Where is Billy?"

"He's on his way to France too, Dennis. He writes to Retta. It's the only way I know anything." She lowered her head, and he took her hand.

"Nora, be brave."

She shook her head sadly. "Yes, I must be brave, like Jack is. The news about Patrick almost killed Jack, but he carries on."

"Yes, and you know, it's the first time I've ever felt sorry for Priscilla. She may be an awful woman, and not much of a mother, but Patrick is her son. She was terrified that he'd die, and she became quite hysterical at the news."

Nora touched his arm affectionately. "Dennis, I'm proud of you, but promise to be careful. Write if you can, and if I find out where Billy is, I'll let you know. Maybe you'll be able to see him. He always liked you so."

He put his hand over hers. He knew that what she was asking for was unlikely to happen, but she, like parents everywhere, needed some shred of hope. "Of course, Nora, dearest."

She saw him off, and watched, sad-eyed, the thousands of troops saying good-bye to their loved ones. The soldiers put on a brave front, joking and laughing, and one group standing near Dennis on the rail sang a popular ballad of the day: "Good-bye, Maw! Good-bye, Paw! Good-bye Mule, with yer old hee-hae! I'll git you a Turk an' a Kiser too—an' that's about all one feller can do!"

Dennis, with a disdainful look, shouted down to her, "Good God, what have I gotten into?"

She laughed and waved. Dear, aristocratic Dennis, confronted with a world he had never known. Mules indeed! God bless him, she thought.

One month later, Sean left for France. His newspaper sent him to cover the Western Front. Rachel did not want him to go, but knowing how strongly he felt, she supported him in his decision. Still, she could not help showing some of her fear, and he tried to reassure her.

"Rachel, darling, I'll be all right. Newspapermen are safely kept far from the lines. Please, don't worry."

"Well then, how did Floyd Gibbons come to be shot in the arm and head?" Gibbons was a well-known foreign correspondent who had received the Croix de Guerre for bravery under fire.

"He went to the aid of a soldier in Belleau Wood, darling."

"Yes, well so would you."

He tried to kiss Rachel's fears away, but as she, Nora and Bridget saw him off, she broke down sobbing. "Come home to us, Sean. Please come home to us."

In September, 1918, Retta had another letter from Billy. His division was gearing up for a big battle, but of course he didn't know where. It turned out to be the Meuse-Argonne offensive, in which three hundred twenty-four tanks helped to break the German lines. They later read in *The New York Times* that the Yanks had charged into no man's land with such rash enthusiasm that, though costly, they had helped to sweep the Allies to victory. Nora searched the war pictures in the rotogravure section of the newspaper every day to see if she could find Billy, but she never saw him.

She was desperate for word about him, and then one

day a cablegram arrived. Her hands shook so much that Retta had to open it.

"Aunt Nora, it's from Ireland."

"Ireland? What in God's name does it say?"

"Received word Billy wounded. Stop. In French hospital at St. Mihiel. Stop. Notified as next of kin. Stop. More when we know. Stop. Love Mother."

Nora collapsed into a chair. "Retta, he's wounded, but Ma doesn't say how badly. He must have listed her as next of kin."

"Oh, Aunt Nora." She held Nora tightly. "They must not know how badly he's wounded, or they would have said."

Nora covered her eyes with her hand. "I've got to know how he is. We're going to Sean's paper right this minute. They'll get word to Sean of where Billy is. Come on."

Grabbing their coats, they hurried down to the *Journal*, where they asked to see Sean's editor in chief.

"You've got to tell him, Mr. Fitzwilliams," Nora told the editor. "Please. I've got to know how badly wounded my son is."

"We'll do our best, Mrs. Desmond, but it won't be easy to get through."

"I know, but please try."

Barely two weeks later, Nora received a cablegram from Sean, telling her that Billy had sustained bullet wounds in his leg, but that he would recover. He had personally gone to see Billy, and he assured her that the lad was not seriously wounded. Nora dropped the cable and sobbed with joy.

Patrick Ryan was sent home in October, 1918, the same month Brian Ryan assured his father in a letter that the war was almost over. Dennis had also sent a letter, which described the indignity of being sprayed for lice, the serving of apple pies to war-weary doughboys, and the horror of wounded and dying men.

On November 11, 1918, the war ended. Nora and Jack were together when word came. They thanked God for sparing their sons, two of whom—Brian and Billy—were still in Europe.

"Jack, it's over, it's over!" They kissed and embraced and danced and laughed.

"Thank God." Jack pulled her to him. "Oh, thank God, Nora, they're all alive."

The following month Patrick called Nora from Virginia. He had been staying with his father, recuperating and resting. His father had become extremely ill with influenza, and he was calling for her.

"Oh, Patrick, how bad is he?" she wanted to know, but Patrick sounded terse, disapproving. Nora, sick with fear, assured him that she would leave immediately. He brusquely told her he'd meet her train.

Influenza had been reaching epidemic proportions, claiming as many lives as had the war. Nora tried to remain calm, but Jack's condition didn't sound good. Arriving in the rain, she pulled her cape about her, looking for Patrick. On the platform, she saw him limping toward her with a cane, and she ran toward him.

As they drove to the hospital, she tried to talk to him, but he was strangely aloof. "Patrick," she finally asked, "what is wrong? Why won't you talk to me?"

"You and my father are lovers, isn't that right?"

She looked him straight in the eye. "That's right, Patrick, we are lovers." Her straightforward answer took him off guard. "We have been, as you say, lovers, for six years now. We are, however, more than that. We are deeply in love, and we are friends as well. Your father means more to me than life itself, and I am very proud of our love."

Her frontal attack confused him. He had expected denials, apologies. "It's—well, it's wrong," he stammered.

"Who are you to say it's wrong? Who are you to judge the lives of others?" Nora was disgusted with the intolerance of youth, first Billy's, now Patrick's. Was I so unforgiving, so unyielding, so certain I was right at that age? she wondered. "Patrick, we take from this world what happiness it has to offer. Maybe you'll find out about that one day. Your father and I hurt no one, your mother included. You know they have despised each other for many years. My heart is breaking at the thought that I might lose the only man I've ever loved, and here you're making your petty judgments on my morals. You needn't have anything to do with me, but spare me your moralizing." She stared straight ahead. "Just get me to the hospital, that's all I ask."

Patrick was too embarrassed to look at her. She had made him feel ridiculous and hypocritical. They drove along silently for a while. Finally, he turned to her. "Mrs. Desmond, I feel like a damned fool. I'm sorry. It was just a shock to me, I guess."

She was still upset, but she softened at his apology. "Patrick, let's forget it. It takes a lot of courage to say you're sorry. Just remember, I love him no less than you do."

Nora was unprepared for the pandemonium at the hospital. Beds lined the corridors, sick people called out for nurses, doctors shuffled here and there with the mechanical quickness of wind-up dolls.

"Patrick, my God, it's awful. Where is he?"

Patrick led her to a small room down the hall in which there had been crammed five beds. Nora ran to Jack's side. He was pale and delirious.

"Jack, can you hear me? It's Nora. Darling, I'm here."

He moaned slightly. She touched his forehead and found that he was burning with fever.

She hurried out into the hall to find help. At the desk, she found a harried nurse. "Just tell me what to do. I'll be staying with Mr. Ryan, so I may as well help the others in the room."

The grateful nurse gave her orders and a smock to put on over her dress. Nora ministered first to Jack, then to the others. She knew Patrick had been sitting with him all last night, so she insisted that he go home.

She found a chair and sat, looking down at the pale, thin face of the man she loved. She couldn't let herself cry. She would need all her energy. She kept changing cold compresses on his forehead and dozed off a little whenever she could. Jack remained delirious all night, occasionally calling out, "Nora, where are you?" She sat for three long nights, sleeping a few hours at a nearby hotel during the day when Patrick came to relieve her. She ministered to whoever else needed help too. When the doctor arrived on the fourth morning, he examined Jack and turned to her. "Mrs. Ryan, he's somewhat improved since yesterday. Don't get your hopes up yet, but he may be over the worst. My advice to you is to get some sleep yourself. You'll be no good to him if you succumb, Mrs. Ryan."

Patrick had entered just at that moment. He put his arms on her shoulders and she turned to him, her eyes red with sleeplessness and worry, her hair disheveled, her smock wrinkled. The doctor left them alone. "You're more Mrs. Ryan than my mother ever was. Thank you, Mrs. Desmond," Patrick said.

"Oh, Patrick." She looked at him with great affection. "Please call me Nora. I just want your father to be well. Let's pray for him."

A few hours later, Jack opened his eyes. The fever had broken. "Nora?"

"Yes, darling, I'm here."

A week later, Jack was released from the hospital. Patrick dropped her off at her hotel to pick up her belongings. Then she went on to Virginia with them. There Nora carefully nursed Jack back to health.

When she arrived home in New York, a letter from Danny was waiting for her. Retta stood nervously by her side, and Mary, who now knew that Billy was her real brother, asked Nora if she could read the letter Nora had finished.

"Of course, darling. But both of you, please leave me alone for a few minutes."

Nora opened the letter from Danny, her heart pounding. She knew through Sean, who had visited the hospital in St. Mihiel, that Billy had decided not to come home to America, but to find his Irish roots instead, and to make his home with his grandparents in Ballygarry. He wouldn't talk about his mother, that much Nora knew.

She had been waiting anxiously to hear about his arrival. It had been over a year since she had last seen him that sad day in Camp Custer.

> Dearest Nora,
>
> Billy arrived in Ballygarry two weeks ago, and Ma and Lord Anthony went to Queenstown to meet him. Ma said that her heart almost broke when he hobbled down the gangplank, weak and pale, but there was no mistaking who he was. It's uncanny how much he resembles William. Lord Anthony must have thought he was seeing a ghost. Ma said a great many sentimental tears were shed, and they

welcomed him warmly, taking him to their hearts immediately. It was decided that he should stay at Lord Anthony's where he would have his own room and all the comforts. Ma has been there with him constantly. Imagine her feelings at seeing her first-born grandchild, a grandchild she never knew existed. And she says Lord Anthony is as happy as she.

We all went to meet him for the first time yesterday, as he was too weak for visitors until then. It was all rather awkward and strange for him, but we liked him very much. He is a fine young man, Nora, a credit to you, and of course, to dear Molly and her husband. He got on particularly well with Terence, who took to him immediately. Next week, Billy will be meeting his half sisters. I don't know if Ma has told you, but William's wife, Margaret, left Ireland right after William died. She was never happy here, and the shock of learning about Billy was a severe one for her. The girls are allowed to visit their grandfather, and Ma says that Billy is the spitting image of the youngest one, Sybil. Ma mentioned that you met her when you were here.

With Ma and Lord Anthony to guide him, Billy has decided to go to school at Trinity as soon as he's well enough.

So, dearest Nora, know that your son is in good hands. And I promise we shall all do whatever we can to change Billy's heart toward you. Be patient, I feel it will happen.

I shall, of course, keep you informed of his life here, and remain yours in Christ.

Your brother Danny

P.S.When Terence first heard about all this, he fumed and raged. "Danny," he said, "I should have killed that bastard, William, years ago. Not because he got our Nora with child, for she had part in that, but that he denied her." Julia and I had a difficult time calming him down. Sure, and I thought he'd go up to Lord Anthony's and kill an already dying man.

Nora unwittingly smiled at the strange way Danny's last sentence had come out. She had been sorry about William's death only because of the pain it caused for Lord Anthony, and she could picture Terence fuming. But her smile faded as she thought about Billy again. She didn't share Danny's optimism, that patience was all that was needed. As time passed, she had learned to live with the pain of Billy's rejection. Just knowing he was alive and well was enough to be thankful for.

At Christmas, Nora gathered the family together. Retta was a beautiful, poised twenty-one-year-old woman. She had just graduated from Manhattanville College. For her graduation, Nora had given her a grand tour of Europe. When she returned, she was planning on joining Nora to learn the lingerie business, and that thrilled Nora.

Mary was now thirteen, still spirited and charming, with lustrous chestnut hair streaked with golden red highlights, and flashing brown eyes. Everyone loved her, and it seemed that she loved everyone in return. She had developed a terrible crush on Brian at Southampton last summer, and everyone kidded her about forgetting Patrick so quickly.

"Why, you were going to marry Patrick when you grew up, remember?" Retta had teased.

"Oh, Retta, I was just a little girl then. He's too quiet

for me. Brian's much more fun. I think perhaps it is he whom I'll marry.''

Bridget and Seamus were happy. They doted on little James, now almost four and the darling of all his cousins. Sarah—Rachel and Sean's youngest child—was just five. She was a pretty little girl, delicate and quiet, with Rachel's dark good looks. Terry, just a year younger than Mary, was obviously Sean's son. He had the same red hair and mischievous eyes, the same sense of fun, the same laugh. Nora adored him and played with him much as she had with Sean, so many years ago. Bridget had insisted on cooking Christmas dinner, though Nora, Retta and Rachel all helped. Seamus finally went into the kitchen and dragged his wife out. ''I want your company, love. I eat your food all the time.''

Annie was there with her nephew, an apprentice architect, who stared longingly at Retta all day. Since he was the only one her age, she chatted amiably with him, but he did look like a lovesick fool, Retta thought. She was seeing several young men, went out dancing several nights a week, and had bobbed her hair. Nora had been dismayed at first, but a week later, she had had her own hair bobbed, and found she liked the freedom it gave her. Other friends dropped by throughout the day, until finally Nora had said farewell to the last of them.

The following night, she and Jack celebrated their own Christmas. They dined at Sherry's, danced at the Fifth Avenue Hotel, and rode through the snow in Central Park in a hansom cab, just as they had on their very first evening together in New York. Then they went to an elegant speakeasy and shared a bottle of champagne.

When they were quite happily tipsy, they returned to his hotel. They couldn't stop laughing, until Jack finally pulled her into his arms. They fell into an embrace, and he was suddenly pressing his lips to hers with urgent desire.

His warm hands gently caressed her shoulders, exciting her. As if in a dream, she followed him into the bedroom, where he undressed her and showered kisses on her soft white skin until she sighed in ecstasy. She trembled with delight as he took her. "It's wonderful," she whispered. "Nothing is more wonderful."

"No, Nora, nothing. Just us, just our love." He held her so close that their hearts beat as one.

It was the Fourth of July in Southampton, 1920. Dennis had come over to help Nora celebrate. They were about to go down to the beach with Mary to bake clams when there was a knock at the door.

Nora went to answer it. When she did not return immediately, Dennis followed her into the hall. "What is it, Nora?"

"A cablegram from Ireland." She tried to remain calm, but she couldn't. "It's Ma. She's quite sick. They don't know what's wrong. Oh, Dennis, I've got to go to her."

"Of course. Let's get you back to the city."

They all drove back into town that night, and by ten the next morning, she was booked on the next ship leaving for Ireland. She called Jack and told him. He couldn't get away to see her off.

Retta was already in Europe, but Ireland was her last destination, and Nora didn't have time to try to contact her. She asked Sean to try to reach her.

"I'm taking Mary with me. I want Ma to meet her. I'd take Terry too, but he's at camp. Seamus and Bridget are going, too."

Two days later, Nora, Mary, Seamus and Bridget were sailing for Ireland on the *H.M.S. George II*.

Chapter 48

Danny came out to meet them at the ship. Bridget and Nora burst into tears at seeing their brother again, now greying and becoming quite portly, but most dignified in his priest's garb. Seamus clasped his hand warmly. Mary was excited to meet her Uncle Danny, the only priest among all her uncles and cousins, and he took an instant liking to her as well.

"Tell me, Danny, how is Ma?" Nora asked anxiously. "When you cabled us—"

"Oh, Danny, is she all right? We've been half crazy with worry!" Bridget interrupted.

"Wait, both of you. Let me get a word in. Faith, I've forgotten what it's like to be among chattering magpies like you. Ma's much better. It's as she was telling us all along, that it was not consumption but a bad bout with bronchitis. Lord Anthony insisted we bring her to Dublin to see a doctor, and she's recovering now at St. Joseph's Hospital. We've all been praying, and I guess God heard our prayers. The Sisters were nearly locking the doors today to keep her from coming out with me to personally supervise the docking of your ship.''

"Thank God, Danny. It's about time we had some good tidings." Bridget gave Danny a big hug.

Then Nora did as well. She found herself wanting to ask about Billy, but she did not. She would find out about him for herself soon enough.

Mary was sitting upright in her bed as they entered the room. She obviously was not enjoying her hospital stay, but she brightened when she saw them, particularly her young namesake.

After they exchanged hugs and kisses and tears, Mary the elder looked over at her suddenly silent, awe-struck granddaughter. "Come here, child, let me look at you.''

Young Mary shyly approached the bed as if being ushered into the queen's presence.

"Why so quiet? Have you none of your mother's gift of gab?''

Nora was astonished at the sudden change in her daughter as she approached the bed and, after a moment's hesitation, threw her arms around her grandmother.

"Oh, Grandma, I've waited so long to meet you. Aunt Bridget and Mommy and Uncle Sean told me all about your fireside stories, your lovely laces, your—''

"I see I misjudged. You do indeed have your mother's way with words. You don't know how happy I am to be with you, at last. Now come sit down and tell me all about yourself.''

As the two Marys became acquainted, Danny took Nora aside. "Lord Anthony and Billy have been with Ma every day. They left this morning. Billy's fine, Nora, but he's been so worried about his grandmother that he's not been concentrating as much as he'd like on his riding for the horse show.''

Nora looked at him in amazement. "The horse show? Danny, do you mean the Dublin Horse Show? Why, I had no idea! No one told me."

"I guess I thought I had mentioned it."

Danny was obviously embarrassed, and Nora guessed that Billy had instructed him not to tell her. The gnawing indecision about whether to confront Billy returned. "Where is he now, Danny?"

"He's back at Lord Anthony's, home from school on summer holiday. Ma will tell you about him."

Bridget, sensing that Nora wanted to speak to their mother alone, discreetly led the others out of the room.

Mary turned to Nora. "Oh, child, what you've been through. I was so sad for you when I found out everything. If only you had told me. How upset Anthony was when he found out. Faith, he had long ago suspected something. He said he feared when first he met you that you and William were involved, and he tried to warn you against him."

"That's all long past, Ma. Don't dwell on it, please."

"And now, Billy being so stubborn," Mary continued. "Anthony and I have tried to reason with him, but he simply refuses to discuss you. Danny has tried as well, and Terence, of course, has tried to browbeat him. In an indirect way, Billy's always asking about you. It's all so sad."

Nora put her head down on the bed, softly crying. "Oh Ma, I lost him once. Must I lose him again?"

Mary stroked her daughter's hair. "He'll come around in time, lass. It takes a while for these wounds to heal."

"What is it about me, Ma? Whatever I do ends in some kind of trouble."

"There's always trouble when you challenge the rules, Nora. But I admire you for that. It's what I always wanted to do, and I'm afraid I'm the one who instilled all those hopes and dreams and ambitions in you, from the time you were old enough to speak. I wanted you to have the life that I never had." She gazed into a distant past. Nora knew she was remembering and remained silent. Mary turned to her, shaking her head, as if to clear away those thoughts. "I only hope there have been compensations for you. There were for me."

"Oh, Ma, of course there have been. Wonderful ones, too. You know, I've cried so often in my life. The sorrows shake me like a gusting wind that blows and upturns everything in its path, and then is as suddenly gone, and afterward, in the calm, I love the life I have. Is that awful, Ma?"

"No, Nora, of course not. Those who never laugh or enjoy or love, those who only dwell on the sorrow never really know what life can be."

"Oh, Ma, I love you. One day I want you to come to America to see what you've wrought."

Mary laughed. "Maybe someday I will, but I'm happy here, Nora. I still have people to care for and things to do."

"Is one of those people Lord Anthony, Ma?"

"Of course, Nora. You've known that for a long time." Nora admired her unabashed response. "We lead a lovely life, separate but together. I loved your father in another way, and I cherish his memory, but Anthony and I are enjoying a new life in our golden years. We read together, take long walks through the meadows and woods, talk endless hours. He has made this part of my life peaceful and full. It's my calm after a life of hardship and those gusting winds you were talking about. And, Nora, I've done the same for him." She gazed into space for a few moments. "But, how I'm going on. That's all in the past now."

"Ma, I'm so glad we talked. You understand me better than anyone. You always have."

Mary pulled Nora to her bosom and held her tightly. The silence and closeness were full of their love.

Mary was released from the hospital within the week, and when the entourage of visitors took her home to Ballygarry, the rest of the family was there to welcome them. Terence ran out the cottage door and grabbed young Mary, swinging her around, exclaiming, "Faith, look what the fairies have brought us." Mary knew instantly that this big, handsome, funny man was her Uncle Terence.

Just then Terence felt himself being lifted off the ground, and turned to see Seamus' face grimacing from the effort. They both collapsed, laughing, to the ground.

"I can see, Terence, that married life agrees with you." Seamus gave him a playful slap on the belly. They both sprang to their feet, and warmly embraced each other as the tears welled up in their eyes.

"Oh, lad, 'tis a miracle that you can see at all." He clasped Seamus' shoulders. "Lord, how I've missed you."

Bridget stood quietly to the side, experiencing mixed emotions at this joyous reunion, for she realized that the last time they had been together, Kevin had been with them.

Julia and Grandma Mary quickly led her inside and chatted away about everything and everyone to take her mind off the past.

This place has ghosts enough for all of us, Nora thought sadly.

A week later, Nora went to Queenstown to meet Retta. Sean had managed to track her down in Italy, and she interrupted her trip to come to Ireland immediately. She was received with the same love and kindness that young Mary had been shown, for everyone had loved Retta's mother, Molly, and they knew that Nora treated Retta as if she were her own child.

Mary held Retta close. " 'Tis another fine grand-daughter I'm having. Child, you're so like your mother.'' She charmed Retta by telling her stories about Molly that even Nora hadn't remembered, and those stories filled in gaps for Retta, helping her feel that she had come to know her mother better.

Nora watched with contentment as these relationships between Mary and her two granddaughters were developing. Bridget, of course, visited Kevin's parents, and while it was a sad visit, she knew it would comfort them. Seamus went with her, for he too had known them.

From the moment she arrived, Retta was eager to see Billy. She had corresponded faithfully with him over the three years he had been gone, and in her own way had tried to make him understand why Nora had done what she had. Grandma Mary was feeling better each day, and one morning at breakfast agreed to take Retta and young Mary to Lord Anthony's for tea so they could be reunited with Billy. Nora, of course, didn't go. She longed to see her son, but she couldn't bear another rejection from him.

Lord Anthony was seated by the fire. A blanket was draped over his knees. He begged them to forgive him for not rising, but he was just recovering from a bad cold.

"I'm certain you caught that cold in Dublin, coming every day to the the hospital in all that rain,'' Mary scolded.

Retta, always observant, sensed that this kind, attractive man was very fond of Mary. His gentleness of tone, his glances and his concern all conveyed great caring. She also noticed how Mary rearranged his blanket and smoothed his collar. How dear they are together, she thought.

Billy came running in from the stables when he heard they were present. His handsome face was alight at their reunion. All three ran into one another's arms, embracing, kissing, laughing, teasing each other with old nicknames. Mary and Lord Anthony sat quietly by, relishing the happy scene. Billy was stunned at how lovely his Retta had become. He touched her red hair lovingly. "My Lord, since when have you become so elegant?" he asked, making ironic use of one of Retta's favorite childhood words. He turned to Mary. "And you, little sister, just look at you—all grown up and perfectly divine."

"Oh Billy, we've missed you so. Please come home." Her eyes began to glisten.

"There, there, little one, don't do that." He tried to comfort her, but to little effect.

Retta, spunky as always, challenged him. "You see, Billy, you've hurt more than just your mother by your selfish behavior." Mary and Lord Anthony tensed. They had been treading so gently with him.

Billy was taken aback. He had forgotten how direct Retta could be. "I'm sorry, Retta. I'd just rather not discuss it."

Retta didn't want to mar their reunion, so she compromised slightly. "No, I guess we shouldn't, now, but we will. Now, tell me all about you. You look taller, Billy, and I had forgotten how handsome you were. Of course, when last I saw you, you were still a boy—my baby brother, actually."

Mary and Anthony took young Mary for a tour around the manor so that Billy and Retta could be alone to talk. As they sat together, so close he could smell her familiar lavender scent, Billy felt all the old passions rising in him. At last, when Retta said she had to be going home, Billy begged her to return on the morrow, and told her he would take her riding. She promised she would come, for she thought she saw a real desperation in his eyes.

As he saw her to the door, and the others were

walking back, she quickly turned to him, blurting out, "Billy, I love Aunt Nora so much, but I know that if God would let me have my real mother back, I'd forgive her anything, no matter what she'd done." She turned away, walking quickly down the path toward Mary and Anthony.

He stared after her. He was angry, for she had used an old ploy of hers to have the last word.

It was warm and breezy the next morning as Retta and Billy rode through the meadows. Retta loved the freedom, the excitement and the sight of her dear Billy again.

"You're still not the world's greatest rider," Billy teased.

"No, I can't compete with you or your mother, but I think I do well enough." With that, she gave her horse full rein and galloped ahead.

Billy was somewhat irritated at her not so veiled reference to Nora, but spurred his own horse on and finally caught up with Retta. They tethered the horses, and as they spread the picnic lunch Mary had packed on the lush meadow grass, with the lovely scent of hawthorn and roses surrounding them, Billy felt the old desire for her returning. "Retta."

"Yes, Billy, what is it?" She sensed the moment she looked at him that something was different. Her eyes widened.

"Oh, God, Retta, I love you. How else can I say it? Don't you know how I've always loved you?"

She held her breath. Billy pulled her to him and he kissed her with the pent-up longing of a lifetime. At first, she resisted, but then she passionately returned his kiss.

After a few moments, she pulled away. "Billy, this doesn't seem right. I'm confused. Please, not right now. I can't seem to think straight."

"There's nothing wrong with it, Retta. My inner being must have known that all along. I've loved you since I was old enough to know what the word meant, even when I believed I'd be damned for that love."

The full realization of what he was saying dawned on Retta. "Oh, my God, Billy, you didn't—I mean, you—"

"All that's in the past. Let's just talk now."

"Billy, I can't. I'm frightened. Let's go back. I need to think."

"Of course, dearest Retta. I'm sorry. I didn't mean to frighten you, I just couldn't help myself. The wonder of the truth overwhelmed me, that it's all right to love you, that we are not sister and brother."

She stared at him. "That's true, isn't it? But you see, I've thought otherwise for a lifetime. Billy, please understand, this is too sudden, too strange for me. I need time. I don't know how I feel. You do understand, don't you?"

Billy gazed at her. "Yes, I understand. But please don't shut me out now, Retta, not without trying."

"Do you mean like you shut your own mother out?" She couldn't help saying it.

Billy stiffened. "You're unfair, Retta. You don't know the pain and fury I feel. You've never been abandoned." He was frustrated, and remembered how she could always make him feel that way. "Damn, what are we arguing for? Come on, let's get the hell out of here."

Nora decided that she couldn't leave Ireland without seeing Billy ride in the Dublin show. She knew where Billy rode daily, preparing himself for the show, and she remembered a place where she could watch him without being seen. So for several days, she unobtrusively hid and watched Billy put his mare through her paces. He was good, she thought, very good, but she noticed a few minor problems that she wished he would correct. If only she could talk with him.

When the day of the show finally arrived, Nora sat in a box apart from the others. Lord Anthony had arranged for her to be in a very good box for viewing, but one which would not expose her too openly to the eyes of her son. All the excitement of the day and the memories it elicited were almost too much for her, and she was glad to be alone.

When Billy rode out, straight and tall in the saddle, her heart almost burst with pride. How perfect, she thought, how perfect! She watched every movement with rapt attention. Oh, Billy, I want so for you to win.

When the judges announced that he had won the first event, she wiped a tear of happiness away. As he rode out for the second event, he passed very close to her box and someone shouted to him. He turned around quickly. Suddenly, he saw her. Their eyes met for a brief moment. She held herself proudly, meeting the challenge in his eyes as he stared at her. Then he turned back to the arena. Her heart was pounding wildly. Had she noticed a softening in his manner? He placed second in the next event, but came back to claim first in the jumping event. She wanted to share his joy, but instead she quickly left when Lord Anthony went to claim the prize.

When she arrived back in her rooms at the Gresham Hotel, she ordered tea and sat quietly, recalling the day's events. The others would be celebrating together, but she was content having seen him ride and win. Just then there was a knock at the door.

"Yes, one moment." She unlocked the door and opened it. There stood Billy. She gasped in surprise. "Billy, I—"

"Oh, Mother, I'm sorry, so sorry. I've been such a

fool. Can you forgive me?'' And at that, he threw his arms about her.

Nora was unable to speak. Three long years had taken their toll, and she wept uncontrollably on his shoulder.

''Mother, this has been one of the most exciting days of my life, and when I saw you sitting there, you, who made it all possible, I suddenly realized all that you had sacrificed so that I could have a better life. I didn't even try to understand, but now I see that you cared for me more than I would have dreamed possible.''

''Oh, Billy, I did so want to explain, but when my letters to you were returned unopened—''

''Don't, Mother. I've been an insufferable idiot. I realize now that I've caused everyone misery in my desire to punish and hurt you. Retta has made me see that. My grandmother and grandfather tried so hard to talk sense to me, and Uncle Terence even called me a jackass.'' He smiled faintly. ''Uncle Terence was right. Can you forgive me?''

Was she truly hearing these words? Were they finally to resume, all these years later, their lost and denied bond? ''Oh, Billy, of course I forgive you. You're my son. I hope you can forgive me, too.''

A sudden storm had driven Mary, Nora and Bridget inside. They sat talking contentedly in front of the fireplace. Danny had been called to Cork on church business, and Seamus and Terence had gone with him. The children were out on a late afternoon excursion.

A wave of melancholy overcame Nora as they sat talking of the past, and she thought of how different her life might have been had her circumstance been other than it was. But this mood quickly passed, as she fondly called to mind her life in America. Queen's Lace, Ballygarry's, Sean and Bridget, her friends, Rachel, Angelo, Dennis, Annie,

Caroline. Ah, Caroline. Nora had learned that the Nineteenth Amendment had recently been ratified, giving women the right to vote. Her heart went out to Caroline, for they had shared much in their struggle for woman suffrage. But the most important person to Nora had been Jack. Although they were apart, Nora suddenly felt closer to him than ever, and silently thanked God for him. Only one cloud dimmed her thoughts—that she couldn't tell her mother about Jack. No, she thought, perhaps someday, but not now. And now, praise God, Billy will be part of my life again. She was content.

Suddenly, the door burst open, and Seamus came staggering in, soaking wet and out of breath, his face red with fury.

"Seamus, my God, what's happened?" screamed Bridget as she and Nora sprang to their feet.

Seamus struggled to catch his breath as they wrapped him in a warm blanket, and Bridget took off his wet boots. "Terence has been hurt, and they've taken Danny," he told them.

Mary leapt to her feet as if struck by a bolt of lightning. "They've what? Our Danny? It can't be!"

"Who's taken him?" gasped Nora, incredulous.

"The Black and Tans, those Protestant bastards. One of them shot Terence in the leg. They're madmen, I tell you. He barely got away. I don't know how he did it."

All the color drained from Mary's face. "Is he all right?"

"Yes, Mary, I'm sure he'll be all right, but Danny—I think they've arrested Danny."

Mary grabbed Seamus by the shoulders. His tear-filled eyes once again saw the pillar of strength and composure she had always been for them. "Now, take hold of yourself, Seamus, and be telling us exactly what happened."

Seamus collapsed in a chair. "We were driving to

Cork, going through Kilcarret, when we saw a young boy and an old woman being pushed around by a Black and Tan. Terence ordered Danny to stop the car, and he jumped out and ran over to the Tan and asked him what he thought he was doing. You can imagine the language he used. Danny told me not to leave the car, that we might have to get away fast. It seems the old lady was suspected of harboring guerrillas. Terence pushed the Tan's hands off the young man and told him and the old lady to be on their way. While they were trying to thank him, the Tan pulled a pistol. Terence knocked him to the ground, unconscious, and grabbed his gun. Just then another Tan came around the corner from behind. Danny yelled out to warn Terence, but the second Tan shot Terence just above the knee. As he was falling, Terence's gun went off and caught the Tan flush in the chest. I don't think he meant to shoot. It was like a reflex. He was taken by surprise.''

Seamus paused to gather his breath and continued. ''By now, I had gotten out of the car, but Danny grabbed me and yelled, 'Get Terence out of here before the others come.' I didn't stop to think. I just put Terence's arm around my shoulder and got him into the car as fast as I could. Danny yelled, 'Go, get out of here fast. God be with you.' It would have done your hearts proud to see his courage. As I looked back, I saw Danny tending to the injured Tan. Terence told me where to take him, and I did.''

''But where is he, Seamus?'' Nora asked in a state of shock.

''Don't tell us,'' Mary interrupted. ''The fewer who know, the better.''

''He's all right. He's safely hidden away. He's lost a lot of blood, but the doctor said he'd be all right.''

The women all breathed easier.

''Julia, my Lord, she's at her sister's. Does she know?''

"Yes, Mary, one of the men went to find her, and they brought her to him."

"Thank God their little boy, Conor, is here safe with us."

"According to the shop owner," Seamus went on, "the first Tan said he hadn't gotten a good look at me, although he said he wouldn't forget Terence."

Mary sat silently for a moment. "Danny in prison, I can't believe it. Tomorrow, we'll find out where they've taken him. My God, will this insanity never end?"

Nora stared into the fire. Nothing had changed. Ireland was still the same. Would it never change?

Lord Anthony found out that Danny was being held in Dublin Castle, and that the bishop was trying to intercede for him. Because they were Americans, the authorities at Dublin Castle had agreed to let Nora and Bridget in to see Danny on the day they were to sail.

Nora realized that she and Terence would have no farewell, for she'd not see him again this trip. Neither could she guess how long it might be before she would come again, so she wrote him a long letter and gave it to Mary to give to Julia.

Nora stared at Mary O'Sullivan working her lace before the fire. How the winds of sorrow had shaken her mother, yet she always remained strong and brave.

Nora thought of this terrible beauty that was Ireland, and how her sons and daughters brought this heritage with them to America. How some, like Uncle Jim, the shrewd orchestrator of people, used their power to help those less fortunate, their sons becoming policemen and contractors and lawyers. How some, like Bridget and she, brought their ancient Irish skills, like their lace-making. And she thought how Sean, with his wonderful Irish way with words, wrote for Ireland and its cause, while making his own way in a new land, and how Jack Ryan, a poor civil servant's son, had become a United States senator. And Seamus, using his way with words differently from Sean, as a lawyer, was also helping his people. And Nora herself, with her fierce pride, making a better life for herself and for those who would follow, in America and in Ireland. All of this was a legacy, she knew, from her mother, a courageous and determined woman.

So much beauty and so much tragedy, Nora thought. She slowly rose, walked over to Mary and kissed her forehead. "Thank you for everything, Ma. Everything you've done for us all these years."

Mary smiled faintly and patted her hand.

"I've learned from you, Ma. I've learned I can make a happy life for myself, even if not a perfect one. I've learned that it's noble to endure, and gratifying to love." She thought of Jack, then. Sweet Jack. She would love him forever, yet endure being apart from him so much of the time, like her mother and Lord Anthony. No, life would never be perfect, but it would be happy.

"If you've learned those things from me, child," Mary said, "you have made your mother a contented woman."

Epilogue

Bridget and Nora went to see Danny at Kilmainham Jail, Dublin, the day they were sailing to America.

"Oh, Danny, how pale you look, and thin," Bridget whimpered.

"Aye, sister, I've not seen the light of day. As for thin, sure, but that won't be hurting me." He forced a smile.

"Danny, the bishop is confident that you'll be released soon," Nora told him. "He says they don't want any more bad press in America, or here."

"Well, that gives me hope. Meanwhile, a few days away from the rich food at Monsignor's table can do no harm. You mustn't worry. I'll no doubt be out to say Mass on Sunday. And besides, the experience has been an educational one." They looked at him disbelievingly. "I understand more now of what Terence is all about, I have new insights, and that won't be hurting a man of God, will it, now? Good-bye, sisters. May the wind be always at your back. Bless you."

The guard was distracted momentarily by someone shouting in the corridors, and Danny whispered, "Is Terence all right?"

"Yes," Nora assured him. "We don't know where he is, but we do know he's all right."

"Thank God, thank God. I've lived in fear. The soldier he shot is still alive. I pray for him to live, you can be sure, for if he dies, there will be a manhunt for Terence the likes of which makes my blood run cold."

They said their tearful farewells and he promised to write often.

"Danny, please know that your letters have been our link with our family, with our home, with our country," Nora said. "They've been so important to us. Thank you. Good-bye, now. Come, Bridget, don't cry. Our Danny will be fine. God will see to that."

They left without turning around. The guard took Danny by the arm and led him away.

Nora stood at the rail as the huge liner docked, her eyes searching the crowd for Jack. The air was full of exhilaration as throngs crushed together, searching to find their loved ones. Suddenly she saw him, and she waved frantically. At first, he didn't see her, and she had a few moments to look at the strong, handsome, intelligent face of the man she loved. So many years had passed, but she was still moved by the very sight of him. Then he saw her, and his eyes sparkled as his face broke into the fabulous Ryan smile, the smile that promised her their world together. He raced headlong up the gangplank, and suddenly this elegant, beautiful, dark-haired, violet-eyed woman whom he loved was in his arms, her lips pressing against his.

Nora's thoughts suddenly flashed back in time, to herself as a young Irish farm girl in a patched blue cotton dress, stepping onto American soil for the first time. Through those years, she had struggled and wept, known tragedy and joy, failure and success, but had, at last, opened her heart to love.

"Jack, oh Jack. You're here. You're here!"

"Nora darling, of course I'm here. I will always be here. Always, sweet one." He gathered her into his arms. "Come, wife of my heart. We're going home."

LOOK FOR . . .

THE FRENCH

An unforgettable portrait of the young and innocent who arrived on America's shores . . . seeking a nation's bounty and the promise of a new beginning.

by W. Maureen Miller

To the French "casquette girls" who came to New Orleans, America was a land bright with the prospect of freedom—a nation that offered them sanctuary from the prejudices of the past. But there were dangers that awaited the beautiful, headstrong Madeleine Boucher. In the arms of the fiercely temperamental aristocrat, Jacques Phillipe Bouligny, Madeleine would find a passion she had never known and she would discover the depths of a man's betrayal. It was a lesson that she and her ravishing daughter Solange would keep in their hearts, as these proud women of a newfound territory learned the limits of their power and the meaning of American liberty.

COMING SOON
WHEREVER DELL BOOKS ARE SOLD

Seventh Powerful Novel in

THE AMERICAN EXPLORERS
Zebulon Pike

PIONEER DESTINY

by Richard Woodley

It was a trail that led ever westward, into the trackless wasteland of the Louisiana Territory. Zebulon Pike began his journey as a young man, yearning for fame and glory, too idealistic to understand the motives of his superior, General Wilkinson. Not even Clarissa Pike could convince Zebulon to turn down the challenge of a courageous mission. Dangers stalk the trail as Pike discovers a traitor among his ranks . . . a battalion of Spanish sharpshooters . . . and a Mexican general who owes a debt of gratitude to General Wilkinson and a man named Aaron Burr. Only the sensuous Juanita Alvarez can tell him the bitter truth—that he has been betrayed by those he trusted most. . . .

Please send me _____ copies of book #7 in the
AMERICAN EXPLORERS series, *Zebulon Pike: PIONEER
DESTINY*. I am enclosing $3.45 per copy (includes 50¢
postage and handling).

Please send check or money order (no cash or C.O.D.s).

Name _____
                              (Please Print)
Address_____ Apt._____

City _____

State_____ Zip_____

Please allow 6-8 weeks for delivery.
PA residents add 6% sales tax.
Send this coupon to:
BANBURY BOOKS, INC.
37 West Avenue, Suite 201, Wayne, PA 19087

THE SAGA OF A PROUD AND PASSIONATE PEOPLE—THEIR STRIVING FOR FREEDOM—THEIR TRIUMPHANT JOURNEY

THE JEWS
by Sharon Steeber

Fleeing from the Russian pogroms, Zavel and Marya Luminov came to a new land, America, not knowing or understanding the test that awaited them. Through hard times and bitter struggles, they planted the seeds of a family fortune. As the abandoned years of the Roaring Twenties gave way to the darkness of the Depression, Zavel, Marya and their children would learn the heartbreak of bitterness and loss as they clung to their hopes, their dreams and their unbreakable loyalties. THE JEWS is the towering novel of their achievements and heritage . . . and of the nation they helped to build with their pride.

Please send me _____ copies of *THE JEWS* by Sharon Steeber. I am enclosing $4.50 per copy (includes 55¢ postage and handling).

Please send check or money order (no cash or C.O.D.s).

Name _____
(Please Print)

Address _____ Apt._____

City _____

State _____ Zip_____

Please allow 6-8 weeks for delivery.
PA residents add 6% sales tax.
Send this coupon to:
BANBURY BOOKS, INC.
37 West Avenue, Suite 201, Wayne, PA 19087

FIRST IN *THE JAZZ AGE* series . . .

NO FUTURE, NO MEMORY

by
Richard O'Brien

**THE SAGA OF A NEW GENERATION, TOUGHENED BY WAR,
GREEDY FOR LOVE AND WEALTH . . .
AND HUNGRY FOR PLEASURE**

In the first, gripping novel of *THE JAZZ AGE* series, Richard O'Brien traces the rising fortunes of John Crain as he returns from the war and begins to search for a new life. His passionate affair with Nadine Berns, his rebellion against the family that would use its fortune to control his life . . . and his final, violent confrontation with the New York underworld . . . all are portrayed in a stirring novel that vividly re-creates the beginning of the Roaring Twenties.

■■■■■■■■■■■■■■■■■■■■■■■■■■■■■■■■■■

Please send me _____ copies of the first book in *THE JAZZ AGE* series, *No Future, No Memory*. I am enclosing $3.75 per copy (includes 50¢ postage and handling).

Please send check or money order (no cash or C.O.D.s).

Name _____
(Please Print)

Address _____ Apt._____

City _____

State _____ Zip_____

Please allow 6-8 weeks for delivery.
PA residents add 6% sales tax.
Send this coupon to:
BANBURY BOOKS, INC.
37 West Avenue, Suite 201, Wayne, PA 19087

BOOK #3 IN *THE JAZZ AGE* series . . . .

Ballyhoo Years

by
Richard O'Brien

MEN AND WOMEN MADE HEADLINES—
AND A CUB REPORTER CHALLENGED THEIR POWER . . .

Joe Flaxton was the chosen man in Hearst's vast empire, a reporter with a reputation for dogging the truth and getting a jump on ballyhoo. But then a hot tip led him to the heart of the Teapot Dome Scandal . . . and to the door of a man named John Crain. As the headlines flashed across the nation—telling the story of the greatest scandal in government history—Joe Flaxton found himself playing a dangerous game, with one beautiful woman on his side. He would have sacrificed everything for her—even his career—but the pull of ballyhoo was strong. And when the moment came, Joe Flaxton would give up the woman he loved for a once-in-a-lifetime story. . . .

■■■■■■■■■■■■■■■■■■■■■■■■■■■■■■■■

Please send me _____ copies of the third book in *THE JAZZ AGE* series, *Ballyhoo Years*. I am enclosing $3.75 per copy (includes 50¢ postage and handling).

Please send check or money order (no cash or C.O.D.s).

Name _____
(Please Print)

Address _____ Apt._____

City _____

State _____ Zip_____

Please allow 6-8 weeks for delivery.
PA residents add 6% sales tax.
Send this coupon to:
BANBURY BOOKS, INC.
37 West Avenue, Suite 201, Wayne, PA 19087

BOOK #2 IN *THE JAZZ AGE* series . . .

BY FRIENDS BETRAYED

by
Richard O'Brien

CHICAGO . . . AND PROHIBITION. BATHTUB GIN FLOWED FREELY, FLAPPERS REIGNED . . . AND GREG MEISTER FELL FOR THE GIRL OF HIS DREAMS

To Meister, the farm boy, Tandy Crain had everything a man could want. She was smart and beautiful. She'd gone to the best schools, knew the right people. It was hard to keep up with a girl like that, but Greg Meister didn't stop trying . . . even if it meant going to Chicago and dealing with a man by the name of Al Capone. Suddenly Greg and Tandy had everything—the big home in Cicero, two beautiful children and everything money could buy. But it was a love built on dreams, and when America went back on its promise, Greg and Tandy Meister faced the shadow of their fading hopes. . . .

■■■■■■■■■■■■■■■■■■■■■■■■■■■■■■■■■■■■■

Please send me _____ copies of the second book in *THE JAZZ AGE* series, *By Friends Betrayed.* I am enclosing $3.75 per copy (includes 50¢ postage and handling).
Please send check or money order (no cash or C.O.D.s).

Name _____
(Please Print)

Address _____ Apt._____

City _____

State _____ Zip_____

Please allow 6-8 weeks for delivery.
PA residents add 6% sales tax.
Send this coupon to:
BANBURY BOOKS, INC.
37 West Avenue, Suite 201, Wayne, PA 19087